LLYFRGELLOEDD CYHOEDDUS / PUBLIC LIBRARIES

Dyddiad dychwelyd		Date due back
08 ~~WITHDRAWN~~		
-2 FEB 2001		
14 APR 2001		
BS		

Awdur / Author: STEPHEN JONES & DAVID SUTTON (ED)

Enw / Title: Dark terrors 5

| Dosbarth Class No. | N | Rhif Acc. No. | 12002842 |

12002842

Dark Terrors 5
THE GOLLANCZ BOOK OF HORROR

Also available from
Victor Gollancz/Millennium

Dark Terrors
Dark Terrors 2
Dark Terrors 3
Dark Terrors 4

Also edited by Stephen Jones
and available in paperback

Shadows Over Innsmouth
Dancing With the Dark
The Conan Chronicles Volume 1:
The People of the Black Circle by Robert E. Howard

Dark Terrors 5

THE GOLLANCZ BOOK OF HORROR

Edited by
Stephen Jones and David Sutton

VICTOR GOLLANCZ
LONDON

This compilation Copyright © Stephen Jones and David Sutton 2000
All rights reserved

The right of individual contributors to be identified as the authors of this work has been asserted by them in accordance with the Copyright, Designs and Patents Act 1988.

This edition published in Great Britain in 2000 by

Victor Gollancz
An imprint of Orion Books Ltd
Orion House, 5 Upper St Martin's Lane, London WC2H 9EA

To receive information on the Millennium list, e-mail us at:
smy@orionbooks.co.uk

A CIP catalogue record for this book is available
from the British Library

Typeset by SetSystems Ltd, Saffron Walden, Essex

Printed in Great Britain by
Clays Ltd, St Ives plc

Contents

About the Editors ix

Acknowledgements xi

Introduction
THE EDITORS 1

At Home in the Pubs of Old London
CHRISTOPHER FOWLER 3

Valentia
CAITLÍN R. KIERNAN 14

Barking Sands
RICHARD CHRISTIAN MATHESON 25

Everything, in All the Wrong Order
CHAZ BRENCHLEY 30

Savannah is Six
JAMES VAN PELT 38

Now Day Was Fled as the Worm Had Wished
BRIAN HODGE 53

Why Rudy Can't Read
DAVID J. SCHOW 68

No Story in It
RAMSEY CAMPBELL 76

Witch-Compass
GRAHAM MASTERTON 92

The Proposal
NICHOLAS ROYLE 116

Changes
C. BRUCE HUNTER 126

The Abortionist's Horse (A Nightmare)
TANITH LEE 137

The Handover
MICHAEL MARSHALL SMITH 150

Pearl
ROBERTA LANNES 162

Beauregard
ERIC BROWN 171

Necromimicos
NANCY KILPATRICK 186

The Bootleg Heart
JOEL LANE 191

Saturday
CHERRY WILDER 200

The Girlfriends of Dorian Gray
GREGORY FROST 214

Bottle Babies
MARY A. TURZILLO 233

Going to Series
KIM NEWMAN 250

Haunts
LISA TUTTLE 277

My Present Wife
DENNIS ETCHISON 300

Alicia
MELANIE TEM 315

The Haunted Bookshop
BRIAN STABLEFORD 331

Starfucker
MICK GARRIS 354

Destroyer of Worlds
GWYNETH JONES 381

The Geezers
PETER STRAUB 393

Honeysuckle
WILLIAM R. TROTTER 411

Final Departure
GAHAN WILSON 460

Pelican Cay
DAVID CASE 464

About the Editors

Stephen Jones lives in London. He is the winner of two World Fantasy Awards, three Horror Writers Association Bram Stoker Awards and two International Horror Guild Awards, as well as being a twelve-time recipient of the British Fantasy Award and a Hugo Award nominee. A full-time columnist, television producer/director and genre movie publicist and consultant (the first three *Hellraiser* movies, *Night Life*, *Nightbreed*, *Split Second*, *Mind Ripper*, *Last Gasp* etc.), he is the co-editor of *Horror: 100 Best Books*, *The Best Horror from Fantasy Tales*, *Gaslight & Ghosts*, *Now We Are Sick*, *H.P. Lovecraft's Book of Horror*, *The Anthology of Fantasy & the Supernatural*, *Secret City: Strange Tales of London* and *The Mammoth Book of Best New Horror*, *Dark Terrors*, *Dark Voices* and *Fantasy Tales* series. He has written *The Essential Monster Movie Guide*, *The Illustrated Vampire Movie Guide*, *The Illustrated Dinosaur Movie Guide*, *The Illustrated Frankenstein Movie Guide* and *The Illustrated Werewolf Movie Guide*, and compiled *The Mammoth Book of Terror*, *The Mammoth Book of Vampires*, *The Mammoth Book of Zombies*, *The Mammoth Book of Werewolves*, *The Mammoth Book of Frankenstein*, *The Mammoth Book of Dracula*, *Shadows Over Innsmouth*, *Dancing With the Dark*, *Dark of the Night*, *Dark Detectives*, *White of the Moon*, *Exorcisms and Ecstasies* by Karl Edward Wagner, *The Vampire Stories of R. Chetwynd-Hayes* and *Phantoms and Fiends* by R. Chetwynd-Hayes, *James Herbert: By Horror Haunted*, *The Conan Chronicles* by Robert E. Howard (two volumes), *Clive Barker's A-Z of Horror*, *Clive Barker's Shadows in Eden*, *Clive Barker's The Nightbreed Chronicles* and the *Hellraiser Chronicles*. Visit his web site at http://www.herebedragons.co.uk/jones

David Sutton lives in Birmingham. He has been writing and editing in the fantasy and horror genre for more than a generation. In recognition of this devotion and achievement in the field, he has won the World Fantasy Award, The International Horror Guild Award and twelve British Fantasy Awards. From producing his own small press magazine and extensive work for the British Fantasy Society during the 1970s, he has been involved in numerous publications, including the multiple award-winning *Fantasy Tales* magazine. More recently he edited and produced *Voices from Shadow*, a small non-fiction anthology celebrating the twentieth anniversary of his magazine *Shadow*. Fiction anthologies under his editorship include *New Writings in Horror & the Supernatural* (two volumes), *The Satyr's Head & Other Tales of Terror* and, jointly edited with Stephen Jones, *The Best Horror from Fantasy Tales*, *The Anthology of Fantasy and the Supernatural*, *Dark Voices: The Pan Book of Horror Stories* (five volumes) and the acclaimed *Dark Terrors* series. His short stories have appeared in a number of periodicals and anthologies, including *Skeleton Crew*,

Beyond, *Kimota*, *Best New Horror* 2 and 7, *Final Shadows*, *Cold Fear*, *Taste of Fear*, *The Mammoth Book of Zombies*, *The Mammoth Book of Werewolves*, *Shadows Over Innsmouth*, *The Merlin Chronicles* and *Beneath the Ground*. Visit his web site at http://ourworld.compuserve.com/homepages/davesandra/

Acknowledgements

Special thanks to Douglas E. Winter, Mandy Slater, Lucy Ramsey, Buddy Martinez, Andrew Smith, John Gordon, Louisa Grimm, Malcolm Edwards and, as always, our inimitable editor Jo Fletcher.

'Introduction' copyright © Stephen Jones and David Sutton 2000.
   'At Home in the Pubs of Old London' copyright Christopher Fowler 2000.
   'Valentia' copyright © Caitlín R. Kiernan 2000.
   'Barking Sands' copyright © Richard Christian Matheson 2000.
   'Everything, in All the Wrong Order' copyright © Chaz Brenchley 2000.
   'Savannah is Six' copyright © James Van Pelt 2000.
   'Now Day Was Fled as the Worm Had Wished' copyright © Brian Hodge 2000.
   'Why Rudy Can't Read' copyright © David J. Schow 2000.
   'No Story in It' copyright © Ramsey Campbell 2000.
   'Witch-Compass' copyright © Graham Masterton 2000.
   'The Proposal' copyright © Nicholas Royle 2000.
   'Changes' copyright © C. Bruce Hunter 2000.
   'The Abortionist's Horse (A Nightmare)' copyright © Tanith Lee 2000.
   'The Handover' copyright © Michael Marshall Smith 2000.
   'Pearl' copyright © Roberta Lannes 2000.
   'Beauregard' copyright © Eric Brown 2000.
   'Necromimicos' copyright © Nancy Kilpatrick 2000.
   'The Bootleg Heart' copyright © Joel Lane 2000.
   'Saturday' copyright © Cherry Wilder 2000.
   'The Girlfriends of Dorian Gray' copyright © Gregory Frost 2000.
   'Bottle Babies' copyright © Mary A. Turzillo 2000.
   'Going to Series' copyright © Kim Newman 2000.
   'Haunts' copyright © Lisa Tuttle 2000.
   'My Present Wife' copyright © Dennis Etchison 2000.
   'Alicia' copyright © Melanie Tem 2000.
   'The Haunted Bookshop' copyright © Brian Stableford 2000.
   'Starfucker' copyright © Mick Garris 2000.
   'Destroyer of Worlds' copyright © Gwyneth Jones 2000.
   'The Geezers' copyright © Peter Straub 2000.
   'Honeysuckle' copyright © William R. Trotter 2000.
   'Final Departure' copyright © Gahan Wilson 2000.
   'Pelican Cay' copyright © David Case 2000.

Introduction

It is another dark and stormy night . . . and for many of us, there is nothing more welcome than getting comfortable with a big book of stories specifically designed to induce the hairs on the back of our neck to stand on end and make our flesh creep.

The horror genre has a long and proud tradition of weighty tomes of terror, ranging from Dashiell Hammett's *Creeps By Night*, J.M. Parrish and John R. Crossland's *The Mammoth Book of Thrillers, Ghosts and Mysteries*, Dennis Wheatley's *A Century of Horror* and Christine Campbell Thompson's *The 'Not at Night' Omnibus*, through Herbert A. Wise and Phyllis Fraser's *Great Tales of Terror and the Supernatural*, Boris Karloff's *And the Darkness Falls* and August Derleth's *The Sleeping & the Dead*, to more contemporary collections such as Kirby Mc-Cauley's *Dark Forces*, Douglas E. Winter's *Prime Evil* and Al Sarrantonio's *999: New Stories of Horror and Suspense*.

The bigger the book, the wider the spectrum of fears which can be explored.

For more than a decade we have been fortunate to have the opportunity to compile a number of well-received volumes of contemporary horror. Within these various titles we have been able to present some of the best and most iconoclastic work by established authors in the genre, as well as introducing a number of new and talented writers to a wider readership. But no matter how many different authors we selected, no matter how much we convinced our publishers to allow us to massage the page-count and squeeze the budget, there were always stories we admired which we had to leave out when making our final selection.

When you receive literally hundreds of submissions, as we do when we begin compiling a volume, it is only ever possible to accept a small percentage of the best manuscripts – and trust that those you have regretfully had to reject will find a home in some other anthology or magazine.

Which is why, when we were offered the opportunity to double the size of *Dark Terrors*, we jumped at the chance. A huge volume of modern horror and dark suspense, published on a regular basis, is exactly what the genre (and we hope the reader) wants. Now we would be able to include more stories by some of our favourite writers; we would be able to give more newcomers a professional forum for their fiction, and we would finally be able to incorporate more of those troublesome novellas, which fall between short story and novel length but which allow writers to flex their creative muscles.

Sure we would.

No sooner had we announced that we were reading than the manuscripts began flooding in. There is no better way than editing an anthology to make you realise that there are simply not enough markets for horror fiction available out there. Of course, much of what we received was unsuitable for one reason or another. But there were still more than enough outstanding stories to fill a big book. And another ... and another. In fact, a list of some of the authors we had to reject would make many other editors green with envy.

And in the end, despite having many more words to work with, we once again found ourselves massaging the page-count and squeezing the budget so that we could include just one more story by a favourite author or a talented newcomer.

Which is why we are so proud of this particular volume. As we have said before, we do not expect our readers to agree with all our choices, but we truly believe that this is as powerful and representative a selection of modern horror as we could compile.

So sit back and relax as the night draws in and the wind begins to howl outside. It is time to feel those nape hairs stiffen and the goosebumps tingle as you once again prepare to lose yourself within those dark terrors which follow ...

Stephen Jones and David Sutton
April, 2000

At Home in the Pubs of Old London

CHRISTOPHER FOWLER

The Museum Tavern, Museum Street, Bloomsbury
Despite its location diagonally opposite the British Museum, its steady turnover of listless Australian barstaff and its passing appraisal by tourists on quests for the British pub experience (comprising two sips from half a pint of bitter and one Salt 'n' Vinegar flavoured crisp, nibbled and returned to its packet in horror), this drinking establishment retains the authentically seedy bookishness of Bloomsbury because its corners are usually occupied by half-cut proofreaders from nearby publishing houses. I love pubs like this one because so much about them remains constant in a sliding world: the smell of hops, the ebb of background conversation, muted light through coloured glass, china tap handles, mirrored walls, bars of oak and brass. Even the pieces of fake Victoriana, modelled on increasingly obsolete pub ornaments, become objects of curiosity in themselves.

At this time I was working in a comic shop, vending tales of fantastic kingdoms to whey-faced netheads who were incapable of saving a sandwich in a serviette, let alone an alien planet, and it was in this pub that I met Lesley. She was sitting with a group of glum-looking Gothic Gormenghast offcuts who were on their way to a book launch at the new-age smells 'n' bells shop around the corner, and she was clearly unenchanted with the idea of joining them for a session of warm Liebfraumilch and crystal-gazing, because as each member of the group drifted off she found an excuse to stay on, and we ended up sitting together by ourselves. As she refolded her jacket a rhinestone pin dropped from the lapel, and I picked it up for her. The badge formed her initials – L,L – which made me think of Superman, because he had a history of falling for women with those initials, but I reminded myself that I was no superman, just a man who liked making friends in pubs. I asked her if she'd had a good Christmas, she said no, I said I hadn't either and we just chatted from there. I told Lesley that I was something of an artist and would love to sketch her, and she tentatively agreed to sit for me at some point in the future.

The World's End, High Street, Camden Town
It's a funny pub, this one, because the interior brickwork makes it look sort of inside out, and there's a steady through-traffic of punters wherever you stand, so you're always in the way. It's not my kind of place, more a network of bars and clubs than a proper boozer. It used to be called the Mother Red Cap, after a witch who lived in Camden. There are still a few of her pals inhabiting the place if black eyeliner, purple lipstick and pointed boots make you a likely candidate for cauldron-stirring. A white stone statue of Britannia protrudes from the first floor of the building opposite, above a shoe shop, but I don't think anyone notices it, just as they don't know about the witch. Yet if you step inside the foyer of the Black Cap, a few doors further down, you can see the witch herself, painted on a tiled wall. It's funny how people miss so much of what's going on around them. I was beginning to think Sophie wouldn't show up, then I became convinced she had, and I had missed her.

Anyway, she finally appeared and we hit it off beautifully. She had tied back her long auburn hair so that it was out of her eyes, and I couldn't stop looking at her. It's never difficult to find new models; women are flattered by the thought of someone admiring their features. She half-smiled all the time, which was disconcerting at first, but after a while I enjoyed it because she looked like she was in on a secret that no one else shared. I had met her two days earlier in the coffee shop in Bermondsey where she was working, and she had suggested going for a drink, describing our meeting place to me as 'that pub in Camden near the shoe shop'. The one thing Camden has, more than any other place in London, is shoe shops, hundreds of the bastards, so you can understand why I was worried.

It was quite crowded and we had to stand, but after a while Sophie felt tired and wanted to sit down, so we found a corner and wedged ourselves in behind a pile of coats. The relentless music was giving me a headache, so I was eventually forced to take my leave.

The King's Head, Upper Street, Islington
The back of this pub operates a tiny theatre, so the bar suddenly fills up with the gin-and-tonic brigade at seven each evening, but the front room is very nice in a battered, nicotine-scoured way. It continued to operate on the old monetary system of pounds, shillings and pence for years, long after they brought in decimal currency. I'm sure the

management just did it to confuse non regulars who weren't in the habit of being asked to stump up nineteen and elevenpence halfpenny for a libation. Emma was late, having been forced to stay behind at her office, a property company in Essex Road. The choice of territory was mine. Although it was within walking distance of her office, she hadn't been here before, and loved hearing this mad trilling coming from a door at the back of the pub. I'd forgotten to explain about the theatre. They were staging a revival of a twenties musical, and there were a lot of songs about croquet and how ghastly foreigners were. I remember Emma as being very pale and thin, with cropped blonde hair; she could easily have passed for a jazz-age flapper. I told her she should have auditioned for the show, but she explained that she was far too fond of a drink to ever remember anything as complicated as a dance step. At the intermission, a girl dressed as a giant sequinned jellyfish popped out to order a gin and French; apparently she had a big number in the second act. We taxed the barman's patience by getting him to make up strange cocktails, and spent most of the evening laughing so loudly they probably heard us on stage. Emma agreed to sit for me at some point in the future, and although there was never a suggestion that our session would develop into anything more, I could tell that it probably would. I was about to kiss her when she suddenly thought something had bitten her, and I was forced to explain that my coat had picked up several fleas from my cat. She went off me after this, and grew silent, so I left.

The Pineapple, Leverton Street, Kentish Town
This tucked-away pub can't have changed much in a hundred years, apart from the removal of the wooden partitions that separated the snug from the saloon. A mild spring morning, the Sunday papers spread out before us, an ancient smelly Labrador flatulating in front of the fire, a couple of pints of decent bitter and two packets of pork scratchings. Sarah kept reading out snippets from the *News of the World*, and I did the same with the *Observer*, but mine were more worthy than hers, and therefore not as funny. There was a strange man with an enormous nose sitting near the gents' toilet who kept telling people that they looked Russian. Perhaps he was, too, and needed to find someone from his own country. It's that kind of pub; it makes you think of home.

I noticed that one of Sarah's little habits was rubbing her wrists together when she was thinking. Every woman has some kind of private signature like this. Such a gesture marks her out to a lover, or an old friend. I watched her closely scanning the pages – she had forgotten her glasses – and felt a great inner calm. Only once did she disturb the peace between us by asking if I had been out with many women. I lied, of course, as you do, but the question remained in the back of my head, picking and scratching at my brain, right up until I said goodbye to her. It was warm in the pub and she had grown sleepy; she actually fell asleep at one point, so I decided to quietly leave.

The Anchor, Park Street, Southwark
It's pleasant here on rainy days. In the summer, tourists visiting the nearby Globe fill up the bars and pack the riverside tables. Did you know that pub signs were originally provided so that the illiterate could locate them? The Anchor was built after the Southwark fire, which in 1676 razed the South Bank just as the Great Fire had attacked the North side ten years earlier. As I entered the pub, I noticed that the tide was unusually high, and the Thames was so dense and pinguid that it looked like a setting jelly. It wasn't a good start to the evening.

I had several pints of strong bitter and grew more talkative as our session progressed. We ate Toad-in-the-Hole, smothered in elastic gravy. I was excited about the idea of Carol and I going out together. I think she was, too, although she warned me that she had some loose ends to tie up, a former boyfriend to get out of her system, and suggested that perhaps we shouldn't rush at things. Out of the blue, she told me to stop watching her so much, as if she was frightened that she couldn't take the scrutiny. But she can. I love seeing the familiar gestures of women, the half smiles, the rubbing together of their hands, the sudden light in their eyes when they remember something they have to tell you. I can't remember what they say, only how they look. I would never take pictures of them, like some men I've read about. I never look back, you understand. It's too upsetting. Far more important to concentrate on who you're with, and making them happy. I'd like to think I made Carol feel special. She told me she'd never had much luck with men, and I believe it's true that some women just attract the wrong sort. We sat side by side watching the rain on the water, and I felt her head lower gently onto my shoulder, where it remained until I moved – a special moment, and one that I shall always remember.

The Lamb & Flag, Rose Street, Covent Garden
You could tell summer was coming because people were drinking on the street, searching for spaces on the windowsills of the pub to balance their beer glasses. This building looks like an old coaching inn, and stands beside an arch over an alleyway, like the Pillars of

Hercules in Greek Street. It's very old, with lots of knotted wood, and I don't suppose there's a straight angle in the place. The smoky bar is awkward to negotiate when you're carrying a drink in either hand – as I so often am!

This evening Kathy asked why I had not invited her to meet any of my friends. I could tell by the look on her face that she was wondering if I thought she wasn't good enough, and so I was forced to admit that I didn't really have any friends to whom I could introduce her. She was more reticent than most of the girls I had met until then, more private. She acted as though there was something on her mind that she didn't want to share with me. When I asked her to specify the problem, she either wouldn't or couldn't. To be honest, I think the problem was me, and that was why it didn't work out between us. Something about my behaviour made her uneasy, right from the start. There was no trust between us, which in itself was unusual, because most women are quick to confide in me. They sense my innate decency, my underlying respect for them. I look at the other drinkers standing around me, and witness the contempt they hold for women. My God, a blind man could feel their disdain. That's probably why I have no mates – I don't like my own sex. I'm ashamed of the whole alpha male syndrome. It only leads to trouble.

I made the effort of asking Kathy if she would sit for me, but knew in advance what the answer would be. She said she would prefer it if we didn't meet again, and yelped in alarm when I brushed against her hip, so I had to beat a hasty retreat.

The King William IV, High Street, Hampstead
Paula chose this rather paradoxical pub. It's in the middle of Hampstead, therefore traditional and okay, with a beer garden that was packed on a hot summer night, yet the place caters to a raucous gay clientèle. Apparently, Paula's sister brought her here once before, an attractive girl, judging from the photograph Paula showed me, and such a waste, I feel, when she could be making a man happy. I wondered if, after finishing with Paula, I should give her sister a call, but decided that it would be playing a little too close to home.

We sat in the garden on plastic chairs, beside sickly flowerbeds of nursery-forced plants, but it was pleasant, and the pub had given me an idea. I resolved to try someone of the same gender next time, just to see what a difference it made. I picked up one of the gay newspapers lying in stacks at the back of the pub, and made a note of other venues in central London. I explained my interest in the newspaper by saying that I wanted to learn more about the lifestyles of others. Paula squeezed my hand and said how much she enjoyed being with someone who had a liberal outlook. I told her that my policy was live and let live, which is a laugh for a start. I am often shocked by the wide-eyed belief I inspire in women, and wonder what they see in me that makes them so trusting. When I pressed myself close against her she didn't flinch once under my gaze, and remained staring into my eyes while I drained my beer glass. A special girl, a special evening, for both of us.

The Admiral Duncan, Old Compton Street, Soho
Formerly decorated as a cabin aboard an old naval vessel, with leadlight bay windows and a curved wood ceiling, this venue was revamped to suit the street's new status as a home to the city's homosexuals, and painted a garish purple. It was restored again following the nail-bomb blast that killed and maimed so many of its customers. Owing to the tunnel-like shape of the bar, the explosive force had nowhere to escape but through the glass front, and caused horrific injuries. A monument to the tragedy is inset into the ceiling of the pub, but no atmosphere of tragedy lingers, for the patrons, it seems, have bravely moved on in their lives.

In here I met Graham, a small-boned young man with a gentle West Country burr that seemed at odds with his spiky haircut. We became instant drinking pals, buying each other rounds in order to escape the evening heat of the mobbed street beyond. After what had occurred in the pub I found it astonishing that someone could be so incautious as to befriend a total stranger such as myself, but that is the beauty of the English boozer; once you cross the threshold, barriers of race, class and gender can be dropped. Oh, it doesn't happen everywhere, I know, but you're more likely to make a friend in this city than in most others. That's why I find it so useful in fulfilling my needs. However, the experiment with Graham was not a success. Boys don't work for me, no matter how youthful or attractive they appear to be. We were standing in a corner, raising our voices over the incessant thump of the jukebox, when I realised it wasn't working. Graham had drunk so much that he was starting to slide down the wall, but there were several others in the vicinity who were one step away from being paralytic, so he didn't stick out, and I could leave unnoticed.

The Black Friar, Queen Victoria Street, Blackfriars
This strange little pub, stranded alone by the roundabout on the North side of the river at Blackfriars, has an Arts and Crafts-style interior, complete with friezes, bas-reliefs and mottos running over its arches. Polished black monks traipse about the room, punctuating the place

with moral messages. It stands as a memorial to a vanished London, a world of brown Trilbys and woollen overcoats, of rooms suffused with pipe smoke and the tang of brilliantine. In the snug bar at the rear I met Danielle, a solidly built Belgian au pair who looked so lonely, lumpen and forlorn that I could not help but offer her a drink, and she was soon pouring out her troubles in broken English. Her employers wanted her to leave because she was pregnant, and she couldn't afford to go back to Antwerp.

To be honest, I wasn't listening to everything she was saying, because someone else had caught my eye. Seated a few stools away was a ginger-haired man who appeared to be following our conversation intently. He was uncomfortably overweight, and undergoing some kind of perspiration crisis. The pub was virtually deserted, most of the customers drinking outside on the pavement, and Danielle was talking loudly, so it was possible that she might have been overheard. I began to wonder if she was lying to me about her problems; if, perhaps they were more serious than she made them sound, serious enough for someone to be following her. I know it was selfish, but I didn't want to spend any more time with a girl who was in that kind of trouble, so I told her I needed to use the toilet, then slipped out across the back of the bar.

The Angel, Rotherhithe
Another old riverside inn – I seem to be drawn to them, anxious to trace the city's sluggish artery site by site, as though marking a pathway to the heart. The interesting thing about places like The Angel is how little they change across the decades, because they retain the same bleary swell of customers through all economic climates. Workmen and stockbrokers, estate agents, secretaries, van-drivers and tarts, they just rub along together with flirtatious smiles, laughs, belches and the odd sour word. The best feature of this pub is reached by the side entrance, an old wooden balcony built out over the shoreline, where mudlarks once rooted in the filth for treasure trove, and where you can sit and watch the sun settling between the pillars of Tower Bridge.

As the light faded we became aware of the sky brushing the water, making chilly ripples. Further along the terrace I thought I saw the red-haired man watching, but when I looked again, he had gone. Growing cold, we pulled our coats tighter, then moved inside. Stella was Greek, delicate and attractive, rather too young for me, but I found her so easy to be with that we remained together for the whole evening. Shortly before closing time she told me she should be going home soon because her brother was expecting her. I was just massaging some warmth back into her arms – we were seated by an open window and it had suddenly turned nippy – when she said she felt sick, and went off to the Ladies. After she failed to reappear I went to check on her, just to make sure she was all right. I found her in one of the cubicles, passed out.

The Ship, Greenwich
The dingy interior of this pub is unremarkable, with bare-board floors and tables cut from blackened barrels, but the exterior is another matter entirely. I can imagine the building, or one very like it, existing on the same site for centuries, at a reach of the river where it is possible to see for miles in either direction. I am moving out towards the mouth of the Thames, being taken by the tide to ever-widening spaces in my search for absolution. There was something grotesquely Victorian about the weeds thrusting out of ancient brickwork, tumble-down fences and the stink of the mud. It was unusually mild for the time of year and we sat on the wall with our legs dangling over the water, beers propped at our crotches.

Melanie was loud and common, coarse-featured and thick-legged. She took up room in the world, and didn't mind who knew it. She wore a lot of make-up, and had frothed her hair into a mad dry nest, but I was intrigued by the shape of her mouth, the crimson wetness of her lips, her cynical laugh, her seen-it-all-before eyes. She touched me as though expecting me to walk out on her at any moment, digging nails in my arm, nudging an elbow in my ribs, running fingers up my thigh. Still, I wondered if she would present a challenge, because I felt sure that my offer to sketch her would be rebuffed. She clearly had no interest in art, so I appealed to her earthier side and suggested something of a less salubrious nature.

To my surprise she quoted me a price list, which ruined everything. I swore at her, and pushed her away, disgusted. She, in turn, began calling me every filthy name under the sun, which attracted unwanted attention to both of us. It was then that I saw the ginger-headed man again, standing to the left of me, speaking into his chubby fist.

The Trafalgar Tavern, Greenwich
I ran. Tore myself free of her and ran off along the towpath, through the corrugated iron alley beside the scrapyard and past the defunct factory smoke-stacks, keeping the river to my right. On past The Yacht, too low-ceilinged and cosy to lose myself inside, to the doors of The Trafalgar, a huge gloomy building of polished brown interiors, as depressing as a church. Inside, the windows of the connecting rooms

were dominated by the gleaming grey waters beyond. Nobody moved. Even the bar staff were still. It felt like a funeral parlour. I pushed between elderly drinkers whose movements were as slow as the shifting of tectonic plates, and slipped behind a table where I could turn my seat to face the river. I thought that if I didn't move, I could remain unnoticed. In the left pocket of my jacket I still had my sketchbook. I knew it would be best to get rid of it, but didn't have the heart to throw it away, not after all the work I had done.

When I heard the muttered command behind me, I knew that my sanctuary had been invaded and that it was the beginning of the end. I sat very still as I watched the red-headed man approaching from the corner of my eye, and caught the crackle of radio headsets echoing each other around the room. I slowly raised my head and for the first time saw how different it all was now. A bare saloon bar filled with tourists, no warmth, no familiarity, no comfort.

When I was young I sat on the step – every pub seemed to have a step – with a bag of crisps and a lemonade, and sometimes I was allowed to sit inside with my dad, sipping his bitter and listening to his beery laughter, the demands for fresh drinks, the dirty jokes, the outraged giggles of the girls at his table. They would tousle my hair, pinch my skinny arms and tell me that I was adorable. Different pubs, different women, night after night, that was my real home, the home I remember. Different pubs but always the same warmth, the same smells, the same songs, the same women. Everything about them was filled with smoky mysteries and hidden pleasures, even their names, The World Turned Upside Down, The Queen's Head and Artichoke, The Rose and Crown, The Greyhound, The White Hart, all of them had secret meanings.

People go to clubs for a night out now, chrome and steel, neon lights, bottled beers, drum and bass, bouncers with headsets. The bars sport names like The Lounge and The Living Room, hoping to evoke a sense of belonging, but they cater to an alienated world, squandering noise and light on people so blinded by work that their leisure-time must be spent in aggression, screaming at each other, shovelling drugs, pushing for fights. As the red-haired man moved closer, I told myself that all I wanted to do was make people feel at home. Is that so very wrong? My real home was nothing, the memory of a damp council flat with a stinking disconnected fridge and dogshit on the floor. It's the old pubs of London that hold my childhood; the smells, the sounds, the company. There is a moment before the last bell is called when it seems it could all go on forever. It is that moment I try to capture and hold in my palm. I suppose you could call it the land before Time.

The Load Of Hay, Havistock Hill, Belsize Park
The red-haired officer wiped at his pink brow with a Kleenex until the tissue started to come apart. Another winter was approaching, and the night air was bitter. His wife used to make him wear a scarf when he was working late, and it always started him sweating. She had eventually divorced him. He dressed alone now and ate takeaway food in a tiny flat. But he wore the scarf out of habit. He looked in through the window of the pub at the laughing drinkers at the bar, and the girl sitting alone beside the slot-machine. Several of his men were in there celebrating a colleague's birthday, but he didn't feel like facing them tonight.

How the hell had they let him get away? He had drifted from them like bonfire smoke in changing wind. The Trafalgar had too many places where you could hide, he saw that now. His men had been overconfident and undertrained. They hadn't been taught how to handle anyone so devious, or if they had, they had forgotten what they had learned.

He kept one of the clear plastic ampoules in his pocket, just to remind himself of what he had faced that night. New technology had created new hospital injection techniques. You could scratch yourself with the micro-needle and barely feel a thing, if the person wielding it knew how to avoid any major nerve-endings. Then it was simply a matter of squeezing the little bulb, and any liquid contained in the ampoule was delivered through a coat, a dress, a shirt, into the flesh. Most of his victims were drunk at the time, so he had been able to connect into their bloodstreams without them noticing more than a pinprick. A deadly mixture of RoHypnol, Zimovane and some kind of coca-derivative. It numbed and relaxed them, then sent them to sleep. But the sleep deepened and stilled their hearts, as a dreamless caul slipped over their brains, shutting the senses one by one until there was nothing left alive inside.

No motives, no links, just dead strangers in the most public places in the city, watched by roving cameras, filled with witnesses. That was the trouble; you expected to see people getting legless in pubs.

His attention was drawn back to the girl sitting alone. What was she doing there? Didn't she realise the danger? No one heeded the warnings they issued. There were too many other things to worry about.

He had been on the loose for a year now, and had probably moved on to another city, where he could continue his work without harassment. He would stop as suddenly as he had begun. He'd dropped a sketchbook, but it was filled with hazy pencil drawings of pub interiors, all exactly the same, and had told them nothing. The only people who would ever really know him were the victims – and perhaps even they couldn't see behind their killer's eyes. As the urban landscape grew crazier, people's motives were harder to discern. An uprooted population, on the make and on the move. Fast, faster, fastest.

And for the briefest of moments he held the answer in his hand. He saw a glimmer of the truth – a constancy shining like a shaft through all the change, the woman alone in the smoky saloon, smiling and interested, her attention caught by just one man; this intimacy unfolding against a background warmth, the pulling of pints, the blanket of conversation, the huddle of friendship – but then it was gone, all gone, and the terrible sense of unbelonging filled his heart once more.

Christopher Fowler lives in London, and he would probably have it no other way. His retrospective collection of twenty-one short stories, *Uncut*, appeared from Warner Books in 1999, and it was followed by *Something for Your Monkey*, a collection of thirteen stories from Serpent's Tail. His latest book, *Calabash*, is a mainstream novel with fantastic undertones which moves between a 1970s seaside town and ancient Persia. It will be followed by another novel, set in present-day London, entitled *Rainy Day Boys*. '"At Home in the Pubs of Old London" follows my continuing fascination with obsessives,' explains Fowler, 'coupled with the realisation that London (Mmm ... London) pubs have probably changed less than anything else in the entire city. This makes them, in some strange way, the most "constant" feature in a fast-changing world. It's odd how pubs largely keep their clientèle through all kinds of social upheavals. I particularly recall the interior of a local pub where I grew up in Greenwich, and went back recently to find that although the furnishings had changed, it held the exact same atmosphere (smoky, raucous, friendly, same mix of people) as it had when I was seventeen. In terms of psychic geography, pubs hold key positions, and they're vanishing fast (something like five a week in London), so it's entirely logical (to me, anyway) that my lead character would feel most at home here.'

Valentia

CAITLÍN R. KIERNAN

All night tossing and turning on the flight from JFK to Shannon, interminable jet drone and the whole autumnlong night spent sailing through ice crystal clouds far above the black roil and churn of the Atlantic. Finally, the ragged west coast of Ireland appearing outside her window like a greygreen gem, uncut, unpolished, and then the plane was on the ground. Routinely suspicious glances at her passport from the customs agent, her short hair still blonde in the photograph and now it's red, auburn, and Anne was grateful when she spotted one of Morris's grad students waiting for her with a cardboard sign, DR CAMPBELL printed neatly in blue marker on brown cardboard. She dozed on the long drive down to Kerry, nodding off while the student talked and the crooked patchwork of villages and farms rolled by outside.

'It's so terrible,' the student says, has said that more than once, apologised more than once, like any of this might have been her fault somehow. Máire, pale, coal-haired girl from Dublin with her tourist brochure eyes, green eyes that never leave the road, never glance at Anne as the car rolls on south and west, the slatedark waters of Dingle Bay stretching away to the north and all the way down to the sea. Past Killorglin and there's a tall signpost, black letters on whitewashed wood, paintwhite arrow pointing the way on to Cahirciveen, still forty kilometres ahead of them and so Anne closes her eyes again.

'Do you have any idea how it happened?' she asks, and 'Ah, Christ. I'm so sorry, Dr Campbell,' the girl says, her voice like she might be close to tears and Anne doesn't ask again.

Two hours later and the blue and white car ferry from Renard Point is pulling away from the dock, ploughing across the harbour towards the big island of Valentia. Only a five-minute crossing, but the water just rough enough that Anne wishes there was a bottle of Dramamine tablets packed somewhere in the Army surplus duffel in the rental car's trunk. She stands at the railing because she figures it's more polite to puke over the side than on the decks, stands with nervous, green-eyed Máire on her left, puffyred, emerald eyes and wringing hands and *None of this feels real*, Anne thinks. *None of this feels the least bit real.* The girl is clutching a rosary now, something shiny from a sweater pocket, silver crucifix and black beads and Anne turns away, watches the horizon, the indefinite confluence of the grey island and greyer sea. The air smells like saltwater and fish and coming rain and she concentrates on the questions she's carried with her all the way from New York, unpleasant thoughts to drown her old dread of seasickness. The questions that began two days earlier with the first news of Morris Whitney's death, with Dr Randall's Sunday afternoon phone call and 'Can you come in this evening, Anne?' he said, sounding tired, sleepless, sounding like all his sixty years had finally, suddenly, caught up with him.

'It's Morris. Something's happened. There's been an accident,' but she didn't want to hear the rest, said so, made him stop there, no more until she took the subway from her TriBeCa apartment uptown to the museum. No more until she was sitting in her tiny, fifth-floor office, listening to Arthur Randall talk. Everything he knew, scant and ugly details and at first none of it seeming to add up – the phone call from the police in Cahirciveen, Morris's body hauled from the sea by a fishing boat out of Knightstown, the vandalised excavation. But Anne listened silently, the old man's shaky voice and her eyes lingering safely on the cover of a back issue of the *Journal of Vertebrate Paleontology* lying on her desk, glossy orange-and-white paper, black print, the precise line drawing of an Eocene percopsid, all safe and sensible things so she wouldn't have to see the wearysad look on Arthur's face.

'Do you have any idea what he was doing out there after dark?' she asks, almost a whisper, and Máire turns her head slightly, her eyes still on the rosary in her hands and 'No,' the girl says. 'None of us do.'

Anne glances back at the mainland, growing smaller as the little ferry chugs diligently across the harbour and she knows now that she shouldn't have come, that Arthur was right and there are probably no more answers here than would have found her in Manhattan. Not if this skittish girl at her side is any indication, and something else, besides, a quiet anxiety beneath the leadweight ache of her loss, beneath the disorientation. A vague unease as the shores of Valentia grow nearer; *He would have come for you*, she thinks, and then Máire is talking again.

'Dr Whitney had us back in Knightstown, you know. Me and Billy both. He said he was worried about whether or not the grants would be renewed. Said he needed the solitude to write at night, to work on the progress report for the *National Geographic* people, but we knew he was havin' bad dreams.'

'So you weren't at the field house Friday night?' and Máire shakes her head, no, 'This last week, we've been riding out on our bicycles every mornin', an' ridin' back again in the evenings. It's only half an hour, maybe.'

And then the ferry whistle blows, shrill and steamthroat bellow to smother whatever Máire said next, and the girl slips the rosary back into the pocket of her sweater.

Valentia Island, seven miles by three, rocky exile cut off from the Irish mainland long ago by the restless Atlantic and the thin, encircling finger of the Portmagee Channel. Sheep and cattle and a century ago strong men mined slate from a huge quarry near the island's northeast corner, mined stone for roofing tiles in London and railroad pavement in Nottingham and Leicester. A small but sturdy white lighthouse where Valentia Harbour meets the ocean proper, once upon a time a fortress for Cromwell's men and its beacon automated years ago. Further west, the land rises abruptly to Reenadrolaun Point more than a hundred feet above the sea, rocky precipice where the rollers have carved away the world, and from there the raw charcoal and ash periphery of the island stretches from Fogher Cliff to Beennakryraka Head. And on these weathered ledges Morris Whitney found the 'Culloo trackway' in 1992; two months in Ireland on an NSF grant to study a poorly curated, but valuable collection of Devonian lobe-finned and placoderm fishes at the Cork Geology Museum and led away to Valentia by persistent rumours of footprints in stone. A local farmer's stories of 'dinosaur tracks' and then a letter to the curator of the museum from a bird-watchers' club, and so he finally took a day off and made the drive from Cork. And not believing his eyes when the old man led him across a pasture to the ledges, gap-toothed pride at the expression on the palaeontologist's astonished face when he saw the perfect, single trail, winding across the slate towards the sea.

'Didn't I tell you? Are they not dinosaurs, then?' the old man asked and Morris could only shake his head, his grin almost as wide as the old man's, clambering down to get a better look as the waves slammed loud against the rocks.

'No, Mr O'Shea, these are definitely *not* dinosaur tracks. Whatever made these tracks lived . . .' and he paused, doing the maths in his head, calculating the age of rocks and the duration of geological periods. 'Whatever made them was walking around a hundred and fifty million years before the first dinosaurs. These are something much, much *better* than dinosaur tracks.' The old man's eyes wide and doubtful, then, and he sat down on the grass and dangled his short legs over the edge of the little cliff.

'Ah,' he said, 'well, now that *is* a bloody wonder, wouldn't ye say?'

And Morris on his knees, a cheap, black plastic Instamatic camera from his backpack and he was staring at the fossils though the viewfinder. 'Yes sir, it is. It certainly is that,' and he snapped away a whole roll of film before following the old man back across the field.

Two hours after dawn and Anne Campbell, jetlagged and shivering in the October gales, stands beside the tracks, a single bedding plane exposed along the thirty-foot ledge, narrow, almost horizontal rind of bare stone to mark this place where the island is slowly being reclaimed by the Atlantic. Overhead gulls and kittiwakes wheel and cry like lost and hungry children. Behind her, Máire is still talking to the constable, redcheeked, potbellied man who escorted them from Kingstown; they speak in hushed voices, as if they're saying things they don't want Anne to hear.

There are still traces of Morris's chalk marks, despite the tides and salt spray, despite everything his killers did to the site. White chalk lines to measure the width of manual and pedal strides, faint reference numbers for his photographs; another day or two and the sea will have swept the ledge clean again. Tears in her eyes and she isn't sure how much of that's for Morris, how much for the ruined treasures, and how much is merely the stinging, icy fingers of the wind.

Over a hundred tracks to begin with, according to Morris's notes, a hundred already exposed when he first saw the ledge and another fifty or sixty uncovered as he and Máire and Billy followed the prints back into the cliff's face, sledges and pry bars to clear away the heavy blocks of Valentia Slate. And now only five or six that haven't been damaged or obliterated altogether. *Desecrated*, Anne thinks, *This place has been desecrated*. As surely as any church that was ever burned or any shrine that was ever looted, and she sits down beside one of the few tracks that hasn't been chipped or scraped or smashed beyond recognition. The gently rippled surface of the rock shimmers faintly, glitterdull interplay of mica crystals and the sun, and she puts her fingers into the shallow depression on the ledge, touches the clear imprint left by something that passed this way three hundred and eighty-five million years ago. She looks up, past the trackway, at the rest of the ledge; patches of algal scum the unhealthy colour of an infection and small accumulations of brown sand, bright against the slate, a few stingy pools of water stranded in the low places, waiting for the next high tide.

'He got everythin' on film,' Máire says behind her, trying to sound reassuring, trying to sound responsible. 'And we have the casts. Dr Whitney sent a set of them off to Cork just last week, and another to the Survey in Dublin.'

'I want to see the photographs, Máire. Everything that's been developed. As soon as possible, okay?'

'Aye,' the girl says. 'They're all back in town. It didn't seem safe to leave anythin' in the field house.' And 'No,' Anne says, as much to herself as Máire, 'No, I guess not.' And then Máire's talking with the constable again and Anne stares past the ledge at the wide, cold ocean.

Her room in Kingstown, dingy plaster walls and faded Catholic icons, the oilyfaint smell of fish, but some place warm and dry against the rain that started falling an hour after sunset. Cold drops that pepper the windowpane and she sat there for a while, waiting for Dr Randall to return her call, stared down at the drenched and narrow streets, a pub across from the hotel and its windows glowing yelloworange through the downpour, soft and welcoming glow and she wished she'd asked Máire to stay. She could have thought of an excuse if she tried, help with Morris's records, questions about the sediment samples sent to Dublin for radiometric tests, anything against the sound of the storm and her loneliness. But the girl made her uncomfortable, nothing she could quite put her finger on, and on the way back from the site Máire leaned close and asked if it was true, that Anne and Morris were lovers, whispered question so Constable Bryce wouldn't overhear. Anne blushed, confused, embarrassed, and 'That was a long time ago,' she replied, nothing else, though, her surprise turning quick to anger and unasked questions about what this girl might know about her, what she might *think* she knew.

So relief when the phone rang, the voice at the other end sounding far away, distance-strained, cablefiltered, but relief anyway. The familiarity something to push away her homesickness for a few minutes, at least, and Arthur Randall asked if she was okay, if she was holding up, and 'Yeah,' she said, 'Sure,' unconvincing lie and he sighed loud; she could hear him lighting a cigarette, exhaling, before he asked her about the trackway, if there was anything at all that might be salvaged.

'Only if it's still buried. You absolutely would not believe this shit, Arthur. I've never seen a site so completely . . . so . . .' and that word from the ledge coming back to her again . . . *so completely desecrated*, but nothing she wanted to say aloud so 'They trashed everything,' she said instead, and 'It just doesn't make sense.'

'Then you *don't* think it was someone after the tracks?'

'No. If this was someone trying to steal fossils, it's the most fucked-up attempt I could imagine. And there's no sign they actually tried to remove anything. Whoever it was, they wanted to *erase* the tracks, Arthur, not steal them.'

And now she sits on her bed listening to the rain on the roof, the rain at the window, and all Morris's photographs are spread out in front of her, glossy $8'' \times 10''$ document of his month on Valentia, every inch of the trackway painstakingly recorded, these photos to back up Máire's maps and diagrams of the ledge, carefully gridded sketches recording the relative position and size of every footprint. And so at least the data has been saved, the fossils themselves gone but not the information. Enough that she can finish what he began, a description of the oldest-known tetrapod ichnofossils, the earliest evidence of the ancestors of all terrestrial vertebrates. Something a little more than a metre in length, no longer fish, but not quite yet amphibian, either.

Anne puts down one of the photographs and picks up another, no tracks in this shot, the fossilised ripple marks from the bed of an ancient stream and for a moment she thinks that's all. Silt and sand shaped by the currents of warm Paleozoic waters and that pattern frozen here for almost four hundred thousand millennia and she's about to put this picture down, too, when she notices something small in the lower, lefthand corner. Something embedded in the slate, glinting in the sun like metal, and she holds it under the lamp beside her bed for a better look.

And her first impression is that Morris has placed an unfamiliar coin in the shot for scale, one of the seven-sided Irish fifty-pence pieces, maybe. She leans closer to the photograph, squints, her nose almost touching the paper now, and she can see that the surface of the thing is smooth, so no coin, and there's no doubt that it's actually embedded in the stone, not merely lying on the surface. She chews at her bottom lip, turns the print upside down and at this angle she can see that it isn't perfectly smooth after all, faintest suggestion of a raised pattern on its surface, ridges and dimples worn almost away by years of exposure to the wind and sea. A crinoid plate perhaps, broken away from the calyx, or some other echinoderm fossil, only a heptagonal bit of silica and a trick of light and shadow to make it look metallic.

No, not a crinoid, she thinks, *Not a crinoid or a cystoid, not a plate from* unclouded sky, no clouds but there is thunder anyway, just as there was Morris Whitney's voice without his body. And she's scared for the first time, wants to wake up now, because there's something moving about in the ferns on the other side of the stream, something huge, and the sound that isn't really thunder from the sky again, the sound like a tear in the sky and it's raining but it isn't water that falls, and Anne shuts her eyes tight, no ruby slipper heels to click so she repeats Morris's name, again and again, while the scalding filth drips down to blister her face and pool red and steaming at her feet.

Morning and the storms have passed, blown away south to Bantry and Skibbereen, the Celtic Sea beyond, and the sky is perfect blue as Anne makes her way back to the cliffs alone. A rusty purple bicycle borrowed from the hotel's cook and she follows the winding road north through the Glanleam woods, on past the lighthouse and then takes a narrower road west, little more than a footpath for sheep, really, past the steep rise of Reenadrolaun and down to Culloo. The sea air chilly on her face, on her hands, and her legs aching by the time she reaches the site.

She sees the girl standing by the cliffs long before she's close enough to recognise it's Máire, tousled black hair and one of her heavy wool cardigans and she's staring out at the foamwhite rollers, something dark in her right hand and Anne stops, lowers the bike's kickstand and walks the last ten or twenty yards. But if Máire hears her, she makes no sign that she's heard, stands very still, watching the uneasy, storm-scarred sea.

'Máire?' Anne calls out, 'Hello. I didn't expect to find you out here,' and the girl turns slowly, moves stiff and slow like someone half asleep and Anne thinks that maybe she's been crying, the red around her eyes, wet green eyes and bruisedark circles underneath like she hasn't slept in awhile. 'I want to ask you a question, about one of the photographs. I have it with . . .'

And then Anne can see exactly what she's holding, the small, black handgun, and Máire smiles for her.

'Good morning, Dr Campbell.'

A moment before she can reply, two heartbeats before she can even look away from the revolver, the sun dull off its stubby chrome barrel, and 'Good morning, Máire,' she finally says. Her mouth is dry and the words come out small and flat.

'Did ye sleep well, then?' the girl asks and Anne nods her head and Máire turns back towards the ledge, back towards the sea. 'I was afraid you might have bad dreams,' she says, 'After lookin' at those pictures.'

'What is it, Máire, the disc in the photograph? You know what it is, don't you?' and Anne takes one step closer to the girl, one step closer to the point where the sod ends and the grey stone begins.

'I didn't kill him,' the girl says. 'I want ye to *know* that. I didn't do it, and neither did Billy.' Her finger tight and trembling around the trigger now and Anne is only a few feet away, only two or three more steps between them and 'It's bad enough, what we've done. But it wasn't murder.'

'You're going to have to tell me what you're talking about,' Anne says, afraid to move, afraid to stand still, and the girl turns towards her again.

'You weren't meant to see the pictures, Dr Campbell. I was supposed to burn them. After we'd done with the tracks, we were supposed to burn everything.'

Fresh tears from the girl's bright eyes and Anne can see where she's chewed her lower lip raw, fresh blood on her pale chin and Anne takes another step towards her.

'Why were you supposed to burn the pictures? Did Morris tell you to burn the pictures, Máire?'

A blank, puzzled expression on the girl's face then, her ragged smile gone for a moment before she shakes her head, rubs the barrel of the gun rough against her corduroy pants. And then she says something that Anne doesn't understand, something that sounds like 'Theena dow'an,' and 'I don't know Irish,' Anne says, pleading now, wanting to understand and she can see the hurt and anger in Máire's eyes, the bottomless guilt growing there like a cancer. The girl raises the revolver and sets the barrel against her right temple.

'Oh God, please Máire,' and the girl says it again, 'Theena dow'an,' and she turns back towards the sea at the same instant she squeezes the trigger and the sound the gun makes is the sound from Anne Campbell's nightmare, the sound of the sky ripping itself apart, the sound of the waves breaking against the shore.

'In the west there is still a tradition of the Fomorii who dwelt in Ireland before the arrival of the Gael. They are perhaps the most feared of all the water fairies and are sometimes known as the *Daoine Domhain*, the Deep Ones, though they are rarely spoken of aloud.'

– Lady Wilde, *Ancient Legends of Ireland* (1888)

Caítlin R. Kiernan lives in Birmingham, Alabama. Trained as a palaeontologist, she didn't begin writing fiction until 1992. Since then, her short stories have appeared in numerous anthologies, including *Dark Terrors 2* and *3*, *The Year's Best Fantasy and Horror Eleventh Annual Collection*, and *The Mammoth Book of Best New Horror Volume Nine* and *Ten*. Her debut novel, *Silk*, received both The International Horror Guild and Barnes & Noble Maiden Voyage Awards for best first novel of 1998. More recently, two collections of her short fiction have been released – *Tales of Pain and Wonder* from Gauntlet Press, and *From Weird and Distant Shores* from Michael Matthews Press. '"Valentia" was written in July 1999,' the author reveals, 'immediately after a visit to the American Museum of Natural History to examine mosasaur fossils (mosasaurs are a group of large marine lizards which became extinct about sixty-five million years ago), and is the sort of story that usually results when I'm in the process of "shifting gears" from my palaeontological studies to fiction writing. The Devonian tetrapod tracks described in the story are real, discovered at Valentia Island in 1992 by the Swiss geologist Ivan Stossel. However, in "Valentia" I have relocated them to Culloo. As of this writing, the Geological Survey of Ireland is in the process of acquiring the actual site so that its fossils may be preserved and protected from looters.'

Barking Sands

RICHARD CHRISTIAN MATHESON

On vacation.
 Hawaii. Where fat, brown people treat flowers like Jesus.
 All us.
 Mommy. Daddy. Grampa Don.
 My brother who came out of Mommy with less brain than a cat. He smiles at everything. I call him Kitty. Daddy thinks it's funny. Kitty can only open his mouth and stare and shake. Like there's a maraca inside him.
 We rented a Toyota Tercel.
 'Cheapest car worth dog-fuck.' That's Grampa Don talking. Mommy hates it when he says dirty stuff. But he's always drinking beer. Loses track of where his tongue is pointing and just says it. Grampa Don's always making trouble.
 We're on our way to Barking Sands.
 It's a beach on the southern tip of Kauai. The sand barks there. Big, bald-headed dunes of it chirping and growling like someone is poking it while it sleeps. The wind does it; like a ventriloquist using the grains of sand as its dummy. It's a very sacred place. They say the ancient tribes are still living on the cliffs way above Barking Sands. I say that inside the Tercel while it bounces over the muddy road. The mud is red and splashes the car so it looks like it has scrapes that are bleeding. Like when Kitty falls down and cries and I just stand and watch him and hope he bleeds to death.
 'There's no tribes still living,' says Mommy, eating an ice cream cone I couldn't finish, making sure it doesn't drip on the upholstery.
 Her tongue moves around it like a red bus going up a twisty road. Daddy breathes in the air and says it hasn't smelled like this in Los Angeles since cave men went to work in three-piece fur suits.
 Grampa Don spits out the window, and the car hops and rocks, having a spaz attack. The Kauai roads feel like the moon. There's no

one going out to Barking Sands but us. It's getting late and the road is lonely.

It is the moon. Just on earth.

The sky will be dead soon. I feel a little afraid but for no reason.

Kitty looks at me and smiles but sees my face and starts to cry. If I had a knife I'd slash his throat. I imagine his dead body lying face-up, in the casket, suddenly awake. Screaming and trying to get out but making no sound. Muted by the birth defect that gave him a busted speaker. I feel bad for him down there, trapped forever under the earth, stuck in his box, screaming. But he'll never do anything with his life anyway.

Maybe it's better to know where he is.

Grampa Don just cut one and all four windows are cranked down. A sweet and sour old-man cloud is sucked out. The blue ocean is starting to seem like a choking face. We're far from the hotel where we're staying and I hate Hawaii. Being here with them.

Last night we went to a Luau and I stared at the pig on the long table. He looked alive. But his eyes didn't move and as I tried to figure out what he was thinking, a big smiling man, in a white apron, cut into the pig with a shiny knife and slid a section of the pig's body right out, like one of those wooden ball puzzles that's made of different sections of wood.

He dropped it on my plate and the pig kept staring forward, unable to fight back. The man motioned me to move on with his bloody knife, and began to cut the pig into more pieces, erasing him.

I looked down at the piece of the pig and felt like throwing up.

Later I brought the piece back and tried to put it where it had been on his body; reattaching his flesh. But by then, he was just bones and a head. The eyes were still facing forward and I pet him a little, seeing my own value as no higher than his, and hating people for what they'd done to him.

Then, Daddy came and dragged me through a bunch of tourists with greasy mouths, lining up to watch the torches and grass skirts. I looked back to see the pig being taken away, its bones passing above the crowd, on a tray, like some terrible crown.

'Barking Sands.' Mommy is pointing.

Grampa Don is already out of the car and looking for a place to dump garbage. But there isn't one and he tosses it on the ground saying it will just rot and become a hotel lobby, over time, with enough rain and 'fucking tourist money'.

He says all the dinosaur bones grew into roads and rental cars after millions of years. He's had four cans of beer since we left the Coco

Palms Hotel, where we're staying, and he's unzipped and hosing down a tree-trunk.

His ancient nozzle sprays Corona on everything like some poison Daddy uses back in Los Angeles. to make snails' heads explode.

Kitty points to a sign that says this is a holy burial ground. He likes words; their shape, worming together to form meaning he doesn't understand. Grampa reads the sign and keeps sprinkling snail napalm like a punctured can.

'This place is too fucking humid.' Grampa Don is wiping his head, like those guys at the 76 station chiselling bugs off the windshield.

Daddy takes pictures even though the sign says no photography 'cause it's a holy place and I guess that's bad. Daddy doesn't care. Mommy smiles and poses under the big cliffs that go up and up and up. Her dress looks like it belongs in a vase. Kitty is crawling on the sand, chasing our footprints like a rabid bloodhound that needs to be shot in the head. I wish I could get away from them all.

It's very windy and sand blows, sticking us with pins you can't see. I cover my eyes and we all lean into the wind. Mommy says we look like arctic explorers going up a snow slope. She wants a happy family. But we aren't.

I hate these trips. Being together.

Grampa Don takes Kitty's hand. Daddy takes Mommy's. A storm fills the sky with black sponges.

Grampa Don lags behind and we all get to the Toyota. It's starting to rain. Daddy starts the car and the mud is turning into dirty, orange glue that grabs our wheels. They spin.

'Zzzzzzzzzzz.' Kitty sounds like a trapped tyre.

The car is a mad dog chained to a tree. Thunder shakes us. Lightning cuts up the sky. Something is wrong. The sky is not happy or pretty any more. The air smells like dead things and angry wind makes all the plants and flowers look like they're bending over to get sick.

There is warm fog. I can't see the ocean any more. It crashes, attacking.

'What's the fuckin' problem?' yells Grampa Don.

Mommy tells him not to talk like that and he curses at her. Daddy tells him to leave her alone. They start to argue.

I hate their guts.

Grampa Don rolls down his window to look at the tyres. I notice something moving through the high sugarcane. He says he hates it here and yells at the mud and the sky and the big sand dunes that bark like wild dogs surrounding helpless animals.

The car tries harder to move. Grampa Don is getting all wet. Mommy tells him to close the window and suddenly he makes a weird noise. An arrow with red feathers is sticking through his neck, sideways. He turns and I see the sharp tip dripping blood on his tanktop. There is mud and blood on his face. He can't breathe. There are wet bubbles in his neck.

Mommy screams.

I see feathers moving through sugarcane. Blue ones. Yellow ones. I see brown skin. Hands, eyes.

Grampa Don tries to scream and blood comes out of his mouth and sprays on everything. Kitty thinks Grampa Don is being funny and laughs, but makes no sound. Daddy screams at him to shut up and Kitty starts to cry. His face turns bright red.

Feathers.

We did something wrong. Something bad.

I am scared as they hide in the sugarcane. I know I'll be dead in another minute. I know I can't escape in this mud and rain. I look at my family. Mommy tries to help Grampa Don and Daddy keeps flooring the gas, too stupid to realise it doesn't help. I say nothing as they ask me to help. I do nothing.

I hate them.

An old man and two people who just argue all the time. A retard brother someone should've cut into little pieces a long time ago.

The car is stuck. No matter what Daddy does. More arrows break the glass. We are bloody. We are dying. Rain is pounding harder, pinning us to the mud, and the tyres bury us deeper, spinning.

Digging us a grave.

As my family screams, I close my eyes and listen to the sand.

Richard Christian Matheson lives in Malibu, California, and he is the son of veteran science fiction writer Richard Matheson. A novelist, short story writer and screenwriter/producer, he has scripted and executive produced more than five hundred episodes of prime-time network TV and was the youngest writer ever put under contract by Universal Studios. His critically acclaimed début novel *Created By* was published in 1993, and his short, sharp fiction has been collected in *Scars and Other Distinguishing Marks* and, more recently, *Dystopia*, published by Gauntlet Press. His 35mm short film, *Arousal*, which he wrote and directed from his own story, was previewed at the 2000 World Horror Convention in Denver, Colorado, and he has recently scripted a four-hour mini-series based on Dean Koontz's bestseller *Sole Survivor*. About his story in this volume, Matheson says: 'There are places untied from time. Ghostly cities, ancient cathedrals. Places in serene recess, where centuries drift unnoticed. And there are places more precious; rarest of all. Places that bear no sign of man's signature, existing within their own exquisite privacy. When I first saw "Barking Sands" beach I was overcome by its beauty: endless, unearthly dunes, misted by miles of primordial waves; somehow dreamlike. It was said the dunes barked; an anomaly of wind which allowed voice. I found it spiritual, oddly troubling. I walked the vastness, listening carefully, imagining what the sand might be saying; if it were invitation or warning. As with all things seductive, there were two answers.'

Everything, in All the Wrong Order

CHAZ BRENCHLEY

There's this disease I heard about, drinking with medics one time, where things get so turned around inside that you end up vomiting your own shit.

Think about that, and bear with me. It's a metaphor, okay? What actually happened was this:

I let him go first up the ladder. I'd thought about that, there were advantages and drawbacks either way, but in the end I waved him up ahead of me. And followed close behind, hard on his heels so that he was barely through the trap before I was following, the bulking shadows of the attic space and my own bulk, my own closeness together serving to disguise and distract him so that he saw nothing, he didn't even ask a question before I was up and the trap was down and I was standing on it.

Then, only then did I lighten his darkness by tugging on the string that lit the lamp behind me; then, only then did he understand.

One of those creaking, angular shadows that had made no sense in the half-dark was his sister. Still kicking, though not swinging much now: twisting rather, this way and that, like a slow clock running down. Her face was purple, and every ligament in her neck stood out against the rope that was taking its time in choking her. Her mouth was stretched wide, gagged by silence.

He was quick, I'll give him that, but I'd always known he would be. He looked, he saw; he twisted himself, faster than his sister, and his hand already had a knife in it. He was uncertain, though, whether to save her life or take mine. Indecision can be lethal, I've seen that time and again; and told him so, told them both, but of course they did not listen. They were children, what did they know of decisions?

I was ready for him, in any case. I kicked him in the testicles; even on a twelve-year-old, that has its stopping power. As he doubled over, I hooked his legs from under him and then stamped on his head.

After that I could take my time in binding his hands behind his back, slipping the ready noose over his head and hauling him up to hang beside his little sister.

I'd introduced myself to the family the year before. Just one short year, summer to high summer, so many dreams I had, all gone to spoil in a single afternoon.

I slipped my way quietly, indirectly, into their consciousness, so delicate a touch that at first it left no mark of mine, no aluminium oxide dusting could have found me out. Plausible deniability, a cynic I suppose would say. I say that it's wisdom to be cautious, to step lightly, to let nothing show that might have stayed hidden; I say that events have borne me out in this. It's always easiest to withdraw early, to leave nothing behind but the fading memory of a sour note. So I was taught, so I have found to be true; so I hope to teach to others eventually. I wasn't given the time this year, alas.

And it had started so well, all the signs were there and I was feeling so pleased with myself and with my targets. Two little children, ten and eleven years old, as I'd discovered, new to the area and thrilling to the possibilities of life, on the verge of great change, great discoveries: they came out of their house one bright morning to find the family cat busy in the garden, licking at what must at first have seemed to be a rag of ancient fur, some discarded tippet.

They came closer and discovered just how wrong they'd been. The thing was quite fresh, wet with blood, gobbets of dark flesh still clinging. After a while they shooed the cat away – no easy task, it was persistent and possessive of its treasure – to crouch themselves in its place and look over what they had. Perhaps they'd been thinking squirrel, thinking this a trophy hunted down and dragged in from the park. Wrong again.

Eventually, at last they will have seen it for what it was, the skin of a skinned little dog, a Yorkshire terrier. No sign of the flayed corpse, they will have seen, only the hide: and that like a message, pegged out on their lawn.

It was a message, and it did its work. They spent five minutes or more just looking, touching, talking, before the girl went with consent to fetch their mother, to show and share this interesting thing.

While she was gone, the boy touched bloody finger to pale lips and curious tongue behind; I knew then that I had him, and that in him I had them both.

That was what I thought I knew, at least; it was all I thought I needed.

The next night, the boy was awakened unexpectedly, perhaps by the strangeness of the light that was falling on his face. He'd left his window ajar as was his habit, but had pulled the curtains hard against the night; now they were drawn back, and something that was not the moon flickered and faded beyond the glass.

It may have taken him a minute, five minutes, even half an hour to find the courage he needed to get out of bed. A boy who likes the daylight, exposure, revelation – such a boy might well allow himself the luxury of fear unobserved.

Eventually, though, curiosity won as it had to; there at least I had not been wrong. He pressed his face tight against the window, and saw an old-fashioned lantern hanging from a branch of the cherry tree that grew in the garden, whose reaching leaves hung just a foot or two short of the house. They must have obscured his view at least a little, but still he will have been able to see the nightlight that burned in the lantern's base, and that something obscure hung above its steady flame. He may have seen movement within the lantern's glass; he may have heard a faint buzzing; he may even have smelled the faint scorching of rank meat.

After a while, there were two faces; he had fetched his sister. Perhaps at her urging, he opened his window wide and they both leaned out as far as they could, as far as they dared. The lantern was beyond their reach, though, and the twigs of the tree offered no support to a climber. At last he closed his curtains, and they both went back to bed.

In the morning, when they looked, they saw nothing in the tree. Neither the night that followed, when they looked again. On the lawn, though, at some distance from the house, a ring of faint light must have caught their eyes, where the lantern hung from a pole set in the grass.

The night after that, there was a figure sitting below the pole.

Attentive children know when they are being summoned; the hopeful, the self-aware respond.

They came down in dressing-gowns and slippers, stepping lightly and breathing hard, holding hands against the mischief and moment of the night. I greeted them with a glance and a nod, before turning my attention back to what I held in my hands.

'What are you doing?' It was the girl who stole the privilege of asking; her brother seemed not to resent it, despite his being the elder.

'Waiting for you.'

'No,' she knew that already, 'I mean, what are you *doing*?'

'Ah.' I peeled my fingers back to show her, to show them both. 'I'm just pulling the wings off this fly, with these tweezers here, to see if it hurts.'

'Does it?' the boy asked in a whisper, as though it were an experiment he'd thought about but had never quite brought himself to the point of making on his own account. Likely it was. Good boys are not wanton.

'Oh, no.' I favoured him with a broad smile. 'It doesn't hurt at all. Want to try?'

A gesture brought their eyes up to the lantern, only a short time before they must have checked it out for themselves; the noise and the smell were both invasive, on that still summer night. It was more than a beacon, set to attract moth-children to its light. I was using it as a vivarium also, breeding a mass of bluebottles in the nightlight's heat, feeding them on what remained of the Yorkie as it ripened.

Some few of the flies escaped from the children's unaccustomed snatchings when I unlatched the lantern's door and swung it open, but there were plenty to spare. The girl squealed in triumph as she snared one; the boy echoed her a moment later.

Neither one needed to borrow my tweezers, their fingers were small and nimble enough for the task. Wings and legs, taken one by one, afforded some little satisfaction but deliberately not enough; their eyes strayed back to the reeking dangle of the dog's body. I smiled, and opened the door again to blow out the little flame.

'Go back now. I will see you another time.'

I let them wait, let them watch in vain for almost a week before my lantern drew them out again. This time I had a rat splayed out on the ground before me, belly-up, its legs pinioned with wire hoops and its tail threshing. Not a street-rat, I'd bought it in a pet shop: white of fur, pink of eye, quivering of whisker.

I showed them a scalpel, wouldn't let them touch either the blade or the rat, not yet; learning is a process, a progress, step by careful step.

Slowly, carefully, I made my incision through fur and skin and into the belly of the beast. Then, with another length of wire bent like a crochet-hook, I began to pull out its intestines and lay them around the creature on the grass.

'You see?' I said, my voice soft but pitched to carry above its agonised screaming. 'It really doesn't hurt at all . . .'

Neither did it. I passed my hook to the boy, and he dabbled and tugged and felt no pain. The girl was a little hesitant, thinking perhaps she might prefer just to watch; I said I had saved the best, the last of it for her. Guided her hand on the little hook, in and twist and draw slowly, slowly: the rat's heart came out amid a tracery of arteries and veins and for a moment, for a brief sweet moment it was beating still as I laid it in her palm.

I never asked them questions, that was not my role, but I did wonder what they thought they had seen, what they expected to find when they came out to join me the first night. Some ancient wild man, I imagine, half seer and half tramp, bearded and elflocked, smelling strangely and speaking of wonders, no doubt, the mystic power of blood and sacrifice.

Not me, at any rate, they cannot have expected me. A young man clean-shaven and smartly dressed, saying little and telling less, mostly showing. Showing and again showing, trying to batter the lesson home by endless repetition: *here is pain, feel its tug; and look, it cannot hurt you, do you see?*

I was, I suppose, just old enough to be their father, though he was older. I was old enough to befriend him, at least, and their mother also; and so I gained the parents' trust where I had the children's already, secretly locked between my fingers. I never let the two intermingle, was never seen in public with the children and barely spoke to them under their parents' eyes. Our private understandings were a thing apart, held separate for safety's sake. I'd warned them not to know me, when we met; they took that to extremes, of course, as children do. They made a game of ignoring me, which I encouraged: *learn through play* I might have told them over and over but did not, never felt the need.

They did that in any case, only not fast enough, or else it was too fast. And so we'd come to this, where I sat on an upturned tea-chest and watched the boy dangle, listened to him strangle and murmured my mantra at him one more time. It was wasted breath, of course, but I had it to waste, which he did not; and it's the first, the last, the only lesson worth the learning, the heart of all teaching. And so I tried once more to drum it into his head, to have him understand that pain is and must be divisible, distributed at will.

'This is hurting you much more than it's hurting me,' I said, seeing how blood sprayed from his torn scalp as he writhed and wrenched against the rope. 'In fact, it's not hurting me at all. Every man is an island, lad: alone, cut off, remote. Aye, and every child too. That's what you've forgotten all this time, playing games with your sister. My fault, I admit it, but it's you that have to suffer for it. That's the division, that's where pain draws the line. I'm here, she's here' – or she had been; I thought she'd gone by now, though certainly she'd taken her time about it, almost too light to choke and I was no poor man's friend to pull down on her feet and make it easy – 'but come right down to it, you're still and always on your own.'

Pain is divisible, and I felt none of it – only frustration, and only at myself. The blame lay clearly with me, that this delight was spoiled. There could, there should have been years of my slow sculpting, bending tender spirits to a new shape, training fingers and minds to a new sensitivity; instead I'd let them slip out of my control, and we all had to pay the separate penalties for my inattention.

Mine was the lightest, by a distance. There would be no consequences to me, from any of what I did that day. I was known only as a casual acquaintance of the parents, worth one interview perhaps, but nothing more than that. The house we were in was isolated, and had long stood empty; it had been I who found it and I who introduced the children to it, as a more private place to play than their garden and easy of access day or night, but I'd worn gloves from the first day that we'd broken in. To them it had been part of my mystique, they hadn't thought to look further. Their own prints would be everywhere, but not mine.

Their parents would grieve, of course, and suffer with it, not knowing that pain is divisible, hurt can be apportioned. It's impossible to teach the old. Give me a ripening child, and I will give you – well, an adult like me. Growth must be guided, from the appropriate age. The right lessons in the right order, that's what counts. I can show them wonders, one by one. I can make a wonder of them.

Give me a child – but no, don't give me two. Therein lay my error, I took on too much without knowing. I have learned, now, and they have paid the price. I took the payment, of course, and enjoyed it, yes; but still my mind makes metaphors of shit and vomiting, which feel apt to me. I had taken these children and trained them to be what they became; they went too far too quickly, they got ahead of themselves and ahead of me, and so it was my task to expel them. That I could do it as I did was a gesture, a generosity of fate, but the overriding feeling was pure disappointment.

I'm hardly the first of us to do this. My own mentor told me that he had several discards before he came to me; no doubt he had others after, I wouldn't know. We don't keep in touch. The thought that he might have discarded me too if I'd been a weaker pupil, or a greedier – that lingers sometimes, a tickling abstraction in my head.

These two were greedy, but only I think because they were two, and siblings. Inevitably they were rivals, they competed. Even in front of me. I'd seen them jealous, I'd seen them egg each other on. I hadn't seen the worst of it, that much was clear now.

I sat and watched until the boy was entirely still, until his blood had ceased to drip. Then – satisfied but unfulfilled, a curious sensation that I'd thought I'd long outgrown – I lifted the hatch and lowered my feet to the ladder, wondering as I left them how long it would be before they were found, whether there would be time for other fluids to drip and dribble, to soak through the boards and stain the plaster beneath, some sign to mark my failure.

I closed the hatch and took the ladder with me, to delay their discovery perhaps a little longer, give the juices perhaps a little chance to flow. I felt that I deserved that sign, I'd earned it.

As I made my way out through the kitchen, I passed what they had left for me on the flagged floor there, what they'd been so eager to show me that afternoon: what had changed all my plans for the day and for their lives, what had led me to take them one by one into the attic and leave them dangling, caught short and out of order, all unfinished.

It was a boy, they'd said, five or six years old and wandering alone, adrift. They'd inveigled him with sweets and promises, the kinds of gift I'd never offered them; they'd held his hand and brought him to the house, to a game they'd played for hours before I'd come in search.

Hard to be certain what it was or had been, that wet mess on the stones. Meat and bone, so much was evident; and there were clothes heaped in a corner, the unfastidious might – must, eventually – pick those over and label him a boy. Whoever that task fell to, I hoped they had the stomach for it. There was other matter that had been tossed there too: skin, largely. Skin and hair, from an inept vivisection.

The body's major organs were laid out beside the faceless corpse, though not in any order. I'd have thought the children better trained than that, but they'd been wild, ecstatic, long past caring. And drenched in blood, and heedless of that too. Careful as I'd been, I'd have to destroy what I was wearing; I could smell this slaughter on me.

Wearily, sorrowfully, I stepped around the body and let myself out of the house, wondering just how long he'd taken in his dying, and glad for once – for the first time ever – not to have been there to see it done. Pain is divisible, and his had been witnessed, not wasted; all the waste had been going on around him.

Chaz Brenchley lives in Newcastle upon Tyne with two cats and a famous teddy bear. He has made his living as a writer since he was eighteen, and this year marks his twenty-third anniversary in the job. A recipient of the British Fantasy Award, he is the author of nine thrillers, most recently *Shelter*, plus a major new fantasy series, 'The Books of Outremer', based on the world of the Crusades. He has also published three fantasy books for children and more than 500 short stories in various genres. His time as Crimewriter-in-Residence at the St Peter's Riverside Sculpture Project in Sunderland resulted in the collection *Blood Waters*, and he is presently writer-in-residence at Northumbria University. Brenchley's novel *Dead of Light* is currently in development with a film company. 'I was saving the title "Everything, in All the Wrong Order" for my autobiography,' says the author, 'before it dawned on me that I had no intention of writing an autobiography, even if anyone had been interested in reading it; at which point, of course, the title was free for general use. It only took about five minutes thereafter to realise that there was a story inherent within it, that had just been waiting for me to drop the possessiveness and the preconceptions and actually think about what it was saying.'

Savannah is Six

JAMES VAN PELT

For as long as Poul could remember, he'd spent the summer at the lake where his brother drowned.

This year, as they climbed in the van, Leesa said cryptically, 'Savannah is Six.'

Poul held his hand on the ignition key but didn't turn it. 'I know.'

Each year since Savannah was born, it got harder to come out. The nightmares started earlier, grew more vivid, woke him with a scream choked down, a huge hurting lump he swallowed without voicing. Poul took longer to pack the van; he delayed the day he left, and when he finally started, he drove below the speed limit.

They pulled into the long, sloping driveway down to the cottage just after noon. Leesa had slept the last hour and Savannah coloured in the back seat, surrounded by baggage and groceries. Her head was down, very serious, turning a white sky into a blue one. She always struck Poul as a sombre child, for six, as if there was something sad in her life that returned to her occasionally. Not that she didn't smile or didn't act silly at times, but he'd catch her staring out the window in her bedroom before she'd go to bed, or her hand would rest on a favourite toy without picking it up, and she seemed lost. She was quick to tears if either parent scolded her, which happened seldom, but even a spilled drink at dinner filled her eyes, the tears brimming at the edge, ready to slip away.

Their cottage sat isolated by a spur of nature conservancy land on one side and on the other by a long, houseless, rocky stretch. He bought the place fourteen years earlier, the year after he married, from Dad, who didn't use it any more.

Only a couple of hours from Terre Haute, Tribay Lake attracted a slower-paced population; county covenants kept the skiers off, so the surface remained calm when the wind was low. From the air it looked like a three-leafed clover, with several miles of shoreline. An angler in a boat with a trolling motor could find plenty of isolated inlets covered with lily pads where the lunkers hung out.

By mid-June the water warmed to swimming temperature – inner tubes were stacked next to the boathouse for a convenient float – and the nights cooled off for sleeping. Poul and Leesa took the front room overlooking the lake. In the first years they'd opened the big windows wide at night to listen to crickets. Lately, though, he went to bed alone while she worked crossword puzzles, or she retired early and was asleep by the time he got there.

Poul knew the lake by its smell and sounds – wet wood and fish and old barbecues and waves lapping against the tyres his dad had mounted on the pier to protect the boat, the late night birds trilling in the hills above the lake, and an echo of his mother's voice, still ringing, when Neal didn't come back. 'Where's your brother?' she'd asked, her eyes already wild. 'Weren't you watching Neal?' She called his name as she walked down the rocky shore looking for the younger son.

Savannah closed her book and said, 'I'm going to catch a big fish this year. I'm going to see him in my raft first, then I'll hook him. But I want to visit Johnny Jacobs and his kittens first.' Over Poul's objection, Leesa had bought Savannah a clear-bottomed raft, just big enough to hold a child, and it was all she'd talked about for weeks.

Poul said, 'They won't be kittens any more, Speedy. That was last fall. They'll be cats by now.' Gravel crunched under the wheels. Leesa didn't move, her sweater still bunched between her head and the window.

Poul wondered if she only pretended to be asleep. It was a good way to not converse, and the lean against the window kept her as far away from him as possible. 'We're here, Leesa,' he said, touching her hand. She didn't flinch, so maybe she actually had been sleeping.

Leesa rubbed her eyes, then pushed her short, black hair behind her ears. She'd started dyeing it last year even though Poul hadn't noticed any grey. His hair had a couple of streaks now, but his barber told him it made him distinguished. At thirty-five, he thought 'distinguished' was a good look.

'I'm going to walk down to Kettle Jack's to see if he has fresh corn for the grill. I like grilled corn my first night at the lake,' Leesa said. Poul wondered if she was talking to him. She'd turned her face to the side, where the oak slipped past.

Poul pulled the car under the beat-up carport next to the cottage. Scrubby brush scraped against the bumper. Leesa opened the door and was gone before he could stop the engine. Savannah said, 'I don't like corn on the cob. Can we have hotdogs?'

'Sure, Speedy.' On an elm next to the cottage, a frayed rope dangled, its end fifteen feet from the ground. Summers and summers ago, there'd been a knot in the end and Neal hung on while Poul pushed him. 'Harder, Poul!' he'd yell, and Poul gave another shove, sending the younger boy spinning. Poul looked at the rope. He didn't remember when it had broken; it seemed like this was the first time he'd seen it in years. With the door open now, forest smells filled the car: the peculiar lakeside forest essence that was all moss and ferns and rotted logs half buried in loam, damp with Indiana summer dew. He and Neal had explored the woods from the cottage to the highway, a half-mile of deadfall and mysterious paths only the deer used. They hunted for walking sticks and giant beetles, or, with peanut butter jars in hand, trapped bulbous spiders for later examination.

Someone yelled in the distance, a child, and Poul jumped. He stood, his hands resting on the car's roof. Between the cottage and the elms beside it a slice of lake glimmered and a hundred feet from shore, a group of children played on a permanently anchored oil drum and wood-decked diving platform, whooping in delight.

'I'd like mustard on mine, and then I'll go see the kittens,' said Savannah. She had her duffel bag over her shoulder – it dragged on the ground – and was already moving towards the back door.

'Sure, Speedy,' Poul said, although Savannah was already out of earshot. Poul arched, pushing his hands into his back. Sunlight cut through the leaves above in a million diamonds. He left the baggage in the car to walk to the shore. To his left, a mile away, partly around the lake's curve, Kettle Jack's long pier poked into the water. A dozen sailboats lay at anchor, their empty masts standing rock-still in the windless day. Partway there, Leesa walked determinedly on the dirt path towards the lodge. Slender as the day they married. Long-legged. Satiny skin that bronzed after two days of sun. He remembered warm nights marvelling at the boundaries where the dark skin became white, how she murmured encouragement, laughing deep in her throat at shared joys.

Poul unpacked the van. Most of the beach toys went around front. He stuck the yellow raft on a high, open shelf in the back of the cottage where rakes and old oars were stored. Maybe she'd forget they had it.

A screen slapped shut behind him. Savannah came down the steps. 'I couldn't find the hotdogs, and something smells bad in the kitchen. I'm going to count fish.'

Poul said, 'Let's go together. Life vest first.' He found one in a pile in the storage chest against the tiny boathouse. It had a solid heft that reassured him.

She pouted as he put it on. It smelled of a winter's storage, a musty, grey odour that rose when he squeezed the belt around her. 'Guess you aren't the same size as last summer? Can't have you grow up this fast. We'll have to quit feeding you.'

Savannah didn't smile. 'Da-ad,' she said.

Minnows darted away when they stepped on the pier. To the left, weeds grew up from the mucky bottom, starting as a ten-foot wide algae belt next to the shore, and waving languidly below after that until the lake became too deep to see them. To the right, white sand began at a railroad tie border six feet from the cottage and reached into the water, a smooth, pale stretch for thirty feet. It cost two hundred dollars every other season to have several dump-truck loads of sand poured and spread to create the beach. A blunt torpedo silhouette a foot long moved towards deeper water. Probably a bass. Most perch were stockers in the lake, and a foot-long blue gill would be a trophy. Only catfish and bass reached respectable size. Poul watched the fish gliding at the sand's edge, perfectly poised between the artificial beach and the lake's invisible depths. Once he'd stood at the same spot with Neal, fascinated by a three-foot-long catfish, nosing its way beneath their feet. Through their reflections, through Neal's glasses and wide brown eyes and sun-blond hair, and through Poul's dark hair and blue eyes, they'd watched its broad, black back. Later they'd baited huge treble hooks with liver or soap, but the fish never returned. Dad had told them some catfish lived longer than men. That same catfish might still be prowling the lake's bottom. Would it remember a summer of two small boys? Or was it now a ghost? Did old ones die to haunt the undersides of piers? Were there places even fish were afraid to go?

Poul shivered and glanced up. Savannah was on her stomach at the pier's end. Her knees not touching wood, her weight precariously balanced. His throat seized up and he walked quickly, almost a jog (although he didn't want to scare her) to where she looked into the water. Poul put his hand on her back, holding her there.

Savannah's hands were flat out, fingers splayed, nearly touching the surface. Without a breeze the lake was smooth as glass. 'Look, Daddy. I'm underwater. Do you think she sees me?' Her reflection stared at her, its hands almost touching her own, the vision of a little girl six inches deep, looking up.

Poul's tongue felt fat in his mouth, and it was all he could do to speak without a quiver in the voice. 'Yes, dear. You're lovely. Now let's go in, and I'll find the hotdogs.'

Savannah held his hand as they walked towards the cottage. The boards creaked underfoot. Through the wide gaps, water undulated in a slow, fractional swell. He shook his head. She'd never been in danger.

Even if she'd fallen in, the life vest would have popped her to the surface, and he was right there. He wished he'd signed her up for swimming lessons during the winter. Poul kept his head down, watching his feet next to Savannah's, her white sneakers matching his small steps. She gripped his little finger and he smiled. After lunch, he'd break out the worms and bamboo poles (anything to avoid the clear-bottomed raft). He'd have to dig up the tall, skinny bobbers and show her again how to mount the bait on the hook.

He remembered fishing with Neal. Dad used an open bail casting reel, sending his lures to splash far away, but they had as much action tossing their bait a few feet from the boat. Poul would stare at the narrow red and white bobber's point, held upright by the worm's weight and a couple of lead shot. The marker twitched, sending ripples away. It twitched again. 'Something nibbling you, Poul,' said Neal, his own pole forgotten. 'Yeah,' said Poul, concentrating on the bobber, which wasn't moving now. He imagined a fish eyeing it below. Could be a bass, or maybe even a pike, like the stuffed one mounted on a board above the bar at Kettle Jack's, its long mouth open and full of teeth.

Savannah cried, 'Help him, Daddy.'

'What?'

She pulled away, dropped to her knees and poked her head over the pier's side, trying to look under. 'Help him!'

'What, Savannah? What?' Poul knelt beside her, a splinter poked his shin. 'Don't fall in now!'

She sat up, her hair wet at the tips where it had dipped. 'Where'd he go? Didn't you see him? He was reaching up between the boards, Daddy. You almost stepped on him.'

The sun dimmed and everything around them faded. Only Savannah was clear. Dimly children shrieked on the distant diving platform. When he spoke, it sounded to him as if they were in a bubble: his faint voice travelled no more than a yard away. 'What did you see, Speedy? Who was reaching up?'

Her lip quivered. 'The boy, Daddy. He was under the pier. I saw his fingers right there.' She pointed. 'He was stuck under the pier, but when I looked, he'd gone away. Where do you think he went to, Daddy?'

Between the boards, the lake breathed gently, the surface smooth and untroubled. A crawdad crept along the muck. Poul watched it through the gap. 'I don't think there was anyone there, Speedy. Maybe your eyes played a trick on you.'

Legs crossed, her hands in her lap, Savannah studied the space between the boards for a moment. Slowly, she said, 'My eyes don't play tricks.' She paused. 'But my brain might have imagined it.'

Poul released a long, slow lungful of air. He hadn't known he'd been holding it. 'If you're hungry, sometimes your brain does funny things.' The sun brightened. Poul shivered and he realised sweat soaked his shirt's sides. 'Let's go in and have a hotdog.'

She nodded. He had to open the porch door for her; it was a high step up and her fingers barely wrapped around the knob. Neal had been so proud his last summer when he could grip it.

Later, while Savannah put mustard on her meal, Poul said, 'Why did you think it was a *boy* under the pier if all you saw was his fingers?' Savannah swallowed a bite.

'He had boy hands. Boy hands are different. I can tell.' She pushed the top back on the mustard.

In the evening, Poul walked to the end of the pier. A breeze had picked up and on the lake two sailboats glided side by side, their sails catching the sun's last yellow rays. Now all the lake was black. If he jumped in here, the water would barely come to his chest – it would be just over a six-year-old's head – but within a couple of strides was a steep drop-off. The wind pushed waves towards him, a series of lines that slapped against the piles as they went by. He could feel the lake in his feet. Deep in his pockets, his hands clenched. Cottages on the far shore glowed in the last light, their windows like mica specks in carved miniatures. Behind them, forest-covered hills rose to the silence of the sky.

They'd found Neal ten feet from the pier's end, his hands floating above his head, nearly on the surface, his feet firmly anchored on the bottom. Poul stood on shore, his fists jammed into his armpits, and watched them load him in the boat, wearing the face mask and snorkel, limp and small, his arms like delicate pipes, his six-year-old skin as smooth and pale as milk, black boots on his feet. They were Poul's snow boots, buckled at the top and filled with sand.

Long after the sun set and the boats disappeared and lights flickered on in cottages, music and voices drifted across the water, Poul came in to go to bed. On the porch, Savannah slept on the daybed. He checked the screens to make sure they were tight – mosquitoes were murder after dark – then locked the deadbolt, taking the key. Sometimes Savannah woke before he or Leesa did, and he didn't want her wandering outside. In the kitchen, he shook as he poured a cup of tepid coffee. A humid breeze had sucked the heat out of him. The cup warmed his hands. Moths threw themselves against the windows, pattering to get in. Leaves hushed against themselves. Years ago he'd sat at this same table, sipping hot chocolate, laughing at Neal's liquid moustache. That day they'd swum. The next they'd fish, and the summer at the lake stretched before them, a thousand holidays in a row.

Poul slipped up the stairs, keeping his weight on the side next to the wall so there would be no creaks. He left his clothes on a chair. Dock lights through the windows illuminated the room enough for him to get around without running into anything. A long lump on the bed, swaddled in shadows, was all he could see of Leesa. Except for his own breathing, there was no other noise, which meant she was awake. When she slept, she whistled lightly on each exhalation. From the beginning he'd found it charming, but never mentioned it, guessing it might be embarrassing. If he spoke now, he knew, she wouldn't reply.

Three years ago when they were at the cottage, she began suffering headaches at bedtime, or sore throats, or stomach cramps, or pulled muscles, or dozens of other ailments. That same summer she went from sleeping in just a pair of boxer shorts to a full flannel nightgown. She'd start complaining about her night-time illness before lunch and after a while he figured they were all a charade. The last time they'd made love had been a year ago, in this bedroom. He remembered her back to him and he pressed against her; he could feel her muscles through the flannel, her hip's still delicate flare. She didn't move away, so he pushed against her again. It had been months since the last time, and the day had been good. She hadn't avoided him. She laughed at a joke. Maybe she's thawing, he'd thought, so he watched her, and when she went to bed, he followed. No chance for her to be sleeping before he got there. But she undressed in the bathroom, came out with the collar buttoned tightly at her neck, didn't look at him and laid down with her back towards him. He didn't move for a while. They'd been married too long for him not to recognise all the ways she was saying, 'No'. Still, it *had* been months. He moved next to her, his erection painful. Outside, waves slapped upon the shore. The boat rattled on its chain.

A third time he pressed against her. Finally, without rolling, she reached back with her hand and held him. He took a sharp breath, moved into her palm, slid against her fingers. She squeezed once, not moving in any other way. When he came a few minutes later, sweat heavy on his chest, his breath quivering, Leesa slowly pulled her hand away and wiped him off on the sheets, as if she were already mostly asleep. It was the most loveless act he'd ever committed. Within moments, her whistling snore began.

That was the last time.

Why was she angry with him? Why had it gone so terribly bad? The closest they'd come to talking about it came that Christmas, after Savannah went outside to play in the snow, and he and Leesa sat wordlessly in the living room. He'd finally said, 'What's wrong?' The sweater he'd given her draped across her hands, she didn't meet his eyes. 'I don't like this colour any more.' Later he found the gift tossed in the back of the closet.

Whatever the source of the anger, it grew worse at the lake. The distance widened and the nightmares came more often. He lifted the covers as little as possible and lay down. Leesa didn't react. Poul looked at the ceiling. A light from a passing boat swept shadows from one side of the room to the other. Its small motor chugged faintly.

Leesa wasn't whistling. He knew she heard the same motor. If her eyes were open, she'd see the same shadows. 'Savannah scared herself on the dock today,' he said into the darkness, the sudden sound of his own voice startling him. Only the cooling cottage's creaks and groans answered.

Hours later, still awake, he heard a noise downstairs. A muted rasp. He propped up on his elbows. Footsteps, then another scraping sound. A bump. Nothing for a long time. His eyes ached with attention, and saliva pooled in his mouth he didn't dare swallow. After minutes he slipped from the blankets and moved from the bed, crept down to the living room, every shadow hiding an intruder, the pulse in his ear like a throbbing announcement. He turned on a light, flicking the room into reality, then into the kitchen where moths clustered against the screens. On the porch, Savannah lay atop her covers, sleeping. Scratch marks showed where she'd pulled a chair to the door. She'd unhooked the chain, but the deadbolt defeated her. Poul tucked her in, then he grasped the doorknob to check the lock again. Slick brass felt cool under his palm. Savannah had sleepwalked. When she was three, she'd done it for a few months, but she hadn't done it since. The paediatrician said it wasn't uncommon; that she'd outgrow it.

Through the porch door's window, the eastern horizon glowed, turning the lake surface purple, but the dock was black, a long, black finger with a black boat's silhouette beside it. A muskrat swam, cutting a long V in the flat water.

The knob turned under his hand. It turned again. Whoever held it on the other side was shorter than the window. Poul slapped his head against the glass. A bare stair. He ran to the kitchen, banging his shin against a stool, breath ragged in his throat, grabbed the deadbolt key from its drawer and stumbled back to the porch. Outside, he looked up and down the shore. A quarter-mile away, his closest neighbour loaded fishing gear into his boat. Poul ran around the cottage. There was no one. Mindless, he sprinted up the long dirt driveway until he stopped at the highway, bent, with his hands on his thighs, gasping. Empty road vanished into the woods on either side.

He sat on the shoulder. A deep gouge in his left foot bled freely and he realised both feet hurt. It took ten minutes to hobble back to the cottage and, wearing only shorts, he was profoundly cold. The sun bathed the cottage's front as he walked to the door. Grass cast long shadows. His own barefooted prints showed in the dew. Poul stopped before going in. Another set of prints led to his door, rounded impressions, small, like a child wearing galoshes, coming from the lake. Then, as if the sun was an eraser passing over the yard, the dew vanished.

Leesa took Savannah into town for lunch and shopping. They needed to stock the refrigerator and freezer and Savannah decided she couldn't live without fruit juice in the squeezable packages.

Poul sat in a lawn chair at the foot of the pier for most of the morning. The sun pressed against his forehead and eventually filled him with lazy heat. Ripples caught the light, sending it in bright, little spears at him. Waves lapped the shore. The boat, tied to the dock, thudded hollowly every once in a while like a huge aluminium drum.

If he shut his eyes, it could be thirty years earlier. The sun beat the same way and the same ripply chorus floated in the air. On the beach he and Neal had talked about deep sea diving and fish. Poul was frustrated. He had a wonderful face mask, fins to push himself along and a snorkel, but the mask was too buoyant. He could dive underwater, but he couldn't stay near the fascinating bottom where the catfish lived. So he had a brainstorm. In the boathouse he found a pair of rubber snow boots he'd left from January when he and Dad had come to the lake to fix a frozen pipe. They were supposed to fit over shoes, so his bare foot slopped around. He held the top open. 'Fill them up, Neal,' he said.

His brother looked at them doubtfully. 'Why do you want to do that?'

''Cause this will keep me from floating.'

'Oh,' Neal said with admiration. He used a yellow, plastic shovel to dump sand in. When it was full, Poul forced the bottom buckle closed. The sand squeezed his leg; he fastened the next one, and it was even tighter. Sand spilled over the top. After the last buckle, there was a strap that cinched the boot closed. It felt like his feet were in grainy cement; he couldn't even wiggle his toes.

Neal laughed when Poul tried to walk. Each foot must have weighed an extra ten pounds and it was all he could do to shuffle forward. Poul adjusted his face mask and snorkel. 'Wish me luck.'

'Luck,' said Neal. 'Find the big catfish, okay?'

Poul nodded as he waded out. The water slapped higher on his body with each step from shore. When it reached his armpits, he put the snorkel in, then slowly squatted, his feet holding firm beneath him. He turned; underwater, the sand held ripples, a sculpture of the surface motion, while the underside of the surface undulated, meeting the beach at the shore. Then he stood, blew water from the snorkel and gave Neal a thumbs-up. Neal waved back.

A few steps deeper and the water line rose on the face mask. Another step and he was completely underwater, breathing through the snorkel. No fish, but a lot of suspended material, bits of algae. Exotic noises. A buzz that must have been a boat cruising along. A metallic clink that might be a chain under the diving platform a hundred feet away. His breath wheezing in and out of the snorkel. Other, unidentifiable sounds. Poul the adventurer, an explorer of undiscovered countries.

Then, a fish just at his vision's edge, much deeper, swam along the bottom. Poul froze, hoping it would come close, but it stayed maddeningly far. He moved towards it, sliding his foot only a few inches. It flicked away, then appeared again, still now, head on, as if it were watching him. An encounter with an alien would not have felt any more exotic. Poul leaned towards the fish, his hand out. A gesture of hello.

Water filled his mouth, straight into his throat and he was choking. It hurt! Eyes tearing, he looked up. He'd gone too deep. The top of the snorkel was below the surface. Blind panic! He flailed his arms, trying to swim up, but his feet didn't budge. He jerked, screaming through the snorkel. No air! No air! He turned towards shore and took a step. He took another, then blew hard, clearing the water and breathed in gasps. Without pause, he continued towards shore. When he was shallow enough, he ripped the face mask off and sucked one huge breath after another. By the time he got to shore, his throat quit hurting, but he wanted to get away, to lie down and cry. He could feel it in his chest, the horrible pressure of no air, the moment when he didn't dare inhale.

'Did you see a fish?' Neal asked. He was sitting with his toes in the water, arms wrapped around his knees. 'Was it totally cool?'

Poul shook his head, hiding his tears by unbuckling the boots. He scraped his feet pulling them out. Later that day Dad would smear first-aid cream on them, his eyes unfocused, his hands shaking.

Poul left the boots on the beach and went into the woods to cry.

He'd never been so scared. He'd never been so scared! And when he returned an hour later, Mom was walking up the shore, calling Neal's name. 'Where's your brother?' she'd asked, her eyes already wild. 'Weren't you watching Neal?'

Poul rose from the lawn chair; he could feel the nylon webbing creases in his backside. Neal was six, he thought. Savannah is six. The two facts came together with inevitable weight. For years he hadn't thought much about Neal's death. Every once in a while, a memory would flare: the two of them talking late at night, after they were supposed to be asleep, the model airplane Neal had given him for his birthday, the words carefully inscribed on the back, *For mi big brother. Luve, Neal.* Neal trusted him, looked up to him, but most of the time Neal didn't exist any more. Then Savannah was born, and Neal came back, a little stronger each summer. Maybe that's what Leesa sensed: the younger brother, dead within him.

Savannah is six, Poul thought, and Neal has been waiting.

He went through the cottage and made sure the screens were tight. It wouldn't do for the house to be filled with mosquitoes when Leesa and Savannah returned. For a moment he held a pen over a notepad in the kitchen, but put it down without writing. A beach towel went over his shoulder and he walked to the end of the pier. Standing with his toes wrapped over the edge, a breeze in his face, felt like leaning over an abyss. Beyond the drop-off, he saw no bottom. The big fish were there, the fishy mysteries he'd left to Neal.

He dove in, a long shallow dive that took him yards away without a stroke. Water rushed by his ears. Bubbles streamed from his nose. He came to the surface, trod water. From his shoulders to his knees, the lake was warm, a comfortable temperature perfect for swimming, but from the knees down it was cold. Neal didn't know how to swim, he thought. To even go on the pier, Dad had made him put on a life jacket, and Poul was the older brother. How many times had he been told to *protect* him, to watch out for him? And it didn't matter what he'd been told, Poul *wanted* to keep his brother safe. At the playground, he listened for Neal's voice. When someone cried, Poul stopped, afraid it was Neal. Loving his brother was like inhaling.

Neal went into the lake; he never came out. Neal must have hated him, Poul thought. At the end, he must have cried out for him, but Poul didn't come. He didn't warn him.

Poul swam deeper, put his face down, eyes open. Without a mask, his hands were blurry. Beyond them, blackness. How deep? Were there pike? He imagined a ghost catfish, its eye as broad as a swimming pool rising towards him.

But try as he might, Poul couldn't drown himself. He floated on his back, letting his feet sink until his weight drew his face under, and just when the time came to breathe, he kicked to the surface. He couldn't let the water in. Swimming parallel to the shore, he passed Kettle Jack's, swam by dozens of cottages like his own until his arms tired. Each stroke hurt, his shoulders burning with exhaustion, but they never quit working. The lake let him live, and Neal never came up to join him. Poul waited for a hand (a small hand) to wrap around his ankle, to pull him down where six-year-olds never grow older. Instead, the sun moved across the sky until Poul was empty. Completely dull, drained and damaged, he turned towards shore, staggered up a stranger's beach, and walked on the lake road towards his cottage, staying in the shoulder, where the grass didn't hurt his feet.

If Neal didn't want him, who did he want?

This far above Kettle Jack's was unfamiliar to him, but the look was the same: long, dirt driveways that vanished in the trees below, or led to cottages camped along the shore. Old boats sprawled upside down on saw horses. Bamboo fishing poles leaned against weathered wood. Station wagons or vans parked behind each house. Towels drying on lines. Beyond, in the lake, sailboats cut frothy wakes; the wind had picked up, although he didn't feel it much here.

He started walking faster. Leesa and Savannah would be home by now. He wondered what they were doing. Leesa never watched Savannah like he did. Her philosophy was that kids take care of themselves, generally, and it's healthier for a child to have room to explore.

He hadn't realised how far he'd swum. Way ahead, the tip of Kettle Jack's pier poked into the lake. Maybe Savannah and Leesa would walk there to see Johnny Jacobs' kittens. But it was hot, and Savannah hadn't swum yet. Yesterday she'd fished. Today she'd want to swim. He could see the scene. Leesa would pull into the driveway. Savannah would put on her swimsuit to go out on the beach. She had sand toys, buckets, shovels, rakes, little moulds for making sand castles. Leesa would set up a chair, lather on sun lotion and read a book. Savannah could be in the water now.

Poul broke into a jog. How idiotic it was to leave the cottage, he thought. No, not idiotic. Criminal. If vengeance waited in the lake, if some sort of delayed retribution haunted the cold waters, why would it care for him? Where would his suffering be if he drowned, like Neal, relieved of responsibility at last? He was running. Kettle Jack's passed by on his left. It was a mile to his cottage. He'd swum over a mile! And maybe that was the plan: to get him out into the lake and away.

Suddenly he felt as if he'd lost his mind. What was he thinking? What sane father would dive into the water away from his daughter? Savannah is six, he thought, and she needs her daddy.

The van was parked behind the cottage. Poul ran to the front, his breath coming in great whoops. Empty lounge chair. Sand toys on the beach. A child's life vest lying next to the boathouse. No sign of her. He yelled, 'Savannah!' as he went through the door onto the porch.

Leesa sat at the kitchen table, eating a sandwich. 'What's wrong with you?' she said.

'Where's Savannah?'

'Puttering around in that raft I bought her. We had a heck of a time finding it.'

'I didn't see her!' he said as he ran out of the kitchen.

Out front, he scanned the lake again. Boats in the distance. No yellow raft. He had a vision: Savannah paddling, looking at the bottom through the clear plastic. Sand, of course; she'd see sand and minnows. Then she'd move further out, her head down, hoping for fish, not aware of how far from shore she was going. The water would get deeper. She'd be beyond the sand, where the depths were foggy and dark green. 'What is that?' she'd think. A moving shadow, a form resolving itself, a face coming from below. The little boy from beneath the pier.

Poul pounded down the dock, scanning the water to the left and right. Leesa followed.

'She was right here a minute ago! I've only been inside a minute!'

At the dock's end, Poul stopped, within an eye-blink of diving in, but the water was clear as far as he could see. Even the sailboats had retreated from sight.

'Maybe she went to see the kittens,' Leesa said.

'With the raft? She wouldn't go with the raft!' Poul's voice cracked.

A bird flew by, wings barely moving. It seemed to Poul to almost have stopped. His heart beat in slow explosions. Leesa said something, but her meaning didn't reach him, the words were so far apart. Then a round shape pushed from beneath the pier. At first he thought it was the top of a blonde head, right under his feet, and it moved a little bit further, becoming too broad to be a head, and too yellow to be blonde. It was the raft. He could feel himself saying, 'No,' as he bent, already knowing Savannah wouldn't be in it. He tugged on its handle. It resisted. Who is holding on? It slid out. No one held it. Six inches of water in the bottom made it heavy.

'Savannah!' Leesa screamed. Then the bird's wings beat twice and it was gone. Poul's pulse sped up. The lake had never seemed so empty.

He remembered Dad, who had stood at the end of the pier, mute, when they pulled Neal out. Now he stood on the same board.

A high voice called from the lake, a child. Poul looked up, his skin suddenly cold. It called again and Poul saw her, lying on the diving platform a hundred feet away, Savannah.

He didn't know how he got there – didn't remember swimming, but he was up the diving platform's ladder, holding his weeping daughter instantly. She nestled her head under his chin and shook with tears. Before she stopped, Leesa arrived in the boat, and they both held her.

Finally, when Savannah's crying had settled into a sob every minute or two, Leesa said, 'How did you get out here, darling? You scared us so.'

Between shuddery breaths, Savannah said, 'I didn't mean to go so far, and I couldn't get back. I paddled really hard, but I fell out. The wind pushed the raft away.'

She looked from Poul to Leesa, her eyes red-rimmed and teary.

'I swallowed water, Daddy. I couldn't breathe.'

Poul swallowed. He could feel the snorkel in his mouth, the solid, leaden ache of water in his lungs.

Leesa gasped, 'Thank God you made it to the diving platform. We could have lost you,' and she burst into tears herself.

Through Leesa's crying, Savannah looked at Poul solemnly. 'I didn't swim, Daddy. The little boy helped me. He took my hand and put me here.' Savannah rubbed her eyes with the back of her arm. 'He kissed my cheek, Daddy.'

Poul nodded, incapable of speech.

'He looked like the boy in your baby pictures.' She sniffed, but seemed more relaxed, her fear already becoming vague. 'My eyes didn't play tricks on me.'

Poul spent the sunset sitting on the end of the pier, his toes dipping in the lake, surrounded by the watery symphony: aqueous rhythms beating against the wood, lapping against the shore. And fish. He sat quietly, and the fish came: a school of blue gill, scales catching the last light in a thousand glitters swirling in front of him and then were gone. Later, when the sun had nearly disappeared, a long, black shape glided by, its eye as big as a quarter, a long row of teeth visible when it opened its mouth. Poul had finally seen a pike.

He sighed, pushed himself up and found Leesa in the kitchen. She'd already put Savannah to bed in their room upstairs.

She looked at her coffee cup dully. It was almost hard to remember what he'd loved about her when they'd first met, then she turned her head a little and brushed back her hair, and for a second, it was there, a picture of Leesa when they were young. Before Savannah. Before coming to the lake had become so reluctant. The second disappeared.

He pulled a chair out for himself and turned it around so he could lean his arms on the back. She didn't speak. Poul shut his eyes to listen to the woods behind the cottage. The air there was always so moist and living, but it didn't penetrate into the kitchen. With his eyes closed, he could swear he was alone in the room.

'I want a divorce,' Poul said.

Leesa looked at him directly for maybe the first time in a year. 'Why now?'

The low, slanting sun cut through the trees behind the cottage, casting a yellow light in the room. He knew that on the lake, now, it highlighted the waves, but didn't penetrate the depths. Fisherman would be out, because the big fish, the serious fish, moved in the evening. The evening was the best time to be on the lake, after a hard day of swimming, of hiking in the woods where he'd played with Neal, and just before they went to bed to tell each other stories until sleep took them, two brothers under one blanket lying head to head, and they dreamed.

Poul said, 'When you realise a thing is bad, you've got to let it go or you'll drown.'

Jame Van Pelt lives in western Colorado with his wife and three sons. One of the 1999 finalists for the John W. Campbell Award for Best New Writer, he teaches high school and college English. His fiction has appeared in, amonst other places, *Analog*, *Realms of Fantasy*, *The Third Alternative* and *Weird Tales*. Upcoming work is scheduled to appear in *Asimov's* and *Alfred Hitchcock's Mystery Magazine*. When he is not teaching, writing or raising kids, he hunts for an agent to represent his first novel. '"Savannah is Six" has some autobiographical roots,' says the author. 'When I was young, my family vacationed on an Indiana lake each summer. Although I never tried the sand in the boots trick, the fish fascinated me, and I spent many happy hours with a face mask looking for them. Now I'm a father with three sons. We haven't been to the lake yet, but I'm stunned by the depth of the relationships between the brothers. All that, a sad divorce, and a love for Ray Bradbury went into the story.'

Now Day Was Fled as the Worm Had Wished

BRIAN HODGE

We would know it as soon as we got there, Vanessa insisted – and more than once. We would know the right place when we found it and not one moment before, so there was no point in second-guessing ourselves. Stop trying so hard. No formal itinerary and that was just the way we should keep it.

'How about here?' Heather had suggested a couple of weeks ago at the Tower of London, before we'd left the city for the countryside. Forty-eight hours before that we would've still been somewhere over the Atlantic.

'Absolutely not, you can't be serious,' Vanessa had vetoed. '*Are* you?'

No reply, just Heather and her puckish little smile, betraying nothing. Even I couldn't be sure, when I'd known her so much longer. It wasn't often you could catch Heather giving away anything more than only as much as she wanted.

'It was the ravens, wasn't it?' I asked her later, on the Tube, starting to feel as though I might be catching on to the way she was thinking here and now, in this world instead of the one we were trying to leave behind. Not that it looked all that different yet – those butt-ugly American fanny-packs and the murderous stress of business commuters look the same everywhere – but we at least felt the potential unfurling before us.

Ravens live at the top of the Tower, we had discovered. Live up there under ceremonial guard. Very serious business, those ravens. Tradition holds that the fate of England hinges upon them. Should the ravens ever leave the Tower, fly away, England will be sure to fall.

'Maybe something about them did make me think of my parents' marriage,' Heather said.

'I thought you wanted to do this.'

'I do. I just don't want to do any of it like they did.'

'In that case, I'd say you're off to a flying start.'

See, the catch with the ravens is that they can't soar away even if they want to. The feathers at the ends of their wings are clipped – prisoners, as surely as any heretic or rightful heir to a stolen throne who'd ever been a guest of the Tower when it was operational. It's possible that if one of them wanted out badly enough, it could tumble off the edge of the parapet and fall like a glossy black stone. But I suppose they're more apt to simply spend their days pecking at the free buffet and eyeing the sky with longing.

Naturally I hesitated to share this insight with her – the considerate thing to do, given the way her mother had leapt from a hotel window when Heather was fourteen, half her lifetime ago. Which hadn't done her father's political career any favours, coming as it did during a re-election campaign. He'd soldiered on in the race, claiming that this was what his poor beloved late wife would've wanted, but even his tarnished silver tongue couldn't sell that one to anyone who wasn't already lining his pockets. By election night, the Senator was a historical footnote.

Heather had told me that it was the only justice she'd ever really seen in the world, but wouldn't you know: it had had to hit so brutally close to home.

Oscar Wilde referred to England and America as two countries divided by a common language. While it may not be the most conspicuous example, this is no more significant than in those words applied to the land. Words that you really don't hear in the States, words like heath and hedgerow, glen and dale, moor and weald and bracken. It's as though in crossing the Atlantic our ancestors undertook some great divestiture, stripping away the luxuriant wealth of how they might speak of what was beneath their feet and tilled by their ploughs. If it could be semiotically reduced, then it might that much more easily be plundered.

But that's America for you. Take what you need, then take as much as you can hold or lock away because God forbid anyone else should have it.

Used to, once upon et cetera, when I thought about Europe and someday travelling there, as soon as I had the time, the only way I could imagine doing the Continent was in as much ostentatious style as possible. Five-star hotels, chauffeurs, restaurants that would break the wallets of everyone I ever wanted to prove I had surpassed, eclipsed, outshone. But now that I could afford it, I found that I couldn't muster up much enthusiasm for this route. These were the dreams of a twenty-year-old, and a decade later as relevant as the telegraph.

One decade later, the only thing making sense to me, to all three of us pale, long-boned Anglos – admittedly, at Vanessa's prompting – was to instead walk this ancestral island of ours, and try to drum up any connection that might still be buried deep in our New World bones, along with the trace elements of cesium and mercury and everything else we ingested without intending to or having much say in the matter.

And so walk we did. We'd bought rail passes to train our way into whichever area we felt like exploring, but once there, it was England at a grass roots level. Naïve dreamers, perhaps, hoping to find something that we feared might no longer exist, if it ever had, but we wanted an England of standing stones and the Cerne Giant and the Uffington Horse, not an England trampled by the same old cigar chompers who would just as soon bulldoze a burial mound as look at it.

And so. We walked. Backpacks on our shoulders, hiking boots on our feet, extra support in Vanessa's – uncommonly high arches, she has – and, just to make it interesting, an additional agenda in our hearts. Figuring for this one we'd be entirely on our own, and just as well, since most people frowned on the sort of thing we had in mind.

At least that's one good thing about lots of money:

You get to say 'Fuck you' like you really mean it.

A grand place for hikes, rural England, as though the glaciers of the last Ice Age had carved the land for feet and walking staves, and nobody can bear to challenge that. You can go virtually anywhere, cut across great tracts of farmland and tarry as long as you like, and with the farmers' blessings, too, as long as you remember to shut the gates behind you so the sheep don't stray out. Just try *that* in the US without risking buckshot or worse.

Denied that level of freedom to roam the eastern county of Suffolk, surely we would never have found the old manor house. Well off any road of consequence, a few miles from the nearest town of Lavenham, it sat entirely by itself, surrounded by a quilt of tilled fields and wild meadows and pastures. It was the sort of place that becomes invisible to those who grow up familiar with it, seen but no longer noticed, as much a feature of the landscape as the oldest yew tree or some far-off tor, and given just as much thought. Even from a distance we could see that it was in ruins, bricks overrun with vines and ivy, one end's outer wall collapsed inwards, and two of its five chimneys crumbled halfway back to the many-gabled peaks of the roof.

'Well, look what we have here,' Vanessa said. 'Stumbling onto a place like this can make an eight-year-old out of anyone.'

And for the moment she reminded me of one, tall and lanky though she was, and older than I was by a couple of years. It was the eager flush of excitement that did it, and how she seemed somehow smaller beneath hair gone mad in the moist air of early autumn. Streaks of colour had been dyed into it these past few months, then thickly braided ... one purple, one green, one the same blue shade as her eyes.

She cupped a hand to her ear and cocked her gaze sideways to the sky.

'Hear that?' she asked Heather and me. 'Hear it?'

'What?' we asked.

'That big booming voice, full of thunderbolts and glee,' she said. 'And it's saying, "Explore ... explore!"'

She sprinted towards the manor house to oblige, sprinting surprisingly well considering the forty extra pounds' worth of backpack and sleeping bag.

Heather and I opted for a more leisurely pace. Because her legs were not nearly as long as Vanessa's, I knew that Heather was afraid how she might look by comparison, that anything less than reminiscent of a gazelle wouldn't be worth the effort.

'Just once I'd like to be the first one to hear the voices,' said Heather. 'Just once I'd like to be the one to tell her what they're saying.'

'Well, don't you think she's probably been hearing voices her whole life?'

'Life is just so weird,' and then Heather laughed. 'All that time you and me thinking we're regular people and then we both fall in love with Joan of Arc.'

'Don't forget, I fell in love with you first,' I told her, and hoped that this would always be enough to sustain us through whatever else we might be lacking. As though, deep down, I didn't suspect that each of us knew better.

Heather's mother, zoned on tranquillisers and launching herself nine floors towards the limousine that had glided up in front of the hotel to whisk her husband to a campaign appearance ...

That was love too. Or at the very least the end result.

Realistically I cannot say that I was expecting this arrangement, this trinity we had formed, to work for a lifetime, or even for a decade. I'd never heard of these things lasting for any duration, everyone's love and affection and ardour bifurcating equally. Such a delicate balance to maintain, able to tip so easily, someone beginning to feel that they're getting the lesser end of the bargain, then demanding one partner or the other make a choice. All right, so there was the poet Ezra Pound, with a wife and a mistress who were crazy for each other, but I couldn't shake this feeling, the laudable attributes of Heather and Vanessa notwithstanding, that I had used up my personal share of good fortune already.

Heather and I had been together for years before Vanessa entered the picture. Heather was the one who met her first, Vanessa temping for a receptionist out on maternity leave at the brokerage firm where Heather gambled on the Dow Jones with other people's money. This was one of Vanessa's quote/unquote respectable phases, when five mornings a week fiscal realities sent her to the end of her closet that she didn't really like to visit, and impelled her to leave her hair one colour, an alien amongst people she could fool into thinking she was no different.

It was talk of suicide that nailed together the bridge between them, the first commonality that they'd realised they shared. Heather's mother, of course, and a couple of years ago Vanessa's younger brother had hung himself two months after his university commencement. He'd run up nearly thirty thousand dollars in credit card debt while a student, more and more companies sending him new cards or raising his limits, and he saw no other way out from under the burden. Ever since, Vanessa had been attempting to sue the banks for wrongful death. As though she could get anywhere in a system so beautifully designed to indenture its slaves at ever-younger ages.

All of which comprised a strange, even morbid, basis for the two of them to start going out for lunch together, but there you go, and as so often happens between co-workers who've begun looking at each other over menus, one thing led to another, and, rather abruptly, a few nights each week Heather started working extra hours. *That* old euphemism.

Once living the lie ballooned up with too much pressure at home – four or five weeks, something like that – she burst into tears and told me what had really been going on. It was far less a confession than a great avalanche of bewilderment, half or more of all the assumptions she'd taken for granted about herself now being called into rigorous question.

And I tried, really tried, to react the way I was supposed to, to get enraged over the betrayal, and had it been another man I might've found it easier, but I couldn't, just couldn't summon the fury, because

I was intrigued and it wasn't so much out of base prurience as suddenly feeling as though I'd spent our years together with my eyes half-closed and now they were beginning to open, and when I looked at Heather and her tears and her confusion all I could think was *I didn't have one clue you had this in you.* But neither had she, so at least we were even.

'I'm not supposed to want her, this isn't the way I'm supposed to be,' Heather said.

'Yeah, who told you that?' I said, but hardly had to ask, so then I said, 'Well, just about everything your parents told you about themselves and each other was a lie, so what makes you think they knew what they were talking about when it came to you?'

Which upset her further for a while, because she was the only one allowed to bad-mouth her family.

'So you're not mad?' she asked later, once this lesser storm had passed.

'I'm too tired to be mad,' I said, and wondered if maybe that wasn't a huge part of all the problems we'd never even stopped to realise we had.

We caught up with Vanessa inside the manor house, this ill-kept hulk gone far down the road to ruin. High-ceilinged and dank within, it was now a home fit for little else but mice and ghosts, although rather than diminish its grandeur, the state of the place only took that grandeur and turned it tragic. You could look at the staircase, dingy and splintered, and envision what it had once been, polished and gleaming in the mellow sunlight from the tall leaded windows. Could look at one of the cold fireplaces, filled now with leaves and grit, and imagine a blazing log that had taken four strong hands to wrestle onto the grate.

'Charming starter palace for young royal newlyweds,' said Vanessa, to no one in particular. 'Needs a little work.'

She'd temped for a real estate agency, too. Have to assume she learned how to read between the lines.

We wandered about, spotting the occasional evidence of prior squatters and steering clear of the unstable end where the wall had collapsed. A yawning, broken-timbered fracture now framed a ragged view of lawn and trees, but the pile of rubble looked too trifling to refill the hole, all the bricks worth salvaging long since hauled away by some frugal herdsman.

It was the gardens out back, or rather what had become of them, that really seized our fancy. Season after season, year upon year, hedges and flowerbeds and ferns had been abandoned to run riot over a couple of acres enclosed within a high stone wall. Vines had woven treacherous mats over flagstones and pathways; moss and lichens had crept up from the bases of statuary and birdbaths. A small fishpond, replenished solely by the frequent rain, had grown thick with algae, resounding with the plop of frogs when we came near. I couldn't remember when I'd ever seen so many shades of green.

Even the walls surrounding the enclosure had succumbed to the onslaught, most of them carpeted in ivy, and Heather pointed to the sleek black shapes perched atop them that watched us or probed for insects under the greenery.

'If anyone tries to clip *your* wings,' she called to the ravens, 'I hope you peck their eyes out!'

They stopped, heads cocked and beaks stilled. They listened, or seemed to. One squawked with its loud, ugly voice.

'You almost get the feeling they understand,' I said. 'It's that damned Hitchcock movie, you know.'

'Well, as birds go, they're sure not stupid, ravens aren't,' Vanessa said. She wrapped her arms around Heather from behind and regarded the ravens with a wistful smile, and why not – consorts of gods and goddesses, eaters of the dead on sword-strewn battlefields, bearers of arcana, these birds and their mystery and their downright pagan mythos were just the sort of things closest to her heart. In her daydreams, I was certain that they whispered in her ear as surely as they were to have whispered into Odin's.

Starting to graduate down to finer details, we converged on a section of the encircling wall that was free of ivy, and, aside from the statues, the only aspect of these gardens-run-amok that alluded to the touch of human hands. Vanessa traced their long-ago labours with her own, fingertips caressing one of several malformed faces that leered from the wall, bulging from the stone in bas-relief.

'God, they look like they could take your hand off in half a second,' Heather said. 'They're worse than snapping turtles.'

'Meaner, maybe,' I said. 'But not a whole lot brighter.'

'Hush, both of you.' Vanessa, doing some snapping of her own. 'You'll hurt their feelings.'

'Oh, go hug a tree,' I said, just to be contentious, only half in play, my elder self swimming up from the depths. In truth, it was still closer to the surface than I would've liked, but I really was trying to be a born-again lackadaisical transient.

The carvings on the wall were the sort of thing I generally associated with churches, and *old* churches at that – cathedrals, really – mediaeval leftovers from Catholicism's gaudier heritage, when popes and priests still condoned a discreet nod towards all things heathen that they'd borrowed, burned, or buried beneath a layer of revisionism. Then again, some people just think they look bitchin'. Hard to say how old these particular fellows were, but they certainly didn't appear to have put up with centuries of weathering. If they'd been carved much before 1900, I would've been very surprised to hear it.

They were almost all head, and their heads almost all mouth. Fierce of eye, they gaped or seemed to bellow. Their arms and legs and compact barrel-bodies looked stumpy by comparison. Some of them reached around to grab their mouths at the corner and stretch them wider still, exposing the depths of their gullets. Giants, I guessed they were, because others grappled with smaller figures of normal human proportion and stuffed these poor unfortunates into their vast maws.

'Fe fi fo fum,' I whispered into Vanessa's ear, quietly, so they wouldn't hear me. 'I smell the blood of an American.' Nuzzling her there and nipping at her lobe until she laughed and pushed me away.

'What do they mean?' Heather asked, defaulting to Vanessa on this one. 'They've got to mean something, don't they?'

'Oh sure. It's like pictures in stained-glass, they have a story to tell, a little lesson in them.' Vanessa shot a playfully bitchy glance at me. 'For illiterates.'

'So what is it these fatheads have to say to us?' Heather said.

'If I'm remembering correctly, they're to remind us that there are always forces out there much greater than we are.'

'Wow, they're absolutely right,' I said. 'For me, it was Microsoft.'

I expected recriminations from Vanessa, but no – something clearly more important had crossed her mind. She glanced about the gardens, then broke loose with a slow, broad smile as she looked at Heather and me.

'We'll do it here, right here, tomorrow,' she told us. 'Haven't I been saying all along we'd know the right spot when we found it?'

And it was fine with me, because the place really was beautiful, and we surely wouldn't be lucky enough to blunder across another like it anytime soon. Heather looked startled for a moment, as if our intentions had never been genuinely real until this moment, and the truth of it was only now sinking in.

'It's perfect,' she said.

'Besides,' and Vanessa swept her hand toward the devouring heads peering from their wall, 'if we're getting married, we really should have witnesses.'

*

The money. Oh, right – that.

There are no better mousetraps any more. These days, if you want the world to beat a path to your door, you'd best come up with something new and improved going on at the other end of the mouse plugged into your computer. While still in college, I founded a little start-up software company called Cerulean Data that grew in surges over the next ten years. Our greatest achievement was developing an applications programming interface that brought the giants calling. Next big leap forward in better-faster-wilder 3D graphics. Simply put, the giants had to have it.

There arose a mighty tug-of-war over how I should handle this, with my accountants and lawyers on one side, my doctor on the other. The former clamoured in favour of licensing the API, since through me, they'd make far more money that way in the long run. But let it be understood they weren't the ones with blood on their toilet paper, the trickle-down effect of my ravaging ulcer. My doctor, who had told me more than once that I was killing myself, voted to sell the company.

In a college business course I had learned that during the development of the original Macintosh, one of Apple Computer's founders gave out T-shirts to his employees that said *90 HRS/WK AND LOVING IT*. That'll never be me, I vowed. Never wear a shirt like that. No. I'm going to have a life.

Ten, eleven years later, anyone who might've heard me back then would have been fully entitled to laugh themselves silly.

Human beings aren't meant to live this way, Vanessa told me, because by this time she had moved into our condo and come to realise that Heather wasn't exaggerating about how little time I actually spent there. Visitor in my own home. Human beings weren't meant to shit blood either, but it happens.

Cerulean Data had gone public two years before Microsoft came knocking, with me as the major shareholder, and the last thing the other shareholders' board of directors was going to do was stand in the way of something like this. All they did was rub their pudgy hands in anticipation, because they knew exactly what would happen with their stock.

So did I. So did Heather. She brokered the deals for herself and Vanessa, the two of them pulling every penny they had out of the bank and borrowing money from whoever would lend it to them to buy up as much stock as they could, then sit back and wait for the windfall. Insider trading, it's called, and plenty of people have gone to prison for it. Worth the risk, though, and I don't know but that only half of it was the money, and the rest of it the thrill of committing a smash-and-grab on a world that each of us wanted less and less to do with ...

Maybe because of everybody we'd found out we had to share the place with.

Since Heather and Vanessa had their hearts set on a noon ceremony, in which we would each profess our vows to the other two with the sun at its zenith overhead, we planned to spend the night in the manor house. We found a ratty old broom and swept clean an area in front of the fireplace in what might once have been the drawing room. A quick test with dry leaves and scavenged kindling proved that the flue still drew smoke, and so we built a fire and spread out our sleeping bags, and it was as fine a lodging as any hotel or B&B where we'd spent a night, as long as you could overlook the lack of running water and a proper bathroom.

Food we had, bread and cheese and apples and wine, and as night fell past the windows, the chill deepened beyond the circle cast by our fire. It was all the light in the world right now, and all we needed. We sat cross-legged or sprawled along our spread sleeping bags and it seemed befitting to tell stories about this place we had found. How it had come to be; how it had got this way.

According to Heather, its decline dated back to the darkest years of World War II, while the Germans were steadily bombing England and Churchill vowed that the British would never surrender. The house belonged to a charmingly proper couple in their late middle years, distant royalty, almost assuredly, but still very far from the throne. One dark night during the Blitz, a stray bomb had taken out the end of the house, but it just so happened that one of the German planes crashed in the nearby woods. They heard it go down, and for hours they waited, until the break of dawn, when the gentleman donned his tweed hunting jacket and brought the shotgun he used for pheasants, and went looking for survivors. He found the pilot alive but injured, and marched him back to the damaged house. But instead of calling the Royal Air Force, the gentleman and his wife, quietly enraged over what was happening to their country, kept the pilot tied captive in their cellar, where they tortured him to death over the next week. Then buried him in the gardens. Shortly thereafter, they went mad with guilt and shame, and, hollow-eyed and searching for absolution, roamed the hallways of the estate until they died. The end.

Overwhelming silence; finally:

'My god,' said Vanessa. 'I had no idea you could be so morbid.'

'Still want to marry me?'

'Yeah, more than ever.' Fingers stroking Heather's inner arm. 'Only now I want to marry you so I can cure you.'

'Does a plan like that ever work?' I asked. 'I mean, wouldn't there be a lot fewer divorces if women would just forget about trying to change who it is they're marrying and accept that it can't be done?'

'Well, we sure changed you, didn't we?' said Vanessa.

'Did we ever.' Heather, backing her up all the way. 'You used to be this hypertensive workaholic I was perennially on the verge of leaving. And look at you now . . . unemployed and a permanent member of the leisure class.'

'We made you what you are today Just admit it and adore us.'

'Don't you have a story to tell us or something?' I asked Vanessa. 'Because I'd sure like to hear it now.'

'Stubborn bastard,' she said to me, but stretched across to kiss me anyway.

And as Vanessa envisioned the history of this place, it wasn't surprising that she would focus on the carved heads. Heather, I couldn't help but notice, had ignored them entirely, but it was only natural that her idea of forces greater than herself should involve things plummeting from above.

In Vanessa's firmament, the house belonged to a renowned sculptor whom the world has long since forgotten. This was during the '20s, in that more optimistic period after the Great War, the War to End All Wars, before the shadow of the next and even greater war began to fall across Europe. Suddenly the sculptor withdrew from his adoring public and the world at large, for reasons he would share with no one, not even his wife, because, well, men are like that. All she knew was that it seemed to follow some mysterious encounter he'd had while walking in the woods, about which he steadfastly refused to say a word. Over the years to come, he spent his days chiselling ancient faces into the garden wall, recreating carvings whose origins were shrouded in the mists of time. And even though he'd turned his back on greater fame and greater fortune, he was much happier now, and then one day he simply walked into the woods and was never seen again, although his wife said that during their final breakfast together he seemed to be holding onto a secret that brought him both joy and sorrow. And so for years and years afterwards, she simply couldn't abide noise, in case she might hear him calling for her to reunite with him at last, at the edge of the trees, and together they would walk into the forest and slip into that much older England, where only a privileged few were now allowed to tread, and where they would join with the elder spirits of the land.

Overwhelming silence; finally:

'But eventually she remarried, right?' said Heather. 'And then some Nazi asshole dropped a bomb on the house?'

'No!' cried Vanessa. 'Just see if I tell *you* any more bedtime stories.'

Me, I was just glad I hadn't been the one to say that.

'Beautiful story, Vanessa,' I said instead, and meant it, wondering if she really could hear voices; if ravens whispered in her ear after all; if, even though she'd made up the details, every word might nonetheless be true.

'And you're absolutely, positively sure you want to marry me?' Heather asked her.

'You know, I'm really not liking the way you keep steering the conversation around to that,' Vanessa said. 'Now what's wrong?'

Heather, rolling onto her back: 'Hasn't the irony of the situation hit you yet? I mean, with the example I had set for me, way back when, I've always thought of matrimony as a kind of prison sentence.' Hands laced behind her head now as she stared at the ceiling. 'And what am I doing? I'm doubling the usual number of jailers.'

Until Vanessa, my idea of other worlds, other realms, had always tended to begin and end with cyberspace – nebulous enough to imbue with a reverential awe, yet ultimately the creation of a binary number system, and therefore not impossible to grasp.

Such arrogance. Such blinkered vision, no better than a horse allowed to see only what stands directly before its eyes.

And my idea of a power greater than myself tended to acknowledge death and only death. Veterans of wars talk of the bullet with their name on it, but since I had no wars to fight, I thought instead of that graveworm underfoot, the worm with my name on it, keeping pace with me through the soil, wherever I might go, patiently waiting for the twilight of my life so that it could begin its work at last.

In moments of insight, of honesty, I would wonder if Heather and I hadn't sucked Vanessa into our lives because she made it easier, somehow, to believe in things we otherwise never would have. Like purpose. Like reassurance that we had not squandered our lives chasing articulated goals only to end up well-fed slaves. Like the existence of doorways to someplace, anyplace, better than those places that had shaped us as children and younger adults . . . a new and welcoming place that had withstood the test of time because time could not permeate it.

And while I was starting to believe in these, that didn't mean I understood the keys that might unlock their doors. Was it faith? Longing? Or need? Was it the energies released before a blazing fire by the Saturnalian couplings of three people whose mouths and loins were so eager to violate the taboos of the only god others had tried to ram down their throats?

Or were the keys never ours to turn at all, those doors opening only for the ones who were most desired by those on the other side?

Fickle and capricious, maybe. Yet since when has life been anything but?

When Vanessa and I awoke, we woke up alone, Heather's spot between us on the sleeping bags empty. At first we thought nothing of it. I'd last roused to tend the fire during the wee hours, while it was yet pitch black outside, and she'd still been there, curled onto her side. Vanessa recalled being awakened briefly sometime after dawn, Heather stepping over her and whispering that she had to go outside to pee.

Smouldering embers now, and chilly mists and morning dew.

We checked the house, calling down its hallways and into its forsaken rooms. Checked the garden, both sides of the wall. Perhaps she had strayed beyond, towards fields or treeline; gone for a walk with a craving for solitude or an impulse to watch border collies run sheep.

'Or maybe it's wedding day jitters,' Vanessa said.

An hour, then two, and after packing and repacking our gear we had done as much as we could to kill time, unless we were to grab the broom and start sprucing up the house as a whole.

Such a peculiar thing, when something feels amiss and you're trying not to allow your imagination to play the worst tricks it knows, the way the obsessions and compulsions take over. A plan of helpless desperation begins to hatch: if you can just dial the same phone number enough times, or look out a window, or down a street, you can eventually materialise someone out of thin air.

With me, it was the garden, patrolling its blossoms and fronds and leaves every twenty or thirty minutes. Had Heather walked here, stood there? What had I missed a half-hour ago that was in plain view? All along envying the ravens their unclipped wings and their sharp eyes.

While walking past a section of the wall, for a moment it was tough to say who had startled whom more – me, or one of the ravens. With a harsh squawk and a flurry of shiny black wings, it came bursting out from behind a veil of ivy, at the same level as my knees, and it was only after it had rejoined its clan along the top of the wall, some tattered morsel glistening in its beak, that the unlikeliness of this struck me: from *behind* the ivy?

Where was there room enough?

I stood before the spot that had disgorged the raven, and even though I didn't want to reach a hand into that dense greenery and pull it aside, this had to be done. And in the cavity newly revealed, there she was, or at least as near as I could tell it was her.

Seconds. Or hours. How long? Goddamned if I know. No matter how many times I bunched the ivy shut, like a curtain, then pushed it aside again, I could not change what I was seeing. Our Heather, *my* Heather, between stone teeth.

It occurred to me to start ripping the ivy away, so I began tugging it free a few tendrils at a time where it had anchored its roots into rock, and while I did this, yesterday's grim little rhyme crawled through my head like the tiniest of worms.

Fe fi fo fum,
I smell the blood of an American

Features revealed – an enormous eye, glaring directly at me as I stripped it bare; a nostril the size of a basketball.

Be she alive or be she dead

The hollow in which she lay crushed was but the mouth.

I'll grind her bones to make my bread.

Hours. Or seconds. How long? I couldn't know, since time did not permeate here, aware only that Vanessa was running across the gardens from the house and I was meeting her halfway, trying to hold her back while shaking my head and telling her, 'No, no, you don't want to go back there and see this,' and of course she did because you can't tell a person a thing like that and expect her to listen.

Hours. Or days. Living by the clock and the sun again, when it seemed that Vanessa and I could only look at each other as if the other were to blame somehow, and finally her voice broke and she said, 'We can't just stay here, and we can't leave her out there, out in that thing's mouth, we have to tell someone . . .'

'You go,' I murmured. 'I'll stay and make sure . . . nothing else happens.'

Alone, then, I returned to the garden, half of me wanting so badly to follow Vanessa into the world of badges and inquests, because I would at least know my way around there, while the other half longed to follow Heather, if only I understood how, and leave Vanessa behind to find her own way, wherever and whenever she was able.

Because I wondered if, in the dawn, heeding nature's call, Heather hadn't finally heard the voice she'd always yearned to hear.

As I waited, I realised that last night we had got sidetracked and I'd never told a story of my own about this place. But for the time being I simply didn't have the heart to contrive one, and decided that Vanessa's tale would do, because in a way I was living it now, listening for

Heather in case she called out for me to come, follow – you won't believe what I've found on the other side of the inside of the wall.

But the only sound I heard was made by some of the ravens, who plainly had more purpose to their lives than I ever did, as their smooth claws found purchase halfway down one blank section of weathered wall, and slowly, with infinite patience and an intelligence I would never have dreamt of, they began using their beaks like chisels to render yet another likeness of their masters.

I was no threat.

Brian Hodge lives in Boulder, Colorado, where he also locks himself away with an ever-growing digital studio of keyboards, samplers, didgeridoos, and assorted noise-inducing gear, in the guise of an alter-ego recording project dubbed Axis Mundi. Its first offerings can be heard on the CD accompanying limited edition hardcovers of the re-release of the author's début novel, *Oasis*. Hodge has written seven novels, most recently *Wild Horses*, published as a lead hardcover by William Morrow, and has recently completed his next book, *Mad Dogs*. He has also published around eighty short stories and novellas, many of which have appeared in the collections *The Convulsion Factory* and *Falling Idols*. About 'Now Day Was Fled as the Worm Had Wished', he says: 'It's the second of two stories written back-to-back whose titles derive from lines in *Beowulf* that I find particularly haunting and evocative. The other was "Far Flew the Boast of Him", and they both, in different ways, indulge a long-standing fascination with the icons and lore of pagan antiquity, and the ways in which – in some places at least – the worlds of then and now seem to intersect.'

Why Rudy Can't Read

DAVID J. SCHOW

Rudy skinned his knuckles on Teresa's teeth when he backhanded her, but it was only a quick spasm of pain and two dots of blood. Teresa would fix things up later. She always did. If he didn't fucking kill her this time.

'Shit! *Puta!* You bang some fucking guy in our own bed?! You're so fucking stupid I see condom wrappers in the fucking bathroom?! Bitch, you're too fucking stupid to live!'

Teresa felt her eye swell shut and tasted her own blood. She registered the blows but did not care about them. Rudy would entertain no protest. He was like that when he got mad, but otherwise he was an okay guy. He stuffed her panties into her mouth and anally raped her. Whenever she twitched or made an unsolicited sound, he chopped her sharply across the back of the neck until her eyes rolled up and she finally swooned into unconsciousness.

She woke up as he dragged her by the hair and dumped her into the shower. 'Clean yourself up, whore.'

Rudy hit the sack and would sleep for at least twelve straight hours. The advantage – sometimes – of Rudy's odd talent was that he needed lots of sleep, to recharge.

Slowly, methodically, Teresa began by touching her split lip. The scab there was gelid, half-formed. It withdrew as the swelling receded. She undid the contusion on her eye by stroking it with her index and middle fingers together. The fingers themselves ceased to throb, and healed. She dealt with her torn and damaged rectum, then repaired her womb. She had done it before, when Rudy had got her pregnant. With a touch, she caused sperm and egg to magically separate. There was no wayward tissue to evacuate. In ten minutes, she was whole again, and well enough to bathe.

Lavishing her power on herself had exhausted her reserves. It tired her out, made her no better than Rudy. She, too, would need sleep.

Her toilet completed, she crawled naked into bed next to Rudy, who grunted and draped one arm over her hipbone. She touched his bloody knuckles and they healed right up. He'd be a different man when he woke up, and they'd probably make love.

She couldn't see any reason to tell him her infidelity had occurred nowhere but inside her own mind.

Sometimes Rudy was happy that he could not actually 'read' people's minds in the mystical sense, that is, inhabit their thoughts, like in pulp stories or movies. What he could do was more akin to skimming the surface of another consciousness – a stowaway, gleaning emotional textures, not a spy, excising deep, dark secrets whole. This made him a great winner at poker, but lousy at the track. He could not tell the future, nor tell you what you were thinking. He perceived tonalities, attitudes, colorations of feeling augmented by the occasional clear snapshot image. It was enough to keep him from working a legit job, or what the flim-flammers would call an honest con. It kept him in snack foods and cable.

It kept Teresa, too, if only by the card logic of two-of-a-kind. With some fast talk, he could keep her convinced that they belonged together for no other reason than they both had special, secret abilities; God-given or accidental or genetic did not matter. Their alignment might achieve, for them, some higher plane or evolutionary plateau . . . whatever was supposed to come next in this world for all the people who lacked even the distinction of a special power.

Rudy had come home after piggybacking the idiots at a poker-and-pan casino. They thought so much about their meagre hands it was simple for him to scrape intentions away as the thoughts rose towards autonomic function. When bad bluffers tried to stand pat, feelings were enough to suffice. Rudy cleaned them out with a smile and wished them well; average losses combined with his affable manner usually inspired well-banked suckers to belly up for at least one more bloodletting.

The work left little room for Teresa, sometimes.

Rudy hated his victims. His rage was a dull, toxic beast inside him, itching to lash out at anything, living or inert, that gave offence. He ached to murder the imbeciles ahead of him at traffic lights. He itched to kill the motherfuckers in the express lane at the market. He wanted to eviscerate anyone who wore a badge or had the authority to say *no* to him. Mostly, Rudy's life was a study of dangerous stress versus thin restraints. Mostly, Rudy held stony, and watched his lip. And mostly, while he raged alone in the private darkness of his own psyche, he was under constant assault by leakage, from the skulls of everyone around him. He sensed the tips and tails of pedestrian feelings ... and raged all the more, because he knew that even total strangers wanted to kill *him*, too.

Except for Teresa.

What restrained him was the innate sense of superiority that came with his power. He obsessed over the reasons for his half-baked ability, this incomplete talent. He wanted a rationale, a 'why-him'. Linking up with Teresa was a matter of common sense. She might help him two steps closer to whatever the goal of his life might be. Possibilities were practically engraved in granite, amongst his aspirations: He was destined to become stronger, and through refinement would realise his purpose. Or: he'd remain this way, partially advantaged. Or: the power was temporary, and might vanish any time. Maybe the Earth had passed through some kind of cosmic belt, or perhaps he'd been dosed or poisoned, and the unintended ability would peter out. If it did recede, then he'd revert to being just like any other schmuck, and would have to survive by his wits – as he had in his previous life – but with the added lessons learned from sneaking into the heads of strangers.

Finding Teresa was proof that he was on the correct track, almost enough to let him acknowledge a higher power, as strangers had once counselled him to do in an anger management group, long ago.

Drama, however, could twist its own way, and when Rudy had returned home, and looked deeply into Teresa's eyes, and seen the passing fancy there, and accelerated to the conclusion that she had fucked another man ... Rudy lost it one more time. It seemed that whenever he strove hardest for control, his temper always sabotaged him. It wasn't his fault, it was people – stupid fucking sneaky small petty goddamn people, always screwing up and never suspecting the approach of a man who could read the signposts of their mistakes and guilt the way a poet reads verse. It was all in the interpretation.

Give me more power, he thought as he fell asleep. *Or take it away ... but please don't leave me like this, halfway, half-assed half-cocked.* It was almost maddening enough to make any other lapsed Catholic pluck up the cross again.

As Teresa neared sleep, whole once more, she thought of the trouble she'd just shared with Rudy. Once she was sure Rudy was asleep, she reflected on what otherwise would have been hazardous thoughts.

Earlier that day, she had watched Señora Espinoza, examining the furrows and lines which bespoke the years of her life. For a moment, she felt as she imagined Rudy must feel, whenever contact was made with another person's emotions. She read pain and loss and strife in the history of Señora Espinoza; a lifetime of reaching, a paucity of attainment, a guttering faith in a Church that promised rewards too late. Where her aged visage should have evidenced rich experience and fulfilment, Teresa perceived denial and disappointment. Years closer to death, Señora Espinoza's face showed her more puzzlement than wisdom, more sadness than wholeness. It appeared that things would only get worse, until all the old woman had was the final betrayal of her chosen god.

'Chocolate?' Señora Espinoza tended a denty pot that had just begun to bubble. She pronounced the word properly, four syllables. 'It's better to have something warm to drink, since I think it's time we talked of a few things.'

Nailed, thought Teresa, who had wrought the same minor miracles too often for the same set of beneficiaries. There was no chance Señora Espinoza would allow her a graceful escape. Teresa was not Supergirl, and had been denied the timely advantage of flying away once her good deeds were done. Now her talent begged an explanation, a quiz whose score could force her into a secretiveness she did not wish to suffer.

'A hundred years ago, you would have been sainted,' said Señora Espinoza. 'I don't want to know how you do it, or why. I need to ask something deeper. I hope you do not take offence at my asking.'

Surprised by this trajectory of enquiry, Teresa shook her head. Agreeability was the bane of her life. She never *objected* to things enough.

'You are a beautiful child. You have a special gift, so much to offer the world.' Bluntly, the old woman fixed her with a clear gaze. 'Why do you stay with that Rudy Paz? He is not a good man. He hits you, he yells, he is – what is the word today? – abusive. I have seen a thousand of his type in my life, and they never come to good ends. No good. He *takes*. He does not give, as you do. I know these things. I do not have to bear witness to know. So, why? Why you?'

The truth had long sought an outlet in Teresa, and her own small measure of hope coerced a confession of sorts. If she had bothered to know Señora Espinoza past her recurrent crippling arthritis, the truth might have come so easily today. She wrung her healing hands. She was searching for the head of the serpent which coiled all around her life; decanting its ambient venom, long felt yet never specified, and words came hesitantly.

'Doña, it is a painful thing to explain. The best way I can think of is this: you know the magic I work for you?'

'You take away the pain.' Señora Espinoza flexed her hands.

'Yes. Rudy has such a pain, too, but he carries it in his heart. His soul is ill. The man you perceive is not Rudy Paz's fault. His family, his upbringing, tragedies. They twisted him into the man you perceive. The hitter, the yeller. And I keep thinking, if I have the power to heal hurt things, I must be able to heal Rudy. To heal him inside, to repair him so he is once again the man with whom I fell in love.'

'You love him still?'

Teresa nodded. She could not actually force the words out. This was more difficult than she had anticipated. Perhaps she should try telling this to an analyst.

Señora Espinoza was full of surprises. She saw right through Teresa, and Teresa, it seemed, could not read people as well as she thought.

Later that afternoon, at the market, she had briefly returned the casual smile of a handsome man browsing in the produce section. It took all of five seconds to engage a brief sexual fantasy about this stranger, a harmless momentary diversion. As a girlfriend had told her, *when you stop looking, you're dead.*

The image was still in her mind when Rudy had come home. The bed, the condoms, the sex had all been components of the fantasy, and he had collected them like books off an easy-to-reach shelf. This raised the unsettling possibility that perhaps Rudy's perceptions were growing stronger.

His sleeping arm was still in contact with her flesh, and that kept her from finding slumber for a few moments longer.

Sexual arousal fogged Rudy's 'read', a factor of Teresa's strategy the next day. If he saw her intent, like a Post-It note on the surface of her mind, he might get mad. She circumvented this hazard by waking first.

By the time his eyes opened, she had already taken him in her mouth, deep and slickly. Teresa knew of no more instant and intimate connection with another human than lovemaking, and what had befallen them both last night could not be called that. This time would be different.

His movements still dopey, his vision unfocused, Rudy exhaled his dreams and drew in air from the new day. His hands found her body with tropistic familiarity and engaged her skin with the warmth of need. She had removed more than his physical hurts, after her own, and now, refuelled by sleep, his touch was nothing but loving, as electric as ever.

Her goal ran further than the temporary removal of the pain, the anger. She knew a Band-Aid fix would only yield more pain for both of them. She had to exert control and not lose her head to lust, not tip over so far that Rudy might glimpse her intent.

She swung her leg over and gave him a splendid view of her ass as she backed onto him, engulfing his cock to the bone. Rudy ground his teeth and alternated between massaging her butt and clenching the borders of the mattress. He was awake now, damned sure.

It was essentially the same position used for rape less than a day ago – rotated ninety degrees, and divested of harm.

Teresa turned again on well-stretched muscles, keeping Rudy inside her, now meeting his gaze and commencing a quick, scooping thrust that shallowed his breath. With Rudy, there was a heartbeat before orgasm during which his entire body would tighten up, as if on the brink of falling off a very high cliff, a sort of diver's tension Teresa knew well. She had to be alert for it. Her own first climax was a teasing little curl of sensation that was busy racing along on its own timetable, and she could not permit it to distract her, just this once.

She felt him tighten up, and broke rhythm precisely on the beat, rising up so he was almost entirely outside her ... then surging definitively down, gorging him as she clasped his head in both hands and, with her mind, *pulled* as hard as she could.

The delirious abrasion and tactile immediacy of Rudy's ejaculation sped her up and, unexpectedly, tipped her over, flooding her nerves with hot electricity. They rarely came simultaneously; that was an unrealistic cliché, a sort of porno movie gag they both mocked. But sometimes it actually happened that way, and this time it was happening *exactly* that way, as she felt his whole body, flexed hard as a fist, giving her everything he had as one of those little-death cries escaped him.

It was like getting hit by a wave and swept down by the undertow. Teresa grabbed him hard enough to leave bruises, and bit her lower lip, freeing blood, and hung on, and cried out herself.

He brought her a towel and a drink and a warm washcloth, and they stayed lazily tangled up for a while, as though the rest of the day did not matter.

She collected her wits and then, purposefully, replayed their lovemaking in her mind, superimposing the face of that anonymous guy in the market over Rudy's. That man who hadn't even been a flirtation, and who had, in total innocence, got her battered.

Rudy just smiled at her, stroking her hair. When he returned her fulsome gaze she felt sure he could see her trick, would plunge quickly towards a different kind of heat. He just kept looking at her, frankly, the way he'd stare if they were strangers and this was love at first sight.

The conceit was nice but Teresa knew that love was a process of learning another person, and that took time, which was why she had stuck by Rudy even through the bitter times, the harsh and hitting times. You needed time, and caution, and tolerance, and if you did it right, you earned love. Surely Rudy understood that, but he just kept looking at her, and it was beginning to irritate her.

'What?' she said, suddenly self-conscious.

'It's funny,' he said. 'Yesterday I was drowning in anger, I was like a lit fuse, and I wished as hard as I could for things to change . . . and I think I got my wish, because I'm trying to read you right now and I can't get a thing.'

'Really?'

He swallowed and nodded. 'For real. You know something else? It doesn't matter. As long as I've got you, the rest doesn't matter.'

Abruptly, she realised the rage had been successfully drained from him. It was like watching a film projected on glass, through which she could perceive Rudy's face. She was reading two inputs. She knew her own expression must be absurdly blank. Not wanting to give herself away, she covered quickly by answering him with a kiss, and retreating to the bathroom.

Her lip still stung from her passion-chomp, and ministering to it would be a light task. She watched her mirror reflection touch healing finger to mouth. Nothing happened.

She tried again, concentrating. More nothing.

What she experienced instead was Rudy's final thought as he dozed off, as clear, to her, as an announcement on a PA speaker. He would never hit her again. He no longer had it in him. He was penitent, and hopeful.

Which kind of pissed Teresa off. Rudy's new attitude did not excuse what he'd done to her, last night and all occasions prior. He had loosened her teeth, blackened an eye, then rammed her until her asshole was bleeding. The big crybaby tragedy of Teresa's life was that she never objected enough when shit was pulled on her, and Rudy had pulled a shitload. How dare that motherfucker beat her up, rape her, and then give her born-again doe eyes as an excuse the very next fucking morning?

Eyes narrowed, she cracked the door and peered out. The asshole was already asleep. Teresa noticed the baseball bat cocked against the jamb, Rudy's idea of budget security. He'd never used it on her. With Rudy it was fists, kicks, backhands, choking. Manual labour.

He'd fallen asleep thinking he would never touch her in anger again.

'That's for goddamn sure,' she muttered.

Rudy's eyes fluttered open just in time to register the fat end of the bat, splitting his forehead. He could fix things up later. If he lived.

David J. Schow lives in the Hollywood hills, where he works as a screenwriter and author. His recent book releases include *Wild Hairs*, a collection of his non-fiction columns from *Fangoria* magazine, a new edition of his 1990 collection *Lost Angels*, and another short story collection due around Hallowe'en. As an editor, *The Lost Bloch, Volume II: Hell on Earth* is published by Subterranean Press, and if you look quickly enough, he turns up in the documentary which appears on Universal's DVD release of *Creature from the Black Lagoon*. '"Why Rudy Can't Read" is one of those wine-cellar stories,' Schow reveals, 'the kind that take years to mature. A large portion of it was handwritten on legal pages sometime circa 1992. It stayed in the files until 1999, whereupon it resurged and practically finished itself.'

No Story in It

RAMSEY CAMPBELL

'Grandad.'

Boswell turned from locking the front door to see Gemima running up the garden path cracked by the late September heat. Her mother April was at the tipsy gate, and April's husband Rod was climbing out of their rusty crimson Nissan. 'Oh, Dad,' April cried, slapping her forehead hard enough to make him wince. 'You're off to London. How could we forget it was today, Rod?'

Rod pursed thick lips beneath a ginger moustache broader than his otherwise schoolboyish plump face. 'We must have had other things on our mind. It looks as if I'm joining you, Jack.'

'You'll tell me how,' Boswell said as Gemima's small hot five-year-old hand found his grasp.

'We've just learned I'm a cut-back.'

'More of a set-back, will it be? I'm sure there's a demand for teachers of your experience.'

'I'm afraid you're a bit out of touch with the present.'

Boswell saw his daughter willing him not to take the bait. 'Can we save the discussion for my return?' he said. 'I've a bus and then a train to catch.'

'We can run your father to the station, can't we? We want to tell him our proposal.' Rod bent the passenger seat forward. 'Let's keep the men together,' he said.

As Boswell hauled the reluctant belt across himself he glanced up. Usually Gemima reminded him poignantly of her mother at her age – large brown eyes with high startled eyebrows, inquisitive nose, pale prim lips – but in the mirror April's face looked not much less small, just more lined. The car jerked forward, grating its innards, and the radio announced 'A renewed threat of war—' before Rod switched it off. Once the car was past the worst of the potholes in the main road, Boswell said 'So propose.'

'We wondered how you were finding life on your own,' Rod said.

'We thought it mightn't be the ideal situation for someone with your turn of mind.'

'Rod. Dad—'

Her husband gave the mirror a look he might have aimed at a child who'd spoken out of turn in class. 'Since we've all overextended ourselves, we think the solution is to pool our resources.'

'Which are those?'

'We wondered how the notion of our moving in with you might sound.'

'Sounds fun,' Gemima cried.

Rod's ability to imagine living with Boswell for any length of time showed how desperate he, if not April, was. 'What about your own house?' Boswell said.

'There are plenty of respectable couples eager to rent these days. We'd pay you rent, of course. Surely it makes sense for all of us.'

'Can I give you a decision when I'm back from London?' Boswell said, mostly to April's hopeful reflection. 'Maybe you won't have to give up your house. Maybe soon I'll be able to offer you financial help.'

'Christ,' Rod snarled, a sound like a gnashing of teeth.

To start with the noise the car made was hardly harsher. Boswell thought the rear bumper was dragging on the road until tenement blocks jerked up in the mirror as though to seize the vehicle, which ground loudly to a halt. 'Out,' Rod cried in a tone poised to pounce on nonsense.

'Is this like one of your stories, Grandad?' Gemima giggled as she followed Boswell out of the car.

'No,' her father said through his teeth and flung the boot open. 'This is real.'

Boswell responded only by going to look. The suspension had collapsed, thrusting the wheels up through the rusty arches. April took Gemima's hand, Boswell sensed not least to keep her quiet, and murmured 'Oh, Rod.'

Boswell was staring at the tenements. Those not boarded up were tattooed with graffiti inside and out, and he saw watchers at as many broken as unbroken windows. He thought of the parcel a fan had once given him with instructions not to open it until he was home, the present that had been one of Jean's excuses for divorcing him. 'Come with me to the station,' he urged, 'and you can phone whoever you need to phone.'

When the Aireys failed to move immediately he stretched out a hand to them and saw his shadow printed next to theirs on a wall, either half demolished or never completed, in front of the tenements.

A small child holding a woman's hand, a man slouching beside them with a fist stuffed in his pocket, a second man gesturing empty-handed at them ... The shadows seemed to blacken, the sunlight to brighten like inspiration, but that had taken no form when the approach of a taxi distracted him. His shadow roused itself as he dashed into the rubbly road to flag the taxi down. 'I'll pay,' he told Rod.

'Here's Jack Boswell, everyone,' Quentin Sedgwick shouted. 'Here's our star author. Come and meet him.'

It was going to be worth it, Boswell thought. Publishing had changed since all his books were in print – indeed, since any were. Sedgwick, a tall thin young but balding man with wiry veins exposed by a singlet and shorts, had met him at Waterloo, pausing barely long enough to deliver an intense handshake before treating him to a headlong ten-minute march and a stream of enthusiasm for his work. The journey ended at a house in the midst of a crush of them resting their fronts on the pavement. At least the polished nameplate of Cassandra Press had to be visible to anyone who passed. Beyond it a hall that smelled of curried vegetables was occupied by a double-parked pair of bicycles and a steep staircase not much wider than their handlebars. 'Amazing, isn't it?' Sedgwick declared. 'It's like one of your early things, being able to publish from home. Except in a story of yours the computers would take over and tell us what to write.'

'I don't remember writing that,' Boswell said with some unsureness.

'No, I just made it up. Not bad, was it?' Sedgwick said, running upstairs. 'Here's Jack Boswell, everyone . . .'

A young woman with a small pinched studded face and glistening black hair spiky as an armoured fist emerged from somewhere on the ground floor as Sedgwick threw open doors to reveal two cramped rooms, each featuring a computer terminal, at one of which an even younger woman with blonde hair the length of her filmy flowered blouse was composing an advertisement. 'Starts with C, ends with e,' Sedgwick said of her, and of the studded woman 'Bren, like the gun. Our troubleshooter.'

Boswell grinned, feeling someone should. 'Just the three of you?'

'Small is sneaky, I keep telling the girls. While the big houses are being dragged down by excess personnel, we move into the market they're too cumbersome to handle. Carole, show him his page.'

The publicist saved her work twice before displaying the Cassandra Press catalogue. She scrolled past the colophon, a C with a P hooked on it, and a parade of authors: Ferdy Thorn, ex-marine turned ecological warrior; Germaine Gossett, feminist fantasy writer; Torin

Bergman, Scandinavia's leading magic realist ... 'Forgive my ignorance,' Boswell said, 'but these are all new to me.'

'They're the future.' Sedgwick cleared his throat and grabbed Boswell's shoulder to lean him towards the computer. 'Here's someone we all know.'

BOSWELL'S BACK! the page announced in letters so large they left room only for a shout-line from, Boswell remembered, the *Observer* twenty years ago – 'Britain's best SF writer since Wyndham and Wells' – and a scattering of titles: *The Future Just Began, Tomorrow Was Yesterday, Wave Goodbye To Earth, Terra Spells Terror, Science Lies In Wait* ... 'It'll look better when we have covers to reproduce,' Carole said. 'I couldn't write much. I don't know your work.'

'That's because I've been devouring it all over again, Jack. You thought you might have copies for my fair helpers, didn't you?'

'So I have,' Boswell said, struggling to spring the catches of his aged briefcase.

'See what you think when you've read these. Some for you as well, Bren,' Sedgwick said, passing out Boswell's last remaining hardcovers of several of his books. 'Here's a Hugo winner and look, this one got the Prix du Fantastique Écologique. Will you girls excuse us now? I hear the call of lunch.'

They were in sight of Waterloo Station again when he seized Boswell's elbow to steer him into the Delphi, a tiny restaurant crammed with deserted tables spread with pink-and-white checked cloths. 'This is what one of our greatest authors looks like, Nikos,' Sedgwick announced. 'Let's have all we can eat and a litre of your red if that's your style, Jack, to be going on with.'

The massive dark-skinned variously hairy proprietor brought them a carafe without a stopper and a brace of glasses Boswell would have expected to hold water. Sedgwick filled them with wine and dealt Boswell's a vigorous clunk. 'Here's to us. Here's to your legendary unpublished books.'

'Not for much longer.'

'What a scoop for Cassandra. I don't know which I like best, *Don't Make Me Mad* or *Only We Are Left*. Listen to this, Nikos. There are going to be so many mentally ill people they have to be given the vote and everyone's made to have one as a lodger. And a father has to seduce his daughter or the human race dies out.'

'Very nice.'

'Ignore him, Jack. They couldn't be anyone else but you.'

'I'm glad you feel that way. You don't think they're a little too dark even for me?'

'Not a shade, and certainly not for Cassandra. Wait till you read our other books.'

Here Nikos brought meze, an oval plate splattered with varieties of goo. Sedgwick waited until Boswell had transferred a sample of each to his plate and tested them with a piece of lukewarm bread. 'Good?'

'Most authentic,' Boswell found it in himself to say.

Sedgwick emptied the carafe into their glasses and called for another. Blackened lamb chops arrived too, and prawns dried up by grilling, withered meatballs, slabs of smoked ham that could have been used to sole shoes ... Boswell was working on a token mouthful of viciously spiced sausage when Sedgwick said 'Know how you could delight us even more?'

Boswell swallowed and had to salve his mouth with half a glassful of wine. 'Tell me,' he said tearfully.

'Have you enough unpublished stories for a collection?'

'I'd have to write another to bring it up to length.'

'Wait till I let the girls know. Don't think they aren't excited, they were just too overwhelmed by meeting you to show it. Can you call me as soon as you have an idea for the story or the cover?'

'I think I may have both.'

'You're an example to us all. Can I hear?'

'Shadows on a ruined wall. A man and woman and her child, and another man reaching out to them, I'd say in warning. Ruined tenements in the background. Everything overgrown. Even if the story isn't called *We Are Tomorrow*, the book can be.'

'Shall I give you a bit of advice? Go further than you ever have before. Imagine something you couldn't believe anyone would pay you to write.'

Despite the meal, Boswell felt too elated to imagine that just now. His capacity for observation seemed to have shut down too, and only an increase in the frequency of passers-by outside the window roused it. 'What time is it?' he wondered, fumbling his watch upwards on his thin wrist.

'Not much past five,' Sedgwick said, emptying the carafe yet again. 'Still lunchtime.'

'Good God, if I miss my train I'll have to pay double.'

'Next time we'll see about paying for your travel.' Sedgwick gulped the last of the wine as he threw a credit card on the table to be collected later. 'I wish you'd said you had to leave this early. I'll have Bren send copies of our books to you,' he promised as Boswell panted into Waterloo, and called after him down the steps into the Underground 'Don't forget, imagine the worst. That's what we're for.'

For three hours the worst surrounded Boswell. **SIX NATIONS CONTINUE REARMING ... CLIMATE CHANGES ACCELERATE, SAY SCIENTISTS ... SUPERSTITIOUS FANATICISM ON INCREASE ... WOMEN'S GROUPS CHALLENGE ANTI-GUN RULING ... RALLY AGAINST COMPUTER CHIPS IN CRIMINALS ENDS IN VIOLENCE: THREE DEAD, MANY INJURED** ... Far more commuters weren't reading the news than were: many wore headphones that leaked percussion like distant discos in the night, while the sole book to be seen was *Page Turner*, the latest Turner adventure from Midas Paperbacks, bound in either gold or silver depending, Boswell supposed, on the reader's standards. Sometimes drinking helped him create, but just now a bottle of wine from the buffet to stave off a hangover only froze in his mind the image of the present in ruins and overgrown by the future, of the shapes of a family and a figure poised to intervene printed on the remains of a wall by a flare of painful light. He had to move on from thinking of them as the Aireys and himself, or had he? One reason Jean had left him was that she'd found traces of themselves and April in nearly all his work, even where none was intended; she'd become convinced he was wishing the worst for her and her child when he'd only meant a warning, by no means mostly aimed at them. His attempts to invent characters wholly unlike them had never convinced her and hadn't improved his work either. He needn't consider her feelings now, he thought sadly. He had to write whatever felt true – the best story he had in him.

It was remaining stubbornly unformed when the train stammered into the terminus. A minibus strewn with drunks and defiant smokers deposited him at the end of his street. He assumed his house felt empty because of Rod's proposal. Jean had taken much of the furniture they hadn't passed on to April, but Boswell still had seats where he needed to sit and folding canvas chairs for visitors, and nearly all his books. He was in the kitchen, brewing coffee while he tore open the day's belated mail, when the phone rang.

He took the handful of bills and the airmail letter he'd saved for last into his workroom, where he sat on the chair April had loved spinning and picked up the receiver. 'Jack Boswell.'

'Jack? They're asleep.'

Presumably this explained why Rod's voice was low. 'Is that an event?' Boswell said.

'It is for April at the moment. She's been out all day looking for work, any work. She didn't want to tell you in case you already had too much on your mind.'

'But now you have.'

'I was hoping things had gone well for you today.'

'I think you can do more than that.'

'Believe me, I'm looking as hard as she is.'

'No, I mean you can assure her when she wakes that not only do I have a publisher for my two novels and eventually a good chunk of my backlist, but they've asked me to put together a new collection too.'

'Do you mind if I ask for her sake how much they're advancing you?'

'No pounds and no shillings or pence.'

'You're saying they'll pay you in euros?'

'I'm saying they don't pay an advance to me or any of their authors, but they pay royalties every three months.'

'I take it your agent has approved the deal.'

'It's a long time since I've had one of those, and now I'll be ten per cent better off. Do remember I've plenty of experience.'

'I could say the same. Unfortunately it isn't always enough.'

Boswell felt his son-in-law was trying to render him as insignificant as Rod believed science fiction writers ought to be. He tore open the airmail envelope with the little finger of the hand holding the receiver. 'What's that?' Rod demanded.

'No panic. I'm not destroying any of my work,' Boswell told him, and smoothed out the letter to read it again. 'Well, this is timely. The Saskatchewan Conference on Prophetic Literature is giving me the Wendigo Award for a career devoted to envisioning the future.'

'Congratulations. Will it help?'

'It certainly should, and so will the story I'm going to write. Maybe even you will be impressed. Tell April not to let things pull her down,' Boswell said as he rang off, and 'Such as you' only after he had.

Boswell wakened with a hangover and an uneasy sense of some act left unperformed. The image wakened with him: small child holding woman's hand, man beside them, second man gesturing. He groped for the mug of water by the bed, only to find he'd drained it during the night. He stumbled to the bathroom and emptied himself while the cold tap filled the mug. In time he felt equal to yet another breakfast of the kind his doctor had warned him to be content with. Of course, he thought as the sound of chewed bran filled his skull, he should have called Sedgwick last night about the Wendigo Award.

How early could he call? Best to wait until he'd worked on the new story. He tried as he washed up the breakfast things and the rest of the plates and utensils in the sink, but his mind seemed as paralysed as the shadows on the wall it kept showing him. Having sat at his desk for a while in front of the wordless screen, he dialled Cassandra Press.

'Hello? Yes?'

'Is that Carole?' Since that earned him no reply, he tried 'Bren?'

'It's Carole. Who is this?'

'Jack Boswell. I just wanted you to know—'

'You'll want to speak to Q. Q, it's your sci-fi man.'

Sedgwick came on almost immediately, preceded by a creak of bedsprings. 'Jack, you're never going to tell me you've written your story already.'

'Indeed I'm not. Best to take time to get it right, don't you think? I'm calling to report they've given me the Wendigo Award.'

'About time, and never more deserved. Who is it gives those again? Carole, you'll need to scribble this down. Bren, where's something to scribble with?'

'By the phone,' Bren said very close, and the springs creaked.

'Reel it off, Jack.'

As Boswell heard Sedgwick relay the information he grasped that he was meant to realise how close the Cassandra Press personnel were to one another. 'That's capital, Jack,' Sedgwick told him. 'Bren will be lumping some books to the mail for you, and I think I can say Carole's going to have good news for you.'

'Any clue what kind?'

'Wait and see, Jack, and we'll wait and see what your new story's about.'

Boswell spent half an hour trying to write an opening line that would trick him into having started the tale, but had to acknowledge that the technique no longer worked for him. He was near to being blocked by fearing he had lost all ability to write, and so he opened the carton of books the local paper had sent him to review. *Sci-Fi On The Net*, *Create Your Own Star Wars™ Character*, *1000 Best Sci-Fi Videos*, *Sci-Fi From Lucas To Spielberg*, *Star Wars™: The Bluffer's Guide* ... There wasn't a book he would have taken off a shelf, nor any appropriate to the history of science fiction in which he intended to incorporate a selection from his decades of reviews. Just now writing something other than his story might well be a trap. He donned sandals and shorts and unbuttoned his shirt as he ventured out beneath a sun that looked as fierce as the rim of a total eclipse.

All the seats of a dusty bus were occupied by pensioners, some of whom looked as bewildered as the young woman who spent the journey searching the pockets of the combat outfit she wore beneath a stained fur coat and muttering that everyone needed to be ready for the enemy. Boswell had to push his way off the bus past three grim scrawny youths bare from the waist up, who boarded the vehicle as if they planned to hijack it. He was at the end of the road where the wall had inspired him – but he hadn't reached the wall when he saw Rod's car.

It was identifiable solely by the charred number plate. The car itself was a blackened windowless hulk. He would have stalked away to call the Aireys if the vandalism hadn't made writing the new story more urgent than ever, and so he stared at the incomplete wall with a fierceness designed to revive his mind. When he no longer knew if he was staring at the bricks until the story formed or the shadows did, he turned quickly away. The shadows weren't simply cast on the wall, he thought; they were embedded in it, just as the image was embedded in his head.

He had to walk a mile homewards before the same bus showed up. Trudging the last yards to his house left him parched. He drank several glassfuls of water, and opened the drawer of his desk to gaze for reassurance or perhaps inspiration at his secret present from a fan before he dialled the Aireys' number.

'Hello?'

If it was April, something had driven her voice high. 'It's only me,' Boswell tentatively said.

'Grandad. Are you coming to see us?'

'Soon, I hope.'

'Oh.' Having done her best to hide her disappointment, she added 'Good.'

'What have you been doing today?'

'Reading. Dad says I have to get a head start.'

'I'm glad to hear it,' Boswell said, though she didn't sound as if she wanted him to be. 'Is Mummy there?'

'Just Dad.'

After an interval Boswell tried 'Rod?'

'It's just me, right enough.'

'I'm sure she didn't mean – I don't know if you've seen your car.'

'I'm seeing nothing but. We still have to pay to have it scrapped.'

'No other developments?'

'Jobs, are you trying to say? Not unless April's so dumbstruck with good fortune she can't phone. I was meaning to call you, though. I wasn't clear last night what plans you had with regard to us.'

Rod sounded so reluctant to risk hoping that Boswell said 'There's a good chance I'll have a loan in me.'

'I won't ask how much.' After a pause presumably calculated to entice an answer Rod added 'I don't need to tell you how grateful we are. How's your new story developing?'

This unique display of interest in his work only increased the pressure inside Boswell's uninspired skull. 'I'm hard at work on it,' he said.

'I'll tell April,' Rod promised, and left Boswell with that – with hours before the screen and not a word of a tale, just shadows in searing light: child holding woman's hand, man beside, another gesturing ... He fell asleep at his desk and jerked awake in a panic, afraid to know why his inspiration refused to take shape.

He seemed hardly to have slept in his bed when he was roused by a pounding of the front-door knocker and an incessant shrilling of the doorbell. As he staggered downstairs he imagined a raid, the country having turned overnight into a dictatorship that had set the authorities the task of arresting all subversives, not least those who saw no cause for optimism. The man on the doorstep was uniformed and gloomy about his job, but brandished a clipboard and had a carton at his feet. 'Consignment for Boswell,' he grumbled.

'Books from my publishers.'

'Wouldn't know. Just need your autograph.'

Boswell scrawled a signature rendered illegible by decades of autographs, then bore the carton to the kitchen table, where he slit its layers of tape to reveal the first Cassandra Press books he'd seen. All the covers were black as coal in a closed pit except for bony white lettering not quite askew enough for the effect to be unquestionably intentional. **GERMAINE GOSSETT,** *Women Are The Wave.* **TORIN BERGMAN,** *Oracles Arise!* **FERDY THORN,** *Fight Them Fisheries* ... Directly inside each was the title page, and on the back of that the copyright opposite the first page of text. Ecological frugality was fine, but not if it looked unprofessional, even in uncorrected proof copies. Proofreading should take care of the multitude of printer's errors, but what of the prose? Every book, not just Torin Bergman's, read like the work of a single apprentice translator.

He abandoned a paragraph of Ferdy Thorn's blunt chunky style and sprinted to his workroom to answer the phone. 'Boswell,' he panted.

'Jack. How are you today?'

'I've been worse, Quentin.'

'You'll be a lot better before you know. Did the books land?'

'The review copies, you mean.'

'We'd be delighted if you reviewed them. That would be wonderful, wouldn't it, if Jack reviewed the books?' When this received no audible answer he said 'Only you mustn't be kind just because they're ours, Jack. We're all in the truth business.'

'Let me read them and then we'll see what's best. What I meant, though, these aren't finished books.'

'They certainly should be. Sneak a glance at the last pages if you don't mind knowing the end.'

'Finished in the sense of the state that'll be on sale in the shops.'

'Well, yes. They're trade paperbacks. That's the book of the future.'

'I know what trade paperbacks are. These—'

'Don't worry, Jack, they're just our first attempts. Wait till you see the covers Carole's done for you. Nothing grabs the eye like naïve art, especially with messages like ours.'

'So,' Boswell said in some desperation, 'have I heard why you called?'

'You don't think we'd interrupt you at work without some real news.'

'How real?'

'We've got the figures for the advance orders of your books. All the girls had to do was phone with your name and the new titles till the batteries went flat, and I don't mind telling you you're our top seller.'

'What are the figures?' Boswell said, and took a deep breath.

'Nearly three hundred. Congratulations once again.'

'Three hundred thousand. It's I who should be congratulating you and your team. I only ever had one book up there before. Shows publishing needs people like yourselves to shake it up.' He became aware of speaking fast so that he could tell the Aireys his – no, their – good fortune, but he had to clarify one point before letting euphoria overtake him. 'Or is that, don't think for a second I'm complaining if it is, but is that the total for both titles or each?'

'Actually, Jack, can I just slow you down a moment?'

'Sorry. I'm babbling. That's what a happy author sounds like. You understand why.'

'I hope I do, but would you mind – I didn't quite catch what you thought I said.'

'Three hundred—'

'Can I stop you there? That's the total, or just under. As you say, publishing has changed. I expect a lot of the bigger houses are doing no better with some of their books.'

Boswell's innards grew hollow, then his skull. He felt his mouth drag itself into some kind of a grin as he said, 'Is that three hundred, sorry, nearly three hundred per title?'

'Overall, I'm afraid. We've still a few little independent shops to call, and sometimes they can surprise you.'

Boswell doubted he could cope with any more surprises, but heard himself say, unbelievably, hopefully 'Did you mention *We Are Tomorrow*?'

'How could we have forgotten it?' Sedgwick's enthusiasm relented at last as he said 'I see what you're asking. Yes, the total is for all three of your books. Don't forget we've still the backlist to come, though,' he added with renewed vigour.

'Good luck to it.' Boswell had no idea how much bitterness was audible in that, nor in 'I'd best be getting back to work.'

'We all can't wait for the new story, can we?'

Boswell had no more of an answer than he heard from anyone else. Having replaced the receiver as if it had turned to heavy metal, he stared at the uninscribed slab of the computer screen. When he'd had enough of that he trudged to stare into the open rectangular hole of the Cassandra carton. Seized by an inspiration he would have preferred not to experience, he dashed upstairs to drag on yesterday's clothes and marched unshaven out of the house.

Though the library was less than ten minutes' walk away through sunbleached streets whose desert was relieved only by patches of scrub, he'd hardly visited it for the several years he had been too depressed to enter bookshops. The library was almost worse: it lacked not just his books but practically everyone's, except for paperbacks with injured spines. Some of the tables in the large white high-windowed room were occupied by newspaper readers. **MIDDLE EAST WAR DEADLINE EXPIRES ... ONE IN TWO FAMILIES WILL BE VICTIMS OF VIOLENCE, STUDY SHOWS ... FAMINES IMMINENT IN EUROPE ... NO MEDICINE FOR FATAL VIRUSES** ... Most of the tables held Internet terminals, from one of which a youth whose face was red with more than pimples was being evicted by a librarian for calling up some text that had offended the black woman at the next screen. Boswell paid for an hour at the terminal and began his search.

The only listings of any kind for Torin Bergman were the publication details of the Cassandra Press books, and the same was true of Ferdy Thorn and Germaine Gossett. When the screen told him his time was up and began to flash like lightning to alert the staff, the message and the repeated explosion of light and the headlines around him seemed to merge into a single inspiration he couldn't grasp. Only a hand laid on his shoulder made him jump up and lurch between the reluctantly automatic doors.

The sunlight took up the throbbing of the screen, or his head did. He remembered nothing of his tramp home other than that it tasted like bone. As he fumbled to unlock the front door the light grew audible, or the phone began to shrill. He managed not to snap the key and ran to snatch up the receiver. 'What now?'

'It's only me, Dad. I didn't mean to bother you.'

'You never could,' Boswell said, though she just had by sounding close to tears. 'How are you, April? How are things?'

'Not too wonderful.'

'Things aren't, you mean. I'd never say you weren't.'

'Both.' Yet more tonelessly she said 'I went looking for computer jobs. Didn't want all the time mummy spent showing me how things worked to go to waste. Only I didn't realise how much more there is to them now, and I even forgot what she taught me. So then I thought I'd go on a computer course to catch up.'

'I'm sure that's a sound idea.'

'It wasn't really. I forgot where I was going. I nearly forgot our number when I had to ring Rod to come and find me when he hasn't even got the car and leave Gemima all on her own.'

Boswell was reaching deep into himself for a response when she said 'Mummy's dead, isn't she?'

Rage at everything, not least April's state, made his answer harsh. 'Shot by the same freedom fighters she'd given the last of her money to in a country I'd never even heard of. She went off telling me one of us had to make a difference to the world.'

'Was it years ago?'

'Not long after you were married,' Boswell told her, swallowing grief.

'Oh.' She seemed to have nothing else to say but 'Rod.'

Boswell heard him murmuring at length before his voice attacked the phone. 'Why is April upset?'

'Don't you know?'

'Forgive me. Were you about to give her some good news?'

'If only.'

'You will soon, surely, once your books are selling. You know I'm no admirer of the kind of thing you write, but I'll be happy to hear of your success.'

'You don't know what I write, since you've never read any of it.' Aloud Boswell said only 'You won't.'

'I don't think I caught that.'

'Yes you did. This publisher prints as many books as there are orders, which turns out to be under three hundred.'

'Maybe you should try and write the kind of thing people will pay to read.'

Boswell placed the receiver with painfully controlled gentleness on the hook, then lifted it to redial. The distant bell had started to sound more like an alarm to him when it was interrupted. 'Quentin Sedgwick.'

'And Torin Bergman.'

'Jack.'

'As one fictioneer to another, are you Ferdy Thorn as well?'

Sedgwick attempted a laugh, but it didn't lighten his tone much. 'Germaine Gossett too, if you must know.'

'So you're nearly all of Cassandra Press.'

'Not any longer.'

'How's that?'

'Out,' Sedgwick said with gloomy humour. 'I am. The girls had all the money, and now they've seen our sales figures they've gone off to set up a gay romance publisher.'

'What lets them do that?' Boswell heard himself protest.

'Trust.'

Boswell could have made plenty of that, but was able to say merely 'So my books . . .'

'Must be somewhere in the future. Don't be more of a pessimist than you have to be, Jack. If I manage to revive Cassandra you know you'll be the first writer I'm in touch with,' Sedgwick said, and had the grace to leave close to a minute's silence unbroken before ringing off. Boswell had no sense of how much the receiver weighed as he lowered it, no sense of anything except some rearrangement that was aching to occur inside his head. He had to know why the news about Cassandra Press felt like a completion so imminent the throbbing of light all but blinded him.

It came to him in the night, slowly. He had been unable to develop the new story because he'd understood instinctively there wasn't one. His sense of the future was sounder than ever: he'd foreseen the collapse of Cassandra Press without admitting it to himself. Ever since his last sight of the Aireys the point had been to save them – he simply hadn't understood how. Living together would only have delayed their fate. He'd needed time to interpret his vision of the shadows on the wall.

He was sure the light in the house was swifter and more intense than dawn used to be. He pushed himself away from the desk and worked aches out of his body before making his way to the bathroom.

All the actions he performed there felt like stages of a purifying ritual. In the mid-morning sunlight the phone on his desk looked close to bursting into flame. He winced at the heat of it before, having grown cool in his hand, it ventured to mutter, 'Hello?'

'Good morning.'

'Dad? You sound happier. Are you?'

'As never. Is everyone up? Can we meet?'

'What's the occasion?'

'I want to fix an idea I had last time we met. I'll bring a camera if you can all meet me in the same place in let's say half an hour.'

'We could except we haven't got a car.'

'Take a cab. I'll reimburse you. It'll be worth it, I promise.'

He was on his way almost as soon as he rang off. Tenements reared above his solitary march, but couldn't hinder the sun in its climb towards unbearable brightness. He watched his shadow shrink in front of him like a stain on the dusty littered concrete, and heard footsteps attempting stealth not too far behind him. Someone must have seen the camera slung from his neck. A backwards glance as he crossed a deserted potholed junction showed him a youth as thin as a puppet, who halted twitching until Boswell turned away, then came after him.

A taxi sped past Boswell as he reached the street he was bound for. The Aireys were in front of the wall, close to the sooty smudge like a lingering shadow that was the only trace of their car. Gemima clung to her mother's hand while Rod stood a little apart, one fist in his hip pocket. They looked posed and uncertain why. Before anything had time to change, Boswell held up his palm to keep them still and confronted the youth who was swaggering towards him while attempting to seem aimless. Boswell lifted the camera strap over his tingling scalp. 'Will you take us?' he said.

The youth faltered barely long enough to conceal an incredulous grin. He hung the camera on himself and snapped the carrying case open as Boswell moved into position, hand outstretched towards the Aireys. 'Use the flash,' Boswell said, suddenly afraid that otherwise there would be no shadows under the sun at the zenith – that the future might let him down after all. He'd hardly spoken when the flash went off, almost blinding its subjects to the spectacle of the youth fleeing with the camera.

Boswell had predicted this, and even that Gemima would step out a pace from beside her mother. 'It's all right,' he murmured, unbuttoning his jacket, 'there's no film in it,' and passed the gun across himself into the hand that had been waiting to be filled. Gemima was first, then April, and Rod took just another second. Boswell's peace deepened threefold as peace came to them. Nevertheless he preferred not to look at their faces as he arranged them against the bricks. He had only seen shadows before, after all.

Though the youth had vanished, they were being watched. Perhaps now the world could see the future Boswell had always seen. He clawed chunks out of the wall until wedging his arm into the gap supported him. He heard sirens beginning to howl, and wondered if the war had started. 'The end,' he said as best he could for the metal in his mouth. The last thing he saw was an explosion of brightness so intense he was sure it was printing their shadows on the bricks for as long as the wall stood. He even thought he smelled how green it would grow to be.

Ramsey Campbell lives in Wallasey, Merseyside. He was presented with both the World Horror Convention's Grand Master Award and the Horror Writers Association's Bram Stoker Award for Life Achievement in 1999. His recent novels have included *The House on Nazareth Hill*, *The One Safe Place*, *The Long Lost*, *Silent Children*, *The Pact of the Fathers* and the forthcoming supernatural tale, *The Darkest Part of the Woods*. An earlier novel, *The Nameless*, has recently been made into the film *Los Sin Nombre* by Spanish director Jaume Balaguero. As the author explains: '"No Story in It" was written around an Alan M. Clark painting – the image the luckless protagonist proposes for his book cover. As with "Never to be Heard" (in *Dark Terrors 4*), the Clark image let me focus ideas I'd already scattered through my notebooks for possible development. I had also recently been writing a memoir of the late John Brunner for my column in *Necrofile*. While there is little of John in my protagonist, I'm afraid that John – were he alive now – would have no difficulty in identifying with him. Nor would far too many writers in our field as well as his.'

Witch-Compass

GRAHAM MASTERTON

On his last night in Libreville, Paul went for a long aimless walk through the market. A heavy rainstorm had just passed over and the air was almost intolerably humid. He felt as if he had a hot Turkish towel wrapped around his head, and his shirt clung to his back. There were many things that he would miss about Gabon, but the climate wasn't one of them, and neither was the musty smell of tropical mould.

All along the Marché Rouge there were stalls heaped with bananas and plantains and cassava; as well as food-stands selling curried goat and thick maize porridge and spicy fish. The stalls were lit by an elaborate spider's-web of electric cables, with naked bulbs dangling from them. Each stall was like a small, brightly coloured theatre, with the sweaty black faces of its actors wreathed in theatrical steam and smoke.

Paul passed them by, a tall rangy white man with short-cropped hair and round Oliver Goldsmith glasses, and already he was beginning to feel like a spectator, like somebody who no longer belonged here.

A thin young girl with one milky eye tugged at Paul's shirt and offered him a selection of copper bracelets. He was about to shoo her away when he suddenly thought: what does it matter any more? I won't be here tomorrow, I'll be on my way back to the States, and what good will a walletful of CFA francs be in New Milford, Connecticut?

He gave the girl five francs, which was more than she probably made in a week, and took one of the bracelets.

'*Merci beaucoup, monsieur, vous êtes très gentil*,' she said, with a strong Fang accent. She gave him a gappy grin and twirled off into the crowds.

Paul looked down at his wallet. He had hardly any money left now. Three hundred francs, an American Express card which he didn't dare to use, and a damp-rippled air ticket. He was almost as poor as the rest of the population of Gabon.

He had come here three and a half years ago to set up his own metals-trading business. Gradually he had built up a network of contacts amongst the foreign mining companies and established a reputation for achieving the highest prices for the least administration costs. After two years, he was able to rent a grand white house near the presidential palace and import a new silver Mercedes. But his increasing success brought him to the attention of government officials, and before long he had been summoned to the offices of the department of trade. A highly amused official in a snowy short-sleeved shirt had informed him that, in future, all of his dealings would attract a 'brokerage tax' of eighty-five per cent.

'Eighty-five per cent! Do you want me to starve?'

'You exaggerate, Mr Dennison. The average Gabonese makes less in a year than you spend on one pair of shoes. Yet he eats, he has clothes on his back. What more do you need than that?'

Paul had refused to pay. But the next week, when he had tried to call LaSalle Zinc, he had been told with a great deal of apologetic French clucking that they could no longer do business with him, because of 'internal rationalisation'. He had received a similar response from DuFreyne Lead and Pan-African Manganese. The following week his phones had been cut off altogether.

He had lived off his savings for a few months, trying to take legal action to have the 'brokerage tax' rescinded or at least reduced. But the Gabonese legal system owed more to Franz Kafka than it did to commercial justice. In the end his lawyer had withdrawn his services, too, and he knew there was no point in fighting his case any further.

He walked right down to the western end of the Marché Rouge. Beneath his feet, the lights from the market stalls were reflected like a drowned world. The air was filled with repetitive, plangent music, and the clamour of so many insects that it sounded as if somebody were scraping a rake over a corrugated iron roof.

At the very end of the market, in the shadows, an old woman was sitting cross-legged on the wet tarmac with an upturned fruit box in front of her. She had a smooth, round face and her hair was twisted into hundeds of tiny silver beads. She wore a dark brown dress with black-printed patterns on it, zigzags and circles and twig-like figures. She kept nodding her head in Paul's direction, as if he were talking to her and she was agreeing with him, and as she nodded her huge silver earrings swung and caught the light from the fish stall next to her.

On the fruit box several odd items were arranged. At the back, a small ebony carving of a woman with enormous breasts and protruding buttocks, her lips fastened together with silver wire. Next to her feet lay something that looked like a rattle made out of a dried bone and a shrunken monkey's head, with matted ginger hair. There were six or seven Pond's Cold Cream jars, refilled with brown and yellowish paste. There was a selection of necklaces, decorated with teeth and beads and birds' bones. And there was an object which looked like a black gourd, only three or four inches long and completely plain.

Paul was about to turn back to his hotel when the woman said, '*Attendez, monsieur! Ne voulez-vous acheter mes jouets?*'

She said it in surprise, as if she couldn't understand why he hadn't come up to her and asked her how much they cost.

'I'm sorry, I'm just taking a walk.'

She passed her hands over the disparate collection on top of her fruit box. 'I think that is why you come here. To buy from me something.'

'No, I'm sorry.'

'Then what is bringing your feet this way?'

'I'm leaving Libreville tomorrow morning. I was taking a last look around the market, that's all.'

'You come this way for a reason. No man comes looking for Jonquil Mekambo by accident.'

'Listen,' said Paul. 'I really have to go. And to tell you the truth, I don't think you have anything here that I could possibly want.'

The woman lifted up the ebony figure. 'Silence those who do you bad, *peut-être?*'

'Oh, I get it. This is ju-ju stuff. Thanks but no thanks. Really.'

The woman picked up the bone with the monkey's head and tapped it on the side of the box. 'Call up demons to strangle your enemy? I teach you how to knock.'

'Listen, forget it. I got enough demons in my life right now without conjuring up any more.'

'Jonquil knows that. Jonquil knows why you have to go from Libreville. No money, no work.'

Paul stared at her. She stared back, her face like a black expressionless moon. 'How did you know that?' he demanded.

'Jonquil knows all thing. Jonquil is waiting for you here *ce soir.*'

'Well, Jonquil, however you found out, there's nothing you can do to help me. It's going to take more than black magic to sort my life out. I'll have to start over again, right from scratch.'

'Then you need witch-compass.'

'Oh, yes? And what's a witch-compass going to do for me, whatever that is?'

Jonquil pointed with a red-painted fingernail to the gourd. 'Witch-compass, genuine from Makokou.'

'So what does a witch-compass do?'

'Brings your feet to what you want. Money, woman, house. Work all time.'

'I see. Never fails. So what are *you* doing, sitting in the street here, if you could use the witch-compass to guide you to whatever you want?'

'Jonquil has what she wants. All thing.'

Paul shook his head. 'It's a great idea, Jonquil. But I think I'll pass.'

'Pick it up,' Jonquil urged him.

Paul hesitated for a moment. For some reason, the pattering of drums sounded louder than usual, more insistent, and the insects scraped even more aggressively. He picked up the black gourd and weighed it in his hand. It was quite light, and obviously hollow, because he could hear something rattling around inside it. Beads, maybe; or seeds.

'See in your head the thing that you want,' said Jonquil. 'The witch-compass makes its song. Quiet when you want is far off distance. Louder – louder when close.'

'Kind of a Geiger counter, then,' smiled Paul. 'Except it looks for luck instead of radiation.'

'Money, woman, house. Work all time.'

Paul rolled the witch-compass over and over in his hand. There was something very smooth and attractive about it, like a giant worry-bead. 'I don't know . . .' he said. 'It depends how much it is.'

'*Il y a deux prix*,' said Jonquil.

'Two prices? What do you mean?'

'*En termes d'argent, le prix est quatorze francs. Mais il y a également un prix moral à payer, chaque fois la boussole pointe sur ce que vous désirez.*'

'I have to make a moral choice? Is that what you said?'

Jonquil nodded again. 'No thing that you truly desire come free.'

Paul gently shook the witch-compass and heard its soft, seductive shaking sound.

'All right,' he said. 'Fourteen francs. If it works, I'll come back and thank you in person. If it doesn't, I won't be able to afford to come back.'

'You will be back,' Jonquil assured him, as he counted out the money. 'Your feet will bring you back.'

It was dry and breezy when he arrived back in New Milford. The sky was startlingly blue and red-and-yellow leaves were whirling and dancing on the green. He drove his rental car slowly through the town, feeling just as much of a ghost as he had on his last night in Gabon. He saw people he knew. Old Mr Dawson, with a new Labrador puppy. Gremlin, his previous dog, must have died. Jim Salzberger, leaning against a red pick-up truck, talking to Annie Nilsen.

The same white-painted buildings, dazzling in the sunlight. The same town clock, with its bright blue dial. Paul drove slowly through but he didn't stop. He didn't want anybody to know that he was back, not just yet. He had been crackling with ambition when he left this town, and his parents had been so proud of him when he made his first hundred thousand dollars in Libreville. But here he was, back and bankrupt, more or less, without even the will to start over.

He drove out along the deserted highway to Allen's Corners, past Don Humphrey's general store. The sunlight flickered through the car windows, so that he felt that he was watching an old home movie of his previous life.

At last he took the steep turn up through the woods that led to his parents' house. It wasn't much of a place: a single-storey building on the side of the hill, with an awkwardly angled driveway and a small triangular yard. His father was out back, sawing logs with his old circular saw, and there was a tangy smell of woodsmoke in the air.

He parked behind his father's Oldsmobile and climbed out. His father immediately called out, 'Jeannie! Jeannie! Look who's here!' and came hurrying down the steps. He was a tall man, although he wasn't as tall as Paul, with cropped grey hair and the slight stoop of somebody who has worked hard in an office all his life, and never quite managed to fulfil himself. Paul's mother came out of the kitchen still carrying a saucepan. She was tall, too, for a woman, and although her hair was grey she looked ten years younger than she really was. She was wearing a pink chequered blouse with the sleeves rolled up, and jeans.

'Why didn't you say you were coming to see us?' asked his mother, with tears in her eyes. 'I don't have a thing in!'

His father slapped him on the back and ushered him up the steps into the house. 'I guess he wanted to surprise us, didn't you, son?'

'That's right,' said Paul. 'I didn't know that I was coming back until the day before yesterday.'

'It's great to see you,' smiled his father. 'You've lost some weight, haven't you? Hope you've been eating properly. All work and no lunch makes Jack a skinny-looking runt.'

'I should have gone to the market,' said his mother. 'I could have made your favourite pot roast.'

'Don't worry about that,' his father said. 'We can eat out tonight.

Remember Randolph's Restaurant? That was taken over, about a year ago, and you should see it now! They do a lobster chowder to die for!'

'Oh Dan, that's far too expensive,' said his mother.

'What do you mean, our son here's used to the best, aren't you, son? How's that Mercedes-Benz of yours running? Or have you traded it in for something new?'

'Oh . . . I'm maybe thinking about a Porsche.'

'A Porsche! Isn't that something! A Dennison driving a Porsche! Listen, how about a beer and you can tell us how things are going.'

'Well, to tell you the truth, I'm kind of pooped.'

'Sure you are, I'm sorry. Why don't you go to your room and wash up? You can fill us in when you're good and ready.'

His mother said, 'How long are you staying for?'

He gave her a quick, tight smile. 'I don't know . . . it depends on a couple of business deals.'

She held his eye for a moment and there was something in the way she looked at him that made him think: she suspects that I'm not entirely telling the truth. His mother had always known when he was lying. Either that, or he always felt guilty when he lied to her, and it showed.

He hefted his bag out of the car and carried it through to the small room at the back. It was depressingly familiar, although it had a new green carpet and new curtains with green-and-white convolvulus flowers on them. His high school football trophies were still arranged on top of the bureau, and there was a large photograph of him at the age of eleven, clutching a shaggy red dog. He sat down on the bed and covered his face with his hands. Eleven years of work. Eleven years of talking and travelling and staying up till two or three in the morning. All of it gone, all of it – and nothing to show for it but a single suitcase and twenty-three CFA francs – not convertible into dollars, and not worth anything even if they were.

His father came in with a can of Coors. 'Here – I'll bet you can't get this in Libreville.'

'No, we get French beer mainly. Or there's the local brew. Okay for cleaning drains.'

He opened up his suitcase. Two pairs of pants, one crumpled linen coat, a pair of brown leather sandals, socks and shorts. His father said, 'You're travelling extra-light. The last time you came, you had so many cases I thought that Madonna was visiting.'

'Well . . . I wasn't given too much notice.'

He took the witch-compass out of the side pocket in his suitcase and put it next to his football cups.

'What the two-toned tonkert is that?' asked his father.

'It's kind of a good-luck charm.'

'Oh, yeah?' His father picked it up and shook it. 'Looks like a giant sheep dropping to me.'

Paul hung his clothes up in the closet.

'You're quiet,' said his father. 'Everything's okay, isn't it?'

'Sure, sure. Everything's okay.'

His father laid a hand on his shoulder. 'I'll tell you who else is around. You remember that Katie Sayward you used to like so much? Her marriage broke up, so she's back here with her aunt, to get over it.'

Paul said, 'What? I didn't even know she was married.'

'Yeah. She married some actor she met in New York. Real good-looking guy. *Too* goodlooking, if you know what I mean. I met him once when she came up to Sherman to see her aunt. So far as I know, he had an affair with some girl in the chorus-line and Katie was totally devastated. If you do see her, I wouldn't mention it if I were you. Not unless she brings it up first.'

Paul went to the window and pressed his forehead against the cold glass. Outside, the yard sloped steeply uphill towards a thicket of dry brown bracken. Katie Sayward. He had always adored Katie Sayward, even when he was in grade school. Katie Sayward, with her skinny ankles and her skinny wrists and her shining brown hair that swung whenever she turned her head. Even when she was younger, her lips always looked as if she had just finished kissing someone. She had grown into a beautiful young woman, with a head-turning figure. Paul had only plucked up the courage once to ask her for a date. He could remember it even today – walking into the home room in front of all the other girls, and saying, 'Katie, how about you and me going out for a burger tonight?' Katie had clamped her hand over mouth, and widened her eyes, and then she had burst out laughing. The memory of it still made him feel hot and uncomfortable.

So Katie Sayward had married. Well, of course she had married, a lovely girl like that. It was just that he hadn't wanted to hear about it. And worse than that, her husband had cheated on her. How could he have cheated on Katie Sayward, when she was the perfect, perfect girl?

His mother came into the room. 'You're sure you don't want anything to eat? I could make you a bologna sandwich. I don't suppose you get much bologna, in Gabon.'

'I'm fine, Mom. Honestly. Let me grab a few zees, that's all.'

'Okay,' said his father, giving him another affectionate clap on the shoulder. 'I'll wake you up in time for dinner.'

Randolph's Restaurant was decorated in the style of an old Colonial inn, with wheelback chairs and softly shaded lamps on the tables and antique warming-pans hanging on the walls. They sat right in the middle of the restaurant, and Paul's father kept turning around in his chair and calling out to people he knew.

'Dick! Janice! Paul's back from darkest Africa! Sure, doing real good, aren't you, Paul? Business is booming! Counting on buying himself a new Porsche, top-of-the-range!'

Paul glanced at his mother. She was still smiling, but he definitely had the feeling that she knew that something wasn't quite right.

His father ordered two large martinis to start, and a mimosa for his mother. Then he opened up the oversized leatherbound menu and said, 'Okay! Let's push the boat out!'

He ordered oysters and caviar with sour cream and blinis. He ordered steak and lobster and fresh chargrilled tuna. They drank Roederer champagne with the hors d'oeuvres and Pauillac with the entrées, $97.50 a bottle.

Paul's father did most of the talking. Paul sat with his head lowered, chewing his way unenthusiastically through his meal. He couldn't even taste the difference between the steak and the lobster, and he left his beans and his broccoli untouched.

'You must be feeling jetlagged,' said his mother, laying her hand on top of his.

'Yes . . . kind of. I'll be okay tomorrow.'

The pianist on the opposite side of the room was playing a slow bluesy version of 'Buddy, Can You Spare A Dime?' and he almost felt like standing up and walking out.

'You know something?' said his father, with his mouth full, and a shred of lobster dangling from his lip, 'I'm so proud of you, Paul, I could stand right up in this restaurant and shout it out loud. My only son, started from humble beginnings, but had the guts to go to Africa all on his own and make himself a hundred million.'

'Well, I'm not so sure about the hundred million,' said Paul.

'You mark my words . . . if you haven't made a hundred million yet, you sure will soon! That's what you're made of! That's why I'm so proud of you!'

They finished the meal with Irish coffees in the cocktail lounge. Paul's father grew more and more talkative and when he started to tell stories about his high school days, losing his shorts in the swimming-pool and falling into the rhododendron bushes, Paul asked for the check.

'That's real generous of you, Paul,' his father beamed. Then he turned to his mother and said, 'How many people have a wealthy young son who can take his folks out for a night like this?'

Paul opened the leather folder with the check inside. It was $378.69, gratuity at your discretion. Suddenly he couldn't hear the piano music any more.

'How is it?' asked his father. 'National debt of Gabon, I'll bet.'

'Something like that,' said Paul, numbly, and reached into his coat with fingers that felt as if they were frostbitten. He took out his wallet and opened it, while his mother watched him silently and his father chatted with the cocktail waitress.

'In Gabon, you understand, they respect Americans. They trust them. Wouldn't surprise me at all if Paul ends up running a big mining corporation over there.'

Paul said, 'Shit.'

'What? What is it?'

'All the money I changed . . . I left it back in my suitcase.'

'You can use your card, can't you?'

'No, no, I can't. It's only for use in Africa.'

'But that's an American Express card. That's good anywhere.'

'Not this one, no. I have a special deal. They bill me in CFA francs, so that I save myself twelve-and-a-half per cent handling charges.'

Paul's father pulled a face. 'Don't you have Visa, or MasterCard?'

'Left them back in my suitcase, too. Stupid of me. Mom's right. I must be jetlagged.'

'Looks like we're going to have to wash the dishes,' said his father.

'I'll tell you what I can do,' Paul volunteered. 'I can come back early tomorrow, soon as you open, and pay you then. How's that? I can leave my watch if you like.'

'Oh, that's okay,' smiled the waitress. 'I think we can trust you, don't you? And what is it they say in those gangster movies? We know where you live.'

They all laughed and Paul tucked his wallet back in his coat and said, 'Thanks.' Shit. Where was he going to raise more than four hundred dollars by lunchtime tomorrow? He could pawn his watch, he supposed. It was a nine hundred dollar Baume & Mercier that had been given to him by the sales director of a French copper company. His ten thousand dollar Rolex had long gone, in legal fees. He just hoped that Robard's jewellers was still in business.

His mother took his arm as they left the restaurant and walked across the parking lot. It was a cold, dry night.

'Winter's coming early this year,' said his mother. His father was weaving ahead of them, singing erratic lines from 'Buddy Can You Spare A Dime?' 'Once I was a bigshot . . . now I'm broke.'

'Well, we don't get much of a winter in Libreville.'

'Is everything all right, Paul?'

'Sure. What do you mean? Everything's great.'

'I don't know. You look – I'm not quite sure what the word is. *Haunted*, I guess.'

'Haunted?' he laughed. 'You make me sound like Hill House.'

'But everything's okay? The business? You're not sick, are you?'

'I got over the dengue months ago.'

'You will tell me, though, if anything's wrong?'

He gave her a kiss and nodded, and then he hurried her along a little faster, so that they would catch up with his father. 'Dad! Dad! Come on, Dad, there's no way that I'm going to let you drive!'

That night he lay in bed listening to the leaves whispering in the yard outside. He felt infinitely tired, but he couldn't even close his eyes. The moonlight fell across the wall as white as a bone.

He ought to tell his parents that he was bankrupt. He ought to tell them that he was never going back to Gabon, couldn't go back. He knew his father would be crushed, but how much longer could he keep up this pretence? Yet he felt that if he told his parents, he would reduce himself to the level of a hopeless alcoholic, finally admitting that he couldn't summon up the willpower to quit on his own.

His parents' admiration was all he had left.

The digital clock beside the bed told him it was 3:57. It clicked on to 3:58 – and it was then that he heard a soft shaking noise, like dry rice in a colander.

He raised his head from the pillow. It must have been the leaves, skittering in the wind. But as he lowered his head he heard it again, much sharper this time. *Shikk – shikk – shikk!* And again, even louder. *Shikk – shikk – shikk!*

He swung his legs out of bed and walked across to the bureau. There, amongst his football trophies, lay the black smooth shape of the witch-compass. It was shivering, very slightly, and as it shivered the beads or seeds inside it set up that *shikk – shikk – shikk!* sound.

Cautiously he picked it up. It felt as pleasant to hold as it always did; yet tonight it seemed to have life in it. It vibrated, and shook again. He pointed it towards the window. It stopped vibrating, and the *shikk* sound stopped, too. He pointed it toward the closet. It vibrated again, but only softly. Next he pointed it towards the door. It gave a brisk shiver and almost jumped out of his hand.

It's guiding me, Paul thought. *It's guiding me to what I want.*

He tested it again, pointing it back at the window, back at the closet, back at the door. As soon as he pointed it towards the door, it became more and more excited.

Supposing it's showing me how to find some money. That's what I need, more than anything.

Hurriedly, he pulled on his shirt and his pants and his shoes. Then, breathing hard, he eased open his bedroom door and stepped into the darkened hallway. He could hear his father snoring like a beached whale, and the clock ticking loudly on the wall. He pointed the witch-compass north, south, east and west. It shook most vigorously when he pointed it towards the front door. It was guiding him out of the house.

He walked as quietly as he could across the polished oak floor. He lifted a nylon windbreaker down from the pegs by the door. Then he eased open the chains, drew back the bolts and went out into the cold, windy night.

The witch-compass led him down the front steps and down the narrow, winding road that led to the main highway between New Milford and New Preston. Although it was only four in the morning, the sky was strangely light, as if a UFO had landed behind the trees. Paul's footsteps scrunched through the leaves at the side of the road and his father's windbreaker made a loud rustling noise. It smelled of his father's pipesmoke, and there was a plastic lighter in the pocket.

And all the time, the witch-compass rattled in his hand with ever-increasing eagerness.

He had just reached the hairpin that would take him down to the highway when he heard a car coming, from quite a long way off, but coming fast. The witch-compass went *shikk!shikk! shikk!* and almost jumped out of his grasp. He began to hurry around the bend and down the steeply sloping road, and as he did so he glimpsed headlights through the branches. A car was speeding along the highway from the direction of New Milford. It looked as if it were travelling at more than seventy miles an hour.

He hadn't even reached the highway when he heard a sickening bang and a shrieking of tyres, and then a sound like an entire junkyard dropping out of the sky. Wheels, fenders, mufflers, windows, crunching and screeching and smashing. Then complete silence, which was worse.

Paul came running around the corner and saw the bloodied body of a dead deer lying in the scrub on the far side of the highway, its legs twisted at extraordinary angles, as if it were trying to ballet-dance. Almost a hundred feet further up, a battered, dented Chevrolet was resting on its roof. Shattered glass glittered all over the blacktop.

'Jesus.' Paul started to run towards the wreck. As he came closer, he saw that the driver was still in his seat, suspended upside-down in his seatbelt. His deflated airbag hung in front of him, and it had obviously saved his life. He was groaning loudly and trying to wrestle himself free.

'Hold on!' Paul called out. He crunched through the glass and then he realised that he was splashing through a quickly widening pool of gasoline.

'Get me out of here,' the driver begged him. He was a heavily built, fiftyish man. His grey hair was matted with blood. 'I think my goddam legs are crushed.'

'Okay, okay, just hold on,' Paul reassured him. He was about to put the witch-compass into his pocket when it gave a high-pitched *shikka-shikkashikka!* that sounded like a snake hissing. Paul looked down and saw the driver's pigskin billfold lying on the road, right in front of him. Even without picking it up, he could see that it was stuffed with money.

'Oh God, please get me out of here,' moaned the driver. 'This is hurting so much.'

Paul reluctantly took his eyes away from the billfold. He took hold of the Chevrolet's door-handle and tried to drag it open, but it was wedged solid. He went around to the other side of the car and tried the passenger door, but that wouldn't budge, either.

He came back to the driver's side and reached into the broken window. He managed to locate the man's seatbelt buckle, but the crash had jammed it and the man's bulging stomach was straining against it. His shirt was soaked in warm, sticky blood.

'Please, I'm dying here. Please.'

Paul said, 'Okay . . . but I can't get you out by myself. I'm going to have to call the fire department.'

'Hurry, please.'

Paul took hold of his hand and squeezed it. 'Just hold on. I'll be quick as I can.'

But in his pocket the witch-compass went *shikkashikkashikka!*

Paul slowly stepped away from the wreck. He looked down and there was the pigskin billfold. He could see fifties and twenties. More than enough to settle his restaurant bill. More than enough to buy him a new coat and a new pair of jeans and see him through the next few days. He hesitated for a second and turned back to the man hanging in the car, and the man was looking up at him, bleeding and broken and pleading with him, get me out of here, for chrissakes. But the worst possible idea came into his head – an idea so terrible that he could hardly believe that he had thought of it. And inside his pocket, the witch-compass rattled and shook as if it were a living thing.

He stooped down and picked up the billfold. The man in the car watched him, unable to comprehend what he was seeing. Paul took all of the cash out of the billfold except for $50. He didn't want to make it obvious that the man had been robbed. He held up the billfold for a moment and then he dropped it back onto the road.

Shikkashikkashikka.

'What are you going to do?' the driver asked him. 'Look, take the fucking money. I don't care. Just call the fire department, get me out of here.'

But Paul knew that it would be different once the man was released. I was trapped, I was dying, and he stole my money, right in front of me.

He walked a few paces back down the road. '*No!*' the driver screamed at him. '*Don't leave me here! Don't!*'

Paul stopped. He lowered his head. In his pocket he felt the witch-compass, warm and thrilling. The witch-compass was guiding him away from the wreck, back to his parents' house. Leave him, what does he mean to you? He was driving too fast anyhow. Everybody knows there are deer on these highways. Supposing you hadn't woken up? Supposing the witch-compass hadn't brought you here. The stupid bastard would have died anyhow, alone.

'*Don't leave me!*' the driver screamed at him. '*I'm dying here, for chrissake! Don't leave me!*'

In one pocket, Paul felt the witch-compass. In the other, he felt his father's cigarette lighter. He turned around. There are two prices, Jonquil had told him. Fourteen francs, and a moral choice, every time the witch-compass finds you what you want.

The driver was suddenly silent. He had seen Paul flick the cigarette lighter, and stand in the road with the flame dipping in the early-morning breeze. The flame was reflected in the gasoline which was running across the road and into the ditch.

Paul genuflected, and lit it.

The fire raced back towards the upturned car. The driver twisted and struggled in one last desperate effort to pull himself free.

'*You could have had the money!*' he screamed at Paul. '*I would have given you the fucking money!*'

Then the whole car exploded like a Viking fireship and furiously burned. Paul gradually backed away, feeling the heat on his face and the cold wind blowing on his back. He saw the driver's arm wagging from side to side, and then it kind of hooked up and bent as the heat of the fire shrivelled his tendons. As he walked up the winding road towards his parents' house he could still see it burning behind the trees.

Afterwards, he sat down on his bed and counted his money. Six hundred and fifty-five dollars, still reeking of gasoline. On top of the bureau, the witch-compass lay silent.

He drove into New Milford the next morning to pay off Randolph's Restaurant. 'Glad you didn't try to leave the county,' smiled the owner, counting out his money. 'I'd have had to set my old dog out looking for you.'

The dog lay in the corner of the restaurant, an ancient basset-hound, snoring as loudly as Paul's father.

On his way home, he took a different route, the road that led up to Gaylordsville and then meandered through the woods to South Kent. He didn't want to go past the scene of last night's auto wreck again. This morning, when he had driven by, the rusty and blackened Chevrolet was still lying on its roof in the road, surrounded by firetrucks and police cars with their lights flashing.

It was another pin-sharp day. All around him, the woods were ablaze with yellows and crimsons and dazzling scarlets. Every now and then he checked his eyes in the rearview mirror to see if he could detect any guilt; or any emotion at all. But all he felt was reasonably satisfied. Not over-satisfied, but the edge had been taken off his anxiety.

He slowed as he reached the intersection where the road led back towards New Preston. About a quarter of a mile beyond it, screened by trees, stood the yellow-painted house where Katie Sayward's aunt lived, and where Katie was staying after the break-up of her marriage. The times he had driven past here when he was younger, hoping to see her. Maybe he should pay her a visit now. But what would he say? 'You thought I was an idiot when we were at school together, sorry about your marriage'?

He drove past slowly, no more than ten miles an hour, ducking his head so that he could peer beneath the branches of the trees. Nobody in sight. But as he pressed the accelerator to move away, he heard a crisp *shikk! shikk! shikk!*

He slowed down again. The witch-compass was inside the glove-box. It started a series of quick, rhythmic rattles. As he drove further away from Katie's house, however, the rattles became less and less frequent. When he reached the next bend, they stopped altogether.

He pulled the car in by the side of the road. The witch-compass remained silent. *It's trying to tell me something about Katie. It's guiding me back.*

He turned the car around and drove slowly back towards the yellow-painted house. Inside the glove-box, the witch-compass started to rattle again *shikkaSHIKKAshikkaSHIKKA* like a Gabonese drumbeat.

Katie's marriage has broken up. Maybe the witch-compass is trying to tell me that she needs somebody. Maybe it's trying to tell me that Katie needs me.

Cautiously he drove in through the gates and up the driveway to the house. Nobody came out to greet him and the place looked as if it were deserted. No vehicles around, and no smoke pouring from the chimneys. Paul climbed out of the car and went up to the front porch and knocked. There was no answer, so he knocked again. He didn't like the knocker. It was bronze, cast into the face of a sly, blind old man. He waited, whistling between his teeth.

No, nobody in. The witch-compass must have made a mistake. He walked back to the car and opened the door. The rattling inside the glove-box was practically hysterical, and he could hear the compass knocking from side to side, as if it were trying to break out.

'All right, already,' he said. He took the witch-compass out of the glove-box and held it in his hand. Then he walked back to the house, and knocked again – so loudly this time that he could hear the knocks echo in the hall. Still no reply.

'There, what did I tell you? There's nobody home.'

Shikkashikkashikka rattled the witch-compass.

Paul pointed it towards the front door of the house, and its rattling died away. He swept it slowly backwards and forwards, and the witch-compass rattled most excitedly when he pointed it to the side of the house.

'Okay, let's check this out.'

He walked around the house, past a trailing wisteria, until he found the kitchen door at the back. He knocked with his knuckle on the window, just in case there was somebody inside, and then he turned the handle. It was unlocked, so he opened it and stepped inside.

'Hello!' he called. 'Anybody home?'

Shikkashikkashikka.

'Look, it's no good shaking like that. There's nobody home.'

Shikkashikkashikka.

The witch-compass guided him into the hall, towards the foot of the staircase. At the top of the staircase there was a landing with an amber stained-glass window, so that the inside of the house looked like a sepia photograph.

Shikkashikkashikka.

'Upstairs? All right, then. I just hope you know what you're doing.'

Paul climbed the stairs and the witch-compass led him along the landing to the very last door. He knocked again, but there was no reply, and so he carefully opened it. The witch-compass was shaking wildly in his hand and he had to grip it tight so that he wouldn't drop it.

He found himself in a large bedroom, with an old-fashioned dark-oak bed, and a huge walnut armoire. The windows were covered in heavy lace curtains with peacock patterns on them, so the light inside the bedroom was very dim. The bed was covered with an antique patchwork quilt; on top of the quilt lay Katie Sayward, naked.

Now the witch-compass was silent. Paul took a breath and held it, and didn't know if he ought to leave immediately, or stay where he was, watching her. She was older, of course, and she had cut her long hair short, but she was still just as beautiful as he remembered. She was lying on her back with her eyes closed, her arms spread wide as if she were floating, like Ophelia. She was full-breasted, with a flat stomach and long legs. *My perfect woman*, thought Paul. *The kind of woman I've always wanted.*

He took two or three steps into the room. The floorboards creaked and he hesitated, but she didn't show any signs of waking. Now he could see between her legs, and he stood transfixed, breathing softly through his mouth.

He took another step closer. He wanted to touch her so much that it was a physical ache; but he knew what would happen if he tried. The same ridicule that he had suffered when he asked her for a date at high school. Shame and embarrassment, and trouble with the law.

It was then, however, that he saw the empty bottle of Temazipan tablets on her nightstand and the tipped-over bottle of vodka on the quilt and the letter that she was holding in her right hand.

He took another step closer, then another. Then he sat on the bed beside her and said, 'Katie . . . Katie, can you hear me? It's Paul.'

Katie didn't stir. Paul gently patted her cheek. She was still breathing. She was still warm. But she was deathly pale. He peeled back one of her eyelids with his thumb. Her blue eye stared up at him sightlessly, its pupil widely dilated.

He lifted her right wrist so that he could read the note. 'Dearest Aunt Jessie. I know this is a selfish and terrible thing to do to you. But a life without James just isn't any kind of life at all.'

Paul felt her pulse. It was thready, but her heart was still beating. If he called the paramedics now, there was a strong possibility that they could save her. She would be grateful to him, wouldn't she, for the rest of her life? There might even be a chance that—

His arm brushed against her bare breast and it gave a heavy, complicated sway. There might be a chance in the future that he and Katie could get together. But if they got together *now*, then he could be sure of having her. Maybe just once. But even once was better than never.

He stood up and very deliberately took off his clothes, staring down at Katie all the time. He had never dared to dream that this could ever happen; and now it was: and he could do whatever he wanted to her, anything, and she wouldn't resist.

He climbed onto the quilt. His body was thin and wiry and his skin was very white, except for his face and his forearms and his knees, which had been tanned dark by the equatorial sun. He kissed Katie on the lips, and then her eyelids, and then her cheeks, and he whispered in her ear that he loved her, and that she was the most desirable woman he had ever known. He squeezed her breasts and sucked at her nipples. Then he ran his tongue all the way down her stomach and buried his face between her thighs.

He stayed in her bedroom for over an hour, and he used her body in every way he had ever fantasised about. He couldn't believe it was real, and he wanted it never to end. He turned her over, face down in the pillow, and forced himself into her, but it was then that she gave a shudder that he could feel all the way through him, right to the soles of his feet.

He leaned forward, his cheek close to hers. 'Katie? Speak to me, Katie! Just let me hear you breathing, Katie, come on!'

She was silent and her body was completely lifeless. He took himself out of her and stood up, wiping the back of his hand across his forehead. *Shikk!* went the witch-compass.

Paul dressed, feeling numb; and then he rearranged Katie as he had found her. He cleaned between her thighs with tissues, and wiped her face. He had bruised her a little: there were fingermarks over her buttocks and breasts, and a lovebite on her neck. But who would ever think that *he* had inflicted them? So far as anybody was aware, they hardly even knew each other.

He left the house by the kitchen door, taking care to wipe the doorhandle with the tail of his shirt. He drove back the way he had come, through Gaylordsville, crossing the Housatonic at Fort Hill so that he could deny having driven back towards his parents' house on the South Kent Road. He even made a point of tooting his horn and waving to Charlie Sheagus, the realtor.

And how do you feel? he asked his eyes, in the rearview mirror.

Satisfied, his eyes replied. Not *fully* satisfied, but it's taken the edge off.

His father was waiting for him in the living-room when he returned. He was wearing a chequered red shirt and oversized jeans and he looked crumple-faced and serious. His mother was sitting in the corner, sitting in the shadows, her hands clasped on her lap.

'Where've you been?' his father wanted to know.

'Hey, why the long face? I went down to Randolph's to settle the check.'

'It's a pity you haven't been settling all of your checks the same way.'

Paul said, 'What? What are you talking about?'

'I'm talking about Budget Rental Cars, who just called up to say that your credit rating hadn't checked out. And Marriott Hotels, who said that you bounced a personal cheque for two hundred dollars. And then I called Dennison Minerals, your own company, in Gabon, and all I got was a message saying that your number was discontinued.'

Paul sat down in one of the old-fashioned wooden-backed armchairs. 'I've been having some cashflow difficulty, okay?'

'So why didn't you say so?'

'Because you didn't want to hear it, did you? All you wanted to hear was success.'

His father jabbed his finger at him. 'What kind of a person do you take me for? You're my son. If you're successful, I exult in it. If you fail, I commiserate. I'm your father, for chrissakes.'

'Commiserate? Those Gabonese bastards took my business, my house, they took everything. I don't want commiseration. I want revenge.'

His father came up to him and laid both of his hands on his shoulders and looked him straight in the face. 'Forget about revenge. You can always start over.'

'Oh, like you started over when you lost your job at Linke Overmeyer? With a little house, and a millionth-of-an-acre of ground, and a row of beans? I had a mansion, in Libreville! Seven bedrooms, four bathrooms, a swimming-pool, a circular hallway you could have ice skated on, if you'd have had any ice, and if you'd have had any skates.'

'So what?' his father asked him. 'That's what life is all about. Winning, and losing. Why did you have to lie about it?'

'Because of you,' said Paul.

'Because of *me*? What the hell are you talking about?'

'Because you always expected me to do better than you. That was all I ever got from you, from the time I was old enough to understand anything. "You'll do better than me. One day, you'll be rich, and you'll buy a house for your mother and me. With a lake, and swans." Jesus Christ! I was nine years old, and you wanted me to give you fucking *swans*!'

His father closed his eyes for a moment, trying to summon up enough patience not to shout back. His mother said nothing, but sat in the shadows, a silhouette, only the curved reflection from her glasses gleaming. In the distance, Paul heard the dyspeptic rumbling of thunder. It had been a dry day, and the air had been charged with static electricity. Lightning was crossing the Litchfield Hills, walking on stilts.

Paul's father opened his eyes. 'Are you going back to Africa?'

'There's nothing to go back to. I'm all washed up in Gabon. I still owe my lawyer seven thousand francs.'

'So what are you going to do?'

'I don't know. Right now, I don't want to do anything.'

'You're going to have to find yourself a job, Paul, even if it's waiting table. Your mother and I can't support you.'

'I see. So much for my fucking four-hundred-dollar dinner then? "Who has a son who takes his parents out for a meal like this?" You didn't even offer to pay half.'

'I'm sorry. If I'd known that you were busted I wouldn't have suggested going to Randolph's at all. We could have eaten at home. And don't use language like that, not in this house.'

'Oh, I beg your pardon. First of all you won't support me, and now you take away my rights under the First Amendment.'

'The First Amendment doesn't give you the right to use profanity in front of your mother.'

Paul was about to say something else, but he took a deep breath and stopped himself. He felt angrier than he had ever felt in his life. But what was the point in shouting? He knew that he wouldn't be able to change his father's mind. His father had almost made a religion out of self-sufficiency. Even when Paul was young, he had never given him an allowance. Every cent of pocket-money had been earned with dishwashing or raking leaves or painting fences. He would rather have burned his money than given anything to Paul for nothing.

'All right,' said Paul. 'If that's the way you feel.'

He walked around his father and went to his room. He slung his suitcase on the bed and started to bundle his clothes into it. His mother came to the door and said, 'Paul . . . don't be angry. You don't have to leave.'

'Oh, but I do. I might accidentally breathe some of Dad's air or flush some of his water down the toilet.'

'Sweetheart, he doesn't mean that you can't stay with us, just till you can get yourself back on your feet.'

'You don't get it, do you? I don't want to get back on my feet. I've spent eleven years working my rear end off, and look what I've ended up with. One tropical suit, two shirts, and a rental car I can't even pay for. I just want to lie down and do nothing. That's all.'

'Do you want to see Dr Williams?'

Paul pushed his way past her. 'I don't want to see anybody. I'm not sick. I'm not disturbed. I'm just exhausted, that's all. Is it a crime, to be exhausted?'

'Paul—' his father began, but Paul opened the front door and went down the steps. 'Paul – we can talk about this. I'm sure we can work something out.'

'Sure,' Paul retorted. 'I can clean out your gutters and mend your roof and you'll pay me in hamburgers. Forget it, Dad. I'd rather go to the Y.'

With that, he climbed into his rental car and backed out of the drive with a scream of tyres. His father sadly watched him go.

By nine o'clock that night the rain was lashing all the way across Litchfield County and the hills were a battlefield of thunder and lightning.

Paul had driven into New Milford, where he spent his last $138 on a steak and fries and a bottle of wine at the Old Colonial Inn. Now he didn't even have enough money for a room. It looked like he was going to have to spend the night in the car, parked on a side road.

He left the inn, his coat collar turned up against the rain, but by the time he reached the car his shoulders were soaked. He wiped the rain from his face and looked at himself in the rearview mirror. If only he had someplace to sleep. A warm bed, and enough money to last him for six or seven months, so that he wouldn't have to do anything but sit back and drink beer and think of nothing at all.

He started the engine, and the windshield wipers flapped furiously from side to side. It was then that he heard the softest of rattles. *Shikk – shikk – shikk.*

A prickling sensation went up the back of his neck. The witch-compass was telling him that he could have what he wanted. A bed for the night, and money. But the question was, how was he going to get it, and what kind of moral decision would he have to make?

Shikka – shikka – shikka – rattled the witch-compass, and Paul took it out of his pocket.

For one second, Paul was tempted to throw it out into the rain. But it felt so smooth and reassuring in his hand, and he knew that it would guide him to a place where he could sleep, and where he wouldn't have to worry for a while.

He nudged his car out of the green onto the main road to New Preston. He turned the wheel to the right, and the witch-compass was silent. He turned it to the left, and the witch-compass went *shikkashikkashikka*.

He was almost blinded for a second by a crackling burst of lightning. But then he was driving slowly through the rain, hunched forward in his seat so that he could see more clearly, heading northwards.

After twenty minutes of silence, the witch-compass stirred again. *Shikk – shikk – shikk*. He had reached the intersection where the Chevrolet had collided with the deer – the intersection that would take him up the winding road towards his parents' house.

'Oh, no,' he said. But the witch-compass rattled even more loudly, guiding him up the hill. Another fork of lightning crackled to the ground, striking a large oak only a hundred feet away. Paul saw it burst apart and burn. Thunder exploded right above his head, as if the sky were splitting apart.

He drove around the hairpin bend towards his parents' house. Now the witch-compass was shaking wildly, and Paul knew without any doubt at all where it was taking him. He saw the roof of his parents' house silhouetted against the trees, and as he did so another charge of lightning hit the chimney, so that bricks flew in all directions and blazing wooden shingles were hurled into the night like catherine-wheels.

The noise was explosive, and it was followed only a second later by a deep, almost sensual sigh, as the air rushed in to fill the vacuum that the lightning had created. Then there was a deafening collision of thunder.

Paul stopped in front of the house, stunned. The rain drummed on the roof of his car like the juju drummers in the Marché Rouge. He climbed out, shaking, and was immediately drenched. He walked up the steps with rain dripping from his nose and pouring from his chin. He pushed open the front door and the house was filled with the smell of burned electricity, and smoke.

'Oh, Jesus,' he said.

He walked into the kitchen and the walls were blackened with bizarre scorch-marks, like the silhouettes of hopping demons. Every metal saucepan and colander and cheese-grater had been flung into the opposite corner of the room and fused together in an extraordinary sculpture, a mediaeval knight who had fallen higgledy-piggledy off his charger.

And right in the centre of the floor lay his mother and father, all of their clothes blown off, their bodies raw and charred, their eyes as black as cinders, and smoke slowly leaking out of their mouths.

Shikk – shikk – shikk rattled the witch-compass.

So this was how he was going to find himself a warm bed for the night. However stern he had been, his father had always told him that he was going to inherit the house, and all of his savings, as well as being the sole beneficiary to their joint insurance policies. No more problems. No more money worries. Now he could rest, and do nothing.

He slowly sank to his knees on the kitchen floor and took hold of his mother's hand, even though the skin on her fingers was crisp and her fingernails had all been blown off. He pressed her hand against his forehead and he sobbed and sobbed until he felt that he was going to suffocate.

'Dad, Mom, I didn't want *this*,' he wept. 'I didn't want this, I swear to God. I'd give my right arm for this never to have happened. I'd give anything.'

He cried until his ribs hurt. Outside, the electric storm grumbled and complained and eventually disappeared, *perpendosi*, into the distance.

Silence, except for the continuing rain. Then Paul heard the witch-compass go *shikk – shikk – shikk*.

He raised his head. The witch-compass was lying on the floor next to him, softly rattling and turning on its axis.

'What are you offering me now, you bastard?' said Paul.

Shikkashikkashikka.

'This doesn't have to happened? Dad and Mom – they needn't have died?'

Shikk – shikk – shikk

'What are you trying to tell me, you fuck? I can turn back the clock? Is that what you mean?'

Shikk – shikk – shikk

He let his mother's hand drop to the floor. He picked up the witch-compass and pointed it all around the room, 360 degrees. 'Come on then, show me. Show me how I can turn the clock back.'

Shikkashikkashikka

The witch-compass led him to the kitchen door. He opened it and the wind and the rain came gusting in, sending his mother's blackened fingernails scurrying across the vinyl like cockroaches. He stepped outside, shielding his face against the rain with his arm upraised, holding the witch-compass in his left hand, close to his heart. He wanted to feel where it was taking him. He wanted to know, this time, what it was going to ask him to do.

But of course it didn't. He stumbled on the wet stone step coming out of the kitchen and fell heavily forward, with his right arm still upraised. It struck the unprotected blade of his father's circular saw and the rusty teeth bit right into the muscle, severing his tendons and his axillary artery. For a terrible moment he hung beside the saw-table, unable to lift himself up, while blood sprayed onto his face and all over his hair. The rain fell on him like whips, and his blood streamed across the patio in a scarlet fan-pattern and flooded into the grass.

Jonquil was waiting for him at the very end of the Marché Rouge. On the upturned fruit-box in front of her stood the carved figure of a woman with her lips bound together with wire; and a rattle with a monkey's head on top of it; and several jars of poisonous-looking unguents.

He walked along the row of brightly lit stalls until he reached the shadowy corner where she sat. He stood in front of her for a while, saying nothing.

'Your feet brought you back,' she said.

'That's right,' he told her. 'My feet brought me back.'

'How is Papa and Mama?' she asked, with a broad, tobacco-bronzed smile.

'They're good, thanks.'

'Not dead, then? Bad thing, being dead.'

'You think so? Sometimes I'm not so sure.'

'You'll survive. Everybody has to survive. Didn't you learn that?'

'Oh, sure. Even if I didn't learn anything else.'

He reached into the pocket of his crumpled linen coat and produced a smooth black object that looked like a gourd. He laid it down on the fruit-box, next to the carving.

'I don't give refunds,' said Jonquil, and gave a little cackle.

'I don't want a refund, thanks.'

'How about a new arm?'

He looked down at his empty sleeve, pinned across his chest. He shook his head. 'I can't afford it. Not at your prices.'

She watched him walk away through the equatorial night. She picked up the witch-compass and put her ear to it and shook it.

Shikk – shikk – shikk – it whispered. Jonquil smiled, and set it back down on the upturned fruit-box, ready for the next customer.

Graham Masterton and his wife Wiescka recently moved to Cork, Ireland, where he is working on a major new disaster novel (as a follow-up to his earlier novels *Plague* and *Famine*), as well as a horror novella and a horror novel set in Ireland. His book *Snowman* is the fourth in a series of young adult horror novels featuring Jim Rook, a college teacher in remedial English with unusual psychic abilities, and his new adult horror novel *The DoorKeepers* was published first in France before appearing in an English-language edition. Much of Masterton's backlist has been republished in France and Belgium, and the year 2000 marked the inauguration of the Prix Masterton, a literary award to the most creative horror authors writing in French. His latest collection of short stories, *Feelings of Fear*, has also recently appeared, and forthcoming is another horror novel for younger readers, *Cut Dead*. *The Secrets of Sexual Play* is a new sex instruction book published in the United States, where the author is a frequent contributor on personal relationships to *Woman's Own*. As he recalls: '"Witch-Compass" is based on a legend from equatorial Africa told to me many years ago when I was editing *Mayfair* magazine by the late William Burroughs, who was living in London and was a regular columnist. William particularly relished the idea that you could only get what you wanted by committing an act of overwhelming immorality.'

The Proposal

NICHOLAS ROYLE

It didn't happen often, but sometimes when Charlie looked at Anne he felt afraid.

'What's wrong, darling?' Anne would ask him.

He just shook his head. What could he say that wouldn't sound stupid?

They'd been looking out for a bed and breakfast for the last half an hour. After leaving St David's around lunchtime, they'd driven up the coast. It was the first time Anne had been to Wales.

'What about that place?' Charlie asked as they passed another sign pointing the way up a little track with a farm at the end of it.

'We'll find a better one,' Anne said, winding her window down and leaning out to let the breeze catch her long mahogany hair. 'If only you'd let me drive, you'd find it easier to look.'

'I'll drive,' he said. 'I make a nervous passenger.' She didn't answer. 'We used to come here when I was a kid,' he said, to change to subject. 'Family holidays, you know.'

'Stop dreaming, Charlie. You're a dreamer. We need to find somewhere to sleep.'

They drove slowly through the little village where he'd queued for freshly baked bread on summer mornings twenty years ago, on the edge of days that had hummed with promise. Then they took the road that went down the side of the estuary, thickets of rhododendrons and beech on one side, vast sands on the other, and beyond the shallow channel the great mountain he'd climbed with his parents.

'Look!' Anne shouted, pointing at a sign already a speck in his rearview mirror.

Hell, he thought, she was right about most things. Why not this?

He swung a quick U-turn and moments later the tyres were crunching uphill gravel. They both got out and the engine ticked as it cooled into silence behind them.

Charlie broke the spell. 'I'm dreaming,' he said. 'Wake me up.'

'Charlie, it's wonderful,' Anne breathed softly into the warm draughts of scent; small blurred clouds of insects chugged like a faraway tractor.

The house itself was almost completely hidden from the road by a lush garden bursting with sudden blooms and thick, knotted trunks, sinewy roots and spiny bushes in vibrant flower that seemed to float off the ground. Something distracted Charlie and he looked up at the first floor of the house, just catching, or so he thought, the dark shadow of a figure moving away from the window. And then abruptly he realised that someone had appeared on the front step, a kind-looking practical woman with hair like a dandelion clock. Her hands moved slowly around one another like a dove preening itself. Anne looked at Charlie and he stepped forward shyly.

'What a beautiful garden,' he said, the words borne on the pollenated air as they were drawn out of his mouth.

The owner just nodded slowly, smiling, and Charlie and Anne found themselves being led into the hall and upstairs.

'There's no one else in at the moment,' the owner said as she turned a corner in the staircase, 'so I can offer you this room.' She reached a door and was already twisting the round, pitted knob.

Charlie had been all over the country, he must have stayed in more than a hundred B&Bs, and he'd never seen such a beautiful room as this. While it wasn't necessarily the sort of room he'd want in his own place, its ancient king-size bed, walnut dressing table with triptych mirror and creaky old rocking chair facing the window were more than you had a right to expect from a guest house. It was top hotel standard and yet it wasn't, because a hotel room would be cold and sterile – no matter how many frilly valences, boxes of apricot tissues and pot-pourri baskets they adorned it with – and the thing that gave this room its warmth and welcoming air was the fact that it seemed lived in. Not that a single thing in the room was dirty – Anne trailed her finger along the window ledge and failed to pick up a speck of dust – but the room had soul.

Charlie opened one of the windows and the heady draught from the garden was intoxicating. Anne was sitting down in the rocking chair when Charlie finally turned around. She was grinning from ear to ear. Suddenly Charlie realised the owner was still waiting in the doorway for their answer.

'Obviously we'll take it,' Charlie said, accepting a key from her outstretched hand. 'It's a dream of a room.'

The owner left quietly. Anne was testing out the bed.

'I'll go down and get the bags,' Charlie offered.

When he returned and had put the bags down by the rocking chair he stood and looked at Anne for a moment. Closing the door rendered the atmosphere in the room even more exclusive and intimate. Anne was lying on her side facing away from him, her thick dark hair falling on to the counterpane.

He teetered on the edge of normal experience for a few soft seconds. Something had frightened him. The scene was too perfect. It would start to break up. Anne was too beautiful. He'd be looking at her and her face would suddenly become covered in fine spidery cracks like an old china doll.

He knew he could either give in to this madness or throw himself back into reality. She loved him; she'd said so several times, and she'd shown him in the way she sometimes looked at him when he was driving or ordering food in a restaurant, and in the way she touched him when they made love. Nothing filled him with greater pleasure than those moments when he felt her soul brushing his.

He lowered himself down on the bed beside her. Eyes closed, she murmured an acknowledgement. They moved quietly the first time, Charlie aware of the owner moving about downstairs. Inside her he felt the tightening, familiar by now of course, yet always a surprise when it finally seized him, and white lights flashed in his head, giving way to huge, grainy images of the deepest, pollen-richest flowers that twitched in the warm air outside the windows.

Anne locked her arms around Charlie's back and wouldn't let him move for at least ten minutes. They drifted off to sleep as if heavily drugged.

Before setting off Charlie had asked her seriously, 'Do you still want to go to Wales?'

'Yes,' she'd said, but without any discernible enthusiasm, so he'd pressed, idiot masochist that he was, arch pessimist in spite of all his protestations to the contrary. Did she *really* want to go? Was she telling the whole truth? Again the indifference. So he asked her what was wrong.

'I don't know,' she said.

So there was something. What was wrong? What had he said or done? The more questions he lined up in front of poor bewildered Anne the deeper the trench he dug under the foundations of their relationship. It crossed his mind to assume the absolute worst and get up and walk away because he'd rather the end be short and brutal than long-drawn-out and spotted with the foul mould of false hope.

But for the first time in his life he realised the enormous stupidity of his actions, the crash course on which he'd plotted their short but wonderful relationship within the space of a few minutes. There was another way. He could step back, ease off, smile for Christ's sake instead of beaming out such misery and resignation.

After all, he'd been pretty wound up the past couple of weeks because of his work. He'd been short with her, sulked when he didn't get his own way, given her a hard time for not calling him.

'Look,' he said quietly, 'I'm sorry.' And he talked about the pressures at the office, said he'd offload some work on to his juniors – that's what they were there for and they'd welcome the extra responsibility – and he and Anne would get over this; it was just a temporary hitch. She nodded, looking unimpressed but mollified. 'We'll go away,' he continued, 'and have a good time. We both need to relax. It'll do us good.'

When he was younger he would have cried self-delusion at this kind of peace-making, because he knew, or thought he knew, that disaster was inevitable. The only variable was the time of its arrival. But these days he was a little less self-destructive and he considered that Anne was telling the truth: she didn't know what was wrong, and maybe nothing was. As long as he acted fairly normally and showed her without histrionics how he still felt about her, the problem would go away.

But still sometimes he was frightened. One of his friends, on meeting Anne, said to him, 'She's far too nice for you,' and deep down he wondered if it was true.

They were getting ready to go out. Anne was leaning over the washbasin to get a good look at her make-up in the mirror, Charlie sat on the far side of the bed. He'd just tied his shoe laces. They'd slept for half an hour, waking when Anne suddenly jumped and sat up. He asked her what had happened. She said it was nothing, a dream perhaps, though she couldn't remember it. Now she was getting her white skirt out of the wardrobe and she left the mirrored door half open. Charlie was ready. He picked things up off the dressing table on his side of the bed, an old hair brush with not a single strand threaded between the bristles, a nail buffer in a horn case, something he hadn't seen since his grandmother had been alive, and a hand mirror with dried flowers pressed behind glass on the back. He turned the mirror around and saw Anne buttoning her skirt.

He also saw, in the mirror in the wardrobe door, an old woman in a grey dress and a shawl sitting in the chair next to the dressing table.

He screamed and dropped the mirror.

Instantly Anne was jumping across the bed, asking him what was wrong.

He felt cold and sick. The chair next to the dressing table, only two feet from where he was sitting on the edge of the bed, was empty.

Anne put her arm around his shoulders. 'What's wrong, darling?' she asked him.

'Nothing,' he said, shaking his head. 'Nothing. I saw myself in the mirror, that's all. In the double reflection.' He laughed nervously. 'Pretty frightening stuff.'

'I thought something terrible had happened,' she said, straightening her skirt.

When she left him, he picked up the hand mirror and looked again at the reflection of the wardrobe mirror. He could see the chair in front of him and it was empty. Still shaking slightly, he replaced the mirror and sat for a moment staring out of the window. The great mountain climbed above the luxuriant trees in the foreground. He wished he was there, within a few yards of its peak with his mother and father; to have the chance to live his life over again and not make the same mistakes.

They drove down towards the coast, skirting the estuary where the tide was beginning to encroach. They passed a sign for the Panorama Walk which he remembered negotiating as a little boy. And there on the left, leading boldly across the sand and the widening channel, was the railway viaduct, hundreds of yards long and propped up by thousands of wooden stilts. He wondered if trains still ran or if the government had closed the line because it wasn't profitable. It was the sort of thing they'd do.

'The bastards,' he said out loud.

'Oh yes,' Anne agreed. 'Who?'

'The government.'

She nodded sagely and they entered the town. He cut his speed and they drifted past boarded-up restaurants and shops. These had been a feature of their trip, which had taken in some of the most depressed backwaters of the country. You heard about it on the radio, read about it in the Sunday papers, but only started to get a real impression of what it was like when you saw it at first hand. Cracks were spreading right across the face of the country, and not just Wales but the whole so-called kingdom. If only the king-in-waiting could be allowed to get on with the job, thought Charlie, as he so clearly wished, things could be different.

Anne didn't agree. 'It's a world-wide problem, Charlie. The world economy is suffering. Mines aren't profitable, so they close. People have to find something else to do.'

'Yeah, 'cause there's so much choice, isn't there?'

She wound her window down. He knew she hated his sarcasm, but every so often it crept out. They didn't agree on politics as on many things, and if she commented on it he downplayed its importance. After all, what did it matter? He'd once gone out with a girl whose list of interests read like the personal section on his CV and it didn't make a damn bit of difference. They enjoyed a high-speed, high-tension relationship for a few months, then crashed into each other. They were both write-offs for a good year or so. If life was a fairground, he was getting a bit tired of the dodgems and fancied walking away from all the noise into the warm night, under strings of coloured lights, with the right person, of course.

'It means we have more to talk about,' he'd once said, and believed it. In any case, she was right. There was a world problem, but he was a romantic and he couldn't bear to witness the litter of so many shattered dreams. Shop after shop boarded up, which when he'd been here as a child were busy and bright as hives.

'What's wrong with being a dreamer?' he asked her suddenly, thinking back to their earlier conversation in the car.

'Nothing, only you have to be careful. Every dream has a blind spot, an area of shadow where the dream can become a nightmare. If you're not careful.'

He thought about this for a moment, realised he didn't really know what she meant, but that she was probably right. They left the car on the seafront and walked back up to the town. Nestling at the foot of a cliff – up there somewhere among the splashes of gorse was the Panorama Walk – the town gave the false impression of being sheltered from the world. Anne took Charlie's hand and they found a homely little pub that served a tasty mild. After a couple of pints apiece Anne was mellow as a warm cat, but Charlie's indignation about the state of the world had been displaced by gnawing anxiety: the old woman he'd seen in the wardrobe mirror had been standing behind the bar for the past half-hour.

Twice he'd suggested to Anne that they leave and find somewhere to eat, but she said she liked it and wanted to stay. Behind her eyes he could see the sparkle of the frost that would form and spread over the evening if he were to insist. This holiday was about showing her he loved her, not pushing her around. So instead he tried to stop her looking towards the bar, absurdly advising her against going to the ladies when she jumped up at one point. But she went, walking right past the bar, and showed no sign of having seen the old woman. He made himself calm down: it was just an old woman, what did it matter if Anne did see her? She'd seen nothing in the bedroom.

But the old woman didn't exactly look like a member of the staff, standing stock still and watching Anne as she returned from the ladies and sat down opposite Charlie.

'Shall we have another?' she suggested, getting out her purse and making as if to get up.

'I'll get them, darling,' Charlie said, already on his feet.

'But it's my turn.'

'Give me the money then.'

She gave him a fiver and sat back, shaking her head and smiling.

Charlie's hands trembled as he handed over the money at the bar. The woman stared straight past him at the back of Anne's head. The publican paid her no attention and Charlie assumed he couldn't see her. Her eyebrows were strips of dead weeds, eyes the colour of an old sheep. Charlie wished her out of existence, but she persisted. He turned and walked unsteadily back to where they were sitting. Once back in his seat he glanced up over Anne's shoulder at the bar.

The old woman had gone.

An involuntary grunt escaped his lips.

'What's wrong, love?' Anne asked, obviously concerned.

He shook his head. 'Nothing.' He placed his hands over his face, rubbed at the corners of his eyes. 'Sorry.'

'You're a bit jumpy tonight.'

'I want to jump on you.' He regretted this instantly. It was crass, not his style, but he *was* jumpy. 'Sorry, darling, I didn't mean that.'

She looked away.

As they left the pub he cast a final look in the direction of the bar. There was only the round figure of the publican waving goodbye, with rather too wide a sweep of his arm. Charlie made a confused sign and hurried to catch up with Anne who was already twenty yards ahead. He looked through the window as he passed and saw that the man was still waving. Charlie broke into a run.

They left the car at the bottom of the path and walked up through the garden, which, in the stillness of the night, smelled even richer and more varied than it had before.

Charlie sat in the rocking chair while Anne used the bathroom. He'd switched the lights off and opened the window as wide as it would go. Anne came in and stood behind him, placing her hands on his shoulders. She bent down and kissed the top of his head. Her hair fell across his face and he breathed in the smell of coconut. He murmured something to her and she walked around the chair so that she was silhouetted against the window. Moonlight caught the soft hairs on her arms and legs. The chair creaked as Charlie moved forward to place his hands lightly on her hips.

'Tighter,' was all she said to him, and outside the window an owl settled on a branch, folded its wings and blinked.

In the deepest pool of the night a noise awakened Charlie. His eyes opened and his body tensed waiting for the sound to come again because he felt sure it would. Anne's body was bent around facing away from him. She liked him to lie behind her and fold his body into the curve of her spine. He would lie like this until she fell asleep, then usually roll over on to his back.

The air in the room was very still, rich in scents from the garden, and oily dark, the moon having moved around the side of the house.

He could hear Anne's low, steady breathing. Then he heard the noise again. A creak. He believed he knew what it was but he had to raise his head a little way off the pillow to be sure.

Another creak.

She had turned the rocking chair around and angled it so that she was facing Anne's side of the bed. Charlie emitted a thin, high-pitched moan and pulled the covers over his head, rolling towards Anne and moulding himself around her, embracing her as gently as his trembling arms would allow. *You won't get her*, he thought.

He woke again and found himself on the far side of the bed, ten inches of cool sheet separating their bodies. The rocking chair was empty. Charlie's body was slick with sweat, his chest tight. Suddenly he jumped out of the bed and ran out of the room. He didn't pause at the top of the stairs. The heavy front door swung open beneath his hand and he charged into the heart of the garden, ignoring the paths. He fought his way through roses, hardly noticing the thorns lacerating his skin, clawing through thick shrubs and swollen, sticky flowers until he stopped dead, panting and sweating in the densest part of the garden. Inches in front of his own face was that of the old woman. Grey, pock-marked and creased, it looked like rotting wood, her eyes like insects with shining wings. Her dry lips hung slightly apart, but he could neither hear nor feel the passage of air between them.

A fit of dizziness seized him and he squeezed his eyes shut and shook his head. When he looked up again the old woman's face was just knots and gnarls on old bark, her grey woollen clothes loose trails of moss and lichen. He sank to the ground and tried to calm his raging mind.

Anne woke as he climbed back into bed. At first she just rolled over and muttered unintelligibly, but then she sat up straight, distressed. 'What's that?' she snapped.

She'd touched Charlie's foot which was still covered with leaves and soil. Anne swept the covers aside and stared in disbelief at his legs.

'You're bleeding,' she said. 'And where's all this from?'

'The garden,' he said lamely.

'Charlie, I don't know what's going on, but it's got to stop because I can't take much more of it. Okay?'

'I'm sorry,' he said. 'I'll wash. I must have walked in my sleep.' He was already at the washbasin switching on the light and wiping his legs with a flannel. 'There's nothing wrong, honestly. I've just been a bit tense, that's all.'

'It's got to stop,' she said crossly and turned away from the light.

When Charlie woke again it was to see the back of Anne's legs disappearing through the doorway. Someone was leading her. He leaped out of bed, but they were already at the foot of the stairs and the old woman's hand was reaching out to open the big door.

'Anne,' he called.

She looked up at him, her face white as the moon itself. 'Charlie, I'm going for a walk. Just let me, okay?' She was naked. He watched her go out of the door and wondered if in allowing her to leave there might be a way to understand.

He walked slowly back to their room and sat on the bed. Straight away he got up again and went to the window. Anne had reached the bottom of the winding gravel path and turned right, the woman like a shadow thrown down on the ground ahead of her.

A shadow; nothing more. Anne wanted to go for a walk, and, even though it was the middle of the night and she was wasn't wearing a stitch, Charlie had to let her. If he attempted to control her she'd perceive his arms as a trap and she'd slip free of it, as simple as that. He forced himself to take deep breaths, then pulled on his trousers and a T-shirt and sat down in the rocking chair. It creaked beneath his weight.

It was still facing towards Anne's side of the bed.

He was out of the room and down the stairs in a flash, tearing down the road on bare feet. He wondered if he should have taken the car, but didn't lose a stride as he ran. Rounding the last curve before the town, Charlie looked left and saw the railway viaduct striking out across the estuary. There was a naked figure walking slowly beside the track. He saw the old woman standing in the channel with an arm out beckoning to Anne. She could have been standing on the sand but that part of the estuary seemed to Charlie to be under water. As he left the road and ran down towards the viaduct the new day's first light was streaking the sky above the hills inland. He clambered up on to the track and skipped from sleeper to sleeper. Anne was on the right-hand side of the line, away from the edge of the viaduct nearest the old woman, but she had stopped and was now looking in that direction. Charlie didn't turn to look, he just ran. Someone somewhere had started to sing, a high-pitched tuneless wail. Still he ran. Anne took a step forward towards the track, which suddenly started to thump and rattle, and a light appeared beyond Anne, growing brighter and bigger like the flowers in the garden.

He reached her just as the train thundered by and he put his arms out, but he only needed to steady her. She was still a step away from the line. As the carriages clattered past, her eyes appeared to come to life and quickly follow the yellow fogged-up windows. In another second the train was gone and they both looked across the track at the estuary. There was only a depth pole standing in the channel with an outstretched boom and a dimly burning navigation light on top.

Her gave Anne his T-shirt and they supported each other all the way back to the guest house.

They didn't stop for breakfast, but the owner smiled kindly when Charlie paid her and made their excuses. As he tucked the last bag into the boot of the car and closed it, he resisted the strong temptation to take a final look up at the bedroom window.

They turned left on to the road, away from the sea and the town, and drove in silence for at least five minutes. When the scenery started to change, Charlie pulled into a lay-by, switched off the engine and asked Anne if she wanted to drive.

'You've never offered before,' she said, turning in her seat to face him and putting her hand over his.

He held the fingers of her left hand and ran his fingertips over them. She wore no rings yet on that hand. He leaned forward and whispered something into her ear.

Nicholas Royle was born in Manchester and currently lives in London with his wife and two children. He is the author of four published novels, *Counterparts*, *Saxophone Dreams*, *The Matter of the Heart* and *The Director's Cut*, and more than a hundred short stories in various magazines and anthologies. He has also edited ten anthologies of short fiction, some of them for the listings publisher *Time Out*, for whom he works fulltime. About the preceding work's locale, Royle says: 'The story is set in Wales, but I've toned the Welshness down a lot. If you made Wales as strange as it really is, no one would believe you. The two main elements of the narrative – intoxication and fear – are the two things I associate most strongly with that small, proud and, in parts, extremely beautiful country. I enjoyed some idyllic holidays there as a child, but these days I make my rare ventures over the Severn Bridge with a heavy heart – and not just because of the standard of driving.'

Changes

C. BRUCE HUNTER

Jennifer winced when she got her first look at the cabin. Not only was it worse than she'd imagined, it was worse than she could have imagined.

Some of the vines growing over it were three or four inches thick, and the only place they showed signs of trimming was around the front door. A couple of the windows were completely overgrown, as was the chimney, and the few clapboards that weren't yet covered had been given only a temporary reprieve. In short, it was the kind of place only a troll could love.

'This is utterly ridiculous,' she said under her breath while she considered getting back into the station wagon and locking all the doors. She didn't mind roughing it. Her lifestyle sometimes made that unavoidable. But this was too Gothic even for her.

'I could use a little help here,' George grunted. He had just hefted one of the cardboard boxes he'd pulled out onto the tailgate, leaving the other for someone else to carry. 'Hurry up, gang. We're going to lose the light soon.'

'If you expect me to clean this place, you're crazy.' Jennifer rested her elbows on the roof of the car, cupped her chin in her hands and continued staring at the cabin.

'It won't need cleaning,' Lee said as he slid the other box off the tailgate. 'We tidied up before we left last year.'

'Men!' she sighed, 'loosely speaking, of course.'

George and Lee carried their things in, while Jennifer took a half step back and sniffed at something very unpleasant. It came on the evening breeze, from inside the cabin no doubt, and she didn't want to know what it was.

But she *had* agreed to come, and a foolish bargain is still a bargain. So she decided at least to see what she'd got herself into.

Leaving the relative safety of the station wagon, she ventured up what in any other setting would have been a fairy-tale path. It was laid out in a broad 'S'. covered with small river stones and bordered by shaped redwood slats, with a menagerie of concrete animals and gnomes scattered around it. Some were posed in the yard, as if they were playing. Others peeked from behind bushes or around rocks. And most still sported fairly good coats of paint.

'I see that *someone* with a little imagination used to live here,' she said, but as soon as she walked through the front door, she regretted the statement.

Compared with the path, the inside of the cabin was a calamity. Perhaps 'insides' would have been a more descriptive term. There was something vaguely intestinal about the array of artefacts that littered the place. They must have accumulated over a period of years, because they were in various stages of returning to nature, some cloaked in a thick covering of green fuzz and looking as if they might move at any moment.

And while the outside got a little air, the inside did not. It sported a mouldering, half-empty cereal box on the counter, a garbage pail that should have been emptied at least a year ago, and a bowl of fruit that any reasonable person should have known wouldn't remain fresh for an entire winter.

All that could be managed, Jennifer thought. But other, more menacing things had insinuated themselves into the cabin. The odour she'd picked up on the breeze came from behind a stack of wood at the fireplace. She would just let the guys take care of whatever *that* was. And the ice chest sitting ominously in the corner was going to remain tightly sealed if she had anything to say about it.

Fortunately, night came so fast that she didn't have to worry about cleaning anything right away. It wasn't so much the darkness that stopped her. The cabin did have a supply of candles. But the mood of the forest after sunset made work impossible.

The full moon cast a bright pall over the mountain, making it look for all the world like a magical wonderland. Everything became colourless, all grey and black, but the brighter hues of grey took on an eerie glow, while the deepest patches of black seemed transparent, as if they were gateways that led to a mysterious, lightless realm.

And it all happened instantly. One minute, daylight filtered through the tops of the trees. Then it winked out, and the whole forest was transformed. No longer sticks and leaves and dirt, the entire place was now an ethereal world of shades that seemed to offer a welcome to those wandering on the dark side but would be a little too foreboding for anyone else.

The only thing they *could* do at that point was build a fire, open a bottle of wine and tell ghost stories while the moon cast patches of light and shadow through the vine-covered windows.

Jennifer kept up with the guys for a few hours. She told the two stories she knew – the one about the hook and the one about a ghost girl hitchhiking back from a prom. And in between, she listened to George and Lee rattle off a succession of tales that were so well honed, the guys must have been telling them for years. But finally she became drowsy, curled up in front of the fire and fell asleep.

The next morning was fantastic, too. A light rain had fallen – not enough to turn the ground to mud, just enough to make everything look and smell clean. The whole mountain sparkled under a big, bright sun that hovered barely above the horizon and was just now peeking through a patch of clouds breaking up in the eastern sky.

It was the one direction where the land dropped away fast enough to provide a view of anything, and the view over there – the valley, the small town with a white church steeple as its most prominent feature and a scattering of white and yellow and blue houses, and the small farms whose cattle, according to the guys, provided the best meat in the state – the view was spectacular. It was the kind of scene Jennifer didn't know existed any more.

When she wandered sleepy-eyed out of the cabin, Lee was sitting on the porch railing, sipping a cup of steaming coffee and looking wistfully at the valley. She stood behind him for a long time, looked past him at the scene Lee had told her about but she hadn't really understood until now, and let the baggage she had brought with her from the city slip away from her mind, just as Lee had told her it would. The scene was so lovely and did such marvellous things to her that it seemed forever before she felt like saying anything at all.

'Where's George?' she finally asked.

'He's gone for a run in the woods.'

Jennifer sat on the railing beside Lee and took the cup from his hand.

'I'm glad I let you talk me into coming this year,' she said between sips.

'Did you finish your project?' he asked.

'No.' She inhaled deeply and stared at the distant town. Somehow work didn't seem to matter any more. 'I'll finish it when I get back to the office on Monday, but I'm not even going to think about it 'til then.'

'I told you you'd like this place.'

'You should have put more conviction into it. I would have come up long ago if I knew it was this perfect.' She handed the cup back and leaned over the railing so she could get a better look at the yard.

'Who did the path?'

'Some of the people who've stayed here over the years. I don't know who started the tradition, but George says it's been going on as long as he can remember.'

'I can see that.'

'What do you mean?' Lee cocked his head to one side, as if he were trying to see whether Jennifer had found something he'd been missing.

'Oh,' she pointed to a well-weathered concrete pagoda. The family of rabbits that surrounded it was obviously a more recent addition. Their paint showed no wear at all. 'I was just noticing. They don't seem to go together.'

'I know. The bunnies weren't here last year, but I think the pagoda may have been the first piece someone brought up.'

'Rabbits and pagodas,' she mused. 'Last night I thought it took imagination to do this. Now I wonder if it wasn't just weirdness.'

'You're looking at it wrong.' Lee took another sip of coffee and went into his I'll-explain-it-to-you mode. 'The way I see it, that path is the heart of the place . . .'

'It's certainly the only thing around here that shows any signs of maintenance.'

'Exactly. So many of us share the cabin, there's no way it can be a home. It just can't be. But some of the guys want to make it at least a little more personal. So they put a critter on the path.'

'I see. That makes it like "home away from home".'

'Exactly. And when they stop coming, they've left something of themselves behind. I know the pieces don't all fit together, but they're not supposed to. Each critter has a story, but no one knows all the stories, so they're destined to remain just out of reach. And the critters have to stay separate, because each of them has a secret it can't tell.'

'Bull!' George wheezed as he emerged from a clump of trees and jogged up the path. He was obviously exhausted and covered with sweat in spite of the cool mountain air.

'Where?' Lee pretended to look around the yard. 'I don't see a bull. Plenty of gnomes and bunnies, though.'

'Has this man been filling your head with nonsense?' George stopped to catch his breath when he reached the front steps.

'He was just telling me about the animals.'

George turned and glanced disdainfully at the concrete menagerie.

'I tripped over that damned pagoda one night,' he said between gasps. 'Almost broke my neck.' He wiped his face with the back of his wrist band and asked, 'Is there any more coffee?'

Lee nodded.

George continued panting for a few seconds. Then as soon as he'd recovered a little, he took the steps two at a time and went into the cabin to towel off. Jennifer followed him in, while Lee stayed on the porch to finish his coffee and watch the sun climb into the sky.

She spent most of the day cleaning, and the work turned out to be lighter than she'd expected. First impressions aside, the cabin was pretty well kept. A little dusting brought the shine back. The dishes had been thoroughly washed and stacked neatly in the kitchen cabinets. They only needed a rinse before being used again. The stove didn't have a speck of grease on it. Even the pots and pans were scrubbed clean.

In fact, it was only the intrusions of nature that had made the place look so dismal. Someone left a window open, and that had given small animals their run of the cabin long enough to make a mess. But it was all superficial. No real harm done.

Jennifer got everything looking pretty good, but when George cooled off from his run, he kicked her out of the kitchen, and she had to turn her attention to the combination living and bedroom while he cooked supper.

She started by scraping the empty beer cans and food wrappers off the low table in the middle of the room. In their place she set out one of the bottles of bourbon George had bought on their way out of the city, and beside it three bowls and as many glasses, which she managed to liberate from the kitchen with only minimal objection from the chef. A candle in an old Chianti bottle became the table's centrepiece. And Jennifer topped the setting off with a loaf of bread on a piece of wood she'd found in the kitchen and assumed was a bread board.

She had just finished arranging everything for the best effect when Lee came in from outside. As usual, he seemed a little wrapped up in something private; didn't start a conversation or offer to help with the housework. Instead, he took his guitar out of its case and after giving it a few minutes to adjust to the room's atmosphere started playing a tune Jennifer hadn't heard before.

Apparently it was something he was trying to learn. He kept getting stuck part way through and spent most of his time looking for a chord that fitted. But it still sounded good, and Jennifer listened to it as she finished her work.

The cabin had several boxes of candles – more than she thought it really needed – so she appropriated a dozen and placed them strategically around the living room. And when everything outside was dark, she lit them and stood back to admire what she'd done. Somehow the candles seemed a perfect accessory for the cabin. They gave it a warm glow that blended with the smells of George's stew to make the place seem every bit as much a home as her own apartment.

It was as if she'd managed to bring in some of the nocturnal wonderland from outside. And that was no small accomplishment.

'This cabin isn't so bad, really,' she said, looking around to survey the results of her labour one more time.

'We like it,' George answered as he brought in a large pot of non-vegetarian stew and set in on the table.

'No. I'm serious. It looks like a dung heap from the outside, but once you get settled in, the place feels pretty comfortable.'

'That's because it's lived in,' Lee said, without looking up from the strings of his guitar. 'We've been coming here for decades . . .'

'Since you were an infant, I suppose?'

'Very funny.' He finally gave up and laid the guitar aside. 'I mean "we" as a group.'

'I was pretty young when I first came here,' George said. 'An old guy picked me up in the Y when I was sixteen. I used to hang out there, hoping to find someone else like me. Then he found me. He brought me here for a week that summer.'

'Does he own the place or something?'

'No, I don't think anyone owns it. And he's dead now.'

'I'm sorry.'

'It's all right,' George said, though something at the edge of his voice hinted that it wasn't. 'We were close for a while, but those days were long ago. I guess that's the way it goes. Everyone dies. Anyway, he told me how his uncle brought him here when he was just a pup.'

'Did they bring up the pagoda?'

George looked confused.

'On the path.'

'Oh, that. They may have. I think someone just put it there to dress the place up. After that, other guys brought up the rest of the stuff over the years.'

Jennifer dished up the food. She ladled out a bowl of stew for George, passed one to Lee and served herself. Then she settled back into a pillow and stirred hers with a piece of bread.

'That's the way this place is,' George went on, pouring some bourbon into his glass. 'The old guy told me I could use it any time I wanted. So I brought Lee here about five years ago. Now we're bringing you. Someday you'll bring a friend. And years from now they'll bring others.'

'Everyone who stays here makes the place a little more lived in,' Lee added.

'Living's better than the alternative, I suppose.' George took a gulp of whiskey and pronounced his approval by pouring another shot.

'You know what I mean,' Lee insisted.

'Sure, but a house is just a house. You got your roof, you got your bed, and if you're lucky you got your whiskey glass.'

'What ever happened to him?' Jennifer asked.

'Who?' Now George looked a little frustrated, as if he wished Jennifer would stick to one subject and ask questions he could grasp the first time out.

'The man who brought you here.'

'Oh. He's buried out back.'

Jennifer didn't ask. She wanted to, but the circles she ran in had an unwritten rule. Everyone was expected to sense which topics were too personal to talk about, and guessing wrong meant getting slapped down.

She wasn't sure, but she suspected she'd drifted into one of those topics. So she didn't ask.

They finished the meal in silence. Then they drank and talked and played harmless games. But it didn't take long for the mountain air and the day's exercise to take their toll, and they were all asleep before midnight.

Sunday started gradually on the mountain. Even in the city, there would have been no need to rush. But here it was unthinkable.

They slept late and woke slowly. There was plenty of time for coffee and doughnuts, which led them out to the porch where they sat for hours, watching the people in the valley emerge in small groups from their tiny dwellings and gather at their big white church and, after a respectable interlude, drift away from it to return home. There was little activity in the town after that, no visible motion at any rate, to show whether the people were doing anything important.

Most of the day on the mountain was like that, too. It passed without incident.

Then came the morose drinking that's often a symptom of being away from home and having too much time to think.

It began in the late afternoon. At least, that's when whatever the guys had been holding in came to the surface.

Jennifer had decided to set the kitchen table for supper, just to add a touch of class. She appropriated some half burned candles from the living room, arranged them at the centre of the table and set out some of the matching Doulton she'd found tucked away at one end of the kitchen cabinets.

But this time, no one wanted to help. After setting the table, she had to cook while the guys stayed outside hacking up firewood they weren't going to use and tinkering with the station wagon, which had run perfectly all the way up from the city. Then when they finally decided to come in, she had to serve the meal.

And when everything was on the table, they didn't appreciate the effort. They passed up the wine she'd set out, drinking straight whiskey instead. The rare steak and scalloped potatoes she'd worked on so hard didn't suit them. Nor did they bother to compliment her table even once. She could accept that kind of behaviour from George, but Lee certainly knew better.

To make things worse, after supper they both refused to leave the kitchen, even when Jennifer snatched the dishes away and whisked the crumbs off the tablecloth. They just sat there, sliding a half-gallon jug of bourbon back and forth between them and swigging it with that macho attitude men seem to adopt when they're feeling down.

Jennifer saw what was coming and did everything she could to stay aloof. First, she busied herself with the dishes – it was her turn anyway – and when everything was dried and put away, she took the scraps outside to scatter them on the ground for the animals.

But when she got back, things had taken a nasty turn. During the thirty seconds she was outside, one of the guys had taken an old Smith & Wesson revolver out of a drawer in the living room. Now it was sitting on the kitchen table beside the jug. That was when Jennifer really wanted to disengage.

She took a glass of wine to the living room, built a nest for herself in front of the fire and started playing solitaire with a dog-eared deck of cards that had shared the drawer with the Smith & Wesson. *Different games for different folks*, she reckoned.

For more than two hours the scene changed gradually but predictably. It started with a little self-pity and a round of whiskey. Then it progressed to questioning the wisdom of the Almighty, who'd obviously made a mistake when he made the world the way it was, followed by another drink. Then more self-pity, this bout steeped in slurred introspection followed by agreement that most parents are ill-equipped for the job.

'I wish you guys would grow up,' Jennifer finally said, speaking over her shoulder but refusing to look around.

'Maybe we have . . . at long last,' Lee mumbled, his words punctuated by the scraping sound of the gun sliding across the table and the less metallic sound of the jug being set down hard.

Jennifer turned her head just enough to see what was going on in the kitchen. She hoped the guys wouldn't notice. She didn't want to encourage them.

George spun the cylinder and raised the gun to his temple. He cocked the hammer, left his thumb on it and tugged at the trigger until the action released. Then he let the hammer down very slowly.

'You know you're betraying your heritage,' Jennifer said, turning back to the cards and shuffling the deck nervously. 'Just accept what you are.'

'That's the hardest part,' George sighed.

'Then gut it out. If I can do it, you can. I'm just a dumb old girl, remember – the weaker half of the species. Isn't that the way you put it once, George?'

She thought if she could provoke them, maybe they'd come into the living room and get their minds on something healthier. But it didn't work.

'Let's do it,' George said.

'Why not.' Lee's voice no longer sounded like him. It was low and tense, with a bitter, icy edge.

Jennifer heard the sound of the cylinder spin and spin again. Then a second of silence followed by a raspy, metallic click and a loud sigh.

She refused to look but heard the ritual repeated twice more. Each time the harsh sounds grated on her nerves. And each time they seemed slower, further apart, as if the guys were losing their nerve. But it was probably just her apprehension that had thrown everything into slow motion.

After the third time, she turned and stared, but she quickly wished she hadn't. The scene was more than she'd bargained for. Lee was pale, his face dotted with beads of sweat. George held the gun. His eyes were closed and his mouth slightly open. He sat completely motionless except for his left hand. It was resting on the table, beside the jug, and moving mechanically up and down in tight jerks.

'I can't believe you two.' That was all she said. She wanted to say more, but it was obviously too late.

George laid the gun on the table, and Lee picked it up. He spun the cylinder and raised the old Smith & Wesson to his head.

Jennifer turned away, unwilling to watch any more of their sick game. To steady herself, she picked up her wine glass and started to take a long pull from it.

The explosion was sharp and much too loud. She jumped so hard the wine splashed all over her blouse, and through the ringing in her ears she thought she heard a short, desperate laugh from George.

She closed her eyes and didn't open them again for a long time. She neither needed nor wanted to see what had happened.

Eventually, a wave of nausea came over her. It's hard when your own kind dies, not like seeing a rabbit or a squirrel lying in the road. When it's one of your own, it becomes a very personal thing.

Her stomach tightened so much she thought she was going to throw up, but it didn't happen. That was good. She needed to be strong, at least for the rest of the night. There was still more to endure before she could go home again.

The last morning at the cabin was beautiful, though sad. By the time Jennifer awakened, most of the shock had worn off. Her hands still trembled a little, but that was normal for the morning after. For the most part, she was able to put it out of her mind while she watched the sun rise and helped load the station wagon.

She and George had run all night. He showed her the path through the rolling hills that led down to the valley. They explored the woods, ate their fill at one of the farms and even circled the town from a safe distance.

The valley was fantastic in the monochrome light of the full moon. All the sounds were happy, while the mingled scents of fireplace smoke and slowly cooking dinners floated on a gentle breeze that made Jennifer's body feel cool and strangely liberated.

It was nearly dawn when they returned to the cabin. They got a few hours of sleep then jump-started with a pot of black coffee, cleaned up and prepared for the drive back to the city.

They laid Lee to rest in the graveyard behind the cabin. He had no relatives, nor anyone who would really miss him, and there was no reason to take him anywhere else.

The revolver still lay on the table in the kitchen. The last thing George did, after he'd packed their things and loaded the car, was to put it in the drawer it had come from and carefully place the box of silver-tipped bullets beside it. Both would be safe there until someone decided to use them again.

While George drove along the winding road that led down to the city, Jennifer curled up in the back seat and tried to get some sleep. The purr of the engine and the gentle beating of tyres on the old blacktop helped her relax. And she consoled herself by holding on to the thought that it would be a month until the next full moon.

Perhaps things would be different then.

C. Bruce Hunter lives in Chapel Hill, North Carolina. The preceding story marks his return to horror fiction after an absence of several years, but he has not been completely idle. He has spent the intervening time exploring esoteric subjects with his colleagues, Andrew and Alison Ferguson. The fruits of their work have appeared in such publications as *Renaissance, The Philalethes* and *Ars Quatuor Coronatorum*, and in a new book, *The Legacy of the Sacred Chalice*, which traces the origins of the masonic ritual to the twelfth century. The author denies any personal knowledge of the events related in this story. Without elaborating, he does admit that it has something to do with experiences he had with a former girlfriend, and adds: 'I hope the readers understand that "Changes" is merely a sensitive and insightful tale about a young woman's monthly cycle. I wouldn't want anyone to think that there's anything supernatural in the story . . .'

The Abortionist's Horse
(A Nightmare)

TANITH LEE

Naine bought the house in the country because she thought it would be perfect for her future life.

At this time, her future was the core upon and about which she placed everything. She supposed that was instinctive.

The house was not huge, but interesting. Downstairs there was a large stone kitchen recently modernised, packed with units, drawers, cupboards and a double sink, with room for a washing machine, and incorporating a tall slender fridge and an electric cooker with a copper hood. The kitchen led into a small breakfast room with a bay window view of the back garden, a riot of roses, with one tall oak dominating the small lawn. At the front of the house there was also a narrow room that Naine christened the parlour. Opposite this, oddly, was the bathroom, again very modern, with a turquoise suite she would never have chosen but quite liked. Up the narrow stair there were a big linen cupboard, and three rooms, the largest of which was to be Naine's bedroom, with white curtains blowing in fresh summer winds. The two smaller rooms were of almost equal size. One would be her library and workroom. The third room also would come to have a use. It, like the larger bedroom and the parlour, faced to the front, over the lane. But there was never much, if any, traffic on the lane, which no longer led down into the village.

A housing estate had closed the lane thirty years before, but it was half a mile from the house. The village was one mile away. Now you reached it by walking a shady path that ran away behind the garden and down through the fields. A hedgerow-bordered walk, nice in any season.

The light struck Naine, spring light first, and almost summer light now, and the smells of honeysuckle and cow parsley from the lane, the garden roses, the occasional faint hint of hay and herbivorous manure blowing up the fields.

You could just hear the now and then soft rush of cars on the main road that bypassed the village. And church bells all day Sunday, sounding drowned like the ones in sunken Lyonesse.

Her Uncle Robert's death had given Naine the means for this venture. She had only slightly known him, a stiff memory of a red-brown August man handing her a lolly when she was five, or sitting on a train with the rest of the family when she was about thirteen, staring out of the window, looking sad at a bereavement.

The money was a surprise. Evidently he had had no one else he wanted to give it to.

The night of the day when she learned about her legacy there was a party to launch the book Naine had been illustrating. She had not meant to go, but, keyed up by such sudden fortune, had after all put on a red dress, and taken a taxi to the wine bar. She was high before she even entered, and five white wines completed her elevation. So, in that way, Uncle Robert's bequest was also responsible for what happened next.

At twenty-seven, Naine had slept with only two men. One had been her boyfriend at twenty-one, taken her virginity, stayed her lover for two years. The second was a relationship she had formed in Sweden for one month. In fact, they had slept together more regularly, almost every night, where with the first man she had only gone to bed with him once or twice a week, so reticent had been their competing schedules. In neither case had Naine felt very much, beyond a slight embarrassment and desire for the act to be satisfactorily over, like a test. She had read enough to pretend, she thought adequately, although her first lover had sadly said, as he left her for ever to go to Leeds, 'You're such a cool one.' The Swede had apparently believed her sobs and cries. She knew, but only from masturbation, that orgasm existed. She had a strange, infallible fantasy which always worked for her when alone, although never when with a man. She imagined lying in a darkened room, her eyes shut, and that some presence stole towards her. She never knew what it was, but as it came closer and closer, so did she, until, at the expected first touch, climax swept through her end to end.

At the party was a handsome brash young man, who wanted to take Naine to dinner. Drunk, elevated, she accepted. They ended up at his flat in Fulham, and here she allowed him to have sex with her, rewarding his varied and enthusiastic scenario with the usual false sobs and low cries. Perhaps he did not believe in them, or was only a creature of one night, for she never heard from him or saw him again. This was no loss.

However, six weeks later, she decided she had better see a doctor. In the past her methods of contraception had been irregular, and nothing had ever occurred. It seemed to her, nonsensically but instinctively, that her lack of participation in the act removed any chance of pregnancy. This time, though, the spell had not worked.

Abortions were just legally coming into regular use. For a moment Naine considered having one. But, while believeing solidly in any woman's right to have an unwanted foetus removed from her womb, Naine found she did not like the idea when applied to her own body.

Gradually, over the next month, she discovered that she began to think intensely about what was inside her, not as a thing, but as a child. She found herself speaking to it, silently, or even aloud. Sometimes she was even tempted to sing it songs and rhymes, especially those she had liked when small – 'Here We Go Round the Mulberry Bush', and 'Ride a Cockhorse to Banbury Cross'. Absurd. Innocent. She was amused and tolerant of herself.

Presently she was sure that the new life belonged to her, or at least that she was its sponsor. With this in mind, she set about finding a house in the country where the child might be brought up away from the raucous city of its conception. The house by the lane looked so pretty at once, the cow parsley and docks standing high, the sunlight drifting on a pink rose classically at the door. When she learned there was the new hospital only two miles away in Spaleby, and besides, a telephone point in the bedroom for the pre-ordained four-in-the-morning call for an ambulance, Naine took the house. And as she stepped, its owner, in over the threshold, a wave of delight enveloped her, like the clear, spotted sunshine through the leaves.

As Naine walked up to the bus-stop by the main road, she was thinking about what a friend had said to her over the phone, the previous night. 'You talk as if it didn't have a father.' This had come to Naine only hours afterwards. That is, its import. For it was true. Biology aside, the child was solely hers, and already Naine had begun to speak of it as feminine.

She realised friends had called her less and less, during the fortnight she had been here. In the beginning their main interest had seemed to be if she was feeling 'horribly' ill – she never was. Also how she had 'covered' herself. Naine had put on her dead mother's wedding ring, which was a little loose, and given the impression she and a husband were separated. Once the friends knew she was neither constantly spewing nor being witch-hunted as a wanton, they drew off. Really, were they her friends anyway? She had always tended to be solitary, and in London had gone out perhaps one night in thirty, and that probably reluctantly. She enjoyed her work, music, reading, even simply sitting in front of the TV, thinking about other things.

The bus-stop had so far been deserted when Naine twice came to it about three, for the 3:15 bus to Spaleby. Today, in time for the 1:15 bus, she saw a woman was already waiting there. She was quite an ordinary woman, bundled in a shabby coat, maybe sixty, cheerful and nosy. She turned at once to Naine.

'Hello, dear. You've timed it just right.'

Naine smiled. She wondered if the woman could see the child, faintly curved under the loose cotton dress. The bulge was very small.

'You're in Number 23, aren't you?' asked the woman.

'Oh . . . yes I am.'

'Thought so. Yes. I saw you the other day, hanging your washing out, as I were going down the lane.'

Naine had a vague recollection of occasional travellers using the lane, on foot, between the stands of juicy plants and overhanging trees. Either they were going to the estate, or climbing over the stile, making off across the land in the opposite direction, where there were three farms, and what was still locally termed the Big House, a small, derelict and woebegone manor.

'Miss your hubby, I expect,' said the woman.

Naine smiled once more. Of course she did, normal woman that she was; yes.

'Never mind. Like a lot of the women when I was a girl. The men had to go to Spaleby, didn't come back except on the Sunday. There was houses all up the lane then. Twenty-seven in all, there was. Knocked down. There's the pity. Just Number 23 left. And then modernised. My, I can remember when there wasn't even running water at 23. But you'll have all the mod cons now, I expect.'

'Yes, thank you.'

'I expect you've done a thing or two to the house. I shouldn't wonder if you have.'

Naine sensed distinctly the nosy cheerful woman would love to come in and look at Number 23, and she, Naine, would now have to be on guard when the doorbell rang.

'I haven't done much.'

'Just wait till hubby gets home. Shelves and I don't know what-all.'

Naine smiled, smiled, and wished the bus would arrive. But she would anticipate Naine would sit with her, no doubt. Some excuse would have to be found. Or the guts to be rude and simply choose another seat.

Two cars went by, going too fast, were gone.

'Now the lane used to go right through to the village, in them days. There wasn't no high road here, neither. You used to hear the girls mornings, going out at four on the dot, to get to the Big House. Those that didn't live in. But the Missus didn't encourage it. She was that strict. Had to be. Then, there was always old Alice Barterlowe.' The woman gave a sharp, sniggering laugh. It was an awful laugh, somehow obscene. And her eyes glittered with malice. Did Naine imagine it – she tried to decide afterwards – those eyes glittering on her belly as the laugh died down. At the time Naine felt compelled to say, 'Alice Barterlowe? Who was that?' It was less the cowardly compulsion to be polite than a desire to clear the laugh from the air.

'Who was *she*? Well that's funny, dear. She was a real character hereabouts. When I was a nipper that were. A real character, old Alice.'

'Really.'

'Oh my. She kep' herself to herself, did old Alice. But everyone knew her. Dressed like a man; an old labouring man, and rode astride. But no one said a word. You could hear her, coming down that lane, always at midnight. That was her hour. The hoofs on the lane, and you didn't look out. There goes Alice, my sister said once, when we'd been woke up, and then she put her hand over her mouth, like she shouldn't have said it. Nor she shouldn't. No one was meant to know, you see. But handy for some.'

This sinister and illogical dialogue ended. The woman closed her mouth as tight as if zipped. And, before Naine could question her further – or not, perhaps – the green bus came chugging along the road.

'Old Alice Barterlowe. Oh my goodness yes. I can remember my gran telling me about her. If it was true.'

It was five days later, and the chatty girl in the village shop was helping Naine load her bag with one loaf, one cabbage, four apples and a pound of sausages.

'Who was she?'

'Oh, an old les. But open about it as you like. She had a lady-friend lived with her. But she died. Alice used to dress up just like the men, and she rode this old mare. Couldn't miss her, gran said, but then you didn't often see her. You *heard* her go by.'

'At midnight.'

'Midnight, that's it.'

'Why? Where was she going?'

'To see to the girls.'

'I'm sorry?'

'Girls up the duff like.'

'You mean . . . you mean pregnant?'

'She was an abortionist, was Alice.'

Naine had only felt sick once, a week after she had moved in. Sitting with her feet up for half an hour had taken it right off. Now she felt as if someone was trying to push her stomach up through her mouth. She retched silently, as the chatty girl, missing it, rummaged through her till.

I will *not* be sick.

I *won't*.

The nausea sank down like an angry sea, leaving her pale as the now hideous, unforgivable slab of cheese on the counter.

'Here you are. Three pound change. Yes, old Alice, and that old horse. Half dead it looked, said my gran, but went on for years. And old les Alice was filthy. And this dirty old bag slung on the saddle. But she kept her hands clean as a whistle. And her stuff. There wasn't one girl she seen to come to harm.'

'You mean – it didn't work.'

'Oh it *worked*. It worked all right. They all got rid of them as wanted to, that Alice saw to. She was reliable. And not one of them got sick. A clean healthy miscarriage. Though my gran said, not one ever got in the family way after. Not even if she could by then. Not once Alice had seen to her.'

On the homeward shady path between the hedges and fields, Naine went to the side and threw up easily and quickly amongst the clover. It was the sausages, she thought, and getting in, threw them away, dousing the bin after with TCP.

Ride a cock-horse to Banbury Cross,
  To see a fine lady upon a white horse—

The rhyme went round in Naine's head as she lay sleepily waking at five in the summer morning. The light had come, and patched beautifully through her beautiful butterfly-white curtains. On a white horse, on a white horse—

And something sour was sitting waiting, invisible, unknowable, not really there.

Old Alice Barterlowe.

Well, she had done some good, surely. Poor little village girls in the days before the Pill, led on by men who wouldn't marry them, and the poor scullery maids seduced at the Big House by some snobby male relative of the strict Missus'. What choice did they have but those clean strong probing fingers, the shrill hot-cold pain, the flush of blood—

Naine sat up. Don't think of it.

Ride a cock-horse, clip clop. Clip clop.

And poor old Alice, laughed at and feared, an ugly old lesbian whose lover had died. Poor old Alice, whose abortions always worked. Riding astride her ruinous old mare. Down the lane. Midnight. Clip clop. Clip clop.

Stop it.

'I'll get up, and we'll have some tea,' said Naine aloud to her daughter, curled soft and safe within her.

But in the end she could not drink the tea and threw it away. A black cloud hung over the fields, and rain fell like galloping.

When Naine phoned her friends now, they could never stay very long. One had a complex dinner on and guests coming. One had to meet a boyfriend. One had an ear infection and talking on the phone made her dizzy. They all said Naine sounded tired. Was there a sort of glee in their voices? Serve her right. Not like them. If she *wanted* to get pregnant and make herself ill and mess up her life—

Naine sat in the rocker, rocking gently, talking and singing to her child. As she did so she ran her hands over and over along the hard small swelling. I feel like a smooth, ripening melon.

'There's a hole in my bucket, dear daughter, dear daughter...'

Naine, dozing. The sun so warm. The smell of honeysuckle. Sounds of bees. The funny nursery rhyme tapping at the brain's back, clip *clop*, clip *clop*.

Naine was dreaming. She was on the Tube in London, and it was terribly hot, and the train kept stopping, there in the dark tunnels. Everyone complained, and a man with a newspaper kept saying, 'It's a fly. A fly's got in.'

Naine knew she was going to be terribly late, although she was not sure for what, and this made it much worse. If only the train would come into the station, then she might have time to recollect.

'I tell you there's a fly!' the man shouted in her face. 'Then do it up,' said Naine, arrogantly.

She woke, her heart racing, sweat streaming down her, soaking her cotton nightdress.

Thank God it was over, and she was here, and everything was all right. Naine sat up, and pushed her pillows into a mound she could lean against.

Through the cool white curtains, a white half-moon was silkily shining. A soft rustle came from the trees as the lightest of calm night breezes passed over and over, visiting the leaves.

Naine reflected, as one sometimes does, on the power of the silliest dreams to cause panic. On its Freudian symbols – tunnels, trains, *flies*.

She stroked her belly. 'Did I disturb you, darling? It's all right now.' She drank some water, and softly sang, without thinking, what was tapping there in her brain, 'Clip *clop*, clip *clop*. Clip *clop*, clip *clop*. Here comes the abortionist's *horse*.' Then she was rigid. 'Oh Christ.' She got out of bed and stood in the middle of the floor. 'Christ, Christ.'

And then she was turning her head. It was midnight. She could see the clock. She had woken at just the proper hour. Alice Barterlowe's hour.

Clip *clop*, clip *clop* . . .

The lane, but for the breeze, was utterly silent. Up on the main road, came a gasp of speed as one of the rare nocturnal cars spun by. Across the fields, sometimes, an owl might call. But not tonight. Tonight there was no true sound at all. And certainly not – *that* sound.

All she had to do now, like a scared child, was to be brave enough to go to the window, pull back the curtain a little, and look out. There would be nothing there. Nothing at all.

It took her some minutes to be brave enough. Then, as she pulled back the curtain, she felt a hot-cold stinging pass all through her, like an electric shock. But it was only her stupid and irrational night-fear. Nothing at all was in the lane, as she had known nothing at all would be. Only the fronds of growing things, ragged and prehistoric under the moon, and the tall trees clung with shadows.

Past all the houses Alice had ridden on the slow old wreck of the horse, down the lane, and through the village. To a particular cottage, to a hidden room. In the dark, the relentless hands, the muffled cries, the sobs. And later, the black gushing away that had been a life.

Why did she do it? To get back at men? Was it only her compassion for her own beleaguered sex, in those days when women were more inferior than, supposedly, during the days of Naine?

Go away, Alice. Your time is over.

It was so silent, in the lane.

Clip *clop*, clip *clop*, clip *clop*, clip *clop*.

Here comes . . .

Naine went downstairs to the bathroom. She felt better after she had been sick. She took a jug of water and her portable radio back upstairs. A night station played her the Beatles, Pink Floyd, and even an aria by Puccini, until she fell asleep, curled tight, holding her child to her, hard, against the filmy night.

The doctor in Spaleby was pleased with Naine. He told her she was doing wonderfully, but seemed a bit tired. She must remember not to do too much. When they were seated again, he said, sympathetically, 'I suppose there isn't any chance of that husband of yours turning up?'

Naine realised with a slight jolt she had been convincing enough to convince even the doctor.

'No. I don't think so.'

'Some men,' he said. He looked exasperated. Then he cheered up. 'Never mind. You've got the best thing there.'

When she was walking to the town bus-stop, Naine felt weary and heavy, for the first time. The heat seemed oppressive, and the seat for the stop was tormentingly arranged in clear burning yellow light. Two fat women already sat there, and made way for her grudgingly. She was always afraid at this point of meeting the awful, cheery, nosy woman. Because of the awful woman, Naine no longer pegged out washing, and had kept the postman waiting on her doorstep twice while she peered at him from an upstairs room, to be sure.

Somehow, to see the awful woman again would be just too much. She might start talking about Alice Barterlowe. Naine was sure that her child, in its fifth month, was generally visible by now. That would set the awful woman off, probably. *No use for old Alice, then.* No. No.

When the bus came, the journey seemed to last for a year, although it took less than half an hour. All the stops, and at every stop, some woman with a bag. And these women, though not the awful woman, might still sit beside her, might say, Oh, you're at Number 23 in the lane. The lane where the abortionist rode by at midnight on her nag.

Exhausted, Naine walked down from the main road. She made herself a jug of barley water and sipped a glass on the shady side of her garden. The grass had gone wild, was full of daisies, dandelions, nettles, purple sage and butterflies.

'I'm so happy here. It's so perfect. It's what we want. I mustn't be so silly, must I?' But neither must she ever speak her fear aloud to her child. Of all the things she could tell the child – not this, never this.

And round and round in her head, the idiotic rhyme, compounded of others that had gone wrong . . .

Clip *clop*, clip *clop*.

She must have been courageous. Alice. To live as she did, and do what she did. Especially then. It took courage *now*. Naine could recall the two girls caught kissing at school, and the ridiculous to-do there had been. Did they *know* what they were *doing*? Dirty, nasty. They had been shunned, and only forgiven when one confessed to pretending the other was a boy. They were *practising* for men. For their proper female function and role.

Naine, of course, was properly fulfilling both. Naine must like men, obviously. Look at her condition. It was her husband who was in the wrong. She had been faithful, loving, admiring, aroused, orgasmic, conceptive, productive. But *he* had run off. Oh yes, Naine was absolutely fine.

She did not want any dinner, or supper. She would have to economise, stop buying all this food she repeatedly had to throw away.

But then, she had to eat, for the sake of the child. 'I will, tomorrow, darling. Your mother won't be so silly tomorrow.'

She had told the doctor she could not sleep, made the mistake of saying 'I keep listening—' But he was ahead of her, thank God. 'The pressure on the stomach and lungs can be a nuisance, I'm afraid. Ask Nurse to give you a leaflet. And you've only moved out here recently. I know, these noisy country nights. Foxes, badgers rustling about. Whoever said the country was quiet was mad. It took me six months to get used to it.' He added that sleeping pills were not really what he would advise. Try cutting down on tea and coffee after five p.m., some herbal infusion maybe, and honey. And so on.

After the non-event of dinner, Naine watched her black-and-white eighteen-inch TV until the closedown. Then she went next door and had a bath.

She had never been quite happy with the bathroom downstairs. It could be grim later, when she was even heavier, lumbering up and down with bladder pressure, to pee. Maybe when things were settled anyway, she could move the bathroom upstairs, put the workroom here.

The child's room, the room the child would have; she had been going to paint that, and she ought to do so. Blue and pink were irrelevant. A sort of buttermilk colour would be ideal. Pale curtains like her own. And both rooms facing on to the lane. It would not matter about the lane, then. By then, Naine would laugh at it, but not the way the awful woman had laughed.

Clip *clop*. Clip *clop*.

After the bath, bed. Sitting up. Reading a novel, the same line over and over, or half a page, which was like reading something in ancient Greek. And the silence. The silence waiting for the sound.

Clip *clop*.

Turn on the radio. Bad reception sometimes. Crackling. Love songs. Songs of loss. All the lovely normal women weeping for lost men, and wanting them back at any cost.

At last, eyes burning, lying down. We'll go to sleep now.

But not. The silence, between the notes of the radio. A car. A fox. The owl. The wind. Waiting . . .

Clip *clop*, clip *clop*.

It was the horse she couldn't bear. It was the horse she saw. Not old Alice in her dirty labourer's clothes, with her scrubbed hands and white nails. The horse. The horse whose hoofs were the sound that said, Here comes Alice, Alice on her horse.

Old horse. Try to feel sorry for the poor old horse, as try to feel proud of courageous Alice. But no, the horse's face was long and haggard, with rusty drooping eyes, yellow, broken, blunt teeth, dribbling, unkempt. Not a sad face. An evil face. The pale horse of death.

'I'm sorry I can't sleep, baby. You sleep. You sleep and I'll sing you a lullaby. Hush-a-bye, hush-a-bye.'

But the words are wrong. The words are about the white pale horse. The night-mare. The nag with the fine lady, the old lesbian. Clippity-clop—

Clip *clop* clip *clop*

Clip *clop* clip *clop*

It was coming up in her, up from her stomach, her throat, like sick. She couldn't hold it in.

'Clip clop clip clop clip clop clip clop here comes the abortionist's horse!'

And then she laughed the evil laugh, and she knew how it had trundled and limped down the lane, its hoofs clipping and clicking, carrying death to the unborn through the mid of night.

'It's my work that's the problem. I didn't realise it would be so awkward.' She was explaining to the estate agent, who sat looking at her as if trying to fathom the secret. 'I'll just have to sell up and get back to London. It really is a nuisance.'

'Well, Mrs Robert . . . well, we'll see what we can do.'

As Naine again sat on the hot seat waiting for the bus, she thought of the train journey to London, of having nowhere to go. She had tried her friends, tentatively, to see if she could bivouac a day or two. One had not answered at all. One cut her short with a tale of personal problems. You could never intrude. One said she was so sorry, but she had decorators in. This last sounded like a lie, but probably was true. In any case, it would have to be a hotel, and the furniture would have to be stored. And then, flat-hunting five months gone, in the deep, smoky city heat. The house had been affordable down here. But London prices would allow her little scope.

It doesn't matter. I can find somewhere better after you're born. But for now. For now.

She knew she was a fool, had perhaps gone a bit crazy, as they said women did during pregnancy and the menopause. Even the kind doctor, when she had vaguely confessed to irrational anxieties, said jokingly, 'I'm afraid that can be par for the course. Hormones.'

To leave the house – *her* house – how she had loved it. But now. Not now.

No one came to look at the house, however. When she phoned the agents, they were evasive. It was a long way out unless you liked walking or had a car. And there had been a threat of the bus service being cut.

Day by day.

Night by night.

Over and over.

Its face.

The horse.

She was dreaming again, but even unconscious, she recognized the dream. It was delicious. So long since she had felt this tingling. This promise of pleasure. Her sexual fantasy.

She was in the darkened room. Everything was still. Yet someone approached, unseen.

They glided, behind dim floating curtains. The faint whisper of movement. And at every sound, her anticipation was increasing. In the heart of her loins, a building marvellous tension. Yes, yes. Oh come to me.

Naine, sleeping, sensed the drawing close. And now her groin thrummed, drum-taut. Waiting . . .

The shadow was there. It leaned towards her.

As her pulses escalated to their final pitch, she heard its ill-shod metal feet on the floor. A leaden midnight fell through her body and her blood was cold.

Its long horse face, primal, pathetic and cruel. The broken teeth. The rusty, rust-dripping half-blind eyes. It hung over her like a cloud, and she smelled its smell, hay and manure, stone and iron, old rain, ruinous silence, crying and sobbing, and the stink of pain and blame and bones.

The horse. It was here. It breathed into her face.

Naine woke, and the night was empty, noiseless, and then she felt the trapped and stifled pleasure, which had become a knot of spikes, and stumbling, half falling down the stairs, to the inconvenient lower bathroom, she left a trail of blood.

Here, under the harsh electric light, vomiting in the bath, heaving out to the lavatory between her thighs the reason the light the life of her life, in foam and agony and a gush af scarlet, Naine wept and giggled, choking on her horror. And all the while knowing, she had nothing to dread, would heal very well, as all Alice's girls did. Knowing, like all Alice's girls, she would never again conceive a child.

Tanith Lee lives on Britain's Sussex Weald with her husband and two cats. She began writing at the age of nine and worked variously as a library assistant, shop assistant, filing clerk and waitress, and had three children's books published in the early 1970s. When DAW Books published her novel *The Birthgrave* in 1975, and thereafter twenty-six other titles, she was able to become a fulltime writer. To date she has published more than seventy novels and collections and nearly two hundred short stories. Some of her recent and forthcoming titles include *Faces Under Water*, *Saint Fire*, *A Bed of Earth* and *Venus Preserved* (the first four volumes in 'The Secret Books of Venus' series); *White as Snow* (an adult retelling of the Snow White legend); a large epic fantasy duet, *Mortal Suns* and *The Immortal Moon*, plus the children's books *Islands in the Sky*, and the trilogy *Law of the Wolf Tower*, *Wolf Star Rise* and *Queen of the Wolves*. About the preceding story, the author explains: 'John Kaiine, my husband, came up with the title. Both he and I tend to get titles out of thin air, frequently without a story attached. (And anyone who's seen much of my work lately, will realise that he has also given me many ideas and plotlines for stories – which, with my own stream of ideas, makes sure I am a seven-day-a-week writing factory.) This title is so threateningly pictorial that of course the story itself arrived swiftly on its heels – or hoofs.'

The Handover

MICHAEL MARSHALL SMITH

Nobody moved much when he came into the bar. From the way Jack shut the door behind him – quietly, like the door of a cupboard containing old things seldom needed but neatly stored – we could tell he didn't have any news that we'd be in a hurry to hear. There were three guys sipping beer up at the counter. One of them glanced up, gave him a brief nod. That was it.

It was nine-thirty by then. There were five other men in the place, each sitting at a different table, nobody talking. Some had books in front of them, but I hadn't heard a page turn in a while. I was sitting near the fire and working steadily through a bowl of chilli, mitigating it with plenty of crackers. I'd like to say Maggie's chilli is the best in the West, but, to be frank, it isn't. It's probably not even the best in town: even this town, even now. I wasn't very hungry, merely eating for something to do. Only alternative would have been drinking, but just a couple will go to my head these days, and I didn't want to be drunk. Being drunk has a tendency to make everything run into one long dirge, like being stoned, or living in Iowa. I haven't ever taken a drink on important days, on Thanksgiving, anniversaries or my birthday. Not a one. This evening wasn't any kind of celebration, not by a long chalk, but I didn't want to be drunk on it either.

Jack walked up to the bar, water dripping from his coat and onto the floor. He wasn't moving fast, and he looked old and cold and worn through. It was bitter outside, and the afternoon had brought a fresh fall of snow. Only a couple of inches, but it was beginning to mount up. Maggie poured a cup of coffee without being asked and set it in front of him. Her coffee isn't too bad, once you've grown accustomed to it. Jack methodically poured about five spoons of sugar into the brew, which is one of the ways of getting accustomed to it, then stirred it slowly. The skin on his hand looked delicate and thin, like blue-white tissue paper that had been scrunched into a ball and absently flattened out again. Sixty-eight isn't so old, not these days, not in the general scheme of things. But some nights it can seem ancient, if you're living inside it. Some nights it can feel as if you're still trying to run long after the race is finished. At sixty-four, and the second youngest in the place, I personally felt older than God.

Jack stood for a moment, looking around the place as if memorising it. The counter itself was battered with generations of use, as was the rest of the room. The edges of chairs and tables were worn smooth, the pictures on the walls so varnished with smoke you'd had to have known them for forty years to guess what they showed. We all knew what they showed. The bulbs in the wall fixings were weak and dusty, giving the room a dark and gloomy cast. The one area of brightness was in the corner, where the jukebox sat. Was a big thing when Pete, my old friend and Maggie's late husband, bought it. But only the lights work these days, and not all of them, and none of us are too bothered. Nobody comes into the bar who wouldn't rather sit in peace than hear someone else's choice of music, played much too loud. I guess that comes with age, and anyway the 45s in the machine are too old to evoke much more than sadness. The floor was clean, and the bar only smelt slightly of old beer. You want it to smell that way a little, otherwise it would be like drinking in a church.

Maggie waited until Jack had caught his breath, then asked. Someone had to, I guess, and it was always going to be her.

She said: 'No change?'

Jack raised his head, looked at her. 'Course there's a change,' he muttered. 'No one said she weren't going to change.'

He picked up his coffee and came to sit on the other side of my table. But he didn't catch my eye, so I let him be, and cleared up the rest of my food, rejecting the raw onion garnish in deference to my innards. They won't stand for that kind of thing any more. It wasn't going to be long before a cost-benefit analysis of the chilli itself consigned it to history alongside them.

When I was done I pushed the bowl to one side, burped as quietly as I could and lit up a Camel. I left the pack on the table, so Jack could take one if he had a mind to. He would, sooner or later. The rest of the world may have decided that cigarettes are more dangerous than a nuclear war, but in Eldorado, Montana, a man's still allowed to smoke after his meal if he wants to. What are they going to do: come and bust us? The people who make the rules live a long ways from here, and the folk in this town have never been much for caring what State ordinances say.

One of the guys at the bar finished his beer, asked for another. Maggie gave him one, but didn't wait for any money. Outside, the wind picked up a little and a door started banging, the sound like an unwelcome visitor knocking to be let out of the cellar. But it was a ways up the street, and you stopped noticing it after a while. It's not an uncommon sound in Eldorado.

Other than that, everyone just held their positions and eventually Jack reached forward and helped himself to a cigarette. I struck a match for him, as his fingers seemed numb and awkward. He still hadn't taken his coat off, though with the fire it was pretty warm in the room.

Once he was lit and he'd stopped coughing, he nodded at me through the smoke. 'How's the chilli?'

'Filthy,' I confirmed. 'But warm. Most of it.'

He smiled. He rested his hands on the table, palms down, and looked at them for a while. Liver spots and the shadow of old veins, like a fading map of territories once more uncharted. 'She's getting worse,' he said. 'Going to be tonight. Maybe already.'

I'd guessed as much, but hearing it said still made me feel tired and sad. He hadn't spoken loudly, but everybody else heard too. It got even quieter, and the tension settled deeper, like a dentist's waiting room where everyone's visiting for the first time in years and has their suspicions about what they're going to hear. Maybe 'tension' isn't the right word. That suggests someone might have felt there was something they could do, that some virile force was being held in abeyance, ready for the sign, the right time. There wasn't going to be any sign. This night had been a while in coming, but it had come, like a phone call in the night. We knew there wasn't anything to be done.

Maggie pottered around, put on a fresh jug of coffee. I started to stand up, meaning to get me a cup, but Jack put his hand on my arm. I sat back, waited for him to speak.

'Wondered if you'd walk with me,' he said.

I looked back at him, feeling a dull twinge of dread. 'Already?'

'Only really came down here to fetch you, if you had a mind to go.'

I realised in a kind of way that I was honoured. I took my heavy coat from the back of the chair and put it on. A couple heads raised to watch us leave, but most people turned away. Every one of them knew where we were headed, the job we were going to do. Maybe you'd expect something to be said, the occasion to be marked in some way: but in all my life, of all the things I heard that were worth saying, none of them were actually said in words. And I ask you: what could anyone have said?

Outside it was even colder than I expected, and I stuffed my hands deep in my pockets and pulled my neck down into my scarf like a turtle. The snow was six inches deep in the street, and I was glad I had my thick boots on. The moon was full above, snow clouds hidden away someplace around a corner, recuperating and getting ready for more. There would be more, no doubt of that. The winters just keep getting colder and deeper around here, or so my body tells me. The winters are coming into their prime.

Jack started walking up the street and I fell in beside him. Within seconds my long bones felt like they were being slowly twisted and the skin on my face like it was made of lead. We walked past the old fronts, all of them dark now. The hardware store, the pharmacy, the old tea rooms. Even in the light of day the painted signs are too faded to read, and the boardwalk which used to run the length of the street has rotted away to nothing. It happened like a series of paintings. One year it looked fine; then another it was tatty; then finally it was broken down and there was no reason to put it back. Sometimes, when I'd walked up the street in recent years, I would catch myself recalling the way things had been, working my memory like a tongue worrying the site where a tooth had once sat. I could remember standing or sitting outside certain stores, the people who'd owned them, the faces of the people I'd spied from across the way. The times all tended to blend into one, and I could be the young boy running to the drug store, or the youth mooning over the younger of two sisters, or a man buying whiskey to blur the night away: switching back and forth in a blink, like one man looking out of three sets of eyes. It was like hearing a piece of music you had grown up to, some tune you had in your head day after day until it was as much a part of your life as breathing. It was also a kind of time travel, and for a moment I'd feel as I once had, young and empty of darkness, ready to learn and experience and do. Eager to be shown what the world had in store had for me, to conquer and make mistakes. To love, and lose, and love again. Amen.

Eldorado was founded in 1850 by two miners, Joseph and Ezekial Clarke: boys who came all the way from New Hampshire with nothing but a pair of horses and a dream. Sounds funny now, calling it a dream, probably even corny. People don't think of money that way any more. These days they think it's a right, and they don't go looking for it. They stay where they are, and try to make it come to them, instead of going off to find it for themselves. The brothers came in search of gold, like so many others. They were late on the trail and worked through the foothills, finding nothing or stakes that had already been worked dry, and then climbed higher and higher into the mountains. They panned a local river and found nothing once more, but then one afternoon came upon the seam – just as they were about to give up and move on, maybe head over to Oregon or California and see if it was paradise like everyone said. It must have seemed like magic. They found gold. When we were young we all heard the story. A kind of Genesis tale. A little glade, hidden up amidst the mountains at over three thousand feet: and there for the taking, a seam of money, a pocket of dreams.

The brothers stayed and built themselves a cabin out of the good wood that grew all around. But news travelled fast, even in those days, and it wasn't long before they had company. A lot of company. The old mine workings have gone to ruin now, but it was a big old construction, I can tell you that. Was a few years when Eldorado was home to over four thousand people, and produced five million dollars a year in gold. The town had saloons and boarding houses, a post office and a fistful of gambling rooms, even a grand hotel. Almost all have fallen down now, though until ten years ago people still used the hotel to board their animals in, when it got real cold. Two walls are still more or less there, hidden amongst the trees, though I wouldn't want to stand underneath them for long. I once showed them to a couple of tourists who came up all this way in a rental car, having seen the town sign down the road. They seemed a little disappointed to find there were still people living here, and were soon on their way again.

That was near ten years ago, and no one's come up to look since, though the town sign's still there. It says 'Eldorado, 15 miles', and stands on a turn of the local road from Giles to Covent Fort, though lately I swear the trees around it have been growing faster. Neither Giles nor Covent are much themselves these days, and the road between them isn't often used. If it weren't for that town sign, there would be no way of knowing we were up here at all.

When the gold ran out there was zinc for a time, and a little copper. The gold fever died away, but Eldorado continued to prosper for a while. There was a Masonic lodge built, and two banks, and a school house with a clock and a bell – the fanciest building in town, a symbol that there was a community here, and that we were living well. I can't even remember where the lodge was now, the banks are gone, and the school closed in 1957. I went to that school, learned most of what I know. Everybody did. It was the place where you turned into a grown-up, one year at a time, back when a year was as long as anyone could imagine, when two seemed like infinity. Probably that was why, for a long time, folks would stop by the abandoned school every now and then, by themselves and on the quiet, and do a little patching up. Wasn't any sense in it, because it wasn't going to re-open, not least because there were no new children – but I know I did it, and Jack did, and Pete before he died. Had to be that others did too, otherwise it would have fallen down a lot earlier than it did.

Now it's gone, and even on the brightest spring day that patch of the mountain seems awful quiet. I guess you could say that no one here has learned anything since then. Certainly what you see on television doesn't seem to have much application to us. I stopped watching a long time ago, and I know I'm not the only one. TVs don't last forever, and there ain't no one around here knows how to fix them. And anyway it just showed a world that isn't ours, and things that we can't buy and wouldn't want to, so what use was it anyway. We've got a few books, spread amongst us.

Eventually the copper ran out, and though people looked hard and long, there wasn't anything else useful to be found. The gambling dens moved on, in search of people who still had riches to throw away. The boarding houses closed soon afterwards, as those who hadn't made Eldorado their home moved on. Plenty people stayed, for a while. My folks did, in the 1920s. Never got to the bottom of why. But anyhow they came, and they stayed, and I followed in their footsteps, I guess, by staying here too. So did some others. But not enough. And nobody new.

Halfway down to the end of Main, Jack and I turned off the road and made our way as best we could up what used to be Fourth Street. I guess it still is, but you'd be hard pressed to find the first three, or the other eight, unless you'd once walked them, and gone visiting on them, or grown up in a house that used to stand on one. Now they've gone to trees and grass, just a few piles of lumber dotted around, like forgotten games of giant pick-up-sticks. You'd think someone might have made an effort to keep the houses standing, even after people stopped living in them. But it's not the kind of thing that occurs to you until far too late, and then there doesn't seem a great deal of point. Spilt milk, stable door, all of those.

The grade has always been kind of steep on Fourth, and Jack and I both found the going hard. Jack had already made the trip once that night, and I let him go in front, following his footprints in the snow. There was another way of getting up to the house, a little less steep, but that involved going past the town's first cemetery, now overgrown, and the notion wasn't even discussed. Ahead of us, a single light shone in one of the upper windows of the Buckley house, which sits alone right at the end, a last stand against the oncoming trees. I felt sick to my stomach, remembering times I'd made the walk before, towards that grand old house hunkered beneath the wall of the mountain.

Hundreds of times, but a handful of times in particular. My life often seems that way to me now. So much of it was just landscape I passed through, like a long open plain with little to distinguish the miles. Then there's like a little bag inside me, which I keep the real things in. A few smells, and sounds, touches like a faint summer breeze. Some evenings, a couple afternoons, and a handful of dawns, when I woke up somewhere I was happy to be, coddled warm with someone and protected from the bright light of day and tomorrow. But it's nights I remember most. Some bad, some good. You fall in love at night, and that's also when people die. Even if their last breath is drawn in daylight, by the time you've understood what's happened, the darkness has come to claim the event as its own. Nights last the longest, without doubt, both at the time and afterwards. They contain multitudes, and don't fade as easily as the sun. They're there, in my bag, and I'll take them with me when I go.

When we got to the house we stomped the snow off our boots on the porch, and then let ourselves in. Over the last few weeks of visiting I had got used to the dust, how it overlaid the way the house had used to be. She'd kept it up as well as she could over the years, but now you could almost hear it running down, like the wind dropping after a storm. The downstairs was empty but for Naomi's cat, which was sitting in the middle of the hall, looking at the wall. It glanced up at us as we started on the stairs, then walked slowly away into the darkness of the kitchen.

I knew then that it was already over.

When we reached the upper landing, we hesitated outside the doorway to the bedroom, as if feeling we had to be invited in. The interior was lit by candles, with an old kerosene lamp by the window. The Doc was sitting on a blanket box at the end of the bed, elbows on his knees. He looked like an old man, very tired, waiting for a train to take him home. Not much like someone who'd once been the second-fastest runner in town, after me, a boy who could run like the wind. He'd gone away, many years ago. Left town, got trained up, spent some years out there in the other places. Half the books in town were his, brought with him when he came back to Eldorado.

He looked up, beckoned us in with an upward nod of the head. We approached like a pair of children, with short steps and hands down by our sides. I kept my eyes straight ahead, knowing there'd be a time to look after the words had been said.

Jack rested a hand on the Doc's shoulder. 'She wake at all?'

He shook his head. 'Just died. That's all she did.'

'So that's it,' I said.

The three of us sighed then, all together. Nothing long, or melodramatic. Just an exhalation, letting out what had once been inside us.

The Doc started to speak, faltered. Then tried again. 'Maybe it's not going to happen,' he said, trying for a considered tone, but coming out querulous and afraid. 'After all, how do we know?'

Jack and I shook our heads. Wasn't any use in this line of thought. Nobody knew how we knew. But we knew. We'd known since the children stopped coming.

We walked around on separate sides of the bed and looked down. I don't know what Jack was looking at, but I can tell you what I saw. An old woman, face lined, though less so than when I'd seen her in the afternoon of the previous day. Death had levelled the foothills of her suffering, filled in the dried streambeds of age. The coverlet was pulled up to just under her chin, so she looked tucked up nice and warm. The shape beneath the blankets was so thin it barely seemed to be there at all: it could have been just a runkle in the sheets, covering nothing more than cooling air. Most of all she looked still, like a mountain range seen from the sky.

Wasn't the first time I'd seen someone dead, not nearly. I saw my own parents laid out, inexplicably cold and quiet, and my wife, and many of my friends. There's been a lot of dying hereabouts over the last few years, every passing marked and mourned. But Naomi looked different.

It's funny how, when you first know someone, it will be the face you notice most of all. The eyes, the mouth, the way they have their hair. Everybody has the same number of limbs, but their face is their own. Then, over the years, it's as if this part of them leaves their body and goes into your head, crystallises there. You hardly notice what the years are doing, the way people's real faces thicken and dim and change. Every now and then something brings you up short and makes you see the way things have become. Then you lose it again, almost as quick as it came, and you just see the continuity, the essence behind the face. The person as they were.

I saw Naomi as she and her sister had once been, the two brightest sparks in Eldorado, the girls most likely to make you lose your stride and catch your breath – whether you were fifteen, same as them, or so old that your balls barely still had their wits about them. I saw her as the little lady who could shout loudest in the playground, who could give you a Chinese burn you'd remember for days. I saw her as I had when Pete and I used to hike up Fourth with flowers in our hands and our hearts in our throats, when Pete was cautiously dating Naomi, and I was going with her sister Sarah, who was two years younger and much prettier, or so I thought back then.

It's that year that many of the nights I keep in my bag came from, that brings faint memories of music to my head. Sarah and I came to a parting of the ways before Thanksgiving, and she eventually married Jack, had no children, but generally seemed content, and died in 1984. Pete and Naomi lasted a couple more months than we had, and then Pete met Maggie and things changed. Five years later, both on rebounds from different people altogether, gloriously grouchy and full of cheap liquor, Naomi and I spent a night walking together through the woods which used to stop on the edge of town. We looked for the stream where the Clarkes first panned, and maybe even found it, and we didn't do anything more than kiss, but that was exciting enough. Then the morning came and brought its light, and everything was burned away. We'd never have been right for each other anyhow, that was clear, and it wasn't the way it was supposed to be. Of course a decade or two later, when I first started to look back upon my life and read it properly, like a book I should have paid more attention to the first time, I realised that this might have been wrong. When I thought back, it was always Naomi's face that was clearest in my mind, though she'd been Pete's and I'd been Sarah's and anyhow both futures were long in the past and dead and buried half a lifetime ago. By then Naomi was married, and when we met we were polite. Almost as if that current which can pass between any two people, the spark of possibility, however small, had been used up all in that night in the woods, underused and thrown away, and now we could be nothing but friends. Naomi never had children either, nor Maggie. None of us did.

Even now, when the forest has started to march its way right up Main Street, I can remember that night with her as if I'm still wearing the same clothes and haven't had time to change. Remember also the way the sisters always seemed to glow, all of their lives, as if they were running on more powerful batteries than the rest of us, as if the one who had stirred their bodies into being had been more practised at the art than whoever did the rest of us. I loved my wife a great deal, and we had many good years together, but as I get older it's like those middle years were a long game we all played, a long and complex game of indeterminate rules. Those seasons fade, and we return to the playground like tired ghosts coming home after a long walk, and it's how we were then that seems most important. I can't remember much of what happened last year, but I can still picture those girls when we were young. On the boardwalk, in the big old house their father built, around the soda fountain when they were still little girls and we were all sparkling and young and blessed, a crop of new flowers bursting into life in a field which would always be there.

Almost all of those people are dead now. Distributed amongst the two cemeteries, biding their time, like broken panes in the windows of an old building. A few of the windows are still intact, like me and Jack and Maggie and all, but you have to wonder why. There's nothing to see through us now.

When Jack and I had looked down on Naomi a while, and nothing had changed, we turned away from the bed. The Doc had quietly got his things together, but didn't look ready to leave just yet.

'There's something me and Bill have to do,' Jack said. 'Only stopped by for the truck. And, well, you know.'

The Doc nodded, not really looking at us. He knew what we were going to do. 'I'll stay a while,' he said. Back in '72 there'd been something going on between him and Naomi. He probably didn't realise that we knew. But everybody did. Then, after her husband died in '85, oftentimes the Doc had taken his evening meal at the Buckley table. I'd always wondered if it might be me who did that. Didn't work out that way.

'What are we going to do about her cat?' I asked.

'What can anyone do about a cat?' the Doc said, with the ghost of a smile. 'Reckon it'll do pretty much what it wants. I'll feed it, though.'

We shook his hand, not really knowing why, and left the house.

Jack's truck was parked around the side. It wasn't going to be a picnic getting down the hill, but it was too far to walk. We got it started after only a couple of tries and Jack nosed her carefully out into the ruts of the street. Fate was kind to us and we got down to Main without much more than a spot of grief. Turned right, away from the bar, away from what's left of the town.

When we drew level with the other cemetery, Jack slowed to a halt and turned the engine off.

We sat with the windows down for a while, smoking and listening. It was mighty cold. Wasn't anything to hear apart from wind up in the mountains and the rustle of trees bending our way. Beyond the fence the stones and wooden crosses marched away in ranks into the night. Friends, parents, lovers, children, in their hundreds. A field full of the way things might have been, or had been once, and could never be again. Folks are dead for an awfully long time. The numbers mount up.

Jack turned, looked at me. 'We're sure, aren't we?'

'Yes,' I said. 'We've been outnumbered for a long, long while. After Naomi, there're only fifteen of us left.'

It felt funny, Jack turning to me, wanting to be reassured. I still remembered him as one of the big kids, someone I hoped I might be like one day. I did grow up to be like him, then older than he'd once been, and then just old, exactly like him. Everything seemed so different back then, everyone so distinct from one another. Just your haircut can make you a different colour, when everyone's only got ten years of experience to count on. Then you get older, and everyone seems the same. Everybody gets whittled away at about the same rate. Like the '50s, and '60s, and '70s and '80s, times that once seemed so different to each other, but are now just stuff that happened to us once and then went away; like good weather or a stomach ache.

Jack stared straight out the windshield for a while. 'I don't hear anything.'

'May not happen for hours,' I said. 'No way of telling. May not even happen tonight.'

He laughed quietly. 'You think so?'

'No,' I admitted. 'It'll happen tonight. It's time.'

I thought then that I might have heard something, out there in the darkness, the first stirring beyond the fence. But if I did, it was quiet, and nothing came of it right then. It was only midnight. There was plenty of darkness left.

Jack nodded slowly. 'Then I guess we might as well get it over with.'

We smiled at each other, briefly, like two boys passing in the school yard. Boys who grew to like each other, and who could never have realised that they'd be sharing such a task, on a far-away night such as this.

Later we'd drive back up into town, park outside Maggie's bar and sit inside with the others and wait. She was staying open for good that night. But first we went down the hill, down a rough track to an old road hardly anyone drove any more.

We got out the truck and stood a while, looking down the mountain at a land as big as Heaven, and then together we took down the town sign.

Michael Marshall Smith is a novelist and screenwriter who lives in London with his wife Paula and two cats. His first novel, *Only Forward*, won the August Derleth Award; his second, *Spares*, has been optioned by Steven Spielberg's DreamWorks

SKG and translated in seventeen countries around the world, and his third, *One of Us*, is under option by Warner Brothers and Di Novi Pictures. His latest novel is *The Straw Men*, and his short stories have appeared in anthologies and magazines around the world and in a collection entitled *What You Make It*. 'In terms of the story itself,' the author says, 'there's not much to say except that I got the idea during a fantastic three-week drive from one side of the United States to the other; that, and a love of the deserted and the ruined so acute that in the end I was actively banned from saying "Oh, look – a fallen-down barn" even just one more time . . .'

Pearl

ROBERTA LANNES

The tumour resides in me like a condominium beside tenements. Its sleek, dangerous sides gleam in comparison with the worn surfaces of my surrounding organs. It pulses with purpose as veins begin to burrow graciously into its foreign body to feed it, along with capillaries whose only intent is companionship in the process. A nucleus throbs at its centre like a heart, growing a fort of malignant cells around it. A thousand minds, all programmed towards one goal, to think it larger, urge it on without conscience, vanquish any and all who seek to destroy it, and order it to spread until the host, me, breathes only for it. Urban redevelopment.

She sits on the edge of the bed, slumped against wakefulness. The new lace curtains flap stiffly in the morning breeze. She feels him lying there, her devoted and painfully needy spouse, silently yearning for attention from her. He's feigning sleep. She has become so separate from him that she feels the distance as a pure weight. The moment his breathing quickens to signal his waking, she pulls herself up and begins plodding towards the bathroom.

She loves the bathroom with its rosy tiles, bright white grouting, fluffy ivy green and celadon towels and cheery framed prints of cottages in gentle gardens. More than these, she adores the scents trapped in the paint and ceramic from years of ablutions: hydrangea, orange blossom, eucalyptus bath oils, hairspray, deodorant, and talc in Lily of the Valley, musk, ylang-ylang and rain. The pot-pourri on the window-sill has gone dry and its gardenia aroma faded to a memory.

Avoiding her reflection, she passes the mirror to the toilet. Lifting her jersey slip gown, she sits down and urinates. The rush of warmth, the relief of pressure, makes her sigh. She wishes she didn't have this thing growing inside her making her have to pee what seems like every hour. She hears him roll over. The bed creaks. Sheets shift. Her heart slams. She waits. The draining discussions that come with his invasions loom outside as unwelcome as that which grows inside her.

It's been ages since she recalled their past together with gratitude and love. This man feels to her now like an ever-present rat she can't quite catch to kill – to give her the peace of mind it will never surprise her in the night or steal her sleep or make her feel dirty – the thing that keeps showing up to remind her she's vulnerable. Once he was everything she'd waited too long to find. Her 'perfect match'. An artist as successful as she, who wasn't the least bit intimidated by her, who shared her values, beliefs, and showed her she could be more than she imagined. They shared everything. Nothing ever went unsaid. Last year on their anniversary, she'd been astonished to find they had created a marriage that had surpassed her ideal, which was the envy of those who circled around them like the homeless around a fire.

But there was one value, one life choice they had never discussed, because at the time it seemed irrelevant. An impossible notion. And when it came up, they were diametrically opposed. And it was too late to compromise.

Within a dark pearl inside a tiny oyster, the thing has begun to grow hair, teeth and a tail. It bites every so often, reminding me I'm not alone. The pain is surreal. As if the tumour grows in an amputated foot and troubles the missing appendage instead of my gut. Its hair is wire, arcing, curling, imbedding itself into clean tissue, cutting, slicing, hoeing the site for brethren. The tail reminds me of a parasite I heard about once at a party. A thing that grew twenty feet long into the host's stomach from the intestines, eating anything that was dumped there for digestion, starving the host. I can feel this parasite travelling up my spine towards my brain. Will it eat my thoughts? Will my body functions go haywire because that thing eats nervous impulses like snacks? Though kindred tumours have not yet grown rampant, they have sprouted. I detect them. Spawn. The mother is so big I have given her a name. *Cybele*.

Standing beside her agent, she considers her oil pastel paintings on the walls of The Culp/Griffey Gallery. They're like a row of windows refusing to open. He tells her 'they are impenetrable', that the gallery owner has somehow imagined what she wants to see in them. What else would possess her to set up this show? She must be going through 'the change', he says with undisguised disdain. He warns her that the critics will say the same things he's saying. Opaque. Dense. Obfuscations so cold that they make you flinch away. Obscure. Uninviting.

They hide nothing! They're the reflections of the darkness in me, she thinks. The darkness born of the growth inside her that evolves every moment into a nemesis. Her demise.

Perhaps, she thinks, the work is of me inside of *it*. Each darkly coloured image is of a fast-faltering light, a weak beam that trains itself into the murky depths only to find indefinite, ill-defined edges. Subterfuge and vagaries. Here, a glimpse of buildings through a fog, warped in a funhouse mirror. There, a faintly glowing figure rushing past at twilight when you're nearly blinded by the remnants of the day. Like dreaming under water, the sun a league above you.

She tells her agent she hates analysing her work, doesn't he know that? She turns from him to the room. Everyone is wearing black in some form – leather, wool, denim, silk. They devour light as they stand about like iron nails pounded into blonde wood. They mutter and chatter over their latest personal acquisitions, ogling her pieces as if doing so was strictly required in order to sip the champagne and consume the designer *hors d'oeuvres*.

Someone asks if anyone knows the artist. Her husband is standing close and turns his bright eager face towards the question. She knows he'll point her out, pride swelling him like a pigeon that's eaten a bowl of uncooked rice, so she excuses herself. Too late. She must stand in the rain of forced adulation or stinging judgment without an umbrella once again.

A fashionable dowager looks her over, says, I was wondering if your series is indicative of the onset of menopause? The woman has a scaffolding of loose skin between her chin and collarbone like a tangle of jungle vines, her face overly lifted so her eyes are catlike. Her chest is flattened by a double mastectomy or gravity beneath a charcoal silk tent and obsidian pashmina shawl. Pearls the size of gumballs fall over that.

The consummate artist avoiding confrontation, she pulls at the hairs that curl onto her cheeks, then lets her hands fall slowly over her swollen, tender breasts to her hips, testing their sturdy presence, daring comparison. The woman sees this, swallows hard, her smile inching into a line perpendicular to the vines of her neck.

No, she says, going for a look that might bring adjectives to mind like *sparkling* and *radiant*, why do you ask?

Her agent has taught her many tricks. Artists are not the best advertisements for buying their work. They need grooming, he's told her. Make the client talk; invite them to see what they will. They buy things they think they understand, especially if they think they understand them better than you.

The woman corrects the drape of her shawl and blinks rapidly under brows that grow closer and down. She is suddenly hard, saying that the pieces say *barrenness*. Fear of incompleteness. Disconnection.

She nods, appearing fascinated. Without reason for defence. Feeling something more sinister viscerally, nearer the objective of the thing inside her. Perhaps from it. *Really*, she says without a trace of rancour, *tell me more*.

He stares at me from across our studio when he thinks I'm involved in my work. I pretend not to notice. I feel so sorry for him, not knowing the truth. But I know him. He'd crumble; make me take care of his misery, his upset, instead of myself. He'd say 'we can see this thing through together', just as he always has, but he has no idea what 'this thing' is. That it's bigger than he and I together.

He's been working on twelve-foot-high paintings lately, where he has to get up on a ladder. He'll make jokes about Michelangelo, a fear of heights, his SissyTeen Chapel, hoping the old me will surface and laugh myself sick on his tarps. There are moments I want to laugh. It won't let me.

It has feet now that kick, hands that grab at my kidneys, intestines and yank. A tumour that uses Kung Fu. I have no defence against such a cunning opponent. Medicaments and interventions of the stealthy chemical or mechanical kind have had no effect. Talking to it when I am alone doesn't still it. No. I can't believe I'm going to be all right. This thing owns me.

I see the malignant thing in my mind. Its children, feral and aggressive, run wild inside me, finding purchase, growing. Calling to each other, *over here – this looks like as good a spot as any to take root – try this tissue, it's succulent and easy!* They are crafty, deceptive. They have to be to resist all I have thrown in their way. They are so many, now. They have tiny faces, and though I can't envision hard, evil visages on children, I know they must look like devils. Their mother has a large ovoid face with an angry vitriolic grimace, teeth sharp as needles, long as stalactites, eyes wide full of vengeance.

I give up. Take me. I don't want a fight.

Elbows hooked inside the sink, she vomits. His hand is on her back, stroking, he's purring words of comfort. She knows he can't imagine that it is his touch that makes her retch. When she's empty and all that comes up is the breath of *Cybele*, she unhooks her elbows and crashes to the floor.

Leave me alone, she tells him. I'm just sick. He sighs. Even his sighs have the effect on her of fingernails on a chalkboard. He threatens to call 999. Go ahead she tells him, knowing he won't do anything to cause conflict between them. Nothing that might increase the distance. He walks out of the kitchen; his footsteps stop sounding on the carpet.

Her body is disappearing to bones that click and rattle like chopsticks in a paper bag. Starving the thing hasn't worked. Still her belly swells full of the *Cybele* and her children, putrefying her insides. Cancerous maggots, roiling there. Reminding her of a life she cannot control, a being that threatens to throw everything that is free and light into an abyss, filling her with the dread of it.

Even as she loathes her husband, she fears he's going to leave. Why not, she thinks? Who would want to live with a woman who harbours a monster so vile, so heinous, it will destroy everything? She sometimes reaches the point when she believes she has to tell him the truth so he'll stay. But it won't allow her to. It holds her tongue and chokes her when the words gather there.

Does she want to save him, or the world? She can't decide if one will lead to the other, or if in saving one, the other must perish. He was once her world. No more. She is now the beast.

She thinks, I am *Cybele*.

I hear him on the phone. He says he knows. It all makes sense now. The dark moods, the distancing, her nausea and lack of appetite, the disappearance of her libido. She's *pregnant*. How does he know? He's found the white plastic stick with its tiny window with screaming red 'plus' sign stuffed into a cardboard tube from the toilet paper, along with the instructions. She'd shoved it between some old magazines and newspapers to be recycled out back. Accident or providence brought him to it. He doesn't know why she couldn't simply tell him. It's not like her. Though she hasn't been his *her* in months.

He says she lies in bed most days. Gets up to draw a while, loses interest, and wanders back to the bedroom. Maybe she *is* ill. Something could be wrong with the pregnancy. But at least now he knows. He smiles wanly at her as she passes him in the hall. She'll only look at him out of the corner of an eye, furtively, as if catching his eye would dissipate her will to keep silent in her secret.

I know he's thinking I *know*. If only.

He says he's determined to confront her. He wants to know when it was she took the damned test. It could have been weeks, or months. She wears baggy things and won't let him see her without clothes any more. She did say several months ago that she didn't want to have a child. That she was too old anyway; it was a moot point. But that if we had one, we couldn't be selfish with our time any more. We'd have someone else between us. He told his friend he thought the idea terrified her.

What if . . . she did something to it? I've found straightened coat hangers and paregorics and strange thin rubber tubing in the bathroom.

I hear him catch a sob in his throat. Oh, God, he says. Oh, God.

It affects all of me, now. My skin is becoming dry, tight, splitting at my heels, around my fingernails. Patches of skin on my face are tinted darker than the rest. My hair is thinning about my face and growing thicker everywhere else, my nails, once pink, look bluish. There's a dark slash from my navel to my mons, like a scar. I wonder if it is a weakness growing on my belly where it will push its way out, like a creature in a thriller. Something plump, livid, and very painful, is bulging from my rectum, dripping blood into the toilet, when I dare to look. It's eating me, my sanity.

Everything hurts. My back. My chest. I think I'm dreaming most of the time. A fever dream. Or a nightmare. I cannot bear to look at myself, not even as I wash, thinking with each glance another flaw will become evident, another defect *Cybele* has cursed me with in her unrelenting battle. I've given up, dear. I submit. Stop this.

Winter has come and she sits at the window. Her breath makes a frosty mask before her, but she stares past it at the icy lawn. She's so weak from lack of food, lack of care, her elbow finds the windowsill to steady her. He piles another quilt on her shoulders, puts one over her knees until she's a caterpillar in a cocoon. She knows there is no butterfly to break free. No magic wife returning from her spiral towards the end.

Outside the window, he's made a snowman with stick arms. Is he mocking her? He whispers that he loves her when he thinks she's asleep, as if telling her will make her love him back. If loving him could save her. She's closed now, all of her willed to the *thing*.

When he taps his boots on the linoleum floor and tells her he's off to the store, she closes her eyes. As the door shuts, she smells the clean scent of him in the wind that rushes in. Once it would have invited her to him, made her cling to his ardour. Now it reminds her of what she'll never have again. Health. Innocence. Nothing to regret. She hates him. Hates him nearly as much as the growth that is slowly eating her life.

She throws off the blankets and quilts. With the strength she finds in her hatred, she pushes up the window. The cold hits her hard and she reels. It caulks her lungs as she breathes it in. She shivers, teeth clattering so hard she tastes fragments of enamel.

Her chest tightens and the pain in her arms and legs makes her wonder if she's having a heart attack. Good, she thinks. If there is no life in me, *you die*. Take this, you motherfucker!

She sees them together; her husband stands beside the psychiatrist looking at her from the doorway. She's lying there as if she's dead, but her vital signs are only weak, not gone. She's hooked up to so many monitors and feeding tubes, she thinks she must look like a dying plant in the garden, pinned to the trellis wall.

The psychiatrist sighs, tells him she's stabilised, but still delusional. It may be as simple as her lacking calcium. That could affect her nervous system, her thinking. After all, she's refused to eat. It makes sense. But she may also simply be nervously exhausted. A euphemism for nervous breakdown. Am I broke down, she wonders?

The psychiatrist asks, will he sign commitment papers? He shakes his head. Why not, she wants to scream! Do it! He tells the doctor that she's simply not prepared to have a child and they will seek outside counselling. His love has made her strong before, it will again. The psychiatrist shakes his head, tells him he risks losing her. No, he tells him. She just needs a few more days in the hospital. Put her back on solid food. She'll rally.

The psychiatrist mumbles something about murder and walks off.

The thing has stopped moving. The pain subsided. Its children have quit their frantic play. The mother has tired of this body and my embargo on her imports. I can't yet allow myself the joy of victory because part of me wonders if this is an ambush in waiting. Or I've lost my mind. Or I'm already dead.

I know the ceiling of this room better than I once knew the geography of my husband's body. I see faces and expressions that change. A Van Gogh's 'Starry Night' kind of image. And the cobwebs dance over the window in the early spring breeze. The light fixture is a great frosted globe with the chafe of dead bugs and dust of the attic in its bowel. I imagine the stuff moving, but I am safe from it down here.

He'll come in now. I turned off the light. He only comes when he thinks something's happened. Like it's *time*. Or I've fallen asleep and stopped breathing because he wasn't there to breathe for me. When he thinks he can save me. *It*.

If he only knew. There is no other choice. My life must take the life of this thing. Maybe then I've saved the world. If it's worked, at least I've saved him. My lost boy, my husband. A man I once loved so much, I was the sun. I was the centre of creation.

Why am I thinking of him now? Because *Cybele* has ceased her assault? She realises I've given up! Yes. I should be thinking of what will come next. Perhaps when all is safe, I can find the sun in me again.

I'm so cold, though. I shut my eyes but see a vast brightness of congealing hues. There, a Kandinsky, a Klee! The colours and shapes! Now I want to paint, to put all the colours into my work that disappeared. I want to be free!

She smiles now. She reaches up to the light, feels as if the bed and the earth are being pulled softly down away from her. She senses he's there, rushing towards the bed, but she doesn't care. Her work is done here. The best work is ahead of her.

The blanket and sheet ruffle, her hair ripples about in an unseen breeze, her face is beatific. The fabric obscures her face a moment as she writhes, then a grunt, a sound like 'aug-huh', stretches out into a sigh. All is still.

His fingertips touch her face, too dry, too cool. His heart is tapping quickly, fear makes his breathing shallow, sporadic. He grasps the blanket and peels it back. His tears come quickly, falling onto her. He kneels onto the bed to hold her, beg her to hold on. She grows colder as his quaking quiets, stops.

He sits up, turns on the light. He wails.

She has curled into a waxen foetal rose, all bones, and dry flesh. There, nestled against her buttocks in a ragged circle of blood is a dark mass of tissue. It's huge, bulbous, with large blue veins and yellow-white strands like long pale fingers, soft bones beneath a thin membrane. He can see faces in the thing, as if there are tiny children trapped in silvery rose bags of jelly, their hair wrapped around their heads. Embryonic cherubs. Horrible and yet benign. Their child. Children. From her. This softens him.

He moves down beside it and tenderly rests his hand on the side. It's warm and moist, like her skin right out of a hot shower. He senses a slight trace of movement. An eye in one of the faces searches. When it finds him, all the eyes settle there, watching him. Waiting. He thinks he sees mouths grinning. The mass shivers and purrs beneath his touch. He smiles. He's a father.

Roberta Lannes lives in Los Angeles with her British husband. She published her first horror story, 'Goodbye, Dark Love', in the 1986 anthology *Cutting Edge*, edited by one of her writing teachers at UCLA, Dennis Etchison. Since then her many acclaimed short stories have been translated into more than ten languages, and her début collection, *The Mirror of Night*, appeared from American independent publisher Silver Salamander Press in 1997. As to her inspiration for the preceding story, the author candidly reveals: 'When I was approached to do the filming of *Clive Barker's A–Z of Horror* as commentator on the letter "U" for Unborn, I was intrigued that I could speak to the profound effect Ira Levin's *Rosemary's Baby* had on me. I read it long before I considered getting married, let alone pregnant. It horrified me and tapped into the very core fear a mother has during her pregnancy of giving birth to something imperfect and, at its worst, possibly monstrous. It was the best birth control imaginable for me. Years later, whilst married, I had to face the real thing. Now, with the end of my childbearing years having arrived, remembering the trauma of a very difficult pregnancy and the child I lost in 1984 at six months, "Pearl" sort of took hold of me.'

Beauregard

ERIC BROWN

He came back into my life on the evening of the first snowfall of winter. In retrospect, the advent of bad weather might have been seen as something of a harbinger. The phone call that interrupted my work – I have never been able to consider the shrill ring of a phone as a summons, only an alarm – was unwelcome, as I was beginning the final chapter of a novelisation that had to be finished by the end of the week. More unwelcome still were the words that greeted me.

'Simon Charrington?' It was my name, spoken in a voice marinated over the years in a fatal combination of whisky and tobacco smoke. 'Simon? Are you there?'

'Beauregard? Christ, is it really you?'

'I'm in the village,' he said by way of a reply. 'How do I find you?'

Numbed, I gave him directions.

He was as laconic as ever. 'See you soon.'

I sat in the armchair in the darkened study, illuminated only by the aqueous glow of the computer screen, and contemplated what I had done. I told myself that I should have lied, said that Simon Charrington had moved away from the village years ago – but then I recalled that you could not lie to Beauregard: he saw through dissimulation and deceit. Such was the acuity of his mind that I fancied, back then, he could read my every thought.

Back then. Was it really twenty years since we had shared a room at Cambridge? In my memory the events of that last term were at once paradoxically clear and maddeningly vague: that is, I have impressions of what happened, but I am unsure, to this day, as to quite how they happened.

I cannot recall how I first met Beauregard, which, considering his singular character and appearance, I consider a strange failing. He seemed to be around our group, hovering on the periphery, for about a term before he introduced himself.

He was a mature student in his late twenties, though he struck me as being even older: he wore a soiled greatcoat, always buttoned, and his aquiline face was emphasised by the recession of his hairline.

He gave the girls the creeps, and even Paul and Dave found his company repellent. He had about him an aura of mystery and dissolute pathos that I considered intriguing. I had recently decided that I wanted to devote my life to the writing of great novels, and I made the beginner's mistake of assuming that I had to actively seek my subject matter, rather than allow it to come to me.

I soon became obsessed with Beauregard. He was that which I had never before happened upon: a true original in a world populated by jejune copies. Although he never said as much in conversation, he disdained the modern world and all its meretricious and commercial trappings: while we were reading Fowles and Pirsig, he would immerse himself for days at a time in crumbling and dusty tomes he brought back from forays to antiquarian bookshops in London and Edinburgh. He was studying mediaeval history, and laboriously compiling a thesis on mysticism of the twelfth century, and in consequence he seemed to inhabit the world in body only: in mind, he was forever elsewhere.

Long into the early hours he would regale me with the results of his studies: he would tell me of worlds within the world we know, of realms that existed in the minds of philosophers, an onion skin series of realities that for him existed because they had been granted brief if incandescent life in the dreams of obscure thinkers and persecuted mystics.

I cannot recall my exact reaction to his hushed, late-night monologues describing the lore of alchemy and abstruse magic. In the company of my other friends I played the sardonic sceptic; with Beauregard I came fleetingly to perceive the disturbing possibility of a truth that existed independently of my quotidian perceptions.

Then he met Sabine, a German girl as strange in her own way as Beauregard: a slim, introverted Classics student, almost pathologically shy. They were seen together setting out on, or returning from, long walks, though they never frequented the usual student haunts. I cannot recall ever saying above a dozen words to Sabine – perhaps I was resentful of her having taken my friend – and I cannot claim to have known her. The others of my group were secretly gratified that his liaison with the German student, as they called her, meant that he had less time for us.

I could not claim to have been griefstricken when Sabine was found hanging from an oak tree in the ancient forest beyond the college buildings, though naturally I was shocked. I tried to talk to Beauregard, but he was even more withdrawn than usual. He left Cambridge not long after, and it was ten years before I saw him again. He called at my flat in London, having obtained the address from a mutual university acquaintance, drank all the alcohol I had in the house and said little: it seemed that the years had built between us an insurmountable barrier. I tried to talk of our time at university, but he had gestured with his hand-rolled cigarette, as if to say the memories were too painful; I questioned him about what he was doing, but elicited little response. He spoke drunkenly of a book he was writing, though his description of its subject made little sense to me. I felt that he despised my materialism, and the shallow books I wrote at the behest of publishers eager for competent prose from someone who could meet a deadline.

That was ten years ago, and I had never seen him since: I had thought of him, though, often wondered what a man so unsuited to the modern world might be doing to get by. It seemed, now, that I might at last find out.

If I considered a phone call more of an alarm than a summons, then a knock at the door was tantamount to an intrusion. I jumped as the hollow thumps echoed through the house. I must have been daydreaming for longer than I thought. It seemed only a matter of a minute or two since I had spoken to him on the phone.

Taking a breath, I moved to the hall and opened the door. The first thing I noticed was not Beauregard, but the fact that a rapid snowfall had lain down a thick sparkling mantle beneath the light of the stars.

Then he stepped from where he had been trying to peer in through the window, and against the effulgent snowfield he bulked taller than I recalled, more stooped; his hair had receded further and his face seemed even more attenuated.

'Simon,' he greeted. He held out a hand, and I shook it. It was icy. I ushered him inside, only then noticing that he was wearing a greatcoat – though surely not *the* greatcoat of twenty years ago?

He stepped past me and paused on the threshold of my untidy study. His gaze seemed to take in everything with a silent though censorious regard, and I was transported back twenty years, to the time when I could not help but feel unworthy in his presence. He seemed to look upon those about him with silent disdain that antagonised many people. Perhaps it was a measure of my own lack of confidence that I felt his censure, then as now, was not wholly unwarranted.

I gestured to an armchair and turned on a nearby lamp. Beauregard winced at the sudden illumination, dumped his battered rucksack into the chair and sat upon the arm, where he proceeded to roll himself an impossibly thin cigarette.

I made some ill-judged comment, along the lines that he reminded me of a dissolute Withnail, though of course the popular cultural reference was lost on him. A line from Horace he might have acknowledged; of film lore he was ignorant.

I babbled smalltalk, asking him how he had travelled here, how he was keeping. As was his wont he made no reply, merely fixed me with an occasional sardonic half-smile.

In the light of the lamp I could see that the passage of years had not left him unscathed. His eyes were rheumy and the skin around them had the thin blue translucence often seen in alcoholics and the ill. His fingers, as they painstakingly manufactured the roll-up, trembled as if afflicted by more than just the cold he had escaped.

'Can I get you something? Tea? Coffee?'

He looked up, fixed me briefly. 'Tea. Black. Don't you remember?'

'Of course. Black tea. I'll be back in a second . . .'

It was with relief that I took refuge in the kitchen. The reality of Beauregard was coming back to me, the essence of the man that was impossible to recreate fully when considering him at a remove of years: he was so unlike anyone else I had ever met, so impossible to locate in terms of where he stood as regards culture and values, that I had the eerie sensation of being in the presence of an alien; that is, of someone not of this world. It was a feeling I had forgotten over the years, but as it returned now I began to sympathise with my friends at university, Dave and Paul, Cathy and Sue, who detested Beauregard and could not abide his presence.

I returned with the tea-tray. He had slipped down into the armchair, his long legs, encased in baggy brown cords, stretched out towards the open fire.

He accepted the mug without a word, took a mouthful, and topped it up with alcohol from a silver hip flask.

I fetched an ashtray as his roving eye sought a place to deposit the foul-smelling ash of his cigarette.

'So . . .' I said, 'it's been a long time – ten years?'

He ignored me. His eye had alighted on the glass-fronted bookcase in which I kept copies of my published work. 'Still writing, Simon?' he asked, as if it had been a passing phase out of which I might have grown.

I nodded. 'Keeps the wolf from the door,' I said, and immediately regretted it. I recalled the disdain with which he regarded those who compromised in order to get by.

He was rapidly thawing out before the dancing flames, and the process brought back another aspect of the man I had conveniently forgotten over the years: Beauregard had a body odour as distinctive as it was strong. I recalled debating with Dave and Sue as to the exact essence of the perfume: I think I described it at the time as something like the reek of an old jungle temple, leaf mould and guano. Now this compost odour filled the room.

'I must say, this is a surprise,' I waffled. 'What have you been up to lately?'

It was some time before he replied. He took a mouthful of his charged tea, then a sharp inhalation of his cigarette.

'Travelling,' he said.

'Anywhere interesting?' I winced as I said this. What was it about Beauregard that made my every comment crass and ignorant? Wasn't *everywhere* interesting, if one approached it with curiosity?

He nodded, his liquid eyes seeing far away places. 'Patna, Kathmandu, Lhasa . . .'

I nodded, as if I were familiar with these cities.

'Working?'

He shook his head. Silly question. 'Studying. Thinking. Reading.'

He always had been a voracious reader of obscure texts. He spoke at least six languages, read six more.

He swung his long head and stared at me. 'I've seen things, Simon. I've seen things you wouldn't believe.'

I nodded again, prepared to believe him, but was aware as I did so that I did not want him to tell me of these things.

Thankfully he seemed disinclined to go on.

'So you've been away for ten years?' I asked, feeling compelled to stoke the conversation.

He nipped the tab of his cigarette and inhaled with miserly economy, and looked at me though the smoke. 'Almost ten years. Walked across Europe, through Greece, Turkey.'

'Walked all the way?'

'All the way, though in eastern Turkey I bought a horse. Rode through Iran, Afghanistan, Pakistan and into India.'

I wondered whether to believe him. He rode through Iran and Afghanistan at the height of the troubles there?

I wanted to ask him how he had paid his way – but there were some things that I had never enquired of Beauregard. I did not know his first name; nor his place of birth; I had no idea if he had brothers or sisters, or if his parents were still alive: it seemed as if the answers to these mundane questions might diminish in stature the man I regarded as something of a myth.

'Years ago I decided never to stop,' he said. 'To settle down, to establish roots – that would be death, Simon. Possessions...' He gestured dismissively at my book-crammed study. 'It isn't what my life is about. I have nothing.'

'And you've been travelling ever since?'

He nodded. 'I have to, Simon. I wish I could explain – I know that if I ever stop, then that'll be the end.'

I nodded myself, at a loss for words.

When I next looked up from my tea, Beauregard had lodged himself further into the armchair and seemed to be asleep. I experienced an immediate relief.

I was washing the cups in the kitchen when I heard him cry out. I rushed back into the front room. He was talking to himself in his sleep, his head turning back and forth. I hovered, considering whether to wake him, when a decision was made redundant. He cried out a name and sat upright, eyes open wide and staring into the flames.

I sat down, embarrassed as he noticed my presence. The name he had shouted aloud had been Sabine's.

'It was a terrible shock,' I said.

He knew what I meant.

I looked at him. 'What happened?'

We had not spoken of it at the time. Beauregard had quit university not long after, without so much as a farewell. One day his rucksack had been on the chair in the lounge we shared, and the next it was gone.

'I showed her something,' he said, and those four words, almost inaudible in his tobacco-wrecked voice, sent a cold shiver down my spine.

'Showed her something...?' My tone communicated my incomprehension.

He nodded. 'You know in any relationship, if it means anything, there has to be a trading of truths.' He looked up at me.

I felt myself colouring. He asked, 'Do you have anyone, Simon?'

I shook my head. 'No... Not at the moment.'

He nodded again. Something in his eyes told me that he understood.

'Well... Sabine meant a lot to me. We were one person. I had to show her what I understood... I showed her that, my reality, and she couldn't take it. She ran. I searched the city. I was worried about what she might do – I knew it had been too much. I think I knew, before the police arrived, what had happened. I woke at midnight with a terrible sense of presentiment. I knew what she had done.' He shrugged, almost casually, and lit another emaciated cigarette with shaking fingers.

I tried to say something, but my throat was too dry. At last I managed, 'What did you show her?'

He looked at me for a long time. 'I don't think I could explain now, and anyway you wouldn't understand.'

I was about to press him, accuse him of patronising me, and ask him again what he had done to drive Sabine to kill herself – but at that second the phone rang, startling me.

It was a friend from the village, asking if I fancied a pint at the Fleece. The thought of a change of venue, of the chance to escape from Beauregard, was a life-belt thrown to a drowning man.

I replaced the receiver and explained that I had arranged to meet someone. 'You could always come along,' I said, knowing full well that he would excuse himself and remain in the house.

'Then I'll show you to your room,' I said, but he gestured to the sofa.

'Simon, I'll be fine here. I'll see you in the morning.'

I nodded, feeling obscurely guilty as I pulled on my coat and said goodbye. The look in his eyes, as he watched me go, told me that he understood my need to get away.

Only as I pushed into the glowing, welcome fug of the tap room did I recall something Beauregard had told me, over twenty years ago: in a rash moment of drunken *bonhomie* he had said that all his life people had wanted to get away from him, though what had struck me as tragic about this revelation was his admission that he understood their reasons.

For the next couple of hours, with the help of the Tuesday night crowd and five pints of Taylor's, I tried to forget Beauregard, and the fact that he was resident in my study for an indefinite period. The effort was too much: from time to time my thoughts would stray. I attempted to recall how long he had stayed the last time, ten years ago. It might only have been a day, though in retrospect it seemed longer.

It was midnight when I made my way back through the snow and let myself into the fire-lit warmth of the house. I looked in on Beauregard in the study.

He was sleeping soundly on the sofa, still wrapped in his greatcoat, illuminated by the orange light of the standard lamp.

I was about to close the door when I noticed the paperback, open and lying face down on the carpet before the sofa. It was a copy of my second book, published almost fifteen years ago – a collection of crime stories which I considered my best work. Something made me cross the room and pick it up, gratified that Beauregard should have chosen this volume from the hundreds of others.

As I flicked through the pages, I became aware of marginalia scribbled in Biro on each page. I carried the book towards the lamp, sat down and studied the tiny handwriting. It seemed that Beauregard had closely read almost a hundred pages, and every one of them was crammed with questions, exclamation marks and bold underlinings.

Simplistic rationale, read one note, and another: *This simply doesn't work – why would she react like this, when on the previous page she agrees to accompany him?* I turned a few pages and read: *The characters of this story are manipulated by the author to propel the improbable plot.*

At the end of each story was a neat summation. In one quick reading Beauregard had seen through the artifice of plot to the tale's fundamental weakness. It was a humbling experience to have the faults of one's hard labour so expertly dissected. At the end of one story, on the remaining blank half page, he had written: *Why the compulsion to achieve such artificial completeness? If art is to reflect life, then in literature a story should not be wholly resolved; there should be threads left which beguile the reader's intelligence and imagination with tantalising and inexplicable possibilities. Charrington's work is yet another reflection of his crass, obsessive-compulsive materialism . . .*

I returned the book to the floor, my face hot with a strange mix of emotions. Beyond rage at the desecration was the beginnings of a shame I found difficult at first to admit to, for while Beauregard's marginalia might have been cruel, not to say callous, it also approached an unpalatable truth.

I retired to my room. It was a long time before I felt myself drifting into sleep, my mind considering Beauregard's words. I hoped that he would not bring up the subject of my literary failings in the morning. I had survived for years with the knowledge of my inadequacy: I told myself that my work was not literature, but entertainment, and that it was popular. For a long time I had salved my conscience, and excused my laziness with the fact that my work sold, and I enjoyed writing it: I would leave literature to minds finer than my own.

I was awakened in the early hours by a sound emanating from the study. I regained consciousness slowly, wondering if I had indeed been woken by a scream, or if I had been dreaming. As I listened, I made out the occasional raised voice. I climbed from bed and pulled on my dressing-gown. As I left the room and descended the stairs, I saw a pulsating blue light leaking from beneath the door to the study.

Still half asleep, I moved towards the door. I paused and listened. I had not been mistaken: I made out two voices. One was a woman's, the other a man's – Beauregard's, I guessed, though he was speaking in so low a tone I found it hard to make out.

I could only recognise the occasional word.

'Then ... here ... impossible!' said the woman. I could not discern the reply.

I reached for the handle and turned, meaning to open the door a fraction and peer inside. However, though the handle turned, the door would not open: it appeared to be prevented from doing so by something placed against it on the other side. Frustrated, I considered knocking and enquiring what was going on. However, something stopped me – some inchoate fear that I would not like what might be revealed if he answered my summons.

Presently the voices ceased, the blue light diminished. I stood for a time, undecided as to what to do next, and finally retraced my steps to bed and soon fell into a deep sleep.

I awoke at eight, as usual, and it was some seconds before I recollected the events of the night before. I recalled finding my book covered with Beauregard's caustic comments, and then I remembered getting up in the early hours ... But had I? In the cold light of day it came to me that the voices, the blue light, had been nothing more than the products of my dreaming mind. For the life of me I could not decide if I really had overheard voices in the front room.

I dressed and made my way downstairs. I reached out to the handle of the study door, and it turned and opened without hindrance. I stepped into the room, expecting to find Beauregard and perhaps his lady friend – but he was not there, and nor was there any sign of a woman.

Then I saw his rucksack on the chair before the dead fire, and stuffed inside it the copy of my desecrated book. At least, then, he planned to steal it rather than have me read his criticism – and this evidence of his dubious charity made me feel irrationally pleased.

I moved to the window and opened the curtains. The snow had continued to fall during the night and my homebound footprints had been all but obliterated. However, leading from the front step, a fresh trail of prints showed darkly in the thick covering. They moved down the garden path, up the hillside and off towards the horizon.

I sat at my desk and for the rest of the day worked on the final chapter of the novelisation, pleased that I was free to finish the work without Beauregard around to distract me.

I took a break at midday, made myself a sandwich and ate it at my desk. More than once I contemplated his rucksack: it had worn well in twenty years, considering the extent of his travels. I recalled how possessive of it he had been in his student days; it was as if because it was his only possession, he therefore had to guard its contents all the more.

I finished my lunch and looked through the window. There was no sign of Beauregard. I moved to the armchair and picked up the rucksack, guilt already pricking my conscience.

I sat on the sofa and, the rucksack on the carpet at my feet, I went through its contents. A baggy jumper, a foetid pair of socks; three books, ancient, leatherbound volumes in Latin. My hand came upon something else, a small pair of Tibetan cymbals which produced, as I lifted them out, a high clear chime. In the bottom of the bag was a folded map on old and jaundiced parchment.

The map was covered in a script strange to me; I thought I recognised the shape of one of the countries, the rectangle of Nepal. To the north was drawn a series of triangles to represent the Himalayas, and beyond that the plain of Tibet. This expanse was covered in Beauregard's small, precise hand, and threaded with a winding route in the same blue Biro.

The route seemed to have taken him from monastery to monastery, the length and breadth of the ancient land. At each monastery, represented on the map by a high-sided, blocky building, Beauregard had written his comments.

Rimpoche Udang v. informative. He suggests I try the phrontistery at Manchang Bazaar. He says my suffering is common, but that Rimpoche Thangan is practised in the ways of relief. He gave me a simple mantra which should provide me with brief respite.

Intrigued, I read on. Beside the northernmost monastery, Beauregard had written: *Rimpoche Thangan listened to my story. He performed a ceremony, with many bells, much incense and chanting. The ceremony involved his cutting my chest, the letting of bad blood requisite if the rite was to be successful. Only time will tell.*

I read the other notes on the map, but learned nothing new. I thought of Beauregard in his ridiculous greatcoat, trekking across the face of Tibet, petitioning lamas and monks, to what end I could not tell. I wondered what ailment he had been suffering from, and if the ceremony ministered by Rimpoche Thangan had proved successful.

I returned the contents to the rucksack, afraid that he should return and catch me going through his possessions. For the rest of the afternoon I worked at the computer, my mind only half on the job of novelising the appalling TV script.

It was dark by the time Beauregard returned.

I had cooked a hot chilli to warm him after his long walk, and at eight he knocked on the door.

His face was blue with cold and his eyes, as they stared into mine, seemed haunted. He brushed past me and moved to the study, where he bent before the open fire and massaged his outstretched hands as if washing them in the heat of the flames.

'I've prepared a meal,' I said. 'You must be hungry.' I hesitated. 'Where did you get to?'

He looked up, as if only then registering my presence. He shrugged. 'I don't know, Simon. Walked for miles. You're certainly isolated out here . . . Yes, I'm ravenous.' He hesitated, then said: 'I hope I didn't disturb you last night?'

'What? Oh, I did hear voices . . .'

He smiled and pointed to the television in the corner, buried beneath piles of books and papers. 'I'm sorry. It was a long time since I last tuned in . . . I hope it wasn't too loud.'

I smiled, shrugged. 'Not at all,' I said. Of course, the blue light, the murmuring voices . . .

But why, I asked myself, had he found it necessary to blockade the door and prevent my entry?

Uncomfortable, I said: 'We'll eat, shall we?'

He looked at me. 'Simon, it's good of you to put me up like this.'

I shrugged, embarrassed, and retreated to the kitchen.

We ate in silence on the coffee table before the fire, Beauregard's hand shaking as he ferried the fork from the plate to his mouth. He emptied a liberal measure of whisky into a mug of black tea and sat back with it clenched in his fist, staring into the dancing flames.

At one point his hand strayed to his rucksack, on the floor beside his chair. His eyes found mine and he said: 'I was telling you about my travels last night. I suppose I was always really heading for Tibet . . . At least, when I arrived there it seemed that way – I knew that this was the place.' He lapsed into silence, cradling his mug, regarding the flames with bloodshot eyes.

'Have you ever heard of the *Bardo Thadol*, Simon?'

'Isn't it some kind of Tibetan religious book?'

'The Tibetan Book of the Dead.' He nodded. 'I'm translating it.'

I looked up, surprised. 'I thought it had already been translated.'

He smiled, a minimalist, sardonic twist of his thin lips. 'It has. Badly. There were things missed out. Things that the translator didn't or couldn't understand . . . I'm attempting to correct that. My version will be definitive.' He said this with such fierce conviction that I could only nod my head in passive agreement.

He looked at me, and his gaze seemed to peer into my very soul, summing me up and finding me worthless. 'I feel sorry for those of you who apprehend only . . .' he gestured with a long, thin hand, 'only this. Oh, there are realities out there so strange and bizarre, if only you could allow your mind to see them.' He shook his head bitterly. 'But you've all been conditioned by the modern world, the crass information media which doesn't allow for any historical perspective other than the immediate. The difficult thing is to decondition oneself, to see beyond what is only superficially apparent.' He paused, then shot me a glance. 'But it's frightening, Simon . . . Believe me, when you begin to see these other realms, at first you are lost, with nothing to guide you, no prior experience to make sense of things . . . Sometimes I am terrified.'

I was aware of my heartbeat. I poured a stiff measure of whisky into my mug and drank. Beauregard seemed on the edge of a revelation. I felt that now he would tell me something that might explain the enigma of himself, but as the silence stretched it came to me that he had said all that he was able: that it was my very lack of ability to comprehend anything other than the here and now that would render his explanations futile.

I opened my mouth to speak. What I had to ask him seemed relevant and yet profane.

'Is that . . .' I began. 'Last night, you were about to tell me what happened . . . I mean, you told Sabine, you showed her *something* . . .'

He turned his head from the flames, his expression devastated. 'I showed her, Simon, and I tried to help her cope with her new understanding, but she wasn't strong enough. She could not bear the knowledge.'

The silence stretched. I took another swallow of whisky, my head swimming. I had a vision of the superficiality of my life, my relationships and my work. It seemed then that I was granted a terrible insight into the fact that what I had known all along amounted to nothing – and that I was equipped to apprehend only this reality. It came to me that what drove Sabine to kill herself might be preferable, however difficult to accept, to an existence of continued ignorance.

I found my voice, at last. 'Can you show me?' I whispered.

His gaze seemed pained and full of compassion. It seemed to me that he wanted to share his burden then, but at the same time could not bring himself to be so cruel. 'Simon, I'm sorry. I know you, and I know that you wouldn't be able to accept . . .' He smiled, and reached out a hand to touch mine in a gesture of intimacy I had always thought beyond him.

We sat in silence, drinking, for what seemed like hours. I roused myself from sleep, sat up and yawned. Beauregard was still awake, staring into the dying embers with an ironic, unamused smile playing on his lips.

'I'm turning in,' I said.

He looked at me. 'Good night, Simon,' he said, and there was something of a farewell in his tone.

I slept soundly, anaesthetised by the drink, until the early hours. As I lay awake, I thought I heard again the sound of voices from down below – and something told me that they did not issue from the television.

A part of me shied away from investigating, afraid of what I might find. Another part knew that I could not ignore my curiosity. I found my dressing-gown and hurried down the stairs.

The same blue light leaked from the gap beneath the door, for all the world like the fluctuating glow of a TV set. I leaned my head close to the door, heard the rapid exchange of voices that might very well have been the charged dialogue of a drama series. I reached for the handle, knowing full well that the door would not open.

I turned the handle and leaned forward with all my weight. Slowly the door gave, opened perhaps six inches. The strange thing was that I felt no scraping resistance, as I would if a piece of furniture had been wedged beneath the handle. Instead, it was as if I was pushing against a constant, forceful pressure from within. I lodged my slippered foot in the opening and peered through.

The light had intensified, bathing my face with a dazzling blue radiance. As I screwed my eyes shut to filter the glare, I heard a woman's voice: 'You didn't think for a minute that you could get away? Even here, in this Godforsaken wilderness?'

Then Beauregard's: 'I hoped, of course. I should have known . . .'

The woman laughed. 'Even *they* couldn't help you!'

'They did, for a while.'

'For a while, yes. It was only a matter of time before I overcame their resistance.'

I choked. I had an awful premonition. I had heard the woman's high, stilted accent before, long before – twenty years ago, to be exact.

My eyes became accustomed to the light, and I stared, and saw at the source of the lapis lazuli radiation the figure of a woman: she was thin, dressed like a hippy, with a cheesecloth shirt and flared denims; she had her hair coiled in familiar braids and wore fastidious, John Lennon glasses.

Sabine . . .

Beauregard was kneeling before her, like a supplicant before some vision. On his face was an expression of such tortured anguish that the features of the Beauregard I knew were almost indistinguishable.

'What do you want from me?' he cried.

Sabine laughed. 'I want to show you what it is like,' she said.

I could take no more. Whether in fright, or an inability to hold open the door against the pressure from within the room, I staggered backwards with a cry. The door snapped shut, and I was pitched into relative darkness. Sobbing, I clawed my way to the banister and staggered up the stairs. I made it to my room, switched on the light and curled myself into a protective ball, shaking with delayed and paralysing shock at what I had witnessed.

I must have slept, against all odds, though fitfully. I came awake often, and always the first vision that greeted me was that of the blue light with Sabine at its centre.

I awoke finally with a bright winter sunlight slanting into the room. It was late. Hurriedly I dressed, fingers fumbling with my clothes. I made my way down the stairs, and as I approached the study I relived the events of the early hours. I knew that this time I had to confront Beauregard with what I had seen.

He was no longer in the study. Not even his rucksack remained. I hurried to the door and flung it open. He had taken his leave, perhaps hours ago. A line of footprints, almost filled in by the new fall of morning snow, led away from the house and up the hillside to the far horizon.

If this were a work of fiction, one of my stories Beauregard so despised, I would take pains to craft a satisfying dénouement; I would explain everything and tie up all the loose ends, in the manner that Beauregard disdained in his marginalia. It would be a ghost story, and I would show the reader what horror he had made manifest to Sabine all those years ago. The apparition of Sabine would be a Tulpa, a spectre from Tibetan lore, returned to haunt Beauregard for showing her what should have remained his own, private secret.

But life is not fiction; there are no neat resolutions and answers, no cosy dénouements to satisfy and entertain. I have presented the incidents as they occurred, and for the sake of my sanity I prefer to think that what I saw last night was no more than the product of my drunken imagination, fuelled by lack of sleep, Beauregard's recollections, and my own confused thoughts of the poor German girl who was driven, for reasons that will remain forever unknown, to end her life.

I often think of Beauregard as I sit here and type my safe, satisfying little stories. I consider the torture of inhabiting a world that ordinary people are unable to perceive, and I see him walking, always walking, through freezing winter landscapes, pursued by the spectre of the young girl who forever haunts his guilty conscience.

Eric Brown lives in Haworth, West Yorkshire, and is perhaps better known as one of Britain's new generation of science fiction writers. He has published nine books – the novels *Meridian Days*, *Engineman* and *Penumbra*; the short story collections *The Time-Lapsed Man and Other Stories* and *Blue Shifting*, plus two children's books, *Untouchable* and *Walkabout*. The first volume of the 'Virex Trilogy', *New York Nights*, recently appeared from Gollancz, and *Parallax View*, a short story collection written in collaboration with Keith Brooke, has just been published by Sarob Press. More than fifty of his stories have been published in such magazines and anthologies as *Interzone*, *SF Age*, *New Worlds* and *Moon Shots*. 'The eponymous Beauregard was extrapolated from the characters of two close friends who both live only marginally in this world,' explains the author. 'Their view of reality is frightening and hellish, as is Beauregard's, though for entirely different reasons. Also, I wanted to write a story from the point of view of a writer who despises himself. And I've always wanted to write a Tulpa story. These three elements came together to produce "Beauregard".'

Necromimicos

NANCY KILPATRICK

The dead bring her life. Since the moment of consciousness of their presence, Amulette, rather than dismiss them, begged the dead to remain. Amulette's mother, father, grand-mère – the lucky one, for whom she is named – two sisters and baby brother, none understand her need for those who have passed. No one understands, really. Only Etienne.

As she matured, her thinking on cemeteries altered. From vast and lovely gardens, they became her personal shopping mall. Wrought-iron gates, stone benches, candles encased in etched glass-and-brass holders, marble angels and cherubs, filigreed metallic crosses ... *Memento mori*. The accoutrements of death, scanned by the eye of a selective consumer. Furnishings for the world between worlds where Amulette resides. The only place where she can exist.

As the sun fades, Amulette leaves the city-din behind: stores dedicated to the here-and-now, or cheap imitations of the past. Inexhaustible vehicles. Food, entertainment, pursuits she cannot understand. People dressed of-a-piece – for a time she enjoyed classifying them: business, casual, post-grunge, retro hippy, neo-rave, Goth – the last those oh-so-sweet darklings in requisite chains, silver crosses clinging to black stretch velvet. To look at them reinforces her yearning.

She turns up a small street and gracefully climbs the mountain with the lit cross atop. The homes en route are stone and wood, the estates of Outremont, where Montréal's wealthy Francophones reside. These edifices oppress her with their blind devotion to one world only. She closes her eyes – this path is a trace memory, a former life, the Karma finally nullified.

Soon she reaches broken sidewalks and barren fields, then the Jewish cemetery on the left, the tombstones too modern to be truly interesting. The graves are blanketed with flowers, the colours muted enough by moonlight to be bearable. Hours ago the gates to Mt Royal Cemetery were bolted, but when the guard naps, the footpath beneath the arched stones allows admittance.

Just inside the Anglo burial grounds, she skirts by the monument to the Englishman killed by the French in a riot one hundred years ago, the inscription bitter. Then the suicides' section of the cemetery – isolated crosses, separated from one another as they are separated from the rest of the graves – she knows she could end up here, or somewhere like it. Then the children's graveyard – tiny sleeping angels, or baby lambs, nestled on low stone Bibles.

She climbs upwards, passes through an arched metal gate. Veterans lie beneath the soil. Rigid row upon row of standardised soldierly markers ... To die undifferentiated, she can think of nothing more painful.

The moment she enters the Cimetière Notre-Dame des Neige, tension lifts from her body like a spirit ascending. Tombstones date back two hundred years. White, grey, patinaed with age. Celtic crosses. Crucifixes. Enormous angels, languid in mourning. Elaborate stone and metal-work, unique when created, nurtured by the harsh elements of a city prone to deep freeze. This is the only place where she feels truly French. Her ancestors knew how to care for those who sired them. Too few of the living have adopted their legacy: blooms decomposing; funereal candles flickering; poetic inscriptions, waiting. 'Remember me, in your arms,' she reads, her voice a call to other stranded souls.

So quiet, amongst the dead. The living talk, move, do what they do for whatever reasons they can convince themselves lend relevancy. Amulette feels their energy – waves of scorching heat, sucking her towards oblivion. Incinerate or flee, there is no alternative, she knows. Only Etienne. But he is ... where? There are no maps in the land of the dead. And so she tends those she finds by night, because someone must, and she is called to. And somehow this allows her to honour him.

She stands silent, listening to crickets, absorbing the rays of the full moon, all the light she can tolerate. Here, on Montréal's mountain, over seven hundred thousand dead exist in three adjoining cemeteries, creating a necropolis. Boxes of bones piled on newer boxes of bones, three and four layers deep, until the boxes burst open and the hungry earth swallows all that the worms refuse. During daylight, caretakers perpetually dig new graves. Pits, open for days, sometimes expose coffins, casket linings, hair and soil-matted death shrouds, human bones. Bits and pieces embroiled in transformation. Amulette climbs into the open graves to rebury these remains. The dirt, so deep, tastes of death-passion. She consumes it like vitamins, daily, an enrichment. Something to keep her going.

In the darkness, back against the hill, dozens of old tombs now abandoned by the living line the higher ground, embedded in this sacred earth like babes cradled in a mother's arms. Ornate iron doors, the complex stonework of the crypts themselves, all buried in grassy mounds. Family names mark the houses of the long dead, but one reads, simply: FATHER. The gate surrounding this crypt has disintegrated. Last winter, the heavy stone cross above toppled and shattered, blocking entrance, or exit.

Much of the grille work of the doors of these crypts exposes to view the centuries-old coffins within. Large black or brown wood and metal chevrons, tarnished handles, and then the tiny boxes for dead babies, or those that were never born.

One tomb draws her. She wonders if Etienne is related – LEBLANC, the family name. He must be, somewhere back in time. Over the door, a dozen feet above ground, a bird, sculpted in dark marble, wings a shroud protecting its body.

Amulette climbs the mound to the top of the crypt. She lies face down, stretched across the earth, and reaches below, blind. Cold-feather wings; beak the hard harbinger of truth. As always, she cries chilly tears. For Etienne.

The soul can linger in grief, lost at the edge of the flesh, paralysed, unable to inhabit any world. The body's instincts to survive barely suffice. The breath of life flows from the mouth in soft moans of lonely despair. Life becomes a stasis and death offers no emancipation.

Her tears wash the *corbeau*, bathing its head with holy water. She clutches its chest, where the heart is, wondering why Etienne abandoned her. She calls on all of the ancient deities to redeem her, but they are deaf.

The dead around her stir. Through the strength of immobility they perceive her anguish in a way the living should but refuse to. Her soul is forlorn, fragmented, the cohesive element lost. But unlike the bones she protects and reburies, no elemental will succour her. She has ceased trying to understand, and has given up imagining. There are no more gods to petition.

The heart of the bird begins to beat. Amulette feels it pulse through her being. Not hope but lack of hopelessness. For moments, what courses through her soothes like a salve to a wound. She breathes as though this is the first moment of life. Air fills her lungs and expands to each cell ... This is the source she struggles to find. The living can no longer nourish her and she must eat of the dead.

The moon beats against her back until she craves more darkness. With an ancient key she found and kept, the door to this home of the dead opens. She re-enters the void.

The scent of corrosion. Air refusing to circulate the planet. Stillness bathed in black compresses her, forcing her to listen. Even the insects are silenced by the maelstrom of nothingness.

Is life its own end? Why must a heart be deflated to receive?

One casket lies apart from the others. Black. Simple. Silver etchings in the ebony, scrollwork she created. The hinged lid lifts easily. She is blind here, and wants it that way. But her flesh possesses eyes that let her remember:

His hair. His face. Lips as incapable of a smile as of a frown. Arms that once held her against the impacted ice that has become her prison, her friend.

Her body trembles, face to face with the shell of him. She screams, powerless to create miracles. The dead listen in sympathy, but they can do nothing.

She lies on top of him – what he hated – and adeptly turns them both so he is on top. The weight is not what it was, and this evokes in her grief. 'Hold me!' she pleads, but the arms do not move.

A cry of despair rips from her chest. He is nowhere. She cannot locate him, cannot join him. And she cannot exist without him. But she does exist, caught in a web of anguish. If only the angel of death would kiss her! She longs for an embrace that will extinguish . . . But that is not her fate.

Then, inexplicably, from this barren womb, an emergence. Beyond the senses, yet incorporating them, like a winged spirit, soaring. Her heart races. Her limbs quiver. She recognises the essence. Quickly it overwhelms her, entering her, forcing her to gasp, red oil sliding through her veins, saturating, soothing. Her chest expands, staked to the moment. Black blood oozes through its chambers, incense through a censer. She hears herself moan in disbelief, feels her lungs pant.

She tastes his lips on hers, feels his body pressing, heavier and heavier until his cells pierce hers. They merge. Her soul, raw, opens. What returns to her soothes her. Her tears blaze hot until finally, she is warm.

Sometimes the dead must be invited back. The darkness must be incorporated or life cannot continue. Sometimes the gods are merciful. Occasionally they hear us.

Nancy Kilpatrick is an American living in Montréal, Canada. Her latest books include the collection *The Vampire Stories of Nancy Kilpatrick*, the anthology *Graven Images* (co-edited with Thomas Roche) and *Bloodlover*, the fourth novel in her popular vampire series 'Power of the Blood'. Her short fiction has also appeared in recent anthologies *Dracula's London*, *Northern Horror*, *Arthur Ellis Awards*, *Over the Edge*, *Whispered from the Grave* and *Mondo Zombie*. '"Necromimicos" blends my love of cemeteries with my anguish from losing love,' explains the author. 'I've always believed that darkness can heal, or swallow you whole.'

The Bootleg Heart

JOEL LANE

My first love was a girl I never actually met. In the autumn of 1984, I came to Birmingham to study psychology at the university. It was the first time I'd lived away from home. My parents were as concerned about my choice of subject as they were about my falling into bad company. They made me promise to attend the university chapel regularly, and to continue my Bible studies as an antidote to Freud's denial of original sin. My first accommodation was a bedsit in a converted house on Gillott Road, close to the city reservoir.

After the uniform greyness and silence of Walsall, living in Edgbaston was something of a revelation. There were half-dressed prostitutes shivering in the streets after midnight, and ugly kerb-crawlers in still uglier cars. Lanky Rastas marched to the slow beat of their ghettoblasters. The same beat was louder in the crowded pubs where packets of weed changed hands for crumpled tenners, beyond what I could afford. Gaunt-looking hotels lurked on street corners. like spivs in old suits. There were teenagers everywhere: boys in tracksuits, their hair cut in wedges or spikes; girls in budgie jackets and white skirts, their hair knotted in or braided out. Bitter kids with nowhere to go, trying out models of adult life.

University was another world again: towering red-brick buildings, crowded lecture theatres, a storm of voices. The girls wore jeans or striped leggings, and cheap ethnic jewellery. I was slow to make friends, especially with the opposite sex. The habits of obsessive studying and solitude hung on even when I'd consciously rejected them. I spent the first term arguing furiously with my lecturers – but only in my head. The psychology course was obsessed with behaviourism and psychometrics. In retrospect, I suppose that was the mood of the time. The liberal humanism my parents had felt so threatened by didn't get a look-in here. They force-fed me Skinner and Eysenck, while asserting that R.D. Laing was 'discredited'. And if I wanted to hear about Freud, I had to go to the English Department.

One Friday night just before halfterm, I was lying in bed listening to the traffic in the street outside. My room was on the second floor. The water-pipes groaned softly through the walls. Then I heard something else. A different groaning, quick and breathless. Was someone in pain? Then I heard the creak of bedsprings, a rhythm that kept pace with the cries. At once, I felt a tension building in my prick. I'd never heard these sounds in real life before. If my parents made love, they did it in silence. I suspected they didn't do it at all.

Of course, I'd heard sounds like this in films. But this wasn't acting. They weren't performing for a camera. They were alone together, and they had no idea that I was listening just a few feet below them. I hardly dared to breathe. The cries became sharper, more frequent. Her voice rose to a taut, helpless scream, then died away again, then built up a second time. Finally, she gave a low laugh of relief and happiness. The darkness around me prickled with stars. I rubbed the semen into my belly.

The next morning, I lay in bed for hours and listened. Eventually, I heard the door to the attic room close and feet rattle on the stairs. That night, I went to bed early, hoping to catch them at it. But I didn't hear them again until the next weekend. In between, I saw the new tenant of the attic room: a dark-haired lad I recognised from university. He was probably a year or two older than me. But I didn't see her. In my mind she was short, with dark hair and a feminine build. She had a dazzling smile, but her eyes were serious. Whenever I saw a girl in lectures or the library who resembled my mental picture in any way, I couldn't help asking myself: *Is that her?*

It happened twice the next weekend. The sounds on Saturday morning, just before dawn, were almost violent: deep, choked cries, driven out of her in a steady rhythm. It was an old house with high ceilings; I was surprised that I could hear so much. There was no traffic outside. The cries echoed around me all day, on the bus, in the library. Late on Sunday night, they had a protracted session. She came four times. I came twice, staining a crumpled handkerchief. Rather oddly, I couldn't hear them talking at any time. I was sure that the different patterns of cries meant different positions, or even different acts.

My other great obsession at that time was music. The small cassette player and box of tapes I'd brought from home seemed hopelessly dull and provincial now. Other students had turned me on to a world of dark passions and unknown pleasures: Lou Reed, Joy Division, Nick Cave. And Bob Dylan in his drug phase. My friend Alan, an English student, had taped *Blonde on Blonde* for me; I played it endlessly, listening for clues to the link between sex and religious enlightenment. One song in particular, 'Visions of Johanna', seemed to explain and justify my obsession with the girl upstairs. I saw something Jungian in the contrast between the real girl in Dylan's arms and the mysterious one in his visions.

Despite the vast amount of time I was spending in my gloomy bedsit, it took me weeks to realise that damp was spreading through from above. One morning, quite by chance, I looked up to see where a spider on the wall had come from and saw a ring of yellow mushrooms around the hall light. More fungus, pale and wrinkled, was growing in a corner of the ceiling. I knocked it all down with a broom. By the time the landlord came for the rent, it had grown back. He was a middle-aged Brummie with wary eyes. When he saw the fungus, he gave a dry chuckle. 'That Trevor's got a cracked pipe under his sink,' he said. 'I've had it fixed, except apparently not. I'll go up and have a look a bit later.' In my next essay, I wrote: *Cyril Burt's influence on Eysenck reflects the latter's reliance on scientific method, except apparently not.* My supervisor commented: *What this subject requires is hard facts, not sarcasm.*

One night, I dreamt that trapped cries of ecstasy were turning to water between the floors, staining my ceiling with the shape of a naked woman. I woke and turned on the light, but couldn't make out anything from the scattered bruises of damp and the cracks in the woodchip wallpaper. As I was about to drift back into sleep, I heard a faint stirring and a dull moan, then a long shuddering wail. I curled into a foetal position as my crotch spasmed uncontrollably, impregnating the dark shape of my dream. In the morning, my supervision partner asked me: 'Are you okay, Matthew? The bags under your eyes, they wouldn't let you through Customs.' I said I had a lot of emotional baggage.

Although the tenement houses around Edgbaston Reservoir were packed with students, they tended not to use the local pubs. The student union had a subsidised bar and a less threatening vibe. Or a group might stock up on cheap sherry and extra-strength white cider at one of the local off-licences before going back to somebody's room. With our heavy coats and bottles of cheap booze, we looked more like sad old men than the hard-faced, overdressed youngsters who crowded the pubs.

One Friday in early December, I completed an essay on 'How Reliable is Eyewitness Testimony?' just in time to hand it in to my supervisor before he left his office. I'd been up most of the night before writing it. I went home, ate a bag of grease-sodden chips and fell asleep. When I woke up, it was nine o'clock. I'd made no plans to see anyone. Feeling disorientated, I pulled on a clean shirt and went out. Highlights of rain glittered in the bare trees. The rusting gates of Edgbaston Reservoir were a cage around darkness. At the foot of the cross made by Gillott Road and Rotton Park Road, there was a low-key pub called the Duck where I occasionally saw people I knew. The rain broke in waves against the curtained windows as I stepped inside, blinking at the smoke.

Two men were playing pool with a studied intensity that broadcast their lack of skill. A middle-aged couple were snogging in a corner, under a blackboard with no message. There was no one here under forty. Still, I bought a pint of Tennant's Bitter and shook the rain off my coat. Then I saw a face at the back, almost in shadow, that looked familiar. I leaned over: it was Trevor, my neighbour. He was blasted. There were two empty bottles of Diamond White on his small table. *Maybe I'll get to see her.* My mouth went dry at the thought. But nobody joined him. His face was blank, hanging over the bottles like a mask on a stick. He didn't see me, though his eyes were open. He was drinking alone.

I went over to his table. 'Hi. I'm Matthew. I'm in the room under yours.' His dull eyes searched for my face. 'Mind if I join you?' He shrugged. 'D'you want another drink?' He pointed to the empty bottle and said, 'Cheers.' I bought two more bottles of Diamond White, one each. The combination, together with my lack of sleep, made me dizzy. We talked about work. He was a medical student, hoping to become a pathologist. I told him I'd decided to go into human resources. Psychology was doing my head in.

Trevor woke up a little as he gulped the white cider, wincing at its antiseptic taste. His eyes refocused every few seconds. His voice seemed to come from a kind of disembodied cavity, somewhere behind him. 'Dissecting rooms ... drugs ... pointless ... no soul to it.' I remember he gripped my hand at one point and slurred: 'When you've cut out the heart and injected it with adrenalin, what happens to love?' I had no answer to that. I wanted to ask him about his girlfriend, but was afraid of betraying my obsession. No matter how drunk he was, I couldn't have asked him what I wanted to know.

At last orders, he got a round in. There seemed no hurry about drinking up. The games of pool continued. The pub was full now: women with perms set like dog turds, men whose beer-slicked mouths shone as they talked. The Gents' stank of chlorine. When I came back, my neighbour was slumped against the long seat. He looked like an empty coat. I shook him awake; he seized his bottle and drained it. As we were leaving the pub, he stumbled and fell over a bar-stool. Luckily, he didn't hit anyone. The barman snapped: 'Get the fuck out of here.' I helped Trevor to his feet and guided him hastily to the door.

Outside, it was still raining. A streetlamp flickered, projecting shapeless faces onto the wall of a closed-down cinema. Young women stalked up and down Gillott Road in shiny black coats, tracked by car headlights. Stains of blood and vomit dissolved slowly in the rain, like a modernist kind of pavement art. Trevor groaned as I helped him along the road, weaving and staggering dangerously close to the kerb – not that many of the cars were moving fast enough to do any damage. He held out a shaking hand, watched it fill with rain, then clapped it to his mouth.

When we got inside the house, Trevor collapsed in the hallway. His dark hair was clotted together, shapeless. I saw bubbles in the corner of his mouth and was terrified that he'd throw up before we reached his room. He muttered something, and I leant over to catch the words. 'Love is the only thing that ... matters ... don't understand ... the only real thing.' Sure. Right. I wanted to know all about love. I didn't want to be manhandling another male up the stairs to his bed. However drunk I was, boys weren't part of the plan. But I didn't mind holding him. We climbed slowly to the third floor. The dusty 40-watt bulbs stayed lit for half a minute, then died. I had to press every timeswitch we passed. I guided Trevor into the bathroom and looked away while he vomited heavily into the ancient ceramic bath. It sounded like breaking glass.

I had to drag him to his room and find the key in his trouser pocket. The lightbulb flickered, then popped. 'Got a torch?' I said.

He shook his head. 'Matches ... on the fire.' The hall light went out. Stumbling in the dark, I opened a curtain. The yellow streetlight showed me a large single room with a bed, a Baby Belling cooker and a table. I glimpsed faces watching me from the walls. The gas fire was framed by a real fireplace; the mantelpiece was piled high with cassettes. I found a box of matches and struck one.

Trevor had slumped on the bed, his face like a wet paper lantern. Books, papers and cassettes were scattered over the floor. A dark stereo was surrounded by piles of LPs: Roberta Flack, Dusty Springfield, Janis Joplin. The faces in the walls were floating, about to speak. Before I could focus on them, the match went out. I lit another one. Trevor groaned; but it wasn't his groans I could hear. The walls of his room were covered with black-and-white photographs of women. Or rather, a woman. She was young, with long fairish hair, a sad mouth, eyes full of light. Most of the shots were face or head and shoulders, but at least one showed her naked above the waist. The match stung my fingers and I had to drop it.

The stark light from outside cast my shadow over the bed. I stood there looking down at Trevor's still figure, no more than a sketch. Then I said, very quietly: 'When she moans like that, what's happening? Are you under her? Behind her? Is your tongue in there? Can you feel it when she comes, or do you only know from the sounds?' He showed no sign of having heard me. I shook the box of matches: one left. I'd better find him a bowl, in case he threw up again. There was nothing in the sink, but a small cupboard was underneath it. I knelt and lit the match.

The first object I touched inside the cupboard was a tall glass jar. It was filled with something like spider's web: long pale threads, looped and tangled. I could see a reddish tinge in the coils, a ghost of flame. Next to the jar was a locked wooden box I couldn't lift. There was nothing on top or behind. I put the jar back and closed the doors. They didn't fit very well. The match burnt down to my fingertips; I blew it out. As I stood up, dazed, the streetlight glinted from one of the photographs, and I realised what I'd seen in the jar.

It was hair. I stepped carefully round the bed to the doorway. Something plastic cracked under my foot. I closed the door behind me. My room smelt of damp, worse than before. Clearly it was getting in from outside.

Shortly before Christmas, a friend of mine threw a party in Smethwick. It was a shared house, more comfortable than the one I lived in. The front room and living-room were decorated with paper streamers and foil stars. The people were mostly English or music students, dressed in black with spiky hair and black eyeliner. The boys too. The music seemed more appropriate to a funeral than a party – I think one of the songs was called 'The Funeral Party', which summed up the mood – but everyone seemed to be having a good time. Cheap wine, cider and lager were ranked in the narrow kitchen. All the coats were in a mound on a bed in the spare room, where couples periodically sneaked off to be alone.

If Trevor was here, I hadn't seen him. Or his girlfriend, whose image hung like a photographic negative behind my eyes. I drank some strong cider, then some wine, then a mixture of the two. A tall girl dressed as Catwoman, with a black cape and whiskers drawn in eyebrow pencil, smiled at me and asked me to fill her glass. Her name was Susan; she was studying architecture. I made some feeble remark about climbing up tall buildings; she just smiled. We drifted into the front room, where a ring of Goths were sharing a joint and talking about Madonna. 'She empowers women by deconstructing the feminine,' one of them said. 'By hiding behind a succession of identities, she proves that identity itself is a mask.' Susan and I sat down together, giggling. I stroked the tight black fabric over her arm. Soon our mouths locked together.

An hour or so later, after several drinks and a furtive grope in the upstairs hallway, I asked her if she'd like to come home with me. 'Okay,' she whispered. 'It's a couple of miles,' I said. 'Are you happy to walk?' She nodded. Outside, frost glittered in the black roadway. There was a cemetery on the corner: grey headstones like books without covers. A dog barked at us from behind railings, but I couldn't see it. Lights shone in the basements of factories where night shifts were starting. It was cold; Susan and I held hands, pretending to be a couple rather than two strangers who'd drunk too much. The city was like a black-and-white film set. I kept seeing faces from the party, melting into shadows or each other. At the bottom of Gillott Road, a truck was being loaded from a curtained building. The wooden crates reminded me of the box in Trevor's room. I could smell the sea.

Back in my room, I apologised for the chaos of books and clothes. 'It's fine,' Susan said. 'But it's cold in here.' I lit the gas fire and turned off the electric light. We undressed each other slowly and stretched out on the bed. Then I heard the floor creak overhead. At once, I froze. I couldn't help myself. But there was nothing. Susan ran her fingers through my hair. 'Are you okay?' she said. I closed my eyes and thought of the bed upstairs, the couple tangled together. As I penetrated her, Susan breathed softly against my face. I thought of the glass-covered photographs. The first time she moved against me, I came hard. Lying beside her, I kissed and rubbed her until she whispered 'Yes, yes,' and my fingers were wet.

Then I curled up with my head on the pillow, listening. I could hear her slow breathing. I could smell perfume and sweat on her neck. Eventually, I knew she was asleep. I strained to hear, but there was still nothing. So this was what it was all about, except apparently not.

At the start of the next term, Trevor and the unknown girl seemed to be making a go of it. I heard them almost every night, and the loss of sleep was more than compensated by the relief. But somehow, I knew this level of intensity was bound to lead to a break-up. It did, but not in the way I was expecting.

My brother's wedding was the start of it. I had to go home for the weekend, only a fortnight into the term. Throughout the ceremony and the long, drunken reception, I kept replaying the cries I'd heard in the early hours of the previous day. *Trevor! Oh – oh, God! Trevor!* It was the first time I'd heard her call his name. Guilt about remembering that in church brought me down all through the evening and the dark, rainy morning that followed. The bus journey back to North Birmingham took a long time, and her voice became clearer with every mile. When I got back to Gillott Road, I sat in the dark and listened to a bootleg tape of Dylan's 'Albert Hall' concert from 1966: the slow, haunting journey through 'Visions of Johanna' leaving the audience baffled; the sneering venom of 'Ballad of a Thin Man' provoking audience fury and a cry of 'Judas!' Then Dylan's enraged 'I don't believe you! You're a liar!' and the raging, desperate finale of 'Like a Rolling Stone'.

At last I slept, dreaming something about Mary Magdalene washing Christ's feet with her hair. The dream ended with a creak of bedsprings from overhead. With the first muffled gasp, I was wide awake. Her cries marked the accelerating rhythm of their bodies. She came fast, then began to approach a second climax. It sounded almost the same as on Thursday morning. *Trevor! Oh – oh, God! Trevor!*

No, not almost the same. It was exactly the same. Note for note, it was a perfect copy.

Thursday, Sunday. Was there a pattern I didn't normally get? Because I'd missed two nights, I'd heard the same tape twice running. Otherwise, I might never have noticed. But even now, with the truth in my veins like ice, my hand was still pumping hard. Semen dripped onto my belly, and the voice upstairs laughed. I knew I couldn't go back to his room.

You probably know the rest, if you saw the papers that Easter. The police interviewed all the tenants of the house. I didn't have much to tell them. Before it came out in the press, my landlord told me what the police had found. Apparently they'd been trying to trace the girl since November. They'd interviewed Trevor at the Medical Centre; he'd claimed not to recognise her bus pass photo. Some other bit of evidence – maybe someone who'd seen them together – had made them visit him in the house, where they'd seen the photographs.

Then they'd found the jar. And the wooden box. I can still remember my landlord's expression, as if he'd felt a sardine come to life in his mouth. A mixture of disgust and awe. 'The police say they found a locked wooden box full of bones. Including a skull. And all the teeth. Can you believe it? Taken apart, like bits of a jigsaw puzzle.' Exactly like bits of a jigsaw puzzle.

The main thing the newspapers picked up on was that he refused to confess or to defend himself. At his trial, they could hardly get a word out of him. I think he ended up in a prison psychiatric unit. What became of his collection of tapes, I have no idea. Maybe I'll visit him one day and ask. What's kept me away is a mixture of fear and jealousy.

I never saw her. Maybe I never truly heard her voice. I hold her in my sleep, feeling her silent terror shake into the core of my hollow flesh. Joanna, her name was. Joanna. And I'm jealous that he had her first. But even more, I'm afraid that if I reach out to him, he'll take her away.

Joel Lane lives in Birmingham, in Britain's West Midlands. His acclaimed short stories have appeared in a range of publications, including *Darklands*, *Little Deaths*, *The Ex Files*, *Dark Terrors 4*, *White of the Moon* and *Hideous Progeny*. He is the award-winning author of a book of short stories, *The Earth Wire*, and a collection of poetry, *The Edge of the Screen*, while his first novel, *From Blue to Black* (which is about drums, guitars and death), was recently published by Serpent's Tail. He has also edited a horror anthology, *Beneath the Ground*, which is forthcoming from The Alchemy Press. According to the author, '"The Bootleg Heart" was influenced by Cornell Woolrich (an unsung hero of psychological horror), Bob Dylan and a nasty bout of 'flu.'

Saturday

CHERRY WILDER

Jack Dixon knew that he had gone mad. The final strand had snapped and he was completely *sans* marbles. He had nowhere to look: he did not trust the Pennsylvania hills any more; the rearview mirror reflected the angry faces of his hosts. He glanced sideways at the driver. Corey was a young black man, very tall and thin, acquired by the family in the West Indies. He was a trusted servant; he often made a fourth at bridge or danced the limbo at parties. Now Corey stared at him and asked in an undertone:

'What did you see, Mr Tenn?'

'Dixon.'

Corey curvetted with the great car on the dirt road; down in the dark valleys, where night had already fallen, Jack could see the glint of lake water.

'I'm sorry, Corey,' he said. 'My name is John Dixon. Mr King is joking when he introduces me as Jack Tenn. Old college joke...'

The glass panel was wide open but communication between the spacious interior of the custom-built limousine and the driver's seat was patchy. Now he heard Elizabeth King say in a drunken harridan's voice:

'You're a jinx! Your stars are vile! You stink of bad luck!'

Jack glanced fearfully out of the window and saw an old man with a scythe. Avery King snarled at his wife:

'If that dog vomits I'll shoot it!'

Corey pressed a button and the glass panel closed. Jack could see the Kings still at it, and now he could see Chung, the chow-chow dog, paws up, peering at Corey and himself.

'What you see, back there, Mr Dixon?' persisted Corey.

Something awful. He had seen something awful, something that convinced him about losing his wits. (*No one, amateur or professional, ever believed what he foresaw, at this moment. Namely that he would be describing what he had seen to them, at some future time...*)

'Big black car parked by the roadside,' he said smoothly. 'You catch a glimpse of it too?'

A hearse, glittering with glass and gold, its doors flung open obscenely, spilling out wreaths of flowers. Against the near side were a man and a woman dressed as bride and groom: they were grotesquely patched with blood as if they had been machine-gunned. The man still lolled half upright against the hearse, but the woman had slid down, leaving her long veil pasted to the *carosserie* with blood.

'... going to *Les Hiboux*,' said Corey. 'Nothing else around here. A few summer places on Lake Grant.'

'Long way out,' said Jack, pulling himself together. 'Can anyone really make a go of a restaurant out here?'

'More of a hobby now,' said Corey. 'For Pierre and his mama. They had a smart place, *Le Coq Vert*, near Stony Brook. Mr King bought them out when his partners put up the new fitness centre.'

In the back seat Avery wrestled the dog to the ground then took a firm grip of Elizabeth's long rope of pearls. She sat back until he released her then seized his hand and tried to bite it. Jack looked out of the window and saw a flock of birds clustered around the branch of a leafless tree. They flew away and left the ragged corpse of a naked black man swinging from the branch.

He sat back and shut his eyes.

'I'm not feeling awfully well, Corey. Is it far?'

'We'll stop up ahead at the lookout, Mr Dixon.'

Jack had a strong feeling of *déjà-vu*. He was back at college in America, driving like this, in the evening, and someone said 'stop at the lookout'. Could almost fill in the details, they were in the Edsel, Avery was driving, two of their best girls were along. Ace King and Jack Tenn and a couple of homecoming queens.

He was overwhelmed with a rush of pure reason, thinking of this harmless scene. A college reunion was a rite of passage; old Ace and old Jack had been dealt a few good hands. Each had succeeded in his own way, as Jack knew they would. Jack could describe himself as a dramaturge, quietly stalking his Chair of Drama at an English provincial university, and Ace had succeeded to the family millions.

The holiday had begun very well. This was some new thing, some kind of nightmare. There had been something in the drinks back there at the Kings' family seat; they were all being gassed here in the limousine. He was going suddenly insane, assailed with frightful images, and with an embarrassment that amounted to hatred. Avery and Elizabeth had never been anywhere near as bad as this before, they were out of their minds.

When the car drew up he sprang out at once but not more quickly than Avery himself, the dog Chung, and Corey, who opened the door for Elizabeth. They were at a crossroads on the shorn summit of a hill and the moon was rising. A resonant bird-cry came from the direction of the lake and further off a dog howled. Chung, the good-tempered tawny creature that Elizabeth had saved from the cooking pot in Hong Kong, when he was a puppy, gave vent to an extraordinary snuffling moan and began to run in circles, black tongue lolling.

Avery came striding up to Jack and looked him over with concern. He put his head back, stuck his hands in his trouser pockets and rocked on his heels, staring at his friend.

'Are you all right?' he asked. 'Saw you looking very squeezed out . . . grimacing away in the front seat.'

'Right as rain!' said Jack, stiffening his upper lip.

Avery was neatly built and fair, a natural sportsman. There was something essentially simple and lovable, for Jack, in a man who could bounce into a room wearing flannels and really say: 'Anyone for tennis?'

'I have a wager going with Corey,' said Ace seriously. 'Here, you must hold the pot.'

Jack took the envelope with a stiff little bow, like a second at a duel, and buttoned it into the breast pocket of his denim jacket. Sporting chances of all kinds were an important part of life in the King household; there was an unhealthy preoccupation with luck, good and bad, and the picking of winners. Jack tried to recall Ace's gambling addiction in college; had his old pal always been so heavily into bloody mumbo-jumbo? The trouble seemed to have carried over into the next generation: when Ace Junior could not be found he was usually in Las Vegas.

The two men strolled along the edge of the dirt road and stared to the northwest, over the boundless tree-girt reaches of mountain and valley. Jack turned his head, looking for Elizabeth, and his blood turned to ice in his veins. He could see her white naked sinewy legs, the folds of her long sequined chiffon skirt, the thrust of Corey's half-covered buttocks: they were up against the car on the other side.

A string of possible reactions flashed before his eyes, but he could do nothing. He looked at the hills and was overwhelmed by a mortal terror that Ace would turn his head. He felt a cold sweat break out on his brow.

'Did you see that?' whispered Ace suddenly.

'What? No! What was it?' babbled Jack.

Ace ran along the shoulder of the road and peered down the narrow crossroad, hardly more than a track in places. Jack stumbled after him and saw a tall figure in a grubby pale-coloured coat, a duster, and a battered black hat. In two long, bouncing steps the man was lost from view behind a tree.

'Did you see it?' demanded Ace.

'I saw a man,' said Jack. 'A tramp or something.'

'Bad luck!' said Ace. 'You missed the possum.'

He turned to call his wife: 'Elizabeth!'

Jack's head snapped around at the same moment. The hilltop was spacious and very light still; Corey, in his modish tan leisure suit, was posed nonchalantly a hundred yards away. Elizabeth stood looking back the way they had come, with Chung at her heels; her long blue-grey chiffon skirt blew backwards, she held a cashmere shawl wrapped tightly about her shoulders.

Now she came swimming through the air of evening, put her powdered cheek next to Jack's for a moment, then said to Ace: 'Let's get on, shall we?'

Jack was convinced by Elizabeth, she was one of the most convincing persons he knew. *His* perception must be disastrously at fault; she had not been coupling with Corey, she had not even been stridently drunk, taunting Ace with his bad stars.

'Ace,' he said, 'did *you* see that chap, just now?'

'No,' said Ace easily, 'can't say I did. But then, I was looking up a tree.'

They were all walking towards the very centre of the crossroads, Elizabeth was leading them, walking faster now. It was dark; the darkness had gathered all around them as they walked, and now there was only a small circle of remaining daylight on the pale earth where the four ways met. A white hen and a black cockerel lay intertwined, dabbled with blood, their throats cut.

Jack felt a light touch on his shoulder; Corey said gently: 'You can see the place from here . . .'

Down the hill the scrubby undergrowth and the spruce plantation gave way to cleared land, fields with fences of split rails. On the right was a low stone building with warm light in its windows. He looked back quickly at the dead chickens to see if they were still there; the hen twitched at his feet.

'Corey,' he demanded, 'what the hell is all this? I saw some character in the bushes just now . . .'

'The lake,' said Corey, acting tongue-tied. 'There's some kind of freaks camping down by the shore.'

There was a sudden drumming on the dusty earth. Elizabeth screamed and overbalanced as Chung butted his way past her legs. He went through the midst of them, his pads drumming, seized the black cockerel and raced on down the hill into the darkness.

'Chung! Baby!'

Elizabeth got up, taking an arm each from Jack and her husband.

'He'll go to the restaurant, Mrs King,' soothed Corey. 'He'll go find Madame Belle.'

'Beast!' said Elizabeth.

She looped her pearls around her neck another time and headed for the car.

'I lay you ten,' said Ace, as they hurried after her, 'that there are at least four people in the place besides us.'

'You mean four other people having dinner?' said Jack warily.

'That's right. Are you on?'

'Yes,' said Jack firmly. 'I say there will be fewer than four. In fact we'll probably be the only people in the place. Timing it from the moment we walk in, of course.'

He hated getting back into the car and was relieved when Elizabeth flung herself into the front seat. He and Ace settled in the nether reaches; Corey had opened the glass panel. Jack did not want to look out of the window, though it occurred to him that perhaps the *other side of the car* was jinxed. He felt an aversion to the back of Elizabeth's head with its perfectly recreated pageboy bob. It was her normal colour, grey-blonde, but he began to think it was a wig; he was troubled by the notion of an ugly seam that ran all the way down the back of the head, like a scar.

He turned his head, looked back at the crossroads, and was able to reach out and tap Ace on the knee. They both looked through the wide rear window. Jack saw the man in the duster standing in the very centre of the crossroads, where the white hen was still lying. He raised a rifle to his shoulder, aimed at the big car, point-blank. Jack gave a cry and ducked his head; there was a light jolt, Corey swung the wheel.

'Sorry, Mrs King!' he said. 'That was some pothole.'

'Something back there?' enquired Ace.

'Did *you* see anything?' countered Jack.

'I saw the water lapping on the crags...' quoted Ace dreamily. 'What was I supposed to see?'

Bearing in mind that he was one of the few people ever to spoof Avery Philpott King III, Jack said in a low voice: 'The *girl*, of course!'

Ace looked back again with mild interest.

'Girl? Where?'

'Gone now...'

He hadn't been able to draw Ace. To prevaricate when one was actually having hallucinations seemed to him the height of madness. Perhaps everyone did it when they began seeing things. Jack called to mind certain scenes in *Hamlet* and *The Tempest* where visions were taking place.

The car drew up before *Les Hiboux* and he followed Avery and Elizabeth up the wide steps between two stone owls with glowing eyes. They passed through two sets of glass doors and Jack could not see the interior very clearly. The room was irregular in shape, with cosy alcoves and a general soft amber light. The décor was new and old, quite nicely done, nothing garish or tatty, the merest hint of French provincial.

Jack saw that he had lost his bet: at least three of the alcoves were occupied. He had the impression of a table full of older people in evening dress, including a woman with some kind of green ornament in her hair. On the other hand there was a couple beside the palm, middle-aged, who had not dressed up. He wore a tweed jacket, rather like Ace, and she wore a twinset, probably cashmere.

'Oh drat!' said Ace. 'You win!'

Before he could query this decision – there were at least ten people in the restaurant, weren't there? How many did Ace think there were? Which ones could he see? – the proprietor, Pierre, came up with open arms. He was a tall, goodlooking, magnolia-skinned individual, running to fat a little. With *his* tweed jacket he wore a single Creole earring and a large pendant of a skull with emerald eyes.

'That'll be fine,' said Elizabeth, choosing between two tables. 'How's Mama?'

'Feelin' the cold per usual,' said Pierre, who never stopped smiling but always had a whine in his voice. 'Keeps gettin' the death cards in her patience. Says we need a new run of luck.'

'You've got one!' said Ace.

He explained the joke about the names: Ace King, Jack Tenn, and Pierre said softly, 'And this lovely lady is your Queen! Oh, we'll have to try and cut ourselves in on some of that luck of yours, Mr King!'

Jack had guessed, correctly, that the place was more *table d'hôte* than *à la carte*. Pierre left them a bill of fare handwritten in copperplate on green note-paper; it was headed for the day of the week: *Samedi*. A single drum began to play so softly that he wondered if it was in the jungle reaches of his mind. The lighting had altered now so that he could hardly see the neighbouring tables: that convincing couple beside the palm had faded into the haze. He could not even be sure that the tree was a palm.

Corey stepped into their circle of light carrying a tray with three glasses in silver holders and a glass jug, twined with flowers. He was in shirtsleeves, showing his fancy vest, like a riverboat gambler.

'Madame B's special punch,' he said, pouring.

'After this,' said Avery, 'we will feel no pain.'

'How right you are, Mr King!' Corey smiled, showing too much gum, spoiling the effect of his capped teeth.

'How many helpers does she need back there?' demanded Elizabeth. 'Corey, make sure you find Chung.'

'He's out back, Mrs King,' said Corey, watching as Elizabeth drained her glass. 'Madame will take care of him till you're done.'

Jack took one gulp of the punch and was flooded with memory. That same stinging dry taste had spoiled his daiquiri, back at the house ... like a pinch of some chemical. He must be sensitive to some damned additive, something that went into drinks. The thing was simply not to touch another drop and to control his paranoia as best he could. He could not see whether Ace had finished his glass or not; Pierre was serving the bisque from a silver tureen.

The rich salmon-coloured soup was delicious; the drumming had grown louder; in the jungle birds were screaming. With an effort Jack pushed back his chair a little, out of the narrowing circle of light, and tried to see where he was. *Les Hiboux* was empty; wherever he looked in his part of the room he could see bare tables, some with the chairs stacked.

A very young girl, brown-skinned, wearing a dusty pink mini-dress, sashayed between the tables collecting the cruets. Her movements struck at Jack like lightning; he forced himself to look away. Elizabeth was making passes with her hands in front of her face as if brushing away spiderweb.

'Not bad at all,' said Ace. 'Bit light on the *langouste*, d'ye think?'

'Mmm,' said Elizabeth. 'Are we going to have some music?'

The tall black man in the duster stood on the little bandstand beside an old upright piano and a set of vibes. He had two little round drums in the crook of his left arm: as the tempo increased Jack felt a rising panic. He looked about for the pink girl and found her sidling out from the kitchen; she went to stand below the platform, in the shadows. Her hips moved rhythmically, she lifted one hand and pulled a clasp from her hair so that it fell down over her shoulders. Jack was shivering now with a painful mixture of fear and excitement.

'Why don't you try it?' said Avery.

He became aware that Pierre had served the entrée: terrine of duck, with white truffles, prettily arranged with watercress.

'No!' said Elizabeth. 'Far too bland. What's the point of the watercress anyway?'

Jack gobbled the pale sliver on his plate and it tasted warm and salty, like blood. The black man was singing in a high, subliminal voice; he stripped off his duster expertly, hardly pausing in his drum beat. He waved his naked brown arms above his head but the drums kept playing, the girl in pink danced in the shadows, flashing her thighs. Now the Master of Ceremonies gesticulated with his left hand and suddenly in his right hand he held a knife. No, worse than a knife, a machete...

'Mama!' screamed Elizabeth.

The old woman advanced out of the shadows near the kitchen door with the same dancing step, keeping the rhythm of the drums. She was small and slight with a very upright carriage; she wore a dark red apron over a long slinky black dress decorated with twinkling bead fringes. Ace and Elizabeth both broke into a chorus of greeting: Jack was introduced to Madame Belle. The light reflected on her steel-rimmed spectacles so that she had no eyes. She still moved back and forth, coming a little nearer to the table each time.

'... been far too long,' said Ace.

'... everyone looking so well!' said Elizabeth.

The old woman, who had not spoken a word, danced right in, drawing her hands out from under her apron. She laid her right palm in the middle of Elizabeth's back, on the grey-blue chiffon of her high-necked dinner gown. She snapped the fingers of her left hand and Corey, who had come from nowhere with a trolley, whisked the plates away.

'Oh, you folks are really getting it all, tonight!' said Madame Belle.

The Kings laughed aloud; Corey and the old woman lifted the casserole on to its warming stand and began to serve the Chicken Christophe. Jack saw that Madame Belle's right hand was wet and discoloured; she wiped it on her apron.

'Just a minute there, Mr Jack!' said Corey, setting down his plate. 'You got a feather!'

He felt a movement at his back, between his shoulder blades. He thought 'They marked two of us, how will they mark Ace?' The old woman danced easily around the table and poised behind Ace's chair, on the way to the bandstand. She danced side by side with the pink girl, below the man with the drum. He wore a black tailcoat now, with red satin lapels, and he played a riff or two on the vibes.

Madame Belle stripped off her apron and flung it to the ground near a pile of other props: the duster coat, the battered top hat, the machete. Her slinky dress had thin rhinestone shoulder straps and showed the paler flesh of her small, slack breasts. The girl's dress had parted at the waist to show her taut, forward-thrusting brown midriff.

'Now this really is good!' said Ace. 'She got it right with the marinade and the extra onions.'

'Yes,' said Elizabeth, 'I must admit . . .'

She wriggled her shoulders, put down her fork and reached far up behind her own back, a movement nearly impossible for a man to make.

'Mama Belle had wet hands or something!'

Corey at once walked behind her chair and dabbed with a napkin.

'Soon dry out, Mrs King, with that light chiffon . . .'

It was the turning point. Jack caught Corey's eye and knew that an error had been made. The young man swallowed hard, tossed his head, and danced away towards the kitchen. Jack said: 'Ace, do you remember our chicken song?'

'What's the matter, sport?' said Ace. 'Don't you care for the Christophe? It's really only a variant of Chicken Marengo.'

'No,' said Jack, still pretending to eat. 'I mean our own particular chicken ditty.'

He hummed a few bars of 'The Skye Boat-Song'. It had got them out of trouble and out of bars several times in the past.

'Good God!' said Ace. 'As bad as that? You really are feeling seedy, aren't you?'

'We're in danger,' said Jack.

The drumming had grown very faint: the tall man and the old woman were poised beside the bandstand like wax figures: the girl lay on the floor, balanced on shoulders, buttocks, bare heels. Now all three began to move in unison; the drumbeat was slowly coming up; the bird-cries sounded. The machete appeared again in the right hand of the tall man.

'Some kind of ceremony!' said Jack. 'They're out to get us!'

'You're out of your mind!' said Ace. 'We know these people. Corey . . . you're not suggesting that Corey . . .'

'Elizabeth,' said Jack, 'could you just manage to turn around without attracting too much attention? We want to see the back of your dress.'

It was hard to tell whether Elizabeth had been following very closely but now she did as she was asked. She bent forward first in one direction, then another, and helped herself to more casserole. Her dress bore the mark of Madame Belle's bloody hand.

'It's blood, isn't it,' said Elizabeth quietly.

She sat back in her chair trembling and pale, as if she were made of grey-blue chiffon.

'They killed my poor baby,' she said. 'If this is one of your gags, Avery, it has gone too far!'

Lips drawn back from her clenched teeth, she seized the heavy serving fork, withdrew a long lump of flesh from the casserole, dumped it on the white tablecloth and doused it with the remains of the punch to wash off the sauce. Jack remembered that Elizabeth was a registered nurse.

'Yes,' she said in a mad, whispery voice. 'Yes, I thought so. It isn't *cooked*, you understand. Just put into the dish.'

She leaped to her feet and shouted: *'Bloody murderers!'*

On the tablecloth lay a medium-sized black tongue with gobbets of adhering tissue: a dog's tongue. Jack felt his gorge rise; the lights went out, flickered back, and the drums filled the world. He saw Ace stand up and put his arms around his wife, restraining and protecting. The pair of them staggered and fell; Jack was dragged down, engulfed by the falling table; he experienced a series of lightning flashes.

He was transported into the ambience of the pink girl, he felt the heat of her body. He saw the jungle clearing, felt the warm moist air, after rain, and smelled the tang of fresh blood. The tall man opened the top of the piano, dragged out a black cockerel and halved it in the air with the machete.

The back of Jack's head hit the floor and everything went into slow motion. (*There was evidence that the back of his head had hit some flat surface; he carried the report from the county hospital about with him, from shrink to shrink, throughout the Anglo-Saxon lands.*) Ace and Elizabeth rose up out of the folds of the tablecloth, legs rubbery, arms extended as if they were trying to fly. The drumbeat was a huge hollow sound. The tall man, naked under his tailcoat, with a necklace of small skulls, leaped high in the air and floated down into the circle of light.

When he moved his arms Ace and Elizabeth began to dance, horribly, like marionettes. Voices swelled in affirmation, calling his name, as their high priest: *'Samedi! Sa-me-di!'* He drew near with the gleaming machete, not touching his victim, and a red line opened from Ace's chin down to his groin, through layers of cotton, silk, cashmere, worsted, epidermis, fat and muscle. Jack heard his own long slow groan of protest as Ace twisted to the floor.

Baron Samedi whisked off Elizabeth's ash-blonde wig and sketched a splitting blow down the back of her skull. She folded down into a soft pile of grey-blue chiffon. Jack saw the girl, he saw Corey, saw

Pierre amongst the worshippers. They danced half-clad, in the darkness, stretching their hands, palm upwards, into the circle of light; Baron Samedi, Lord of the Crossroads, flicked at them with his magic blade until a red line marked each one . . .

He was shivering with cold and trying to get more of the fur rug, which whimpered beside him. When he moved the skin of his face hurt terribly, runners of pain spread through all his limbs . . . He slid backwards along the ground on his bottom, like a baby, in total darkness, smelling blood, grass, petrol, wet dog. He hugged Chung's neck and ungummed his eyelids painfully but still saw very little. They were free of the car now and he was beginning to see its position.

'Yes, yes, old chap,' he croaked to the distraught dog.

He was pleased, for some reason, to find Chung *licking* his face. He turned his head very slowly and saw a tree on the shoulder of the road. Up above was the starry heaven. There was a dreadful silence; no one else groaned or sighed. *Run off the road at the Lookout.* Jack tried to shout but all that came out was a feeble, hoarse sound hardly above a whisper.

He kept on trying as he inched painfully towards the tree. He clung to its trunk and dragged himself upright. Chung moaned and howled, butting his knees. The car had rolled over and come to rest against a larger tree. *On the way back to town.* Avery. Elizabeth. Corey. Jack made a very great effort: '*Help!*'

The old man strolled towards him with an awful lack of urgency. He made his own light. Jack could see sparks of blue fire at his lapels, on his bony wrists, on the brim of his battered top hat.

'Help's coming.'

The voice was half in, half out of his head.

'In the car . . .' gasped Jack. 'Mr and Mrs King . . .'

'Corey,' added the old man. 'He's there too.'

'Are they . . . ? Can't you see to them?'

'No, Jack,' said the old man, smiling sadly. 'I only seen to you.'

He did something with his eyes so that they turned white; the bones of his skull shone through the taut, black skin of his face. Jack heard the raunchy rhythm of the drum, the roar of the jungle; he smelled the reek of blood.

'*Help them, damn you!*' he shouted.

'You're a wonder,' smiled the Baron. 'You are a natural. Just a leetle pinch of the obi medicine and you see all that there is to see and then some. It will all come back to you.'

Jack heard the wail of a siren, somewhere along the dark road through the hills. Help coming. He tried to make out the restaurant, down the hill, but all its lights were out.

'What was the plan?' he demanded. 'Why would those people want to gang up on some rich customers with a . . . a voodoo ceremony?'

'How 'bout vengeance?' asked the Baron. 'Or a sacrifice to bring gambling luck?'

He was suddenly holding up five diamonds: ace, king, queen, jack, ten. He folded them away into his skeletal black hand and blood oozed between the fingers.

'Conjuring tricks!' said Jack through set teeth.

'That's the very word!'

'Chung wasn't hurt . . .'

The old man chuckled and buried his fingers in Chung's thick fur. 'We take pity on dogs,' he observed, 'even when we might have to find some poor dog already dead. Colour up his tongue a little . . .'

'That's enough!' said Jack.

He tried to stand alone, without clasping the tree, and began to weep for pain and weakness.

'It ain't no use to go down there,' said the old man.

But Jack was stumbling, crawling, back down to the wrecked car. Chung came with him a little way then would go no further. His eyes had grown accustomed to the darkness: he was able to make out the body of his old friend, Avery Philpott King III, skewered and gutted, in the ruins of the back seat. Elizabeth was worked into a very small space beside him. When Jack touched her hand, pulled gently at her cold wrist, the whole wreck seemed to shake.

He scrambled backwards, lurched against the car again and cried out in alarm as it rocked crazily. He found that if he bent sideways he could see Corey, head and shoulders bulging the windshield.

'They take Corey out first,' whispered the old man, in his head. 'Then the wreck will fall down and burn . . .'

'Murderers!' said Jack.

He remembered Elizabeth leaping up from her chair.

'The magic became too strong,' said the old man.

He reached down a solid, skinny, old man's hand and helped Jack back up the slope. The ambulance and a police car, with sirens blaring and flashing lights, swept on to the dark hilltop.

'Sometimes it happens that way,' he went on. 'The magic becomes too strong and Baron Samedi swoops down to do some death-dealing . . .'

He propped Jack up against the tree, like a zombie, with Chung at his feet. He left him with a final word: *'Remember, you got an Ace in the hole, boy!'*

Jack saw him walking away over the crossroads, through the crowd of helpers all converging on his tree. He could not tell if any of them were aware of the old man or not. Jack was wrapped in a blanket and given treatment for shock. He saw the body of Corey, still with a spark of life left in it, being carried past on a stretcher. Corey's left arm hung down; the palm of the hand was marked with a thin red line, like a cat-scratch.

(The psychiatrists he consulted in the United States and in Britain showed interest in various aspects of his story. The American woman was interested in the possible misuse of hallucinogenic drugs. The Scotsman was distressed by the racist element. The English woman was impressed by his sexual reaction. Everyone was relieved to hear that Chung made a complete recovery. None of them trusted Jack; he could not decide whether they found him too mad or not mad enough.)

There was a shout from over the edge of the road as the wrecked car crashed down and burst into flames. One of the policemen – would he be a deputy sheriff? – was struck by a piece of burning debris. He ran blazing across the summit of the dark hill and the ambulance attendants rushed out with more blankets to smother the flames.

In the light of the burning man Jack caught a glimpse of Pierre, Madame Belle, a girl that could have been the pink girl, huddled together. There was a bunch of youngsters, campers, the freaks from down by the lake. Next morning, in the county hospital, wherever that was, he remembered the 'pot' that Ace had given him to hold for 'a wager with Corey'.

The envelope in his jacket pocket bore his own name, *John Dixon*, in Ace's handwriting. Inside, folded in sheets of green tissue paper, he found a cross made of dark stained wood, carved with a skull and a phallus. Yes, of course Ace had been in on the thing somehow. But had the cross been passed to Jack with malice or for his protection? He wondered if Elizabeth had received any kind of a fetish.

Corey had died during the night so Jack had no chance to talk to him again, except in the way that he talked to all of them again: in his dreams. He wrapped up the fetish and kept the horrid thing by him for years, showing it only to a few close friends.

In fact he was never able to scrape up more than a very few close friends, but his luck was phenomenally good from that time forward. It was said that J.D. had the golden touch; that his taste in women was exotic; that he was addicted to psychotherapy. In the end he gave the voodoo cross to the young actress who played First Witch in his famous *Macbeth* with the Haitian setting.

Cherry Wilder recently returned to her native New Zealand after living in West Germany with her late husband and two daughters since the mid-1970s. She published poetry, short stories and criticism before making a commitment to genre writing – science fiction, fantasy and horror – and her short fiction has appeared in many magazines and anthologies, including *Interzone, Asimov's Ghosts, Best SF 16, New Terrors, Dark Voices, Skin of the Soul* and *Best New Horror*. Her novels include the 'Torin' trilogy (*The Luck of Brin's Five, The Nearest Fire* and *The Tapestry Warriors*), the 'Rulers of Hylor' trilogy (*A Princess of the Chameln, Yorath the Wolf* and *The Summer's King*), the 'Rhomary' series (*Second Nature* and *Signs of Life*), and the horror novel *Cruel Designs*. Her collection *Dealers in Light and Darkness* was published by Edgewood Press, and she is currently working on the first volume of a new 'Hylor' trilogy for Tor Books. As she explains, '"Saturday" recalls a visit to a real restaurant in the Pennsylvania Hills in 1983. The district is called Twin Lakes and at the time this suggested the atmosphere of the occult work, *Twin Peaks*.'

The Girlfriends of Dorian Gray

GREGORY FROST

With his fork, he cut through the layers of crisp philo dough, lifted and placed in his mouth the slice of *bisteeya*. The flavours of cinnamon, coriander, butter and almonds flooded his senses – a sweet and tender orgasm to which he gave himself completely, eyes closed, fingers curled tenderly around his utensils. When he opened his eyes again, he was staring right at Alison.

She sat across the table. In front of her was a white bread plate and a glass of spring water with a slice of lemon floating in it. The plate contained three saltine crackers. Alison was trying to look disinterested and unaffected by his meal. But just then her stomach gurgled and he had to keep himself from smiling at its betrayal. She could have had the same meal he was eating, or anything else on the menu: he would have been more than willing to order her something, anything. The choice to starve was hers. He could not concern himself with it.

A single rose stood in the small vase between them. It was his particular flourish, that rose. He began his conquests with the rose, knowing that so simple a gesture was an arrow to the heart of the romantic. He promised elegance, thoughtfulness, taste, but above all, romance. After their first date – the first night they'd met after she answered his ad – Alison had confessed that the rose made her toes curl. Tonight, however, it stood as an emblem of distance, a cenotaph of her feelings for him, already buried elsewhere. He knew this would be the last night, knew already exactly how it was going to end. It had ended this way dozens of times before.

He was elegance himself – tall, smoothly groomed, with perfect teeth and long slender hands. He took extra good care of his hands. 'The hands of an angel,' one of the women had told him. Wasn't it Tricia? Yes, that seemed right. Tricia was always alluding to Christian iconography: hands of an angel, face of a saint, heart of the devil. An annoying habit, actually – he never could have married her. But of course he wouldn't; just as he wouldn't be marrying Alison.

He'd taken her to only the finest restaurants in the city. A night out with him ran to hundreds of dollars, and he never skimped, never hesitated to order the finest meals. Maître d's knew him. Chefs came out of the kitchen to the table and discussed dishes with him. Dining with him was like dining with a celebrity. 'If we are going to eat, then we should only ever eat the best,' was his mantra. Never would he have dipped below a four star establishment. He was like someone who had just stepped out of a magazine ad for Rolex watches or Dom Perignon, a real live James Bond without the silly devices and world-dominating villains. A man who'd been bred to know the best and settle for nothing less. And by association, what did that make the woman who accompanied him?

How many dinners had they shared before she noticed the first signs of the change? It was three before he saw, but he was watching. Six or seven for her, by his reckoning. When you're in love, you overlook and deny so many seemingly insignificant things.

Like the fact that he was a gourmand.

He not only liked the finest cuisine, he liked as much of it as he could possibly consume in any one sitting. Four courses, six courses: pâté de fois gras, bisques thick with cream, lobster-stuffed squid-ink ravioli in a tomato-cream sauce, soufflés, quiches, duck à l'orange, prime rib of beef, cherry compôte, tiramisu, bottles of champagne, carafes of wine. Single-handedly he could take out a whole menu.

For all that, his manners were impeccable. It wasn't that he sat slobbering and gnashing, drawing attention to himself as some deranged Neanderthal with a fork might have done. No, he ate demurely, quietly, chatting with her, truly interested in what she had to say (or at least feigning interest so well that she would never notice the difference). Dinner with him lasted the entire evening. The courses came and went – soups, hors-d'oeuvres, first course, main course, cheese course, desserts and coffee, liqueurs. She would not have noticed right away that he had eaten an extra course, or more than one dessert, or consumed an entire bottle of wine on his own and helped her with half of another. Simply, he ate. And ate. And ate. And ate.

He wondered if any of them would have stayed with him. He supposed it didn't matter, since he never intended to stay with any of them. But he liked that they always called it quits. Alison was going to call it quits tonight. When they got to the saltines stage, they always called it quits.

He'd been surprised that first night how petite Alison was – the smallest woman he'd had so far, her head barely reached his nipples. And very healthy. She exercised hard, and was proud to show him her abdominals, her perfect, smooth, taut and round rear, and her well-muscled legs. She was certainly the only woman he'd met who claimed she enjoyed stair-climbers and rowing machines. Such strict attention to her physique included diet, and so she hadn't been prepared for the cream sauces, the nights of sheer ecstatic indulgence in all things edible, the ease with which one got hooked by rich, buttery fattening foods. He supposed it had been something like springing a trap on poor Alison. By the time she'd mentioned to him – a gentle reproof – that she thought he over-indulged when they went out to dinner, he could only laugh. She told him as if he might be unaware of it himself. In all other ways he was the personification of charm and compassion; a wonderful, thoughtful lover. Of course when he'd offered her the ring she had accepted. On the first date he showed it to her. On the second date, he placed it on her finger. His eating habits didn't dissuade her from accepting his offer of a more significant relationship.

Then the tummy had arrived.

Suddenly she didn't fit comfortably in her electric blue Lycra. Where she had been hard muscle, she began to bulge. The solution, of course, was to increase her workout and decrease the number of times she ate out with him, both of which she did. She promptly gained another dozen pounds. Soon he had to coerce her into going out, and when she did, she ate the lightest fare – a salad, or something high in protein like fish, while avoiding all starches, breads and pastas – while he devoured half the planet with his usual zeal, but always solicitous, always asking if she minded that he ate a regular meal, exhibiting such concern that she could say nothing except 'of course not'. There were many nights when she begged off dinner and he went out alone. It didn't matter. Once she'd handled the ring, she didn't have to be with him.

Now five months had passed and the engagement had run its course. The longest it had ever run was eight months, but Anita had been a much taller woman to begin with. At four months, while expressing continued desire for her company, he ceased to exhibit any for the physical relationship they'd shared. Without saying anything directly, he reproached her for her size. He found her 190-pound physique as repugnant as she did. *He* didn't weigh that much. She was only five feet tall. She couldn't remotely carry this kind of weight around. Just climbing the steps to the restaurant left her labouring for breath. He held her hand and waited for her with the utmost patience and consideration. Never would he give her cause to doubt the sincerity of his concern. Treadmills and rowing machines fell by the wayside. Alison couldn't bend forward enough to row, and she complained of back aches when she used a stair-climber. At five months, the skin sagged on her arms, flowed around her elbows and knees. Her calves literally hung over her ankles. She was gelatin, marshmallow, not human at all. He found it all terribly disgusting, especially as he sat there indulging himself with a raft of the most glorious foods and never gaining an ounce.

She had tried every diet and gone so far as to experiment with acupuncture and hypnosis. He suspected she had become bulimic. She couldn't become anorexic. Not quite yet anyway.

Nothing had worked. Nothing was ever going to work.

So while he finished the *bisteeya*, Alison told him that she had to stop seeing him, that her world was out of control and she needed to get away for awhile. She was going to a clinic in upstate New York where they could help people with her kind of disorder. It was – it had to be – hormonal.

He set down his fork and let her see that he was stunned, crestfallen, horrified. 'I do understand,' he said. 'You have to take care of yourself. Why, it must be awful to have to watch me enjoying food when it's become so miserable for you to eat. That's so awful, Alison. I can't imagine what it would be like to have to stop enjoying food. I don't think I could do it. I'll – I won't have another thing. I'll call the waiter right now and cancel the main course. You should not have to sit here like this.'

She agreed with him on that point. But rather than making him end his dinner, she insisted he just allow her to go. 'It's better if I don't see you again, either. I'm afraid—' her eyes glistened with her first tears '—I can't separate you from what's happened to me. I'm sorry.' Sobbing, she slid his ring across the table.

She rose to leave the restaurant, but swayed dizzily, and he leapt to his feet and caught hold of her pudgy arm to brace her. He moved as swiftly as someone who had foreseen that she would become light-headed.

He guided her into her coat, then hailed a cab and helped her struggle into the back of it. She clutched his hand, kissed it, then turned her face away. He gave the driver her address and a twenty dollar bill, wished her well, and sent her off.

Once the cab was out of sight, he returned to his table and proceeded immediately to eat the rest of his meal as if nothing had happened, as if there was not – and could not have been – a care in the world. Some of the other diners glanced at him with disgust. He ignored them. The waiter asked if the lady would be all right, and he answered, 'Eventually. She's having digestion problems.' The waiter eyed him peculiarly, and he took that as his cue to say loudly enough for those nearby to eavesdrop: 'We've just broken up. So, while I'm sorry that she's feeling ill, I'm not full of tea and sympathy just now. You understand? She's broken my heart and I'm not going to cave in. I refuse.' That seemed to satisfy the waiter. At least it lent some justification to his insistence that the dinner proceed. People ate their way out of misery all the time. Didn't they?

Thus he ate and ate as if Alison were still there, as if she or her phantom were being served a portion of everything, too, as if no amount of food could salve his conscience. As if he had one.

In the morning he called the paper and placed a new ad. He needed a new vessel.

The most difficult part was this limbo in between. He had no vessel and he wanted desperately to binge; but he knew that, if he succumbed to his lust, the repercussions would be his alone to bear. That was how the spell worked. It wasn't under his governance. It hadn't really been his idea in the first place.

The whole thing was Rebecca's fault. She'd irritated him into it. At the time, of course, he'd only half-believed in it, and that half was drunk. Magic was silly – Penn & Teller pulling the audience's collective pants down. That was magic to him.

He'd been drinking ouzo, but as Manny had said, 'What else ya gonna drink in a bar in Canea on Crete, dude?' In his cups, he'd been complaining to Manny and one of the local men about Rebecca's vanity, her obsession with her model's figure, which included denial of most of the foods he loved, and her complaints about his own softening physique. If she was to deny herself these pleasures, then she expected him to do the same. He wasn't even married to her yet and already she was instituting changes in his life. 'Come all the way here just to eat Melba toast? My God, it's hideous!' he'd exclaimed. Mummy and Dad were footing the bill for this trip – his reward for graduating with honours – and he wasn't about to spend their money on a diet of figs and yogurt. There was more to it, of course. She'd complained the whole trip about how pathetic and stupid the native population were, these poor little people without even cell phones. The next thing he knew, he and Manny were in the company of two locals on a narrow street with a name like Iepela Odoc or something. Well, the word in Greek that *looked* like *odoc* meant 'street' but that was as far as he could get with his sloshing vocabulary.

He had the money to buy the spell. He could have bought a dozen. He remembered joking to Manny that there was 'a special on love potions in aisle five'. He didn't so much as feel the amount he was paying, although to the woman – the herbalist or witch, or whatever she was – it must have been a jackpot sum. In her corner of the world, that much money was a fortune. 'Travel broadens the mind, not the girth,' he'd announced. It was all a lark.

'You don't believe, but yet you pay?' she'd asked. She clearly thought him an idiot. He never got to answer. She asked him to give her something to use to focus the spell upon, and he fumbled in his pockets and pulled out the antique ring he'd bought for Rebecca in Athens – he intended it to be her engagement ring. At least, he had intended that before she started telling him what he could and couldn't eat.

The next thing he knew, he'd been presented with a small chalice and he was thoughtlessly drinking the contents. Whatever it was, it made him double over in pain. His brain cleared enough for him to experience fear – to think she might have played a trick on him and now he would die in a little shop on a back street in one of the oldest cities of the world, murdered by a woman who looked about as old as the city. He had time to hiss, 'Manny, you stupid bastard,' before blackness shot with stars scooped him up and deposited him back in his hotel room. He opened crusted eyes beneath a spinning ceiling fan, on his bed; it was as if the entire adventure, the whole day, had been a wild dream. He was still dressed. He checked his money belt. The cash he remembered giving the woman was in fact gone – but only that much. The other thousand he had was still there, and so was the antique ring. If it hadn't been for that he might never have believed the journey had happened at all.

He felt no different. He looked no different. Whatever she'd given him, it hadn't killed him. The whole thing was just a mean, drunken digression. Despite which, he gave Rebecca the ring at his first opportunity, and then watched to see what would happen.

Of course it had worked. He couldn't believe how well it had worked. Over her shrill protests, he finished his holiday eating whatever he wanted, as much as he wanted. Within a month, Rebecca had developed a double chin. Dear, vain, conceited Rebecca was swelling up like a balloon and could do nothing to stop it. His pudginess, on the other hand, was vanishing. By the time they left for home, he looked positively trim. That was when he knew.

Once they returned home, it continued. Rebecca tried everything from yoga to liposuction. The latter vacuumed fat off here and there, but couldn't slow down its reappearance. She saw specialists in diet, hormones, metabolism. No one could account for the changes. No one could reverse them. She ate in the zone, adhered to the Atkins diet, and finally, humiliatingly, joined Weight Watchers. The latter thought she lacked the will to lose. She was cheating.

She became reclusive, and within the year was institutionalised. Never for a moment did anyone save Manny have the slightest suspicion what was really happening – and Manny, the instrument of the spell, couldn't say a thing. It was all too sublime.

Finally, Rebecca's clogged arteries had given her a stroke. She hadn't lived long. After the funeral, the family returned his ring to him; it was only proper – he had stuck by her the whole time. At least, when he wasn't eating.

The moment his fiancée was gone, any overindulging he did came back on him as it would have on anyone. He made himself rein in his appetite. The trouble was, by then he'd discovered he *liked* to eat that way. His body had grown used to rich sauces and huge quantities of food. It ached for more.

Rebecca had a sister, Midge, who liked him. She had always been waiting in the wings, jealous of her older sister. It was the element of sibling rivalry, stealing the boyfriend away from her dead sister, that made his part easy. Within weeks they were engaged, and he started eating again. He did so warily, with an eye to Rebecca's replacement, because at that point he wasn't certain the magic would transfer. But Midge wasted no time in following in her sister's elephantine footsteps. The difference was that Midge somehow figured out he was responsible. He suspected that Manny told her, and thereafter he and Manny parted company. Midge soon rejected him. Although she never could have understood what was happening, he had learned never to involve people who knew one another.

And so he had come to the personals page, where potential fiancées abounded – a thousand women of all persuasions looking for the right man, for romance and adventure. He looked for the ones who proclaimed their thinness, their great physiques. He tailored his own ad to attract them. It was easy. They were ducks on a pond.

Two days later, when he looked to check that his ad was listed in the personals, he found Cerise. Her ad was across from his on the page. The title caught his eye.

THE WAY TO A MAN'S HEART. WiOF, in the middle of life, slender, attractive, loves good food, trained chef, ISO delicious male, 35–45, who wants to savour the flavour. BOX 2356.

The silly 'savour the flavour' rhyme ought to have made him dismiss the ad, but instead it crawled inside his head like some tiny, obnoxious nursery rhyme, helixing in singsong around and around his thoughts. 'Trained chef' was a taunt, an invitation, a tantalising dare. He started imagining all sorts of things – of taking her to the best restaurants in the city, watching her pass judgment on the culinary delights as he devoured each one. Letting her pick out the courses one after the others, selecting his sauces, hobnobbing with the various chefs. Choosing the very shape of her own undoing.

What was the 'O' for, he wondered. Old, maybe, Oriental. Widowed Oriental? Slender? Well, for the time being, maybe. He would change that.

He replied to her ad immediately, calling the 900 number and leaving his name, his phone number and particulars. He finished by saying, 'Good food is necessary for all things sensual. How can anyone be a sensualist without appreciating food? You, with your training, can't help but *be* sensual. Of that, I'm certain.' He didn't know why, but he was sweating by the time he finished – a case of nerves. Having made the call, he found himself worried about losing her to someone else. The ad spoke to *him*. He wondered if his own ad had affected the women who answered that way.

He'd never had a problem inducing them to accept the ring, which meant that they came to the date with some illusions, some ridiculous hopes that worked to his advantage. And he always began with the rose, that romantic hook. He remained attentive, cultured, never angry or even irritated; he was, he felt, a good lover, always solicitous, as hard, soft or vocal as they desired. He never looked at another woman, not even when the ballooning began. He was obsessed with watching the changes as he reshaped and distorted her. It was like peering into a funhouse mirror, witnessing a transformation that should have been his own. Behind the rapacious joy of eating and the visceral pleasure of controlling and destroying, he couldn't imagine what he would have looked like by now without the ring, without the magic.

Responses to his ad trickled in, but he didn't answer any of them. He waited for the woman to call him.

As the days ran on, he convinced himself that he'd been rejected, he had lost her. Maybe she'd had an answer before his. Her ad might have been in place for ages. He dug out the section and looked at it again, noting the 'Exp. 2/19' date at the end. His own ad didn't expire until the 23rd, so she must have been bombarded with calls well before his own, how could she not have been? Someone had beaten him to her and there was nothing he could do, no way to get her to consider him instead. He thought of calling again, but knew how desperate that would make him sound, and he refused to be desperate. He sank into a depression, and thoughtlessly ate a huge meal to take his mind off her. Of course it did just the opposite, and he gained five pounds on top of everything else. Defeated, he returned to his mailbox and listened to a dozen unappetising answers. What could he do? He needed a vessel. He was starving without one.

After two weeks she called. A husky, lightly accented voice asked to speak with him. Her name, she said, was Cerise, like the colour. 'I loved your reply. You seem to know me just by imagining my cooking. You made food sound as if it were your one consuming passion.'

'It is,' he said. His palms were sweating. 'You – you're a chef?'

'Yes. Oh, not professionally. That is, I don't work as one. But I have been trained here by the CIA, and also in France awhile ago.'

The CIA – only someone with his fixation would know to render that as a reference to a cooking school and not a collective of spies.

'What was your specialty?' He felt like an idiot asking it. What had happened to his refinement, his sensibility? His whole façade had deserted him.

'Mediterranean dishes.' Then she added, 'So, would you like to sample my art?'

He'd intended to ask her to come to Figaro's with him – that had been his original plan, the one he'd used on all the others. Instead he found himself saying, 'I would love to,' and writing down her address and promising to be there that night.

He hung up the phone and then sat still, his mouth dry, his penis as stiff as if she had just performed a striptease before him. There was something truly wonderful about her. *Absurd*, he thought, *but I believe I'm in love*.

He considered that he might even regret what had to happen to her.

He arrived at 8:00 p.m. sharp. She had a midtown flat overlooking the park, an address that announced her wealth. The doorman called her and he heard her voice answering to let him in. The doorman touched finger to cap and held the door as he entered.

He'd brought a fine Bordeaux with him from his cellar, one that he never would have brought along on a blind first date. It seemed terribly important to make a good first impression. He had his single rose, and the ring was in his breast pocket. He never knew when he was going to convince his vessel to wear it. What was important was that the magic start – that she handle the old ring sometime during the first meal. By the second or third date, he would propose, give her the ring to wear, and then let the rest happen. He'd done it enough times that the process was scripted, events pre-ordained before the first course had been cleared.

The elevator was an old-fashioned cage, and he rode up rigid with apprehension, staring through the bars but seeing nothing beyond his own desire.

Even before he'd reached her door, he could smell spices and sea scents. His stomach fluttered with anticipation at the same time as he realised the wine he'd brought wasn't going to work. He ought to have asked what she was making. It would be interesting to see if she appreciated the gift; they could always drink it the next time.

He lifted the knocker and rapped quietly. She opened it at once.

The moment he looked at her, he knew what the 'O' had stood for. 'Olive,' he said aloud.

As though she understood his meaning, she smiled when he said it; and he thought he would go blind with lust. For a moment he actually forgot about food.

Her flesh was a deep, deep olive colour. She was as tall as he, and her bearing could only be described as regal. Her cheekbones were high, and as sharply defined as her jaw, which ought to have been too large, too pronounced on such a face but was unaccountably beautiful. Her eyes were lighter than her complexion, nearly golden. Her hair was jet black, yet where the light in her entryway sparkled in it, the hair seemed highlighted with gold, as if she'd looped thin strands through it. Her eyes looked him up and down as she spoke his name and offered her hand. He, utterly besotted, raised it to his lips and kissed it. She smiled again as he gave her the rose, and looked at him a moment over the petals. There were lines of experience beneath her eyes, but they laughed at him, promised joy.

She ushered him in, took his overcoat while commenting on the cold weather, accepted his proffered bottle. As he'd hoped, she noted its vintage with satisfaction: she knew her wine.

She wore a sort of loose, red, ochre and purple dashiki, belted in gold at her narrow waist, slit along the sides. When she reached to hang up his coat, he glimpsed her breast and realised that she was wearing nothing at all beneath the gown.

She had a bottle decanted already, some cold and golden aperitif, and she poured him a drink, then led him on a tour of her apartment. It was simply decorated in the style of a Mediterranean villa. The walls had been glazed, treated in rough imitation of old plaster. There was a mosaic built into the dining room wall of a fish creature – a kind of seahorse with a bearded human head. It looked like something that might have been uncovered at Pompeii. Whoever had died and left her a widow had provided for her very well.

'I hope you like paella,' she said. She placed herself on a divan across from him. Her feet, in sandals, crossed at the ankles. He couldn't help staring.

'You made a paella?'

She shrugged as if to say it was nothing. 'I selected the ingredients this morning myself.' She sipped her wine. 'It's important to have fresh ingredients.'

'Absolutely.'

'So, please, tell me about yourself.'

'Well,' he said, and launched into a longwinded autobiography, surprising himself as he told her about his first sexual encounter, about growing up with a sense of superiority over the average citizen because he could read a wine list, because he could recognise quality in objects, in places. In people. At least, that was what he found himself saying. He described his trip to Crete with Manny and Manny's girlfriend and Rebecca, calling it 'the transforming event of my life'. He very nearly blurted out that he'd purchased a magic charm there – very nearly gave away his secret to a woman who was about to become its next victim – and decided that he'd best go light on the wine.

The dinner became immediately one of the greatest meals he had ever eaten. She had struck the perfect balance among the fish, shellfish and mussels, the *herbes de Provence*, saffron rice and chorizo. Each mouthful was like an island floating on an orgasmic ocean, so good that his eyes closed half the time. He had to eat slowly. She plied him with more wine, a lovely Sauvignon Blanc, and flat bread, and conversation. She described her life as nomadic. She had, it seemed, lived all over. She told him about cooking classes in Paris with artists whose names he'd never heard; about living in Venice with her late husband; about travelling finally to 'the New World' for a change not only of scenery but of lifestyles, of attitudes. Of people. She made it sound as if it had all taken centuries. And who had she found but a man who had himself gone to the old world? To Crete. A lovely place.

She talked and he ate, slowly, steadily, ready to die for another mouthful. He lost count, but she must have fed him three portions. She seemed only more and more delighted as he devoured the food, relishing and groaning and repeating how incredible she was. He would have eaten four or five helpings if his body allowed it, but even with the spell it was still his stomach.

Finally, sated, he sat back, saying, 'I believe I have never in my life eaten anything at all to compare with this.'

Cerise collected his plate. After a few minutes she emerged from the kitchen with a slender, Turkish-style coffee pot. She set it on the table. It smelled wonderful. His head lolled while he studied the filigree etched into the pot. He fingered the ring in his pocket, drunk with the idea of marrying her tonight. It was absurd, he had to remind himself. He didn't want a wife, only a receptacle, a fiancée. But, dear God, how could he allow her to slip through his fingers? Whether she swelled up like a human blowfish, where on Earth would he ever taste another meal to equal this one? How could he deprive himself of her culinary art?

He mulled it over to no avail. It was a conundrum. Finally, he said, 'You are divine, Cerise, your meal was just . . . breathtaking.'

'I'm happy to have robbed you of breath,' she said, and laughed lightly. She poured the coffee then. It was sweet and strong, an intoxicant to smother the last of his will. He took the ring out and set it on the table.

'This will – this will sound mad, but I am mad, I think. I am madly in love with you.' He couldn't quite make it more comprehensible than that, but he pushed the ring towards her.

She saw it and her teeth flashed again in delight. It was a beautiful ring. She took it, slipping it on her finger and admiring it as she said, 'I knew when you answered my ad that you were the one I was looking for. The *only* one.' She slid around the table, perching beside him. The smell of her was more heady than the scent of the meal had been.

'Oh. Oh, my, my . . .' He couldn't find the right word and embraced her instead. His hands slid like snakes inside her clothing.

She made love as she made food. Everything was fresh, full of spice, hot and overwhelming. He thought of the sea god on her wall and he imagined the face as his own. He was drowning in pleasure, letting himself go completely. He was a ship, she was a storm, and he rode the tempest, too lost to look for bearings, just spinning, spinning, rising and falling.

In the morning when he awoke, he was alone in her bed. This room, like the others, had a sense of antiquity about it. A bronze sun with a capricious face looked at him from the wall. The mirror beside it was edged in verdigris and copper, the reflecting surface marbled with imperfections. When he got up and stood before it, he gasped.

Gasped and looked down.

His belly was swollen. He turned sideways, twisted his face, looked at the reflection, then down at his stomach, then back again. He craned his neck and patted the slight jowl under his chin that hadn't been there the night before.

He looked as if he'd gained ten pounds.

Something was terribly wrong. He couldn't understand it – he'd given her the ring, hadn't he? He thought so, but he'd been intoxicated by her food and drink. By Cerise herself. Maybe he'd just imagined giving it to her.

He checked in his clothing, patted the pockets. Then he turned and circled the bedroom until he spied the ring on her dressing table. He snatched it up. So, she hadn't worn it? But what difference did that make? All the others had had to do was touch it for the spell to take hold, the transformation to unfold. He crumbled under self-doubt: maybe he'd given it to her too late. Could there be a time limit that he just hadn't encountered before? Damned if it didn't look like the whole thing had been flipped back on him. As if he'd gained for both of them.

Uncertain, he dressed, assuring himself that, yes, the food was superb, more than superb, but not good enough to warrant this. And maybe that was it – maybe it had to be someone else's cooking. He would go home, listen to the women who had answered his ad, select one and start over. Give the ring to some other woman as soon as possible.

He walked out of the bedroom, his mind made up, his story already arranged – walked into a cloud of olfactory bliss: Cerise had baked, poached, cooked, and it was ready and waiting for him. As was she.

The sight of the Eggs Benedict smothered in hollandaise made the blood pound in his temples. She'd brewed more coffee, baked some sort of braided bread that glistened with honey, filled bowls with fruit. Around the corner in the kitchen, she looked up from pouring him a mimosa.

She was naked: she'd cooked breakfast in the nude! She offered him that alluring smile once again, and proudly carried the fluted glass to him. Which he accepted. Her hands slid around his neck, into his hair. She kissed him, tasting of strawberry. Her tongue snaked along his own. His will dissolved.

They ate breakfast in almost complete silence. She treated it as if it were a silent sharing. He tried to remember between bites of egg and ham and buttery sauce what he was going to say to her. He began to wonder if he couldn't continue seeing Cerise. Pick some new Alison or Sandra or Jill or Rebecca to take on this cooking, too! He could have it all – Cerise *and* a vessel – and why not? They never had to meet, or even know the other existed. His eating picked up speed. He ate now almost as a test, just to make sure the spell hadn't taken late. So long as that chance remained, he didn't want to do something rash.

When he had eaten, she served him more coffee, then led him back to her bed. He followed docilely, in something of a daze. His body responded to her touch as before; he grew hard and let her ride him into near exhaustion. It went on longer than he would have thought possible. He couldn't believe that after half an hour he was still erect, still going, still unreleased. Tension, he told himself. Tension.

Finally, after she had experienced repeated orgasms of her own, he joined her. She sat awhile, then lay beside him. He sprawled, twitching like a galvanised frog's leg, unable to coordinate his muscles enough to stand up. His whole body smelled of her now. Even the scent of her sex worked on his appetite, making him hungry for more. He dozed, then woke with a start from a dream of having fallen, to find her sleeping beside him with feline contentment upon her features.

He rose unsteadily, glanced at the time, found his underwear and socks. Before he dressed, he stepped in front of the old mirror again. If anything, he looked fatter than just a few hours before. That wasn't possible, was it? It had to be an illusion – his fear working on him. No one got fat this fast . . . except for his vessels. As if to drive the point home, his pants had to be coerced into meeting. He sucked in his gut and used his belt to keep them together. All right, then, there it was – the spell didn't work on her. Now there was no question. No tempting fate further; he had to get out of here before she cooked another meal for him.

Cerise made a noise deep in her throat, not a moan exactly, more like a few notes from a song being hummed below his hearing. She didn't move, but her golden eyes tracked him. 'You are going, my darling?'

'Ah, you're awake. Yes, I have to. That is, I have business that I should have taken care of this morning, and now it's late afternoon, and if I don't do it today, I'll have to wait until Monday.'

'Oh.' The sound of disappointment. 'You'll come back tonight?'

'Well, I—' He could think of nothing to say by way of an excuse. 'Of course. Unless there's a problem. If there is, I'll call you.'

'All right.' She stretched languorously, her black hair reaching all the way to the dimples above her buttocks. Her legs were slightly spread. With her smell clogging his nostrils, all he could think of was how much he wanted to push them wider apart and dive in between.

He made himself turn away. 'I'll call,' he repeated, but she had fallen asleep, and he fled from his returning arousal and the accompanying fear that if he gave in, he would never get away.

Back home, he stripped and showered, scrubbing hard to rid himself of her maddening scent. He put on fresh clothes, leaving the others in a heap beside the laundry hamper. He would have to bag them, take them to a dry cleaner's and get the smell removed.

Comfortable but exhausted, he sat on his couch and dialled his account box and listened to the list of those who had responded to his ad. There were five, and from that list he culled two who sounded the most promising and self-absorbed. He wanted someone vain and stupid right now; someone he could manipulate without having to work hard at it.

The first woman he called was named Gwen. She giggled when he made the simplest joke, said she had never eaten anything like he described and couldn't wait to try. He made a date with her, hung up and called La Parisienne. By luck they had a table. The maître d' knew him of course and was delighted to hear from him. He sat back, sighed with relief, then curled up on the couch and fell asleep. His descending thought was that he had escaped from something terrible.

The new vessel was perfect. She had artificially dyed red hair, and wore an outfit which she undoubtedly thought appropriate for an evening of fine dining but which was just a few steps shy of a hooker so far as he was concerned. Her jewellery was cheap and gaudy. His ring would be lost within the trappings. Still, it was the easiest thing in the world to ask her what she thought of it, if she liked it. She turned it over, studied the stone – 'This is a real one, isn't it?' – and tried it on. He let her wear it all through the soup course. He listened to his body as he ate the rich mushroom bisque, but sensed nothing. Convinced that the bisque wasn't touching him – that it was going where it was supposed to go – he relaxed and anticipated the rest of the meal.

Gwen babbled about her job – something clerical in a photo-mounting company where her manager kept finding ways to touch her. It was all accidental, according to him, but she knew better: the man was a sleaze. She was thinking about filing a suit.

He tried to seem interested, nodding, giving her warm smiles of sincere support. His mind, however, refused to focus on her. The main course arrived – he'd ordered a wonderful fillet of beef in a sauce of wine, shallots and Dijon mustard. When he closed his eyes at the first mouthful, he saw the dining room of Cerise's apartment. It was dark, cold. Leaves were blowing, swirling around the empty room. Startled, he opened his eyes, swallowed. Glanced around himself at the restaurant. The noise of a dozen conversations seemed to echo the hiss of the leaves. Gwen asked, 'Are you okay?'

He said, 'Of course,' and to prove it took another bite. Again, he couldn't help closing his eyes with pleasure, and again the instant he did, he was whisked away to the empty table. But it wasn't empty. Cerise was sitting in the chair across from him, motionless, like a corpse, her face hidden in the shadows.

He opened his eyes and found that he'd dropped his knife. A number of people were looking his way, and Gwen said, 'Honey, I think you need an aspirin or something.' This opinion seemed to be shared by the maître d', who along with the waiter appeared at his side to ask if everything was all right. He laughed lightly and replied that it was nothing – simply, the meal was so good that he'd been transported by it. The maître d' bowed slightly at the compliment and retreated. The waiter replaced his knife.

'It *is* really good, isn't it?' said Gwen.

This time when he ate, he was careful not to close his eyes. This significantly diminished his pleasure in the meal but he had no choice. He ate thereafter a subdued dinner. When Gwen couldn't finish her Suprêmes de Volaille Basquaise, he didn't even attempt to eat it for her, even though the sautéed chicken breast looked and smelled so wonderful. He ordered dessert over her protest that she couldn't touch another bit; after all, he didn't care what *she* ate, but he presumed that her early satiety meant that the magic was working better than ever. So smug was he over this that he forgot himself again at the first taste of the coffee crème caramel. He let his eyes close.

A fierce wind circled him in the cold dark dining room. The cadaverous Cerise rocked in her chair, as though buffeted. Her hand, crablike, reached for his across the polished surface. Her voice, a rasp, asked, 'How can you leave me? How can you leave me like this?' The final sibilance went on hissing. Her hand caught him and he tore himself free of her grip.

He came to, on his feet, moving, the chair already falling back from him, Gwen with her hands up as if to ward him off. There was crème caramel on her forehead, her arm. He couldn't find his spoon.

The whole restaurant was watching. Silent. He'd only closed his eyes for a fraction of a second, how could so much have happened? He sat down, confused, terrified. When the waiter came this time, he asked for the check, added a generous tip and apologised quietly, explaining that he was on a new medication and was obviously reacting badly to it. This did not remove the worry from the waiter's eyes, but at least it might serve to protect him so that he might return another night, after a few months. Once he'd seen through this ... this whatever it was.

He apologised to Gwen, who suggested that maybe they should call it a night. She handed him back the ring. He knew she would have nothing further to do with him. He'd thrown food at her, like some sophomoric fraternity twit.

Not far from the restaurant was a small café where he could get a drink. That, he decided, was exactly what he needed. He sat at the bar and ordered a double of Glenmorangie, his favourite Scotch. He huddled over the glass, inhaling it, trying to calm down. The smell was, as always, intoxicating. His guard came down for only a moment, but that was all it took to transport him again.

Her bony hand gripped his. 'You are mine,' she said. 'Only for me. You swore. You chose.' She leaned towards him and the light from outside fell upon her face – the face of the gorgon. Her golden eyes seared him.

He screamed, lunging back from the bar, pouring Scotch over himself. He slid from the stool and fell heavily. The back of his head struck the floor, bounced and hit it again.

The next thing he knew, someone was helping him to his feet, and a voice asked, 'What *bit* you, there, fella?' He heard other voices saying, 'Seizure' and 'drunk'.

'I'm all right,' he insisted. 'All right.' Although his head ached and he felt nauseous. 'Sorry, sorry. Medication. Bad reaction.' He slapped a twenty on the bar and fled. Four doors away, he doubled over and threw up his dinner. *So much*, he thought, wheezing, *for needing a vessel*.

After that he walked without destination, without purpose, lost in a fog of pain and fear, stinking of Scotch, the smell of which reactivated his gag reflex twice more until all he could vomit was air.

Finally he stumbled inside. There was nothing for it but to sleep off the whole experience.

Head hanging, he rode the elevator up and was halfway down the hall before he smelled the food. His stomach rumbled, and he stopped dead and looked around himself. This wasn't his building. His hallway.

It was hers.

He knew where the smell of cooking came from. Somehow he had slipped right past the doorman without noticing, been let in – no, been *brought* in. He turned and lunged back into the elevator, slamming the cage door closed; then he stood inside, his hands on the bars, the odour of cumin and cloves, coriander and cardamom spinning around his head the way the wind had spun about the table in his vision of her. The smells – how could he ignore the rich – the divine – smells?

He had only to relinquish control and his body took over. His body, now divested of all extrinsic food, wanted desperately to fill itself again. It led him step by step to her door.

He raised the knocker, and the force of it dropping was enough to push the door open further; it had been ajar, waiting for him. He walked in. She was standing in the kitchen, wearing nothing but an apron and her golden sandals, her body the colour of wheat toast, and he went to her, his arm outstretched, the ring between his thumb and forefinger. She turned as if on cue, her own hand raised to let him slide the ring into place. Once she had it on, his arm dropped and he stood, transfixed, unable to move or think, bound to her utterly.

'You love your food too much to do without me, don't you? Even on the telephone, I knew you were the one. You're so like Odysseus's men. They loved their food and drink to excess, and so were halfway to being swine before they even set foot on my island.' She turned the ring with her thumb, admiring it. 'Complementary magics. Of course, mine is the stronger for being the older of the two, so I can use yours as you have done. *Of course*, you are my vessel and my pleasure, my piggy. For so long as you last. Now, go sit down and I'll serve you.' She said it all without malice or cruelty, but gently, with affection.

She turned back to her cooking, to the huge clay pot she'd removed from the oven.

He shuffled past her and into the dining room. Took his seat. A bouquet of roses stood in the centre of the table. There were dry, dead leaves on the tabletop. Circe brushed them aside as she set his plate before him – a mountainous biryani sprinkled with *varak*. 'There, my darling, now eat to your heart's content.'

Staring at the rice and meats, inhaling it, his terror drowned beneath the ocean of his appetite. He looked into her eyes as his own flooded with tears. It was all going to be his.

Gregory Frost lives in Merion Station, Pennsylvania, and he has been writing and publishing stories of fantasy, horror and science fiction for two decades. His story 'How Meersh the Bedeviler Lost His Toes' was a finalist for the 1998 Theodore Sturgeon Memorial Award for Best Short Science Fiction. He has twice taught in the Clarion Writers programme at Michigan State University, of which programme he is also a graduate. He teaches fiction writing courses occasionally at the University of Pennsylvania, works as a publications designer, and is a student of aikido (where he wears the 'angry white pyjamas'). He is currently working on two fantasy novels, neither of which knows that the other exists. '"The Girlfriends of Dorian Gray" owes a debt of gratitude to two friendly dinner tables,' reveals Frost: 'first to that of Michael Swanwick and Marianne Porter, where the idea manifested; second to that of David and Karen O'Connell, where the story found an ending. I'm sure it had something to do with the wine.'

Bottle Babies

MARY A. TURZILLO

Allie first saw the fairies in the flower garden beside the driveway, and they were naked. But maybe they would be her friends. She didn't have any friends because Mom and Dad didn't want people to come into the house and discover Bobby.

How to make friends with them, when they were almost invisible?

She thought the spicy-fragrant petunia blossoms were small enough to make skirts for them; she knew they were girl-fairies because of their long hair, lavender, pink, and pale green, but her eyes weren't good enough to see if they had nipples, like her own, which must be concealed. Perhaps a tiny cloverleaf could cover each breast, though she wasn't sure how to keep them in place.

'Mom,' she said, 'may I borrow some thread?'

Mom's sharp grey gaze flicked away from the needlework scene of a Japanese garden she was doing. Mom had all sorts of hobbies. 'You may have that black spool that's almost gone.'

Allie chewed the end of her braid. 'Colours would be better.'

Mom threw down her needlework in annoyance.

'I want to make little clothes.'

Dad came in. He was carrying one of Mom's bonsai plants. A little dwarf maple tree, just right for the fairies. 'Little clothes for who?'

'Not for Bobby. Bras.'

Allie was pretty sure she really had seen the little people. She also knew she had better not say any more about them. Some things, like Bobby, were not discussed even in the bosom of the family. 'For pretend little people.'

Dad spoke over her head to Mom. 'The child needs glasses, Sara. She's been seeing fairies in the garden again.'

'My daughter,' said Mom, taking the bonsai from him, 'will not wear glasses. My daughter is perfect.'

Men don't make passes at girls who wear glasses, Allie thought. Mom always said that. Allie felt no need for glasses. School was out for the summer. Anyway, she could see fine when the teacher put her in the front row.

'Black thread,' said Mom, and began to lay out the bonsai tools, scissors, wire, tweezers.

The black thread was so old it came on a wooden spool, but Allie didn't mind. It broke easily so she wouldn't have to use her kindergarten scissors, which didn't cut.

She carefully selected six petunias, two each of pink and white, one purple, and one purple-and-white striped. She snapped these off close to the stem and removed the stamens, making flared skirts. Next, she selected twelve cloverleaves and laid them in pairs on the walkway. A breeze stirred them. 'Darn,' she said softly, trying to line them up again.

A fairy darted out and placed the cloverleaves back in place.

Allie was too startled to say anything. She sort of believed in the fairies, but she also knew that she couldn't see very well, and as Dad said, was maybe making them up.

'Thank you,' she said, her voice softer than the rustle of the breeze through the zinnias. She broke off sections of thread, each two inches long, and glued them to the cloverleaves. The black wasn't all that bad, she decided. It looked like trim, like the white collar on her plaid church dress.

'Here you are,' she told the fairies.

Nothing happened.

Well, of course. Nothing happened while you were looking. It was like Bobby growing up and getting big enough to fill that whole bottle, when at first he had been just a baby. Carefully, she got up and walked away. She sat on the grass, eyes squeezed shut, while she counted to a hundred.

She opened her eyes.

The skirts and tops were still there.

'Well, have it your way.' She knew she couldn't stand counting to three hundred, or however much it might take, so she went into the house and read a book about a mouse that rode a motorcycle.

When she finished the book, she came outside and the six little skirts and tops were gone.

Elated, she ran all the way upstairs to Bobby's attic room.

Bobby was in his bottle, of course. She had watched the slow growing process that forced his body to conform to the bottle shape. His shoulders came up around his ears. His knees were wedged either side of his chin. His head was moulded into a cone-shape, to fit the neck of the bottle. He was naked, of course, but his crossed ankles covered his sex parts. Anyway, she had got used to his nakedness.

Lately he hadn't wanted to talk to her very much. He said he couldn't breathe.

'Bobby, *fairies*. In the garden!'

Bobby twisted his head away from her as much as he could. It was getting pretty tight in that bottle, which had originally been a thirty gallon dispenser for spring water, with a hole Daddy cut in the bottom just big enough to insert Bobby, who was then an infant. At least that's what they told her had happened. Bobby was thirteen, and she was only eight, so she had to believe what she was told.

'I wish I could take you down to see them,' she continued, knowing that her words were both kind and cruel. Kind, because Bobby had no other entertainment. Mom came up and read to him sometimes, and Dad would talk to him while he was flushing the bottle out, but they wouldn't even get him a television. They said radio was good enough, tuned to one of those light classics stations. Very boring.

But Allie knew she was being cruel, too. Bobby must really feel annoyed that he couldn't go down to the yard and watch the fairies.

Still, what could she do? When Allie had been four she had lugged her tricycle all the way up the stairs for Bobby to see. Dad had been really mad over that. Said she'd chipped the paint and banged holes in the staircase wall.

'They were just the right size to have a picnic under one of Mom's bonsai trees. Maybe the wisteria one.' Mom sometimes brought her hobbies upstairs to work on to keep Bobby company. 'They won't let Mom and Dad see them,' she continued conversationally. 'But you're a kid, so they'll come out for you.'

'My propinquity might differ,' said Bobby.

'Hm?' Sometime she didn't understand Bobby.

'I said, I am not your garden-variety rug-rat.'

'Well, I think they'd realise you were a kid. They might even be special nice to you because of your Williams syndrome.'

'The ordinariness-challenged have no advantage in life, Allie, despite what Mom and Dad and that teacher of yours feed your cranium.'

'But fairies are different.'

'Very well. Show me the gollldurn cluricaune.'

Allie put her face very close to Bobby's, so only the glass of the bottle kept them from touching. 'I can't, Bobby. They don't come inside. They belong in the garden.'

'Allie, you're losing it,' said Bobby. 'Delusional. Fairies, even I know, are unreal. Spawn of imagination.'

'I'll bring you one. They can be your friends. They're going to be my friends.'

Bobby made a face so hideous that Allie jumped back, making the bottle rock slightly. 'We have no friends. I'm a geek and you're a geeklette.'

'I don't live in a bottle,' said Allie, rubbing her elbow, which she'd scraped as she jumped back.

'Yes, you do. You just can't see it.'

Allie spent hours outdoors, much to her parents' satisfaction. 'Put bloom in those cheeks,' said Dad.

'Keep her nose out of a book,' said Mom, and went cross-eyed, mimicking Allie with her nose in a book.

The fairies came back and talked to Allie. *We like the clothes*, they said. *So amusing. But just the skirts. The bras had man-made stuff in them.*

'It was just cotton,' said Allie. 'I checked the spool.'

It had been passed through a steel needle. And there was the glue.

'This means you won't like me, doesn't it?'

Not necessarily. Do you have anything else for us? said the largest fairy.

'Like what?'

But they were gone.

'Bobby, they liked the skirts! But they want more stuff before they'll be friends with me. Help me think what I can get them.'

Bobby was in one of his moods. He just stared coldly at her.

'Please, Bobby! If they make friends with me, maybe they'll come and be friends with you. Wouldn't you like that?'

'Obfuscate,' said Bobby. 'Brunhilda. Prosencephalic equitation.'

'Stop it!' Nobody knew where Bobby got these words. He couldn't get at books to turn the pages. When Mom read to him, she always read stupid, simple children's books. Allie herself couldn't read well enough to be entertaining, and she certainly hadn't read him words like *prosencephalic*.

'Okay, sis, how about cornflakes and Cheerios? Tell them they're potato chips and doughuts. Throw a junk food pooka-picnic.'

'I don't know. They wouldn't wear the bras because the thread had been passed through a steel needle.'

'Maybe they wouldn't wear them because the bras were *ugly*.'

Next day, while Mom was carefully cutting the roots off a pretty little red maple sapling to make it a dwarf, Allie stole some Cheerios, which she dampened and dipped in powdered sugar, and some cornflakes. She tried to get salt to stick to the cornflakes. When she saw that the grains were too large, she crushed them between the bowls of two spoons, then sprinkled the pulverised salt over the flakes.

Heart pounding, she stole the cap from Mom's tube of glue and filled it with orange juice. She placed the tiny snack on a coaster, went out in the garden, and plunked herself down next to the lily-of-the-valley leaves, where she had first seen them.

After long minutes of waiting, she realised she would have to leave the food. They didn't like for her to see them too much.

The food was gone when she came back after lunch.

Thank you, said the fairies. *That was very strange.*

'Did you enjoy it?' asked Allie.

We didn't eat it. We fed it to toads we use to draw our gourd-carriage.

'Why—'

It burned our fingers. It had been touched by machinery.

Allie looked up and realised her father was squatting only a few feet away, weeding the marigold patch.

Why can't he hear you? she asked in a tiny whisper.

The fairies just laughed.

'Am I the only person who can hear you?'

Your neighbour's dog, Bandy, can hear us. If we like we can sing loud enough and high enough to poach his brain like a swallow's egg.

'But I can't really hear you.'

No.

'Then how do I know what you're saying?'

She knelt in the sunlight holding the empty coaster for a long time, but the fairies were gone.

'Bobby! They liked the cereal. They fed it to their horses.'

'Equitation,' said Bobby wearily. 'What mounts are these? Dragonflies?'

'Toads.'

'Don't tell Mother. She'd shit a manticore if she knew we had toads in the garden.'

When she went downstairs, Mom and Dad were having an argument.

'—not a bottle, it's a Skinner box. Don't make me tell you again,' said Dad.

'But germs get in there.'

'No, they don't. How would germs get in?'

'Carried by insects, Doug.'

'He's perfectly safe. You have to be careful with a child who has Williams syndrome.'

'He's old enough to switch him to an orgone box.'

'Sara, he's not even fourteen! An orgone box is more appropriate for children at puberty.'

'But he's got sores on his rump! You can see them. The orgone box is—'

'Sara, I will hose the bottle out *twice* a day if that will set your mind at rest. Now, shouldn't you be investigating—'

Allie ran upstairs to Bobby.

'Bobby, Dad is talking about hosing your bottle out twice a day.'

This bottle-washing – the equivalent of a daily bath – was bitterly unpleasant for Bobby, because it involved dumping several gallons of water mixed with disinfectant into the bottle. The water drained out the hole Dad had cut so long ago in the bottom, but sometimes the water level came up to Bobby's chin, and he feared drowning. Also, the water was often icy cold or scalding hot.

Still, the process was necessary, or Bobby would be up to his neck in his own wastes.

Bobby screamed, loud and long. Usually the bottle muffled his cries, but this time, Dad and Mom came running up the stairs.

'What have you done to him?' Dad snarled at Allie.

'Nothing. I just told him—'

'Nice girls don't tell. Nice girls mind their own business,' said Mom, hauling on Allie's pigtail so that Allie had to stand on tiptoe to avoid having her hair pulled out by the roots.

'Make them stop! Cease! Holy moly! Halt!' screamed Bobby, but it wasn't clear who he was screaming at.

Allie ran all the way downstairs and hid in the garage. She couldn't hear anything from there, even the voices of the fairies.

When she went upstairs again, Bobby's wispy, long hair was wet and he looked exhausted.

'Cryogenic lancination,' he whimpered. 'Could you turn on the heater?'

'They took the heater away when summer came.' She embraced the bottle and pressed her body against it.

'Mercy buckets, sibling.' Bobby closed his eyes and took a ragged breath. 'But your body-heat doesn't get through the glass much.'

'They're mean,' she said. 'Mean parents. I don't think any of the kids at school have such mean parents.'

'I'll warm up in time. It gets right califactive in here in the afternoons.'

'What would happen if I told my teacher you were here?'

'I don't know. Mom would pull all your hair out and make you wear a Dolly Parton wig, and Dad would pour peroxide in my bottle.'

'I could tell the fairies.'

'The fairies hardly like you anyway. They'd probably never come back if they realised you came from such kinked kith and kin.'

When Allie slunk down the back stairs, she heard Mom say, 'The point is, he's *growing*. And he's a bad influence on Allie. I say separate the two of them. Allie can go live with my mother, and we'll shift Bobby to the cellar. He'll be happier down there, with less to distract him.'

Allie sat down on the stairs, next to two of Mom's less successful bonsai, a hemlock that was tied almost in a knot and a rhododendron that refused to bloom.

'I disagree, Sara. Allie shows signs of being disturbed. It's not just that she needs glasses.'

'Please don't start that again. You know how I feel about doctors.'

'And the influences at her school are not exactly wholesome. But say she went into the Skinner box in the fall. You could home-school her. She'd still get an education—'

'Not another bottle-baby, Doug. She hasn't a thing wrong with her. And she's going to be my beauty queen, you'll see.'

'You win. The orgone box, then.'

'Bobby, what's an orgone box?' she ask her brother.

'Why?' His voice reflected deep suspicion.

'They think I'm crazy because of the fairies. And because I cried when Dad put ice-water in your bottle.' She hushed her voice and put her mouth at the very lip of his bottle. 'I think they want to send me away. Or put me in an orgone box. With a lock.'

Bobby banged his head against the glass of the bottle. He had less than a quarter inch to move his head in, but he banged it hard, and tensed his body as if trying to crack the bottle. 'I will kill them,' he said finally. 'I will think of a way to kill them.'

Allie wished she hadn't told him.

Allie explained the situation to the fairies.

None of them said anything for a long time. *Some of our kin have been captured by humans and put in bottles*, they said finally. *But it hasn't happened in a long time. We're too invisible for them.*

'I just wanted you to be friends with us,' Allie said. 'But Mom thinks I'm beautiful, and Dad thinks I need glasses.'

What have you to trade? asked the fairies.

'Little trees,' said Allie reluctantly.

We have all the trees we need, big and small.

'These are special little trees. My mother made them out of saplings, by cutting their roots off and twisting their branches. They're very beautiful. They look like trees in a fairy garden. You could have little picnics under them, or put swings in them and play.'

Would your mother be very angry if we took them?

'Oh, she would be horribly angry. She would—' Allie almost said that Mom would get spray made specially to exterminate fairies, but thought better of it. 'She would punish me if she found out.'

Mmmmmm, mused the queen fairy. *Mustn't get our little friend in trouble, eh, ladies? And yet—*'

'I could drink coffee and stay up late at night. Then I'll bring them out to you. But I'd have to take them back on the upstairs porch before dawn.'

Clever child! said the queen fairy. *Very well. We'll go see your brother and we'll divert your parents' attention so they won't put you in a bottle.*

'Divert them?'

Do not trouble yourself. We are the fairies. We dazzle women's minds.

'And you'll be our friends?'

The fairies laughed, musically. *Of course, clever child! We are the soul of conviviality.* And they began to sing, higher than Allie could hear, but very loud. She had to clap her hands over her ears. Her head hurt so badly she wanted to scream.

When Mom was in the bathroom next morning, and Dad had already gone to work, Allie poured the remains of the morning coffee into a large mayonnaise jar and hid it in the closet of her room. All day, she wanted to tell Bobby she had solved their problems. But Bobby was acting very strange and kept saying that he would kill his parents. He didn't say how.

At night, she went to bed and lay in the dark, listening to the fairies laughing outside. Strange that she hadn't heard them until just last week. Their voices were very sweet, but so high and loud that her ears rang.

She knew her parents and Bobby couldn't hear them, but all the dogs in the neighbourhood bayed. How would her parents fall asleep so that she could sneak the bonsai out to them? She began to cry, big racking sobs, hot tears and snot running onto the pillow. And then the fairy laughter stopped, and the dogs settled down. She checked her clock, and it was midnight.

In bare feet and white pyjamas, she went to the closet. She had left it open so it wouldn't creak when she got the coffee. She drank it and lay down, listening to hear if her parents were asleep yet.

Ready, said a voice, jarring her awake.

She sat up, rubbed her eyes, and looked at the clock. Three o'clock! She had fallen asleep.

Grimly, she plodded downstairs to her mother's hobby room.

The hobby room was a wonder: exquisite needlework scenes of ladies in flowing gowns and veils, lampshades made of jewelled buttons and beads, macramé dresses on porcelain dolls with gauze wings. Most of the bonsai lived on the upstairs screened porch, but mother had left several in the hobby room for further pruning and potting.

Allie picked out two, a pyracantha just coming into bloom, and a juniper with miniature bamboo grass and a stone lantern the size of Allie's thumb. The juniper was supposed to be very valuable. It was over fifty years old. Both smelled sweet and earthy, like the grave in which Dad had buried a dead robin. With one in each hand, she tiptoed out into the kitchen, down the back steps, into the garden.

The garden was flooded with moonlight, and nightfrogs warbled. The neighbour's dog Bandy yapped once, then was silent.

'Fairies,' she whispered. 'I'm here.'

Ahhhhh, said the queen fairy. *Very lovely. Your mother is clever, clever.*

'What about me?' Fairies swarmed out of the lily-of-the-valley leaves and from under the periwinkle. They climbed into the containers that held the bonsai, scrambled up branches, swung from limbs, rolled in the moss, and plucked blossoms.

If you were clever, human child, would you be here?

'You promised,' said Allie.

Sooooooothe, sang all the fairies.

When Allie woke, sunlight was beating down on her left cheek, and her right was ground into the grass. Her parents were standing over her.

'Now are you willing to listen?' asked her father.

'She's going to be my little beauty queen,' said Mom, that whiny tone in her voice. 'Bobby wasn't right, but my little girl is perfectly all right.'

'Sleepwalking!'

'Other children have done it.'

'It's the children at her school.'

Allie could no longer pretend to be asleep. She sat up and rubbed her eyes.

'What have you done to my bonsai?' said Mom.

The containers held only churned earth and stumps.

Allie was ashamed to visit Bobby that day, and afraid to go into the house. Mom had not yet decreed a punishment for the destruction of the bonsai. Dad went to work and Mom stayed in the house, never even calling Allie for lunch. So Allie hid in the garage, gloomily inhaling the smell of gasoline from the lawnmower and wishing the fairies would come back. But the fairies never came in buildings. That was a strict rule. Wasn't it? There had to be some explanation.

She got hungry, but not hungry enough to go into the house. She was thinking of running away. But how could she leave without Bobby? He really would go crazy if he didn't have her to talk to.

When dusk fell – very late, because it was summer, Allie knew – she crept out into the yard and crouched beside the geraniums. Dad's Studebaker was in the drive, but neither parent had come to find her, nobody had called her for dinner. She was very hungry now, even a little sick. The geranium leaves smelled like carrots, so she nibbled one, but it was bitter and she spat it out.

'Fairies,' she called tentatively. Abandoned by humanfolk, maybe she was now one of their kind, and they would answer.

Human girl, said the high voice, just as she was ready to give up.

'How did you chop down the little trees?' she asked. 'I thought you were not allowed things of steel.'

There was a long silence, then a *whir* as a fairy flew by her face. Instinctively, Allie batted it away. But when she touched her face, her fingers came away smeared with blood.

The light was on in the kitchen, and through the window she could see Mom and Dad eating dinner. Carefully, so the screen door would not squeak, she stole onto the back stairs and listened.

'—come back when she feels like it, the scheming brat. I told her—'

Allie squeezed her eyes shut. She must run away now, she was sure. Whatever punishment they had devised would be too horrible to imagine. And the fairies were no help – on the contrary, they were bad; they had killed a fifty-year-old bonsai tree that Mom had paid a lot of money for.

The door between the stairwell and the kitchen was ajar. If she crawled, she could make it to her bedroom to pack and from there to the attic to say goodbye to Bobby.

She had an idea. She would go first to the basement and get a brick. She would shatter Bobby's bottle, and he could run away with her.

Where would she go? To an orphanage, maybe, or perhaps she could get some kindly couple with a baby to take her in as a nanny. She would be very sure they were a nice couple, and not planning to bottle or box their children. Bobby could get a job mowing lawns, or perhaps teaching vocabulary lessons.

Allie pushed her bedroom door open and immediately knew something was wrong. There was a damp smell, like the peat moss Dad put down in the garden, or like the humus Mom mixed with the soil of her bonsai.

In the centre of the room, blocking her access to the closet, was a big box, like a coffin, with the lid open. It was lined with damp, green carpety stuff that had little stems sticking up from it. Some of the stems had flowers or berries on them. She placed her hand on the pillow-like hummock at one end. It was cool. Live moss.

On the outside, opposite the hinges, was a hasp with an open padlock dangling from it.

If they put her in that box, she would never, never have friends, and she would never be able to rescue Bobby.

She decided she didn't need to take clothes with her. She carefully opened the bottom drawer of her dresser and took out the tin Easter egg in which she hid her life savings. Without counting the money – she remembered that it was over twenty dollars – she slipped it in the pocket of her pinafore.

The brick was heavy and awkward, but she dragged it to the attic.

'Bobby!' she hissed. 'Bobby, wake up!' She brought the brick down on the shoulder of Bobby's bottle with all her might.

Bobby shrieked, but the bottle was tougher than she thought. It didn't break.

'Be quiet! We're going to run away!' she whispered. She brought the brick down again, but nothing happened except that the bottle clanged like a gong.

She brought the brick down a third time, and Bobby screamed, 'Stop! The glass will cut me, and I'll bleed to death!'

Footsteps pounded on the stairs. Mom's strong hands ripped the brick out of her hand. Dad hoisted her over his shoulder. She dangled there, screaming, dizzy with the height of the stair, as he strode down, down, to her bedroom.

She kicked and fought, tears streaming like blood from her face, but the two of them packed her into the mossy coffin, threw the hasp, and slammed the padlock shut.

There was, she discovered, plenty of air. It was cool in the coffin (this must be an orgone box, she realised), and the dirt-smelling moss tendrils tickled her face. She flexed her arms against the sides, and tried to draw her knees up to kick, but there wasn't room. There was, maybe, just room for her to grow a few inches. She gave over to crying, softly and hopelessly, and the moss drank up her tears.

She cried for a long time, then dozed, dreaming that she was a bonsai tree, or a funeral arrangement, something expensive and cool Mom had brought home from the florist.

Someone was cutting her roots, and it didn't even hurt.

She had no way of knowing how long she had been in the box, breathing dew-moist mossy air. It might have been an hour. It might have been weeks. But she heard someone turning the tumblers of the lock. By this time, she was too overcome with the scent of the moss and the coolness that had sunk into her bones to think of escape. Even if Mom threw the box open and invited her to step out, would she have the energy?

The lock fell away, and nothing happened. The lid did not open. Mom and Dad's big faces did not peer in with their toxic concern for her. She was glad, for she was certain that they would have scissors and wires and potting soil, to change her into Mom's beauty, the beauty that Mom planned to make her.

She just wanted them to lock it again, leave her alone. Tomorrow she might fight. Tomorrow, or a week or a month from now. Fall. That was plenty of time Perhaps she would start fighting when fall came.

Open it, human.

'What? Mom?'

We certainly don't have the strength to open it for you. Open the lid. Or stay there and rot.

Allie pushed feebly with her arms. The lid creaked back. She turned and heaved with her whole body.

'I thought fairies were not allowed in human buildings,' she said.

The orgone box drew us. Still, it is a power we find unsuited to a young girl, so we free you from it. Run, now girling. The grey large ones are in the top of the house stealing the one who lives in glass.

'Bobby? Somebody is stealing Bobby?'

The large ones. Run from them. They are too dead for us to kill, and they are not part of our world. We have no power over them.

Allie sat up, and nearly blacked out. The orgone box seemed to have drained all her strength. She managed to roll over and balance on her hands and knees. From there, she carefully put a foot on the ground and heaved herself out.

She sat on the floor for a long time, hands over her eyes.

'Fairies?'

No answer. She willed herself to climb to her feet and stand, supporting herself against the dresser. She was afraid if she touched the orgone box she would fall back into it and never get out again.

She took a few shaky steps to the door and opened it a crack.

Heavy footsteps sounded on the stairs from the attic. She jerked the door closed again just as she saw a shadow – Dad's shadow, she was sure – on the hall landing.

Why were they going so slow?

They must have Bobby! She had to do something, anything. Even the fairies knew something had to happen, and fast.

There was a telephone in Mom's room, by her bed. If she waited until Mom and Dad had dragged Bobby in his bottle to the stairs from the second to the ground floor, she could get to the bedroom phone, she was sure.

She lay on the floor and peeked under the door. She couldn't see Mom and Dad from this angle, except just when they rounded the landing and started down the lower staircase.

Then she waited and listened to make sure they were down far enough so she wouldn't be seen.

Holding her breath, she slid through the door, tiptoed down the hall, and wrenched the knob to her mother's room.

Someone was in the room. A ghost in white.

No.

It was her reflection in her mother's full-length mirror.

She darted over to the bed and picked up the phone.

She stared at the big black dial. Who could she call?

O!

'Can you please please help me?' she begged, when the operator came on the line.

'You have to dial information,' said the operator, politely enough.

'No! I'm alone in the house and something awful is happening. I need—'

'You need the police?'

Police? They might help! 'Yes, please!'

Four long rings, and a woman's voice answered, 'Is this an emergency?'

'Yes, oh yes, it is!'

'What is your address?'

'I don't know! I can't remember! Please, they have my brother in a bottle and they're taking him to the basement. He'll die in the basement!'

'Little girl—'

Allie squeezed shut her eyes, and bright spots pinged in her vision. Why wouldn't anybody take her seriously?

'Little girl! Listen, I need your address. I can't send help if I don't know where you are.'

Allie tried to think. 'Asphodel Street.'

'The house number. Do you know your house number?'

'No.' Allie wept. She couldn't remember the house number or her phone number.

'Little girl, what's your name?'

Allie told her.

Rustling of pages. 'Ah! That's 222 Asphodel. Does that sound right?'

'Yes.'

'Now tell me what's wrong.'

'My brother. They put him in a bottle, and now they're going to put him in the basement. They locked me in a box with moss in it, but the fairies let me out—' The minute Allie said it, she realised she shouldn't have brought the fairies into the story.

'Allie. Your name is Allie? Allie, you know you shouldn't tell stories to the police.' A deep breath. 'But somehow I think you're not just acting. You sound horribly upset about something. The question is, what? Can I speak with one of your parents?'

'*No!*' Allie screamed. 'They'll kill me. They'll put me back in that box and I'll never get out again.'

'Hold on.'

Allie let the receiver sink into her lap and wiped her nose on the tail of her pyjama top.

A shadow fell across the floor in front of her.

Mom said, 'Now how did you get out?' She grabbed Allie's arm and wrenched her to her feet. Allie went limp – a trick she had seen older children use in the schoolyard – then twisted away. She slithered under the bed.

'Doug!' screamed Mom. 'Doug, leave the bottle down there for a minute and come here. We have a problem.' Mom's face, dark with fury, peered at her from the edge of the bed. Allie scuttled as far away as she could.

Faintly, from the telephone receiver, Allie could hear a voice: 'We're sending a patrol car right now. Tell me where you are in the house.' Then, softly, 'Better safe than sorry. Crazy kids.'

Mom's voice: 'That really isn't necessary. We have everything under control now. Sorry my daughter bothered you. No, no, of course we'll go easy on her. She's just a child, after all.'

Dad's voice: 'How the hell did she get out?'

The bristles of a broom poked under the bed, nearly stabbing Allie in the eye.

'Oh, for heaven's sakes!' said Mom's voice. Sounds of bedding being yanked aside. 'Help me, Doug!'

In a moment, the mattress and springs shifted and were tipped sideways beside the bed. Allie, completely exposed now, screamed. Dad lunged over the bedframe and grabbed her, his huge hand clamped over her mouth. 'Atta girl. Just calm down, Allie. Nobody's going to hurt you.'

'*I'm* going to hurt her,' said Mom. 'What in the world do you mean, making prank calls to the police? Don't you know that's a serious crime in this state? In any state! Back in the box until we figure out an appropriate punishment. For this, *and* for what you did to my two best bonsai.'

Dad's big hand was stopping Allie's breath. She struggled to scream, to breathe! Tears and snot ran onto Dad's hand, and she bit him.

He was so surprised that he let go. Allie hadn't meant to bite her father, but when she saw she was free, she ran towards the door. Mom caught her pigtail and yanked. 'For God's sake, Doug, how can you let a little imp like this defeat you?' She caught Allie's ear in a grip like a pair of pliers. 'Back to the box, you little demon!'

The doorbell rang.

Mom and Dad froze.

Mom tightened her grip on Allie's ear. 'Doug, just go answer it. You don't have to let them in. They can't have a search warrant this fast. By the time they can come back, we'll have everything tidied up.'

Dad clumped down the stairs and went to the front door. Allie could hear muffled voices. She drew in a breath to scream, but her mother stuffed a corner of the bedspread into her mouth.

Allie heard male voices, but couldn't understand enough to know what was going on. The voices all sounded friendly, almost apologetic.

'No, she's gone to bed. Fell right asleep, poor little tyke. We shouldn't have let her stay up this late. She gets over-excited and pulls these pranks. You can come by in the morning if you like, although I hope you won't file a complaint against her. She's a good girl, basically, just full of the devil.'

More inaudible words, then the front door swung shut. A sound like the closing of a coffin lid, thought Allie, like the closing of the orgone box lid.

The loss of hope was almost more than Allie could bear. It had been so close! The police had been right there, at the door, and they had believed Dad instead of her. She would spend her life in a moss-lined box, Bobby would go insane in the basement with nobody to talk to, neither of them would ever have a friend, not even one, not even each other.

'Fairies!' she shrieked. Mother snorted in impatience. Dogs began to bark.

First only the neighbour's dog Bandy, then the dogs across the street, then more dogs, hundreds. Above the howling, Allie could hear the sound of fairy voices. Not laughing now, not singing.

Screaming at full volume.

Allie screamed too, not because she wanted to, but because of the pain in her head. Her mother twisted her ear, then suddenly let go and began screaming. Then her father bellowed. Both had their eyes squeezed shut, their hands over their ears.

Glass shattered.

And Bobby screamed.

Bobby had probably been screaming all along, but the bottle muffled his voice.

'Bobby! Bobby, I'm coming, Bobby!' Allie, suddenly free, jerked away from her mother and ran down the stairs.

Bobby lay among shards of glass, blood running from cuts on his arms, torso, legs, face, all over.

She had always thought of Bobby as, well, *short*. He would never be any taller than the bottle he was in, she thought. But now he lay, a grey-white snail free of its shell, on the kitchen landing. His legs, twisted as they were, were long. His hands lapped uselessly at the end of rubbery, snake-like arms. In the uncoiling, his sex parts were revealed, and Allie was deeply embarrassed to see that he had hair and genitals just like those in a marriage manual she had sneaked a peek at once.

Bobby flailed, yelling and weeping, trying to coil up into the protective unborn shape in which he had spent his whole life. Allie knelt amidst the broken glass and tenderly picked shards out of Bobby's face.

Someone was pounding at the back door now. Mom and Dad

shuffled down the stairs and, holding hands tightly, gazed in uncertain dread as two policemen kicked the door in.

The dogs stopped barking.

Mary A. Turzillo lives in Ohio, where she once taught art and theatre students at Kent State University. She quit teaching four years ago to write full time. She has published two volumes of criticism, two chapbooks of poetry, and had stories in such magazines as *Interzone*, *The Magazine of Fantasy & Science Fiction*, *Science Fiction Age*, *Weird Tales*, *Asimov's* and *Redbook*, along with appearances in various anthologies. She placed second in the 1997 Rhysling Awards and was a finalist for the British Science Fiction Association Award and a winner of the 1999 Nebula Award. She is currently working on a novel about a Martian serial murderer. About her contribution to this volume, the author reveals: 'This story is autobiographical. The fairies were real; I saw them. And although I don't have a brother, my mother's best friend did have Williams syndrome. I admit the bottle came out of a history textbook two of my students showed me. My parents would never do that to me or my sister.'

Going to Series

KIM NEWMAN

MEMO
From: Tiny Chiselhurst, producer/creator
To: April Treece, junior researcher
Re: Untitled Docusoap/Gameshow Pilot

Here's final draft of the flyer. Every word approved by Dr Wendel and Miss Lark as calculated to reach the cross-section of personality types we need.

EVERYDAY MEGASTARS WANTED
Is this you? 18–45, sexy, extrovert, killer body, unconventional, tagged 'difficult' by lesser mortals, ambitious, unattached, competitive, 'bonkers', up for anything? Apply: Mythwrhn Productions, Box 101, Leech Pyramid Plaza, London Docklands.

As a classified ad, this is to go into the following periodicals: *Big Bazookas*, the *Sunday Comet*, the *Nazi Atrocities* part-work, *Young Offender*, *Pop Hitz* and *Shy Girl Monthly*. As a flyer, it is to be distributed via inner city clubs, comic shops, student union buildings, social security offices and police stations. We agree that we should target especially the waiting rooms of probation officers and court-approved psychotherapists, the business places of drugs and weapons dealers, abortion and VD clinics, all-night casualty wards, Young Conservative meetings, and pubs that cater to the motorcycle, rugby football, slag-on-the-pull and stockbroking communities. Word from the top of the Pyramid is that Cloud 9 (Derek Leech!) is really hyped on this project, so let's get things moving.

SERIES PROPOSAL
This seven-part (initial run) series combines three of the most popular (and, let's face it, economical) TV formats of the last ten years: fly-on-the-wall docusoap, slags-on-holiday mock doc

and sci-fi/adventure gameshow. A group of charismatic, sexy young chicks and chaps, strangers to each other, are brought together in a luxurious, Bond-style environment (country estate, mountaintop hunting lodge, beach house) and have to spend a week together. Cut off from civilisation, the contestants (subjects, stars?) are in contact with a host – we think we can get US smartmouth obonxio-comic Barry Gatlin, but other options are Ruby Wax or someone off *Star Trek* – who communicates via video-link each evening and sets tasks and competitions, which range from puzzle-solving exercises through treasure hunting on the grounds of the luxury retreat and harmless combat games to how-low-can-you-go? gross-out or endurance dares. Meanwhile, the stars are on camera day and night; we trust that days of strenuous competition will be followed by evenings of unwinding in wild, entertaining and provocative manners. Over the course of the week, we will see how each contestant scores, in every imaginable way.

Tiny Chiselhurst, Creator and Owner

[NB: THIS IS FOR SENDING TO THE APPLICANTS ONLY, AND SHOULD UNDER NO CIRCUMSTANCES BE CONFUSED WITH THE REAL SERIES PROPOSAL, WHICH IS AVAILABLE ON AN EYES ONLY NEED-TO-KNOW BASIS TO SECURITY-CLEARED INSIDERS AT MYTHWRHN AND CLOUD 9 – TINY]

Dear Potential Megastar,

Thank you for your interest. Please fill in the attached form and return it to me at Mythwrhn Productions.

This isn't an exam: the answers you give aren't right or wrong, but will help us determine whether you are the type of person for our show. Don't think too hard or try to give answers you think we want. Be yourself.

All forms are confidential.

Best wishes,

April Treece, Researcher

ARE YOU A MEGASTAR?

1: Please write your name, age, contact details, next of kin, and rough annual income.
2: Sex?
   ... male.
   ... female.

... yes, please!
   ... don't know.
3: How many jobs have you had since leaving school?
4: Do you feel yourself to be ...
   ... attractive to the opposite sex.
   ... unattractive to the opposite sex.
   ... attractive to the same sex.
   ... horny.
   ... a love god/goddess in the flesh.
5: How many sex partners have you had per year, on average, since the age of twelve?
6: Do you feel yourself to be ...
   ... more intelligent than the average.
   ... less intelligent than the average.
   ... of average intelligence.
   ... too intelligent to be measured by this stupid question.
   ... a real Brainiac.
   ... a spoon.
7: If attacked in your home, what household items would you use to defend yourself?
8: Which of these describes you?
   ... a conformist.
   ... a maverick.
   ... a team-player.
   ... scary.
   ... a tosser.
   ... a leader.
   ... a nurturer.
   ... a bitch.
   ... the best there is at what you do.
   ... a disappointment.
9: Have you ever broken a law and not been caught? If so, please give details.
10: Would you be willing to do severe harm to ...
   ... an enemy soldier on a battlefield.
   ... a violent criminal threatening your mother.
   ... a Member of Parliament.
   ... a spastic.
   ... your mother.
   ... a wounded animal.
   ... a stranger.
   ... no one at all, under any circumstances.

... a television personality.
... a former boy or girlfriend who treated you badly.

11: Would you have sex with someone unappealing just because they were famous, notorious, physically unusual, or on television? If you have, please give details.

12: When Bambi's mother was shot, what was your reaction?
    ... it was very tragic and sad.
    ... the bitch got what she deserved.
    ... venison pies, yum!
    ... Bambi ought to avenge his family.
    ... Who's Bambi?

13: Have you ever written an anonymous letter or made a prank phone call? If so, please give details.

14: When you broke up with your last boy or girlfriend, was it ...
    ... just one of those things.
    ... all for the best, really.
    ... your fault
    ... their fault.
    ... a prelude to revenge.
    ... one more fucking thing on your plate.
    ... never had a boy or girlfriend, and don't much like the sound of it.

15: Would you play a computer game called *Dunblane Massacre*?

16: Have you ever ...
    ... performed in a karaoke pub.
    ... had sex with two or more partners simultaneously.
    ... experienced memory loss after alcohol or drug intake.
    ... been on television.
    ... considered joining the armed forces.
    ... had sex in a public place.
    ... used terms of racial ('nigger', 'chink') or sexual ('cunt', 'queer') abuse in general conversation.
    ... deliberately botched a job interview.
    ... stalked a celebrity.
    ... got your own back on someone who had done you a wrong.

17: Which of the Spice Girls would you most like to rape?

18: Do you believe in ...
    ... UFO abductions.
    ... Our Lord, Jesus Christ.
    ... other people's pain.
    ... microwaves.
    ... ghosts.
    ... an eye for an eye.

... Swedish Sin.
... yourself.
... turning the other cheek.
... capital punishment.

19: When was the last time you were really happy? Please give details. If never, please give details.

20: Could you take a week off from your life/work/family to star in a television series? Please answer honestly, to save time later.

PRODUCTION SUB-MEETING, No. 19.

PRESENT, for MYTHWRHN PRODUCTIONS: April Treece (Featured Researcher), Claire Bates (Minion), Davinda Paquignet (Recording Angel).

BATES: Can I just say, off the record, how much I *hate* this proposal.
TREECE: Get in the queue, Claire. Tiny's got this bonnet bee that they love it at the top of the Pyramid. It's all the things Derek Leech, our ultimate lord and master at Cloud 9 Television, is supposed to be keen on. Cheap, crass, cruel and compulsive.
BATES: And crap!
TREECE: You might say that. I couldn't possibly comment.
BATES: Dav, stop writing this down!
PAQUIGNET: Sorry, force of habit.
BATES: Ape, have you sorted through the completed forms?
TREECE: God, yes.
BATES: Where did we find these sickos?
TREECE: Milling about in general population.
BATES: 'Which of the Spice Girls would you most like to rape?' What sort of question is that? A bit sex-specific, surely.
TREECE: The responses are 75 per cent male.
BATES: Sur-prise.
TREECE: So far as we can tell. Those who ticked 'yes, please' for 'sex?' are sometimes hard to work out. And those are our pass applicants.
BATES: They'll be men. Or really dim tarts.
TREECE: A frightening number of women responded. Some skipped the Spice question. Some didn't. A few nominated male equivalents. You wouldn't think anyone could have those fantasies about Frank Dobson or ...
BATES: Ugh! Don't say any more! I don't want to know!

PAQUIGNET: I didn't think it was possible to have the amount of sex most of these people say they have.
TREECE: Not if you work in television, it isn't.
BATES: Too bloody right.
TREECE: Dr Wendel says to divide that answer by ten to get a proper figure. Except for the ones who claim to be virgins. Half of them aren't lying.
PAQUIGNET: What about the lad who gave names and addresses? Are we supposed to phone the victims up to check him out?
TREECE: No wonder he can't keep a steady girlfriend.
BATES: If you had a party, would you want any of these people to come?
TREECE: God, no. But this is Tiny's baby, and we have to carry it to term, no matter how we feel. Look, Claire, it's a looney idea and even Derek Leech wouldn't seriously consider putting it out. We're more likely to see live bullfighting on British TV than this horror, so we won't get hurt. Let's go as far with it as we have to before Tiny, inevitably, changes his mind.
BATES: I don't want my name on any of the documentation, or a credit on any proposal or pilot. I'm serious. I don't want a paper trail connecting me to this . . . this atrocity. Dav, stop bloody writing!

```
Dear Loser
Thank you for your interest. Unfortunately, you are not the per-
son we - or anyone else - are looking for at this time.
   We wish you joy in your continued obscurity.
       Sincerely,
          April Treece, Rejecter-in-Chief
```

```
MEMO
From:   April Treece, senior researcher
To:     Tiny Chiselhurst, producer/creator
Re:     Horrible People Pilot
```

We sent out entry forms to the first 5,000 people who responded to the ad or the flyer and got 2,389 completed returns. I passed on the 968 papers with 'yes, please!' ticked for Question Two – the famous 'trigger signal' – to Dr Wendel and Miss Lark, who have evaluated them all and selected 178 'possibles'. I'm astonished not only at the number of people out there who have sent anonymous letters but are proud enough of the fact to boast about it at enormous length, continuing onto the other side of the paper, to strangers. As requested, I've sent a curt rejection letter to all 178 and ignored the rest.

I still don't believe this is going to fly, or that even Cloud 9 will broadcast it if it does. That said, reading over the completed forms, I'm starting to understand why audiences might actually enjoy watching the show. Are real people really this awful? The runners have stuck up their favourite forms on the message board. At the moment, the champion is the Sporty Spice fan who would see off an attacker by taking a mouthful of bleach and offering a blow-job, though my clear winner is the 'nurturer' guy or girl (ambiguous name and no helpful answer to Q2) who claims to have shagged seven of Dr Who's companions (not including K-9, I trust). Do we have a title yet?

MEMO
From: Tiny Chiselhurst, producer/creator
To: April Treece, chief researcher
Re: Bedlam Unplugged

Any of the 'possibles' who get back to us to complain about the 'Dear Loser' letters should be invited for interview. Please note whether applicants complain via e-mail, telephone or the post, and pass print-outs, recordings and photocopies to Dr Wendel and Miss Lark. Anyone not classed as a 'possible' who complains we haven't got back to them should also be considered for interview if the complaint shows the proper character type. Taking the usual wastage into account, we only need a dozen or so strong candidates.

I know the troops have their doubts about this, Ape, but I've got a gut feeling that it is going to be a winner! At present, Cloud 9 is inclining towards a neutral title like *A Week Off* or *Microcosm*, though I'm all for something as blunt as *It's a Madhouse!* or *The Pit* and cleverclogs Bender has voted for *The Raft of the Medusa*. How does one go about offering someone a blow-job if one has a mouthful of bleach? Sign language. And if you threw a brick in the Soho House, you'd be lucky to hit someone who hadn't shagged seven of Dr Who's companions. Onwards and upwards!

INTERVIEW TRANSCRIPT, NO. 17.

APPLICANT: HARRY 'DONGER' BENNETT, 32.
FOR MYTHWRHN: Tiny Chiselhurst, Dr Vernon Wendel, Myra Lark, April Treece.

LARK: Harry . . .
BENNETT: Everyone calls me 'Donger'. Ever since school.
LARK: Ah, Donger . . . first, we must apologise for the mix-up with the letter.
BENNETT: So you should. Nearly missed your chance there, didn't you?
LARK: Indeed.
BENNETT: But I like your whole approach, really. 'Dear Loser'. No poncing about there. Puts the losers right in their place. The real losers. I like to see that.
LARK: You describe yourself as competitive?
BENNETT: No. I would describe myself as a winner. It's just a fact of life. Ever since school.
LARK: You did well in school?
BENNETT: Too right. Fighting them off, I was. Had half the Sixth Form, and a couple of the younger teachers. The beginning of a great career.
LARK: And academically?
BENNETT: Rugby, football, basketball. Everything. Except cricket. That's for poofs.
LARK: You don't like, uh, homosexuals?
BENNETT: Show me a bloke who says he does and I'll show you a poof. It's not a natural thing, is it? Whatever they say these days.
LARK: You've never been married?
BENNETT: I've been engaged a couple of times, if that's what it takes to get the cork to pop.
LARK: It's important that you be unattached, for the show. Do you have a girlfriend?
BENNETT: A couple, actually. But no one I can't chuck if something tasty comes along.
LARK: You understand, then, that there's a certain standard of, ah, wildness expected on shows like this.
BENNETT: I've seen my share. Holidays in the sun. Drunken tarts gagging for it. Is this like that?
LARK: There's an element of that format, but there's also a game aspect, a competitive streak. Physical competition.
BENNETT: *Blind Date Meets Gladiators?*

LARK: You might say that. You look as if you could look after yourself.
BENNETT: I've had my share of scrapes. I come out on top. By any means necessary, if you know what I mean and I think you do.
LARK: You work for an estate agent?
BENNETT: I work *as* an estate agent. It's just what I do in the days. History is made at night.
LARK: Do you like your job?
BENNETT: I like helping people. Setting families on the road to home-ownership.
LARK: Really. Really?
BENNETT: Well, no. You're sharp That's what we're supposed to say. I like the push and the commission. There are so many ways to make something work to your advantage. That side of it is fun, but there's always a problem with the pillocks.
LARK: The pillocks?
BENNETT: Buyers, sellers, the lot of them. Pillocks. Always pulling out at the last minute, or screaming that they've been rooked, that they weren't told something it was their business to find out. You know the sort. Pillocks.
CHISELHURST: Donger, do you find April attractive?
BENNETT: Phwoarr!
TREECE: Really, Tiny.
BENNETT: No, fair question. You look very good for your age, Miss Treece. April. Smart. Good clothes. I like that. Not like some of the shag-slags. Some women put on a suit and look dikey, but not you.
CHISELHURST: If Dr Wendel came at you in a pub with a knife, could you take him?
BENNETT: No offence, but yes.
WENDEL: You might be surprised.
BENNETT: Like I said, I'm a winner. If he had a knife and I didn't, I'd bottle him. End of story. It's not even that he's older and smaller, but it's that he hasn't got the heart. Most people haven't. Too squeamish.
CHISELHURST: Thank you, Harry . . . ah, Donger. We'll be in touch.
BENNETT: Have I passed? Is there anyone behind the mirror?
CHISELHURST: We have enjoyed this interview.
BENNETT: I'm in, aren't I? I bloody knew it. You won't regret this. You need me. I'm a natural for your show, what's it called?
TREECE: Provisionally, *It's a Madhouse!* It may change.

BENNETT: *It's a Madhouse!*, yeah. I like that. Anything can happen in the next half hour. Anything.
CHISELHURST: April will show you out, ah, 'Donger'.
BENNETT: Excellent. I'll be back. Ka-poww!

INTERVIEW TRANSCRIPT, NO. 34.

APPLICANT: SHONA MURTAUGH, 24
FOR MYTHWRHN: Tiny Chiselhurst, Dr Vernon Wendel, Myra Lark, April Treece.

WENDEL: So, Shona . . .
MURTAUGH: [high-pitched giggles]
WENDEL: I beg your pardon?
MURTAUGH: 'So, Shona'. Sounds funny like that. [high-pitched giggles] Are you all right? Look like you've swallowed a lemon, you do.
WENDEL: It'll pass.
MURTAUGH: [high-pitched giggles]
   [noise of glasses and bottles rattling on table]
WENDEL: I beg your pardon.
MURTAUGH: You're funny, you are. You've got to have a laugh, haven't you, though. [high-pitched giggles]
WENDEL: It's not actually a physiological necessity, but there may be some psychological explanation.
MURTAUGH: You what? You talk mental, you do. [high-pitched giggles]
CHISELHURST: We were interested in your sexual history.
MURTAUGH: [extremely high-pitched giggles]
CHISELHURST: Well, Shona, we were. You seem to have been an unusually busy girl.
MURTAUGH: I just like . . . [high-pitched giggles]
WENDEL: We're not here to judge you.
MURTAUGH: Yes, you are. To see if I'm right for your show.
   [noise of bracelets clattering]
WENDEL: Well, of course, in that sense, you're right.
MURTAUGH: You should watch what you say. People might think you were taking liberties. People might not like that. People might not like that at all, thank you very much indeed. I should cocoa.
   [thump on table]

WENDEL: I apologise.
MURTAUGH: So you should, so you should. [high-pitched giggles] I can't help it. It's your face. You look like a bearded collie. I think I'll wet my knickers. I'm mad, me. You must think I'm dreadful. Sorry.
   [faint grinding of teeth]
LARK: Others have noted the, ah, resemblance between Dr Wendel and a dog.
MURTAUGH: [high-pitched giggles] I'll do myself an injury at this rate. You're a funny mob, aren't you? Not outright funny like Jim Davidson, but it's the way you say things, all sly and clever but with hidden meanings. It's all there, isn't it? You must have enough cleverness to get to the moon in this room, eh? All to get to the bottom of me. It don't seem right. I should be trying to get to the bottom of you.
TREECE: You're not working at the moment.
MURTAUGH: I was sacked from my last place, at the DSS. Went from one side of the counter to the other. Something will come along. It always does. I'm good at getting jobs, not so good at keeping them. [high-pitched giggles] This is like a job interview, isn't it?
WENDEL: There are simlarities. But there are differences.
MURTAUGH: That sounds cryptic. [high-pitched giggles] So, do I get it?
CHISELHURST: You're shortlisted, certainly.
MURTAUGH: [high-pitched giggles]
CHISELHURST: April will show you out.
MURTAUGH: Ta ta for now.
   [noise of leaving]
TREECE: What was that girl on? Laughing gas?
LARK: Every time she went off, I felt it in my fillings. It's quite extraordinary.
TREECE: All the dogs in the area have gone mad.
CHISELHURST: I think she's a natural for *It's a Madhouse!*.
TREECE: You can't put Shona on television, Tiny. There'd be bomb threats.
CHISELHURST: Ape, that girl is a star. Her funeral will be bigger than Diana's.

EXTRACT FROM INTERVIEW TRANSCRIPT, NO. 41.

APPLICANT: MARTIN LEIGH, 39
FOR MYTHWRHN: Tiny Chiselhurst, Dr Vernon Wendel, Myra Lark, April Treece.

LEIGH: Prison's not so bad, once you've made your mark. You just have to let them know where you are on the totem pole. You pick out some old villain, some big nob from years ago who still thinks he's got it, and you take him apart. Mark his face, put him in the infirmary, get the boot in. Then you take what was his, make it yours. Earn some respect. You can come out ahead, if you've got good currency. Fags and smack, mostly, but you can build an empire on a good source of chocolate.
TREECE: You have a lot of tattoos.
LEIGH: More than you can see. Turns you on, does it? All the birds like ink. And, inside, some of the fellers. You'd think it'd make a difference, but after a while . . . Well, one hole's as good as another.
WENDEL: And so, how long were you a warder?
LEIGH: About five years. After the Paras and the SAS wouldn't have me, it seemed a decent option. You wouldn't think the Paras and the SAS would be soft, would you? I've had ex-Paras on my block and made them whine and beg. Shows you how much tests and interviews count for anything.

EXTRACT FROM INTERVIEW TRANSCRIPT, NO. 72.

APPLICANT: ANDREA D'ARBANVILLIERS-HOLMES, 19
FOR MYTHWRHN: Tiny Chiselhurst, Dr Vernon Wendel, Myra Lark, April Treece.

LARK: What are you looking for in a man, Andrea?
D'ARBANVILLIERS-HOLMES: Good shoes are a sign.
LARK: Of what?
D'ARBANVILLIERS-HOLMES: Status, you might call it. There are other giveaways. Like, if he has a good post code but only owns a flat. I mean, if he hasn't got enough to buy a house by now, things are hardly likely to get better.
LARK: Do you believe in romance?
D'ARBANVILLIERS-HOLMES: Yes, of course. But it's easy to come by, isn't it. There are always blokes falling over their willies to get to

you. After a while, you have to impose stricter criteria. It's not money in and of itself, it's the things that come with it.
LARK: Do you believe in marriage?
D'ARBANVILLIERS-HOLMES: Absolutely. That's why I'm so careful about who I get married to. And about who I hop into bed with. It can't be just anybody, you know.
TREECE: Andrea, why do you want to be on television?
D'ARBANVILLIERS-HOLMES: Well, it's advertising, isn't it? I hope to make an impression on the right people.

EXTRACT FROM INTERVIEW TRANSCRIPT, NO. 108.

APPLICANT: DONOVAN WYKE, 27
FOR MYTHWRHN: Tiny Chiselhurst, Dr Vernon Wendel, Myra Lark, April Treece.

WENDEL: I put it to you, Donovan, that you are a habitual fantasist, a chancer who drifts through life dreaming of the big scores but inevitably botches even the petty scams, a bloodsucker who has exploited and betrayed every human connection you have ever made, a man unable to understand even the concepts of honour and fidelity, a compulsive liar with no conscience about wild promises made and broken, a congenital screw-up who is lucky not to have been knifed in an alley or wound up living on the streets begging for spare change to feed your crack habit.
WYKE: Well, I suppose if you were being hardcore about it, but there are explanations.
CHISELHURST: Welcome to *It's a Madhouse!*, Donny.
WYKE: You won't regret this. I can promise you that.

EXTRACT FROM INTERVIEW TRANSCRIPT, NO. 125.

APPLICANT: PETRA KIDNER, 22
FOR MYTHWRHN: Tiny Chiselhurst, Dr Vernon Wendel, Myra Lark, April Treece.

KIDNER: There's just something sexy about fire. I feel it in my clit, in my nipples, in the scar tissue on my inner thigh and upper back. I love everything about fire. The smoke, the flames, the heat, the

crackle. Every month, I take off my eyebrows. See. The pain is there, a part of it, but very minor. I just like to see things burn.
LARK: Things?
KIDNER: Things, *mostly*. But there's nothing like it, you know. The smell, the texture, the taste. Burning flesh. It gets to me. Does that make me weird? I'm not, you know. I like a cup of tea and *Eastenders* and always send my Mum a box of chocs on Mother's Day. Some girls love one particular pop group or a particular type of bloke. With me, it's different. It's fire.
LARK: So what is your favourite pop song?
KIDNER: [laughs] What else? Jose Feliciano, 'Come on Baby, Light My Fire'.

EXTRACT FROM INTERVIEW TRANSCRIPT NO. 128.

APPLICANT: JOSHUA BREW, 22
FOR MYTHWRHN: Tiny Chiselhurst, Dr Vernon Wendel, Myra Lark, April Treece.

CHISELHURST: You complained that we hadn't responded to your entry form?
BREW: IT'S NOT *RIGHT* THAT PEOPLE SHOULD BE TREATED THAT WAY.
CHISELHURST: We explained that your form was lost in the post.
BREW: YES, I ACCEPT THAT *NOW*.
CHISELHURST: But when you phoned the duty officer, you made quite an impression. That's a distinctive voice you've got there.
BREW: WHEN YOU'RE USED TO PREACHING THE *WORD OF OUR LORD JESUS CHRIST AT HEATHEN POP FESTIVALS*, YOU NEED A BIT OF *LUNG POWER*. I DO BREATHING *EXERCISES*.
CHISELHURST: You'll forgive me for saying this, but you don't seem like the normal type of young person we've been seeing for this show.
BREW: JUST BECAUSE I'M A *CHRISTIAN* DOESN'T MEAN I DON'T LIKE A 'GOOD TIME' AS MUCH AS THE NEXT YOUTH. I OWN MANY *CLIFF RICHARD* COMPACT DISCS. I CAN JIVE WITH THE BEST OF THEM. SOME OF OUR *CHRISTIAN YOUTH MOVEMENT* EVENINGS ARE EVERY BIT AS *WILD* AS A RAVE. WE PLAY CHARADES AND DRINK *CIDER*.

TREECE: Kickin'.

BREW: OH YES. BUT MY MAIN INTEREST IS BATTLING *THE DEVIL* WHEREVER I FIND HIS *EVIL WORKS*. I WON'T TOLERATE *SATAN* IN ANY OF HIS MANY FORMS. THAT I CAN *GUARANTEE*.

> MEMO
> From: April Treece, production associate
> To: Tiny Chiselhurst, producer/ creator
> Re: *It's a Madhouse!*

Disaster! Donger Bennett, our prize plonker, the man we most want to see on *It's a Madhouse!*, has found 'true lurve' and wants to back out. Apparently, there's someone out there blind stupid enough to marry him. One Maxine Evenson, another estate agent. They'll probably breed! It's too horrible! We have a contract, we could sue, but that could lead to publicity, which might lead to Derek the Antichrist having us killed. NB: that last bit was a joke! Please advise.

> MEMO
> From: Tiny Chiselhurst, producer/creator
> To: April Treece, assistant producer
> Re: *It's a Madhouse!*

Make an appointment for a house viewing with Miss Evenson, and claim to be Donger's last fiancée – I know that's going to be disgusting for you, but maximum Brownie points are involved – with only her best interests at heart. Play her a snippet of the initial interview tape, to wit:

> LARK: You've never been married?
>
> BENNETT: I've been engaged a couple of times, if that's what it takes to get the cork to pop.

Then present her with the background check dossier we assembled before offering him the contract. You might highlight in pink the more significant sentences. Tell her you had the dossier done when he proposed, like a survey before buying a house. If she's another bloody estate agent, she'll understand. If this is handled quickly, the crisis will fizzle. Trust me.

MEMO
From: April Treece, co-associate producer
To: Tiny Chiselhurst, producer/creator
Re: *It's a Madhouse!*

Maxine Evenson is out of Donger Bennett's life, lucky girl. On my own initiative, I ordered Claire to call on the Donger for a follow-up interview, which means we owe her hazard pay. While fighting him off and, we trust, not lying back and thinking of television, she let him see suitably cropped and doctored photographs of Andrea Double-Barrel, Miss Giggly and Petra the Pyro. Donger is extremely keen to climb back into the Madhouse. It's my hope he gets on especially well with Martin 'Lockdown' Leigh.

PRODUCTION MEETING, NO. 54

PRESENT, for MYTHWRHN PRODUCTIONS: Tiny Chiselhurst (Producer), Phil Bender (Director), Barry Gatlin (Presenter), Constant Drache (Designer), April Treece (Production Assistant), Claire Bates (Researcher), Davinda Paquignet (Researcher).
PRESENT, for CLOUD 9 TELEVISION: Derek Leech (Supremo), Heather Wilding (Executive Expediter), Basil Quilbert (Security).

CHISELHURST: You've all seen the highlights reel we put together of the video interviews. Incidentally, you'll notice we got coverage of the room from three angles. The traditional behind-the-mirror shot was augmented by prototypes of the secret cams we'll be using for *Madhouse!* None of the interviewees spotted either gadget, and here we had to install the equipment in an existing environment rather than being able to dress the set from the ground up as we will on location.
WILDING: One is in the light fitting. As for the other, I give up.
CHISELHURST: Behind the fire regulations notice.
WILDING: You're recording now?
CHISELHURST: No. Davinda is taking minutes.
WILDING: Derek?
LEECH: That is acceptable.
CHISELHURST: So, how did you all like the tape? Do you see the potential?
GATLIN: MY FAVOURITE IS THE *CHRISTIAN*!
PAQUIGNET: Ouch, my ears!
WILDING: We see potential, Tiny. The tape represents your best prospects for *Madhouse*?

CHISELHURST: We have a couple in back-up, but yes. Dr Wendel?
WENDEL: It's not just a matter of getting the right people, but of getting the right mix. They can't all be too samey. There has to be a demographic spread of class, age and sex types among the subjects.
WILDING: But, ugh, no oldies, right? This is yoof you're giving us.
WENDEL: No one over thirty-five, indeed. And eighty per cent under twenty-five. We built that early into the parameters of the experiment.
WILDING: Experiment?
CHISELHURST: It's how Biffo the Boffin thinks. Heth, believe me, this is Light Entertainment, not Heavy Educational.
WILDING: Educational worries me. It's a zapper prod. And so, frankly, are a lot of these people. Where did you get them?
CHISELHURST: They're real people, Heth. They came in of their own accord.
WILDING: You must have recruited the prison guard . . . what was his name?
TREECE: Martin Leigh. Lockdown Leigh.
WILDING: Yeah, him. He's a Central Casting Psycho.
CHISELHURST: He's our borderline choice, actually. Miss Lark thinks he's a bit obvious. Those tattoos might scare off some of the others too early.
LEECH: I like Leigh. He'll be a leader. For a while.
CHISELHURST: My thoughts exactly, Derek. He's a star in the making.
BATES: The one I hate most is Arabella Thingy-Thingy. The gold-digging posh bird.
BENDER: She's my favourite. That voice. It's not on a level with the LOUD CHRISTIAN or Miss Giggle, but there's something awful about it. Almost Thatchery.
GATLIN: Looks like a horse, though. I don't want to fuck her.
BENDER: Enough people will. You're a Yank, Barry. You don't understand this nanny thing we Brits have.
GATLIN: I don't want to fuck her. But I do want to hit her.
BATES: Is that how you divide them? Into ones you want to, uh, have sex with, and ones you want to hit?
GATLIN: Them? People in general?
BATES: Contestants, participants, subjects, victims, whatever we call them.
GATLIN: It's a fair enough system. Now, the Flame-On Chick. I *definitely* want to fuck her. I could light her fire, baby-cakes. You can take that to the bank and cash it!

TREECE: You're a sick man!
GATLIN: That's why you hired me, cherry-bee. You ain't gonna get Alastair Cooke to present *It's a Madhouse!*
TREECE: There's still Craig Charles.
GATLIN: [laughs] Get the fuck outta here!
CHISELHURST: We're off-topic, space kiddettes. Back to our mad people, please.
PAQUIGNET: I don't think they're mad.
CHISELHURST: What do you mean, Davinda?
PAQUIGNET: They're just . . . ordinary. Even the pyromaniac girl. I don't see them as any worse than the people I meet in clubs every night of the week.
WENDEL: Miss Paquignet, you are a junior assistant minion, I am a senior forensic psychologist. I assure you every one of these subjects is suffering from a severe, probably incurable personality disorder.
LEECH: Incurable?
WENDEL: By conventional means.
CHISELHURST: It's possible that *Madhouse!* will have some therapeutic effect.
WILDING: Oh, give us a break, Tiny. This is docusoap shit, not *On the Psychiatrist's Couch*. If we even thought you were sneaking something with content past us, you'd be off the air faster than a Girl Guides *Tribute to Gary Glitter* concert. We're not funding this for therapy. The point is that the people you've selected don't *deserve* help. Right?
TREECE: I certainly don't want to see 'Donger' Bennett get in touch with his inner self and accept it.
BATES/PAQUIGNET: Donger the Plonker!
TREECE: He made a big impression on the girls in the office.
WILDING: And our office too. And we only saw the tape.
TREECE: You should meet him in person, get the full-strength Donger. Someone must have died and made him Bumgroper General. And he has this . . . smell. I think he uses rhino semen as an aftershave.
BATES: If nothing else, *Madhouse!* is the show that will tell the world Donger Bennetts are no longer acceptable.
GATLIN: So, none of you wanted to fuck him?
BATES/PAQUIGNET/TREECE: [retching noises]
GATLIN: Just asking, kittens. I thought he made some solid points, myself.
TREECE: [laughs] Are you sure you don't want to be a contestant rather than the presenter?
GATLIN: [laughs and shivers] No way, Ape.

WILDING: As ever, we're concerned with costs. How have you been coming along with the location?

CHISELHURST: That's Constant's department. Care to report?

DRACHE: Clearly we need isolation, and also a certain ambience of luxury. There's a lifestyle element to the series, a subliminal trace of *Fantasy Island* or the 007 films, so we want a touch of class to set off the anticipated behaviour of the participants. First, we looked for country houses within the United Kingdom, but that proved impractical. Besides the liabilities of renting somewhere we all expect to sustain quite a bit of damage during the recording, our mainland is too small, too crowded. There's nowhere, even in the wilds of Scotland, more than half a day's hike from civilisation. It's important that the players not have the option of just quitting and walking off. In the end, we've settled on an island. Several possibilities in British waters have come to light, but we favour the Med.

WILDING: That'll cost.

DRACHE: Not in the end. We think the climate, the traditional association of the Mediterranean with 'fun in the sun', will significantly add to the show's appeal. Never make the mistake of underestimating the fuck factor.

BENDER: *Baywatch* was a joke in the States, but a huge ratings hit here. That's not all down to tits. If you live in Bolton and it's drizzling over the gasworks, you want to switch on the telly and see sun-drenched beaches, azure seas, drinks with a mess of fruit in them and skimpy bathing suits. It's a can't-miss proposition.

CHISELHURST: And international waters will help with some of the legalities. That's always been a concern for Cloud 9, I know.

LEECH: It makes sense.

WILDING: Then it'll be authorised. But we've worked with you before, Constant. I want no overruns on this. Don't kit the set up with so much fucking décor that the animals get lost. This is a people programme, remember.

DRACHE: We have definite ideas on the look of the show.

TREECE: Abstract sculptures. Lots of sharp metal edges. Heavy candlesticks. Agricultural implements as ornaments.

CHISELHURST: You see the possibilities, Derek.

WILDING: No need to spell it out, Tiny. Now, our other concern. Clearly, we're in a cutthroat business and the competition can't get wind of this. The format'd be too easy to clone.

CHISELHURST: We're already thinking of licensing it to the States. Look how *Who Wants to Be a Millionaire?* took off. And it's a natural for the Japanese market.

WILDING: Our main concern isn't plagiarism, though. It's backlash. You all know Mr Quilbert?
CHISELHURST: Basil, hi.
WILDING: He'll be heading up our security operation. As of now, he owns you. Understand.
QUILBERT: Good morning, Mr Chiselhurst, Miss Treece. And those I haven't met. We'll have one-to-one sessions scheduled soon. It is a condition of the involvement of Cloud 9 in this project that all matters concerning security be channelled through me. There will be no exceptions. We have prepared acceptable cover stories as to the nature of the programme, based on the mock proposal you sent out to the applicants, and these will be leaked steadily to the trades. We're building the cover stories around Mr Gatlin's track record in extreme stand-up and the well-established 'adventure game' style of show. The truly radical nature of *It's a Madhouse!* should not become evident until we are ready to broadcast. I have prepared various strategies for dealing with the cries for suppression we envision as inevitable. Cloud 9 will preface the premiere with a week of anti-censorship programming, with our tame 'intellectuals' debating with the less coherent and attractive members of various censorious or regulatory bodies. The purpose of this is to defang those most likely to object to a show which we consider will have the widest possible audience. If columnists have just spent an hour on Cloud 9 crying for freedom of speech and expression, they can hardly turn round and say we should not broadcast a show they consider to be objectionable. We used this basic strategy very successfully last year with the launch of the Lolita Channel and a variant is currently in play to pave the way for our 24-hour War and Gore strand.
CHISELHURST: So I take it you're giving us a go. Derek?
WILDING: Cloud 9 will take *Madhouse!* to series. Make us television history, Tiny.

THE FINAL SELECTION

```
Harry Bennett
Joshua Brew
Andrea D'Arbanvilliers-Holmes
Petra Kidner
Martin Leigh
Shona Murtaugh
Donovan Wyke
```

NOTES, by MYRA LARK

The optimum number of participants was set at seven early in the planning stages. An odd number ensures that, in the event of factionalisation, there will be an uneven split, with shifting loyalties or connections making for an unstable, potentially eventful series of relationship storms. In the event of heterosexual liaisons forming, one of the men will be left out. The most obvious candidate would be Mr Brew, because of his religious persuasions. More interesting from our purposes would be Mr Bennett, whose self-image is constructed entirely around his ability to coerce sex from females. It has been a subject for concern that Mr Leigh is too obviously dominant amongst the group, being habitually used to attaining his personal objectives through violence, but Dr Wendel and I have conferred and we see avenues around this 'problem'. If a blunt solution is required, Mr Leigh could be handicapped in some manner and forced to a great extent to rely on the goodwill of the others for his continued comfort. A subtler way out would be to arrange matters so that, from the outset, Mr Wyke is in a more commanding position. His record suggests that he can for a short while at least project the image of a confident, born leader.

After running simulations and role-play scenarios with fully briefed substitutes, these eventualities occur in every single variation of the basic situation.

a) After three days, multiple sexual exchanges will have taken place. There will also have been betrayals, extensive verbal and minor physical abuse and the development of very deep, though shifting, attachments and dislikes within the group.

b) At the six-day stage, a danger point is reached as the group turn against the experiment. We believe they will make an effort to destroy all recording devices in sight, and repeat our suggestion that these be dummies. Some of the 'hidden' cameras should be easily discoverable and disablable too. It is vital that we keep the subjects' attentions on each other and not foster a group paranoia directed at external bodies (eg: the production company), so we must insert into the scenario the idea that one or more of the subjects are in fact 'plants' working for us. You will recall that at an early stage of development, we rejected the idea of actually having a 'mole' in the group as unnecessary and unsatisfying. We believe these subjects are capable of creating and starring in their own paranoia/entertainment scenario with very little help from us.

c) Once the imaginary 'plants' have been dealt with, the programme will continue as before. Food, sexual favours, soft drugs and basic services will become currency. It is to be stressed that we should not go out of our way to make things difficult for the subjects – by withdrawing or tampering with the food supply, for instance – since the purpose of the show is to let them be themselves. Their own personality types are what is at issue here, are the factors that will make them stars. We have every confidence in them.

d) Most of the variables become extreme on the eighth day, when the subjects realise the experiment is not limited to the week they thought they had committed themselves to. Then the communications from Mr Gatlin should become more cryptic or mocking, playing on the knowledge of the survivor personalities we have gained in the course of the first week. It is possible that the group will forge together to attempt escape, but the inherent instabilities of the personality mix make this a highly unlikely and unworkable venture.

NB: Our amended psych profiles and the medical details of the subjects are attached. Note especially Mr Bennett's asthma, Miss Kidner's understandable high degree of tolerance for searing pain and Mr Wyke's clinical sociopathy.

MEMO
From: Tiny Chiselhurst, producer/creator
To: April Treece, co-associate producer
Re: *It's a Madhouse!*

We have our madhouse! It's three miles or so from St Helena, and we've bought it outright so it's our own country (what should we call it?) and we can write the law-book. It was a refuge for the idle rich in the 1920s, and comes complete with a villa Drache is having restored to its original condition at great expense to Cloud 9. From the snaps I've seen, it's very Agatha Christie. The hidden cams are being installed as I write. We're taking advantage of the restoration to build a lot of versatility into the cams. There will be no blind spots on this island, though the stars will be told that there is one room set aside for privacy. Naturally, that's where we expect a great deal of the action to take place, so it's bugged from here to there and gone.

Just in case our stars take too long to find out about each other, we're planting scrapbooks about each of them in the villa library. For the first week, Barry will transmit instructions nightly via a two-way TV hook-up to set out games and contests we've designed to be uneven and unfair, to sow discontent amongst the stars, and string them along the game aspect. Dr Wendel and Miss Lark disagree about when or if they will tumble to the 'real' nature of the show, but both are sure it won't come until well after we have got the good stuff going. I sense Satellite Awards in the making.

MEMO
From: April Treece, associate producer
To: Tiny Chiselhurst, producer/creator
Re: *It's a Madhouse!*

Mr Q reports Shona Murtaugh is really Judy Burke, a freelance journalist for *Scam* magazine. The bitch is undercover doing an exposé on rigged docusoaps. She must be imagining headlines along the lines of TV TEAM FORCED ME TO HAVE SEX WITH PLONKER.

MEMO
From: Tiny Chiselhurst, producer/creator
To: April Treece, co-executive producer
Re: *It's a Madhouse!*

Shona or Judy? It doesn't matter. What I want to know is whether the meltdown giggle is real or fake?

MEMO
From: April Treece, executive producer
To: Tiny Chiselhurst, producer/creator
Re: *It's a Madhouse!*

The shriek is real. I've got that from three sources. Probably why she got the assignment. No one can stand to have her in the office.

Going to Series

MEMO
From: Tiny Chiselhurst, producer/creator
To: April Treece, co-producer
Re: *It's a Madhouse!*

If the giggle's real, the girl's in. Have Mr Q disable any mobile phone or computer up-link she might contrive to get to our island (that goes for the others too, BTW). Miss Lark considers someone genuinely hiding her name will be a shoo-in to get tagged as the 'plant'. If the scenario runs as expected, I doubt Judy the Journo will ever file copy.

REQUEST FORM No. 69

Re: *It's a Madhouse!*
From: Constant Drache, Production Designer
To: April Treece, producer

It is vital that my team be supplied with the following as soon as possible:

1: A set of Sabatier kitchen knives. The sharpest in the world, and the most stylish. The full set runs to eighty-five pieces, and includes special blades for paring apricots, shelling crabs, etc.
2: Traditional tools for the shed. Nothing electric or rubber-gripped, just plain old wooden-handled hammers, screwdrivers, saws, awls and axes. I want that rough, honest-work, *Waltons* feel for this location.
3: Matches (books, boxes, Art Deco containers), cigarette lighters, flints, candles, magnifying glasses, tapers. Every room, almost every surface, will be fully equipped with little temptations. Also: fire-lighters, paraffin, brandy.
4: Paintings. We're concealing the video com-link behind a print of Edvard Munch's *The Scream*. It's a cliché touch, perhaps, but effective. Miss Lark and Dr Wendel have come up with a list of artworks appropriate for every participant, and we can make sure their rooms are designed to reflect, intensify or provoke their particular quirks. Bennett's room, for instance, will be furnished with erotic prints of male nudes.
5: Ill-hanging doors. The villa is being refitted from the ground up. It is appropriate, given the title and the intent of the show, that none of the doors or windows be fitted properly. Every angle

will be a few degrees out of right, every oblong almost imperceptibly a parallelogram. The house is almost an eighth player in our game, and it gets billing on the title so I'm sure even the tightwads at the top of the Pyramid will be pleased to allow the expenditure.

MEMO
From: April Treece, meister producer
To: Claire Bates, senior researcher
Re: *It's a Madhouse!*

Much as I like the idea of Donger Bennett being woken up at three in the morning every night by an hour of Barry White played full blast through the speakers in his room, I think you're missing the point. *Madhouse!* is not about what we do to them, but what they do to each other. Ideally, we should be able to sit back and let them get on with it. That was what all the psycho-babble was about, to harp on Dr Wendel's favourite tune, 'to get the right mix of personalities'. However, thanks very much for the contribution: Tiny does see potential in the music. What we've decided to do is, in effect, put JOSHUA BREW in charge of the entertainment. The CD library will be equipped with every recording Cliff ever made and the player will be set up so that it can only sound out full blast and in every room in the house, plus outside speakers that cover the whole island. If JOSHUA wants to listen to his favourite God Bothering chart-topper, then the rest of them have to as well. That should be an interesting frill, and comes out of the personality mix rather than being imposed on it.

PRODUCTION SUB-MEETING, No. 109

PRESENT, for MYTHWRHN PRODUCTIONS: April Treece (Next to God), Claire Bates (Senior Researcher), Davinda Paquignet (Researcher).

PAQUIGNET: So, Ape, who's your fave?
TREECE: Fabu fave or urgh fave?
PAQUIGNET: Fabu, first.
TREECE: Weirdly, it's Petra the Pyro.
BATES: Me too.
PAQUIGNET: Why?

BATES: She's the human one. If it weren't for her kink, she'd be just like us. I hope she comes out of it.
TREECE: So do I. She should be the one who surprises the others. I'm betting on her as the star-in-the-making. She could have a scourge-of-God thing going for her.
PAQUIGNET: And as for the urgh fave? Donger Bennett?
TREECE: At first, but after a while he just gets to seem sad. Probably something about his childhood.
BATES: That's just a strategy, Ape Donger Bennett is filth in a human skin, a dinosaur penis dragging a walnut brain around.
TREECE: Claire, you *didn't* . . .
BATES: Give me a break, Ape. I'm not that desperate to rise in the industry.
PAQUIGNET: Easy for you to say. You're out of minion class now, darling.
TREECE: I'm with Claire now. It's Andrea I hate most. I remember girls like her from school. Always taking things away from you.
BATES: I've switched too. The real monster is Wyke. The more they dig into his past, the worse he gets. Lark says he's the true sociopath in the pack. Do you know he ran a bogus charity marathon for Eritrea? Organised it, rather. Couldn't run for a bus, if you ask me. And he's the one who picked up the initial flyer in the VD clinic.
TREECE: No, that was Leigh. Wyke came from the Young Conservatives. He's never voted in his life, because he doesn't like to give a fixed address. He was buttering up some Andrea clone, trying to get her to invest in a bogus Internet service for dimbo debs. Bastard.
PAQUIGNET: Petra the Pyro is coming for them all, retribution with a flick-lighter.
BATES: Ape, would you watch this show?
TREECE: I don't want to think about that. In the end, I don't think I could resist it. You're still an anti, though?
BATES: No. I cracked when you sent me after Donger. I hate myself for this, but I wouldn't miss it for the world.
PAQUIGNET: It's going to be very popular. I think we're all going to do very well out of it.
TREECE: So, Claire, do you want to change your mind about the credit? After the Donger Affair, Tiny said you could go from Senior Researcher to Junior Producer if you want. It's a Hell of a way to get it, but . . .
BATES: Ape, I'll take it. Where do I sign, and in what?

CONTINUITY ANNOUNCER SCRIPT, CLOUD 9 TELEVISION.

```
Seven very special people. One very unusual house. An island
paradise.
    What happens?
    You can find out tonight, exclusively on Cloud 9 TV, the Derek
Leech Channel. To subscribe to this pay-per-view premiere, call
our numbers now!
    The show everyone will be talking about tomorrow!
    It's people. It's real. It's raw. It's struggle. It's surprise.
It's life. It's Something Else.
    It's a Madhouse!
    Coming up next . . .
```

Kim Newman lives in London. His recent book releases include the novels *Life's Lottery* and *An English Ghost Story*, the collections *Seven Stars, Unforgivable Stories* and *Where the Bodies Are Buried*, and the non-fiction volumes *Millennium Movies: End of the World Cinema* and *BFI Classics: Cat People*. His award-nominated novella 'Andy Warhol's Dracula' was one of a quartet collected in Peter Crowther's anthology *Foursight* and also forms part of *Johnny Alucard*, the fourth volume in the author's popular 'Anno Dracula' series. About the preceding story, he says: 'This is part of a loose series of stories I've been doing about the world of media mogul Derek Leech, which includes "The Original Dr Shade", "Organ Donors" (some of whose characters recur here), *The Quorum*, the "Where the Bodies Are Buried" series and other items. The real-world precedents for the story are horribly obvious, and have become more so since I wrote it. A good rule of thumb for ordinary folk dealing with the media these days is "don't sign the release form".'

Haunts

LISA TUTTLE

John Hutchinson was a haunted man. Not bad – I'll never believe that – and not mad, as others think, but haunted. Driven to what he did by a ghost. You can't blame him for what he did; I honestly believe that. Of course, he didn't believe in ghosts. But in the end belief doesn't matter a damn. Things happen that make no human sense. Trying to make sense of them could drive you mad – or worse.

I probably knew John Hutchinson as well as anybody. He was one of my best friends in high school – Hutch, John Wayne Barlow, Greg Hainey and me. We called ourselves the Big Four, sometimes the Famous Four. In some ways, it was an unlikely alliance. Greg and Hutch were budding scientists, engineers-in-training, devoted to rationality, practical and smart, whereas John Wayne and I loved the arts, the psychological and the weird. Really, we should have hated each other, and maybe at a bigger school we would have. But we were all misfits growing up in a small town in Texas. To everybody else, we were geeks and losers. We didn't have any other friends. So we tended to kind of get lumped together – bookworms, hopelessly unfashionable, no good at sports – and learned to like each other.

For three years we hung out together, wasted time, and helped each other at school, both socially and academically. It was Greg who kept me from flunking out of Algebra, it was John Wayne who turned him on to Mervyn Peake and Aubrey Beardsley and Edward Gorey, it was Hutch who got me to take an interest in science, it was me who helped him with his English essays, and tried to teach him there had to be more to life than the strictly rational.

We used to go on ghost-hunts. Mostly, I guess, they were an excuse to huddle together in a graveyard or an abandoned house at night and try to scare each other, but we were serious about it as well. Greg and Hutch were complete unbelievers, rationalists who bemoaned the fuzzy-minded attitude which allowed me and John Wayne to reckon that there just might be 'something' there. John Wayne and I wanted to see a ghost, for real, to experience what we'd read about so often. Greg and Hutch wanted to prove that there are no such things as ghosts, to force me and John Wayne to admit that they were right and we were wrong.

Well, we never saw a ghost. And since Hutch disallowed self-reported 'creepy feelings' as evidence, there were never even any close calls, although we did have a couple of really weird sessions with my mother's old Ouija board. We ended our brief career as psychic investigators with our established belief-systems unshaken: Greg and Hutch were still rationalists, John Wayne and I still hoping.

After graduation we went our separate ways – Hutch to the West, John Wayne to the East, Greg and me to the University of Texas in Austin. We kept in touch, and got together at Christmas when we could escape from our families.

I might as well admit right here that I used to have a crush on Hutch. But I kept my feelings to myself, and I'm sure he never knew. My self-esteem was low. I was a skinny, flat-chasted girl with glasses and a bad home-perm, and I felt that the survival of the 'Big Four' was dependent on my sexuality being kept as hidden as John Wayne's. Like him, I pretended to be 'one of the guys' to survive. I had a lot of fantasies about Hutch one day waking up to my presence, really *seeing* me for the first time – but I couldn't do anything to try to make it happen. If I *made* him see me differently, what if he didn't like what he saw? It wasn't just that I couldn't face rejection. If I declared myself, the balance of power would shift. The Big Four would crumble. I couldn't risk destroying it for all of us.

Then we went away to college. Although we stayed in touch, the old *raison d'être* for the alliance had gone. Life at the university was totally different from a small-town high school. I found new friends, intellectual soulmates, and also lovers. I let my hair grow long, put on a few pounds in strategic places, borrowed my roommate's clothes, gained confidence. I felt that I was completely changed.

That first Christmas when I saw Hutch again – saw the new assurance in his skinny, slouching stance, saw the way he filled out his Gap T-shirt and chinos – I felt a fluttering in the pit of my stomach and realised that here was one thing which hadn't changed: I still wanted him. In fact, I wanted him more than ever – and now there was no reason, I felt, why he shouldn't want me.

So, after Mr and Mrs Hutchinson had gone to bed, and Greg and John Wayne had staggered off home to their parents', I stayed on. Hutch got out another six-pack and we settled down on the flowered chintz sofa in the enclosed back porch for more personal conversation.

By way of checking that the path was clear, I asked if he had a girlfriend at college.

He grinned, and told me of his conquests. There were nearly a dozen already; he was averaging one a week. A different girl each weekend. He didn't like to repeat himself, because if you asked a girl out two weeks running, she'd start making assumptions and talking about a *relationship* for God's sake!

'The problem with girls,' he told me, as if I weren't one, 'is they're hard-wired for monogamy, which guys aren't. Girls screw around, sure they do. But if they screw the same guy regularly, then after a certain point, which I reckon is about a month, it's like some switch in their brain gets tripped, and they get flooded with these chemicals, you know, serotonin and that, and suddenly they're *in love*.' He did the fingers-for-quotemarks thing in the air with his hands as he spoke those dire words in a tone dripping with irony.

The attraction – why not be honest and call it *lust* – which I'd been feeling for him, died inside me.

'The problem is,' he went on, after pausing to chug some beer, 'a month is about the time when the average guy stops feeling so horny for her and starts to get kind of bored. His genetic imperative is to move on to fresh pastures, try to knock somebody else up. Even if, you know, you're not intending to knock anybody up, ever – well, that old urge is still there, genetically encoded.'

'So in other words,' I interrupted him, trying to make my own voice just as ironic as his, 'the answer to my question is, no, you don't have a girlfriend.'

He grinned at me. 'I couldn't be that cruel, Becky! Breaking their little hearts? No, but it's hard. When I find somebody really hot, you know, and think it would be great to get together with her again – well, I just have to resist the urge, and go out to look for somebody new. I always make it pefectly clear that what I want is sex, not a relationship.'

'What about love?' I demanded. 'Don't you ever think about that?'

He shook his head. 'Love's a con. It doesn't exist. There's body heat, there's hormones, there's the genetic imperative – and there's social myths about romantic love. That's all it is. It's not real, just because people believe in it.'

I was reminded of all the conversations we'd had in high school, when Hutch and Greg would put forth the rational, materialistic argument, and John Wayne and I would try (and fail) to shoot it full of holes with alternatives from the arts, from books, from philosophy, from *feeling*. I suddenly wished I wasn't alone with Hutch. John Wayne had told me – had he confessed the same to Hutch or Greg? – that he was in love with his roommate. But I didn't want to use John Wayne's private feelings as ammunition, and I had no great love of my own to argue from. I'd never been any good at arguing, anyway, not like the boys, who would say anything to score a point. Occasionally, when John Wayne and I were flailing too badly, one of them would switch sides to argue our position, to make it a fairer fight. I knew Hutch could wipe the floor with me, and I'd never be able to believe in love again . . .

'Gosh, it's late,' I said looking at my watch. 'I'd better go home.'

The years went by. John Wayne did postgraduate work in set design, then moved to New York, where he seemed to be always on the fringes of the theatrical and/or art world, barely surviving, but happy. I worked for a free-sheet in Austin, and then got offered the chance to start up an arts and entertainment paper in Galveston. Hutch had a job with one of the big oil companies based in Houston; I think he had something to do with designing drilling equipment. Greg was the most successful of us all. The little software business he'd started up in college took off in a big way, and by the time we were in our mid-twenties, Greg was a millionaire. He settled in Austin in a big, beautiful house, married a doctor named Linda and became a leading light on the charity fundraising circuit. Despite all the demands on his time, he kept in touch with his old friends.

I'm not sure I would have stayed in touch with Hutch but for Greg. Although I'd thought of myself as being the very heart of the group when we were in high school, now he was the one who forwarded my replies to his e-mails to Hutch, and vice-versa. It was only his efforts which kept alive the ghost of the Big Four.

Even though Houston and Galveston are very close together, I never saw Hutch from one year to the next except at Christmas, when our visits to our parents overlapped, or up in Austin at one of Greg's parties. He threw great parties, especially at Hallowe'en. Even in Austin, a city where Hallowe'en is taken seriously, Greg's Hallowe'en parties were the stuff of legend.

I was surprised, and flattered, when Greg invited me to Austin one weekend in April, to discuss plans for that year's Hallowe'en party. He said he wanted to pick my brain; he desperately needed my help to create a unique and unusual experience.

He sent the same invitation to Hutch and John Wayne. He even paid for John Wayne's plane ticket.

So there we were, suddenly, the Famous Four reconstituted, with the addition of Greg's wife, Linda. We stood in their living room, grinning uneasily at each other.

'You should have brought Luke,' Greg said. 'I hope I made it clear Luke would be welcome?'

He had. I nodded and explained, 'I didn't want him overwhelmed with our shared nostalgia.'

'Who's Luke?' John Wayne asked. 'There was no "Luke" mentioned in your Christmas card!'

I could feel Hutch staring at me, and I hoped I wasn't blushing. 'We're not actually living together yet,' I said carefully.

Greg rolled his eyes at my coyness. 'Luke is her fiancé,' he announced. 'At least, she told *me* they were engaged.'

'Tick-tick-tick,' said Hutch.

'I think you'll find that men have biological clocks, too,' I said, trying not to sound annoyed.

'Not in the Hutchinson theory of life and love,' Greg said, grinning. 'There, women have but a short shelf-life, while men are the eternal hunter-gatherers.'

Hutch shrugged. 'It works for me,' he said.

John Wayne looked him up and down. 'It might work now, but what about when your visible assets start to go?' He struck a pose. 'Madame Fortuna predicts: a lonely old age.'

'Oh, I'll probably get married eventually,' he said. 'Becky's right—'

I nearly dropped my drink as he nodded this acknowledgement to me.

'—men can afford to leave it till later, but we've got the same urge to procreate. And I don't actually want to be a bachelor forever. Studies show that married men are happier and live longer than singles. I figure when I'm in my late thirties I'll start shopping around for a wife.'

Linda snorted. 'God, Hutch, you make it sound *so* romantic! How could any woman resist you?'

'I don't know, but many have,' he told her, grinning.

'Luckily he's not too picky,' said Greg, putting his arm around her. 'When the time comes, he'll just head for the Generic Wife aisle at Wal-Mart—'

'Target, surely,' I objected, giving it the French pronounciation.

'Come on, let's move to the dining room,' Linda interrupted.

Hutch had been barely nineteen when he'd formulated his theory about men, women and love. But it seemed that nothing which had happened to him during the next eight years had made him change his mind. I knew from Greg that Hutch no longer picked up and discarded women with the rapidity of his college years. Probably, he didn't find it so easy off-campus. More recently, he'd gone for longer-term, yet easily broken, liaisons with married women.

Behind me, as we walked through to the dining room, I heard John Wayne quizzing Hutch. 'So you're just going out to shop for a good little wifey when the time is right? I know you like to be Mr Unemotional, but get real. What about that crazy little thing called love?'

'He doesn't believe in it,' I said, taking the seat the Linda motioned me to.

'Belief has got nothing to do with it, believe me! Is that true?' When Hutch nodded, John Wayne said thoughtfully, 'Boy, you are really ripe for a fall! I just hope I'm around to see it when you fall head over heels for . . . whoever.'

He was looking, very thoughtfully, at me, as he spoke. I didn't know why, but I could feel myself blushing. I dreaded Hutch's rejoinder, his devastating deconstruction of the fraud of romantic love.

Greg rescued us all from that. 'Let's talk about this Hallowe'en party,' he said firmly.

'That's what we're here for,' John Wayne said. 'I'm sure once we four put our heads together, we'll come up with some great ideas. What do you want?'

'I want a haunted house,' Greg said.

'Not the *whole* house,' Linda objected quickly.

Greg shrugged and shook his head. 'No, Linda's right. I can only give you the west wing to work on.'

'This house?' I asked.

'No, we've got a new house under construction on a lot overlooking Lake Travis. Figure it should be ready for a Hallowe'en house-warming. And I'd like to do something really special with it – with the west wing, anyway.'

'Creepy Gothic décor?' John Wayne suggested.

Greg nodded. 'Yeah, that's part of it – I was hoping I could leave that part to you and Becky. Hire artists or decorators, buy whatever you need – I want it to be scary, but subtle. Disturbing, but not so severely that nobody could stay there. And I want Hutch to provide the ghost.'

'Thank you,' Hutch said, bowing his head gravely. 'However, honoured though I am to be proposed as a sacrificial victim, I should warn you that, if murdered, I will not return to haunt you or your house!'

'Hutch, this is your old pal Gregory talking to you. We both know that ghostly phenomena are not caused by the spirits of the dead.'

'Right, right. So what kind of a con-trick do you want from me?'

'Not a con-trick. An experiment.' His eyes were bright, his round face glowing like a jack-o'-lantern. He paused as a waiter came in to deliver the first course.

'A couple of guys in England did some research into the effects of low-frequency soundwaves on human physiology. The results were reported in several places – I can't believe none of you guys read about it!'

'Well, we didn't, so you'd better tell us,' I said, tasting the bright green soup. Leek, creamy and delicious.

'They found that if you set up a standing wave of about nineteen cycles per second, a person in it is going to start feeling more and more uncomfortable: shivery, oppressed, frightened, just completely creeped-out.'

'And in that state, they're very suggestible, maybe start imagining ghosts,' I guessed.

'The human eyeball has a resonant frequency of eighteen cycles per second,' Greg explained. 'Infrasound just above that frequency will cause sympathetic vibrations in the eyeball—'

'And you'd start seeing weird things,' said Linda. She shuddered.

Greg was already positively vibrating with excitement as he gazed intently at Hutch. 'Could you repeat the experiment for me? I mean, set up a standing wave which would make the west wing seem to be haunted?'

'If you're paying for it.' A slow, wide grin cracked Hutch's usually solemn face. 'God, I'd love to try something like that!'

'I thought you would!' Greg rubbed his hands together. 'I'll put you in touch with the architect and Bud, my contractor, so you can all work together. I'll tell Bud to give you whatever you need. This takes priority. If we have to change the layout of the house, so be it.'

'Just as long as the ghost can't get out of the west wing,' Linda said. 'I don't want the infrasound affecting anybody anywhere else in the house. There could be health implications.'

'It'll be a completely localised phenomenon,' Greg assured her. He looked at Hutch. 'Bear that in mind – and that there has to be an off-switch, so the west wing doesn't have to be haunted *all* the time.'

We all got caught up in the excitement of planning. It felt almost like old times. Although of course there were differences. Greg was paying for it all. It was real work for John Wayne, but Hutch, who said he couldn't afford to be caught moonlighting, would design and build the machine for producing the sound in his spare time, for expenses only. As for me, well, I was really just an onlooker, although both Greg and John Wayne were good about asking for my input. I couldn't contribute anything to what Hutch had to do, and he said flatly that there was no point in trying to explain anything to a liberal arts major, I would just have to wait and see.

This I got to do, finally, in September, when I flew up to Austin for a private view. There was no way I was going to wait for the formal unveiling on Hallowe'en like some ordinary, gullible member of the public!

Luke went with me; he wanted to see the house. It was impressive, since Greg had plenty of money and was willing to let the architect have his way rather than insisting on imposing his own (frankly, rather primitive) notions of style, but I was really only interested in the west wing, and seeing the results of Hutch's experiment. So we left Luke wandering around quite happily while Hutch led me and Greg to the site of his experiment.

I was shivering as I stepped through the last door (the gallant gentlemen let me go first), but whether I was already responding to the atmosphere or just anticipating, I have no idea. The room was big, like all the others in the house, but seemed to have been built on a different scale. It was long and narrow, more like a hallway than a room, and although it was perfectly spacious and airy (the ceiling was very high) and light, there was something oppressive about it. I'm not usually claustrophobic, but I started getting a prickly, trapped feeling, as if I'd wandered into a closet by mistake. There were no windows. I must spend half my life in windowless rooms without giving it a thought, but for some reason, it bothered me here. Although I knew perfectly well I hadn't gone down any steps or ramps, I started thinking that this room was underground. The real problem was that the air-conditioning and ventilation system weren't working properly. The temperature had dropped – I was actually shivering with cold – but the place was so airless that no matter how much I gulped I couldn't get the oxygen I needed.

I was just about two beats away from a full-blown panic attack when I turned to my friends. Hutch was standing and gazing at nothing with a small, proud smile on his lips, and Greg's bright eyes were darting everywhere. The freckled skin of his bare arms had sprouted goose-bumps, but what parted his lips and made him breathe faster was anticipation, not anxiety.

Of course. We were *meant* to feel like this. As soon as I'd realised that it was Hutch's standing wave which was making my pulse race, I stopped being afraid. There was nothing to fear. I still felt uncomfortable, but now that I knew why, I could deal with it.

Greg and Hutch had moved further into the room, and I went after them. I thought I heard someone come through the door right behind me, and I turned, expecting to see Luke.

He wasn't there, but *someone* had just slipped past me – from the corner of my eye I caught sight of a slim, grey figure speeding past.

'There, look!' cried Hutch, and I whirled around, saw him pointing at the wall, saw – I blinked, narrowed my eyes, struggled to make sense of it – a woman, in a long, grey, hooded coat, backed up against the wall. I had the sense that she was frightened, cornered, with nowhere to run, and then she was gone.

We all sighed simultaneously.

'So this is the haunted west wing?' Luke entered, and we all looked to see his reaction. He shivered. 'Creepy. Really oppressive. That's not just your standing wave, Hutch, it's the lighting, the shape of the space.' He prowled up and down, checking it out. Finally he stopped and looked at us. His eyebrows raised. We were all staring at him so strangely, I guess. I went over and slipped my arm around his waist, feeling better for the contact immediately.

He gave me a squeeze and looked at Hutch. 'Is it just this creepy feeling, or is anything else supposed to happen?'

'It might,' said Hutch. 'Visual disturbances. Tell us if you see anything weird, huh?'

Luke nodded. We all waited in silence for a bit. I looked at the door, because that was where I'd been looking when I'd first seen something, but Hutch and Greg were both staring at the wall where the figure had disappeared. I could feel Luke's tension in his arm around me, and he kept jerking his head around.

'See anything?' Hutch asked him after the third sudden movement.

'No – yes – maybe, I don't know. Just out of the corner of my eye, a sort of grey shape, blurred, like something moving. But when I turn my head, it's gone.'

'Some*thing* or some*one*?'

Luke shrugged. 'No idea. Just a blurry, moving shape. Could've been an animal, I guess.'

For some reason his comment really spooked me – I think it was the image it conjured of the grey woman metamorphosing into a beast. *She* had seemed to me frightened, not frightening, but the idea of a shapeshifting monster was terrifying.

'Let's go,' I said.

'Fine with me,' said Luke, walking me towards the door.

'I'm going to stick around for a while longer,' said Hutch. 'Just to see what happens. How about it, Greg?'

I expected Greg to agree; I'd thought the haunted west wing was going to be his new toy. But he was looking oddly pale. He shook his head. 'No, I don't think so, man. I've got kind of a headache . . . I got to get out of here for a while. And I really don't think you should stay too long.'

Hutch shrugged. 'I just want to check something out. I'll meet y'all out front in about fifteen minutes.'

What a relief it was to leave that empty room. I began to feel better immediately.

'My headache's gone already,' said Greg, sounding surprised, as we stepped outside the front door. He sighed happily, inhaling the scent of sunbaked earth and cedar. 'Whew, I feel like I just came back from some dungeon in the Middle Ages!' Then he looked at me. 'You don't think Hutch will do himself any harm?'

'There are health implications,' I said cautiously. Since Hutch wouldn't tell me, I'd looked into the literature about infrasound research myself. 'But no, I really don't. And I'm sure it'll be safe enough for your party guests. Nobody's going to be in there for more than a few minutes at a time.'

'Only Hutch. And don't forget, this isn't his first time.'

I nodded. 'But it's not likely to do him any lasting harm. I'm sure there are factory floors which are worse.'

Greg took us on a tour of his property. We even went down the rough hillside path – 'there'll be steps the next time you come' – to the lake and a wooden dock. We were away for more than twenty minutes, but when we returned to the house there was still no sign of Hutch.

'I guess I'd better go get him,' said Greg.

My heart gave a flutter. 'Let's all go.'

He gave me a look, then dead-panned, 'Of course. What *was* I thinking? In the movies, they always get into trouble when they split up. Oh, my God, we should never have left him alone!'

'Don't look be-hiiiiind you.' It was Hutch, of course, grinning sardonically. 'Some friends *I've* got – leaving poor little me all alone in the infamous haunted west wing.'

'Since you're the one who haunted it—'

'Oh, great, so now I discover my so-called friends think I'm a ghost?' His hand shot out and gripped my arm. I think the movement was meant as a punch-line, but as his fingers, icy cold against my sun-warmed flesh, dug into me, I lost it, and screamed.

The men – even Luke – looked at me as if I was insane.

Hutch yanked his hand away as if I'd burned him.

'Sweetie, Sweetie, it's okay,' said Luke – a little belatedly, I thought, but better late than never.

I hugged Luke to hide my blushes. I felt like a complete idiot. I began to babble. 'Sorry – sorry – I just – I don't know, Hutch, you startled me! After-shock, I guess. I mean, even knowing what it was, the whole thing was just so creepy! Really got my adrenalin going. Sorry, Hutch.'

'That's okay. You were supposed to be scared. It's good – means I succeeded.' Hutch twitched his shoulders. 'I won't say I was scared myself, because I wasn't, but my body sure thought I ought to be. It wanted me out of there! If I wasn't shivering, I was sweating like a pig. Thank the Lord I've still got a clean shirt in my case in the car!'

'So, did the ghost come back after we'd left?' Greg wanted to know. 'Did he have anything to say for himself?'

'He?'

'The ghost,' Greg explained.

I looked at him in surprise.

'What did you see?' Hutch was frowning.

Greg shrugged. 'A grey figure in a long cloak, with a hood, so I couldn't see his face. I thought he was like a monk.'

'I saw a woman,' I said.

'So did I,' said Hutch. There was something in the way he said it, looking at me, that made me tingle.

I shrugged irritably. 'But it's not like there was anything there to see – there's not a ghost. We didn't see anything, really – it's about perception, not vision. Our eyeballs vibrated, and our brains were just trying to make some kind of shape out of that blurriness.'

Hutch shook his head slowly. 'It has to be more complicated than that. In so-called haunted houses people see the same ghosts again and again.'

'Because of tradition,' Greg put in. 'People see what they expect to see.'

'And you expected to see a monk?' Hutch said sceptically. 'Doubtless one of the world-famous Lake Travis brotherhood.'

'Sure, the Indians wiped them out, burned the monastery to the ground, in ought eight,' Greg said. 'I always build my houses on sites of historical and religious significance, didn't you know that?'

'There isn't any tradition here, yet,' I pointed out. 'We didn't know what to expect. So our minds were free to make their own connections. For Greg, obviously, grey ghosts have got to be monks.'

'Whereas for you and Hutch, it's the sexier option of a dead woman,' Luke said.

I made a disgusted face at him. 'Dead women are *sexy*?'

'Hey, not to *me*. But according to Edgar Allan Poe and everybody else who follows that route.'

'I don't think somebody who saw an animal ghost should talk about sexy.'

Hutch ignored us. 'I'd like to interview more people about their experience in the west wing,' he told Greg. 'See if some kind of consensus starts to emerge. Maybe at the party.'

'Yeah, okay,' said Greg. 'But try not to get too heavy. Remember, they're my guests, not your experimental subjects.'

'Well, hey. I wouldn't have to bother anybody at the party if I could run an experiment beforehand. If I could bring some people out here, you know, and then ask them to describe their experience.'

'*Mi casa es su casa*,' Greg agreed. 'I'll get another set of keys cut for you. There'll be decorators and such-like coming and going for the next few weeks – that won't bother you? Good.'

'You don't mind if I camp out here for a night or two? I'd really like to find out what happens on repeat visits; you know, does the whole thing cycle through again? Do you get habituated to it, more or less sensitive? All sorts of questions.'

Greg nodded, looking admiring, looking, maybe, a bit envious. 'I might join you,' he said. It was as if he'd forgotten this was his house – his ghost. But this was how it had been in high school, when Hutch always had the best ideas – or, at least, the ability to convince us they were his.

Later, at the airport, Hutch asked me if I could sketch a portrait of the ghostly woman I'd thought I'd seen.

'Oh, I don't know, Hutch – it was only a glimpse – I'm really not sure. Maybe, if I see her again—'

'We don't know that you'll see the same apparition twice. I need some hard evidence. God knows, most people are completely incapable of describing what they've seen in any kind of detail . . . I don't want to rely on what people think they remember. *You* have a talent, Beck. You can draw. Your portraits are really good.' He turned to Luke. 'My mom framed the portrait Becky did of me in high school. She's still got it on the living room wall, says it's more like me than any photograph!'

I felt myself blushing, both pleased and embarrassed. I'd given up any serious attempts at drawing while in college. The art teachers there did not admire my work. It lacked flair and individuality. I could copy – but computers could do that sort of thing *so* much better.

I bought pencils and a pad of paper in the airport shop, and while

Hutch, Greg and Luke drank coffee at the next table, I struggled to produce an image of the woman I'd imagined I'd seen. Her figure – coat open over a loose dress – and posture, cowering fearfully against the wall, were what I remembered best about her, and were the easiest to capture. It was her face that was difficult. I did the best I could to sketch the features I thought I remembered, while not making them too individual. Result: generic pretty young woman backed up against the wall by (unseen) threat.

Hutch grinned broadly. 'That's her! That's what I saw!'

'You know, I think I saw her too,' Luke drawled. 'On the cover of a book in the newsstand over there where Becky bought her paper.'

Luke's sarcasm didn't register on Hutch. 'May I keep it?' he asked.

I nodded. Of course, what else, I had drawn it for him. But I suddenly wished I hadn't.

The Hallowe'en party was supposed to be the main event, but for me it turned into something less than a sideshow.

Things hadn't been going well between me and Luke, and for some stupid reason we ended up sniping at each other nearly the whole of the drive from Galveston to Austin. At the party I spent about ten minutes talking to John Wayne, who was in a snit because Hutch didn't appreciate what he'd done to the west wing – he just flat didn't like it, if you please, because it *distracted* the visitors from what John Wayne called 'Hutch's special effects'.

I went down to the west wing to see for myself, but there was such a long line of people waiting to get in that I gave up. I meant to go back later, but that never happened. I never even saw Hutch that night. Instead, I found Luke, and the tension which had been building between us suddenly exploded. We left the party to have our fight in private, and we thoroughly demolished the relationship. By the time Hallowe'en had given way to All Saint's Day, our engagement was off, and we never wanted to see each other again. I made him drop me off at the bus station because I couldn't bear another four hours of his company on the drive home.

I e-mailed Greg and Linda to apologise for walking out on their party and to explain about the break-up. I sent a similar note, only more grovelling, to Hutch. Knowing how proud and possessive he was of 'his' haunting, I figured he'd be furious that I'd disappeared.

Greg's reply was practically instantaneous, concerned about my emotional state, offering me the lakehouse as a retreat if I wanted to get away from Galveston for a while. From Hutch, nothing. After a week, I e-mailed him again, this time quizzing him about the results of his 'experiment'.

I'd chosen the right topic. He couldn't resist a reply.

I'm going to write it all up and submit it as an article somewhere. Till I manage that, here's a quick breakdown of my findings: Roughly 60 per cent thought they saw some sort of human figure; another 10 per cent saw 'something moving' which they thought might have been an animal or a person; 5 per cent thought they just glimpsed something but couldn't say anything positive about it at all, another 5 per cent 'heard', or 'sensed' something they couldn't see; and 20 per cent experienced no ghostly or inexplicable manifestations at all.

Of the (most interesting) 60 per cent, slightly more than half described the figure as female, usually as wearing a long gown, but otherwise their descriptions varied widely. Of those who saw a male figure nearly half described the figure as a monk or a priest! (The long gown again?)

Guess I'll have to try to make sense of the data, draw some kind of conclusion. Might be good to have your input on that; how would you feel about collaborating?

Nobody else saw our woman.

Our woman. The phrase sent a thrill through me. I was warmed by it, and felt closer to Hutch than I had in years. And he wanted to collaborate! I replied right away, letting him know I was eager and willing to help.

But I didn't hear from him again for a couple of weeks. It was early December when he phoned and asked if I could come and meet him in Houston.

He didn't sound like himself. There was something in his voice I'd never heard before. 'What's up?'

'I've found our ghost,' he said.

'What do you mean?'

'Come and see for yourself.'

I met him in Houston the next day. It was the middle of the week and should have been a working day for both of us, but there we were, playing truant. He'd given me explicit directions for how to find a restaurant called The Black-Eyed Pea, where he would be waiting for me.

I couldn't figure it out. The scenario I imagined centred around old newspaper clippings, maybe the story of a murder in Travis County, maybe the discovery of a young woman's body in the lake. I surely wasn't expecting Hutch to greet me, when I joined him in his booth beside a window, by pointing out at a high-rise bank building across the street and saying, 'She works there. She'll be coming out of the building for her lunch break in about . . .' he checked his watch, 'thirty-five minutes. You should get a good view of her then.'

I looked at him. He didn't look well. I could tell he wasn't sleeping, or eating right, and he was drinking too much coffee. 'Who are you talking about?' I asked, although I already knew.

He waited for the waitress to take my order, and then he told me. 'Her name is Melanie Caron. She's twenty-six, single, works for First City National over there and lives by herself in a townhouse in a little subdivision off the Gulf Freeway. Not a rental; I think her parents bought it for her – there's money in the background, I think.' He paused, seeming to lose track of what he was saying, and ran a hand over his face.

'But why?'

'Oh, the car she drives, the townhouse—'

'No, I don't mean the money! I mean, why her, why are you so interested?'

'Wait'll you see her.'

'No. I don't remember what I saw. Not well enough to be sure.'

He slammed his hand down on the table, making the silverware judder. 'Don't say that! You drew her picture!'

'It's a *drawing*. I'm not a camera.'

'I know it's her,' he said quietly. 'The second I saw her – sitting at a table just over there,' he canted his head. 'As soon as I set eyes on her it was like little *things* just crawling all over me ... the creepiest sensation. I *knew* it was her.' He raised his haunted eyes to mine. 'I don't know why. I don't know what it means. But I saw her ghost. It has to mean something.'

'Why? Why does it have to mean anything?' This was *his* line when I'd tried, in my clumsy way, to argue for the existence of God, an afterlife, or even the significance of coincidence.

'Don't be an asshole, Becky,' he said irritably.

'Don't *you*. You want to know what it means? Okay, I'll tell you: you don't want to know. It's a warning.'

He became more alert. 'You really think so? I need to tell her?'

'*No*. You need to keep the hell away from her.' The way he looked when I said that told me everything. My heart sank. 'You've told her?'

'Not about the ghost, no, not about seeing her – but *you* could. Maybe she'd believe you.'

'And she wouldn't believe you, because why?' He didn't answer; he didn't have to. 'Because you came on to her, and she didn't want to know. And instead of letting it drop you've been following her around, spying on her.' I turned to gaze out the window at the bank where this unknown woman worked. I felt a horrible, cold dread filling me up from my feet to my head. 'Oh, lordy. You're stalking her.'

'Becky, come on!' He gazed at me, anguished. 'I thought you'd understand! It's not like that. If you'd help me . . .'

I prayed that I could.

'Look, Hutch,' I said gently. 'Think about the ghost. Think about how she looked. I don't just mean her face, I mean her, whaddayacallit – her affect.'

He frowned at me. I spelled it out. 'She was *terrified*. Somebody was after her. Maybe you?'

'I wouldn't hurt her.'

'So how's she supposed to know that? Telepathy?'

Just then the waitress arrived with the food I no longer wanted to eat.

'Would you like to order now, sir?' she asked him, but Hutch shook his head. 'Just some more coffee, please.'

He turned his attention back to me as soon as the waitress had gone. 'You could tell her the truth. You could just recognise her and go up to her, tell her about the ghost. I bet she'd believe you. Why shouldn't she? And I bet she's heard of Greg. If he invites her to a party she'd probably be thrilled.'

'What if she's not? What if she doesn't believe me? What if—'

He held up his hand to stop me. 'Quit borrowing trouble. We can deal with any problems when—'

'No.'

He blinked at me in disbelief. 'You won't help me?'

I was trembling, but determined. 'I'm trying to, believe me. This is insane, Hutch. Look at what you're doing – try to look at it from her point of view—'

'But she doesn't know about the ghost!'

'What difference does that make?'

He sighed and shook his head. 'Becky, it's the whole point! I'm not trying to *woo* this woman – I'm not in love with her; she's a mystery I'm trying to solve!'

I swallowed hard. 'The mystery is all in your head.'

'And yours,' he shot back. 'You saw her too – don't you care why?'

Before I could begin to answer, he froze. His head came up like a hunting dog's and he stared through the window. 'Here she comes.'

I followed his gaze across the street. But he must have sensed her before she appeared because all I could see were a couple of grey-suited men just emerging from the building. Behind them, a second later, a slim blonde woman in a salmon-pink suit came pushing through the heavy glass doors.

'See? It's her.'

'She's not wearing a grey hooded coat—'

'Look at her face.'

I tried, but from that distance she was just a generic pretty young businesswoman. I'd already made up my mind how to play it, though, so I said, definitely, 'That's not who I saw.'

'What! You're lying!'

'I am not. That's not who I saw.'

'Wait. Maybe she'll come in here for her lunch, and you can see her close up.'

For a minute it did look like that was her plan. She crossed at the light and seemed headed straight for the restaurant. But as she came nearer, she looked nervous. I saw her eyes flickering across the cars in the parking lot, and over the big window where we sat, watching.

I think she caught a glimpse of Hutch, and that decided her. Because instead of approaching the entrance she turned abruptly and walked past.

I spent the next half-hour doing my best to argue him out of his obsession, then pointing out how dangerous it was. But he was no more convinced by my attempts at putting forward the rational viewpoint than he'd ever been by my emotion. Even the irony of our reversed positions was, I think, lost on him.

Well, you know the rest of the story. Nothing, not my refusal to help, nor my attempts to make him see reason could stop what was to come.

Hutch became ever more obsessed with Melanie Caron. When charm, reason and persistence all failed, he finally just went after her, to take her by force. His gun wasn't loaded – after all, he didn't want to hurt her, only to make her go with him – but she didn't know that. He didn't know she had her own gun, that she'd started carrying it with her always, against the threat he posed. But, of course, he didn't think he was a threat. Even after she'd shot him, as she believed, in self-defence, even as he was dying, did he understand what he had become?

Yet wasn't he still the same Hutch I'd known and loved?

Everyone else seems to think he'd changed, become a monster, monstrously pursuing the object of his desire.

Even Greg, even his parents, seem to have written him off, sadly, as mad.

Yet if he was mad, it was with the same madness which had always driven him: that of the single-minded scientist, the engineer in pursuit of a practical solution to some material problem. He wasn't 'in love' with Melanie Caron in the sick, obsessive way of stalkers; he just wanted to know what she *meant*.

And so did I.

After his death, seeing the image of Melanie Caron on TV and in the papers, I became convinced that she *was* 'our ghost'. I felt awful because I could never tell Hutch I'd been wrong, could never apologise . . . I'd completely screwed up the real chance I'd had of helping him.

I felt horribly guilty. Of course, I'd thought I was doing the best, by warning him away from her – and I *had* been right about the danger. But I should have known he wouldn't listen to me. He couldn't walk away from an unsolved problem; it just wasn't in him. I should have known that, and tried to avert this horror in some other way. Maybe, if I'd done what he'd asked, and approached Melanie myself, I could have talked her around, reached some peaceful accommodation. Would it have hurt her to spend a little time with him, with us? To help us solve the mystery of her haunting?

The mystery remained, and, after all, it was *our* mystery. Solving it felt like one last thing I could do for Hutch.

Although my intuition that the ghost had been a warning to stay away from Melanie Caron turned out to be horribly right, that didn't solve the mystery. The logic was circular, like a time paradox: the ghost we saw was a clip from the future, when Melanie had cowered in fear from her stalker – but that future could never have come into being if Hutch hadn't first seen her cowering in fear. I couldn't accept the idea of a totally predetermined universe, that our fates were scripts written before our births, so that brought me back to Hutch's original question. Why her?

I took my time and thought carefully. I couldn't afford to blow what might be my only chance.

I decided to approach her as a journalist, and told her I was researching a story on the subject of stalkers. She wasn't a Galveston resident, so had no idea how unlikely a topic that was for the weekly *Shore Times*. And although she told me she didn't want more publicity, when I swore I wouldn't use anything she didn't approve, and said I just needed some 'insider detail' to help me understand the experience of being stalked, she agreed to meet me, suggesting a Starbucks' near her office. People do like to tell their stories.

I made the most of our first meeting. I've never worked harder to make somebody like me. Never felt so desperate for acceptance. But it worked. I racked up a lot of miles on my old car, pretending urgent business in Houston so that I could take her up on her invitation to 'call, if you happen to be in town'. To keep her talking to me about Hutch, I told her that although my editor had spiked 'our' story, I was considering writing a book about stalking.

I sucked up to her shamelessly – and it all paid off, finally, when she invited me out to her house for dinner. She knew I would have a long drive back to Galveston, and one of the things we had in common was a liking for good wine with our dinner, so she invited me to stay the night.

I had been afraid that she might have sold her house and moved, unable to bear to go on living in the place where she had killed someone, but no, she was still there, in the house where Hutch had died.

Why not? she asked me, shrugging. She liked it there. Why should she let 'that bastard' drive her out? Since 'that business' she'd had an alarm system installed. She felt as safe here as she could feel anywhere.

'So you don't feel the house is haunted?' I held my breath waiting for her answer, hoping. Maybe, despite his determined materialism, Hutch's spirit was still hanging around.

But she shook her head firmly. 'I'm sure it's not. I had this psychic, she's supposed to be really, really good, come to check it out, and she said there was no evil here, nothing but good vibrations, lots of love.'

I felt my heart turn over. Poor Hutch.

'But I did get the kitchen completely redone, just to be on the safe side, and I had a Feng Shui expert advise me about the energy flow . . .'

'The *kitchen*?' That was where we were sitting now, with glasses of wine and bowls of olives, nuts and taco chips set out. I gaped at her. 'Why the kitchen?'

She stared at me, obviously suspecting my journalistic credentials. It must have been publicised, or maybe she'd told me when I wasn't listening. 'Because this is where I shot him, of course! He actually died in the laundry room, just there—' she pointed across at a louvred shutter, painted sunflower yellow, which screened off the narrow back hallway from the rest of the room – 'but there's not much to redesign in there. It's not like I ever spend much time in there, anyway, not like I do in the kitchen. But I did everything I could. I had the carpeting taken up, of course, put down Mexican tiles instead, and had the walls repainted blue, a very harmonious colour, instead of white like they were before, because white's the colour of the dead in China, after all, and—'

I got up. 'Do you mind if I look?' I was already walking away from her as I spoke. I didn't want her to see the tears which had sprung to my eyes at the thought of poor Hutch dying all alone in that cramped space while his killer sprinted out the front door to safety.

It was a tiny little room, all right, tightly packed with a big washing machine and even bigger dryer; cupboards overhead held the usual sorts of cleaning stuffs. I tried with all my might to get some sense of Hutch, some lingering trace of his personality, in that little room, but there was nothing. Maybe the Feng Shui had got rid of his hungry ghost. Or, more likely, what Hutch had always believed was true, and there was nothing left of us after death; ghosts were just vibrations aided by imagination and the hope that springs eternal.

I got myself under control and returned to the kitchen, where Melanie was starting to get our dinner together.

The evening dragged on. I'd never realised how exhausting it could be to be constantly 'on', always on my guard, like a spy, having to pretend to like someone I would rather have hated. Not that I did hate her, actually, because I understood too well that, in similar circumstances, under seige in my own home, I would have done my best to kill my stalker. What difference would it have made to me to be told that he was somebody else's beloved friend? At least I didn't have to pretend to be interested in her. I did, genuinely, want to know everything there was to know about her. Somewhere in that mass of personal detail must be the answer to what had happened to Hutch. I had no idea what I was looking for, but I was determined to find it.

Yet somehow the more I knew about her, the less I understood. Melanie was becoming deeply familiar to me, almost a part of myself. Not like the friends we make by choice, but like the playmates forced on children by proximity or family. I thought she was like the boring cousin, a year younger than me, I'd had to play with whenever my mother or my aunt wanted a day off. I knew every detail of her life, knew her room and her toys almost as well as my own, and yet I knew nothing at all about her. When, halfway through college, she dropped out and became a Moonie, I couldn't say I'd seen it coming, but neither could I be genuinely shocked, because, after all, why shouldn't she? I had no idea who she was inside.

Was Hutch as mystified as me, or would being in Melanie's presence have given him what he needed, answered all his questions? As she chatted on, I tuned out, my thoughts drifting back to Hutch, the pain of his loss, the endless regrets . . .

'Becky, what's wrong?'

She reached across the table to touch my hand and I jerked away, spattering fresh tomato sauce all down my shirt.

We both cried out in dismay.

'Oh, gosh,' Melanie said, jumping up as I began to dab at myself with my napkin. 'No, don't do that! You'll set the stain – the best thing is to take it off right away and put it under cold, running water. Take if off, take it off now.'

I looked up at her and she blushed. She turned away. 'I'll go get you something else to put on, of course,' she said in a strained voice. 'Put it straight into the sink, put the cold water hard on it, you hear?' She kept her back to me as she spoke, and hurried out of the room.

By the time she got back I had remembered: there are no coincidences in this life. Every action is meaningful. Suddenly it made sense to me: I had been thinking about Hutch. This might be a way of getting closer to him, of finding out more.

'Could I wash this? Really wash it in the machine, I mean?'

'Uh, if you want. Sure. There's a couple of towels in it now, they'll be okay with it.' She held out her hand but I kept a grip on my dripping shirt.

'I can do it. Just tell me where the soap is.'

'Oh, well, if you look in the cupboard just above the machine – are you sure? Okay then, put it on half-load.'

I performed the simple actions slowly, like a ritual. The little room was like a chapel, high-ceilinged, bare, stone floor ... My naked arms goose-pimpled. I'd been over-warm in the kitchen, but it was freezing out here.

'Are you okay?' I'd taken too long, and she'd come to check on me.

'Sure, I'm fine.' I managed a smile, took the T-shirt she offered, followed her back to the table.

About twenty minutes later, as we were still sitting there, sipping wine, I felt it: a sort of low rumble like an approaching storm, and the fine hairs on my arms prickled with electricity. There was a high-pitched whine like a plane taking off.

'Oh, that *machine*. ' Melanie said crossly. 'You can't hear yourself *think*.'

As she got up and walked towards the laundry room door – which I'd left open – I followed her. I wanted to get back into the little room, sure that he would be there, invoked by the nearly palpable noise.

But I didn't get in, because of course Melanie wasn't going in, she'd only gone to close the door, and I was behind her. When she stopped, I ran smack into her.

We were there on the threshold between the two rooms, possibly on the very spot where he'd been shot. I felt a presence, unmistakable, absolutely electric, as we collided. She gasped, and then gave a sort of helpless little moan and turned around – a tight little turn, more a rotation, which kept her pressed against me, only now it was her breasts I felt, soft and firm against mine.

An absolute imperative brought our lips together. I'd never been attracted to a woman before in this way, but I didn't question it. I couldn't. It was the most natural and necessary thing in the world to kiss her. And as I did, I knew that this was what Hutch had wanted. And now it was what I wanted. In this feeling between us was all that was left of him.

If he'd been alive, Hutch would have been horrified, I'll bet, by my ignorance in thinking that an ordinary domestic washing machine could produce infrasound waves powerful and concentrated enough to haunt a room. But he'd never shared the specifications of his ghost-machine with me, so why shouldn't I think it?

I still thought it as, still kissing her, I pushed Melanie through the doorway, against the vibrating machine, and moved slowly down her body, kissing her through her clothes and then beneath them. I think I imagined that I was doing this for Hutch, or that he was working through me.

But he'd been just as ignorant, just as foolish, in imagining that he could solve the mystery that was Melanie by pursuing her, and forcing himself on her.

I know otherwise now.

She's still a mystery to me, although I know her better, inside and out, than I've ever known anyone before. And she knows me, even about my connection to Hutch. I've told her everything. And yet the mystery remains, which I think we'll forever try, and probably fail, to solve. It's called love.

Lisa Tuttle was born in Texas, but has lived in the United Kingdom since 1980. She currently resides in Scotland with her husband and daughter. Her novels include *Familiar Spirit*, *Gabriel*, *Lost Futures* and *The Pillow Friend*, along with several titles aimed at younger readers. Her short fiction has been collected in *A Spaceship Built of Stone*, *A Nest of Nightmares* and *Memories of the Body*, and she has edited the anthologies *Skin of the Soul* and *Crossing the Border*. She has recently compiled a new short story collection, *My Pathology* (the title story is from *Dark Terrors 4*), and is currently working on a dark fantasy novel called *The Changeling*. 'The theory about infrasound and ghosts is absolutely real,' explains the author. 'I based my story on a newspaper article (the *Sunday Telegraph*, June 28, 1998) about research done at Coventry University. Although I haven't heard about anybody actually attempting to create a "real" haunted house on this basis, I wouldn't be surprised to learn that it had been done. And Austin, Texas, strikes me as one of the more likely venues for such an attempt. Like the narrator, I grew up in Texas and in my youth hung out with a group which was into ghost-hunting and semi-scientific psychic research. So far as I know, I've never seen a ghost, but I've encountered weird atmospheres where the appearance of a ghost felt pretty immanent.'

My Present Wife

DENNIS ETCHISON

The road was wide and well-lighted for the first mile or so, then narrowed to a single lane and led into the foothills, where the signs were impossible to read even with her high beams. That was almost enough to make Lesley turn around and go home, especially when the other car sped up and began to close the distance. It had been on her tail since she left the freeway.

She tried to ignore the headlights and stopped under the first streetlamp in several long blocks, took the invitation out of her purse and looked at it one more time.

The hand-drawn map on the back was useless. It might have been a child's sketch of a tree made with black crayon, the branches leading off the page into unknown territory. The lines were not labelled and there was only an X at the top, a house number and the words *Saddleback Circle*.

When the headlights glared in her rearview mirror she had to glance up.

The other car slowed, pulling even and hovering for a moment. Her side window was milky with frost. She reached for the button and rolled the glass down.

'Richard,' she shouted, 'leave me alone or I'll call the police! I mean it this time!'

Then she got a good look at the other car. It was a brand new Chrysler, shiny black and heavy with chrome fittings, so dark inside that she could not see the driver. Embarrassed, she held up the invitation and waved it, accidentally brushing the controls by the steering wheel.

'Sorry, I – I thought you were someone else. Do you know where—?'

But now her wipers were on, skittering back and forth across the windshield, drowning out her own voice. The tinted passenger window on the other car remained closed.

'Wait, please! I think I'm lost . . .'

The Chrysler glided silently past her to the next corner, a plume of white exhaust billowing up behind it.

She spotted the same car a few minutes later, its turn signals winding uphill in a pattern that vaguely resembled part of the hand-drawn map. Then there was an entire row of red taillight reflectors ahead, stopped along both sides of the road, so many that there could be no doubt she had finally found the party. It took a few minutes more to locate a parking space next to the split-rail fence on Saddleback Circle.

A sharp wind blew out of the canyon, gathering force and turning back on itself as if chilled by the cul-de-sac at the end. Lesley walked towards the glow of a big house, while heavy steps sounded beyond the fence and white breath condensed in the air between the trees. A riderless horse, pale and steaming against the darkness, stood snorting and pawing the earth. She closed her collar and hurried on.

The house shone like iced gingerbread, all the doors and windows sparkling with colour and movement. The gravel driveway was still full of cars. Someone stepped forward from the shadows and she put her hand up to shield her eyes from the glare of Christmas lights over the porch.

'Hello?' she called out, shivering.

'Les, you made it.'

'Coral? It feels like it's going to snow!'

'Don't say that in LA. It's bad luck.'

'Am I too late?'

'Come on in, for God's sake.' Coral led her up the wooden steps. 'Get yourself some eggnog and I'll introduce you around.'

A dozen people were jammed around the coatrack in the foyer, the faces of the taller ones blurring as they moved aside for their hostess. The air was warm with body heat but Lesley's fingers trembled as she undid the button at her throat and smoothed her collar.

'I can't stay.'

'You have a late date?'

'Right, Coral.'

'Then stick with me. I'll fix you up.'

'No, really, I'll just mingle . . .'

Lesley squinted in the sudden brightness, gazing through crêpe paper and popcorn strung from the vaulted living room ceiling. The party was close to breaking up but a few tanned women in satin and denim stood talking to men with cowboy boots and silver belt buckles, while long-legged teenagers whispered behind a table full of empty pie tins and half-eaten cookies. When she turned around Coral was not there.

She rubbed her hands together and wandered into the hall, past matted photographs of her friend in a black hunt cap and coat jumping a chestnut mare over hurdles. A man's voice droned from one of the bedrooms, describing how he had broken his ankle during a flying dismount the previous year. Only his broad shoulders and pressed Levi's were visible through the doorway. Three women sat on the edge of the bed, listening with lips parted. Lesley continued down the hall before he could roll up the leg of his jeans to show them the scar.

In the den, Coral took her arm and led her to a balding man on the sofa.

'Ed, you remember Les, from the Tri-Valley meet. We went out for dinner after.'

'Oh, right,' he said, half-standing, the top of his head a pink smear. 'Did you ever sell that Hermès saddle?'

'Not yet,' said Lesley.

'How much do you want for it?' asked a drunk woman on the other end of the sofa.

'I haven't decided.'

'Where's your friend?' said the balding man.

'Who?'

'Big guy, longrider coat. What's his name?'

Coral said in a low voice, 'Honey, that was last summer.'

'Richie, that's it.' He looked around. 'Is he here?'

Coral rolled her eyes. 'They're not together anymore.'

'Oh. Too bad. Nice fellow.'

'Sit down, Ed.' When they were back in the hall, Coral whispered, 'I'm so sorry. I told him, but he doesn't listen.'

'It's okay. I'm over it.' They passed the bedroom, now empty. 'Who was that man?'

'You know my husband!'

'I mean in there, with those women.'

'What did he look like?'

'I couldn't see his face. Tall, black hair . . .'

'Sounds familiar.'

'I don't know what you're talking about.'

'Don't you?' Coral steered her toward a table of *hors d'oeuvres* in the dining room. 'Do yourself a favour. Try a different type, for once?'

Lesley blinked and lowered her head, fumbling for a paper plate.

The first chafing dish contained a few wieners floating in water. Before she could open the next one small feet thundered behind her and five or six children ran to the table and filled the last of the hot dog buns. When they were gone she set her plate aside, reached for a cut-glass cup and dipped some punch out of the bowl.

'Do you have any vodka to go with this?' she asked, but Coral had already gone on to the living room.

Lesley explored the rest of the downstairs.

She passed several couples. There were a few single men leaning in doorways or working the halls, their faces indistinct as she squeezed by them with her head down. In an enclosed back porch the teenaged girls were busy rehearsing a skit of some sort. The yard was illuminated by floodlights and the trees shook silently beyond the glass, teasing a view of absolute darkness. She listened to the girls for a minute, then found her way to the TV room.

A young mother held her sleepy son on her lap, stroking his forehead as they watched a tape of *The Man from Snowy River*, and a woman in a short black cocktail dress stood in the corner talking to a slim, sandy-haired man. Lesley was about to move on when the woman spotted her.

'Les?'

'Hi, Jane.' Lesley started out of the porch, but the woman was already at her side.

'I haven't seen you in so long!'

'I don't ride any more.'

'Why not?'

'I moved.'

'So where are you taking lessons?'

'Nowhere. I can't, till my arm heals.'

Jane seemed not to hear her and turned to the man in the corner. 'Do you know—?'

'I was looking for Judy,' said Lesley as he came over to join them. 'Is she . . . ?'

'This is Les,' the woman told him. 'Ask her. She has a fabulous horse.'

Lesley avoided his eyes. 'I used to.'

'What happened?' the man asked.

'I had to sell him.'

'You should have seen her in the Tri-Valley Finals,' said Jane.

'That was one of Suzie's horses. She let me take him out for the day.'

'Who paid?' he said. 'Or did you go Dutch?'

Jane laughed too loudly and said, 'Have you met—?'

'Michael.'

'I don't think so.' His fingers were soft, smooth and unknotted. She withdrew her hand and reached for her purse, but it was not at her side. She had left it on the coatrack in the foyer.

'Where do you ride?'

'Shady Acres. I mean, I did.'

'How do you like it?'

'Beautiful!' said Jane. 'You'll have to come out sometime.'

'I should. My wife wants to ride, but I'm afraid I'll get rug-burns.'

Jane cracked up.

Lesley could not quite meet his eyes, which stood out in an otherwise ordinary, almost uncompleted face. 'Hunters and jumpers?'

'Not that advanced. She's only been on a horse a few times.'

'Well,' said Jane, 'I can show you some easy trail rides. It's right by the State Park.'

'Great. I'll tell her all about it.'

'Where is your wife?'

'She's on her way She had to work late.' He turned his attention to Lesley again. 'What does a decent horse go for?'

She averted her gaze. 'That depends on what you're looking for, I guess.'

'Well . . .' Jane pulled at her lip as she waited for his eyes to fall on her again. 'I'm not supposed to talk about it, but Suzie told me about a steal up in Ventura County. An eight-year-old, A-circuit champion, for—'

Just then a bell clanged.

Lesley went to the hall, following the sound.

Coral held up a metal triangle and beat it with a soup ladle as though calling ranch hands to a chuckwagon dinner. When the remaining guests had assembled in the dining room she announced a special treat, a one-act play written and performed by the Junior Class girls. Lesley saw the teenagers through the open kitchen door, waiting with hand-written notebook pages, practising their lines one last time. She took a position along the wall nearest the living room, as a pretty blonde girl stepped in front of the buffet table and began speaking.

'Kind ladies and gentlemen, I pray you, do not judge me! I was but a poor maid who lost her way . . .'

The girl held out her arms, palms up, in a gesture of supplication. From the foyer came the rustling of coats as a few more couples took this opportunity to slip away. Lesley watched the girl, not looking at the hall to see if Jane and the fair-haired man had followed her.

'... so when *he* came to Sparta and offered me such a fine mount, how could I resist?'

Now a crude horse's head bobbed out of the kitchen, followed by a second half made of brown paper with a real horsehair tail. A high-pitched whinnying came from under the paper and the two halves of the horse reared up and bumped the girl, who fell onto her back.

Next to Lesley, a woman nearly spilled her glass of wine.

The audience giggled and applauded. The horse took a premature bow. The woman held her husband's arm to keep from losing her balance.

'Is this R-rated?' she said, convulsed with laughter. 'Her mother's going to die!'

'It's all right,' said her husband behind the brim of his Stetson. 'I think it's *Equus*.'

'I think it's the Trojan Horse,' said another voice.

Lesley raised her eyes and saw that a man wearing a camel's hair sportcoat and a bolo tie had squeezed in next to her.

'Don't you?' he asked her, leaning closer.

'I really don't know.'

'What are you drinking, little lady?'

She shook her head. 'Nothing, thank you.'

She let herself out onto the wide front porch and felt for her purse, but it was still inside. Couples walked down the steps to the gravel, blowing on their hands, jingling keyrings, unlocking cars in the driveway. Headlights flashed and for a second the blonde girl from the play was silhouetted against the split-rail fence, imprisoned by the arms of a teenaged boy. The headlights moved on and there was the sound of laughter in the dark. Lesley leaned on the railing as footsteps passed behind her from the other end of the porch.

'Excuse me,' she said without turning, 'but do you have a cigarette, by any chance?'

'Well, let's just see here once.' It was the one Jane had introduced as Michael. He checked his shirt pocket and came up with a crushed pack of Marlboros. 'Hey, you scored.'

'I don't want to take your last one.'

He straightened the cigarette for her. 'My wife says I should quit, anyway. You can help me get rid of the evidence.'

She cupped her fingers around the flame, careful not to touch his hand. 'Did she finally make it?'

'She'll be here. She promised.'

'What does she do?'

'Legal work,' he said.

'I'd like to meet her.'

'You need a lawyer?'

She inhaled and blew out a cone of smoke. 'Oh, I guess not.'

'Sexual harassment, or a quickie divorce? Let's see, you keep the house and car . . .'

'I'm not married.'

'Palimony? That's easy. But first you have to stop calling and hanging up. Leaving notes on his car.'

'It's not me.'

'You found a dead horse in your bed?'

'Not yet.' She smiled at him and coughed.

'Smooth, huh?'

'This is the first one I've had in a long time.'

'Why did you stop?'

'Someone I know – knew – didn't like it.'

'He should meet my present wife.'

'How many times have you been married?'

'Only once. It's a joke. I used to call her my first wife, but she didn't like it. So now I introduce her as my present wife. She doesn't think that's funny, either.'

'I wonder why.'

'You're a lot like her.'

'What's her name?'

'Sometimes I forget,' he said with a twinkle in his eye.

A burst of whistles and applause from inside the house.

'I'd better go in,' she said. 'Thanks.'

'The first one's free.' His eyes shone out of the shadows. 'Seriously. She can get you a restraining order.'

'Who, your present wife?'

'If that doesn't work, we'll tie him up and dump him on a trail somewhere. State Parks are always good.'

They laughed.

Mothers hugged their shiny-faced daughters, who made desperate hand signals to each other across the dining room. Lesley touched the blonde one's arm.

'You were wonderful.'

'Thanks!' the girl said in a sweet, breathless voice.

'You're Tara, aren't you?'

'Um, yeah.' The girl looked over her head, scanning the room with restless green eyes. She had a broad forehead and skin that almost glowed.

'You probably don't remember me,' said Lesley. 'I helped you train for your first Junior Class meet.'

The girl pretended not to hear and swept by her to the hall, where the two halves of the horse, now in riding clothes, led her away. They were all legs and gangly arms, their silken hair pinned to the backs of long necks above collarless dressage shirts, their clean faces mouthing words that could almost be read from across the room. Lesley smiled after them and went into the kitchen.

Coral and three other women were putting food into stainless steel bowls.

'Well, it's about time,' said the one with the short haircut.

'Judy? I was looking for you!'

'We had a bet you wouldn't show.'

'Michelle! And Jeannie . . .' Lesley embraced them. 'Sorry I'm late. I saw Tara – she's adorable. What a great Helen.'

'Next week she'll be Joan of Arc,' said Michelle. 'All she does is watch that movie over and over.'

'Does she still ride?'

'She will, if I get her some chain-mail.'

'Judy has a bone to pick with you,' said Jeannie, covering a bowl with plastic wrap.

'What about?'

'When's the last time I saw you at Shady Acres?' asked the one with short hair.

'A few months.'

'Try six. Right?' she asked Jeannie, pouring the leftover eggnog back into a carton.

'I had to sell Kahlua when I moved out.'

'That's no excuse. You're the best rider I've ever seen.'

'No, I'm not . . .'

'And you know darn well you can ride Jack any time. All you have to do is ask.'

Lesley blushed. 'That's really, really nice of you, Jude. I will, as soon as my arm's healed.'

'It's healed now, and so are you. Got it? You dumped the jerk and you're back in the mix. What are you doing Saturday?'

'I'm not sure yet.'

'The Grand Prix at Oak Ridge. Box seats.'

'I'll call you.' Lesley glanced over Judy's shoulder at the kitchen window, as a tall dark figure passed in the yard outside. She put her hand to her throat. 'Who else did you invite?'

'Friends only.'

'I mean tonight,' she said to Coral.

'Is it cold in here?'

'No, I'm fine.'

'Then why are you shivering?' Coral put the last bowl away and closed the refrigerator door. 'Come on. I can't let you leave like this.'

There were plates, half-eaten hot dog buns and torn wrapping paper on every surface. A few sportcoats and plaid Pendletons still prowled the edges of the living room. Coral led her upstairs, past small children bundled like teddy bears for the ride home. She thanked the mothers and fathers for coming, then steered Lesley into the master bedroom.

'I'll help you clean up.'

'No, you won't.' Coral rummaged in the closet, pulled out a suede jacket with sheepskin lining. 'Here. Put this on.'

'I'll bring it back.'

'Saturday. The old gang will be there.' She helped Lesley get her bad arm into the jacket and looked at her. 'I know it's been a rough year for you. But it's over.'

'I guess so.'

Lesley turned away and opened the curtains above a table that held Coral's trophies and ribbons, just enough to see down into the backyard.

'Did you ever find out who she was?' said Coral.

Below, the yard was empty, the gate latched. There was no one on the side of the house next to the kitchen. In the distance taillights wound slowly up the canyon road like blood cells through a clogged artery. She let the curtains fall closed.

'He never admitted it. He told me I was paranoid, and after a while I almost believed him. But I know I did the right thing. It's just that sometimes . . .'

'You don't call him, do you?'

'He calls me.'

'What does he say?'

'Nothing.'

'Then how do you know?'

'Well, if it's not him, then that means he was right. And I *am* paranoid.'

'My God, Les.'

'Sometimes I think he's following me. Like tonight.'

'I definitely did not invite Richard!'
'There was a car behind me, on the way.'
'If he's stalking you—'
'It wasn't even his car. But when I saw it I thought . . .'
Coral sat her down on the bed.
'Listen. There are plenty of men out there. You could have met a few tonight, if you'd take those damned blinders off.'
'I don't want another relationship.'
'Who's talking about that? Take them for what they are: fun and games. I'll tell you a secret. The rest of it isn't that great.'
'Then why did you get married again?'
'Ed's a good man. And I love our new house. But there's only one first time.' She pressed Lesley's fingers. 'You're lucky. Everything's still right there in front of you, like a candy store – all you have to do is enjoy. Like the song says, love the one you're with, right? What's the first thing you do when you get thrown? Pull yourself together and get back on! So give yourself a chance. For me?'

At the foot of the stairs her husband was busy picking loose popcorn out of the rug. His body was thick around the middle and when he got up he had to hold the banister for support. Coral helped him stand.
'Leave that,' she said, resting her head on his shoulder. 'You're such a neatness freak.'
He kissed her with a noisy smack. His pink face was detailed in this light, with kindly lines etched around the eyes.
'I'll do it,' said Lesley. She found a paper cup and began collecting the popcorn.
'It can wait till morning.'
Michelle and Judy came in from the dining room.
'Who's here?' Coral asked them.
'Just some guys,' said Judy. 'The kind that never give up.'
'Jeannie's in the kitchen,' said Michelle. 'She drank too much eggnog.'
'Put her in the guest bedroom. She can sleep it off.'
'The junior girls are there.'
'What are they doing?'
'Talking about boys and horses.'
'Are there any boys?'
'Only that trainer, with the story about his leg. He has one boot off.'
'Pervert,' said Ed and headed for the back of the house.
Lesley crossed the dining room. There were candy canes and sugared peanuts on the carpet, cookie crumbs folded in napkins by

every chair. As she gathered them up colourful holiday sweaters and turquoise watchbands flashed beyond the arches. The faces of the men who had stayed were no longer blurred but easy to see now, weathered and tan or pale but interesting, professionals and jocks from the city or the country, each with a story to tell. Easy laughter lilted from every direction. It would take a few more minutes for them all to say their goodbyes. She grabbed as much trash as she could and took it to the kitchen.

As she emptied her arms, a low moaning came from the floor by the butcher block table.

'Jeannie, what are you doing down there?'

'Sitting.'

Michele and Judy came in with a crumpled paper tablecloth. They stepped around Jeannie and found the trash can.

'How are we going to get her on her feet?'

'Tell her Hap Hanson's in the other room.'

'He's too old.'

'He's not, is he?' said Lesley.

'Too old?'

'No, in the other room.'

'Sure.'

'Who is?' Lesley asked.

They both turned from the sink and looked at her. Michelle winked at Judy. 'There might be a couple of single guys out there.'

'Like?'

'Chris, from the barn. And Jason the baby doctor, and that guy from Westlake Village, the lawyer—'

'His wife's the lawyer,' said Lesley.

'Which one is he?' asked Judy.

'Curly hair, five-eight or nine . . .'

'That's him. He's definitely married.'

'To his first wife!'

'I know. I was just wondering.'

'If he fools around?'

'*No*. He's nice, though. Funny. Is he a friend of Coral's?'

'She didn't invite him.'

'His wife, then,' said Michelle. 'She rides.'

'Not yet,' Lesley told them. 'She wants to take lessons.'

'I heard she works for a TV station.'

'She's a vet,' said Judy.

'They just moved here,' Michelle said. 'From Phoenix.'

'Texas,' said Judy.
'He told me San Diego . . .' Jeannie mumbled from the floor.
'Maybe he crashed the party.'
'Why would he do that?'
'Looking for his present wife!'
'Remember, he's off-limits.'
'I *know*,' said Lesley, 'okay?'

She made coffee and helped her friends walk Jeannie to a sofa in the living room, then left them and joined Coral and her husband. The front door was open just enough to show the blonde girl at the edge of the porch, kissing someone goodnight in the shadows. It was not the same boy she had been with earlier. Lesley lingered in the foyer as the last guests put on their coats. Michelle made her promise to meet for lunch next week, then went outside to find her daughter.

'You finally stopped shivering,' said Coral.
'I feel better now.'
'Good.'
'Glad you could make it,' said Ed.
Lesley met his eyes without flinching. 'Thanks for inviting me. You don't know.'
'Any time,' said Coral and held her. 'I mean it,' she whispered. 'See you Saturday?'
'I'd love to.'
She went back to the living room. Judy would take Jeannie home and bring her back to pick up her car in the morning. Then Lesley remembered her purse. It was on the rack, behind a long black leather coat.
'Whose is this?'
'Mine,' said Ed.
'It was my present to him,' Coral said. 'Because he's my sweetie.'
'Oh.' Lesley hooked her arm through the strap of the purse.
'You drive carefully, now,' Ed told her.
Lesley started out, then came back and hugged him, too.
'I will,' she said.
She closed the door. Now the moon shone down like a huge streetlamp, illuminating the fence and the tops of the trees beyond the front yard. There were no more cars or shadows in the driveway. She started down the steps.
Behind her, the boards squeaked and a man's voice said, 'Need a ride?'
'No, thanks.'

'Sure?'

'I have a car.'

'Where? I'll drive you.'

She noticed a black Chrysler still parked by the curb at the end of the driveway and walked faster, digging for her keys. She shook her purse but nothing jingled. When she stopped to open it he bumped into her and the purse fell to the ground.

'Let me get that, little lady.'

'I can do it.'

She knelt before a pair of snakeskin boots. They belonged to the one with the camel's hair coat and bolo tie.

'Wonder what happened to those keys?' he said with a grin.

'How did you know . . . ?'

'I got it, honey,' said another voice.

'Over here,' she called as the sandy-haired man came down from the porch. 'Where were you, Michael?'

'Looking for you.' To the tall man he said, 'We're okay here, pardner.'

When the other man left she said, 'You have wonderful timing.'

'You, too.'

'I feel so stupid. Now I can't find my keys.' She kept sifting through the gravel with her fingers. 'I left my purse for a while. You don't suppose that man . . . ?'

'Let's just see here once.'

He put his hand in his pocket and clinked his own keys. Then he leaned down and raked the gravel, and suddenly her keyring glinted there in the moonlight.

'Oh, God, thanks!'

'Where are you parked?'

'All the way at the end.'

'I'll walk you.' He helped her up. 'Do you have a long way to go?'

'A few miles. Once I get to the freeway I'm okay.'

'Left at the first street, then follow it till you see the on-ramp.'

'Got it.' When he patted his pockets she reached into her purse. 'How about a menthol?'

'Just like my wife.'

'I thought she didn't smoke.'

'She used to.'

'I hope she's all right. Did she call?'

In the flare of the lighter his hair was red and his smile ironic. He cupped his hands over the flame, enclosing her fingers.

'She wouldn't know the number here.'

'Does she have a cell phone?'

'No. She doesn't want people bugging her when she's away from the clinic.'

Lesley lit her own cigarette and blew out a cloud of smoke, white as frost from the chill in the air. 'I thought she was a lawyer.'

'The office, I mean.'

They came to the end of the driveway. Ahead the trees were so tall that the rest of the canyon was black.

'Do you mind if I follow you?' she said.

'Sounds like a plan.'

'In case I get lost again.' She fingered her keys, took a deep breath, held it and finally let it out. 'Look, would you like to have coffee or something? It's so cold. I was thinking about stopping, before I get on the freeway.'

'There's a Denny's by the underpass.'

'Is that the only place open?'

'Something wrong with Denny's?'

'I just meant . . .'

A car drove out of the canyon and he turned to her, the headlights blazing in his eyes. 'Not good enough for you?'

'What?'

'Nothing's ever good enough, is it?'

She tried to step back but he had hold of her wrist, the one that was almost healed.

'You're hurting me!'

'Sometimes I wonder why I married you in the first place,' he said, his breath steaming until his face was only a blur again. 'Well, listen up, bitch. Tonight you're going to do exactly what I tell you and like it! Got that? I might even take you to the State Park afterwards. There's never anybody around . . .'

Then, jerking her so violently that her feet left the ground and her toes scraped the dirt and the rocks, he dragged her the rest of the way down into the cul-de-sac.

Dennis Etchison lives in Los Angeles. He is a winner of both the World Fantasy Award and the British Fantasy Award. *The Death Artist* from DreamHaven Books is his fourth collection of stories illustrated by J.K. Potter. 'The late Robert Bloch had a deliciously mordant sense of humour,' the author recalls. 'Always the wicked jokester, his mischief found expression in public and private conversations as well as in his writing. I once heard him introduce his lovely spouse Elly, to whom he had been happily married for many years, as "my present wife", a remark she somehow did not find amusing. When I followed his example and tried to introduce "my first wife" (first and only, I should add) on a couple of occasions, for some reason mine did not like that one any better. So, since I do not share Bloch's love of risk in matters of domestic harmony, I decided that it might be safer to write about a character given to such remarks. What if an unfamiliar man showed up at a social gathering and spoke glowingly of a wife who was not there? Would his married status cause the single women in the room to let down their guard? Would it actually make him more appealing? To carry the idea further, what if the man used this as a technique of seduction – or worse? He might even be, say, a psychopath who no longer differentiates between the one he is married to (or was, if she is even still alive!) and the one he is with. Sounds like a story to me . . .'

Alicia

MELANIE TEM

Puberty hit Alicia early and hard. After two other daughters who'd been more or less impossible in their early teens, we'd been hoping for a late-bloomer, but when she had noticeable if asymmetrical breast buds by the time she was ten and got her period well before her eleventh birthday, we knew we were in for trouble.

'She's growing up so fast,' became my husband's refrain. At first he'd sound more plaintive or ironic than seriously alarmed; alarm came later.

This annoyed me, because I didn't want my daughter to be afraid of her adolescence, even if her parents were. I needn't have worried. 'She's growing up at exactly the pace she's supposed to,' I'd say a little testily, meaning to be reassuring to both Alicia and her father. But as time went on I wasn't so sure.

Soon the older girls started pointing out, with equal parts envy and annoyance and with sly glances in our direction, that their little sister had a more respectable cleavage than they did. She started getting hips, couldn't buy pants to fit her in the girls' department any more.

The spring she turned twelve, she grew a good six inches between Christmas and the end of school; you could practically see her legs elongating with every lope across the soccer field. For a little while it was obvious from the sidelines that she suddenly wasn't familiar with her body or her emotions: elbows flew all over the place; when the action was at the other end of the field her attention visibly spumed away like little curls of steam; once she kicked the ball into the opponents' goal and burst into tears so hysterical she had to be pulled from the game. But it didn't take her long to get herself together, and before that season was over Alicia was the best forward on the team, because of a truly formidable concentration she learned to bring to bear.

Suddenly ninety per cent of the phone calls were for Alicia, from giddy, snotty girls and boys with squeaky voices; a few boys who sounded alarmingly older didn't call more than a few times, so I restrained myself to a raised eyebrow. Her big sisters reported that she would say things – statements, never questions – obviously intended to draw them into discussions of sex and love. Her tender age made them decidedly uncomfortable with this; they were just old enough for a dawning perception that parental worries and rules might not be completely arbitrary, but still sufficiently close to Alicia's age to think maybe they ought to ally themselves with her against us. I must admit I took a certain ignoble amusement in their discomfiture, remembering how difficult they'd been.

A sense began to gather of something impending – not doom, exactly, but something threatening. My husband and I both became vigilant. We analysed Alicia's every state of mind, her every action. We wondered what she was thinking, even when she seemed to be telling us. We talked about Alicia so much and so fruitlessly that I, beginning to resent her ubiquitousness, would try to change the subject, but my husband was even more obsessed with her than I was and he'd bring it right back to her. It became hard to think of anything else.

Whereas the older girls had been moody – bursting into tears if a waiter brought them regular instead of cherry Coke; having to be sent from the dinner table to get a giggling fit under some semblance of control – Alicia remained relatively even-tempered. The most noticeable change was in her relationship with her father. She'd always been Daddy's girl. Now she'd talk to him in a tone she'd never use with me, just this side of disrespectful, or she'd give him a rather skilful cold shoulder at his slightest unresponsiveness, actual or imagined, to her slightest desire, whether or not he could possibly have known what it was. At the same time, she was more overtly affectionate with him than usual, often snuggling against him on the couch or grabbing his hand as they walked across a parking lot, and she was openly flirtatious, sauntering past him just out of the shower wrapped only in a towel, soliciting his opinion about whether she could still decently wear last year's bathing suit.

My husband, a sensible man, tried to remember what he knew from raising the older girls, to give her feedback and set limits for her without taking things personally. I tried to stay out of it, to let them work out their relationship themselves and trust that he had his own ways of dealing with it. After a confrontation with her, overt or subtle, he'd often retreat to his garden, which for some time had been a source of solace and inspiration for him and, now that he was skilled enough to try things like topiary and cultivating more exotic plants, functioned as distraction, too.

But often I couldn't stand it and would step in to protect him from her. This was, after all, the man I loved, and this nubile young woman was treating him shabbily. Besides that, I was aware of a kind of primal jealousy, the intensity of which shocked me; this was *my* man, and she couldn't have him.

One day it came to me what she was doing. She was practising on him, trying out various ways of behaving with men, testing her power. This was all perfectly normal behaviour for an adolescent girl with a trustworthy father, and the older girls had done some of it, too, but something about Alicia's concentrated version was chilling.

Our house was positively awash in female hormones. I'd started the hot flashes and emotional lability of menopause. Our oldest daughter, living with her new husband in the basement apartment, was pregnant. And Alicia, beautiful and poised and not even officially a teenager yet, exuded a sexuality that took us all aback, at first even her. Palpable as an electromagnetic field, it charged the air, gave her a sort of aura. It changed her voice, her skin tone, the way she sat in a chair and walked across a room and lounged in a doorway. Something new had come into this daughter, and it excited and worried me deeply.

Long accustomed to being the only male in a house full of women, pampered and revered and out of a particular sort of gender-based fondness sometimes not quite taken seriously, my husband was nonetheless finding this almost too much for him, and he'd threaten to run away for the next few years He was joking, but not entirely.

'Men have hormones too, you know,' one of us would jibe. 'Men have midlife crises, too. Where's your red convertible? Gonna go have a tummy tuck?'

'Who's got time for a midlife crisis in this family?' he'd grumble.

Once Alicia took the banter to a quite different level by saying coyly, 'I bet you've got a bimbo on the side, don't you, Daddy? Somebody young enough to be your daughter? Maybe one of our friends?' She named two or three of her sisters' friends and even one of her own who'd been wearing a lot of make-up and very tight tank tops since grade school, and fixed her father with a decidedly grown-up leer.

She'd gone too far. She'd pushed an edgy playfulness over into some darker, sleazier territory. There was a thunderous silence. Then her father, face flushed and lips pressed into a hard white line, left the room.

'What'd *I* do?' Alicia asked, with an innocence that could have been genuine, and I didn't know what to say.

'She's too young!' he kept insisting, as if taking a stand on principle would change what was happening with Alicia. 'She shouldn't even be thinking about such things.' But she was. We did hold the line on the accoutrements of sexual development like make-up and braless midriff tops and anything close to dating, but the currents of erotic energy still roiled.

Part of the difficulty for us was language. We heard her saying 'I love you' to virtually every boy to whom she took a fancy, however fleeting. She spoke of 'going out with' or 'being with' somebody when all they were doing was seeing each other at school and talking on the phone. She referred to whatever boy she liked at the moment as her boyfriend and seemed not at all fazed when her boyfriend was somebody else the next week. She'd say with satisfaction, 'I guess I'm popular, huh?' and I'd try to gauge whether this was anything more than a healthy self-image awkwardly expressed; I began uneasily to think that it was.

Increasingly bothered, I tried to engage her in conversations about the power of words to shape reality, and she didn't actively shut me out, but she didn't say anything, either, and I couldn't tell whether she'd taken my point or not. Of our three daughters, Alicia was turning out to be the hardest to read; I wouldn't have called her secretive, exactly, but her private self was virtually unassailable, a cache of thoughts and feelings and knowledge about herself and the world that she guarded like the dangerous treasure it was.

Alicia was a few months into seventh grade when Todd appeared on the scene. Actually, she told me with a hint of smugness that I didn't at the time understand, they were in the same class and had known each other for a couple of years, but neither had found the other particularly worth notice until now. 'What's different?' I enquired, trying for the right degree of maternal interest. 'Is it that he's grown up?'

She shook her head, her sun-streaked brown hair shining. 'Not really. But I have.'

Todd's mother told me later, before I realised enough about what had happened between our children to stop talking to her about it, that she was a single mother and Todd was her only child; they'd always been really close. He was such a good kid, a straight-A student, track star and serious artist, never in trouble of any kind, never having needed any but the mildest discipline, kind and responsible and happy. He'd been showing no signs of interest in girls until suddenly one day he fell head over heels for Alicia. It was, she said somewhat wistfully, as if he'd been pulled out of childhood into adolescence overnight, before she was ready for it and, she worried, before he was.

When I told her Alicia was the youngest of three, she said in all seriousness that she'd defer to my experience in this. 'Oh, my, don't do that,' I protested. 'I don't know any more than you do.' She laughed, as though I were being falsely modest. And, in fact, what I said wasn't entirely accurate; I did know enough about kids to realise that there was something outside the normal range about Alicia.

Todd's mother and I chuckled wryly together about the power of love, and commiserated with each other about the interesting next few years in store for us both. I was to remember that conversation more than once as the Todd-Alicia story unfolded; in retrospect, wistfulness and amusement, however wry and knowing, came to seem shockingly off the mark, and commiseration a woefully inadequate reaction. But even if I'd been more aware then of what was going on, what would I have said to Todd's mother? 'Tell your son to beware of my little girl'?

It started one autumn Saturday when Alicia was out raking leaves. This was not a chore she did willingly, but, unlike her sisters, she didn't waste time on pouting or tantrums; once it became apparent to her that she couldn't talk her way out of something odious, she'd set her jaw and do it. If I'd been the one to insist, that would pretty much be the end of it. If it had been her father, she'd make him pay by barely speaking to him for the rest of the day or, if it was late, going to bed without saying goodnight, which especially vexed him. It wasn't that she thought she'd make him stop telling her to do things she didn't want to do or saying no to things she did, but she knew her coldness bothered him, and she seemed to relish the excuse to demonstrate her influence over him. I didn't like this pattern much, but it was fascinating to observe.

Todd came by on his bicycle that morning, as he often did since our house was on the least direct route possible between his house and the grocery store where he was often sent. He sped past as usual, not stopping, probably hardly even glancing at Alicia. I was out in the yard myself, and I saw her follow him with her eyes, though the motion of the rake didn't falter. Todd came back around the block. In his laboured pedalling and downcast eyes there was a strong hint of reluctance, and I had the distinct impression that Alicia had willed him back, just to see if she could.

He pulled over to the curb, childishly dragging one sneaker in the leaf-filled gutter. They exchanged a few words, inaudible to me. Her sweet high giggle made my heart race, and I could only imagine what it was doing to Todd. Then he rode off. The interlude hadn't even been long enough for me to complain about her not getting her work done.

But it accomplished its purpose. Todd wandered back again that afternoon, this time ringing the bell and keeping his voice from cracking long enough to ask for Alicia, whom I discovered waiting at the top of the stairs out of his line of sight.

Very soon it became obvious that her feelings for this gangly, awkward kid, a few weeks younger than she was, were something new. It was quite as though she'd *decided* this would be something new. Nearly all of her formidable attention was brought to bear on Todd, which made me pity him and wonder about his stamina.

Alicia did her homework quickly and correctly, but minimally and without interest, using only the thinnest surface layer of her mind. Despite our remonstrances and the coach's complaints, she hardly ever went to soccer practice, and I wished she hadn't turned out to be right, that he'd let her play anyway because she was far and away his best player. At dinner she scarcely interacted with the rest of the family, her mind clearly elsewhere.

'Earth to Alicia!' her sisters would tease, or, a trifle snidely, 'Oooh, little sister's in love!' But she'd hardly notice.

Not infrequently we'd come upon her sitting calmly in a chair somewhere, grey eyes very bright and focused on the middle distance, lips and hands moving slightly. Even if we spoke to her or touched her shoulder, it would take a few seconds before she was aware that we were there. 'Was I like that?' her sisters asked incredulously, and we said yes, but in truth there was something quite different about this youngest child.

We limited her phone time. We let Todd come over on his bicycle no more than a couple of times a week for only an hour or two at a time, made sure one of us was in close proximity whenever he was there, insisted they leave the door to the family room open and do something other than sitting on the couch listening to music. Alicia didn't seriously protest any of these constraints. When we'd say no he couldn't come over today, she might frown or roll her eyes. When we'd tell her to get off the phone, she might push it a little, stay on five minutes longer, but she wasn't openly defiant, and I had no sense of underlying rebelliousness, either.

'What do you like about Todd?' I tried one afternoon when Alicia and I were alone in the house. 'How is he different from Peter or Javier or, what was his name? Jimmy?' Jimmy was a stretch; in first grade he'd brought her roses from his mother's garden.

She smiled and answered without hesitation, 'I have power.'

Something about the way she said that sent a shiver up my spine. 'What do you mean by power?' I asked carefully.

'I mean, like, he says can he call me tonight and I say no and he doesn't. Or he asked if he could kiss me and I said we didn't know each other well enough so he didn't.' I risked a direct glance in her direction. Her lovely face was made both lovelier and a little sinister by the flush in her cheeks and the sparkle in her eyes.

I was somewhat relieved to hear that she felt in control, but now there was another concern, a broader moral issue having to do with the character of the woman she was becoming. 'You be nice to Todd,' I admonished. 'You have the power to hurt him, you know.'

'Oh, Mom, please. I *know*.' But she looked newly thoughtful, and I found myself wondering, with some trepidation, what I'd just done.

Todd started bringing her presents. Flowers from what I assumed was his mother's' garden until I discovered they lived in an apartment without one. A rosy lidded soapstone heart, not wrapped and not in a box, from the back of which I glimpsed her peeling what was probably the price tag. A ring with a clear stone she insisted on calling a diamond, though of course it had to be paste; she wore it prominently on a chain around her neck. Her older sisters had dubbed such things 'friendship rings', a concept my husband and I had never quite grasped. Alicia said, 'It shows he belongs to me.'

'He doesn't belong to you!' I objected. 'Alicia, you don't own him.' She just smiled.

The late-night phone calls began sometime in November. We'd decided Alicia wasn't ready for her own phone though her next-older sister helpfully reminded us in front of Alicia that she'd got one for her twelfth birthday; we said it was because Alicia would be on it with her friends all the time, whereas our other daughter had been pretty much a loner so the phone had been more symbolic than practical to her and not much problem for us. Unspoken, even between her father and me, was the apprehension that Alicia'd be using the phone for unspecified nefarious purposes. When we denied her request, she frowned and started to sulk like any thwarted adolescent. Then a supercilious smile crossed her lips and she shrugged, declaring in every way but verbally that our intransigence was a pain in the butt, but basically irrelevant.

The extension in our room was on my side of the bed, so I was the one who answered it. 11:45 p.m., nearly three o'clock in the morning, less than an hour before my alarm was set to go off so I had no hope of going back to sleep – every time, I'd catapult from unconsciousness to disorienting hyperconsciousness, adrenalin geysering, certain our oldest daughter had gone into premature labour or there was some other sort of bad news, since good news is rarely delivered in the middle of the night. My husband would have shot awake, too, and I'd feel his tension whether I was touching him or not. Often we'd hold hands.

The first time, Todd asked politely for Alicia and seemed surprised and then miffed when I informed him brusquely that she wasn't allowed to receive phone calls after nine o'clock and that he'd awakened us. He said sorry, minimally. The next few times, he asked for her in a hoarse, urgent whisper, sometimes saying no more than her name, and once he begged me to call her to the phone, which I refused to do on the theory that if he got what he wanted he'd be even more persistent.

This was getting old. I told both kids that if he didn't stop it I'd call his mother. My husband threatened to take away Alicia's phone privileges altogether, whereupon she wouldn't be in the same room with him for several days.

Finally I did call Todd's mother. This conversation didn't go well. She listened without comment, and then said icily, 'My son is no angel, but I know he wouldn't do something like this.'

'I'm not accusing him,' I hastened to say, although I was. 'I just wanted you to be aware—'

'Hey, you know something?' Startled by how quickly her tone had heated with indignation, I wondered if there was more going on here than I knew. 'I'm really tired of my son being blamed for all this. It's your daughter who's chasing him.'

'She doesn't call him in the middle of the night,' I retorted, though I'd sworn I wouldn't get into this kind of maternal debate. It was apparent that we were no longer on the same side, and I regretted that.

'She tells him to. Todd says she tells him to call her, and he doesn't want to, but he can't help it. He's not sleeping much. He looks awful. I'm taking him to the doctor.' I could tell she'd just now decided to do that.

'Maybe they should stay away from each other for a while,' I ventured, wondering even as I said it how we'd ever enforce such a ban.

Todd's mother, having settled on a plan, was calmer now. 'I don't think that's necessary. They're just kids. Alicia is a lovely little girl. Todd really likes her, and I do, too. Let's just help them work this out.' I agreed, with new hope.

For a while then we got heavy breathing, once or twice a week; we couldn't prove it was Todd, since Caller ID showed 'private name private number' and *69 revealed only that the number was blocked, but we knew it was and Alicia didn't deny it. We felt harassed, of course, and vaguely threatened. We considered calling the police. By Christmas, though, the calls had stopped. To me there was something slightly ominous about that, too, though sleeping through the night was undeniably a relief.

Soon after Christmas break, Alicia started alluding to behaviour problems Todd was having in school. Offhandedly she'd say something like, 'Todd got in trouble again today,' or, 'I don't know what I'm going to do with that boy.' Then she'd laugh, or there'd be an expression on her averted face that could be called gratified. Whether I pressed or tried subtly to draw her out, she wouldn't give details. When we saw Todd during this time, he looked haggard and his eyes were wild.

'Does it seem to you that Alicia hasn't been having much homework lately?' My husband was frowning at her grades, which were not stellar, as in the past they'd sometimes been, but were certainly acceptable.

'She says they aren't assigning anything, or she gets it done in class.'

'No wonder the public education system in this country is such a mess,' he fumed.

At mid-year school conferences, where they told us Alicia was charming, never a behaviour problem, doing fine although she didn't seem to take school very seriously, we ran into Todd's mother. My husband kept edging away, and I found myself decidedly uncomfortable around her by now, but she hardly would let us go even when the teacher was ready for her. 'Todd has been having an *awful* lot of homework lately,' she complained. 'Has Alicia?'

Before I could say anything, my husband gave a non-answer, 'I'm always glad to see them having homework.'

'He hardly has time for anything else. Except your daughter, of course.' She smiled nervously. My husband and I avoided each other's eyes until we were out of her sight, then exchanged a long, worried look.

It was the middle of the night on a cold snowless Tuesday, when my husband shook me awake. 'Todd's mother's here.'

I sat up. The dread that we'd been floating in for some time and that had been in my dreams, too, in the form of dangers just out of my grasp, seemed about to coalesce, and I struggled to make sense of it. 'Why? Where's Alicia?'

He looked very vulnerable standing there in his pyjamas. Love for him spouted clear and strong out of the swirl of deep troubled sleep and adrenalin in my head. 'She's asleep in her bed. But Todd's missing.'

'Is he here?' I had visions of twelve-year-old lovers trysting under our roof, and my sense of sexual morality, not easily offended, prepared to be outraged. Acute anticipatory guilt also swept through me when I thought of facing Todd's mother; there wasn't any doubt in my mind that my daughter would have been the instigator.

'He's not with her, but I haven't searched. He took his mother's car.'

I stalked to Alicia's room. Despite the anger and anxiety that made me want to shake her, I decided to rouse her gently; believing this to be strategic, I was shaken by the tenderness I felt for this daughter of mine in the moments before I woke her. She was heartbreakingly beautiful, pale lashes against dewy skin, pearly bare shoulder, graceful hand clutching like a talisman the ring Todd had given her.

On a hunch, I bent and whispered so close to her ear that I could feel its whorls against my lips, 'Alicia, honey, where's Todd?'

She stirred and murmured something I didn't catch. Her eyes stayed closed and her breath shallow and even; she appeared to be still asleep.

So I pressed, feeling I was taking a chance though of what I couldn't have said. 'Alicia. You know where Todd is. Tell me.'

'Driving.' Now she sounded like someone in a trance, or someone pretending to be. I thought of drugs, of course, and of practical jokes.

'Driving where?'

'Here,' she said, and sat bolt upright. Her eyes were glazed. Her chest heaved. She didn't seem really to know I was there. Her face was set in sheer determination, a look characteristic of her since toddlerhood but alarming now in this distilled form.

I risked grabbing her by the upper arms. Her skin was very warm, her strong young muscles clenched. 'How do you know he's driving here?' Now I did indulge myself in a small, hard shake, which dislodged her from her altered state.

She looked straight at me and, somehow, I was compelled to let go of her, though I didn't want to. She pushed me aside and was at the door of her room when the front doorbell rang. On her way out, though, she did pause long enough to turn and say to me, 'Because I sent for him. Cool, huh?'

Todd and his mother, Alicia and her father and I, plus both her sisters who'd heard the commotion, sat in our living room nearly until dawn. The story had many variations, and I still don't know which if any was the whole truth, but the gist of it was this:

Todd had been having trouble sleeping for weeks, and that night he'd been unable to sleep at all. He'd been tossing and turning, listening to music, thinking of Alicia. His blush at this last admission seemed to me more shame than embarrassment; I saw a little smile cross Alicia's lips, and I thought she looked proud of herself.

Then, Todd said – and this took a long time and many false starts to emerge – he'd felt her calling him. Not heard; felt. He said it was like being famished and having to get something to eat, or – more furious blushes – like having to go to the bathroom really bad. Except that there were words to it: 'Todd. I love you. Go get your mom's car keys and drive over to see me. Right now.'

To which Alicia simply said calmly, 'I was asleep. I was in bed asleep,' which the others seemed to take as irrefutable proof of her innocence in the matter.

When it seemed we'd gathered all the information there was to gather – or, at least, all that was accessible to us – my husband wrapped things up. 'Alicia,' he began, glancing at me for confirmation but then fixing her with his most level gaze, which she met unhesitatingly. I knew what he was going to say and I could have intervened with a dissenting opinion, but I didn't disagree. Looking back now at that portentous moment, I still don't see what reasonable alternatives we had. 'You and Todd will not be seeing each other any more.'

Alicia sat up straighter, and her face glowed dangerously, but she said nothing. It was Todd who looked stricken and gave a pitiable little cry of protest. His mother started to say, 'I'm not sure—'

My husband, though, was sure. He got to his feet, an imposing figure, to continue. 'They are twelve years old. They're too young for this. It's gone too far. She's not to see him any more. Todd, you're not to call here or come to the house. It's over. Do you understand me?' Todd was crying. Alicia was not. 'Alicia? Do you understand me?'

'Oh,' she said sweetly, 'I understand you, Daddy,' and the back of my neck tingled.

The next day, our VCR and camcorder were stolen. The doors and windows were locked and there was no sign of forced entry. The detective asked if anyone could have got hold of a key. Though we didn't say so to him, my husband and I shared gut-wrenching suspicion of Alicia, but she'd spent the night at a friend's across town and she didn't have her own key. The detective said it was probably kids, in and out in a hurry, taking whatever they could grab quickly. Probably somebody who'd been in our house and knew what we had.

Then a pet mouse that Alicia said was Todd's appeared on our doorstep, slashed throat encircled with a blood-soaked pink ribbon to which was attached a disturbing love-note: 'I love you more than I love myself.'

My daughter and I stood together on the porch looking at the bizarre offering. I could hardly speak. 'Alicia, is this from Todd?'

'Dad said I can't see Todd any more, remember?' There were flashes of purple and silver as she cut her pretty grey eyes at me; her irises had always picked up and incorporated ambient colours.

'Something's going on,' I said, an understatement.

'Like what?' It was a challenge.

'I don't know. But I think you need to see a counsellor.'

'No way.' She backed off. 'Not a chance.'

Not expecting much in the way of support or ideas on how to handle this, I nevertheless tried to call Todd's mother again. Their number was now unlisted.

I asked Alicia about that, too. 'I'm not allowed to talk to him on the phone, remember?' Her pinked upper lip was drawn back in the subtlest of sneers. 'Why would I have his number?'

For a week or so then, Todd seemed to have been effectively banished from all our lives. Alicia never mentioned his name. I kept thinking about him, hoping he was all right; he'd unexpectedly touched my heart. Alicia'd been too much for him, I feared. Girls notoriously mature faster than boys; he just hadn't been ready for her.

Then Todd set fire to our house. Alicia was in school when it happened; I called later and was able to verify that she'd been in every one of her classes that day. I came home from work to find the firefighters already there, and my husband holding Todd, who was so ravaged I thought at first he'd been burned. His body, always thin, was positively gaunt, his skin mottled. His hair hung scraggly over his face, with actual bald patches at the temples and crown. His clothes were torn and dirty; I'd often noted how carefully he'd dressed. He was hysterical, not trying to escape but clinging and sobbing, 'I didn't mean to do it! I swear, I tried not to do it! But she made me!'

The damage to the house turned out to be structurally minimal, though the contractors declared it complicated and therefore exorbitantly expensive to repair. Nobody was hurt. Most upsetting was the loss of my husband's tulip tree, burned to the ground. Once shortly after the fire, Alicia and I happened to both be standing at the kitchen window at the same time, and we saw him crouched by the charred stump, mourning. 'Sometimes,' she observed dreamily, 'you have to make sacrifices for love.'

'Alicia,' I said, as steadily as I could, 'he's your father.' I wasn't entirely clear about everything I meant in saying that, but Alicia nodded as if she knew perfectly well.

Todd killed himself on Alicia's thirteenth birthday. It was a cloudy, chill spring morning, streetlights still on when she came down to breakfast, all of us groggy and rushed. The hyper-vigilance I'd developed over the past year alerted me the instant she came into the room and took her place at the table that something had happened, but I'd learned not to ask directly, instead to watch and listen and create cautious openings until she divulged whatever she had already decided to divulge.

'Todd's dead,' she said, and took a long, shaky drink of orange juice.

Her father said, 'Jesus.'

Her sister said, 'Alicia, you are too *weird*.'

I said, 'How do you know?'

Her face glowed with tears now, but her weeping had a soft, romantic quality eerier than if she hadn't been crying at all. 'It's for my birthday,' she told us, her voice breaking. She stopped short of anything like, 'Isn't that beautiful?' or, 'I told him it was what I wanted for my birthday,' but I heard those things as clearly as if she'd said them aloud, and I thought her father did, too.

He sprang around the table and jerked her out of her chair. She made no noise and didn't fight back, just clenched her fists against his chest and narrowed her eyes. He shook her. 'What's going on, young lady? You tell me right now what's going on!'

'Todd's dead!' Now she collapsed into his arms, sobbing like a child, and after a moment of blatant bewilderment he held her, soothed her, stroked her hair.

I couldn't watch. I left the room, left the house, considered leaving altogether but was held back by commitment to my family, which included my youngest child.

Todd had asphyxiated himself in the family car in the locked garage. Beside him on the seat was a note: 'Happy Birthday, my love.' I read about it in the paper.

Alicia is eighteen now, though with her model's carriage and worldly self-possession she seems much older. There have been numerous other boys since the hapless Todd, none of whom seemed to make much of an impression on Alicia, more than a few of whom hung around long after it was obvious she'd utterly lost interest. One of them, while he was still in hopeless desperation calling, sending letters, ringing the doorbell, parking by our curb for hours at a time, was arrested for raping another girl; Alicia gave every appearance of having known about it before her sister told her, and when my older daughter demanded to know if this guy had been a creep with her, she answered readily that he'd never seemed interested in anything like that. Then she added, 'Guess this'll teach him,' and her sister and I could not meet each other's eyes.

Then there was a girl named Molly whose devotion to Alicia was quite unrequited. My curiosity as to whether the relationship was sexual seemed almost irrelevant. For a time Molly virtually lived at our house, doing Alicia's bidding so thoroughly and eagerly that it was hard to watch. She'd get her a glass of ice water. She'd clean her room. She'd fix her hair in beautiful, elaborate styles, while her own hung stringy and untended. At first Alicia would issue orders, no less direct for being phrased politely: 'Go get me a large ice tea with lots of lemon, would you, Molly?' Then she had only to express a preference: 'It's chilly in here,' and Molly would rush to close the window my husband had just opened for fresh air. As time went on, their need for ordinary communication was extinguished altogether and Molly would do what Alicia wanted without being prompted in any way apparent to anybody else. This accomplished, Alicia got bored. From one day to the next, Molly vanished from our lives.

'What's happened to Molly?' I ventured to ask.

Alicia shrugged. 'I guess she dropped out of school. I haven't heard anything else.'

'I thought she was your friend.'

My daughter gave a crisp laugh. 'What made you think that?' Molly's name has never been brought up in our house again.

Molly and the boys were just diversions. Practice. Alicia's real quarry was more intimate and her pursuit of him, I see now, all but lifelong. It was subtle, though, and subtly cumulative; every time I thought I saw something worrisome, a half-dozen reasonable explanations came into my mind at the same time. She was the youngest child. It was good for a girl to be close to her father. And what if I had understood what was happening? Alicia always had been Daddy's girl.

Always interested in all the girls, my husband gradually became obsessed with Alicia. He hung on every word she designed to say to him. He brought her little treats. He began leaving work to pick her up from school, and I began to suspect he often didn't go back. He took to buying her impulsive, expensive presents – a brand new white sports car, real diamond earrings – without consulting me, always swearing we had discussed it and I must have just forgotten. It became easier and easier for her to manipulate around every rule we'd ever set for her – curfew, chores, provocative attire, minimally civilised behaviour – and she did it for sport, because he couldn't bring himself to discipline her; when I complained, which for a while I did bitterly, he'd talk about choosing your battles and keeping your priorities straight.

I'd enter a room where they were together and there'd be the strong aura of a conversation abruptly suspended, though I wouldn't have heard them talking. On the increasingly rare occasions when she went out, he'd always wait up for her, and I had the impression they spent time alone together before either of them went to bed. Each of us had always made a point of doing things alone with each of our kids; eventually Alicia and her father were going out every Saturday night, and the time he and I had together devolved from seldom to never.

Alicia graduated from high school last June. She has no career or educational goal, though it wouldn't be accurate to say she has no plans. She's never asked if she could stay here; we've all just accepted the ongoing arrangement, Alicia as though there'd never been any question, I with decidedly mixed feelings, my husband with palpable, even pitiable relief. I doubt she'll ever leave.

I miss my husband. I scarcely recognise him any more; he acts hardly at all like the man I thought I knew, and he's aged, paled, greyed. He takes interest now in nothing but Alicia. He lost his job some time ago, is nothing more than dutiful towards anybody else in the family, doesn't garden or read or even watch television. We haven't shared a bed in a long time; I couldn't say exactly when he started using the guest room at the end of the hall, next to Alicia's. Often I hear footsteps at night, but there seems no point in rousing myself to investigate.

At the same time, I have come to feel closer than ever to Alicia. This is odd, but I am too pleased to allow myself real worry. She has been concentrating on her father, and I've been occupied with a new grandson, our middle daughter entering college and a job promotion of my own, so we're rarely in each other's company, but when we are I am caught, not to say trapped, in the warm beam of her attention. Gradually I've come to crave it, even as I sense in it something beyond a normal mother-daughter bond.

She works me. I ought to feel manipulated, I suppose, but what I feel is chosen. From the other side of a room crowded with family, I'll suddenly feel her gaze on me and, as if on command, raise my eyes to hers. She smiles. My breath catches with something I can only call gratitude, though why I should be grateful to my own child for nothing more than smiling at me I couldn't say.

'I'm glad you're my mom,' she'll say in passing, just touching the small of my back, and I'm aglow for days.

This morning, my husband and I were in each other's presence without her, a rare thing and, for some reason, dangerous. He looked at me with haunted, sunken eyes and whispered, 'What's happened to us?'

'Ask Alicia,' I heard myself say.

'I don't mean to do these things. I don't want to. She makes me.' I affected incredulity and concern for his mental and physical health, but I knew what he meant.

We heard Alicia coming down the stairs then, and I had to get to work. It was with a certain savage relief that I left them alone together.

But throughout the workday, I've been able to think of little else. Restlessness vivified by jealousy has been building. I hear my daughter's voice in my mind, no words but with inflection and timbre whose intent is unmistakable. I feel a persistent tug, as though her hands were on me, or her gaze. She wants me. Alicia wants me. There are knives in the kitchen; I feel the heft of the butcher knife across my palm, and revulsion only adds an erotic limn. Alicia wants me. I'll go home at lunchtime and get rid of the man who's between us, and Alicia will be pleased.

Melanie Tem is a writer and social worker who lives in Denver, Colorado, with her husband, author and editor Steve Rasnic Tem. They have four children and three grandchildren. Her novels are the Bram Stoker Award-winning *Prodigal*, *Blood Moon*, *Wilding*, *Revenant*, *Desmodus*, *The Tides*, *Black River* and, in collaboration with Nancy Holder, *Making Love* and *Witch-Light*. Several dozen of her short stories have appeared in various anthologies and magazines, and she has published numerous non-fiction articles. The author was awarded the British Fantasy Award for Best Newcomer in 1991. '"Alicia" was inspired by my own experiences as the mother of teenage girls,' reveals Tem. 'The story came to me in the mother's voice; I wasn't interested in Alicia's experience so much as in her effect on other people as observed by her mother, and especially her effect on her mother, who after all was once a teenage girl herself. Teenagers can sometimes seem, to themselves and to people around them, like creatures of another species – humanoid, struggling to be fully human, but with thought processes not quite like ours and powers they can't control – and in our society girls often play this out through sexuality. Adolescence can be such an exhilarating and terrifying time of life, for the teenager and for those who come into her orbit, that it didn't take much metaphorical extension to cast this story as a dark fantasy.'

The Haunted Bookshop
BRIAN STABLEFORD

I was putting the final touches to the introduction to a new edition of C. D. Pamely's *Tales of Mystery and Terror* when the phone rang. I picked it up with my left hand while my right forefinger finished pecking out the last few words of the sentence.

'Hello.'

'Brian? Lionel, Cardiff.'

Lionel Fanthorpe rarely uses his surname when identifying himself to his friends in outward calls, preferring his place of residence.

'Hi, Lionel,' I said, attempting – unavailingly, of course – to match the cheerfulness and ebullience of his tone. 'How's fame treating you?'

Lionel had recently achieved a measure of celebrity by virtue of being appointed the presenter of *Fortean TV*, a magazine programme devoted to the not-entirely-earnest investigation of weird events and individuals. This had caused a certain amount of controversy in the broadsheet press, some of whose columnists had thought it unbecoming of a minister of the Church of Wales to lend his dog-collar to such irreverence.

'It's marvellous,' he assured me. 'Actually, that's what I'm ringing about.'

'You want me to appear on *Fortean TV*?' If I sounded sceptical, it's because I am – and it's because I'm universally renowned for my scepticism that I have every right to be sceptical about the possibility of ever being invited to appear on *Fortean TV*.

'Oh no, we're full up for the next series. It's just that ever since the first series I've been deluged with calls from all kinds of people clamouring to get on. You wouldn't believe some of the stories they tell.'

'Actually, Lionel,' I said, 'I wouldn't believe *any* of the stories they tell – but I do believe that you've been deluged with calls. What do you expect if you set yourself up as the front man for rent-a-crank?'

'That's exactly why I thought you might be a valuable addition to our team,' he told me, refusing to take the slightest offence. Lionel's geniality knows no bounds.

'You want me to be *Fortean TV*'s resident sceptic?'

'No, no. Forget *Fortean TV*. It's because Martin watched the show that he got in touch, but he doesn't want to be on it. He wants me to exorcise a supernatural presence in his bookshop.'

If it had been anyone else on the other end of the line I'd have been perfectly certain that the word was 'exercise', no matter how nonsensical the containing sentence might have become, but this was Lionel.

'Do you do exorcisms?' I asked.

'It's not something I do lightly,' he assured me, 'but if I'm convinced that it will do some good, I'm prepared to employ any of the Church's rituals. I believe that exorcism is a legitimate weapon in the war against evil.' Lionel is what the Victorians would have described as a *muscular* Christian – not so much because he has a black belt in judo as because he believes that the power of active evil has to be countered by an equal and opposite reaction. He is the only man I know who could say 'Praise the Lord and pass the ammunition!' with perfect sincerity.

'Why do you need me?' I said. 'The presence of a strident atheist is hardly likely to help the party go with a bang. Assuming, of course, that departing demons *do* go with a bang, as well as the obligatory whiff of brimstone.'

'I don't need you for the exorcism, even if there is one,' said Lionel, cheerily. 'I just thought you might be interested to sit in on a preliminary investigation – an all-night sitting – so that we can try to figure out exactly what we're dealing with. I read your thing in Steve's anthology.'

'Ah,' I said, as enlightenment dawned. Steve Jones had edited an anthology for Gollancz which consisted of famous horror writers' true encounters with the supernatural. Not wishing to miss out on the opportunity I had supplied a piece entitled 'Chacun sa goule' which offered a scrupulously accurate account of a real event: the coincidental discovery of a rare book by Maurice Maeterlinck, of whose existence I had been unaware until a few days earlier, at an antiquarian book fair I had stumbled across by chance. Typically, I had supplemented my record of the bare facts with a philosophical rhapsody about the existential significance of the continued permeation of the world by the carbonaceous matter which once made up the bodies of the dead. I had observed that the carbon dioxide in every breath we take contains atoms which might once have been part of the people of the past, whose minds also echo in the pages of their writings, so that the dead do indeed retain a 'ghostly' presence in the present. Although graveyards were doubtless replete with such ghosts, I had said, the most significant of my own ghostly encounters invariably took place in bookshops. It was perhaps not unnatural, therefore, that on being told about a haunted bookshop – a bookshop whose resident supernatural presence was so discomfiting as perhaps to require exorcism – Lionel would think of me.

'Well?' said Lionel. '*Are* you interested?'

'What bookshop?' I parried. 'Where?'

'It's a second-hand place – just down the coast, in Barry.'

'There isn't a second-hand bookshop in Barry,' I said, confidently. I once lived in Swansea for several years and I still visit my children there on occasion. If there had been a second-hand bookshop in Barry, I would have found mention of it in *drif's guide* and made the effort to visit it.

'It's not been there long,' Lionel told me.

'And it's haunted already? Who by?'

'Martin's not sure that it's the premises. He thinks it might be the books.'

I nearly came out with some crack about Martin presumably having picked up a copy of Abdul Alhazred's *Necronomicon* at a jumble sale in Tiger Bay but I hesitated. The idea of haunted books was not without a certain appeal – in fact, the mere mention of *books* was inevitably appealing to a man of my kind. Even the newest second-hand bookshop needs old books to dress its shelves. Most people anxious to move into the trade use their own collections as bases, but hardened collectors are usually so reluctant to put out their old favourites that they shop around for anything that can be bought in bulk at a reasonable price. I knew that there had been a time in the nineteenth century when the coal industry was booming and Cardiff was a busy port. The middle class had had aspirations in those days – C. D. Pamely's father had been a mining engineer in Pontypridd but he'd harboured greater ambitions for his sons – and it was possible that there were some nice caches of good antiquarian stock lurking in a place like Barry, which had been a haven for the South Wales gentry before slipping way downmarket to become a third-rate holiday resort.

Haunted or not, there was just a slim possibility that the mysterious Martin's shop might have some interesting contents – and if it had opened too late to obtain an entry in the latest issue of *drif* the professional vultures might not have had the chance to strip the shelves clean of tasty meat.

There is nothing that gladdens the heart of a book-collector like the thought of virgin stock. 'It sounds interesting,' I said to Lionel, effortlessly switching into earnest mode. 'When do you propose to hold this investigative vigil?'

'Monday,' said Lionel.

It was short notice, but I assumed that it would have been even shorter if Lionel hadn't been otherwise occupied on Sundays.

'Suits me,' I said, firmly hooked and avid to be reeled in. 'Name your time and place.'

Lionel picked me up from Cardiff Station in an old Cortina whose funereal paint job seemed appropriate to the occasion. He already had two passengers in place so I had no choice but to take a back seat. There wasn't a lot of space for me, let alone my overnight bag, but I squeezed myself in.

'This is Martin,' Lionel said, indicating the middle-aged man whose claim to the front seat had obviously been secured by reason of dimension as well as opportunity, 'and this is Penny, from the Society for Psychical Research.'

'Is that still going?' I asked, nodding politely to a thin, thirtyish woman with spectacles whose lenses were almost as powerful as mine. My relentlessly antiquarian mind inevitably associated the SPR with its late Victorian heyday, and the investigations of Katie King and D. D. Home mounted by the likes of William Crookes and Oliver Lodge. The woman seemed slightly resentful of my ignorance.

'Yes it is,' she said, in a severe manner which suggested that she'd been warned about my sceptical tendencies – and also, perhaps, that she thought that taking a back seat to a man who presented *Fortean TV* was slumming it a bit.

'Penny's done postgrad research at Duke,' said Lionel, proudly, as the car pulled way into the last remnants of the rush-hour traffic. 'In the selfsame labs where J. B. Rhine once worked.'

'I thought you could do that sort of thing in the UK now,' I said. 'Didn't Arthur Koestler leave a bequest to set up an established chair in paranormal studies? Somebody took the money in the end, didn't they?'

'There isn't a *course* here,' the woman explained. 'I wanted to do a proper course.'

I didn't want to offend her further by challenging her use of the word 'proper'. Instead I cast an appraising eye over the equipment with which she had surrounded herself. I recognised the fancy temperature tracking-gauge and the video camera easily enough, but most of the rest was in leather cases, and it wasn't obvious what the ammeter on her knee was supposed to be connected to.

'Are we the whole squad?' I asked.

'For now,' Lionel said. 'If Penny gets anything interesting, she'll call in some of her associates for a more thorough investigation – with Martin's permission, of course.' The way he added the qualifying clause made me wonder whether Martin's permissiveness might already have been severely tested by Lionel's insistence that a preliminary investigation would be necessary before deciding whether an exorcism might be required. I could understand why; even though the traditional silly season wouldn't be under way for another two months, the *Fortean Times* was hot enough nowadays to have all its best stories followed up by the *Sun* and the *Daily Star*, not to mention the *Sunday Sport*. That kind of coverage might boost the sales of a haunted bookshop for a week or two, but the embarrassment might last a lifetime.

'I hope the Reverend explained to you, Mr Stableford,' the bookshop proprietor intoned, in a broad way-up-the-Valleys accent, 'that this whole business is confidential.'

'No one will hear a word of it from me,' I assured him. 'My lips are sealed.' I can be very pedantic when giving out promises; while I type this page not a sound is escaping from my lips. I have not, of course, changed any of the names in the interests of protecting the innocent – or even the guilty – but you will doubtless have noticed that I have withheld the surnames of the minor characters.

'Perhaps you could fill Brian and Penny in while we're on the road, Martin,' Lionel suggested. 'Give them some idea of what to expect.'

Martin did not seem overjoyed by this prospect. In fact, he looked as if he might be having second thoughts about the wisdom of having approached Lionel in the first place – but the incumbent at his local chapel was unlikely to do exorcisms, or to look kindly upon anyone who broached the possibility. The great majority of Welsh Methodists tend to the view that a man who imagines himself to be troubled by ghosts or demons is a man with an unusually guilty conscience, who should look deep into his own soul for the source of his disquiet.

'Would you rather I did it?' Lionel asked, his generosity as boundless as his geniality.

'No,' said Martin, his mind quickly made up. 'Best if . . . well, see, I'm from the Rhondda originally. In the industry till the pits closed – not a faceworker, mind, always above ground. Middle management, I suppose, is the phrase they use nowadays. Anyhow, I was over twenty years in when the axe came down, an' the redundancy was a nice package. I'm only forty-three, so I knew I had to *use* the money – start a business, like. Well, I'd always been a reader, an' it just so happened that I was still in the office, tidying up, when one of the old boys we'd kept on to do the clearing up came in to ask what we wanted done with all the books from the old colliery library.

'I didn't even know there'd ever been a colliery library, but when the boys had found all these boxes of books in a storage-loft the old-timer had recognised them – said he'd often seen the like around his house in the old days, when his father and grandfather had been regular borrowers. It had fallen into disuse in the fifties, I suppose, what with paperbacks an' all, an' the room it was in had been turned into an office. So I said, it's all right, boys, I'll look after those – put what you can into my car, and pile the rest up in the bike-sheds. I'll ferry the boxes home a few at a time. Well, nobody else wanted them, did they?

'I thought at first I'd just look through them, like – sort out anything I wanted to read and give the rest to Oxfam – but when I got the old boy to help me stow the second batch he said that if I'd got a good home, he knew where the books from the old Workingmen's Institute had been put away when they turned it into a club an' the library was turfed out in favour of a snooker table. That's when I got the idea. Ours couldn't have been the only pit in Wales with its own library, nor our village the only one with a Workingmen's Institute, an' we're not the kind of folk to *throw things away*. Why not scout around, I thought, see what I could dig up, an' open a bookshop?'

Why not indeed? I thought, sympathetically.

'I knew there was no point doing something like that in the Valley, mind,' Martin continued, 'or even in Merthyr. I thought of Caerleon first, but the wife wasn't happy about moving to what's practically *England*, an' I knew Cardiff already had *two* second-hand bookshops, so I thought of Barry, which the wife has always liked. It turned out that a lot of stuff from the old colliery libraries had been sold years ago to old Ralph in Swansea or that shop that used to be in the Hayes before it all got torn down, but I found four more sizeable lots that I picked up for next to nothing.'

'How many books altogether?' I asked, impatient for hard news.

'About twelve thousand, give or take.'

It wasn't as big a total as I'd hoped. Given the educational mission of nineteenth century Workingmen's Institutes, I guessed that at least half the books would probably be non-fiction and half the rest would probably be religious texts. Even if there were only three thousand volumes of fiction, however – and even if the bulk of those were standard sets of Scott and Dickens, there ought to be *something* of interest. None of the books had seen the light of day for at least twenty years, and some might not have been inspected for the best part of a century – and the most exciting fact of all was that Martin didn't seem to have a clue. In a business full of sharks, he was pure whitebait.

'How long, exactly, has the shop been open for business?' I asked.

'Open for business?' Martin echoed, incredulously. 'It hasn't been *open* at all. Didn't the Reverend . . . ?'

'Sorry, Martin,' Lionel interposed. 'When I phoned Brian I didn't realise that you hadn't got that far.'

My heart was still busy leaping. Not just virgin stock but extra virgin stock, untouched by sharkish fin!

'Do you think,' Penny put in, resentfully, 'that we could get to the *paranormal activity*?'

I had quite forgotten, in my excitement, that this was supposed to be a *haunted* bookshop. I remembered J.W. Dunne's theory that ghosts are images displaced in the fourth dimension from parallel worlds where time might be running ahead of or behind our own. If so, Martin's as-yet-unopened bookshop might easily be haunted by the shades of dozens of bookdealers, all impatient to get into it.

'Yes,' I said, trying to sound supportive of our collective mission. 'Tell us about the ghosts.'

'I never said *ghosts*,' said Martin, his voice suddenly infected by a note of pedantic caution. 'I never saw a *person*, you understand. Whatever it is, it's not *people*.'

'Poltergeist phenomena, then?' said Penny, eagerly. 'Books moving by themselves – pages turning. Or is it a matter of sudden chills, changes in atmosphere?'

'Bit of that, like,' Martin conceded. 'Wouldn't mind, if it were *only* that – cold, creaking an' so on.'

'So what *is* it, exactly?' Penny wanted to know.

'Don't know, *exactly*. You're the expert, I suppose – you an' the Reverend. I didn't notice anything at first – even the wife thought the place was all right, when it was empty. It's a lock-up, of course; we weren't planning on living there although it's got what the estate agent called living accommodation on the first floor. *Modern* family couldn't live there, even if their kids had long gone – too small by half, an' the bathroom facilities are woefully inadequate. I decided to use the so-called bedroom as a second stockroom, put shelves in an' everything. Plan was that when I'd got the shop going steady we'd both move down to a nice house overlooking the sea, but there's not much chance of that now until it's properly sorted – by the Reverend, I mean. It's not so bad in daylight, of course, but even then . . . well, the wife's only been in there by day, an' she swears she'll never set foot in it again, even at high noon. *I've* been in there past midnight, putting up the shelves – but only the once, since I started putting out the stock. Seems as if the *presence* came with the stock, like, although it wasn't there when the books were all in boxes piled up in my hall an' front room. It's a real mystery.'

'If it were a single haunted book,' Lionel mused, 'you might be able to solve the problem just by getting rid of that one volume.'

'If it is,' said Martin, darkly, 'an' you can figure out which one, you can have it for nothing.'

Given his account of how he'd acquired his stock, Martin could probably afford to be generous. Given that his stock had been on the shelves of private lending libraries for many years, though – and stored in various lofts and cupboards for many years more, without anyone complaining about any kind of haunting – it was difficult to see how the problem could be one of the books, or even all of them.

My preliminary judgment, inevitably, was that the problem was probably in Martin's mind. If he'd lived all his life in the Rhondda, heir to hundreds of years of mining tradition and having spent all his own working life in the industry, it must have been a terrible wrench to be forced to contemplate entry into an alien way of life. Reader or not, he was obviously no book-*lover*; he'd seen an opportunity and he'd felt obliged to seize it, but he must have thought himself caught between the devil of new endeavour and the deep blue sea of unemployment. Was it so very surprising that the devil in question had indeed turned, in his fearful mind, into a tangible force of darkness?

Lionel was still following his own train of thought. 'What kind of book might that be, do you think?' he asked, of no one in particular. For a moment, I thought he was really going to bring up the *Necronomicon*, but he took the second worst option. 'A grimoire, maybe? A copy of the *Key of Solomon*?'

'Sure,' I said, sarcastically. 'Every colliery in the Valley used to have its resident wizard, who kept his secret lore on the top shelf of the library, bound up to look like records of coal-production. You shift sixteen tons, and what do you get? Another day older an' deeper in debt. Jesus don't you call me, 'cos I can't go – I owe my soul to the pithead whore.' I was content to recite the words with only the faintest lilt; I have the singing voice of a crow with laryngitis.

'Actually,' said Penny, 'it wasn't unknown for eighteenth-century mines, and even for early factories, to have luckmen – wizards of a sort. Miners, especially, were very superstitious. It was a high-risk industry, you see. The transition from forced labour to wage-labour wasn't as long ago as you might think, even in these parts, and the transition from superficial workings – actual *pits*, that is – to deep-shaft mining was a step into unknown territory. The activities of the luckmen would have been vital to the morale of their fellow-workers.'

'Did they teach you that at Duke?' I asked, in a neutral tone.

'No,' she said. 'The LSE. I did a degree in sociology before I did my master's in parapsychology.'

I'd been a lecturer in sociology at Reading for twelve years before I quit to write fulltime, but I'd never heard of luckmen. On the other hand, I'd done my first degree in biology, so I'd never studied industrial sociology at all. 'And were these luckmen in the habit of consulting books of protective rituals?' I asked.

'I don't know,' she said.

'If they did,' Lionel put in, '*moving* the book might have been the crucial disturbance – like moving bones laid to eternal rest. Didn't M. R. James once say that all his stories were variations on the theme of *curst be he who moves my bones*?'

'If it's a case of *curst be him who moves my books*,' I opined, 'we're more likely to be dealing with a dyed-in-the-wool book-collector than a black magician. I'd come back to haunt anyone who creased the dust-wrapper on one of mine. Hell hath no fury like a collector who finds a shopping-list scribbled on a flyleaf.'

Lionel laughed, probably to be polite. Neither of the others cracked a smile. It looked as if it was going to be a long night, but I consoled myself with the knowledge that I could keep myself busy for hours with that much stock – fool that I was, I had no inkling of the horrible shock that was to come.

Martin's shop wasn't in a prime position, even by Barry's standards, but it was close enough to the seafront to catch a certain amount of passing trade during the holiday season. He was enough of a business-man to realise that his bread-and-butter business would be selling paperback pulp to people who needed something to occupy their eyes while they lay around on the beach, so the wooden shelves he'd erected in the window were stocked with best-sellers that looked as if they'd been culled from all the charity shops in South Wales.

When Martin unlocked the front door Penny and Lionel had enough respect for the alleged supernatural presence to pause for a moment, so I was first in. Although the sun hadn't quite set it was hidden by the houses on the far side of the street and the window display blocked out most of the light that was left, so I had to wait for Martin to switch on the electric light before I could actually set to work. It was not until the light came on that the full horror of the situation hit me.

I shouldn't have been surprised, of course, but rampant acquisitiveness generates the kind of optimism which allows inconvenient realisations to slip through the cracks of consciousness. One sweep of my gaze across the shelves on the back wall was sufficient to tell me what I should have guessed the moment Martin started going on about old colliery libraries and the innate reluctance of honest folk to throw anything away. Maybe if his name had been Hywel or Dai the awful datum would have clicked into place, but Martin was an English name. Alas, the books he'd picked up for 'next to nothing' – the great majority of them, at least – were in Welsh.

What Martin had managed to acquire wasn't the *entire* stock of the old libraries, I realised, but merely that fraction of it that had been left behind when the readily saleable stuff had gone – mostly texts whose utilitarian worth had been severely compromised by the fact that it was printed in a language falling swiftly into disuse.

If the bookshop really is haunted, I thought, bitterly, *the culprit is more likely to be a dead language than a dead man.*

'Do you get many Welsh speakers in Barry?' I asked, mournfully.

'Welsh is taught in all the schools,' Martin said, proudly. 'Legal requirement, see. Not so many speak it at home nowadays, of course, except up north – but people from Gwynedd go on holiday like anyone else. Can't keep a language alive without books, can you?'

By this time I had quick-scanned all eight of the shelves against the back wall and had turned my attention to the books behind the desk where the ancient cash-register stood. Most dealers keep their best stock – or what they think of as their best stock – behind their own station, to minimise the risk of theft. Not all the books behind the cash-register were in Welsh, but eighty per cent of them were, and the rest were evenly divided between books on mining and religious texts. This seemed to me to be a sad comment on Martin's values as well as his stock.

'Didn't the library stock include *any* English literature?' I asked him, plaintively. 'Or any illustrated books, perhaps?'

'Some,' Martin conceded. 'I put the old fiction upstairs. That's standard practice, isn't it?' He'd obviously done a little market research and observed that most second-hand bookdealers relegated the dross of ancient bestsellers and book club editions to the remotest corner they had. My spirits recovered a little; it was in such neglected corners that I always found my best bargains: rare works of nineteenth- or early twentieth-century fantasy whose specialist significance was unappreciated by dealers whose own expertise was in railway books or natural history.

'The luckmen would have been Welsh speakers, of course,' observed Penny, who was bringing in her second load of equipment and supplies while Lionel went back to the car for his third. 'All their spells and incantations would have been handed down from time immemorial.'

'They must have been true descendants of Merlin and Owen Glendower, mustn't they?' I put in, insouciantly. 'The last custodians of the authentic Druidic tradition.'

She looked at me as if I were a caterpillar in a salad sandwich. 'Yes,' she said, simply. 'That's exactly what they were.'

Diplomacy compelled me to refrain from making any clever remarks about Taliesin, the Bardic motto, Eisteddfods or male voice choirs. I eyed the rickety staircase that led up to the first floor, carpeted in what had once been red felt but was now almost completely black. 'Is there a switch for the upstairs lights?' I asked Martin.

'There's one at the top on the left,' he informed me, 'and another just inside the door of the front room. You shouldn't need them, though – the windows up there let in more light than this one.'

As I headed up the stairs I could feel renewed optimism putting a spring in my step. The uncluttered windows of the short corridor and the 'so-called bedroom' did indeed let in more light than the window downstairs, but they were also a lot smaller, so the advantage was not as marked as I could have wished. Even so, I let the electric switch alone as I stepped through the open door into the room directly over the shopfront.

As soon as I had moved into the room the feeling hit me. It took me completely by surprise, and the impact was sufficient to make me catch my breath.

I had been in that room before.

I had, of course, experienced the commonplace sensation of *déjà vu*, but never so intensely as to make me doubt the conventional explanation that it arose from an illusion generated when the same sensory information was accidentally duplicated in the brain, having been transmitted there by two distinct neuronal pathways. This was different, not just because of its intensity but because I knew – vaguely, at least – when and where I had had the experience that was being so carefully and so improbably reproduced by the present moment.

Most people, it is said, have recurring dreams. They may dream repeatedly of houses, of sexual encounters, of flying, or of appearing naked in public. When they have such dreams – or, at least, when they become conscious that they are having such dreams – they know that they are revisiting scenes already familiar: that the house is one they have previously visited in dreams, or that their power of flight is something which they are *re*discovering. Some such dreams may be enigmatic, perhaps because they are symbolically disguised, but others are trivially literal; mine have always been perfectly understandable. My own recurrent dreams are of second-hand bookshops.

I have never considered it at all unusual that my long-standing addiction to combing the shelves of second-hand bookshops should be reflected in my dreams. Nor have I ever considered it unusual that such dreams should often be attended by the sense of *returning* to familiar haunts – because that, after all, is the form that the vast majority of my actual book-hunting trips take. It is only to be expected that when I dream of bookshops – or, at least, when I become conscious that I am dreaming of bookshops – I usually feel that they are familiar bookshops. Interestingly, however, they are *never* bookshops that really do exist in the everyday world; they are always imaginary bookshops. This means, of course, that when I have the sense of having visited them before, I know that I can only have done so in other dreams. It is as if the virtual geography of my private dream-world numbers amongst its fixtures a series of shops, some fascinating and some not-so-fascinating, which I visit at irregular intervals: a population parallel to that with which the geography of the real world is dotted.

Sometimes, when dreaming of bookshops, I become conscious that I am dreaming – but I resist waking up, because I know that when I do I shall have to leave behind any interesting books I might have found. When my bookshop dreams become lucid in this fashion I often become conscious of the fact – or at least the illusion – that the shop I am in is one of which I have dreamed before.

Just as I had never dreamed of entering an actual bookshop, so I had never actually entered a bookshop of which I had dreamed. That I seemed to be doing so now was more than a cause for astonishment; it seemed, in fact, to be a violation of natural law, as threatening in its fashion as any conventional apparition or ominous shadow. I stood transfixed, appalled by the thought that I – a great and hitherto worthy champion of scepticism – could be assailed in this rude and nasty fashion.

Mercifully, the moment did not last. The shock of awful discovery was replaced soon enough by a struggle to remember what, if anything, I had found in this room when it had only been the figment of a dream. The mental reflex of the book-collector was powerful enough to drive away the alarm of revelation; I ceased to worry about the *how* of the mystery and focused my mind instead on the truly crucial question of what there might be to be found, and whether the illusion of having dreamed about the room – I was already content to dismiss the sensation as an illusion – might somehow assist my search.

No sooner had I begun to scan the nearest shelves, however, than the force of reality began to reassert itself upon my senses. The proportion of Welsh texts here was considerably smaller than on the shelves below – no more than half, and perhaps a little less – but that did not make the remainder seem significantly more promising. There were several sets of standard authors, more poetry than prose, in horribly shabby pocket editions. My expert eye immediately picked out a number of yellowbacks, but their condition was so awful that it would hardly have mattered had they been more interesting titles than they were. A few bound volumes of old periodicals turned out on closer inspection to be *Sunday at Home* and *Pick-Me-Up*, not even *Longman's* or *Temple Bar*, let alone anything more interesting.

In brief, it looked like the kind of stock over which a collector might toil for hours in order to turn up a couple of items whose significance to his collection was marginal at best. Not, of course, that I could contentedly let it alone; I knew that I would indeed have to inspect every single shelf, lifting every volume whose title was not clearly inscribed on its spine, in order to make perfectly certain that nothing evaded me. No matter how laborious the task became, I would have to stick to it come Hell or high water – but first I had to return downstairs, in answer to Lionel's urgent call.

All Lionel wanted, it turned out, was to hand me a cup of tea and ask my opinion as to what kind of pizza he ought to have delivered.

There is nothing like a four-way debate about pizza toppings to bring a ghost-hunting expedition right down to earth; by the time we had settled on two mediums, one with bacon, mushroom and tomato and the other with olives, anchovies and pepperoni, mundanity had such a secure hold on Martin's bookshop that even Madame Arcati at her most lunatic would have been hard-pressed to find the least hint of spirit activity.

By this time, of course, Penny and Lionel had set up all the SPR's apparatus. The video camera was on its tripod, ready to be spun around in quest of the kinds of things that one glimpses in the corners of one's eyes. A quaint little pointer was inscribing a record of the room's temperature on a slowly rotating drum. (I was glad to note that since we had entered the shop our combined bodyheat had contrived to raise the temperature by a whole degree Celsius to a reasonably comfortable sixteen.) I still wasn't sure what it was that the ammeter was hooked up to but whatever it was had not yet succeeded in generating a flicker of current.

Lionel asked Penny to tell him a little more about luckmen and their role in the mines of yore, but Penny had already run to the limit of her information on the subject so she tried to pump Martin about residual superstitions in the modern industry – a subject on which he was not at all forthcoming.

'I was always above ground, see,' he said. 'The boys at the face had their own little community – they'd tell you tales for a laugh, like, but they'd never let on that they took any of it seriously.'

'What tales?' Lionel wanted to know.

'*You* know. Not a pit in the Valley has a clean sheet mortality-wise – not any that's been open longer than twenty years, anyhow. The eldest are full of worked-out shafts and old rockfalls, an' there's always talk of voices – voices of men killed by gas or crushed, you see. Offering warnings as often as not; I've heard far more tales of men being saved than men being lost. Nobody goes down a pit needs scaring, see; work's dangerous enough without that.'

'Judging by the dust on some of the books upstairs,' I said, 'one or two of them must have made a good number of trips down into the shafts.'

'I doubt that,' Martin said. 'No time to read down there, nor light good enough to read by. The dust on the bindings is the kind that gets in everywhere – the fine stuff that hangs about in the air and never quite washes out. Almost like a liquid, it is, or a *miasma* – smears and clings and blackens even if you never set foot in the cage or a hand on a hopper.'

I had to admire the way he pronounced 'miasma', lingering over the vowels as only a Welshman could.

'The dark spirit of the pit,' said Penny, softly. It would almost have been enough to make us look over our shoulders if we hadn't heard the delivery boy's moped rattling over the potholes in the street. We fell upon the pizza-slices with the kind of eager rapacity that only competition can generate, even though we all knew perfectly well that we were only entitled to four apiece.

While we ate, darkness fell – and shadows crept upon us in spite of the electric light. Martin, born and bred to the economy of the Valleys, had only fitted sixty-watt bulbs.

Martin was watching us now, alert for any sign of tension or unease. As with many Celts, his eyes were pale even though his hair was dark, but they weren't blue; they were as grey as slate. Although Penny was a very different physical type – ectomorphic rather than endomorphic – she had very similar colouring. Her eyes did retain a slight hint of blue, but her complexion lacked the hint of rosy pink that Martin's had. Lionel must have been at least twenty years older than Martin and thirty years older than Penny but he looked more robust than either of them. He was originally from Norfolk, which probably meant that he – like me – was a descendant of Viking settlers. *Our* ancestors had never been bards or Druids; our family trees were as devoid of luckmen as of mistletoe.

I was prepared to feel a slight pang of regret about that; I knew that if I were going to find any real treasure in that dust-caked morass upstairs I was going to need some luck. Even while we ate, my restless eyes were checking and rechecking the downstairs shelves, unable to find anything worth lingering over.

The pizza was as mediocre as could be expected, but the tea was better. It seemed *much* better until I got to the dregs, when I began to notice an odd aftertaste. I noticed, too, that the air in the shop had a peculiar texture to it. All bookshops are dusty, of course, and when books that have been a long time in storage are first set on shelves they often release a little dampness into the air, faintly polluted with fungal spores and bits of dead silverfish. Book-lovers learn to savour that kind of atmosphere, or at least to ignore it – but this texture was slightly different from any I'd encountered before. This gave the impression of being *vintage* dust – a real *grand cru*. Martin's pronunciation of the word 'miasma' echoed in my mind as I tried to measure the dust's quality more precisely, but it didn't seem dismissable simply as coal dust any more than it warranted elevation to the status of 'the dark spirit of the pit'. It was something more teasing than either.

I couldn't help thinking of the sceptical kind of occult detective stories, where the intrepid investigators eventually find that alleged hauntings are merely noxious vapours released from bad drains or unusual chemical reactions. Was it possible, I wondered, that the redistribution of books kept so long in close confinement really had set free some disturbing vapour that had been patiently building up in the inner recesses of the boxes for decades? I didn't like to suggest to the others that perhaps we should have brought a canary.

'Well,' I said, as soon as I had bolted my last allotted slice of bacon, mushroom and tomato. 'I'm going to get started on the upstairs stock. If you need me, just scream.'

'Will you be all right up there on your own?' Martin asked, as if he sincerely believed that I might not be.

'If I'm not,' I assured him, '*I'll* scream.'

'If you find any of mine,' said Lionel, 'let me know.' Long before he got religion Lionel was the most prolific writer of science fiction and supernatural fiction in Britain, producing over a hundred and eighty volumes for the late unlamented Badger Books at the princely sum of £22 10s a time. His one longrunning series had consisted of occult detective stories starring the redoubtable Val Stearman and his lovely female associate La Noire. Stearman had, of course, been modelled on the young Lionel, and his spirit was doubtless still active even though the containing flesh had suffered a little. It required an extremely optimistic eye, alas, to find the slightest hint of La Noire in Penny-from-the-SPR.

'I will,' I promised.

This time, I had to use the electric lights. I made a mental note to bring my own hundred-watt bulbs if I ever got involved in a similar vigil in future. I started my search in the top left-hand corner of the shelf-unit to the left of the door and began to work methodically across and down, across and down.

If you've ever browsed the less popular shelves in the London Library you'll know how dust from the red leather bindings that are gradually rotting down will stain your hands and your shirt, so that a long session in French Fiction can leave you looking suspiciously like Jack the Ripper. Exploring these shelves was not dissimilar, but it was an order of magnitude worse. Within ten minutes my hands were absolutely filthy and my green corduroy jacket was beginning to turn black. My shirt and my jeans had started out black, but that didn't spare them any manifest effect, because the dust was so fine as to be *slick* and it soon made itself felt in their texture. If the dust had been pure carbon it would, I suppose, have been graphite, but even the best Welsh anthracite isn't anywhere near pure carbon. This was *impure* carbon, and its impurities were enhancing its ability to form a *miasma*.

I couldn't help wiping my hands periodically on my jeans even though I knew that it wasn't helping the situation. Nor could I help occasionally touching my hand to my face, my forehead and my hair, even though I knew that such touches would leave smudges. By the time I'd done twenty feet of shelves – without finding a single book that I'd have been happy to pay more than 50p for – I knew that I must be a real sight, and what Martin had said about the woeful inadequacy of the bathroom facilities suddenly began to seem more relevant.

Despite the aforementioned inadequacy, my companions stumped up the staircase one by one to use the facilities. Lionel was the only one who looked in to see how I was doing. When I stopped for a break myself I took the opportunity to inspect my features in the mirror, and I managed to scrub off the worst of the stains with toilet paper, but even a thorough soaping failed to shift the worst of the grime from my fingers.

As I resumed my labours I remembered what I'd written in 'Chacun sa goule' about our breathing in the carbon dioxide relics of the dead every time we fill our lungs. To the extent that the dust-particles on the books were coal they were presumably the relics of creatures that had roamed the earth in the Carboniferous Era: the flesh of early dinosaurs compounded with the mass of gymnosperm tree-trunks and the chitin of giant insects. That ancient carbon must, however, be mingled with echoes of more recent lives and deaths: the lives and deaths of the men who hewed the coal, or that minority amongst them who had tried, valiantly, to improve their minds with the aid of the written word.

Once, at the university of Reading, I had attended an open lecture in which A. N. Wilson had argued that the rich inner life of thought and feeling, which we now take completely for granted, is largely a product of books, and most especially of novels. Men who lived and died confined by oral culture, Wilson argued, had not the mental resources to build a robust inner monologue, a pressurised stream of consciousness. If that were true, I thought, such men could hardly be in any position to leave ghosts behind when they died and decayed. If dust really could retain some kind of spirit, it would, of necessity, be the spirit of *readers* – in which case, book-dust ought to be the most enspirited of all.

As I formed that strange thought the sensation of having been in that room before returned in full force, swiftly and irresistibly.

I did not pause in my routine of plucking the books off the shelves, inspecting their title-pages and returning them, but the automatism of that routine suddenly became oppressive and seemingly unnatural. Before, when the sensation had come over me, I had thought it an anomaly: a sensation that I should only have been capable of feeling in a dream – but now it did not feel anomalous at all, because it seemed *now* that I really was *in a dream*, where I was perfectly entitled to remember bookshops visited in other dreams, and to dwell in the curious nostalgia of discoveries barely made before being lost in the moment of awakening. As in all such episodes of lucidity, I had not the slightest desire to wake; indeed, I had the strongest possible desire to remain as I was, potentially able to grasp and hold any treasure that wishful thinking might deliver into my horrid night-black hand.

The light of the sixty-watt bulb grew dimmer, and the walls of the room drew closer. The spines of the books grew darker, and the air became thicker and heavier. Because I knew that I was in a dream-state, I wasn't unduly worried – to the contrary, I was intent on preserving a state in which the power of desire might be adequate to lead me to a precious find. It occurred to me that the room had become uncannily like a pit, both literally and metaphorically. The dross on the shelves was the stone of the imagination, inert and useless, while the texts for which I was searching were pregnant with mental energy that only needed to be read in order to warm and illuminate my inner being.

Because I already possess twenty thousand volumes, my want list has been shrinking for years, and the works which I yearn most desperately to find nowadays are so rare that it would require a veritable miracle of luck to locate affordable copies. Without any magical ritual to aid me in my search through Martin's stock I had only honest toil to bring to my task: a simple, straightforward determination to make certain that nothing would escape my notice. I searched with relentless efficiency. I worked methodically along the shelves, ignoring the miasmic dust, in the frail hope that somewhere beneath its obscuring cloak a treasure trove might be waiting: a copy of *Gyphantia*, or *Omegarus and Syderia*, or *The Mummy!*, or *The Old Maid's Talisman*, in any edition and any condition provided only that the text were complete.

It soon became so difficult to draw breath that I felt slightly dizzy, and so dark that I had no alternative but to pause in my work. I was already kneeling down, inspecting the lowest shelf in a unit, but I had to put out a hand nevertheless to support myself against the shelves. My eyes began to play tricks on me; phosphenes lit up the black air like a cluster of stars, and the darkness itself began to flow and shift, as if it were alive with a host of bustling shadows: a host so vast and so crowded that its individual parts were jostling for presence in a narrow corridor that was growing narrower by the instant.

The dust that lay upon the air now seemed so dense that the air was indeed *liquid*. My trachea closed reflexively and I found myself gulping, *swallowing* the air and the intoxicating spirit which possessed and saturated it.

I was not afraid. I was secure in my conviction that an instant of panic would be enough to bring me out of the dream-state and back to wakefulness, and I had dreamed far too many dreams of this frail kind to allow panic its moment of opportunity. I drank the spirits of the dead, and drank them gladly. I drank them *thirstily*, because I knew that they were closer to me than any mere kin. What was my own spirit, after all, but a compound of all that I had read and inwardly digested? Even if A. N. Wilson were mistaken in his estimate of the majority of men, he was surely right about himself and he was right about me. *My* inner life, *my* pressurised stream of consciousness, was the product of texts and the love of texts. I had been a ghoul all my life; what had I to be afraid of in that dark room full of clamorous spirits? The greater part of my life, and the greater part of my emotion, had been spent and generated by intercourse with the dead; what need had I to feel threatened, or to suspect the presence of maleficent evil?

I drank deeply, avid for further intoxication. The dust was, after all, a previously untasted vintage.

I felt slightly stirred, as if moist wind and cloying warmth were washing over me but leaving no impresssion. I felt the fading gleam of the Celtic twilight in my lungs and in my heart. I felt the heritage of Merlin and Taliesin and the force of Druid magic in my brain and in my groin. I heard the musical voices of luckmen intoning their spells, mingled with the strangled cries of hewers choked by gas or crushed by falling stone, all echoing together in the empty spaces of my mind.

It was a delicious fantasy, a haunting dream: a fantasy so delicious and a dream so haunting that I would dearly have liked to maintain it against the cruel penetration of lucidity – but I could not do it.

My supporting hand moved along the wooden shelf and my senses reeled. It was only the slightest of adjustments, but the little finger picked a thin splinter out of the distressed wood, and the tiny stab of pain made me gasp. The gasp turned to a cough, and then to a fit of coughing – and a cataract of black dust cascaded out of my mouth into the palm of my hand.

The sixty-watt bulb buzzed and flickered, and its light became noticeably brighter. I hauled myself to my feet, blinked away the moment of drowsiness and went to the bathroom to rinse my hands again. Having done that, as best I could, I went back to the place at which I had paused and started scanning the top shelf of the next unit.

I didn't curse myself for losing the dream. Dreams are by nature fragile and fugitive, and only death can free us, in the end, from the everpresent duty of waking from their toils.

It took me a further three-quarters of an hour to finish searching the upstairs room. The best items I found were a couple of bound volumes of *Reynolds' Miscellany*, including the serial version of Reynolds' *Faust*, and battered copies of Eugene Sue's *Martin the Foundling*, George Griffith's *A Criminal Croesus* and Mrs Riddell's *Fairy Water*. They were all in poor condition, but they were all titles that I'd be glad to add to my collection. Considering that the hunt had started so unpromisingly it didn't seem to be a bad haul, and there was still a slight possibility that I could add to it from the ground floor stock.

Lionel, Martin and Penny were sitting downstairs, all as quiet as church mice. I thought at first that they might be asleep, and I took care to tiptoe down the last few steps, but Lionel looked around and said: 'There's more tea in the pot. We've all had a second cup.' His voice was slower than usual and a little thicker.

'I'm okay,' I assured him. 'Seen any sign of *the presence*?'

'Not *seen*, exactly,' he told me, 'but we definitely felt something, didn't we?'

'It's not as bad as it has been,' Martin said, evidently disgruntled by the failure of his shop to come up with the goods, 'but I *can* feel it.'

'How about you?' I said to Penny.

'Nothing objective,' she said, looking sadly at her various instruments. 'But I can feel *something*. It's faint, but it's there.' I could tell from the tone of her voice that she was disappointed. It's hard to impress people with subjective feelings; she knew that unless she could carry away some kind of tangible record – a clip of film, a trace on her rotating chart or a leaping needle on the ammeter – she'd have nothing to interest the punctilious inquisitors of the Society for Psychical Research.

'Anything upstairs?' Lionel asked, obviously expecting a negative answer.

'Just books,' I said. 'Hundreds and hundreds that no one will ever want to read – and a few dozen that someone might. I've only found a few, but they won't just sit on my shelves unread. I feel sorry for the rest, in a way. All that thought that went into their creation! All that *effort*! If they only had voices, they'd be clamouring for attention, don't you think? They'd be excited, wouldn't they, at having been taken out of their coffins at last and put on display? They probably thought that the Day of Judgment had come at last when Martin first unpacked them – but disillusionment must be setting in by now. How long do you think it takes a book to give in to despair? Not long, I expect, if it's a book from a colliery library – a book which has already had a taste of the darkness of the abyss.'

'You're not taking this seriously, are you?' Martin said, without undue rancour. 'It's all a joke to you.'

'The trouble with sceptics,' Penny added, taking care to couch her remarks in general terms, 'is that they're too enthusiastic to accept their own insensitivity as proof that there's nothing to be sensitive to.

They're like blind men denying that sight is possible. Not everyone's the same, you know. Everybody's different, and some of us can feel the presence of things that others can't.'

'Perhaps you're right,' I said, mildly. 'You don't mind if I move about, do you? I'll try not to disturb you.'

'Feel free,' said Lionel, with typical *bonhomie*. 'There's no need for us to sit still or be quiet. There's a long night still ahead of us – plenty of time for the presence to make itself felt more keenly, if it cares to.'

He was absolutely right, of course – the night that stretched before us was very long indeed. I did my bit, and never closed my eyes for a moment. Once I'd finished checking the downstairs stock I perched on a wooden chair and chatted to Lionel about anything and everything except religion. We remembered a few old times and a few old friends; he told me all about *Fortean TV* and I told him about all the stories and articles I'd written lately. I expect the others found it more than a little boring, although Lionel kept bringing them into the conversation at every possible opportunity. He likes to be the life and soul of every party, and he sometimes succeeds in that, even when it seems to be an uphill struggle. He was the commanding presence in the bookshop now; his was the personality which filled it.

All the while, I watched the three of them. I watched them *watching*, waiting for something that always seemed to be on the brink of arriving but never quite did. They *did* feel another, darker presence – of that I was sure, although they made no elaborate attempt to describe or discuss it – but they had no idea what it was. They wanted it to become more clamorous, not so much because that would reveal it more fully and more clearly, but because they thought that the clamour might somehow contain its own explanation – but it never did. Its brief hold on the atmosphere of the shop was loosening; it needed no exorcism to persuade it to slip away into oblivion. Hour by hour and inch by inch, Martin's haunted bookshop became *dispirited*.

So far as I could tell, we did nothing to encourage the slow decay of the presence, but we did nothing to prevent it. None of us had the least idea how to encourage it, and none of us would have wanted to had we known how.

As the time passed I watched my three companions become sleepier and sleepier as habit tested their resolve. I heard their voices slow and slur as dreams reached out for them even while they struggled to stay awake – but wakefulness won the war, and the dreams that might have claimed them had they been alone evaporated into the increasingly empty air. The dust stirred up by Martin's exertions was already beginning to settle out and to settle down, adsorbed on to the surfaces of wall and window, carpet and ceiling. Even when I first sat down the air was no longer vintage air; as the morning progressed it became flatter and more insipid, increasingly soured by the faint odours of living flesh.

By the time dawn broke, Martin and Penny were agreed that the presence had gone – that its hold was broken. Martin was slightly anxious that it might return as soon as it could find him on his own again, but Lionel assured him that he would be more than willing to come back if Martin thought it necessary, and would be happy to spend the night alone on the premises if that were the only way to bring the presence out. The way he said it told me that he didn't expect any such thing to occur; without quite knowing how he knew it, he was convinced that the presence had loosened its grip and lost its hold.

We had breakfast in a café before starting back to Cardiff. Lionel drank lots of black coffee to make sure that he was in no danger of falling asleep at the wheel, although he was no stranger to all-night vigils. In the event, we got back to the railway station without the least hint of alarm.

'You didn't have a wasted journey, anyhow,' Lionel said, as I got out of the car. He was looking at my overnight bag, which was bulging with the books I'd bought at a pound apiece – a perfectly reasonable price, considering that they were only reading copies – from the parsimonious Martin.

'Not in the least,' I said. 'To tell you the truth, I don't think any of us did. Sometimes, all it takes to exorcise a presence is to fill a place with people and talk of ordinary matters. Perhaps Martin will feel more at home in the shop from now on.'

'Let's hope so,' said Lionel. 'Thanks for coming down.'

I waved goodbye as the car pulled away. I slept on the train, dreamlessly, all the way back to Reading.

When I got up to leave the train I noticed that the orange upholstery was stained with black. I knew that my jacket would have to go to the dry-cleaners and my jeans into the washing-machine, but I had every faith in the ability of modern technology to clear away the last residues of the dust. Ours is an inhospitable world for matter out of place and mind out of time.

Lionel called me a week later to say that Martin had had no further trouble with paranormal phenomena and discomfiting presences, but that he'd decided to get rid of the shop anyway.

'He reckons that he's not cut out to be a bookdealer,' Lionel informed me, sadly. 'He says there's a world of difference between being a reader and being a *real bookman*, and that he's obviously just a reader. He thinks he might look for a little newsagent's shop, or a pizza franchise.'

'Good luck to him,' I said.

'Penny's gone up to Scotland to investigate an old mansion. It's only the Lowlands, she says, but it's still more promising ground than Barry. The Scots are more firmly rooted in their native soil, she says. They're more closely in touch with their ancestors, and they're far too wise to doubt the nearness of the Other World.'

'Good luck to her, too,' I said. 'How about you?'

'Still skating on that thin crust called reality,' he assured me, quoting the catch-phrase he uses in every episode of *Fortean TV*. 'You won't believe some of the stuff we've got lined up for the next series. Be sure to watch it, won't you?'

'Actually, Lionel,' I told him, 'I won't believe *any* of it. But I'll tune in religiously just the same.'

Brian Stableford lives in Reading, England. In 1999 he was the recipient of the Science Fiction Research Association's Pilgrim Award for his contributions to SF scholarship; this completed his set of the four major awards available in that field. The author's fiftieth novel (and seventy-fifth book), *Year Zero*, was recently published by the Welsh small press imprint Sarob Press, for whom Stableford has also translated and edited the obscure nineteenth century French Gothic parody *Vampire City* by Paul Féval. He has also published *The Fountains of Youth*, the third volume in a future history series which began with *Inherit the Earth* and *Architects of Emortality*, and is set to be continued in *The Cassandra Complex*. About 'The Haunted Bookshop', Stableford says: 'As the story itself makes clear, the idea arose from the piece I did for Stephen Jones' *Dancing With the Dark* – and, of course, from watching my old friend Lionel Fanthorpe introducing *Fortean TV*.'

Starfucker

MICK GARRIS

I was the bastard son of Art and Commerce. Hollywood chewed me up and swallowed me whole, and when it had digested me, evacuated me like watery excreta from its overloaded bowels.

You'll have to excuse the unlovely imagery; I have no reason to be bitter. Everything that happened was my own damned fault.

It wasn't just the studio system. The independent world is almost as dire; it's just a smaller list of talentless moneychangers who have to justify their existence. The only reason you don't get rewritten by a list of hacks is not because of some kind of integrity inherent in the scruffy independent system; it's because they'd rather not pay all those dogs to piddle on your papers.

Well, there's no Movie Police forcing you to lie down and spread 'em for Hollywood. You don't like it, go back to the night shift at Vidiots.

There are many reasons to love an industry unburdened by morality. Primary amongst them is Forgiveness. A Hit forgives us all our trespasses, in fact, *rewards* us for them. One *Titanic* and you're allowed to scream and rant and fire and pull guns and fuck anybody who'll prance to the crook of your finger. And they forget all about *Piranha II: The Spawning*.

I had my big shot, my X-wing Fighter to Alderaan, my major studio break . . . and I bombed out big-time. It wasn't big-budget, but it was high profile. The trades were filled with the saga of the film school prodigy who jumped right out of the gate and into studio features, even without a load of music video shit on his résumé. And how that first-time Hollywood Helmer never even finished the movie. The studio wouldn't even Alan Smithee the damned thing; they just flushed their investment away . . . and I followed it down the drain.

I learned a big lesson, and I'm ready to share it with you, free of charge.

Never work with puppies, kids or mutant babies.

*

My own mutant kept me underground, feeding off my bodily fluids like Bernie Brillstein before meeting its untimely end as In-Sink-Erator chum for the Studio City sewer gators. As Asta's grue spattered the rusted porcelain of my kitchen sink, so did I. But I got over it. I even began to bathe again.

And work.

Well, when I say work, you won't find it on my résumé.

I wrote and wrote and wrote some more. And when I finished, I wrote some more. But the padlock had rusted shut. Nobody wanted to buy the stories I had to tell. Fair enough. Again, nobody's forcing me here. I serve of my own accord. So I wrote and wrote and wrote some more.

But I never sold any of it. And I can't blame anyone but myself. I thought that my experience had deepened me, and that my writing had matured, and reflected new reaches of insight into the human psyche. In truth, I was just jacking off.

But between then and now, I *did* shoot another feature length film, though I haven't told my new best friends at CAA. And it made a fortune, though not for me. I say film, but it was shot on MiniDV video, for a Valley company called Vivid. The San Fernando Valley is the red-rimmed sphincter of 'Adult Entertainment', and for a shining moment – though I hadn't sported an erection in close to two years – I was its king. If you've spent way too many nights alone with your VCR and your left hand, you may be intimate with my timeless classic, *Gulp!* Yes, the exclamation mark is part of the title, your guarantee of artistic merit.

The two-day shoot had only one real disaster, though 'disaster' is a subjective term. Patty Petty had just been implanted eight days before the shoot with massive bags of mammarian come-hither, topping her slender frame with enormous globes that stretched her fine alabaster skin so tight that, during a particularly energetic (and award-winning) coupling that involved five men, two women, and one excessively randy orang-utan, her breasts just split right open, dropping the silicone bags to the floor like unwanted Gerber's from a baby's mouth.

It was beautifully lit, and the camera was in the perfect position to see it all. It may be my most memorable scene.

With an investment of eight thousand dollars – and one thousand of those crispy green boys were all *mine* – *Gulp!* has grossed close to eight million dollars. Thank God for insurance. It swept the Adult Film Awards (Best Feature shot on Video, Best External Orgasm, Most Orifi Filled, and a host of others) and almost made me wish I'd used my own name on the damned thing. Almost.

Gulp Two! was a certainty. But I left that to other hands. Been there, porked that.

It's funny, if not really all that amusing, how one thing leads to another in this berg. In the afterglow of *Gulp!*'s transcendental performance, Patty was cast as a Wise-Beyond-Her-Years Stripper, a featured role that required Tasteful Nudity in an otherwise unmemorable Artistic Endeavour known as the Untitled Independent Feature. The Sterling Stripper Story crashed and burned before the first week was in the can, but pretty, petty Patty introduced me to its producer, who had actually seen and enjoyed *Words Without Voices*, and he hired me to write his Magnum Opus ... for the princely sum of two thousand American dollars. That was exactly double my *Gulp* fee, so I wrote my little tell-tale heart out. It was a grim, violent, Urban Drama, spattered with Red Humour and Brotherly Love. Well, our Masterwork of Renegade American Cinema stepped into mucky post-Columbine legal entanglements that kept it from even being midwifed on video.

But two years after it was collecting dust on the Payment Due shelf at the lab, Mr Producer hijacked his finest hour (and forty minutes) and managed to book it illegally into the Slamdunk Festival. For the uninitiated, Slamdunk is the scruffy alternative to Sundance and Slamdance. where loft-living men in black get their tawdry little celluloid stories that no legitimate human will have anything to do with projected onto the big screen once before being consigned to a K-mart video transfer with felt marker labels that sit with pride on the apple crate next to the dying Korean TVCR and the Tarantino collection.

Luckily, Sundance stank on ice that January. People had grown tired of the sensitive as well as the insensitive. Cinematographic ennui blanketed Park City with eleven inches of dull snow. And, with a bit of help from unnamed sources, word began to creep out about the lesbian nipple-tonguing scene in our Masterwork. It is said in the Bible of American Independent Cinema that if you blanket raw Eros in artful light and gorgeous surroundings, they will come. Give them guilt-free art-house erotica, wanking material for the intelligentsia, and the kilos to the kingdom are yours.

We played to a full house, breaking the legal logjam, and leading to an eleven-week run at the Nuart. It's still running midnights at the Angelika Center, even though it's been on video for months. Sure, most of the attention went to the snotty little auteur in the backwards cap and the baggy Hilfigers, but you know, somebody writes this shit. And this time, that somebody was me, and that shit was *mine*.

So now I'm working again.

I mean, I'm not Kevin Williamson, but I'm doctoring a couple of Gramercy scripts at ten grand a week, sold a spec to Fox Searchlight for the low six figures, and made an overall with Bob and Harvey over at Miramax that includes directing my third script for them. If and when.

But I've been through this before, and if you can't learn from experience, you are less than human, and consigned to a life as detritus. You exist to fail and provide an example to those who *can* learn from your mistakes.

So ... no Porsche and big house for me. I'm driving a TT, with a condo at the Marina City Club. Leave the pretensions to the backwards cap crowd. I'm letting my hair grow out brown.

There's even been a rebound in the social world. Invitations to screenings and parties are ubiquitous, and I don't bother to RSVP. I haven't paid for a meal since Slamdunk. And that was a year and a half ago.

I wasn't even going to bother with the American Cinemateque opening party, except that I'd never seen DeMille's silent *Ten Commandments* before. Hell, I'd never seen *any* silent film before ... or any DeMille, either, for that matter. But I'd heard about the grand old Egyptian Theatre, and there was a live orchestra, and my tickets were free, but they'd have cost *you* a hundred bucks apiece ... *if* you could get them. I was at a meeting at Paramount in the neighbourhood anyway, and it was better than fighting traffic to the Marina. Well, the Cinemateque completely ruined Hollywood's first and greatest movie palace, cramming a hideously ugly high-tech architectural disaster into its beautiful shell, and I slept through the dusty old harridan of a movie.

But the party afterwards made the evening more than worthwhile.

Oh, it was littered with the usual suits and poseurs and perfect specimens at both ends of the Hollywood rectum spectrum. There were the witty and famous, the witless and gorgeous, the rich and the stitched, the sparkled and the spackled, the cream and its curdle. Milling about the cramped, crimson lobby were Golden Age Movie Star lookalikes serving drinks and the latest trendy Biblical edibles from Along Came Mary. It was mildly clever. They did, however, manage to find some pretty good doubles: a Gable and a Lombard, a magnificent Monroe, a mammarian Mansfield. There was a remarkably unhaltered Harlow sheered in a *Platinum Blonde* satin gown that chilled and hugged her alabaster breasts with static electricity that made her nipples point shamelessly all the way to Heaven.

It was almost enough to make me give a shit about Old Hollywood. It was fully enough to feel my first post-Asta stirrings Down There.

The tight marcel of her white-hot hair, the anachronistic, unathletic voluptuousness of her unfettered hips, the sea-bottom near translucence of her milky – no, *creamy* – skin enraptured me in unexpected ways. Everything old was new again. My fascination did not go unnoticed. A publicist for the Cinemateque, ever alert to the needs of Her People, smiled at my obvious rapture, sidled up to me and gripped my elbow with her manicured claw, sipping champagne from a plastic flute from the other. Her lipstick smeared the rim a muddy, dried-blood colour.

'Pretty, isn't she?'

Pretty. Meg Ryan is pretty. A nice day is pretty. A fucking *nose* is pretty. Harlow II was something way beyond that. I don't know that they've even got a word yet for what she was. Really, it's been a couple of years since I last gave a shit about sex. I mean, it was ruined for me, I thought, for good. And Madame Publicité only bittered the batter. Though her high, domed forehead was stretched tight and shiny, her telltale hands were creepy and crêpey. Her thinning hair was course and wiry, her collagen lips bloated like a flounder's, her eager eyes trapped in a look of constant surprise. She was the sexual Antichrist.

But what the Antichrist taketh away, Harlow II gave back a thousandfold. Hallelujah, I am reborn.

The publicity monster stroked the inside of my arm with her talons and released a string of intimate words in my ear in a voice I know she felt was sultry, but to me was a gaseous nicotine croak.

'You can have her, you know,' she exhaled, wilting the rented flowers around us. 'Let me introduce you.' And the Publicity Pimp, gripping me so tight I feared blood loss, led me to the Goddess.

Well, suddenly realising the woman was a professional wilted me a bit . . . until we were face to face. It turned out I was the proverbial man who needed no introduction. She knew who I was, had seen the Masterwork during its Nuart run, even *bought* the video, though it still hasn't come out at sell-through. She even knew about *Words Without Voices*.

Had to be an actress. Damn it.

But who else works these Hollywood gigs? Professional servers? Beautiful People entirely uninterested in the performing arts? What the fuck did I expect? It was a disappointment, though it did nothing to fade her glory. She was magnificent, one of a kind. And the wattage from her smile could run a thirty-plex projection booth for a year and a half.

The Pimp winked and left us, with a smutty exit line that dangled huskily in the air of her wake: 'If you need a third party, you know who to call.' I'd rather lick Michael Jackson's star on the Walk of Fame clean.

When the tendrils of her reeking Giorgio finally receded and I could draw the semblance of a breath, I laughed uncomfortably. 'Seen any good movies lately?'

Her smile never broke, even with her simple answer. 'No.'

I was falling hard. They haven't made a good film in years. All they make are Crybaby Movies, no real guts or glory. Tobe Hooper can't get a studio picture set up. Gus Van Sant reshot fucking *Psycho*. It's all crybaby shit or comedies that aren't funny or send-ups. There hasn't been a real movie in the '90s, and the new Millennium seems just as bleak.

But she had an addendum: 'Not since your picture at the Nuart.' And then her smile went sideways with the extra-added attraction. She whispered, 'Gulp.' Not like a title, or anything. Just the word. Gulp. Without the exclamation point. Just to let me know that she knew. And still, she never lost her smile.

I could only stare at her in admiration. 'Same to you, but more of it.' It was a lame retort, I know, but I had to say *something*. And she laughed, a tinkling shower of delight that prickled the hair on the back of my neck. Gulp, indeed.

'If you weren't an actress, I'd ask you to marry me.' Chicks dig that.

'If you weren't a director, I'd slap you for that.' But I was, so she didn't. 'I like directors . . . especially the young, talented ones.'

'If I meet one I'll be sure to introduce you.' The self-deprecating stuff always hooks them. And I wanted her hooked. Gaffed. Boned.

'Oh, we've already met.'

Her wet, crimson lips glistened, and I watched them stick together and peel apart as the 'm' made its way through her mouth in slow motion.

'Will you be at the after-party?' she asked. After-party? What after-party? Was that on my invitation?

'Will *you*?'

'I have to be.'

'Then so do I. When and where?'

'It's a secret.' And then she leaned close, offering a bud-tipped alabaster view, and shared her secret with me.

The rain was Biblical, but the directions very specific. The little roadster and I headed up Laurel Canyon, past Joel Silver's Frank Lloyd

Wright masterpiece on Hollywood Boulevard, turned left on Wonderland and slid through an aquarium of eely estuaries and sobbing oaks. We groped through the rare midnight storm, ever upwards, evading the cracks of lightning that drew closer as we drove higher. At the applause of a particularly splendiferous hand of electrical fingers in the sky, I turned to look down at the Basin below and behind, just in time to see its voracious maw go dark.

It made little difference to my slithering drive. Here in the jungle of the Hollywood Hills, there were no streetlights. The moonlight was my guide. I was so close to my destination. I could not give up my quest, even if the party was called off when the lights went out.

So I continued, the heart of Indiana Jones beating within my chest.

At last I emerged at the crest of the mountain, and I saw Xanadu. Not the Olivia Newton-John bowl-filler, but the Orson Welles original, done Southern California-style. It was vast and pink and Spanish-tiled, probably built in the twenties when this acreage could be had for pocket change. And though the dozens of windows were dark, red-vested car chimps were jockeying the Benzes and Beemers into place. I parked the TT myself, and let the rain submerge me as I walked to the door.

Cool.

Security was tight, but I didn't need a ticket. The enormous Polynesian totem at the door let me right in without even a word passing between us. Either a fan or he'd been primed.

I walked inside this Old Hollywood mansion, and found myself submerged in darkness. I squinted through the twisting hallway, choking on the musk of history, and stepped into the spider's parlour. It opened up into a giant room filled with overstuffed furnishings and the glow of pale candlelight. It was a step into another era, one you only see on the screen, and even then only in black-and-white. This place was an education in early cinema, the kind I flunked out in at film school: an education I did not want, but could not avoid. The whole house was dressed in the elegance of a Hollywood long gone, like an Ernst Lubitsch drawing room comedy, dressed by William Cameron Menzies. The ceilings were high and scalloped, the maroon velvet draperies belted into place by gold ropes. It all looked so wrong in colour.

This was a Hollywood for which I had no nostalgia. It had grown long in the tooth on quaintness and manners and dust and censorship. It was far removed from real life: cornball artifice with heavy make-up and jerky special effects. It looked like Cary Grant should step in and offer me a drink.

Which is exactly what happened.

His black hair oiled into a perfect, shining part, a pearly grin that rounded the dimpled chin into an undersized apple, he poured me champagne and wished me well before disappearing into the candlelit gloom.

As my pupils adjusted to the light, I realised that I stood in a room filled with perfect specimens of an age gone by. Elegant in their evening clothes, many of them had been at the Cinemateque gala. But none of the icons from the fifties or beyond were here. These replicants were strictly of pre-war vintage. Most of these had *not* served at the Egyptian; they were *special*: the very most beautiful recreations of Hollywood's so-called Golden Era. Not really being a student of celluloid history, there were a lot of lookalikes I didn't recognise at the time. You know, if a movie was made before the birth of Michael Bay, I wasn't interested. But some of them you just couldn't avoid, so great was their status as pop culture icons.

Even the new generation of filmmakers that comes after me would have recognised the young John Wayne, that woman with the big monkey in *King Kong*, Kate Hepburn, Jimmy Cagney, Jimmy Stewart, Lana Turner in a bright red sweater, that woman who always had her blonde hair hanging over one eye, that Thin Man guy with the moustache, the old lady from Big Valley, who was a lot better-looking young, but still no babe. Except for Lana's show-off sweater, all of them were in the most elegant evening clothes of the era: white tie and tails, satin gowns, real classy stuff.

But what really looked out of place, even more than seeing these facsimiles in full, living colour, was watching what they were *doing*. The place was foetid with body heat. Those elegant clothes slid off of bare shoulders and dropped into elegant little pools of silk at the feet of the guests being serviced. I mean, it wasn't like everybody was whanging and banging in the middle of the room or anything; it was a little subtler than that.

But the Hollywood Hills were alive with coupling. Each massive easy chair, divan or settee was occupied with at least one gorgeous specimen treating the guests to a taste of Old Hollywood. A hand cupped a puddle of breast here; a flesh probe reached between tight buttocks there. Lips met teats and groins lubricated to the gentle strains of the string section in the other room. This glamorous repast of bodies on bodies was still elegant, passionate yet ethereal. It was my first appreciation of Hollywood Past.

I felt out of place, like a child, apart from the party, a guest but not a participant . . . until tapered porcelain fingers rested on my shoulders from behind. I turned, and joined the celebration. Harlow II touched her scarlet lips to my cheek and gently slid her fingers between mine. 'I was waiting for you.'

Jesus!

The words eased over me on her gentle breath, and every body hair prickled to attention. In the candlelight, she was even more luminous, practically digitally enhanced. Her fingers wrapped around mine, and it was as if we had melted together at the hand.

'Nice party,' I managed, but my voice cracked the 'nice' into two syllables. I couldn't imagine a modern woman as beautiful as my Jean ... and I told her so.

'You should see me on a weekday.'

I shuddered. The veil of imagination lifted for a moment, and for just a slice of that moment I could see past the platinum hair and the period lipstick, and saw her as just another beautiful actress in LA. Everything suddenly darkened in a crash of artifice, and my pulse dropped. The arousal waned, and I struggled it back in time, but without success. Jean was a working girl, another gorgeous face in the Academy Players Directory, with a wannabe résumé and an attraction to randy directors. I went limp.

She noticed.

'What's the matter?'

'Nothing. I just imagined you without the wig, having lunch with your agent at the Ivy and checking your pages every hour on your cell phone. In the real world.'

She looked at me, figuring me out. 'This is my real world. Here. Now. With you. This is no wig; go ahead, feel it.'

I did. I ran my fingers through the curling-iron waves, and she closed her eyes, enjoying the journey. 'Pull on it.' I gave it a little tug, and her lips parted, releasing that intoxicating breath. It was not a wig.

'I don't have an agent, I eat lunch at Musso and Frank's every day, and I hate cell phones. In fact, that's how I tell good people from evil people. If you talk on a cell phone in a restaurant, you're evil. Period. No way around it, no second chance. One strike and you're out. Cell phones in restaurants or talking in a movie theatre: the true signs of human slime.' I hoped nobody would choose this moment to reach out and touch me via the PacBell digital in my coat pocket. 'This is me, the real me, the ever me. Just a little less dressy on weekdays. So mind your manners, or you'll have to be spanked.'

Oh, please, not that. I apologised, and she forgave me.

'What would you like?'

'Are you kidding?' Uncharacteristically, her face flushed and she looked shyly down under my hungry gaze.

'You want something to drink?'

'Cary Grant gave me champagne, which I don't drink. I'll take a Coke, if you've got it. But I just want to be with you.'

She smiled at me, all girlish and genuine. 'That's so sweet.' And she led me by the hand. We walked through dim caverns of candlelight, each containing bodies in rhythmic heat. I was not startled to see Cary lying beneath an energetically hyperventilating Madame Publicist, her eyes rolled back in her head in ecstasy, her nails gouging red rivers down Cary's chest. I tried to sneak past, but her eyes found me, and she gave me a yellow wink. Her words reached me on a wave of dragon breath: 'Have a nice time . . .' And then she came. Loudly.

Ugh.

Other couplings were more visually appealing. There were fantasies fulfilled throughout the house, animus cloaked in an historic glamour. Dead movie stars brought back to life by the vigour of our desire. I can't tell you how exciting these violations of the Hays Code were to watch.

Laid out in the elegance of the location, the perfect grooming and formal wear intensified the heat to an amazing degree. The power may have been off, but the house was filled with electricity. I had always seen that Old Hollywood shit as dull and historic and musty and grampy. But now it was making me sprout wood.

I'm a director, so I observe. I felt no guilt staring at the couplings as Jean led me through them. It was a symphony of flesh, and each of the players was first chair. And I was being led to the podium to conduct a little ditty of my own.

I couldn't believe that the dark room she eased me into was anchored by a heart-shaped bed. That image would have worn a beard even in one of those old thirties movies. But it did, and the bed was made up in pink satin, as if art-directed to set off Harlow II's peach gown. The high-ceilinged room was lit only by a shaft of blue moonlight through a curtain of rain. The chill of the moonlight was tempered by the heat of our bodies. When she slid lightly onto the corner of the bed, tiny arcs of static electricity crackled between her and the sheet. As she sat in the shaft, highlighted by the moon, I could only gasp. She lifted her arms to me, and I dropped down next to her. I knew this had to go slow. It had to be drawn out. This might only happen once.

She stroked my face with her delicate fingertips, a Mona Lisa grin tugging at her scarlet lips. Those lips moved slowly in, and I wanted them to just devour me: wrap around my head and work their way down to my toes until I was dinner. Instead, they eased against my cheek, pausing there before peeling wetly away and leaving their crimson imprint. She grinned at the lipstick she'd left on my face, and lunged in to lick it off in a swift wipe of her tongue. Then she laughed.

I put my hands up and gently held her face in them, as if it might shatter. Her skin was as smooth and white as an egg. She let me draw her face close to mine, and finally we kissed. No suction, no open mouths, just our lips touching each other, gently at first, breathing each other's breath. I kissed her upper lip, her lower lip, then tilted my head to kiss them both at a vertical angle. Then I got hungry. I started to pull her lower lip into my mouth, nursing on it. Soon, the tiny pink tip of her tongue ventured into my mouth, tracing my teeth and gums. There was the faintest taste of chocolate on her tongue, and I savoured it. I wrapped my mouth around her tongue, and she slid it deeper inside, soon moving it to a samba rhythm. Then she took my tongue and nursed on it. I'm sure my eyes rolled back in my head in idiot abandon.

When finally we broke for air, we just looked unbelievingly into each other's eyes and breathed. And then we both just broke into laughter with the delight of it all. She nestled into the base of my neck, kissing it wet and warm, and I carefully lowered the satin strap that held in Nirvana. But I wasn't about to go right for the good stuff. I wouldn't be the pig with the hands that only wanted to grasp the tits and the clutch. For the first time in my life, I pleasured in the getting there. I felt the rich gloss of her neck and shoulders, stroked the clean, perfect whiteness of her deliriously long back. I kissed down her neck, tasted her wrists, even lifted her arm to cradle my head under it and kiss her pit. I tasted the slightest hint of salt and loved it. There wasn't even a trace of stubble.

And she, too, was happy to take her time with me. Her lips brushed lightly over my neck as she unbuttoned my shirt. I could feel the heat of her breath as she nuzzled my chest, her teeth lightly tugging on the hair around my nipples. She sucked easily on mine as I wanted hers. But I'd get there soon enough.

My hands went all exploratory, gently excavating the secrets of her body. I eased the satin down off of her breasts, and there were little sparkles of static electricity introducing them in a fanfare of tiny fireworks. Her happy little breasts were as white as the rest of her body, not surgically enhanced, and capped with tiny pink roses that almost disappeared in the moonlight. I first felt their heft with a light stroke of the underside with the back of my hand. I slowly closed in, palming them, holding them, clutching them. I nuzzled them, but that was it. Soon I had drawn them hungrily into my mouth, and I wanted to feed off of her: milk, blood, anything. I just wanted to swallow her fluids.

At that point, it wasn't long before I was atop her, the globes of her ass clutched tightly in my hands. Her legs scissored me tightly as she chewed voraciously on my earlobe. And as her body was wracked in orgasm, I was pumping two years of dormant seed endlessly into her. I thought it would never stop . . . but finally it did.

When the new sun peered into the bedroom window, the old movie was over. Jean was gliding into jeans and a T-shirt, and brushing her hair out of her eyes. She wasn't Jean any more. I bet she lived in the Valley. I heard the leaden thump-thump of techno-disco booming through the old house, and a ripple of nausea curdled me. It took me a while to come to. The 2000s had fully replaced the 1930s. And I didn't like it.

I watched the muscles of her chest heave as she brushed her platinum hair and tried to figure out what came next. 'Um . . . what do I owe you?'

'Don't worry about it. Last night was all taken care of.'

Nice party.

I couldn't take my eyes off of her, and she winked at me in the mirror.

'When can I see you again?'

She turned to me. 'Anytime you've got fifteen hundred bucks. Or a part you might think I'm right for. I'm a very versatile actress.'

I tried to smile back, but I'm sure she saw my face crash. Jean was gone. This stranger gave me a mock pout. 'Aw, baby misses Jean Harlow, doesn't he? I can be Jean anytime you can afford it.' And she handed me a business card with her pager number on it. She kissed me hard on the lips and toodled.

What a crash. I don't know why I felt so devastated, so abandoned, so cheated. But here I was, hollow and deflated, still sticky from last night, inside and out. All I had left was the drive home.

Home.

I stared out at the sewage bobbing along the beach from my tenth floor condo. I hated the present. A second-stage smog alert hung heavy over the effluent, and the traffic on the boulevard below was blocked like a bowel. I had the Criterion *Armageddon* on the DVD player, enveloping me in full Dolby Digital surround, but even that couldn't bring me out of it. Normally its twenty-cuts-a-minute exhilarated me;

today it merely enervated me. It just felt like a bunch of frantic, noisy crap, a cinematic nagging mother-in-law, screeching in my ear. I missed the past . . . and I'd never even been there.

So I decided to visit.

I made a sojourn to the dreaded San Fernando Valley to Dave's Video, a beacon in the midnight of Ventura Boulevard. I loaded up on every black-and-white DVD made before the Great War and charged it to my Gramercy account. Research, you know. Let them pay for my education in the classics.

I lugged the tonnage of my cinema booty back to the Marina, and vegetated in front of the new HD screen from the Good Guys. Tendrils of beard sprouted as I reached back into the ghosts of the past. First, I made my way through every Jean Harlow film I could find, from *Hell's Angels* through *Saratoga*. She'd made a couple dozen pictures in the course of a half-dozen years, then up and died. But Jesus, what a legacy she left! Through Harlow, I discovered Howard Hawks, William Wellman and Victor Fleming. The movies spoke to me in an eloquence I'd never known before. They just plain *spoke*! The words sparkled, the scenes played out without cuts, the camera observed, rather than led the characters! What a revelation!

I worked my way through the Harlow collection, hungering for her crumpled little expression, lusting after her pale, ever-braless form. *Dinner at Eight* led me to George Cukor; Cukor led me to Ernst Lubitsch, who led me to Preston Sturges, who led me to John Sturges, who led to me John Ford, on to Hitchcock and Huston, David Lean and Frank Capra, Tod Browning and James Whale. And through the filmmakers I met some new dead friends: Jimmy Stewart, Robert Donat, Gene Tierney, Donna Reed, Ava Gardner, Rita Hayworth, Jean Simmons, Glenn Ford, Ann Savage, Veronica Lake, Boris Karloff, Fay Wray.

Who knew these creaky old grinders would be so filled with wit and beauty and humour and tension and revelation? Who knew that a film could be more than a barrage of flash-cut imagery, digital animation, and DTS explosions?

Maybe you did, but I didn't.

I know, I'm sounding like some old fart film instructor who can't let go of a past that's practically been buried alive, but it's true. I don't mean to preach here – I really don't – but I was born again. I guess I'd only seen the old shit. I didn't find the jewels. That would be like judging today's movies by the latest Adam Sandler.

The best of the old stuff was elegant and smart and breezy and entertaining and, well, *engaging*. And the worst of it was ... well, the worst of it was like most of the movies today. Bankrupt and boring.

I got it.

Bleary-eyed and exhausted, but also wonderfully recharged after a dozen weeks of nonstop watching, I turned off the set. I'd forgotten the world was in colour, and it startled me. The cleaning lady had vacuumed around me for the last couple of months, and thrown out all the food delivery cartons, but the place was still a litter of videos and detritus. As I stood, my head reeled. My eyes had stared at a fixed focus for so long that they found it difficult to hone in on anything else. My hair was a couple inches longer, and I had the semblance of a Fu Manchu beard tickling my chin.

I slid the glass door to the balcony open and stepped out onto the cusp of the real world, and let it breathe on me. It was noisy and argumentative and its breath stank. I liked the movies better. Reality bathed me in ugliness, and I shivered. It reeled around me and my mind drifted away to beauty.

I remembered what brought this on in the first place. I opened up my wallet, and pulled out her card. It didn't have a name on it, just a number. I dialled it, got the system's nervous beep-beep-beep, punched in my number and waited. This time, as I looked out into the vast Pacific, I couldn't discern the turds floating out there. Maybe they cleaned them out again; maybe they were just hiding. But the sea was as blue as the veins on Cher's forehead. If only the sky matched. Instead, it was congealing into a disgusting mauve solidity.

Her call booted me out of my coastal reverie. She knew who it was from just my 'hello'. She was good. I needed to see her. I wanted to share what I had found with her, and needed to siphon some of it off of her, so I invited her over. She came.

By the time she called up from the lobby, I was showered and shaved and reborn. My eyes could focus near and far again, and my breath was kissing sweet. My expectant erection tugged me like a divining rod to the door at the sound of her gentle rap. Oh, my lovely embodiment of the past, my alabaster testimony to all that once was beautiful and elegant and witty and desirable. My link to another, better world, the only world that mattered, a world without corruption or darkness or despair.

My Jean.

I pulled the door open ... and wanted to cry.

This was not my Jean. This was that girl in the Jeans and the T-shirt and the Reeboks and the backwards Nike cap, fresh from the gym. This was all the girls I'd read and dated and sampled and discarded and been discarded by. This was now, and I wanted – *needed* – then.

She saw it and knew. She lifted a shopping bag from Trader Joe's and pulled out a bottle of wine. 'I brought wine.' I tried not to look so let down, and she dug deeper in the bag. 'And Jean.'

She held up the peach satin gown with a twinkling little smile that did its best to win me over. 'Which way to the bathroom?'

Unable to speak, I merely pointed, and she scurried through the condo and locked herself in. No matter what she looked like when she emerged, I had seen behind the façade. I knew it was fake now, and that it wasn't going to work. It was so perfect, that night at the Cinemateque, until the fateful morning after. I wouldn't see Jean any more, merely the actor playing her. It wasn't the same thing.

Still, when she emerged, the gown clinging to her like hot breath, she was stunning. The lips were sanguine, the hips unfettered, the breasts at full attention. But now, having experienced the real Jean Harlow in every one of her films – even the one with Laurel and Hardy – I realised she didn't really look all that much like Harlow. Beautiful, desirable, yes. Harlow, no.

'Forget about that girl at the door,' she told me. 'I sent her away. I want you all to myself.' She gave me a sharp little bite on the lip. I tasted my own blood.

She stepped into the middle of the living room and appraised the place, knowing I would appraise her in the light of the picture windows. The room basically consisted of open space, the giant TV system and a view of the murky Marina. And now, her. She startled me with a sudden squeal of delight. 'Look!' she said as she knelt at the pile of silver discs littering the floor. 'You've got all my movies! Let's watch one!' She picked up a copy of *Red Dust* and held it out to me in front of the stack of electronic hardware. Then, in a baby-doll voice: 'How do you work this thing?'

I popped the disc into the machine and fired up the monitor, filling it with the true Harlow and Clark Gable.

'Do you have any popcorn, Clark?' she asked me. I had to disappoint her, but she was goodnatured about it all and pulled me into a pile of pillows with her. It was a strange experience looking from the screen to the siren curled in my lap. She mouthed all the dialogue that Harlow spoke as the sun outside sank into the Marina.

As the movie continued, she slid up against me like a cat, and the contact was all warm and comfy and even arousing ... but that's not what I wanted. I wanted the woman on the screen. The Jean in my lap started to purr, her engine ignited and accelerating. She pushed me back into the pillows and climbed atop me, I drowned in her body.

Her skin as smooth as the discarded satin gown, she flowed against me like butter on a frying pan, melting on me. Her talents spread throughout her body, but mine resisted. I tried closing my eyes, but could not keep the girl at the door out of my home. She drew me into her and we coupled ferociously, but it was nothing like that night. And I know it wasn't her fault, but I couldn't help but focus on the tiny red pimple sprouting on her chin. The *real* Harlow would never be so blemished. We united wetly and energetically, and our mutual release finally jettisoned enough unspilled juice to cramp my sphincter. But I was not satisfied, and she knew it.

'You know, I try my best to be her for you, but I can't really *be* her.'

I couldn't say anything. I was spent and sweating, and just couldn't come up with an answer. I felt like the king of movie geeks, pining for a movie star who died before my parents were even conceived. What a fucking goober.

She just watched me, her mind working, and I felt like a twelve-year-old. My heart had been broken by an image on television. Her gaze just embarrassed me. Mama, make it stop. She just kept looking at me, judging me, shrinking me with her eyes. Meanwhile, the movie had come to an end.

Without saying anything, she walked across the room, still spectacularly naked, and picked up the phone. Her eyes still pinning me to the floor like a butterfly specimen, she started dialling and walked into the kitchen. I heard her dulcet, off-screen voice, but not the words. I heard her sign off before she re-entered the room and cradled the phone, shameless in her sheath of flawless ivory flesh. She gently took me by the hand and took me to the glass doors overlooking the water. She stared out for long silent minutes before speaking.

'How much would you pay to spend the night with Harlow?'

I figured it was time to pay up. I guess fifteen hundred wasn't a lot to pay to discover what a retard I was.

'I'll get your money.'

I went to the desk and brought her the cash.

'I didn't mean me,' she said as she took the bills and folded them into her dainty Bakelite purse. 'I meant Harlow.'

'I think you're as close as I'm ever going to get.'

That made her laugh. 'I'm not.'

I was sick of her laughing at me. Think again about me casting you in anything, I thought.

'I mean Harlow, Jean Harlow, exactly who we were watching on the screen.'

'What are you talking about?' I didn't want to play this game.

'What would you pay for a night of connubial bliss with Jean Harlow?'

'The real Jean Harlow? If it were possible?'

'If it were possible.'

'I don't know. I can't go that far into the abstract.'

'Come on, think about it. If you could have one night with her, how much would it be worth to you?'

I thought about it. 'Fifteen hundred?' I thought it would compliment her.

'Shit, you can get *me* for fifteen hundred. Come on, for real. An entire night with Jean Harlow, exactly as you've seen her in the movies. How much?'

'I don't know . . . ten thousand dollars?'

'Cheapskate.'

'Twenty.'

'Jesus.'

I gave up 'Then let's stop doing this. I couldn't fuck Jean Harlow for all the money in the world, so let's just stop this. She's been rotting since 1937.'

She just smiled sweetly and shook her marcelled little head. '*I don't think so . . .*'

Where the fuck was this going? 'Well, if she's a hundred years old and living in Argentina or something, I don't think I want a piece of her.'

That fucking smile again.

'Would you pay a hundred grand to spend the night with the Jean Harlow of your dreams? The 1937 Jean Harlow? If you could. For real.'

Just for the hell of it, I thought about it. Would I? The decision was a bit more difficult in the wake of the powerful orgasm I'd just experienced minutes ago. But with the Gramercy and Miramax deals set in hard copies, I had some disposable income. Is that how I'd dispose it? A hundred grand? Hell, I could spec out a script in a month for double that. So that's like two weeks' pay. Of course, you can't crank out a dozen scripts a year, but Jesus, even if it's a couple months' pay . . . would it be worth it? I didn't have a wife or kids or anything: just me and my TT. I'd pay a hundred thousand dollars to sleep with Harlow.

If it were possible.

So I said yeah.

And she said really? And I said yeah, I think I would. And she said that was interesting and slid into her jeans and that fucking T-shirt again, kissed me goodbye, and fluttered away.

It was another week before she called me back. I was immersed in *Saratoga* when the machine picked up. I never answer the phone, especially not when I'm viewing, and *especially* not when it's Jean onscreen. But it was her voice: 'Are you there? It's Jean.'

The voice, I had to admit, was perfect. I picked up.

'Hi.'

She giggled, sounding like New York in the thirties. 'Go to the bank,' she whispered.

'What for?'

'It's time.'

'Time for what?'

'You know. Hundred-thousand-dollar time. Cash or traveller's cheques.'

Well, you and I both know what that meant. But what it meant was impossible. I didn't know how to respond to her, and just sat there with that porcelain face basting my brain, probably breathing funny.

'Are you still there?'

'I'm here.'

'Can you get to the bank today? And meet me at Union Station tonight at eleven?'

I didn't understand. 'I don't understand,' I told her.

'Like heck you don't.' And then, with another tinkling little titter, she hung up, as the real Jean smiled at me from my 62-inch Pioneer, enhanced for sixteen-by-nine.

I'd spent a couple of nights sharing skin with this phenomenal creature, reaching a Nirvana Kurt Cobain never dreamed of, but what did I really know about her? That she could set me to palpitating was a given ... but what kind of idiot would go to the bank, pull out a hundred grand, and meet this angel in the middle of the night at a train station in the cesspool of downtown Los Angeles? Surely this was a set-up; obviously this, well, I'll say it, this *prostitute* had found a malleable mark, a sucker just dying to toss off his ill-gotten gains. She and her pierced and tattooed cohorts would beat me up and take my cash. *You* would never have gone for a crack-brained scenario like this one, and I would never have dared writing such a silly plotline. If I'd turned it in to Sid Fields, I'd have flunked Screenwriting 101.

But, you know, I did have a hundred grand. It was pretty much all I had at the moment, but, you know, I had more coming in. And I was unburdened by investments. What was the worst that could happen to me? Other than having my money stolen and my throat slashed, what did I have to lose? My soul? Yeah . . . *that's* worth a lot.

Was it really that preposterous to think that I might be able to have . . . *Jean*?

Well, the answer was obvious, but I sped down to Washington Mutual anyway.

Still grand but ageing and missing a few teeth, Union Station reached coldly into the scuffed, blue-brown night sky. Mine was the only car in the desolate lot and I parked as far as I could from the three creased, ruddy faces sharing hits off a bottle of violet rotgut. The sound of their retching was a perfect contemporary counterpoint to the timeless architectural elegance that reached out to embrace me. I was, as usual, anally punctual. Eleven distant chimes hung sweating in the muggy night air.

As I stepped into the empty vastness of the old dowager, it was like stepping into an evacuated Capra epic. I could imagine the post-war homecomings, the reunited sweethearts spotting one another through the teeming masses of humanity, the brass-band sendoffs to the senator's last hurrah. But the monochrome crowd evaporated and the cracked leather seats and the gang-gouged woodwork brought me back home. It was an empty Art Deco barn strangling on its memories. I would be one of them.

Then the tip-tap tip-tap of high heels echoed around me, and I turned just as an unmistakable silhouette rounded the corner. She stepped into a shaft of light, and its reflection off of her platinum hair ignited the room in yellow fire. She stood there, letting the spotlight caress her perfection.

'Hi.'

'Hi back.'

I walked to her, my heart suddenly racing in anticipation, the cash in a shoulder bag, suddenly weighing a hundred pounds. What the fuck was I doing here?

'What the fuck am I doing here?' I asked her.

'Dreaming. Give me your keys.'

'Where are we going?'

'Heaven.'

I followed her out of the cavernous, empty building and back to my car, unable to pull my eyes from the lift and ripple of the perfect globes of her rear as she walked.

The thick summer night laid on us like an oil change, even with the top down. She caromed through the dank darkness, the empty downtown Los Angeles streets choking on their past. Broadway was a desiccated corpse, the klieg lights of the grand Million Dollar, United Artists, and Los Angeles Theaters long extinguished. A handful of zombies lumbered like cancerous cells through her clogged artery. We were on our own Fantastic Voyage through Innerspace when Jean suddenly pulled off behind the old Times Mirror building and guided us down a long, dark, seemingly endless alley.

That alley led to the decaying backside of a once-grand edifice, a cracked granite frown slowly settling into the sinking subway horizon. She pulled us into its gaping, festering maw, and kept driving like a drill into the ground. The corkscrew drive was seemingly Hellbound as it dug us deeper into a quakephobe's sweatiest nightmare. But as we plunged down beneath the city, lit only by headlights and the dim, browning sconces that studded the concrete wall, the temperature grew much cooler.

In moments, my grinning little TT peered into a grand open lobby, its flawless white-veined black marble gleaming in the shine of its headlights. A giant stone Thinker sat contemplating us in the middle of the vast room as Jean killed the engine and tip-tapped across the gleaming mirror of marble floor to the centre pair of sculptured brass doors. The elegance of the lobby was impressive, and of another world: overstuffed leather and cherry sofas and chairs, vast WPA murals of noble working people on the job, a heavy walnut reception desk the size of a Beverly Center screen. It had all of the chi-chi quiet snootery of a Beverly Hills face-tightening clinic.

Jean said 'I'm here' to nobody and nothing in particular, and the giant, wizard doors opened up to Oz.

The hallway was of impressive length and faded grandeur, lit by the dull Cocteau glow of *faux* lantern sconces. It was a soft, warm, but dim light ... and in it, Harlow II was even more ravishing. She led me down the length of the hallway, and as we reached its end, the dark wood double doors opened up to us, revealing the Man Behind the Curtain.

The man was tiny, certainly not over five feet, with a venerable, dried-apple countenance tightly sheltered with a thick, pomaded landing strip of artificially boot-blacked hair. A ghost of cataract and eyelids that drooped like sagging breasts almost hid the sparkle of his rheumy grey eyes, and his osteoporosis curled him into a tiny question mark. He looked up at Jean, apparently unwilling to make eye contact with me until getting her approval.

'He's good,' she told him, and the little lawn gnome finally looked up at me, manufacturing a smile that revealed perfectly straight white teeth that were way too big for his crêpe-paper mouth. He reached out his right hand – which was missing the thumb – and I shook it. I don't know if you've ever shaken hands with a guy without a thumb, but it just doesn't feel right. His other hand was tucked out of sight in his pocket, and I wondered if the little gremlin was born without opposable thumbs at all.

After I shook his hand, he kept it reaching out at me. I thought he was stuck on pause or something until I realised that he was waiting for me to hand over the shoulder bag with the cash in it.

'Who are you?' I asked, and he looked back up at Jean, who turned to me with a smile.

'No names.'

That made the little homunculus grin, and his smile, even in the dim light, was blinding. I handed over the bag to PeeWee, who zipped it open and started carefully counting the bills. This was going to take a while. Jean leaned in to stick a kiss on my cheek.

'Have a great night.' And she turned back down that long, lonesome hallway.

'Wait.' She turned back with an expectant look. 'Can this guy even talk?'

That made the withered little manikin testy. I thought he was going to bite my kneecap. 'Of course I can talk! Oh, shit, I've lost count!' And he started over. From one.

With a 'Nighty-bye,' Harlow II was down the hall and out the door, leaving me with my own private Dr Loveless. I waited in the doorway while he counted it all out: one hundred thousand dollars in hundred-dollar bills.

Eventually satisfied that I wasn't a piker, Mr Subspecies turned and led me down the newly revealed corridor. I had to move slowly to keep from overtaking his baby steps.

We took another turn and he reached up on tippy-toes to flip a light switch, revealing a long, antiquated chamber that opened out onto several apartments. Each of them had a large picture window that looked into the central chamber, and each window was draped with ornate wine velvet curtains on the inside. Most of the curtains were closed, but not all of them. As I followed in my Munchkin's eensy steps, I was able to see into a drape that lolled lazily open. Inside was an ornate bedroom, decorated as if by Menzies: heavy wood pieces, a high moulded ceiling, and a vast silk-sheeted bed against the wall. The only light was cast by the dim chamber sconce, but even in the shadows I could see that the bed was unmade.

Just as we passed the window to the clip-clop of teeny feet echoing through the otherwise silent chamber, a face suddenly appeared like a spotlight in the opening of the curtains. I jumped, I admit it, startled by its abrupt appearance, and the golden halo that surrounded her familiar face in the struggling, limp light reflected off her bottle blondness. But most unnerving of all was how her eyes were locked on mine, just a foot or so away from me. This was most definitely not Jean.

The face was enormous, a round, fleshy visage under a marigold mane, exquisitely painted in white-hot Helena Rubinstein beauty. The eyes, though – they were huge and liquid pale, drilling right into my own. But the spark was out behind them; they were gorgeous but empty, lifeless, shining husks of eyes. I wasn't sure she could even see me through them.

But boy, could I see her.

Striking in her red satin wrapper, she was an uncaged housefire. That huge moon of a face rose over an alarmingly ample décolletage and a waspy little waist I could circle in two hands. This was a woman you could only see in colour: the red of her lips, the electric gold of her hair, the flamingo pink of her tongue, and – even though bound behind the thin red wrapper – the evident, nursed-dark muddy brown howdies of her vast, reaching nipples.

The Little Man gripped my hand in his gnarly, four-fingered tug, trying to pull me down the hall, but I couldn't move, not now that I recognised her. This incendiary explosion of boobs and blondness had been immortalised most spectacularly by Frank Tashlin in *Will Success Spoil Rock Hunter?*, but that's not how I recognised her.

No. The little relentlessly yipping dog at her feet was a clue, but what finally led me to put it all together were the tiny, nearly invisible tell-tale sutures that circled her neck.

I was eyelocked with Jayne Mansfield.

Obviously, some assembly had been required, since she was decapitated in a car wreck in 1967. But that was Jayne. The real deal. Alive. Breathing. Her impressive water wings heaving with each breath. I could barely even blink as I riveted into her glassy, vacant orbs. She didn't blink at all, not once. It was unsettling, at the very least. I'd only seen eyes like that once before, and I didn't want to remember it, but now she made me.

When I was five years old, my dad was teaching me how to ride a bike without training wheels for the first time. He'd just taken them off without even telling me, and I was roaring down the street, oblivious to my new mastery of two-wheeled travel, when he shouted out for me to look that I was riding without training wheels. I looked down, saw that it was true, and panicked. The handlebars shimmied and I lost control. Dad came running to help me, just as an ancient, wheezing Impala roared around the corner on a tail of grey exhaust, and slammed him into the phone pole. I skinned my knee through my jeans as I fell off the bike and ran to see my father, who was shattered and pinned between the empty grin of the Impala's grille and the cracked Phone Pole Tower of Pisa. Our eyes were cinched as his life beat away with his slowing heart, leaving the flesh husk and the glazed, sightless eyes reflecting my own. I could see, even then, when his life had left him and his eyes gone blind.

And now Jayne gave me the same vacancy sign before pulling the curtain shut.

'Come on,' the tugging little gnome croaked as I allowed him to pull me from the blockaded showroom. 'She's not for you.'

'Was that Jayne Mansfield?' I asked him.

'No, it was Jane Pauley. What the fuck do you think?'

'You're a cranky old asshole, aren't you?'

'I'm actually very sweet once you get to know me.'

I didn't believe him. But I followed him down the seemingly endless chamber anyway.

He stopped me at the very last room.

'You didn't bring flowers, did you,' he said in a judgmental sneer. 'She likes flowers.'

'Nobody told me.'

'It's breeding, common decency to bring a woman flowers. Now . . . you know the rules.'

I looked at him. How should I know the rules? 'Not really.'

'Just be gentle. Thoughtful. And no rough-housing.'

And then he was off, no doubt back to his place behind the curtain. His walk took him forever.

I gently rapped on the ornate door and waited, my heart trying to climb up my throat. I kept waiting, the mystery and marvel and anticipation shrivelling my nerve as well as my manhood. I felt like a turtle pulled back in its shell. When it became evident that no one was coming to answer my knock, I reached out and gripped the doorknob. It was greasy with palm-sweat, but wasn't locked. It opened, and I entered in quiet, tiny steps.

The room was hushed and dark, but so were my desires, I guess. But the dim light from the candle guttering on the nightstand couldn't extinguish the glow that Jean Harlow – the real Jean Harlow, alive and in full living breathing colour – cast. She sat on the edge of the peach satin bed, draped in shadow and a fine silk chemise. She turned to face me, but the curtain of shadow blacked out her features. I was frozen in place, my mouth gawping; I hadn't the strength to take a breath. The hairs at the nape of my neck curdled and a shimmer of gooseflesh traversed my body. Jean. Jean. Roses are red. And all of my guts have gone green.

After a big slice of eternity, I made the next move, taking a step towards her and the bed. Jean glided back a few inches on the satin quilt, lifting her face into the warm, gentle caress of the candlelight. It was at that moment that it became obvious that Harlow II looked nothing like my Jean, the real Jean. The *faux* Harlow had been sandblasted by modernity, corrupted by the modern age, while Jean – milky, creamy, elegant Jean – was above all that passage-of-time nonsense. I don't know how she was here sitting on this bed in this room with me after dying in 1937, but she was. This was no imposter. Somehow, she had been rescued from the ravages of death, had earned a station in eternity, and for a hundred thousand dollars I had bought a share of that station. A night with my forever Jean. A taste of eternity. Whatever science or magic made it possible, I was its slave.

And Jean's.

Unlocking the invisible shackles that bolted me to the floor, I moved to the bed and looked down at her longingly. She looked up into my eyes and gently patted the space on the bed next to her with her palm, once, silently inviting me to sit. Her eyes, though pure and startlingly blue, were ringed in black mascara, and as vacant and unblinking as Jayne's, though larger and more inviting. Her mouth was painted in a rose red so dark it was almost black, and it shone in the pale candlelight. Her lips eased open, just a sticky little fraction of an inch, releasing the softest, curious sound from within. She was purring a constant, sensual little rumble, her own internal combustion engine.

'Jean?'

Without blinking or moving her eyes from me, she nodded. I sat next to her and took her pale ice cream hand in mine. The hand was cool and soft, limp, barely motivated, and I drew it to my face. I touched the back of her hand with my lips, I couldn't help it, and she let me. Her skin tasted like vanilla and fresh hand soap. She watched me kiss her hand through barren, staring eyes, and I laid my hand on her cheek and turned her face towards me. Her eyes turned sluggishly to mine, and we were face to face. Her purr was more distinct now, though no less sensuous. I could feel her breath stroke my face in cool even waves. Its scent was a bit pungent, but no more than it might be after a plate of penne arrabiatta. But it sure didn't smell like vanilla.

She neither resisted nor encouraged me, so I bent in and kissed her. She kissed me back, and my eyes closed in exultation. Her full, soft lips parted, and her chilly pink tongue sought mine. She sucked it into her mouth and began to nurse off of it, and there's no way I was going to stop her. I sneaked a peek as she milked my tongue, and her eyes were wide open, still unblinking, her mouth sucking mechanically, almost painfully, on my tongue.

I pulled away to look at her, and she looked back, gorgeous but empty. No resistance, no encouragement.

'What would you like?' I asked her. She just looked back at me. No words. Never any words. I knew the lights were out, but it didn't keep my libido from raging. My fear was that, presented with a dream, my physiognomy might recede and that junior might chicken out, but *au contraire, mon ami, au contraire*. The passive, alabaster icon on the bed with me ignited my hormones and overcame my stupefaction. The ample voluptuousness of one of Hollywood's greatest stars awaited me; the dream of a lifetime was at my fingertips, and if it wouldn't come to life to a symphony of Preston Sturges dialogue, if it would instead be my own personal silent epic, well, shit, so be it.

I reached out and gently lifted the strap of her chemise from her shoulder and let it drop, revealing the delicate sundae of her breast to me. Her eyes locked shamelessly on mine, and I reached over to cup it in my palm. As her feline engine accelerated, I bent down and took her breast in my mouth. It yielded, its cool marshmallow vanilla a creamy treat. The nipple stayed relaxed, unresponsive, never flexing to attention. Her arms curled about me and limply came to rest on my shoulders. I looked up from her breast and she watched me nursing on her with those clear blue unblinking eyes. It stopped me. I raised my face to hers, tried to see beyond the pupils, but was blocked by absence.

She moved, in, eyes still wide open, and kissed my mouth. The hum from within was soothing and welcoming. I let her kiss me, closed my eyes, and ran my fingers through the tight marcels of her platinum hair. Her hair felt like weaves of satin, glossy and slippery, and my fingers got lost in it. My thumb tangled in one of her waves, and I gently tugged it free.

Her breath caught in a gasp and I opened my eyes, afraid I had hurt her. Her eyes were even wider now as I lifted my hand from her hair ... pulling a patch of it away with my thumb! There was a clot of greyish reddish brownish skin at the base of the tangle of spun gold wrapped around my thumb, and she reached for it, unable to take it in her own sleeping fingers.

'Oh, God, I'm so sorry, I'm so sorry!' I tried to calm her, but she just kept quietly and unsuccessfully reaching for her curls. There was a dark brown square on her scalp where the patch had pulled free, and a few drops of a dark fluid that could only have been blood wept to the surface.

'Are you okay?' She didn't answer me, of course. She had given up trying to retrieve her hair and was suddenly reaching for my groin with curious, less-than-dexterous fingers. I couldn't help it; the boy had a mind of his own. As she fumbled to release me, I helped her with the zipper, quickly forgetting about our little experience with the hair. The same mouth that had locked so successfully to my tongue now found succor in the netherworld.

The suction was remarkable considering the fragility of her other movements. I had never felt anything like the cool, muscular, rhythmic suction her mouth incurred. I couldn't help but grip her hair in my hands as I approached a bucking, uncontrollable orgasm that jolted through my body, emptying me of weeks of celibacy.

I jerked violently in fulfilment, and her head bobbed off and back onto my convulsing tissue. It was irresistible impulse; I didn't mean to pull away the handfuls of flaxen hair and grey, preserved flesh. And when she screamed – the first vocalising she'd released since I entered her room – I looked down to see that one of those fragile, ice blue, vacuous eyes had been punctured, and wept a clear tide of thick tears.

Her inhuman screech echoed through the silence and in moments the little gnome was charging into the room in hunched-over horror. '*Jeeeeeaaaaaannnnnnnn!*' he howled. It was the longest single-syllable word I'd ever heard. He yanked me away from her in an incredibly powerful four-fingered grip, and in a cloak of guilt I climbed back into my khakis.

The little professor tended Jean with incredible gentleness, his own eyes going glassy as he dabbed her leaking eye socket with his hanky. '*I said no rough-housing!*' he told me as he soothed her delicate body. 'You'd better get out of here.'

I agreed. As I made my way to the door, I heard his plaintive, melancholy words evaporate into the velvet night: 'Daddy fix, Baby. Daddy fix again.'

My hundred-thousand-dollar half-hour was over.

I've tried several times to return to the House of Harlow, but it is long gone, and without a trace. I've called and called Pseudo-Jean, but that number is no longer in service, and there is no new number. Now all I have to remember Jean are her movies. I've seen them so often that I know them all by heart, but it isn't just the movies themselves that so entrance me. It's the time long past, the dream long remembered. And I had a piece of that before I put its eye out.

Mick Garris lives in California's Studio City. Best known as the director of such movies and TV mini-series as Disney's *Fuzzbucket*, *Critters 2*, *Psycho IV*, Stephen King's *Sleepwalkers*, *The Stand* and *The Shining*, King and Clive Barker's *Quicksilver Highway* and Peter James' *Virtual Obsession*, he has also directed several episodes (including the pilot) and served as the supervising producer on the Steven Spielberg series *The Others*. As a scriptwriter, his credits include *Coming Soon!* (with John Landis), **Batteries Not Included*, *The Fly II* (with Frank Darabont and Jim and Ken Wheat), Disney's *Hocus Pocus* (with Neil Cuthbert), ten episodes of Spielberg's *Amazing Stories*, an episode each of *New York Undercover* and *Tales from the Crypt*, and with Tom McLoughlin he created the series *She-Wolf of London*. His short stories have appeared in anthologies and magazines including *Hot Blood*, *Silver Scream*, *Splatterpunks*, *Midnight Graffiti* and *Carpe Noctem*, while Gauntlet Press recently published his collection *A Life in the Cinema: Eight Stories and a Screenplay*, which includes a foreword by Stephen King and cover art by Clive Barker. As Garris explains: '"Starfucker" is the sequel to a short story called "A Life in the Cinema", which achieved some degree of notoriety when it was first published in David Schow's anthology, *Silver Scream*. With that story, I wanted to see if I could remove the choke collar of self-censorship that never seemed to fetter favourite authors of mine like King and Barker. Well, I guess it was a success in that matter, for it has embarrassed friends and family members for several years. I'd always wanted to revisit this character (who was inspired by, if not based on, a real Hollywood hotshot right out of film school, but I'm not telling who), and this story, which came well over a decade later, is it.'

Destroyer of Worlds

GWYNETH JONES

I'm trying to create in my mind the image of a little boy. He's four years old, his hair is brown and not clipped short; it's long enough to curl in the nape of his neck like a duck's tail. He is wearing a blue jacket with green facings, green lining to the hood. Little red mittens dangle on a woollen cord from the cuffs of his sleeves, his little hands are bare. I remember him clearly, but it isn't enough. I want to *see* him. I'm walking around the park, called Delauney's Park, though who Delauney was no one has any idea. There's a playground with squishy asphalt so the children won't break their heads. There's a gravel football pitch, there's a shelter with toilets (always locked), and a space of turf, greenery, shrubberies, trees. The park is small, tired, urban. It was all the world to us. We used to come here, not every day but very often, right from the beginning. I remember playing hide and seek. It was a winter's day, the winter before he started school, the rosehips bright red vase-shapes on the bare bushes. I saw him walk out from behind the shelter, having failed to find me, those little mittens hanging pitifully. Head down, so utterly lost and bereft, oh dear sweet child. I was hiding behind a tree.

I walk around and around, a woman alone, staring at toddlers. I'm not trying to control myself, I know that the expression on my face looks frightening, but I have licence. I don't have to make that slight constant effort we all make in public, maintain the barrier, don't let your emotions leak out. Tell any one of these mothers-with-small-children, and even fathers-with-small-children, what has happened to me, and whatever I do, they will accept. If I lie down and kick my legs and scream and mash my face into the ground, that will be fine. As if I was three years old.

He never did that. He was a sweet child.

And out of the tail of my eye I see him. He's there, *there* he is. I turn my head, very very slowly. I can hold him in place, *I can see him*, the little boy standing by the corner of the shelter, looking to and fro, looking for me. I don't have to concentrate, he's there independently, no effort, *I am really seeing him* ... It lasts only a fraction of a second, like the existence of a rare, fragile element in a scientific experiment. Then I'm fighting the whole weight of reality again. He's there still but it's an effort to hold the image, quivering like a stilled frame on a TV screen, and that's no good. It was my imagination.

Up in the back of the park, furtherest from the road and the playground, there's a certain bend in the path, a corner that is always in the shadow of tall laurel bushes. A place you think dogs wouldn't pass, they'd crouch with hackles raised and back away. He was afraid of that spot. We used to tell each other maybe it was haunted. He liked to be frightened, children do like to be frightened, *just a little*. Really it was the deep shade he didn't like, I'm sure; but a child's uneasiness is convincing. You think they must know something they haven't the words to tell. I'm walking around and around, mad woman staring. I come to the murky corner because I must, and I see him again. The little boy is there, completely without my volition.

I went home. My husband was curled in a foetal position on the couch in the living room, daytime on the screen. My mother had left the day before. She'd been wonderful, bearing up with a brave face, cooking meals for us and so on. I think we were both relieved to be alone again, although there is no relief when a thing like this has happened. But her departure means we have moved into the next phase. We've brought the baby home from the hospital, we've had the few days' buffer state of importance and fuss, we've reached the point when we are on our own and the task opens up, limitless: this time our baby is his death. I'm trying to recapture this little boy: putting him to bed, his bathtime, his sweet little body, he's giggling, running all wet and rosy from the towel that's trying to catch him, minuscule little erection. I want him here, I want to see him here.

'I saw him,' I said. 'In the playground. Eric, listen. I saw him. I really did.'

My husband said, 'What's the use in that? You didn't lose him anywhere near the park.'

I sat down on the armchair, the old one with the leaf-pattern in black and white on the upholstery, the leaves he used to trace very seriously with baby fingers. 'You think I'm mad.'

'I think in your state of mind you can easily force yourself to see a ghost. I just don't understand why you're doing it.'

'I want *to know what happened to him*. I want to see it.'

'That's disgusting,' he said.

My child, called Christopher after his grandfather, went out with me to the shops. In the Post Office I looked around and he was gone. I ran out into the street. He was nowhere. And when I was sure he was gone, you can imagine. You can imagine how I ran up and down, calling his name, how I flung myself at passers-by, how I was shaking from head to foot, how terror possessed me. We always called him Fery, it was his own name for himself. He's gone to the fairies, he's gone. It's eight days. He's dead.

In cases like this, suspicion always falls on the family, especially on the man. The police were going to be suspicious of us as a matter of course. I think we made it worse for ourselves by being certain, straight away, that he was dead. I think I made it worse for us by my terror. But how could we believe anything else? The child is gone for an hour, for three hours, he's been missing for a day and a night. How are we supposed to unknow what everyone else in the world knows, about what happens to a child snatched away like that? . . . just because it is our child, this time, not a story on the news. They told us not to give up hope. Children have funny whims, he might have wandered off, taken a bus, decided to run away from home. Paedophiles often are not violent, he might turn up safe in some sad bastard's miserable bedsit. Fools. We can't give up hope, we will hope forever: but we know he's dead. I think of him, when we had the builders in before he was two years old. My baby goes up to the foreman and takes hold of the man's big, plaster-ingrained hand, wants to show him a Lego house. It's potty-training summer, the little boy is dressed merely in a blue T-shirt that leaves his round middle and his little bum bare. 'You'll have to watch him,' says the builder-man to me, very seriously. 'He's too friendly.'

A child must not be friendly, that's provocation. A child must not smile, must not take an adult's hand, that's flirtatious. I shake with fury. They're saying it was his fault. They're saying he brought it on himself. I try to imagine him here, giggling and wriggling amongst the cushions, very small. But all I see is something like a great sky folding into itself from horizon to horizon, bellying and billowing into a vast ochre mushroom cloud that rises and fills the universe. A million megatons of death, nothing can be saved, destroyer of worlds.

'I'm going to go back to work,' said Eric. 'Do you want your sister down?'

By work, he means that he'll return to his office at the back of our house, the room that overlooks the garden where he teleworks on his computer. Projects, consultancies. I have no more idea of what he does, in detail, than if I was the child myself. He makes good money. I don't have a job, which means I have nowhere to go. My sister has offered to take unpaid leave, desert her family, come and be with me. I don't want her.

'No,' I said. 'I'll be fine.'

A policewoman comes to visit the house, with a uniformed constable, also a woman. They ask me if they can have a look around. Would I mind? They want to search our house, and I'm supposed to say well of course, please, step this way. My face serene, a little polite smile, as if they've come to read the gas meter. I am not supposed to resist, or question. I am not supposed to say, *you think my husband killed our son.* It's such an insane charade, dealing with the police. The WPC in uniform sits there holding her mug of tea, (I offered: they accepted). She has her face arranged in a solemn look of sympathy. I think she's really sorry, how could she not be sorry, but it's like tissue paper. Any move I make, anything I say will tear it and reveal the police agenda. Any sign that I've ever read a tabloid report on a child's disappearance, or watched the news, or seen a TV mystery drama where *it was the father, of course it was the father, you can see the solution a mile off . . . It was the mother, you can see she's disturbed . . .* will be an admission of guilt.

The superior officer searched the house. The WPC sat with me. Strange, I'd have thought it would be the other way round. Eric stayed in his office. When she came back the superior officer started to ask me a few questions.

I said, 'How can you think my husband had anything to do with this? He's desperate. He's sitting up there out of his mind with grief. He doesn't eat, he doesn't sleep—'

'Mrs Connors,' she said. 'Hazel . . . I'm still hoping Christopher will be found. Believe me, it does happen. Children are found, more often than not. But don't you think a man who had killed his seven-year-old son would be distraught?'

It was as if she'd hit me. Seven years old. My image in the park was wrong, completely wrong. He doesn't look like that any more. His ghost can't look like that. Three years. *I'd forgotten a whole three years.* This is what happens to you when the Destroyer of Worlds has filled your mind, blanking everything out. Your whole memory unravels, crumbles, you can't hold it together. I stared at her, and the mug of tea in my hands dissolved. I couldn't feel it any more, it fell to the floor and cooling tea spilled all over my feet.

She looked at the mess. I didn't. I was thinking of how much work I had to do, recapturing: getting him to appear to me not as a four-year-old but as he was the day I lost him. That's the only way I'll find out what happened. She took my hand, and I let her do that.

'Hazel, why wasn't Christopher in school that day?'

'He had a cold. I kept him at home, but he seemed well enough to come out with me.'

'But your husband was at home?'

'He works at home. He does his share of looking after Fery, but he works office hours. Am I getting points for answering the same questions in the same words fifty times over?'

A pause, a look of reproof. I'm tearing the tissue paper.

'Christopher's seven years old. Did you ever think of having other children?'

'No,' I said. 'I'm planning to go back to work. But it wouldn't make sense, at the moment. Wouldn't have made sense. When Eric isn't working at home, he has to travel. He's away often. I would have gone back to work, when Fery was old enough to be home alone.'

What the superior officer is really asking about is our sex life. No children? Why? Don't you sleep together? So, what does your husband do instead? I won't tell her anything.

When Fery was two, he buried a wooden train in the sandpit at Delauney's Park. It was red and blue, it had yellow wheels, it was called Thomas. He didn't tell me that Thomas was missing until we were about to go home; and it was winter and getting dark. I searched, as well as I could. I couldn't find that little train at all. I didn't have a chance, the sandpit was too big and Fery could not tell me where I should dig. We went back the next day, and we still couldn't find Thomas. We never found him. But all that year, and longer, Fery went on looking. Stranger than that: wherever we were, including when we were on holiday in Italy, if we passed a playground he must go in. If there was a sandpit, he must dig. He was looking for Thomas. Long afterwards, he still remembered. I'd be in Delauney's Park, the mothers sitting together the way we do, on the edge of the sandpit: I'd see my four-year-old casually get hold of a shovel and start turning over the cool, dirty, lollipop-stick infested sand. I'd know he was looking for Thomas, but he didn't want anyone to know because he knew it was silly. And I'd want to help him. As if any day could be that winter's day, and we could tear the tissue paper and step back, undo the wrong we did, catch up the dropped stitch, make the little red and blue train appear.

I walk down to the row of shops. The pharmacist, the bakery, the bank on the corner. The greengrocers. They will vanish soon. The only shops in the world will be inside shopping malls, nothing but To Let signs blossoming on the High Street. The mothers-with-children, and the occasional fathers-with-children, queue up in the Post Office with the foreign students and the pensioners. I look inside. I am trying to make him appear, there by the carousel of cheap greeting cards. He's looking at the cards, investigating the dirty jokes, lingering with tender emotion over sugary cartoon animals. He's at an age where the attraction is equal, either way. This is the way I'll find him. Not by running and sobbing, not by marching in a line across waste ground, searching the back alleys, pulling up floorboards. Not by looking up the paedophile register. I will walk along this row of shops, pushing the doors and glancing in. This is where he was lost, this is where he will be found. Where else could he be? Lost Thomas logic. I'll take his hand, I'll say *there you are*, exasperated: and we'll go home together. Years from now, as long as the same shops are still here, as long as I can find anywhere little shops that remind me of these, it could happen.

What was he wearing? A boy, his body no longer blurred by the chubby disproportion of babyhood, not even a small child any more. A boy nothing like the sweet baby with the red mittens, in Delauney's Park. I need a different ghost. (I need all the ghosts.) He was wearing trainers and tracksuit trousers, black with white stripes. He was wearing red boxer shorts and a green T-shirt, and grey socks. He was wearing a grey hooded sweater with some sporting logo on the front, and a black quilted jacket. He was carrying nothing. He was too old to be visible in mothers-with-children world. He was not holding my hand. We've asked and asked, the police have asked and asked. No one saw him that morning. No one remembers me except as the mad woman, running up and down, distraught, flying up to the counter at the bank, demanding wildly *have you seen a little boy?* I don't remember him myself.

That day was scheduled to be like a thousand other lost days, all its millions of precious images discarded, mislaid, never filed. Even now, I have forgotten most of it.

I'm trying desperately hard, and then suddenly I let go. I can't help myself, it's like a muscle failure. I turn away, defeated; and there he is. Glimpsed, corner of my eye. I turn my head slowly, slowly, inching it round ... He's there, crystal clear, no effort. He is standing by the greeting cards, sideways to me, the soft curve of his cheek, his eyes intent and a little furtive.

And then what happened, I beg of him.

Fery looks around. He isn't looking at me. He's looking at something that isn't in my memory, no matter how I struggle to recover it. I want to look where he's looking, towards the opening door of the Post Office, but wanting will do me no good, because surely I did not look that way. I never saw whoever it was, whatever, the monster, the horror that took my child. I try to turn my head anyway, but there's an awful barrier ... and suddenly I'm on the floor, thank God I'm wearing trousers, retain some dignity sprawled there, sobbing, fighting off hands that try to raise me up. The shock was physical, the shock of knowing I saw him. I really saw him. I have forced myself to see a ghost.

When I found he wasn't with me, and he wasn't in the street, I hurried home. He wasn't there. Eric wasn't in, either. I called Fery's best friend's mother: no reply. Another friend's mother, no reply. I went to Delauney's Park, no sign. That part lasted about an hour. The running up and down and sobbing – that lasted I don't know how long. I called my husband on his mobile, I left a message. I called the police. I ran up and down again, by this time meeting everywhere the concern of the street, it was an incident room already. The man in the Post Office, the young girl with the stringy hair in the bakery, the cashier at the bank. If this was a soap-opera I would have known their names but I didn't. We knew each other viscerally, like animals using the same pathways in some natural environment, we didn't need names to get along. That's all changed. I'm a celebrity now.

The man behind the Post Office counter called Eric. He came and took me home.

I told him that I'd seen a ghost again. He said, 'Would you like to go away? Far away? If the police will let us? I think that might be the best thing.'

'No,' I said. 'You don't understand. I forced myself to see a ghost, but the ghost is real.'

The husband gets interviewed at the police station. He hasn't been arrested, he's nowhere near being arrested, but he's in an interview room. The interviewing officer has a chaperone on hand, like a male doctor about to examine a woman patient's intimate parts; everything is being recorded on video. I know about this interview because Eric told me.

They asked him about our sex life.

'Would you say you and your wife had a good physical relationship?' asked the policeman.

Let it be recorded. 'Off and on, satisfactory. I mean, fine,' said Mr

Connors. 'Sometimes good, sometimes not so good. Like most people. We've been married ten years, you know.'

'Was she ever maybe a bit too much for you? Too demanding?'

'I wouldn't have said that was a problem.'

He was trying to guess what I might have answered, and hoping our two stories would agree. That's the charade the police force on you, with their insistence that it's up to you whether you answer or not. With their tissue-paper sympathy and their watchful eyes.

'D'you ever stray, I mean, have you ever had an affair?'

'No.'

'What about your wife?'

'Not that I know of.'

'She was your first girlfriend, wasn't she? You've never looked at another woman?'

'Looked? I don't know about looked. I'm happy with the relationship we have—'

They have investigated our lives. They have found amongst our books and videos adult movies, arthouse movies that they construe as pornographic. They have invented a sour, twilight existence for the woman who stays at home although her son is seven years old, and the man who works at home except when he goes on mysterious trips away. The man who finds the adult workplace and his adult wife too demanding. Everything looks bad in their light.

'Don't you see what they're doing?' I yelled at him. 'They're setting you up as some kind of pervert, and you can't stop them. Damned if you answer, damned if you don't.'

'They won't find any evidence,' said my husband, shrugging, 'will they?'

We looked at each other for a long, long moment, until I could see nothing but the mushroom cloud, boiling and silently thundering up into the sky. What can happen? What does it matter? It doesn't matter if they call Eric a pervert, it doesn't matter if I scream in the Post Office. Nothing can be worse than this.

Destroyer of Worlds.

'I'm going to follow him,' I said, 'I want to know everything. I don't care how bad it is.'

Nothing hurts. You could saw my leg off, I'd feel nothing. Being 'hounded by journalists' is not a torture, being interviewed by the police is not a torture, making appeals on the TV is not a torture. Don't pity the families in these cases, pursued by the greedy, prurient media. We feel nothing. I've felt more outrage over an unwanted piece of junk mail, long ago, than over a tabloid reporter on the doorstep, or the sting of a camera flash in my eyes. I couldn't care less. I walk out. I go and stand in the street. I lean against the wall of the bus shelter, waiting.

I see a boy in a black quilted jacket and black trousers coming out of the Post Office. I know why nobody saw him, he is totally anonymous. There is no sign of the baby's body I loved, no sign of the sweetness of his smile. When he was five he once confided in me *I keep getting stiffies* ... Where on earth had he picked up that expression? In the classroom, obviously, other children have older brothers. Had he any idea what he was saying? I don't think so. Once, I lost him for ten minutes in our public library. When I found him he said he'd gone to the toilet for a wee. He'd gone into the Gents alone because he thought he couldn't go in the Ladies without me. Very proud, very independent. There was a man in there, he said. Who looked at me, and I was scared. The Gents at the Public Library is unsafe for little boys. Thinking like this is a disgrace, but what is to be done? My blood ran cold. I said, don't go there again.

But I can't keep on going in the Ladies, he said. Not all my life. So what will I do?

I'm following my ghost down the street. There must be someone with him, taking him away, but I only see my child. He's walking aimlessly, oh how I love to see him when he doesn't know I'm watching. To see him look into a shop window, to see him bend down over a piece of litter, studying it, hope springing eternal, has he won a million pounds? He walks on, carrying this old crisp packet, his companion: little boys need to have something to hold. A stone, a ball, a pencil, an elastic band; a boiled sweet furred in pocket-grime. Of course I won't tell him but of course I know ... this affection for the object is easy to read. I am not repelled. When he gets older I will remember these days and I will understand a young man's obsession with his favourite toy, his faithful companion, his treasure. Having a son will explain the whole sex to me, at long last.

The boy on the street stops and half turns: a stilled frame, quivering. He's looking back, seems to look at me with an expression of intense malignity, eyes narrowed, inhuman rage—

He has read my thoughts.

He will never be a young man. He is dead.

I saw him again at the railway bridge. He was up there, crossing the line. I still could not see who was with him. I was in the car park, all the suburban commuters' cars in rows. Everyone has their place, I imagine. Eric doesn't like to drive, he walks when he comes to take the train. The boy on the bridge looked back at me, with incredible hatred.

I followed him, we climbed over the fence and into the wasteground beside the line. Brambles, unkempt winter grass, weedy sycamores, naked straggling buddleia thickets with dead flower spikes. Rusting cans, rotted litter, slugs and snails, blackened ballast, the view from a train window. A path like a grey snail's trail, a little boys' path. Is it true that he came this way, or is the ghost lying to me?

Who brought him here? What happened?

There's a hut by the track, the roof of tar paper, the slatted walls obliterated by crusted grime. It's a den, a hideout, it's somewhere things can happen out of sight. My path is heading towards it. No ghost now . . . but then suddenly there he is. I don't understand what I see, then I realise he's naked. A flash of pitiful white arms and legs, a face blank oval, and in the quivering frozen frame he's running, brambles whipping his little ribs, rusty cans bruising his bare feet, I can't hear him but I know he's crying, terrified and shamed. He's running and running, crying for help, but there's someone catching him—

How do you kill a little boy? By accident, is my best hope. You want him to stop screaming, you're afraid someone will come. You took him to a lonely place but it had to be somewhere nearby and now it isn't lonely enough. Big adult hands, squeezing the child's throat, or throwing him down, and his fragile temple crashing against stone. Something like that, in a moment. He was fighting for his life and he didn't know he was going to lose until he'd lost. He didn't die helpless, he didn't die smothered, pinned, held down, knowing the whole world had betrayed him—

I found myself crouched by the snail path, fists in my pockets, head bent, dizzy and nauseous. The vision had gone, but I was seeing in my mind's eye my baby's skin darkly marked, printed with the pattern of that black jacket, clear as frost flowers. I'll tell the police, I thought. They won't believe me, but they'll come here and search. They'll leave no stone unturned. I listened to the distant hum of traffic, and looked at my watch. The ghost had led me where I wanted to be led. I knew that, really. I stood up and went on down to the track.

I was beside the railway line, walking up and down, looking at my watch, shivering, oh God, how long between these suburban trains, when Eric arrived. I saw him coming, I didn't try to get away. 'Come home,' he said. 'Hazel, come on home.'

'How do people kill themselves? I don't know how to do it. But I'll find a way.'

He nodded, and took my arm. I didn't resist. He ought to say please don't leave me or all we've got left is each other, or someday we'll make a new life. But ideas like those don't come. There is nothing left, no human need, regret, affection nor pity. Destroyer of Worlds.

'You know how I felt about Fery,' I said.

'I know,' said my husband, leading me away. He has never reproached me, he has never said it was your fault, you lost him. How could you. Ideas like that don't come either. Not yet.

'I loved him too much.'

'Yes. You loved him too much.'

What a cruel thing to say.

I have committed a grave crime. I have given birth to a child, and made him my whole world, in a society where children are not safe, where little boys can be taken from the street and never seen again. Now there's another turn of the screw, they are taking away from me my last memories. They are saying he was already lost, before I ever went out to the shops that morning. They are saying he never walked beside me, he never peeped at the greetings cards in the Post Office with that furtive, tender attention which I remember so clearly. No, they destroy that world. He was lost already, he was long gone. Where did I lose him, and when?

In Delauney's Park the mothers-with-children, and occasional fathers-with-children, are in possession until school is over. They talk to each other, they play with their toddlers, they nurse their babies. They sit like cows in the grass, silently ruminating over the weariness of broken nights. Then the schoolchildren appear, first from the nursery then from the primary school classrooms. They yell, they run around, they play with dolls or footballs, they pose and swagger and compare the prices of their trainers; they are cruel to each other. But the light changes and the shadows grow. The mothers-with-buggies all go home, except maybe for one lost soul, smoking a cigarette, naked ankles, skirt too short, her baby grizzling vaguely.

When the light has changed the park has a different clientèle. Bloodstained needles, used condoms, teenagers and derelicts: all of them no more than decayed and broken-down kids themselves, that's why the after-dusk playground is their home. They sell illegal drugs, and they bandy words with the schoolchildren, the bold, inquisitive ones who have lingered. Fery was one of those. Always ready to run, he promised me, at the first sign of trouble. Did he stay out too late one evening and I didn't notice? Did he fail to come home, and my husband was so wrapped up in his work he didn't know? Eric tells me they are going to search the park again, because of something I said or something someone remembered. The police will walk through the shrubberies in a line, working like a single machine, picking up every scrap of detritus. They will reach into the dark by that bend in the path, where the laurel bushes make their permanent shade, and they'll find ... I don't know what. Maybe they'll find out why it has always felt bad. If a ghost can exist after death then why not before? My son and I used to be sure that spot was haunted.

I won't watch the search. I think I'll stay here, in his bedroom, with the soft toys that he'll never consign to oblivion, the pictures of cartoon animals, the battered childish things that he would have abandoned. I'm lying on his bed, where we used to cuddle together, bedtime, storytime, I'm saying now I have to go and he's saying, no, stay, stay with me not with Daddy; just for once. He doesn't know what he's saying, soft arms holding onto me. He's only a baby. I don't have to be in the park, this is the foul place, the place that dogs wouldn't pass. This is where I lost him. This is where he destroyed all the worlds.

Gwyneth Jones lives in Brighton. A writer of science fiction and fantasy for adults and teenagers (under the name 'Ann Halam'), she was co-winner of the 1991 James Tiptree Award, for science fiction exploring gender roles. Her young adult novel *The Fear Man* won the Dracula Society's Children of the Night award in 1996, while the same year her fairy tale collection *Seven Tales and a Fable* was awarded two World Fantasy Awards. Recent publications include *Deconstructing the Starships*, a collection of essays and criticism on SF published by The University of Liverpool Press, and a futuristic thriller for teenagers entitled *The N.I.M.R.O.D. Conspiracy* from Orion Children's Books. As the author explains, '"Destroyer of Worlds" was inspired by a newspaper report I read several years ago, about a little boy killed in the same way, or one of the ways, suggested in this story. I had a child of the same age, and the details stuck in my mind as a parent's worst nightmare.'

The Geezers

PETER STRAUB

'Clyde was a hell of a shock,' Ray Constantine said to Gus Trayham, the man on the next bike.

'Shock to us all,' Gus said. 'You weren't shocked, you wouldn't be breathing.'

'I mean, besides that,' Ray said. 'The whole thing reminds me of Paolo. It brings it all back.' Nine years earlier, Paolo Constantine, a student at the Rhode Island School of Design, had died of a drug overdose. Ray's wife, Fabiana, whom he had met during his Fellowship at the American Academy in Rome, had eventually packed up everything she chose to salvage from their marriage of twenty-five years and returned to Italy.

'Don't you think it brought Linc back to me? All that misery when he went upstate? Linc passed three years ago, this April.'

'*I* remember,' Ray said. Neither he nor the other three men who met every weekday to exercise in Dodge Gymnasium at Columbia University and lunch together afterwards had known Lincoln Trayham. Gus's elder brother, but it was an article of faith with them that although Linc may have done some bad things and made some bad choices, as Gus put it, he had been falsely convicted of second-degree murder and railroaded into a life sentence.

For a time, they continued pedalling furiously, though perhaps a touch less so than the three teenage sylphs beside them. One of the sylphs wore a Philips Exeter T-shirt and Spandex shorts and, Ray noted, had not once lifted her stunning little face from a hypnotic perusal of the book propped on the console before her, *Killer Diller* by Grant Upward, a onetime friend or semi-friend who by dint of writing the same book over and over had entirely eclipsed Ray's own, less frequent fictions. 'Maybe we shouldn't have come today,' he said.

'Do us good,' Gus said. 'Sweat out some pain before we talk to the Man.'

Dismounting more gracefully than Ray, Gus strode past the sylphs and ejected a panting, long-haired beanpole from the bicep curl machine by the simple mechanism of standing before him, lowering his head, and glowering. After the boy muttered an apology and slipped away, Gus adjusted the weights from 50 to 120 pounds, positioned his upper arms on the pad, settled into the seat, wrapped his fists around the handles and began smoothly raising and lowering the stack of weights. Gus Trayham's father had coached football and swimming at Fisk, and despite the distinguished appearance given him by the bald head, grizzled white beard, and spreading waistline he had assumed as he approached sixty, Gus was the strongest and most athletic of the four friends.

Ray walked over to the lat pull machine located next to the stationary rower, where blond, still nearly boyish Tommy Whittle was going through his reps while answering the bemused smile of a dark-haired girl moving towards the water fountain. Tommy's acting career was recovering from the layoff imposed by a three-year-old mugging that had put him in the hospital for a month, but people who had watched a good deal of television during the late eighties and early-to-mid nineties often imagined him to be an acquaintance whose name they had temporarily misplaced. Tommy referred to this sense of baffled recognition on the part of strangers as his 'infamy'. Now he watched Ray lower the seat of the lat pull and said, 'How do you think they'll handle it? One on one, or all at the same time?'

'One on one,' Ray said. 'That captain – what's his name?'

'Brannigan,' Tommy said. 'Like the John Wayne movie.'

'What John Wayne movie?'

'*Brannigan*,' Tommy said. 'He played a Chicago cop who goes to London to bring back a suspect. Mid-seventies. Not bad, not bad at all. But I'm a freak for the Duke.'

'Tell me about it,' Ray said. He set the pin for 175 pounds and straightened up to grasp the long bar attached to the weights.

'One on one, huh?'

Ray let the bar ascend, carrying his arms with it. 'Brannigan is going to park us in a room somewhere and call us out individually. We'll tell him whatever we know. Are you nervous, Tommy?'

'Sure I am. Clyde, that was a hell of a blow. Will you take a look at Leo? There's a guy who is really *upset*.'

Ray agreed with Tommy Whittle's assessment. Leo Gozzi was executing half-hearted abdominal crunches with long pauses between each one. His olive face had a grey tinge and purple bags drooped beneath his eyes. After Leo's report of dubious financial practices on the part of his employer, a computer company, had been leaked to the press, first his job, then his marriage had disappeared, and he had moved twenty blocks north into an apartment on West 107th Street, only a block from Clyde Pepper's two rooms on West End Avenue. It was Leo who had introduced Clyde into their group.

When Ray finished his reps, he moved across the aisle and slid into the back press, the machine next to Leo's. He had adjusted the weights and begun to push backwards before Leo glanced over his shoulder.

'Hey, Ray,' Leo said.

'I hate to say it,' Ray said, 'but you look like shit.'

'This thing with Clyde has me tied up in knots. I got about ten minutes' sleep last night. I just lay there, feeling my muscles getting tighter and tighter. It's amazing I can stand up straight.'

'Do your laps, and we'll relax over lunch. Everything will be fine.'

Leo performed another desultory crunch. 'Does Sally know what happened?'

For a little more than a year, Ray had been on-again off-again with an attractive, deeply messed-up editor at Ballantine named Sally Frohman. Currently they were on again, though indications such as the frequent usage of the word 'relationship' led Ray to anticipate a period of sexual drought within a matter of weeks, perhaps even days. 'Why?'

'I guess I was wondering what you said, and what she thought about it, how she reacted, that's all.'

'Is that right?' Ray asked.

'Well, you know,' Leo said.

'Okay, Leo. Sally was pissed off about something. She was sitting on the sofa, staring at the floor with her hands pushed into her hair, and I was at the kitchen table, doing revisions. The phone rang. That detective, Brannigan, told me about Clyde, probably the exact same way he told you. When I hung up, Sally said, "Am I allowed to know who you're meeting tomorrow afternoon" "Yes, Sally," I said. "I have to talk to a detective at the 26th Precinct. About two hours ago, one of my friends from the gym, Clyde Pepper, was found in Riverside Park with his throat cut and his head bashed in. You never met him, but Clyde was a nice guy, and for some reason I'm having trouble believing he was murdered while you and I were sitting here ignoring each other." "Oh, honey," she said, "I'm so sorry." She started to cry. I made a drink for her and a drink for me. Then Gus and Tommy called. Sally and I went to bed, and for some reason we had the best sex we've had in months. Afterwards, I began to tell her a few things about Clyde, and I choked up. Pretty soon, we were both crying.'

'I called Tommy and Gus,' Leo said. 'I would have called you, but I figured Sally was spending the night at your place.'

'Your tact is greatly appreciated,' Ray said.

The four of them proceeded through their rounds of the exercise machines and returned to the locker room to change into bathing trunks. Four flights below, a utilitarian passage led to a scarred grey door and the labyrinth containing the swimming team's lockers and two small, green-tiled chambers lined with shower heads. After brief, obligatory showers, they padded up a cement ramp and two by two, goggles swinging from their hands, went down a narrow corridor and through a metal door into an echoing underground vault.

Eight lanes wide, the Columbia University pool was open to the general student population, faculty, staff, and alumni every weekday afternoon from noon to two p.m. Red plastic cones and wall plaques clamed the central lanes for 'fast' swimmers, the two at their left for the 'medium', and the first two and the eighth, long ago dubbed the 'geezer lanes' by Gus Trayham, for slowpokes. Within each lane, a blue stripe at the bottom of the pool divided inbound left from outbound right, and its occupants swam in circles. In the past, unless the presence of too many other swimmers forced them to alter the pattern, Leo and Clyde Pepper had taken lane 1, Tommy Whittle lane 2, and Ray and Gus wider, deeper lane 8.

Composed more of faculty, alums, and staff than students, the fifteen to twenty swimmers who shared the pool with them separated out into the unobjectionable (those who did their laps in a steady, businesslike manner), the tolerable (who swam too slowly but were reasonable about it), and the offensive (people who barely moved at all, strayed out of their lanes, kicked up geysers of spray while mooching along, charged into people instead of detouring around them, and those whose ugly, ungainly strokes made them appear to be crippled). In the latter category were 'the Monitor', whose floundering crawl suggested that one of his arms had been amputated; 'Cruella', an elderly woman with a permanent sneer who did not actually look too bad until she followed a deliberate blow from a passing foot with a death-ray delivered through her radioactive blue goggles; and 'Creeping Jesus', a mournful character thought to be a Professor of Biblical History given to crouching in silent prayer by the end of the pool for fifteen minutes before crawling in and thrashing, apparently in utter panic, from one end to the other.

Ray noticed the Monitor and Cruella making life miserable for the two Japanese girls also in lane 1, so he was not surprised when Leo announced that he would take the far lane today, although he secretly thought that Leo would have done the same had only the Japanese girls, ordinarily a great attraction, occupied the first lane. Tommy slipped into the water and joined two sturdy middle-aged women who were churning back and forth like horses. Ray, Gus, and Leo wandered past the diving boards to the far end, where a crop-headed blond lifeguard whose piglike face always reminded Ray of a dissolute peasant in a Dutch tavern painting looked up from his perch and said, 'The big guys!' He glanced at Leo Gozzi, then back at Ray. 'What happened to your buddy?'

Leo came to an abrupt halt and recoiled, as if he had bounced off a wall.

'He dropped out,' Ray said.

'Suddenly called away,' said Gus.

'Sorry to hear it,' said the boy. 'For an older guy, he had major pecs. Hey, you're all in great shape. I hope I look the same at your age.'

'Be enough to get to our age,' Gus said. 'What with putting your life on the line three days a week.'

'Hah,' the boy said.

One by one, they lowered themselves into the pool and breast-stroked towards the far end, Gus in the lead, then Ray, Leo behind him, each of the latter two waiting until the man ahead reached the middle of the pool before pushing off. For the first four laps, Gus was rolling into his return just as Leo ducked underwater and started back up to the far end. According to the same custom by which Gus invariably led off, thereby setting the pace, they did not break rhythm to stop and rest until after the tenth lap, but after Ray dipped into the turn for the back half of his sixth, he saw Leo floating down at the other end, one arm over the rope lane-divider, the other propped on the splash ledge. Gus ploughed through the water and executed his turn without saying anything to Leo. When Ray came to the end of the pool, he looked at Leo, who waved him on. Ray spun under and kicked off.

His shoulder muscles stretched to meet the resistance of the water, seeming nearly to take in breath. There was always that moment when you and the resistance locked together and you felt your relationship with the water change from unconscious acceptance into a working partnership in which the resistance became a springy, yielding support. The difference had to do with consciousness, with being awake to your context. This moment of contextual awareness, Ray thought, resembled those periods when, immersing himself for the fiftieth time in a new book's early scenes, he finally noticed how greatly his conception of certain characters diverged from the selves announced by the actual words they spoke. Supposedly sympathetic characters said things like, 'Roger acts like he's cynical and cold-hearted, but down deep he's a real monster.' While writing his seventh novel, Ray had learned at last how to listen to his characters; a decade later, consciousness of this other context had come to him only after months of reporting to Columbia's pool. You had to pay attention to the medium through which you moved: if you did not, you were blind and flailing.

Leo was still clinging to the rope when Ray swam back. He said, 'Keep dragging your ass, you might as well get in with Cruella and the Monitor.'

'I needed a rest,' Leo said.

Ray set off again for the top of the pool. Halfway there, he looked back and was relieved to see Leo swimming towards him.

After Ray's and Gus's tenth lap and Leo's eighth, they took a breather, bobbing in the water and holding onto the ledge. 'Leo,' Gus said, 'I gather you had a rough night.'

'You didn't?' Leo asked.

'Well,' Gus said, 'Thursday is Ruth's night. We had dinner at Jezebel and went back to my place. I stood on Junior. After Lieutenant Brannigan woke me up, *you* talked to me for half an hour. Then Tommy called. I sent Ruth home and talked to Ray. I kept thinking about how you brought Clyde in, how we all hooked up with him. I was trying to get my head around what happened. Took me hours to get to sleep, all the crazy shit that was going though my mind. We all had a rough night, and now we got to carry on, hear what I'm saying?'

'I know, I know,' Leo said. 'But I was closer to him than the rest of you.'

'Then you got to deal with that,' Gus said, and swam away.

Carrie, their waiter (or 'waitress', as the geezers would have put it) at The Heights, said, 'What happened to your buddy?'

The pig-faced boy who guarded the watery realm of Cruella and the Monitor three days a week had used the same words, and although the question had not been addressed to him, Ray answered as before. 'He dropped out.'

'The man took a hike,' said Gus, putting a more active spin on the concept that Clyde had been called away.

Leo turned his head to the long second-floor window looking down on Broadway and muttered, 'You could put it that way.'

Carrie awaited further clarification. She was a slender, small-boned young woman, and her waiting had an open, expectant quality. A couple of seconds passed while the four men at the table examined the silverware, the chalkboard listing the day's specials, the mixture of Columbia students and neighbourhood funk milling on the sidewalk.

'*Ohh*-kay,' Carrie said. 'Four spinach salads and two Cokes, coming up.'

They had the same lunch every day, and their regular waiters, Carrie, Troy the Boy and Melissa, had been trained to add extra bacon and blue cheese to the salads. Ray suspected that they just went into the kitchen and said, 'They're here.'

'Leo,' Gus said, 'I'm a little concerned about you.'

'Don't be,' Leo said. 'I'm not supposed to open my mouth?'

'Open it all you like,' Gus said. 'But don't put your business on the street. Say, Carrie reads about this business in the paper. Say, she sees his picture on the news. Until that happens, and I don't think it will, because I never heard Carrie indicate she gives a damn about the news unless some movie star gets his tit caught in a wringer, but until it does she's better off thinking Clyde moved out of town. Why spoil her day?'

'I get it, I get it,' Leo said.

'All of us have to deal with what happened to Clyde, but we don't have to drag other people into the process.'

'Gus,' Leo said, 'please stop lecturing me.'

'You'd learn what a lecture was, I ever gave you one,' Gus said. 'This here is friendly advice.'

'Try keeping the friendly advice to yourself for once,' Leo said.

Gus held up his hands, palms out, and smiled at Leo.

Carrie set their plates before them and went through the routine with the pepper grinder. Ray and Tommy Whittle got the Cokes. All four men ran their knives through the salads half a dozen times, cutting the spinach leaves into smaller and smaller sections, and began eating.

When the silence became unendurable, Gus said, 'Who saw Clyde last? I guess it must have been you, Leo.'

'As far as I know,' Leo said. 'After the three of you got into a cab, Clyde and I went down Broadway to 107th. He dropped me at my building and kept walking towards West End. That was the last time I saw him.'

'Anybody call him that evening?' Gus asked.

'Not me,' Leo said. 'Did you?'

Gus widened his eyes. 'I don't think I called Clyde but twice in the past two years. Once when you had to spend all day tinkering with some movie star's computer, and once when I had an extra Knicks ticket and couldn't get any of you to go with me. He turned me down too, so I wound up taking Louise, my Tuesday regular.' Gus Trayham had long ago evolved a complicated system which allocated certain days of the week to the inner core of his sexual partners, most of them married women operating on tight schedules. 'Did you two talk to Clyde last night?'

'No,' Ray said. 'Outside of this, I never saw Clyde that much. We had dinner a couple of times last year. One day when the gym was closed for Christmas break, we went to a movie together. And about two weeks ago, he called up around nine, ten at night to say he was down the block from my place, and I invited him over. We had a few beers.'

'The same thing happened with me,' Tommy said. 'Last Friday, the phone rang. It was Clyde. He said he was out for a walk, noticed he was in my neighbourhood, and wondered what I was doing. I told him to come up. We shot the breeze, and he started looking though my videotape collection. "I guess you do like John Wayne," he said. "Have you got *She Wore a Yellow Ribbon?*" "You bet," I said, and we watched the whole thing. Great movie.'

'That's interesting,' Gus said, 'but you didn't say if you talked to him last night.'

Tommy's head snapped forward. 'Last night I didn't talk to anyone until Brannigan gave me the bad news. He said he got our names from Clyde's address book. Right away, I called Leo, but I guess he was talking to you, because I tried you next, and both lines were busy.'

'Clyde should have wandered back to our neighbourhood instead of getting stupid and going to Riverside Park,' Gus said. 'Time to settle up and pay a visit to the Man.'

A bored uniform glanced through a pane of bullet-proof glass that looked as though someone had once tried to shatter it with a brick. He listened to Gus's explanation of why they were there. He asked him to repeat it, then he looked wearily at Ray.

'Lieutenant Brannigan asked us to come here at 3:00 in connection with the death of Clyde Pepper,' Ray said.

Although he was wearing a watch, the uniform consulted the wall clock and observed that the time was 2:58. He shook his head and loafed to the door to request, very slowly, that another officer conduct these gentlemen to Lieutenant Brannigan's office. Without saying a word, the second officer got to his feet and began slouching down the corridor.

At the back of the station, the officer led them into a squad room where prematurely jaded men and women in their early thirties sat at desks crowded with papers and cups of coffee. He flapped a hand at a wooden bench and a row of plastic chairs. Ray and Gus took the bench and Leo and Tommy dropped into the chairs. The officer knocked once at a wooden door, slouched inside, and returned a moment later, followed by a tall, balding ex-fullback wearing a handsome Italian suit, a sparkling white shirt and a lustrous silk necktie. His eyes were the colour of wet cement, and his lipless mouth had all the warmth of a mail slot.

The geezers stood up as the ex-fullback strode towards them and introduced himself as Lieutenant Brannigan. The mail slot lengthened into a deathly smile as Brannigan shook their hands. His mushroom-coloured teeth seemed too numerous and surprisingly small.

'This is what we're going to do,' Brannigan said. 'You were Clyde Pepper's only friends in the world, looks like. I want to pick your brains, see what you might be able to tell me. Chances are, his assailant was a mugger, and we're doing everything we can on that front, but the degree of violence here exceeds ninety per cent of muggings, including those that result in homicide. So we have to keep our minds open. We have to consider other options. I want to find out a few things about you, hear whatever comes into your mind about the deceased. You never know what might give us a lead, no matter how insignificant it seems to you. The procedure shouldn't take much more than an hour. Are we in agreement?'

Each in his own way, the four men assented.

'Thank you for your co-operation. Let's begin with you, Mr Constantine.'

Brannigan pointed Ray to a chair, sat behind his desk, and opened a notebook. For a moment, the wet-cement eyes bored into Ray's. 'Are you comfortable about having this conversation, Mr Constantine?'

'Absolutely,' Ray said. 'I guess I was assuming that a mugger must have killed Clyde, so I wasn't sure how we could help you. I'm happy to tell you everything I can, though.'

'I appreciate that. Were you aware that before taking retirement your friend was a homicide detective assigned to this precinct?'

'All I knew was that Clyde was a retired police officer.' Ray paused, but Brannigan simply sat behind his desk, watching him. 'Did he work here a long time?'

'Twelve years,' Brannigan said. 'Most of that time, Detective Pepper lived out on the Island. After his divorce, he moved into a high-rise in Riverdale. Right after he retired, he came into the city and took the place on West End.'

'He must have missed his old neighbourhood,' Ray said.

Brannigan displayed another deathly smile. 'What kind of work do you do, Mr Constantine? Most people can't take two, three hours off in the middle of the day to work out in a gym.'

'I'm a writer.'

Brannigan tilted back his head and raised his eyebrows. 'That so? What do you write?'

'Fiction. Novels.'

'What kind of novels? Anything I might have heard of?'

'Thrillers,' Ray said, steering around the words 'crime' and 'detective'. He named his last three books.

Gentle Death, *The Iceman*, and *Dying Fall* seemed to have flown beneath or above Brannigan's radar. The Lieutenant said, 'Do you know Grant Upward? I like his stuff, but he writes books so fast I can't keep up with the guy. Two of my detectives out there, they read Grant Upward's books as soon as they come out.'

'Actually,' Ray said, 'Grant and I are old friends.'

'I'm impressed. Now, tell me about this group of yours. How you met, what the other men do, your connections to Columbia, things like that.'

'We're all neighbours,' Ray said. 'I met Gus Trayham in 1980, '81, something like that, when we used to go to the same bar on Columbus Avenue. He works as a grip for companies that film commercials. Gus took some classes at Columbia in the late sixties, I think, and he started using the gym before the rest of us. I got an MA at Columbia in 1966, so one day I went with him and signed up. That was in the spring of 1990.

'Around that time, my computer started going haywire, and a writer friend of mine, in fact it was Grant Upward, said I should talk to a guy named Leo Gozzi, who helped writers with their computers, setting them up, doing upgrades, hand-holding, whatever they needed. I called Leo. He came to my place and straightened everything out. He was great. After that I called him every time I needed advice. Leo and I spent so much time together we became friends, which was a good thing, because half the writers in the New York area wound up hearing about him. Later on, through Tommy he began getting calls from actors, too. If he didn't already know you or like your work, you were out of luck. Turns out Leo graduated from Columbia. When he said he wanted to start exercising, I thought, why not?, and introduced him to Gus. That's how he got in.'

'What about Mr Whittle?'

'Tommy's an actor who lives on my block. He grew up in our neighbourhood, and Tommy and Gus are old friends. After I started going to the gym, Gus and I told Tommy all he had to do was say he was an alum, and they'd let him buy a card, because they never check.'

'Do you work out five days a week?'

'If we can. I might have to meet a deadline, and Gus sometimes has a string of twelve-hour work days. Leo gets stuck in Westchester or New Jersey with a client who's flipping out because his system just crashed. The actors Tommy put him in touch with introduced him to some famous actors, and those people are like babies, they want everything right now. Tommy goes to a lot of auditions, so he can't make it every day, either. Clyde was pretty regular, though.'

'How did Clyde Pepper come into your group?'

'He and Leo lived about a block away from each other. After they started hanging out, Leo arranged for us to meet Clyde for dinner one night, and he fit right in. For one thing, Clyde looked like he'd been working out all his life. He certainly wasn't going to be an embarrassment or slow things down. Besides that, he was an interesting guy. In some ways, Clyde fit in better than Leo.'

'Oh?' said Brannigan.

'Well, Leo's a friend of mine, and if you need someone to hook you up with an Internet provider or lead you through the ins and outs of a software program, he's your guy. And by working out with us all these years, he managed to get himself into good condition, but that's not really where he's coming from. Leo went to Bronx Science.'

'I'm not sure I follow you.'

'I'm talking about involvement in athletics. Do they even have sports at Bronx Science? Computers are Leo's whole life. Right out of college, he was hired by one of those outfits where everybody wears jeans and works twelve hours a day. A few years later, the company took off, and Leo did very well until he discovered the owners were screwing their suppliers. When he spoke up, they dumped him. He went freelance because he couldn't get another job, and then he came into our group. But he didn't have the same background.'

'An athletic background?'

'Yes,' Ray said. 'It makes a difference.'

'Did Clyde Pepper have an athletic background?'

'Clyde grew up in Inwood, and he played basketball and ran the half-mile in high school.'

'What about the rest of you?'

'Gus played football and basketball at Fisk. Tommy was an all-conference guard his senior year at New Trier, in Illinois, and he made the football team his first year at Carleton, before he got interested in theatre. I did varsity football, basketball and track all though high school. The point is, Clyde had worked under coaches, he'd been through a sports programme. He knew about discipline. He set goals for himself.'

'His death must have come as a shock to you.'

'It still is a shock,' Ray said. 'If he had to take a walk, I wish he'd come down to our neighbourhood, called one of us up, stopped in for a beer or something. Clyde did that, sometimes. Who goes into Riverside Park late at night?'

'That's an interesting question,' Brannigan said. 'Was it a habit of his, do you know?'

'You got me,' Ray said. 'But you'd think a guy who used to be a homicide detective would know better.'

'When was the last time you saw him?'

'About an hour after we left the gym. We always have lunch at a place down on Broadway. When we're done, Gus and Tommy and I get into a cab, and Leo and Clyde walk home. The last time I saw Clyde, we were hailing our cab.'

'Did you talk to him yesterday evening?'

Ray shook his head. 'Last night, I was with my girlfriend, Sally Frohman. Around midnight, whenever it was, you called and gave me the news. I talked to my friends for about an hour. We could hardly believe what happened. You don't expect a friend of yours to get killed.'

'You were with your girlfriend all night?'

'Depends what you mean by all night,' Ray said. 'Sally rang my buzzer about 11:00, maybe a little later. She was worried about something. Well, she was pissed off at me and wanted to make sure I knew it. Hold on.' He smiled at Brannigan. 'Are you checking to see if I have an alibi for the time Clyde was murdered?'

'I'm asking you what you did last night.'

'What time *was* Clyde murdered?'

'According to the Medical Examiner, sometime between 10:00 and 12:00.'

'Then I have half an alibi.' Ray said. 'But I didn't do it, if you had any doubts about that. I was fond of Clyde, I liked him a lot. After Sally and I finally got to bed, I cried. I really did, I cried like a baby.'

'Murderers cry all the time, Mr Constantine. Don't take this the wrong way, but I've seen dozens of people who committed murder break down and weep. Some of them were sitting right in that chair. They cry because they almost always killed a friend, a spouse or a child of theirs. You should put it in one of your books.'

Remembering a scene near the end of *Dying Fall*, Ray said, 'Now that you mention it, I already did. Funny, isn't it? Sometimes you write things you weren't aware of knowing. Grant Upward and I used to talk about that. He said it was one of the reasons he wrote – to discover what he knew.'

'You get the same thing in police work now and then,' Brannigan said. 'If we could bring Clyde Pepper back to life, I think he'd agree with me. The man had one of the best records in this precinct, maybe *the* best. Not a man who gave up easily. Did he ever talk about his work?'

'Not that I remember,' Ray said.

'He never mentioned a boy named Charles White? Charlie White?'

Ray looked up and brought the tips of his fingers together. 'If he did, I've forgotten all about it.'

'Three years ago, the case attracted a lot of attention in the press. It wasn't as big as Robert Chambers and Jennifer Levin, but it was almost in that league. I'm surprised you don't remember it, being in your line of work.'

'This was something Clyde was working on?' Ray asked.

'It was one of his last cases. Around 3:00 one morning, a Barnard student and her boyfriend saw a kid lying on the ground inside the gate to the Columbia campus on 116th Street. He was curled up behind his backpack in the dark, off to one side. If his white polo shirt hadn't caught her eye, the girl would never have spotted him. They thought he was drunk, and they went in to see if they could help him. After they got a good look, the boyfriend called 911 on his cell phone. The kid had been beaten to death. That was Charlie White. He was in his last year of pre-med at Columbia, and he lived in a fraternity house on the other side of 116th Street, a couple of doors down. Ring any bells?'

'Maybe,' Ray said.

'In one of his pockets, our pre-med frat boy was carrying five grams of cocaine in individual packets. The backpack was even better. A rock the size of a walnut wrapped up in a plastic bag was rammed down next to his books. Turned out Charlie White had a reputation for dealing coke to his fraternity brothers. Plus other interested parties.'

'Oh, yeah, Charlie White,' Ray said. 'Sure. He was from a well-off family in the Midwest, wasn't he? His father had a big job in the Carter administration.'

'Missouri,' Brannigan said. 'His father was Under-Secretary of the Treasury during Reagan's first term.'

'He must have been killed over a drug deal,' Ray said.

'Your friend Clyde didn't buy that theory. I've been looking through his records, and I wouldn't be surprised if he was right. In the end, Pepper came up empty-handed. Must have been frustrating for a guy like that.'

'Well, yeah,' Ray said. 'But what makes you think he was right?'

'A couple of things. To beat someone to death, you have to keep coming at him, keep putting in the effort. Drug-related murders are like executions. Turning a guy's face into mush takes anger, it takes passion. It's personal.'

'Maybe the kid burned one of his customers,' Ray said.

'Could be. But I suppose it would be the first time in history that a guy killed his dealer and didn't rip off his stash.'

'Uh huh. That makes sense.'

'Do you see what I'm thinking, Mr Constantine? Clyde didn't want to give up that case. Who knows, maybe he moved out of Riverdale to keep working on it. So I was interested if he ever talked about this to any of you. Anything he might have said could be useful to us.'

'No, he never did,' Ray said. 'Not to me, at least.'

'Well, I had to ask,' Brannigan said. 'Thank you for your cooperation. Would you send in Mr Gozzi, please?'

Ray left the office, closed the door behind him, and went over to the side of the room. 'Your turn in the barrel,' he said to Leo, and when Leo stood up, Ray said, 'Did any of you ever hear Clyde mention an unsolved case he was still working on?' None of them had. 'Too bad,' Ray said. 'We might have been able to give them some help.'

Ray watched Leo Gozzi enter Brannigan's office, then sat down beside Gus to wait until the last man came out.

'I'm sorry, but I think we're at a dead end,' said Sally Frohman. 'I really wish I didn't, because I like you a lot, Ray, and I thought we had a relationship that was going somewhere. You're a good writer, too – I never had any doubts about that. When I got my first job, some of the women told me never to get involved with writers, it didn't take me long to learn why, but I always thought it could be different if you respected the guy's work. I guess I was wrong. Or there might be some other problem, one that has nothing to do with your being a writer, I don't know, at this point everything seems connected to everything else, but what I do know is, this thing isn't working, and I think it would be better if we stopped seeing each other.'

She had left two messages on Ray's machine, arrived at his door toting a manuscript-laden briefcase, shared take-out Thai food and a bottle of Beaulieu Vineyards chardonnay at the kitchen table, adventurously and with a hint of desperation observable only to an experienced Sally Frohman-watcher strewn her clothes here and there on both floors of his brownstone apartment, and concluded her farewell performance in a *bravura trifecta*, most of which, Ray hoped, had been genuine. Presently, which is to say at 10:35 p.m., they lay recumbent between daisy-printed sheets. The fragrantly chromatic harmonies of Faure's *Second Quartet for Piano and Strings* drifted about them, courtesy of WNYC.

'Gee,' Ray said, 'you respect my work?'

Sally gave him a dark, deeply reproving look. Her hair fuzzed out electrically around her head, and the distance between her eyes seemed about an inch wider than usual. 'Is that your final comment?'

'No, sorry. Just an ill-advised attempt at levity. You never told me anything like that before.'

'*Didn't* I?' For a moment, she seemed stricken. 'Well, maybe not in so many words. But you're changing the subject. Tonight was lovely, and I'm going to miss you, but we're not going anywhere, are we? This is as much as there's ever going to be, and it isn't enough.'

'Sally,' he said, 'your timing is incredibly bad. One of my closest friends was killed yesterday. Clyde didn't have a heart attack, he wasn't wasting away from some disease, he was *knifed*. Some creep cut his *throat*. The guy smashed in Clyde's *skull*. I don't see how you can ... Aaah, hell.' He flattened his palms over his eyes, then dropped his hands at his sides. 'If you want to know the truth, Sally, in a way – and take this however you like – it's like my son died all over again. This is not the moment to start whining about our relationship, all right?'

'No,' Sally said. 'It isn't all right. I'll overlook the part about whining, because I know none of this is easy for you. Ray, I am very, very sorry about your friend.' She sat up straight and wrapped the sheet around her. 'Do you know why I came here tonight? I wanted to do whatever I could for you – I wanted to help you get through this. I thought you might *need* me, Ray.'

'I'm glad,' he said.

'But did you talk to me about your friend? Did you let me know what you were feeling? Ray, you completely shut me out. Before dinner, I asked you about what happened at the police station, and you said it was nothing. During dinner, you said that your friend Leo looked distressed at the gym today, and I gathered you were concerned about him, but when I asked, you clammed up. You wouldn't have said anything if I hadn't forced the issue. You're like this glassy, frozen surface – you never open up. In the entire time we have been together, you never told me any more about your son than that his name was Paolo and he died of an overdose. I don't know how old he was, or where he was when it happened.'

'He was twenty,' Ray said. 'It happened, as you put it, in his apartment, during his third year at RISDE. RISDE is an acronym for the Rhode Island School of Design, located in Providence, Rhode Island. Is that what you wanted to hear? Do you feel more informed?'

'You're never going to let anyone in,' Sally said. 'I feel sorry for you. Even more than that, you make me sad. You have nothing but those guys at the gym and your work.'

'You'd be surprised at what I have,' Ray said.

The telephone rang. Sally did not take her gaze from him, and the telephone kept ringing.

'What happened to your answering machine?'

'I turned it off,' he said, and leaned sideways and picked up the receiver. After a short time, he said, 'No, I haven't heard from him.' Ray listened to his caller some more and said, 'Okay, yeah. I'll be right there.' He hung up.

'Don't take this personally, but I have to leave. That was Gus Trayham. He's been trying to talk to Leo all night, but Leo isn't answering, and Gus is worried. He and Tommy are up on 107th Street, trying to convince the super to let them into Leo's apartment. I should be there when they get in.'

'Why? What do you think is wrong?'

'I don't even want to say.' Ray got out of bed and began hunting for his clothes. 'Talk about lousy timing. What do you want to do, stay here?'

'I'll wait for you to get back,' Sally said. 'Unless you want me to come with you.'

'No, no,' Ray said. 'With luck. I won't be gone more than half an hour. If it's going to be later, I'll call.'

A few minutes after midnight, Ray let himself back into his apartment. Fully dressed, Sally was seated on his sofa, dividing her attention between the stack of pages on her lap and Channel One, the 24-hour local news station.

'Well?' she said.

Ray shook his head and walked into the kitchen. He took a glass from a shelf, dropped in ice cubes from a bowl in the freezer, and half-filled the glass with whiskey. When he turned around, Sally was leaning against the counter just inside the entrance, part of the manuscript still in her hands.

'I see you need a drink,' she said.

'That's nice,' Ray said. 'I appreciate your support.' He sat at his table and swallowed whiskey without taking his eyes from her.

Sally took a step towards him, then stopped moving and tucked the pages under one arm. 'I assume you got into Leo's apartment.'

'Yes,' Ray said. 'That we did. It took a little heavy-duty persuasion, but the super finally opened the door to Leo's disgusting pigpen. The results were unsatisfying. They lacked a certain resolution. The pigpen was empty. In the sense of its tenant being nowhere in sight. Looked at another way, the place wasn't empty at all, since garbage was piled up everywhere you looked. We waited around until we were about to pass out from the stench, and then we gave up.'

'Do you think he killed himself? Is that what you were worried about?'

Ray leaned back in his chair and gazed at a spot on the wall five or six feet to her right, pretending to consider her words. He appeared to be mildly amused. 'I would say . . . I would say that your question is too narrowly framed. Our anxieties are free-floating and essentially undefined. They are of an inclusive nature.'

'That's not—'

He interrupted her, still contemplating the spot on the wall. 'I will say this, however. If I had to live in that filthy dump, thoughts of suicide would never be far from my mind. Seeing his apartment puts Leo in an entirely different light. I had no understanding, none whatsoever. Of the way he lived.'

She looked at him in silence for a suspended moment. 'Have you had any new thoughts about us?'

'Now?' Ray took another swallow of whiskey. After a few seconds, he shifted his gaze to Sally. 'Do you know how ridiculous that question is? That doesn't mean you can't spend the night here, by the way.'

'Here's another ridiculous question,' she said. 'How would you describe the way you're feeling at this moment? Or, if you are uncertain about your feelings, what are you thinking?'

'Oh, I'm completely clear about my emotional condition,' Ray said. 'It's as though a huge explosion just went off a yard or so away from me. Chunks of metal and parts of bodies are flying all over the place. People have begun to scream, and the screaming is going to continue for a long time. I'm still on my feet, but as yet I don't know if I have been injured. I almost have to be injured, but I'm afraid to look. That's how I feel.'

Sally quivered.

Ray tilted the last of the whiskey into his mouth and thumped the glass on the table. 'And what I'm thinking is this. Betrayal is the ugliest, most repulsive thing I can imagine. I hate being betrayed.'

Sally wavered backward. 'We have nothing more to say to each other. Stay there, don't walk me to the door.' She spun around and left the kitchen.

'For God's sake, Sally,' Ray said. 'I wasn't talking about you.' He stood up and poured more whiskey into his glass. From the living room came the rustle of papers being stuffed into a briefcase. 'Sally?' The next sound he heard was the closing of the door.

Peter Straub lives in New York City. He is the author of *Ghost Story*, *Shadowland*, *The Talisman* (with Stephen King), *Koko*, *Mystery*, *The Throat*, *The Hellfire Club*, *Mr X* and other acclaimed novels. He has won two World Fantasy Awards, the British Fantasy Award, two Bram Stoker Awards and the International Horror Guild Award. In 1998, he was named Grand Master at the World Horror Convention. His second collection of shorter fiction, *Magic Terror*, was recently published by Random House. '"The Geezers" is the product of a lengthy period,' says the author, 'extending from roughly October 1998 to February 2000, during which I reported four days a week to the gymnasium at Columbia University in the bracing company of my friend and neighbour, Hap Beasely, a native of Nashville and former paratrooper, former policeman, fellow jazz connoisseur and clotheshorse, also a wondrous raconteur and *bon vivant*. Beasely and I did stretching exercises, walked around the track, worked out on the torture machines, swam laps in the pool, sweated in the sauna, then daily repaired for lunch – the same lunch, every day – to a little second-floor student restaurant called The Heights, located four blocks south of the Columbia campus on Broadway, where we soon became familiar with everyone on the staff. My efforts at coasting through the exercise-units amused and outraged Hap in about equal measure. (His father had been a coach at Fisk University, and he could have been a great coach, had it not meant taking so much time away from being a *bon vivant*.) When the time came to contribute another story to the ongoing series of anthologies from the Adams Round Table, a group of mystery writers including Lawrence Block, Susan Isaacs and Mary Higgins Clark that meets once a month for dinner and conversation, I decided to place my contribution in the familiar world of the Columbia gym. The character called "Gus Treyham" is drawn in part upon my friend Hap. My purpose in this story was a kind of radical indirection – I wanted to leave the essential point unstated.'

Honeysuckle

WILLIAM R. TROTTER

The green-eyed coed had written a slick little story about teenage angst in a small southern city in the late 1980s, tagged with a politically correct ending that put yuppie greed in its place. Halfway through the story she had included (quite calculatingly, I suspected) a startling sex scene. True, there have been sex scenes in about half of the stories I'd read for this workshop, but there were turns of phrase and allusions in this girl's treatment that hinted of interesting personal proclivities.

Now she was staring at me expectantly, waiting for me to make a pass at her, in the guise of literary criticism, or for me to tell her how gifted she was; I suspected that in the yeasty crucible of the mind crouching behind that *Cosmopolitan*-cover face, the two were intertwined. I knew what my lines would have to be if I wanted to score with her, and for an instant my 49-year-old ego was tempted. She'd probably been told, by more than one English instructor who wanted to get into her pants, that she was *very* talented, and if tonight was the night she got to Fuck a Famous Writer, some degree of confirmation would be hers, some small professional magic transferred by the act.

Suddenly feeling mulish and weary, the only thing I wanted to do was slap her perfectly made-up cheeks with the cold mackerel of reality. Somewhere along the way, whether from reading too many articles in *Writer's Digest* or from the encouragement of too many horny professors, this young woman had become convinced that she would be able to earn an actual living by writing proper little stories like the one that lay on the table between us. She could churn out stories like this by the dozen, I was sure, and as long as she stayed in graduate school, she would thrive. Out in the great marketplace, however, this kind of MFA-realism was a debased currency.

'It's a good story,' I began.

Her face fell, then snapped back into the same lacquered smile. Good teeth, sweet breath, a satiny tongue – I was probably going to miss her by the time midnight rolled around.

'But...' she encouraged, grittily determined to show that she could Take Criticism.

'But nothing. It's a good story. Polished, effective, self-assured. Technically speaking, it's one of the best I've read during this workshop.'

'But I sense you're still holding something back,' she prompted, leaning forward.

'Well, this is a purely subjective reaction, you understand, but it's just like a thousand other stories that writing students are grinding out all over the country. God knows I've read enough of them. You've been told to "only write about what you know", and the problem is that you and all the others who write like this have taken that advice literally... and I'm afraid you all "know" the same stuff.'

Say this for her: she didn't give up easily. Changing the subject, she leaned back and threw out a question as big as a fishing net. 'So, then, what advice would *you* give to somebody who wants to write as much as I do?'

'Don't.'

'I beg your pardon?'

'Don't. Not to the exclusion of having a real life and a real job. Learn computers, get a licence to sell real estate, or find somebody rich to marry. Just don't leave this university thinking you're going to earn a living writing short stories. It will not happen.'

'I think I have what it takes,' she fired back.

'Maybe you do. What you don't have is any real conception of what the odds are against you, how big a part blind stupid luck is going to play, and how vast the competition is when it comes to the kind of stories you write. At least learn a tolerable trade, my dear, because the market for short stories is microscopic and the kind of magazines that print them usually pay in free copies. You might consider broadening your range to include romance novels, advertising copy, travel writing, or some such thing that will enable you to pay the bills while you practise your craft.'

That tore it; she wouldn't go to bed with me now on a Vegas-sized bet. She gathered up her manuscript, thanked me for my time, and sashayed out of the conference room with enough of a swing in her fine tennis-playing ass to let me know I had just talked myself out of something memorable.

Still, I was more relieved than regretful when she snapped the door shut behind her. Her story had been the last one in the pile and this had been the last conference of the week-long workshop I had contracted to give at my old Alma Mater. I'd presented my obligatory lecture the previous afternoon and coped – graciously, I think – with a book-signing in the student union and a two-hour cocktail party afterwards, where I had listened to a lot of senile drivel from antique professors who swore they remembered having me in their classes, along with a surfeit of trendy educational babble from middle-aged academics of my own bewildered and increasingly irrelevant generation. God save me from ex-radicals with tenure; they are equal to the worst of Stalin's commissars.

Now the afternoon stretched before me like a blank page. I repacked my briefcase, downed the last inch of tepid coffee in the Styrofoam cup I'd been nursing for an hour, and left, for the last time, the office the college had loaned me for the duration of my four-day sojourn. My plane didn't leave until tomorrow morning, and I had turned down all offers for dinner and drinks. As I left the building and stepped into the bright spring sunlight, I had some vague notion of buying a bottle of bourbon and spending a monastic but tranquil night in my hotel room, surfing the premium channels for a decent movie or just enjoying the luxury of reading something I *wanted* to read.

It was one-thirty in the afternoon, most of the kids were in class, so the campus was pretty much deserted. As I started to walk to the parking lot where my rented Taurus waited in a VIP slot, I was suddenly cold-cocked, nearly overwhelmed in fact, by a sneak-attack wave of nostalgia. Although Davidson College had doubled in size since I had graduated in 1965, gone coed, loosened the hammerlock of Calvinism that had made the school conservative even by the standards of the Bible Belt, the campus itself had not lost the remarkable beauty of its nineteenth century landscaping.

Even during my moments of deepest discontent with its stiflingly reactionary curriculum and hypocritical 'traditions', I had always loved the look of the place: beautifully groomed lawns, roomy sidewalks, groves of towering elms and seasonally magnificent magnolias which created a palette of Turneresque light-effects at twilight; and the stately, if slightly pompous, façades of its Greek Revival architecture. Few places in America, in the mid-1960s, could have looked and felt so protected from the turmoil that had begun to rack the nation elsewhere.

And this was one of those picture-perfect late-spring afternoons that seemed to distil every enduring beauty of the North Carolina Piedmont into a kind of sensual banquet potent enough to slow the very tides of Time: mellow and generous sunlight, warm enough for shirtsleeves yet still hinting of the evening cool to come. Every random sound – a dog barking, the rustle of a squirrel leaping from one tree to another, the lazy but purposeful footsteps of students heading for the library, a distant whoop of sheer youthful exuberance from one of the dormitories – was made vivid and full of significance by the specialness of the springtime air I breathed. The intensity of the moment was unexpected, and it opened a vault of long-suppressed memories.

For about five minutes, I just stood there, rooted, in the centre of the quadrangle, breathing slowly and letting the mood take possession of me. Enlightenment quickly came: I knew that I was going to spend the rest of the afternoon in its grip. I had tricked myself, it seemed; subconsciously, I had arranged things, including, probably, my unnecessarily rude remarks to the girl, so that just such a fallow period of time would be available to me. I accepted the possibility I had tried to put in the back of my mind: I would, after all, make the pilgrimage I had sworn to myself I would not make.

Once behind the wheel, I went on autopilot; the little town that surrounded the campus had not grown all that much. Beyond its limits, I ignored the signs pointing west to the big new highway that led to Charlotte and turned in the opposite direction, on to an old New Deal-era two-lane country road that meandered through the cornfields and woods to the east.

The memory of the first time I had travelled this road came surging back so vividly that, for an instant, my youthful self seemed to merge with my middle-aged persona, so that I could see and hear and smell with senses that had not become brittle, selective, guarded.

It was on a May afternoon in my Junior year. I had just taken my final exam in a required course I detested, and I was still bristling from forty-eight hours of Dexedrine and coffee-fuelled cramming. Too wired to sleep or even relax, I climbed into my ratty old '58 Chevy and started driving aimlessly. The big highway to Charlotte was still six or seven years in the future, and so when I found myself at the first significant intersection, I turned towards the country, for no more compelling reason than the fact that I had not ever driven in this particular direction before.

The instant I did so, I experienced a remarkable sense of having done exactly the right thing, as though I had subconsciously caught a scent or felt the tug of an importuning current. There was little traffic – two or three cars passed going the opposite way, but otherwise the road was all mine. Cornfields stretched out in both directions, tenderly green, bordered by stands of trees close to the road, so that I passed through alternating bands of sunlight and shade, which created a soothing rhythm. Exactly where I was going or how long I would be driving, I did not know, nor did I particularly care. The wind streaming over my bare arms smoothed out those exam-time tensions.

After perhaps twenty minutes, I saw a sign announcing the imminent appearance of a place called 'Haynesville, Unincorporated; pop. 500.' The name was not unknown, though I had never actually been there; just a dot on the road map, one of those tiny Piedmont farm towns one drives through on one's way to a larger dot on the map. Don't blink as you pass through or you'll miss it. A couple of gas stations, a feed-and-hardware store, a cinder-block post office, some tree-shaded houses set back from the road. A single four-way intersection with a yellow blinking light defined the centre of town. I scrupulously maintained the speed limit and made sure to come to a complete stop at the intersection – this place looked like the very archetype of a rural speed trap.

Which way to go? I was about to continue in the same direction when I saw, half-obscured by weeds, a small hand-painted sign: an arrow pointing left towards something called 'The Gardens'. The sign could not have been placed there to get the attention of travellers or tourists – of whom there were precious few on this half-forgotten old highway; rather it seemed to be a reminder to local people who presumably already knew what The Gardens were.

Responding once more to that subconscious magnetic tug, I made a slow left turn and decided to check out The Gardens. For the first two or three miles, I saw nothing but more farmlands, pine groves, hedges, and gently sloping fields flowing with a late-afternoon patina of dusty gold.

Then, quite suddenly, the car seemed to enter a cloud of aromas so dense, so overwhelmingly rich, that my first inhalation made me as dizzy as the first toke I'd ever taken of really good pot. At first, the dominant scent was that of honeysuckle. That's what hooked me, I guess. Growing up in Charlotte in the 1950s, I had experienced a secure, comfortable childhood, long before the city became a sprawling, traffic-choked Atlanta-clone. Every family I knew had a house with a big backyard, and the lazy summers were blissfully endless. Aside from the generic hormonal changes and confusions, even my adolescence had been a savoury, romantic time. And if there was one sensory input guaranteed to land me in a dewy-eyed trance of nostalgia, it was the sweet, seductive smell of ripe honeysuckle blossoms – in that aroma was distilled the essence of a thousand summery afternoons and lingering twilights.

At that moment, I felt as though I had suddenly driven into a river of honeysuckle, so thick and narcotic was the scent, and without realising it, I slowed the car to a crawl, leaned my head into the slipstream, and drank it in gratefully. Several intoxicated moments went by before I grew accustomed to the honeysuckle smell and began to register the complex symphony of other scents it had initially masked.

Later on, when I had time and cause to relive that moment a thousand times, I would reflect on how impoverished our vocabulary is when it comes to the olfactory senses, despite the importance of scent in our lives. Fifty million brain receptors are assigned to the sense of smell, and when they fire, they zap the same set of neurons that stimulates the canyons of our brain that Evolution has made the seat and source of pure emotion. Later on, I would have plenty of time and motivation for studying 'aromacology', and I would even learn the clinical term for what I experienced at that moment: 'hypersomia', the condition of being overwhelmed by scent.

At the time, however, I felt both disoriented and curiously, embarrassingly, aroused; as though I were bathed in an erotically charged kind of aromatic music, a rich, many-layered chord of scent that seemed to blend, in perfect proportion, the essence of every ingredient of a perfect spring afternoon. I breathed in the tawny gold of sunset, a meadow-sweet hint of new-mown grass and hay, an overripe syrupy hint of gardenias, and a hundred other blended essences: rustic, sultry, powdery, pollinated, fungal, pheremonic, resinous, roseate – sharps and flats, bold flourishes and subtle harmonic progressions. My senses grew overloaded to the extent that I verged on an out-of-body climax, as disturbing as it was seductive. Some tiny part of my rational mind ruefully admitted that it was a good thing there was no traffic on this old highway, for I was surely Driving Under the Influence...

I knew I had found The Gardens. Too curious, and too close to stoned to continue driving, I coasted to a place where the shoulder of the road levelled out. I was barely aware of opening the car door and gave no thought to locking it. At that time, in that part of the state, people seldom bothered even to lock their front doors. Then I began walking slowly away from the road into a dense maze of shrubbery, pine trees, and wild flowers. I followed the current of scent like an inner-tube drifter on a lazy, spiralling river. The profusion of flowers and herbs around me was luxurious, baroque and seemingly haphazard, yet I sensed there was order to it, on some larger scale than the one I could perceive at ground level. Perhaps if I had been able to rise above it in a helicopter, some great rococo symmetry would have become obvious.

I could no longer see the car, but knew I could home-in on its location when I needed to. Despite the dizzying opulence of the foliage and its myriad scents, I was moving as purposefully as a compass needle swinging north. After some moments I arrived at the edge of a rutted dirt driveway. As I paused to catch my breath, I was startled by the sound of movement, a rustling in the underbrush on the other side.

As soon as she stepped forward into full view it was apparent that she had been aware of my presence, or at least my proximity, long before I had become aware of hers. She gazed at me, unflustered by my sudden appearance, appraising me with eyes of cool, dark hazel. She had pale, roseate skin, fine-grained as expensive vellum; high cheekbones, a generous mouth the colour of strawberries, and a cascade of cornsilk golden hair. She wore no make-up, and needed none. Her cotton dress clung to her in a sudden breeze, outlining long, coltish legs and sprightly apple-sized breasts, and she clasped in front of her a large wicker basket overflowing with herbs and flowers of many kinds. I judged her to be, at most, seventeen.

She smiled. 'Hello. My name's Virginia.'

I stammered my own name and stepped forward awkwardly. I had been driving past, I explained, when I suddenly felt compelled to stop and explore these gardens, these groves . . . then I stopped – there *was* no more of an explanation. But she only smiled more warmly, as if to reassure me.

'People come here all the time,' she said.

'What sort of people?'

'Every now and then, people like you, who see the sign and get curious. But mostly folks from around here, who already know about the place.' She shifted her basket to her left hand and stepped closer. We shook hands. Her touch was quietly electric. She tilted her head to her left, away from the highway. Sunlight brushed her hair and was at home there.

'Why don't you come up to the house? You look like you could use something cool to drink, and Mother always keeps a pitcher of lemonade in the fridge. It's the best you'll ever taste.'

I fell in beside her and we walked along the dusty driveway. The grounds on either side now took on a more orderly appearance: I was fleetingly aware of tended groves, small plots of exotic herbs and flowers, shade-giving canopies of plastic sheeting, small greenhouses, and occasional clapboard sheds, not unlike small tobacco-curing barns. These things seemed to radiate out from an as-yet-unseen central point.

Which was, of course, her home: a rambling old country house, many-windowed, framed by a broad and comfortable porch with wicker rocking chairs, dignified by a number of white columns. No matter how numerous my subsequent visits, I never could see the entire outline of the building, so hidden were portions of it by vines and shrubs and thickly matted trellises.

I never could recall what we talked about during the ten minutes or so it took to walk the length of the driveway to the front steps of the house. I only remembered how easy and pleasant it was to converse, and how we had already become friends by the time she ushered me into the long, shadowy front hall and led me into the kitchen. The lemonade, as promised, was delicious.

'This is so good.' I said, after my second tall glass. 'I'd like to thank your mother. Can I meet her?'

There was something sad in her smile, although at the time I attached no significance to it.

'Mom's a little bit shy. She has a throat condition, you see, that makes it hard for some people to understand her. That's why I'm the one who takes care of our visitors. Please don't think she's being rude if she doesn't come out to meet you – I'm sure she knows you're here and I'm sure it's just fine. Here, take another glass and we can sit on the front porch and talk.'

And just like that, we did. Reflecting later, I guess I understood from the beginning that this was the strangest household I had ever visited, but when I was with Virginia, when I was under the spell of the place, it seemed more natural than any of the upper-middle-class homes I had known when I was growing up. The Gardens was a place apart, evolving to its own rhythms, governed by its own natural laws. Virginia, through her warmth and innocence and sweetness, eased my passage into her world and made me feel at home there.

This property, she explained, had been in her family since before the Civil War; each generation had improved and added to the gardens, planting new species, crossbreeding, patiently learning the secrets of flowers and herbs, leaves and mosses, even fungi. It was the same with the house – each patriarch had added a wing or a room, a greenhouse or a shed, until the original configuration of the building was hidden like the nub of a pine cone.

In the early decades of the century, Virginia explained, the family had been quite large, but now there were only herself and her mother. Some of the men had died in wars; many of their wives had borne few, if any, children. She also alluded, briefly, to an unidentified illness that had shortened lives. At the time, her recitation of family history seemed not so different from the kind of generational ups and downs that could afflict any large family that, by habit or choice, relied on a fairly restricted genepool to replenish its ranks; such genealogies were not rare in the rural South. To me, the saga seemed deliciously Faulknerian, even though her speech and manners were not those of a typical Red Clay rustic. In the space of one afternoon, I had already mythologised her into a rare wild flower, a beautiful child of nature whom I had somehow been destined to discover.

As twilight thickened around us, and The Gardens became shadowy, more mysterious, I began to sense a change in the diapason of scents that surrounded me. Aromas of sunlight and photosynthesis began to fade, replaced gradually by heavier, darker scents. Some I recognised – gardenia, mint, sage – many others eluded recognition. The Gardens were composing their own nocturne.

So what, exactly, *was* the family business?

'We sell plants and flowers, just like any other gardeners,' she replied. 'But the family has always focused its attention on scent. Certain aromas have certain effects, on people and on animals. We mix aromas like pharmacists mix medicines. There are compounds that cure hay fever and diminish the effect of allergies, and others that cure depression. There are mixtures that make livestock more fertile, that help chickens lay more eggs and cows give more milk. When folks around here have a problem, they come to us. We have a large inventory of specific mixtures – after all, we've been doing this for more than a century – and if we don't have a remedy, Mother and I try to develop one. Everything we create is organic; natural oils and essences. Mother says they contain the Life Force. We can't help everybody, but we succeed more often than we fail, and people in these parts have come to trust us.'

Not until twenty years later, when New Age concepts came into vogue as the last spiritual refuge of ageing hippies, would I encounter the term 'aroma therapy', but Virginia and her clan had been practising its precepts for generations and, through trial and error and intuition, had actually created an extraordinary olfactory pharmacopoeia.

Sitting there on her darkened porch, listening to the sultry music of her voice, immersed in rare, exotic and evocative scents, everything she told me seemed to make perfect sense. I was young, romantic, ready to believe in the evidence of my senses. The coming of night made me feel simultaneously disembodied and filled with an earthy vitality. As the last saffron glow of sunset faded in the treetops, fireflies began to glow. With the coming of full night, they began to gather in vast multitudes, more than I had ever seen before, so that their illuminations pulsed in silent waves, bright enough to read by, like atoms of moonlight.

'Isn't it a bit early for fireflies to be out?'

'Their mating season peaks in June, yes. But here in The Gardens, they always show up early. Mother says that this is the place where all the fireflies in the South start their seasonal cycle – they radiate out from here in a great spiral. Something about the place gets them charged-up. It's funny to think of firefly lust, I guess, but I have this lovely image in my mind of a great vortex of living light, gathering energy here like a cyclone, then spreading all that beauty across the land.'

Suddenly, her hand was in mine and its softness, its warmth, the grace of her long, elegant fingers, evoked a thrill of intimacy in my whole body.

'Come with me,' she whispered, 'and we'll walk in the heart of The Gardens. On nights like this, it is very beautiful.'

What followed was dreamlike. Neither on the morning afterwards nor on any of the many times I tried to reconstruct the episode in detail, could I summon more than an Impressionist memory of the walk I took with her. Anchored to my flesh only by the touch of her hand, I followed her around the house and into a great expanse of orderly groves and fields, each with its own whirlpool of scent. Thousands of fireflies swarmed around us, escorting us, making the very leaves and vines and night-blooming flowers phosphorescent. I had never seen anything more beautiful or more mysterious; the very air we breathed seemed to be imbued with some undiscovered sensory dimension. Virginia herself appeared to glow softly, as though her flesh were kin to the nocturnal blossoms whose now-soothing, now-arousing scents flowed over us as we explored.

How many hours passed, I cannot say. Nor can I remember the names and properties of the orchids, vines and nectars she described for me. Not only time, but also the world beyond this place had ceased to exist for me. And try though I later did, obsessively, I could never remember the exact moment when we first embraced, when I first tasted the rich, nocturnal sweetness of her mouth.

I only know that, if someone had asked me during the week that followed, if I believed in Magic, I would have answered, passionately, 'Yes!'

At some point, we ended our circumnavigation of The Gardens and I could see the dark outlines of her house again. Dim light showed in several windows, and the back door was open. Suddenly, a thick, soft, oddly distorted voice uttered a single word, not loud, but curiously penetrating: 'Virginia?'

Instantly, she squeezed my hand and let go. The spell that had surrounded us faded quickly, leaving me again disoriented, suspended between two worlds.

'That's Mother, calling me in. I have to go now.'

'I'll come in and meet her,' I stammered, reverting to the middle-class manners I had been taught. 'I don't want her to think I'm rude.'

Virginia put her hand to my lips and stared at me with luminous eyes.

'It's all right. She understands. But she's shy. Perhaps some other time.'

I was suddenly desperate to stay near her. 'Can I come back? Can I see you again?'

'Of course. Come back a week from tonight.'

'I don't know if I can wait that long. What about tomorrow night?'

She shook her head. 'Mother and I have a lot of work to do this week. She's experimenting with some new things, exploring some new directions. I'm the only help she has. But I *will* be waiting for you, a week from tonight.'

And with that, she blew me a kiss and went inside. Stumbling like a drunk, I groped my way back to the front of the house, found the driveway, and eventually regained my car.

I returned to The Gardens one week later, at twilight. Virginia was waiting on the front porch when I parked. The sight of her, gracefully gliding down the front steps, rewarded a week of mounting anticipation, during which I could hardly keep my mind on classwork. There was just an instant's hesitation when I got out of the car and faced her, then she came into my arms and I smelled the sunlight lingering in her hair and the evocative woody aroma of whatever herbs she had been working with earlier.

She led me into the kitchen, where her mother – nowhere in sight, but that did not surprise me any more – had put out a lavish supper for the two of us. I remember lamb chops grilled with herbs, fresh corn, biscuits, and, predictably, a monumental salad whose strange and subtle flavours bespoke the local origin of its ingredients.

It was dark by the time we finished. I helped her wash and dry the dishes, effortlessly falling into a domesticated routine, just happy to be standing beside her. As she finished putting away the last plate, she turned and said: 'Would you like to see where I do my work? It's my lair, really, my own private mad scientist's laboratory.' Of course I did; if she wanted to spend the evening playing canasta, that was fine with me.

So hand in hand we threaded through the foliage to a secluded corner of the grounds until we stood before a surprisingly large building. Inside were numerous boxes, pots, and trays filled with plants and flowers, some of them bathed in the light of fluorescent fixtures hanging from the ceiling. The far wall was lined with shelves and cabinets, all filled with gardening tools, glassware and stoppered, labelled jars. Nearer the entrance was an area furnished like a study, with desk, bookshelves, even a bed. Of course I noticed the bed right away; in retrospect, I think I was supposed to.

Virginia gave me a tour, and I hung on every word. Inside the jars were exotic essences, powders and oils from all over the world, imported or grown here in The Gardens under special conditions: coriander oil from Russia, lavender from England, sandalwood from India, nutmeg oil and patchouli from Indonesia, bergamot oil from Sicily, bitter orange from Egypt; anise, valerian, chamomile, lemon, spikenard, clove, champak and ylang-ylang ... I remember but a few of the names of what she showed me. The commingled scents, until you got used to them, were close-to-overwhelming, a fugue of such complexity that its individual strands overloaded the ear. From their effect, and from the nearness of the girl herself, I became intoxicated, transported to the same dreamlike state I had experienced on our first nocturnal walk, when we had watched the fireflies weave their sarabandes of light.

Her study shelves were lined with notebooks and esoteric volumes, some of them, I supposed, quite valuable. Their titles had an arcane ring to them: *Libellus de Distillatione Philosophica*, Garcia da Orta's *Colloquies on the Simples and Drugs of India* (Goa; 1563), Giovanni Roseto's *Secreti Notandissimi dell'Arte Profumatoria* (Turin; 1555), and so forth. Some were modern reprints; others were antique leather-bound tomes. All bristled with bookmarks, showing that they were consulted (or had been, by her forebears) on a regular basis. I was impressed, and told her so.

'It's our family calling; what else could I devote my time to? You really don't need a fancy laboratory, or research grants – just seeds and patience and time. My mother says that we've been successful because there aren't any courses in aromacology, no textbooks, no rules, no dogma. And thus no inhibiting roadblocks from the conscious, verbal mind. No critical static. We do what we do and find out what works, we distil, we blend, make powders and elixirs, write our own recipes; above all, we're patient. There are hundreds of formulas in those notebooks, and I'm adding some new ones from my own research.'

She looked up at me with those wide, pure eyes and seemed suddenly to get an idea. 'Can I show you something I've been developing? It's a compound that relaxes you physically but also makes you mentally alert. No drugs, no FDA approval needed, just Mother Nature's own ingredients. I'm rather proud of it.'

'I'd love to see, or smell, anything you want me to.'

'Careful,' she teased, quickly kissing the tip of my nose. 'A girl might take advantage of such an open invitation.'

I settled into a comfortable chair and watched her perform a ritual of preparation, quite ready to be taken advantage of in any way she wanted. She moved amongst her shelves and implements like some improbable alchemist purifying from the gross to the subtle, measuring powders and oils into a pair of heated thurifers. As a final step in the process, she scraped tiny amounts of resins into the mixture, using a spatulate knife with the bold confidence of Van Gogh working his palette. A silken, ghostly vapour began to rise from the censers as she finished and knelt beside me, grasping my hand.

'What do I do?' I asked, already becoming more lightheaded.

Again she laughed, musically and with just a hint of prideful anticipation. 'Oh, just do what comes naturally. But first, just breathe.'

Thus began our first 'trip' together. I must perforce use the terminology of the sixties, for these shared rituals with her would acquire the ceremonial quality I later saw amongst dedicated acid-heads trying to synchronise their vibes before the molecules reached critical mass: choosing the records to play, the swatches of cloth to rub, the psychedelic artworks to peruse, preprogramming themselves. Yet no matter how many such events I witnessed, I doubted that many of them had the opium-eater intensity, the sheer sensuality, of the chemical adventures I shared with Virginia.

After a few breaths, I could feel the changes starting. On one level, I was quite aware of my surroundings – I was in a big shed in the backyard of a most unusual family farm, part of me still worried that her mother might come in and create a scene – but on a higher and more resonant plane of consciousness, I was drifting into another place altogether. No, *we* were. This was not simple 'smell' in any way; the carefully mixed aromas permeated my entire being, and those fifty million olfactory receptors were all kicking into overdrive.

We were now in a mental and perceptual space that evoked a windswept seashore: ocean breezes, tangy yet not exactly salty . . . warm white sand . . . weathered timber with a faint tarry resonance. I felt utterly at peace, yet fully energised, my skin so sensitive it was almost painful. Her hand burned exquisitely. Her face, at that moment, was that of a Pre-Rafaelite Madonna – transfigured with beauty, but also smouldering with desire. When I bent over and kissed her, our flesh melted into one essence. How we moved from that first kiss into her bed, I cannot remember. We were following currents that flowed outside of normal time.

She was still a virgin, but she knew, instinctively, what to do, and at the time I could only marvel at my good fortune. That first sexual encounter made every other in my young life seem callow and fumbling. By simply responding to her movements and words, by following the hidden instructions in her small cries and moans, I did the things she wanted, when she wanted them, and inhaled for the first time the scent that would be the most precious of all: the deep marine sweetness that rose from between her flawless thighs.

How long, how many times, we made love, I do not know. The entire night was a continuum, one long unfolding melody of touch, taste, texture. She and her magic became my only reality. At some point, of course, we passed into sleep, tightly spooned against each other, our shared moisture drying like new skin layered over the old.

She woke me at dawn. My mouth was dry, and my body reluctant to move. She brought me a cup of coffee.

'You should probably go before it gets light. Before Mother gets up. As long as we don't flaunt ourselves in front of her, she'll mind her own business – I often spend the night here, if I've been working late – but it wouldn't do for her to find us in the same bed.'

I accepted that explanation; why not? I still felt a little trippy and disoriented, but I also felt like the luckiest young stud alive. Whatever the ground-rules were, I would abide by them – anything, anything at all, to prolong this idyll. As I groggily pulled on my shoes, I looked at her in wonder, observing the preternatural brightness of her eyes, the bruised, endlessly kissed flesh of her wonderful mouth, and asked: 'Why did you choose me? I was a stranger who just happened to wander into your life. Surely every guy within a ten-mile radius of here has come to court you.'

In perfect seriousness she answered: 'I chose you because you *did* just "wander into my life", at exactly the right time, and in exactly the right place. That's how all of the women in my family have chosen their mates: by instinct. That's how my mother found my father, twenty years ago – one day, he just appeared in The Gardens, looking for something to cure a sick horse, and as soon as she saw him, she knew. It was the same with me.'

I should have thought long and hard about those words, but now that the spell was wearing off, and the light was growing brighter outside, I accepted the more mundane imperative of getting my horny young ass out of there before her mother appeared and accused me of deflowering her daughter. One last embrace, a willing promise from me to return next weekend, and I was gone, into the dewy grey dawn, circling around the house through groves of cobwebbed bushes and backing my car, as quietly as it would go, away from The Gardens.

Until that moment, I had entertained vague plans of getting a summer job while living with my parents in Charlotte; classes were over for the year, and I was in fact one of the last students still inhabiting the dorms. On the spur of the moment, I decided to stay on campus and register for some elective Summer School courses, just so I could be closer to Virginia. My parents made no objections, and coughed up the registration fees without complaint, even though my sudden dedication to academic betterment probably puzzled them.

So the summer went, and then, in September, I began my Senior year. My course-load during the summer was light, and I was so full of energy, so overflowing with vitality, that I began writing my first novel. By mid-July, I had fifty thousand words on paper, and was taking new chapters with me when I drove to The Gardens for my weekly trysts with Virginia.

Our meetings assumed the quality of ritual: I would arrive in the late afternoon, we would take long walks in the woods and fields surrounding the old house, eat the supper her still-invisible mother prepared for us, then adjourn to Virginia's quarters. At her request, I began to read my book to her, and she always listened intently, encouragingly. And I, in turn, followed, as best I could, the progress of her own research and experimentation. At some point in the evening, always, she would prepare one of her aphrodisiac aroma-cocktails and we would begin to make love.

In my mind, gradually, a fantasy began to take shape: we would marry and I would live with her in this beautiful place, writing my books while she tended her beloved plants. This was a vision she seemed to share, and if it differed from my own in any details, she never spoke of them.

When I later became so cynical about the drug-and-music culture of the sixties, it was partly because nobody I observed during those years enjoyed a 'trip' comparable to the ones I took with Virginia. She was a virtuoso in her field, all right. Sometimes the set-ups were as simple as lighting custom-rolled sticks of incense, and other nights they were quite elaborate. She used censers, small fans, a kind of vapouriser, some glass gizmo that resembled an alembic, even a rotating fragrance-wheel with different pockets of compounds that spun slowly past a fan pointing in our general direction. I never knew beforehand what the conjured ambience would be – delicate and evanescent (putting us in the mood for slow, patient, Tantric sex), or raw and earthy (turning me into a young stallion and Virginia into a growling, insatiable, slut) – but it was always powerful, all-consuming and filled with wonder.

Her mother never interrupted us; if I had been thinking straight, I would have wondered a little more about that. Instead, I simply accepted it as part of the pattern. Her mom would not be the first parent I had known who voluntarily chose to ignore the evidence of her daughter's sexual activity. As long as she didn't actually catch us 'doing it', Mother could pretend we weren't. Or so I reasoned it, and Virginia said nothing to indicate otherwise.

Months rolled by. I studied enough to keep up my grades, continued pounding away at my novel, and measured time's passage only from one visit to The Gardens followed by the next. I remember only one moment of personal friction during the entire autumn of 1964, and that was when I casually said to her: 'There's a really good concert at the college next Friday night. Would you like to come with me?'

Her eyes grew hard for a moment, and her smile forced. 'I can't do that. I belong here.'

'But don't you and your mother ever get out, go into town, even for groceries?'

'Mother's not able to travel, even a short distance. When we need groceries, someone brings them to us.'

'But your mother is an adult – surely she can take care of herself for one evening! I mean, Jesus, we've been seeing each other for almost eight months. and I'd like to show you off to my friends.'

Suddenly her nostrils flared with something close to anger, an emotion I had never before seen on her lovely face. 'I told you Mother is not well! Why do you think I spend so much time in this place? Just so I can make cow-laxatives and sleeping teas for the local granny-ladies? I'm working on something that might make her better, and I can't just interrupt that work. I make time for us on the weekends because I love you, but I love her too, and I'm dedicated to helping her, as much as it's in my power do to so. You've *got* to understand that.'

By the time she finished speaking those words to me, she was actually trembling. I did not know why my simple request should have opened a fissure in the hitherto perfect surface of our relationship, but obviously it had, and the very thought sent an icy tendril of fear through me. At all costs, even if it meant accepting some fairly eccentric attitudes on the part of my beloved, I wanted to preserve the idyll we shared ... forever, if I could.

There was another uneasy moment on the weekend before the start of Christmas vacation. I had kept in touch with my parents with regular phone calls, but had neglected to pay them a long visit since the end of Summer School. As much as I would have preferred to spend more time with Virginia, I knew it was incumbent upon me to go home for Christmas. She understood, or at least gave the appearance of understanding. And that last night before Christmas break, she made love like a madwoman.

In the morning, as I prepared for my now-customary predawn departure, she kissed me rather sadly and said: 'I've made something for you. Keep it with you, and when you want to remember The Gardens, or me, just open it and smell.'

She handed me a pot-pourri bag about the size of a tennis ball, closed off with a drawstring. I started to open it and take a sniff, but her hands prevented me. I marvelled briefly at their strength, wondering whether I could have forced them open without having to break some fingers.

'Not now!' she said fiercely. 'When you're away, and when you want to be reminded of me. Only then. Promise me.'

Of course I promised her, as I always did, without really thinking about it.

Rather to my surprise, I enjoyed going home. I had not spent a night in my room in almost a year, and I was pleased to rediscover some of my own artefacts. I also renewed contact with some high school friends, one of whom had just been drafted into the Army and was feeling decidedly nervous about it. I started reading the papers and watching the evening news again, and became uncomfortably aware of the widening war in Vietnam, of the first wave of student unrest, of the seismic disturbances looming in the world of pop music, fashion and attitude.

On the night before Christmas Eve, I and my friends held an impromptu high school reunion party at someone's parents' vacation home on the Catawba River. Two dozen ex-classmates showed up. We rented two kegs of beer and every other person in attendance, it seemed, brought either a bag of pot and a pipe or a cigarette case full of pre-rolled joints. I'd smoked before, of course, like virtually everyone else I knew, but it had been almost a year. By spending every Saturday night since May with Virginia, I had missed most of the partying around the college, and, of course, she and I had no need of dope – the stuff we inhaled was every bit as potent as any *cannabis*.

So I took a few sociable tokes for *auld lang syne*. And then a few more. Pretty soon, I was stoned as a bat and so were most of the others. As we all got higher, the inhibitions got lower. I began to notice that one of the girls was coming on to me – a peppy little brunette, ex-cheerleader, on whom I'd had something of a crush during my Senior year. She hadn't paid much attention to me then, probably because she was the main squeeze of the Student Council President, but her priorities had obviously changed during the interim. She had heard that I was writing a book and wanted to hear All About it. Under the circumstances, I was happy to oblige.

One thing led to another, while the party-buzz swirled around us and the Rolling Stones growled on the record player. Before I knew it, her hand was on my knee and she was leaning closer, an unmistakable predatory gleam in her eye. Part of my mind was already rationalising: I was not, after all, engaged to Virginia, not in any formal sense, and I was tempted not just by my previous adolescent lust for this girl, but by the looming chance to put some of my newfound sexual expertise to the test. Ten long days remained of the Christmas break, enough for me and the cheerleader to have some good times, not long enough for any real commitment.

While I was marshalling these arguments, I was also acutely aware that I needed to piss like a racehorse. I excused myself, promising to return soon. Don't go anywhere, I said to the former Miss School Spirit. Oh, I wasn't planning to, she chirped.

But the bathroom was occupied and there was a line. So I sneaked out the back door and wandered down to the boat dock. The night was cold and clear, windless, and the sudden drop in temperature had a momentary sobering effect. I went to the edge of the dock, unlimbered, and enjoyed a long meditational pee, fascinated by the concentric ripples I was making on the slick, black, surface of the old river.

Then here came Old Man Conscience, just when he was not wanted: Virginia and I *had* made a commitment to each other; I took her faithfulness as a given – after all, I had never seen another young man in her company, nor heard her speak of any – and she obviously felt the same where I was concerned. Our lovemaking had been epic, deeply satisfying; there had not been a routine moment. Did I really think the cheerleader had anything new or exciting to offer, other than the guilty pleasure of novelty for it own sake? As I zipped my fly, the cold of the winter night suddenly struck me deep and I began to shake. I knew, with utter certainty, that if I went back inside and consummated the evening's flirtation, that Virginia *would know*. No matter how many showers I took, she would be able to smell the effluvium of another woman on my skin, in my blood. To Virginia's hypersensitive nostrils, the coldest ashes of guilt would leave a murderer's spoor.

Resolved to be strong, I reached into my pocket and took out the pot-pourri bag she had given me. Just before re-entering the house, I stood in the shadows, untied the drawstring and took a deep hit. In these ingredients, somehow, magically, she had trapped the essence of our nights together. Memories flooded me with painful immediacy: nocturnal gardenias, jasmine, roses, the scent of sunlight in Virginia's hair, the roseate milk of her skin after a night of love.

I staggered back into the muggy warmth of the house, into the reeking banks of cigarette and pot smoke, and with my first breath became violently disoriented: as in 'bad trip', my senses going into hyperdrive and taking me places I did not want to go. I held on to the side of a kitchen counter and tried to fight down the nausea that threatened to engulf me. Perhaps it was just a chemical reaction between Virginia's pot-pourri and the marijuana fumes, or perhaps my own perceptions had grown much keener than I'd realised until that moment, trained (so to speak) by all the olfactory adventures I had experienced in The Gardens.

There was a garbage can nearby, and I could smell everything in it: stale beer in the bottom of cans, wet cigarette butts, old popcorn, coffee grounds, the brown remains of a salad. Even worse was the vile, urinous stink of a litter box tucked away beneath the kitchen table. One of the revellers walked by, on his way to the beer kegs, and I could smell the failure of his deodorant, the sulphurous wisp of a silent fart. And, with shocking and disturbing intimacy, the rusty odour of tampons. I could look around the crowded living room and tell which of the girls was having her period – including, I was surprised to learn, the one I had been flirting with.

My system could not process any more of this unwanted information. I retreated into the backyard and violently puked all over some azalea bushes. The stench of my own vomit made me even sicker, and for a moment I thought I was going to pass out. Gradually, however, the cold air washed the worst of the smells from my head and I began to crawl out of the mood. I knew better than to attempt another re-entry; what if I had a flashback and disgraced myself in full view of my friends? And as for the cheerleader, all desire had been quelled by that sickeningly intimate whiff of her menses – not to mention the fact that I was now liberally splattered with up-chuck.

With unsteady gait but a pristine conscience, I navigated back to my car and drove, very carefully, to my parents' house. Safe in my old room, with its comforting momentoes of a more innocent time, I briefly considered flushing the contents of Virginia's magic bag, but decided that it had not been the pot-pourri's fault – the scents that came from it were all pure and sweet and powerfully evocative of the finest nights I had ever known. No; the problem was the context in which I had impulsively opened it, creating a violent dissonance of mood and triggering an allergenic sensitivity in all those fifty million olfactory receptors. I put the pot-pourri bag on my dresser and went to bed. I did not sleep well.

1965 came in clear and cold; there was a New Year's Eve party, but I stayed at home with my parents and watched the big ball fall in Times Square. The decade – *my* generation's decade – was at midpoint and history was at a watershed. Even my parents sensed as much, for during our last dinner together, the night before I was scheduled to return to college, my mother casually enquired as to whether or not my draft deferment was still in good shape. I assured her that it was, as long as I adhered to my plan of entering graduate school, and as long as I kept my grades up, there would be no problem doing that. My dad grew uneasy during this conversation: he had been in the Navy in World War II, executive officer on an LST in the Pacific, and was fittingly proud of that service, but I knew from our conversations during the holidays that he had grave misgivings about the unfolding adventure in Vietnam. Crushing a peasant uprising was not easy to equate with stopping Hitler or avenging Pearl Harbor.

Six days into the new year, I returned to campus and began my final semester. At first, things were as they had been at the beginning of my affair with Virginia: our first night together, after the unaccustomed abstinence caused by the holidays, was memorable – we all but devoured each other. Whatever doubts I had about the longterm implications of the relationship, whatever inconsistencies and quirks there were about her secluded life in The Gardens, all were swept away from the moment I embraced her and inhaled the new and potent aromatic cocktail she had prepared for our reunion.

But by the end of winter, there were troubling occasions; not when I was with her, of course, but during the week, when I strove to complete my undergraduate responsibilities and to lead the normal life of a Senior. I began to have periodic flashbacks, like the one that had ambushed me on the night of the party. These could be triggered by something as ordinary as the chance whiff of fresh dog turds near a sidewalk, or the body odour of a passing student who hadn't had a shower in five days. I would become dizzy and nauseous, overpowered not by seductive, floral, sensual aromas, but by sharp and disturbing signatures of decay, filth and the lesser functions of the human body. The episodes might last a few seconds or a few minutes, but they always left me uneasy, oddly insecure, and plagued with severe headaches.

I understood, logically, that my long and regular exposure to the rarified olfactory banquets of Virginia's world had sensitised me, rendered me vulnerable to the baser, uglier odours of the world as well as its finer, subtler essences. It was as though I had developed a peculiar set of allergies to complement my heightened senses.

From these episodes there surfaced an unwelcome awareness of the sheer weirdness of Virginia's existence. All my invitations to go on a 'real date' – to a movie, a dance, an off-campus party – she deflected adamantly. There were rules to our relationship that now seemed confining rather than deliciously exotic. A year ago, I had fantasised about marrying her and settling down with her, learning something of her family trade, making a secure and hermetic life for us inside her world. Now, I began to feel somewhat boxed-in. Her seeming indifference to the greater world outside The Gardens puzzled and, on occasion, irritated me.

Everything was beautiful and serene so long as we stayed within the pattern that had been established. I still read to her from my manuscript, and she was still the perfect audience – attentive, rapt, flattering in her reactions. 'Your writing makes me sad for things I can never know,' she once remarked, after I had read a particularly Kerouacian rhapsody.

'Why can't you?' I asked, a little more sharply than I intended.

'I've told you,' she answered with bland indifference. 'I have to stay here and help Mother with her work.'

'Seven days a week?' I said, raising the ante. 'What's so important that you can't even go out to dinner with me? And where does your invisible mother do this work of hers?'

Virginia gestured vaguely towards the house. 'She has her own workshop, her own place, in the house.'

'Yeah, okay, but what the hell is she working *on*, a cure for cancer?'

For just an instant, the youthful innocence of her features hardened and her eyes, still the loveliest and most expressive I had ever seen, flashed with impatience.

'I told you once before, there's been hereditary sickness in our family. It killed my father not long after I was born, and my older brother when he was still a baby. Both Mother and I are working on therapeutic compounds to counteract its effects. In addition to the things we do for our customers.'

'Why don't I ever see any of these customers?'

'Because everybody in these parts knows we're only open for business during the week. The weekends are for ourselves. And for you,' she added quickly.

Before the conversation could evolve further along these patently uncomfortable lines, she removed my arms from around her shoulders, stood up, and quickly added a big dollop of compound to the censer that was smouldering on a nearby lab table. Quick as flashpowder, a cloud of powerful aroma filled the air, and as it reached my nostrils, she watched me closely, observing with almost clinical detachment, waiting to see what effect it would have.

Instinctively, I held my breath, but the scent got into me nevertheless, not just through my nostrils, but through every pore of my flesh. In seconds, all my doubts and questions faded into a muddled vagueness, and I was once more helpless with desire for her. My hands ached to be filled with her breasts, my mouth would shrivel and turn to dust unless moistened by her lips and tongue. She smiled as my arousal became visible, then slowly, tantalisingly, removed her clothes and came to me with open arms. I surrendered, as I always did, to the ecstasies of the moment.

One Saturday evening in May, when The Gardens were flooding with the urgencies of spring, I drove up to the house and was mildly surprised to see that Virginia was not in her usual place of welcome on the front porch. I closed the car door forcefully, figuring that she would appear as soon as she heard the sound. But she didn't, not this time. In the softening light of late afternoon, the house loomed immense and shadowy. The atmosphere of The Gardens, usually so rich and verdant this time of year, seemed preternaturally still, as though a vast breath were being held.

Curious, I climbed the front stairs and knocked on the door. Then I called her name. After a few more minutes of strained silence, I shrugged and went inside. My first intention was to go straight down the hall and into the kitchen, where I expected to find the usual well-prepared dinner on the dining table. But when I peered into the kitchen, I saw only empty plates and glassware; no food had been set out, although there were simmering pots on the stove and the aroma of a roast browning in the oven. I coughed politely. There was no response.

For a moment, I was at a loss; so unvarying had been the pattern of our trysts that I did not know what to do next. I retreated down the hall and observed as I did so that the living room door was ajar – at least, I presumed it was the living room, although the door had always been closed before as we made our ritual journey from the front porch to the kitchen. It occurred to me that I had never before seen that part of the house and just now, for some reason, I wanted to. Feeling a little bit guilty, I went in.

It was a perfectly ordinary living room, with comfortable but nondescript furniture that looked to have been bought in the late forties or early fifties. There was no TV, but then, I had not expected to find one. There was a telephone, however, on a table near the front window, which was covered with curtains. The telephone was not surprising – after all, these people ran a business – but the fact that Virginia had never given me a telephone number *was*. Beside the phone was a notepad, with a list of crossed-out orders jotted down. The last one read: 'Granny Wilkerson: quart of jasmine tea – grandson will pick up Thursday a.m.'

I felt vaguely disappointed, as though I had expected the contents of this hitherto sealed-off space to reveal something important about Virginia's family. I made a quick circuit of the room, through dim subaqueous light. Only one thing caught my eye: a line of framed photographs on the mantelpiece.

Here at last were some images of my beloved's family, about whom she had only spoken in generalities. I examined the older pictures first: stern-faced men with muttonchop whiskers and handsome women in late-Victorian gowns of black. A man in the puttees and campaign hat of a World War I doughboy. And a newlywed couple dressed in the style of the 1940s: the woman was tall and blonde, with eyes and cheekbones that resembled Virginia's. Her expression was one of satisfaction and repletion, as though she had just achieved some major goal in her life.

The stiffly dressed man beside her bore rather a different expression: one of resignation, I thought, rather than newlywed bliss. A man who took his duties, whatever they might have been, very seriously indeed. These, then, were Virginia's parents; of that, I had no doubt.

But the longer I stared at the image, the more disturbing it was. The dutiful husband bore at least a generic resemblance to *me* – his features seemed a fast-forward projection of my own as they might turn out to be in full manhood. The same dark eyes and rumpled hair, the same jawline and aquiline nose. My older brother, perhaps, if I had had one. With renewed interest, I went back and examined the older photos. Despite the dramatic changes in dress and facial hair, all the men were at least of the same general physical type as myself, just as all the women bore a passing ancestral resemblance to Virginia. Either I was looking at a record of true Southern Gothic inbreeding, or a remarkable case of coincidence. What was it Virginia had said to me on the first night we made love? Something about how the women in her family picked their mates instinctively, at first sight? Perhaps there was more to that remark than I knew.

Lost in thought, I did not hear her enter the room. When she spoke my name, I jumped. And as I turned to greet her. I could not help noticing that the manteltop space next to the photo of her parents was occupied by an identical, but empty frame. Was it reserved for a similar newlywed image of us?

She was not pleased to find me there, but she hid it well and quickly, distracting me with as warm an embrace as any she'd ever given me.

'Mother and I were working on something important,' she quickly explained, 'and the time simply got away from us. Come on back to my place while she finishes making dinner.'

I hooked my arm through hers and let her steer me towards the porch again. We always went from the kitchen to the porch, and then around the house on the outside; we had never gone *through* the house in order to reach her lair. This time, I balked.

'Let me help in the kitchen.'

She tugged on my arm impatiently. 'No, no. Mother has everything under control.'

'I'm sure she does, Virginia, but I also think it's long past time for me to meet her.'

'I told you,' she insisted, 'Mother's very selfconscious about her condition. Please, let's just go to my place and relax until the food's ready. I've got something special for you tonight.'

Her face was so extraordinarily beautiful in the twilight, her expression so pleading and insistent, and the promise of 'something special' so alluring, that I yielded and followed where she led.

Once we reached her quarters, she busied herself (with what would later seem to have been unusual haste) mixing some new compound in her favourite thurifer. She chatted nervously while she bustled, moving some large, extravagantly flourishing potted plants close to our chairs. ('These will increase the effect,' she explained, and as always, I accepted her explanation.) I tried to relax; a considerable portion of me was already feeling that wonderful erotic ache for her. But some recalcitrant part of my mind remained tense and on guard, and compelled me to say: 'Why do all the men in your family look like me?'

'Do they?' she forced a laugh. 'Well, I guess it's a predilection for brown eyes and curly hair. Just like some men get turned on by redheads more than brunettes. You're *my type*, my love, whatever that means. Just accept it as I have. We're together because we were destined to be. You've said so yourself, many times.'

Of course I had. Because our love had indeed seemed predestined, and because I was young enough, romantic enough, and horny enough to find the idea marvellous.

So I remained silent and willed myself to relax as Virginia performed her alchemy and the room began to fill with yet another new and potently effective scent. She settled into my lap, hugged me close and began kissing my closed eyes with hot, delicate lips. My erotic response to her was by now Pavlovian, and I was damned if I would let my doubts and unanswered questions spoil what promised to be an exceptional sexual adventure, even by our standards.

Whatever she had concocted, it was one of the most powerful recipes yet. After a few minutes of breathing a tart, slightly mossy fragrance, none of whose ingredients I recognised, I began to feel warm and tingly, disembodied, anchored to reality only by the intensely arousing sensations she was giving me with her full yet subtle lips, the satiny tip of her tongue. I no longer cared whether I ate supper or not. Nothing mattered except her caresses.

I have no idea how long we kissed and petted and fondled before I lost consciousness. I was never aware of *losing* unconscious – the erotic dream was its own continuum, and I did not know, until I woke up from that dream, that I had passed out. The last thing I remembered, for certain, was Virginia unbuttoning my shirt, running her fingernails through the hairs on my chest, and swirling her tongue around my nipples.

Considerable time had passed, because I opened my eyes to darkness and a pale column of moonlight streaming through the windows that faced the depths of The Gardens.

At first, I thought she was still beside me: I felt a pleasant tingling in my arms and chest, as though her wonderfully skilled hands were still caressing me. The scent of her potion lingered in the air, but it was stale and faint. Instinctively, I tried to raise my left arm and look at my watch, but something restrained my movements. In an instant, I was fully awake, and alarmed to feel myself enmeshed, everywhere, by thin filaments that clung to me like ropes. Had she been planning a little bondage as part of the evening's scenario? *That* was a specialty she'd never mentioned before, albeit an intriguing one.

Outside, a cloud moved past the moon and by the sudden brightness, I could see my arms, legs, and torso covered with vines that had grown, with unnatural rapidity, from the plants she had positioned around my chair. I was immobilised, like a bug in a spider's web. When I struggled, a dozen flashes of pain erupted from my exposed flesh, and I saw that the vines not only bound me in place, but their tips had penetrated my skin, and from the obscene sucking sensations that accompanied the pain, they seemed to be feeding on my blood, either that or – and this seemed even more horrible – they were passing some hideous substance from their barbed tips *into my flesh*.

Shouting and cursing, I began to tear at the vegetation. It was as though I sought to pluck a horde of leeches from my skin, for as each vine tore free, it left a raw, bloody puncture-wound. The vines began to writhe, like a nest of snakes, with a hideously malevolent awareness. As I freed myself, they lashed at me, furiously trying to regain their purchase on my flesh. I kicked over the pots and stamped on them. When I was finally free of their ghastly embrace, streaming blood from a dozen lesions, I grabbed a hoe and smashed the pots, chopping each wriggling worm of vegetation until I saw no more movement. Then I fled. Past the dark and now-sinister house, into my car and back to the campus.

As the cool night air streamed over my raw face and arms, I began to feel like a man who has broken free of a strange and terrible enchantment. What Virginia's purpose had been in subjecting me to such a horrible experiment, I could only guess. But now that her spell was irrevocably (or so I thought) broken, I could see that, from the moment of our first encounter in The Gardens, she had been *cultivating* me as she did her exotic plants and essences. Oh, yes, she had instinctively 'chosen' me, because I was indeed 'her type', just as those sombre-faced men in the photographs had been her mother's type, her grandmother's type, and back through all the generations that had lived on that land. And what of the mysterious 'sickness' that had plagued the males of her clan? Had it been the by-product of some cruder but equally unholy symbiosis between their flesh and the plants that, for whatever loathsome reasons, required human blood or tissue to complete their life cycles?

How long would she have kept me there? Was there some terrible bargain to be made for continued access to her body? If I had stayed with her, married her, would the price of that union have been the periodic loan of my body to her damned plants?

By the time I reached my dorm room, I was one mass of heartache. Not to mention the fact that I looked as though I had been mugged by a giant octopus. As I was unlocking my door, a friend stumbled by on his way to the bathroom.

'Jesus Christ!' he exclaimed when he saw me. 'Where the hell have you been and what the hell happened to you?'

'Went to a party that got a little rough,' I muttered.

'Must have been some fuckin' party. You missed at least three final exams, you know.'

'Impossible. I don't have my first final until Monday afternoon.'

'Oh, man, don't you know what day it is?'

'I thought it was Sunday night.'

'Sorry to break the news, pal, but it's almost Wednesday morning. You've been gone four days.'

How I got through those final days of my Senior year, I don't know. I took make-up exams, of course, but my mind and heart were elsewhere and I did poorly in every subject. Enough to drop my grade average from a B-plus to a C-minus. Enough to jeopardise my plans for graduate school. Enough to make me prime fodder for the draft board.

To this day, I remember nothing about graduation, except my parents' troubled displeasure at the way my scholastic career had nose-dived. I was like an addict who had suddenly been deprived of his drug of choice. Nothing could erase the horror of what I had awakened to in Virginia's room, but neither could I get her out of my mind. Perhaps, just perhaps, there had been some explanation, which she'd had no chance to give, that would have enabled me to live with this new and bizarre element in our relationship. Part of me was now afraid of her, but larger and more primal parts of me ached for her, for the voluptuous rapture her presence filled me with. I knew, with a woeful certainty, that I would never find another woman who could conjure such erotic magic.

I lost track of days and nights; I hung out in my parents' house, partied some with my old friends, made a few desultory passes at my manuscript. In my own way, I had 'dropped out' before the phrase became a cliché.

When the draft notice came in the mail, in late June, I accepted it stoically. I suppose, looking back on it, that I held fairly conventional ideas about the Vietnam crusade. As an avid student of history, I was under no illusions about the purity of Communist causes – I knew how much blood dripped from the mandarin-thin hands of Ho Chi Minh; and as a writer, I knew the old bastard was at best a third-rate poet. I fancied myself something of a military history expert, and I was curious to see if we could do what the French had failed to do: put a lid on the ideological ant-heap. But in the end, I guess, I submitted to the United

States Army's call more or less for the classic reason men enlist in the Foreign Legion: I wanted to forget. I wanted a distraction big enough to cure me of Virginia. I figured it would take something on the scale of a war to do that.

But before I entered the embrace of the Green Machine, I wanted to pay her one last visit. I guess I had some bullshit notion of letting her know it was due to her that I was going off to war and maybe going to get my young ass shot off, not to mention some other parts of me that she had been very fond of. I wanted some kind of apology, some kind of explanation, some kind of closure.

Be careful what you wish for.

I drove to The Gardens on a muggy windless Wednesday night, a couple of days before I was scheduled to embark for basic training at Fort Bragg. On impulse, I shut off the headlights and coasted quietly into the parking area in front of the house, not wanting to spoil the impact of my sudden appearance at the door. All around, the groves and fields were in full summer riot and when I inhaled that opulent mixture of fragrances I felt not unlike an alcoholic who's taking his first belt of bourbon after months of sobriety. Memories washed over me. I was a bit unsteady when I silently closed the car door and mounted the front steps.

After waiting a few minutes for someone to answer my knock, I tried the door. It was not locked. There was dim light spilling from the kitchen into the hallway, but otherwise the place was dark. I heard no sounds of activity. It was too early for the inhabitants to be asleep, and I was quite sure they were not out watching a movie or eating at a local café. I walked down the length of the hall and paused before entering the kitchen. I knocked again, rather timidly, on the doorframe. Again, no response. The kitchen was empty.

But now that my ears had grown used to the silence, I did hear Virginia's voice – distant and too muffled for me to make out any words. It seemed to come from within the walls. I circled the room, trying to home-in on the sound, until its volume increased slightly. I was standing in front of what I had always assumed was the door to a storage closet or a pantry.

After a moment's pause, I also became aware of a new and altogether unpleasant set of aromas: dank, heavy, suggestive of mould and fungi, even of rot. Part of my mind was urging me to forget the whole business, turn my back forever on this part of my life and just drive away. Another part of my mind was intrigued: was this perhaps the entrance to Mother's private lair? If it was, and I managed to get a look at what was going on there, I might at least come away from this journey with answers to a few of my questions.

This internal debate did not last long, and, of course, the curious part of me won it. I turned the door knob, and slipped through the opening. As I did so, the foetid, fungal smells grew oppressively stronger: organic, heavy, full of slow, unpleasant moisture. I fought down an impulse to gag and tried to breathe through my mouth.

I was standing at the top of a narrow rickety flight of stairs that made a sharp righthand turn about fifteen feet below the door. There was enough light to see by, but it was a type of light that corresponded to the smells emanating from below: greenish and sickly and thick enough to verge on mist.

Now I could hear Virginia's voice clearly. She was talking eagerly about whatever experiments were being conducted, horticultural terms mostly, and her words were punctuated by the sounds of glass and metal implements. It took a moment or two of hard listening to realise that the conversation was two-sided.

Some of Virginia's remarks were answered by monosyllabic grunts that seemed to come from a throat stopped with phlegm, the words barely intelligible to me, as though they bubbled up from underwater.

Carefully, I descended the last few steps and peered around the edge of the entrance to this subterranean den.

I only got a glimpse before I turned and ran back upstairs and out of the house, but I remember every detail, flash-frozen on my retinas: beds of glistening moulds and fungi, some of the growths extruding waving fronds that looked very similar to the vines that had fastened upon me in Virginia's workshop; Virginia in a stained lab smock, transplanting a vile-looking lump of matter that shuddered and humped in her hand as though it were not merely alive, but sentient; creepers and vines writhing on the ceiling, turning the room into a living cavern; tubes filled with circulating fluids that were being pumped from one obscene growth to another.

And Mother, of course.

Mother still retained a human shape, if you could call it that: an immense, shuddering bulk of distended and puffy flesh, mottled with unhealthy greens and charnel greys and pocked with scabbed-over sores, some of them oozing a dark yellow ichor. Mother, whose fingers had fused into some unholy amalgam of flesh and vegetable matter. Mother, whose face, when she turned it more fully into the greenish light, was a mass of pendulous polyps. Mother, who moved to hand her daughter a glass beaker, and who did not step so much as slosh forward, as though the simple act of movement brought her flesh – if that's what it was in her condition – to the verge of liquefaction.

I made a sound, more a groan of disgust than anything else, and fled up the stairs as fast as I could go. Most of my mind shut down from the impact of what I had seen, but one rather incongruous thought did keep surfacing as I drove recklessly away: that woman, or whatever she had become, had fixed my supper. Dozens of times.

Lucky me: I got to Vietnam just in time for the Ia Drang Valley campaign, in November of 1965. Actually, I *was* pretty lucky in a sense: my unit did not participate in the main battle in the mountains just east of the Cambodian border, where more than five hundred men of the First Cav were killed or wounded in a vicious, close-up encounter with about two thousand North Vietnamese regulars. But I was on the fringes of the battle, participating in numerous patrols and ambushes in the vacinity of Duc Co. My unit didn't have any stand-up fights with the NVA – not in November, at any rate – but we lost men almost every day to mines, mortar attacks, and snipers.

Every man took his turn at point on those patrols. My CO gave me a few weeks to get acclimated before giving me that assignment. That day's operation promised to be hairy: we were to scour an area of particularly thick jungle south of Route 19, where some of the enemy units decimated in the Ia Drang fight were thought to be regrouping and licking their wounds.

Visibility under the forest canopy was dangerously limited; I could see, at best, maybe twenty metres ahead of my M16 barrel and I kept turning around to make sure the rest of my platoon was still behind me. We'd gone about a kilometre when we came to a slight clearing that bordered a stream. On the opposite bank were some mammoth trees with roots the size of a small car, surrounded by dense underbrush. The thought crossed my mind: if I were the enemy, I could not ask for a better place to mount an ambush.

I'll cop to it: I was scared shitless. I'd never been this close to the enemy before, nor been in a close-range firefight. Without thinking, I reached for the only talisman I had: Virginia's little pot-pourri bag, which I carried in one pocket of my blouse. My fingers closed over it, and it released a slight, comforting fragrance. I sniffed my fingers, just as I had on the morning after we'd first made love, hoping to obtain some magical connection with a simpler, sweeter time.

As soon as I did that, I experienced the first major olfactory flashback I'd had in months. It came over me like the first rush of a hit of bad speed. My skin prickled, my vision blurred and I was suddenly cognisant of the rainforest smells, in all their wet, fecund, richness, just as if I had inhaled some of Virginia's custom blends. It was overwhelming: orchids and vines, earth and mould, the silvery scent of the creek, even a passing feral hint of a tiger somewhere in the deeper forest.

I knelt behind cover and signalled for the men behind me to do the same. I tried to ride out the sensations, sort out the smells, get myself together. With this kind of sensory overload, I was worthless as a point man.

Or was I?

After the first blast of scent, my mind began processing the input in a more rational manner, and beneath all the jungle odours, I began to discern – as sharp and keen as woodsmoke on a winter night – the smell of human flesh, and the unmistakable odour of the fish-sauce the Vietnamese love to put on their food. And I knew with absolute certainty that the enemy was on the opposite bank of the stream, waiting for us to come into the open.

I crawled back to the platoon and told the lieutenant what I thought.

'How do you know they're over there?' he whispered. 'Did you see movement?'

'No sir. I *smelled* 'em. And I'm not just guessing – they're *there*.'

The lieutenant stared at me for a moment, weighing his decision. I didn't blame him for being sceptical – I was still considered an FNG (Fucking New Guy) and this was, after all, my first time as point man. Then he made up his mind, pulled out a map, and signalled for our radioman to scuttle closer. Two minutes later, the radioman was bent over the handset of his PRC-25, calling in a fire mission from a battery of 155s that were on call to support us.

Then the lieutenant and I crawled back to a point where we could observe the other side of the stream. The first round fell a little short, throwing up a huge geyser of muck. The radioman adjusted the range and called for a barrage. The far bank vanished in a whirlwind of fire, smoke and debris, and as the big shells chewed things up, we heard screams and observed body parts and pieces of weaponry flying through the air.

If there were any survivors among the would-be ambushers, they fled long before we crossed the water and started counting the bodies. Well, 'estimated' is maybe the word, because the barrage had left only bits and pieces. The lieutenant finally decided, somewhat arbitrarily, I thought, that we had zapped at least twenty NVA, and after he radioed that information back to headquarters, he slapped me on the shoulder and said: 'Ya done good, son. You must have a golden nose!'

Of course, the tale of that patrol grew in the telling, and some of the other guys started looking at me funny, as though I had some kind of supernatural penumbra glowing around my head. Like it or not, I was stuck with the nickname 'Golden Nose' from that day until the day I finished my tour.

But the funny thing – well, it really wasn't *funny* so much as weird – is that from the moment of that olfactory flashback, my sense of smell became permanently hypersensitive and my ability to control it, to turn it on and off, grew with practise. Of course the very experience of combat heightens all the senses, adrenalises the reflexes, causes time to dilate (many a firefight registered on my eyes in Sam Peckinpah slow motion), and generally reinforces the notion that life itself is experienced most keenly when you're in danger of losing it. All of us felt such things.

Only I had an extra sensory edge. Whatever Virginia and her potions had done to my chemistry, to the very meat of my brain, I was blessed/cursed with a nose that would have done credit to a K-9 tracking dog. Danger and adrenalin made my aroma-perceptions bloom. It was a blessing in the sense that I could literally smell an ambush or an otherwise undetectable enemy bunker complex. My CO was wise enough not to give me the point *every* time we went into the bush – a man can only do that so many consecutive times before he burns out and turns into little more than a quivering bundle of ganglia – but when we went tunnel-hunting or when there seemed a good likelihood of enemy contact, I was usually up front, nostrils flared, antenna twitching, filtering out the now-familiar rotten-ripe scents of the forest or the rice paddies, trying to pick up the smell of the enemy – the rice he ate, the bunkers he slept in, the hidden places where he buried his shit. I was good at it; I saved some lives and caused some serious hurt to the gooks.

As for the 'curse' part, well, I learned about that a week or so after the 'Golden Nose' patrol. My platoon went into billet for a few days, while some other poor bastards went out and beat the bushes in our stead. We got a chance to catch up on sleep, write letters, take showers, eat steaks, drink beer, walk to the local native town and pay for a perfunctory blowjob.

We also got a chance to smoke pot. Shit, everybody did it except some of the officers, and most of them just looked the other way. The rule of thumb seemed to be: get stoned when you're off duty, if you want to, but stay clean when you're in the field. I had not partaken of the weed since that disastrous Christmas party when it triggered my first, and so far worst, olfactory flashback. But when the corporal in the next bunk handed me a reefer of Thailand's Best, I figured what the hell?

Big Mistake.

Oh, it felt good enough at first: a nice mellow buzz followed by idle thoughts of walking into the village and getting my ashes hauled. Going with the flow, I brushed my teeth, juiced my pits, and put on the one shirt I could find that was not fouled with sweat. Then I went outside and I got as far as the wire perimeter when the bottom fell out of the world.

That first wave wasn't so bad. The thing about Vietnam, once you discounted the heat, the monsoons, and the fact that about half the population wanted to kill you, was that it was a damned beautiful country. That first deep breath bequeathed me the essence of that lush green beauty: the delicacy of rice fronds waving in the wind, the richness of the jungles, the stern granite of the nearby mountains, the vast and sinuous pictogram of the Mekong River.

Then I inhaled again and I smelled everything – and I do mean *everything* – which lay beneath that beauty. I smelled the decay of fifty thousand corpses, even the dry powdery effluvium of the bones of those Frenchmen who had died here in the 1950s. It was as though I had become suspended over a vast charnel pit where each and every victim of that tragic country's endless wars had been gathered in one stinking mountain of human offal: the stale-shroud scent of the long dead along with the ripe fluid-and-tissue reek of the newly killed.

I reeled and gasped again, and yet another layer of scent invaded my pores: the sour and devious reek of corruption emanating from the governments in Saigon, and the sly taint of hypocrisy pooled in the armpits and under the tongues of our own politicians and generals. I smelled the char of napalmed flesh, the palpable stink of fear from those about-to-be-tortured. I smelled the earthy wriggling of maggots. I smelled jet fuel and the cordite of a million fire-missions.

Even now, after many years of trying to find the vocabulary to do justice to the experience, I can only adumbrate the palest echo of what it was like. My nostrils burned with violation, my brain began to seethe, unable to contain the input. With no other possible outlet, I began to scream. Those who witnessed me in the throes of this moment later told me I looked like a man who had been struck by lightning. Several guys ran over to where I lay, writhing on the ground in a foetal ball, clawing at my skull. I remember nothing that happened after I hit the ground, and that's just as well, but one of the soldiers who reached me first later told me that the only intelligible words I said were: 'Virginia, you bitch, what did you do to me?'

I went into deep catatonic shock and just lay there, trembling, a thin stream of bile trickling from my mouth. The medics were puzzled, of course, and finally just diagnosed it as a case of total, sudden burn-out (a not-unheard-of phenomenon in men who had been out in the bush one time too many). I was sent to the base hospital at Plei Me 'for observation'. They pumped me full of Valium; I slept a lot; the symptoms faded rapidly. After a week, the doctors could find nothing wrong with me. Neither could the shrink who spent a few hours prodding my psyche – if I had tried to tell him the truth, he would probably have thought I had just concocted a fantasy in the hope of getting a psychiatric discharge. So they declared me fit for duty and I went back into the bowels of the Green Machine.

Where I performed my soldierly duties well enough to earn a Bronze Star. My lieutenant kept a close eye on me for a few days, to make sure, I suppose, that I didn't suddenly start foaming at the mouth or speaking in tongues, and then, because he needed the Man with the Golden Nose, he put me back on point whenever there was an especially hairy mission to perform.

But something had profoundly changed in me. That apocalyptic vision of death and corruption had altered my perceptions. I did what I had to do out of loyalty to the men I served with, but all illusion was now stripped from me. I knew we were not going to win this war: I had quaffed the stench of defeat on a psychic wind, I had turned over the biggest rock in the country and seen the maggots crawling on the underside. I knew now that every death, on either side, was one more drop in a tidal wave of futility and waste. And there were times when that knowledge tore at my heart, for there was nobody I could share it with.

For the rest of my tour, you may be sure of it, I smoked no more pot. And as these things have a way of doing, my inability to share its benign balm made it all the more desirable to me. Time after time, when the other guys were passing joints or fellating the bore of a shotgun while someone else poured smoke into the breech, I cursed the chemical peculiarity that was Virginia's legacy to me. I felt shut out of the camaraderie that made our miserable existence tolerable. I longed to join them in the communal high, but was terrified at the thought of what even one toke might trigger. When the fumes got thick, I had to leave. Another olfactory visit to that vast charnel house might really drive me nuts, and I knew it.

What did I do instead? I began to drink. Not just the lukewarm beers that were plentiful in any base camp, but Jack Daniels, straight out of the bottle. Oh, I never did it on the night before we were scheduled to Go Out, at least not in the beginning, but when the other guys lit up their Thai sticks and pipes full of Laotian Brown Lung, I reached into my locker for the bourbon and sought out an empty bunker for another ride on what Willy Nelson called, in one of his greatest songs, 'The Amber Current'.

By the final weeks of my tour, I was walking a thin line indeed. Off duty, I had become a drunk, and there were days when I went into the field nursing God's own wrath of a hangover, which did nothing to increase my chances or my usefulness to the other guys. The lieutenant knew, and sometimes when he talked to me, I could see him weighing his decision: should I ground this guy before he gets himself or someone else zapped, or does he still have enough left to be of value?

It was getting harder and harder to pull myself together, especially there at the end. I was now a short-timer, subject to all the traditional fears of getting my ass shot off just before it was time for me to leave, and I was a borderline alcoholic to boot. Things were made even worse by the fact that we were now patrolling a region that had been in enemy hands for months and was known to be riddled with tunnels. Guess who was the Designated Tunnel Rat? Yes sir, it was Mr Golden Nose himself.

About ten days before I was due to rotate home came the mission that won me the Bronze Star and finished me as a soldier. Things were hot in our zone: lots of scrappy little clashes with NVA regulars, our resources stretched thin putting out tactical fires, and incessant demands from headquarters for the sort of intelligence one is more likely to find in a tunnel complex than on the body of some ordinary dead gook.

The one I sniffed out on that particular morning gave every promise of being a monster, a labyrinth that went God-knew-how far back inside a massive jungle-covered ridge.

There was a ritual to preparing for a tunnel-crawl. I stripped off everything except my basic clothing, took a flashlight, shouldered an empty pouch, and drew a special silencer-equipped .38 revolver (if you fired a regulation .45 in the confines of a tunnel, there was a good chance you'd rupture an eardrum). I felt like a matador donning the Suit of Lights before entering the bullring. Then I shook hands all around, trying not to observe those I'm-glad-it-aint-me expressions on the other guys' faces, got down on my belly and slithered in.

A few feet from the entrance, I paused to let my eyes become adjusted to the dark. The dank brown walls stretched ahead of me like the coils of an intestine. As silently as I could, I began to lever myself forwards with my elbows, keeping the flashlight in my left hand and the revolver in my right. At the first fork in the tunnel, I paused again. Which way to go? I needed some advance warning if there were live people down here. So once again, ritualistically, I reached for Virginia's magic bag and took a whiff.

Instantly, my smeller prickled with new sensitivity. The scents from the righthand tunnel were old and stale, but from the left came a trace of recently boiled rice – an underground kitchen, perhaps, or even a command post. I went that way, the tunnel broadening slightly. I discovered the command post by falling into it. Whoever had been living here, they'd had time to fix things up rather comfortably: desks and chairs, a couple of cold lanterns, a radio set, crusted rice bowls, some sleeping pallets. All the comforts of home, VC style. After untangling myself, I shone the light around and found what I was hoping to find: a cardboard box full of what appeared to be old radio messages, a couple of folded maps with marks on them (no booby trap; I could smell those, too), the sort of stuff that gave the intelligence analysts a hard-on.

But as I gathered up this bounty and stuffed it in the pouch slung over my shoulder, I was blasted by a new wave of scent: hot, fleshy, sanguine, tainted with fear, sweat, and pain. Somewhere in the tunnels ahead was a hospital. If I could force myself into that loathsome reek, I might find more documents, perhaps fresher and more timely than the relics I had already bagged.

Moving very slowly now, I entered the tunnel that led away from the command post, the smell of the hospital becoming almost unbearable as I advanced. There was candlelight ahead. The tunnel went upwards and beyond the lip of earth, I sensed an expanded space. I could smell human habitation, too, but the scent of blood and bandages and sweat was so powerful that I could not tell if it came from occupants recently moved or still there. A wounded VC could be very dangerous. I shut off my own light and decided I needed some more precise olfactory input. Time for another hit off the pot-pourri bag.

This time, I got more than I bargained for when I raised my head over the entrance and peered in. Christ, what an abattoir was there! Five or six cots, all of them rusty with old blood, a dented operating lamp connected to a dead generator, a pile of basic surgical instruments near an old-fashioned boiling-water steriliser, rolls of bandages, a few jars of ether. And a big corrugated washtub full of putrid human parts – arms and feet and blackened lumps of tissue. It looked positively mediaeval.

Then the full wave hit me, with so much force I almost fell back into the tunnel. I smelled, and *felt*, the agony of every wounded man who had been brought here. Suddenly I saw this whole war as my enemy must have seen it: endless effort, endless pain, endless suffering, endless hiding from our planes and artillery, years and years of it, and still burning fiercely beneath all that, a raw, primal determination to be rid, once and for all, of the foreigners who had held this land in bondage since antiquity. It was a staggeringly simple perception, but it turned my mind inside-out. I felt the hopelessness and suffering of every man who had been treated in this room, and I also felt their pride, the determination of those men to bear any pain, any suffering, if by doing so they could move their cause forward by a single inch. The hospital I had been in was no Disneyworld, but it was a suite at the Plaza compared to this primitive butcher shop. What a foe they were! How could we hope to outlast them?

Then I smelled, and saw, the wounded man. He rose from his cot like a wraith: emaciated. terrified, his face consumed by two black-lacquer eyes that burned with fever. Now I was belted by the char of the gangrene that was devouring him. His torso was wrapped in slime-covered bandages, and I was sure they were the only thing holding his guts inside. I got a burst of his pain, too, and it was almost more than I could bear. Maybe his comrades would come back for him when our unit had left the area, although it didn't seem likely that he had that much time left. One thing for certain: I could not shoot him like a dog.

'It's okay,' I said, shaking my head and pointing at my pistol. 'I won't kill you. Just lie back down and I'll leave.'

Of course, he didn't understand a word. I held up both my hands and made placating gestures. I was going to back out of the room and his existence would be our little secret. There was a pile of ragged, torn, bloody uniforms in one corner of the room, but I had already decided not to look for any more papers in their pockets – it would have been too much like sticking my hands into other men's gaping wounds.

As I started to back away, I spotted the AK-47 he'd been hiding by his side. Though it must have cost him immense pain to do so, he was slowly swinging it in my direction, his eyes glowing like coals.

'No! It's not necessary!' I yelled to him, but even as the words came out, my hand swung up and the .38 barked twice, its reports muffled by the silencer. And I felt, *almost as hard as he did*, the impact of the bullets as they tore through his ruined body; I also felt the last dying flicker of determination that made him pull the trigger of his own weapon, emptying the whole clip in one long roaring burst that blew the bed next to his in half. And I felt him die, still hating me.

How long after that I lay there, I don't know. Long enough for the lieutenant to send somebody in after me. When they dragged me out into the sunlight, he took one look at me and knew I was finished. But the stuff I brought out in my satchel, along with the other odds and ends my rescuers had filched from the pockets of those bloody uniforms, actually proved to be valuable information, so he wrote me up for the medal.

I stayed in the base camp until my time was up, drinking heavily, staring into space mostly, trying not to relive that moment when I felt the impact of *my own bullets* snuffing out the existence of a brave man who had been keeping himself alive by sheer willpower and consuming hatred for his enemies. I was so hungover on the morning I was lifted out that I puked out of the helicopter – my last contribution to the soil of Vietnam.

The rest, as they say, is history – literary history, anyhow. There was money put away for graduate school, but I took it and moved to New York instead, just as the city was turning into one of the nation's two biggest hippie meccas. For the whole time I'd been with Virginia, and during odd moments of nostalgia during my 'Nam tour, I'd kept working on that huge, romantic, Thomas-Wolfeian novel – fanciful autobiography, most of it – whose avowed theme was to capture the essence of that Ball-Before-Waterloo period of the late fifties and early sixties, before the death of innocence and the collapse of the American Dream as my parents had lived it, and I had absorbed it, during my early adolescence.

The writing was (need I even tell you?) a gushing amalgam of Kerouac, Wolfe, Fitzgerald, Hemingway, and every other writer whose work had given me a hard-on during my formative years. With my graduate-school grubstake and a part-time job, I figured I would be all set to do the Young-Writer-in-New-York bit for two or three years, and at the end of that time, naturally, give birth to a great novel.

I arrived in Manhattan near the end of 1966, still suffering from periodic 'Nam-mares and bad flashbacks, but still young and so grateful to have survived combat that I felt, on my better days, not unlike I had during my affair with Virginia: freshly laundered nerve endings, pumped with Possibilities, ready to drink in the scene and spew out the words.

Trouble was, I expected to find the *same* New York I'd read about in Wolfe and Kerouac: Bohemian cafés with chequered tablecloths and drippy Chianti bottles, great jazz, wild poets reading their sequels to 'Howl', and hip intellectuals sitting up all night discussing books, movies and music.

What I found instead was a three-year block party thrown by a chaotic alliance of cultural anarchists, political zealots who harboured all the good will and tolerance of Joe Stalin's favourite judges, puffed-up media pundits, and greed-crazed record company executives. I was armed with a theoretical knowledge of what Young-Writers-in-New-York were *supposed* to do with their careers, but that aspect of my book-learnin' was hopelessly out of date. Nobody gave a shit about big, romantic, traditional novels any more. In my small southern college, I had been regarded as a rebel; in the Big Apple in late 1966, I was hopelessly middle-class.

Off-balance from the start, I foundered. I had, God knows, as much reason to loathe the Vietnam War as anyone, but I boiled with rage every time I saw the TV images of protestors vilifying or even spitting on returning vets whose only crime – like mine – was that they had survived their tour.

But as 1967 dawned and the bloodbath increased, I, too began to oppose it, at least in my mind. The war had started to stink (as I knew all too literally) like fish gone bad in the sun. By then, it lacked even the tragic existential grandeur of the French débâcle, that operatic, Foreign-Legion-to-the-front sense of a once-great empire dying like an old Gauloise butt hissing-out in the mud. It was not just the bull-headed stupidity of our 'body-count' tactics that offended me, it was also the deplorable lack of *style* that characterised the whole American effort on any level above the regimental: thousands of young men just like me being fed into a meatgrinder by generals who specialised in management theory instead of honest-to-God warfare and who probably had cement deer in their yards at home.

Work on my novel sputtered, then died. That 'innocence' I had wanted to capture now seemed as remote as the Court of Versailles. I decided to make an all-out effort to plunge into the milieu in which I was stranded, and forget about trying to find what Wolfe and Kerouac had found in the city. I grew my hair long, bought some fashionably outlandish duds, and tried to blend in. Everybody I knew was awash in hedonistic abandon, grooving on the music, turning on, living for the day, etc., etc., the whole Party Line. Not to mince words, there was enough good fucking going on to exhaust a dog with two dicks.

Problem was, it was *all* fuelled by pot. In the words of my sometime-friend Norman Mailer, 'Sex has got to be pretty goddamn great to match even a quickie on pot', and, as he so often was in those days, Unca Norman was right. If you smoked, you flowed. You could participate in marathon conversations whose contents would stupefy with their banality if you were straight; you could wallow in music you would ordinarily consign to the cultural midden-heap after the first eight bars; you could laugh a lot, get the munchies, and score with any nearby chick who happened to look at you with even a flicker of interest.

And I wanted all that, wanted to immerse myself in What Was Happening; if I could not write like Thomas Wolfe any more, well then, I could become the madman chronicler of the craziest, horniest, yeastiest era since flappers and bathtub gin.

But – *God damn you, Virginia!* – every time I tried to get high, every time I toked on a soggy passed-around joint, I suffered an attack of hypersomia so close to clinical schizophrenia that I had to lurch out into the night and heave my Nachos into the nearest alley, leaving me sodden and slow and disoriented for days afterwards. Whatever she had done to my metabolism, the changes were permanent. While the circulating fumes of other people's tokes only made my eyes burn and my appetite for junk food increase, the first touch of cannabis on my own lung tissue always, always, threw me straight to the vestibule of my private Hell.

Imagine yourself a poor but goodhearted child, confronted with a vast display of toys and candy – all the things you'd ever wanted Santa to bring you, but your parents could never buy. And all that separates you from this bounty is a membrane as transparent as glass and the society around you has given you blanket permission to reach in and grab anything your heart desires. But every time you press your hands against that invisible barrier, it's like sticking a wet finger into a light socket. Imagine the frustration, the longing, the gnawing bitterness.

On every side, the century's greatest party was going full blast, and to groove with it all you had to do was smoke a little reefer and check your mind at the door. How I ached to join the dance! Because I could not, however, I became consumed with directionless anger and jealous envy of all those who were lustily soaking up enough memories of sensual pleasure to keep their hearts warmed up in the old-folk's homes, decades later.

At the age of twenty-five, then, I had become as crabby and cynical as the crustiest *NY Times* columnist railing against the excesses of youth. Jesus, I *wanted* those excesses to be mine, too, and I burned to write about them from the *inside*. There were weeks when I felt like a man with a permanent erection who could not, for the life of him, achieve a decent climax.

Damn you, Virginia!

What jolted me out of my funk – and led me down a creative path I had never contemplated before – was the legendary March on the

Pentagon, in October 1967. If I had not been able to lose myself in the hedonistic swirl of the times, I had at least been sharpening my sense of their politics. The word on the streets, as the event drew nigh, was close-to-Apocalyptic. The Johnson government was mobilising massive force to protect its symbolic Bastille; there might well be blood in the streets, and the radical crazies from the Left seemed hellbent on making sure there would be copious amounts of it. I wasn't sure just where I stood in the ideological spectrum, but if the Revolution really was about to happen, I was as well-positioned as anyone to be its John Reed. So I packed a notebook, a secondhand movie camera, and a vial full of uppers and hitched a ride – in a VW microbus full of tie-dyed Dead Heads who seemed to think it would be a lark to have their heads cracked by police batons – to Washington.

By sheer accident, I ended up in the vanguard of the horde that made the march. Even more: I managed to end up on the very steps of the Pentagon, with only two or three rows of protestors between me and a double row of bayonets. Believe me, this was not the vantage point I would have chosen. If the SDS lunatics really did try to storm the building and shooting did break out, I was ten feet from the muzzles and utterly held in place by the pressure, behind me, of approximately one hundred thousand people. I looked nervously over my shoulder: simmering in the ripe afternoon sunlight was a restless sea of people, waving banners, playing guitars, lofting effigies and all manner of weird cultic fetishes. Before me loomed the guarded ramparts of Power. And off to the side, on the edge of a parking lot, Allen Ginsberg and the Fugs were chain-dancing, chanting their Pentagon Exorcism: 'Out, demon, out!'

Then, as I looked around at the snipers posted on the roof and the CIA types in sunglasses muttering into their headsets, at the banks of TV cameras and lights and microphones, while the multitude behind me chanted *'The whole world is watching!'* I felt a sudden breakthrough to exaltation. At that instant, the whole damned world *was* watching, and I was at Ground Zero. The historian in me came wide awake, even as the rational part of me was half-sick with fear. No, it was not really the Bastille, or even the Palace Square in Petrograd, but there were enough similarities to get my adrenalin pumping as it used to when I was pulling point in the jungles.

It was, as they say, A Moment, and during that measureless interval, the writer in my soul stirred vigorously to life.

Suddenly, from around the flanks of the main steps, two flying wedges of gas-masked MPs charged into the crowd. Tear gas canisters popped and clubs began thudding into flesh. They were obviously under orders to move the mass of people back and simply to spread fear, and I instantly recognised, behind the lenses of their gas masks, a look I had seen all too often in combat. Knees drove into groins, and hippy-length hair was yanked out by the fistful. You can bet your ass the crowd dispersed, or tried to. I saw an opening to the left and wormed my way out of the mêlée, doing a bit of groin-kneeing myself, my eyes streaming tears from the gas.

And as I stood gasping for breath and groping for my handkerchief, I found myself standing a few feet away from Norman Mailer. He looked as wild as a bull with three pies in his hump, head lowered, ham-sized fists clenched, those tangled trademark eyebrows practically grinding together with determination. Taking a deep breath, he marched defiantly into a line of US Marshals blocking his path.

Christ, I was with Thoreau at the moment he was choosing to let himself get hauled off to the pokey! Without thinking, I ran forward and dove into the knot of people surrounding a man whom I considered America's finest living writer.

The marshals, evidently, had been warned to look out for Mailer and not to rough him up. They were under no such instructions with regards to myself, however, and by the time we found ourselves sitting in the same sweatbox of a police van, I was nursing a loose tooth, a split lip, a cauliflower ear and a bruised right hand from the one good punch I'd managed to land during the fracas.

At first, both of us were too winded, too speedy with adrenalin, to do more than nod. After a while, though, Norman stuck out his hand and introduced himself.

'I know who you are, man. What you did back there took some guts.'

'You too, unless my personal magnetism is greater than I supposed it to be.'

Jesus, he actually talks like he writes! I thought.

'Call it research. I'm a writer, too, and there's a story in all this that somebody's got to write.'

Norman looked at me sternly, pulling rank.

'That's why I'm here as well, sonny.'

I shrugged. I was a second-rate club fighter suddenly thrown into the ring with the heavyweight champ. No contest.

'It's all yours, maestro,' I managed to croak.

As though by way of consolation, Norman patted me on the arm and said: 'That was a pretty fair right hook you got in, I'll say that. Where'd you learn to fight?'

'Army.'

He studied me with renewed interest.

'Infantry, I'll wager.'

'How'd you know?' I responded, forgetting, for a moment, that this was the man who had authored *The Naked and the Dead*.

'For a flash there, you had That Look. I saw it often enough in the Philippines.'

The authorities took their own sweet time booking and fingerprinting us, and while we waited, we swapped war stories, grunt to grunt. I even told him about the Golden Nose business, although of course I did not tell him about *how* I came to acquire that metabolic anomaly. He seemed genuinely fascinated.

'The sense of smell is unjustly neglected, much maligned by being written about only in connection with vaginas and toilets' (he pronounced the word with the gnarly Irish brogue he was then affecting in his public speech, 'ter-let'). Then he startled the hell out of me by writing his unlisted Brooklyn Heights address on a scrap of paper and saying: 'Write a war novel, kid. If you can write it as good as you talk it, you'll have something. When you've completed the first hundred pages or so, send 'em to me and I'll tell you if they're worth a shit.'

So as soon as I bailed myself out and got back to New York, I did just that. I fussed with outlines and chronologies and made some false starts, but then, one lonely night when I was about to crack the seal on a fresh bottle of bourbon and hammer myself to sleep, I remembered Virginia's pot-pourri bag. I had not even fondled the damned thing since 'Nam, except to pack it away in a bottom drawer. But the instant I remembered it, clarity enveloped me like a gilded halo on a Byzantine icon.

My hands shook as I retrieved it, untied the drawstrings and put my nose down into whatever essences still brooded there for me, compounded to match the profile of my soul by a woman who had become, in my rational mind, almost a myth.

One hit was all it took, and I was back in Vietnam, on a trip as vivid as anything the acid-heads could have conceived. It was as though my senses had become transposed: nose for eyes, scent for touch, turning me into one big quivering dousing-rod of a receptor.

But there was one crucial difference: along with the rot, pain, terror, blood and corruption came the bronzen scent of pure courage, the plough-horse-stubborn effluvia of endurance and stoicism from the warriors. Not only my comrades, but those at-the-time faceless little men who outlasted every massive horror our technology could throw at them, who could march twenty miles and still fight a battle, fuelled by nothing but a few handfuls of congealed old rice.

It would be an exaggeration to say that the novel 'wrote itself' in that moment of epiphany, but the sculptural outlines of it manifested themselves like a bronze by Rodin. I was visited, almost palpably, by the two main characters: one would be an amalgam of every brave American I had ever fought with, and the other would be a fleshed-out version of the gaunt, pain-ravaged enemy soldier I had killed in that reeking tunnel-complex. The story would be *theirs*, their lives and deeds and sufferings and ultimate deaths, as intertwined as Yin and Yang. I would grind no axes, make no apologies, follow no agendas. My model would be *The Iliad*, nothing less.

Six months after that night, I sent Mailer the first three hundred pages. Two weeks went by before I got a growly-voiced telephone call from him: 'Come over and let's get drunk together, you son of a bitch! You've written a great book.'

As soon as I'd hung up, I whispered: *Thank you, Virginia!*

Thanks to Norman's recommendation, the completed manuscript landed right on the desk of Putnam's senior fiction editor. They bought it, but warned that it could not actually be published until 'the political climate' was right. I never quite understood that (and Mailer fulminated about it in commiseration), but for once in my life, my timing was perfect: six months later, the film *The Deer Hunter* came out, to extravagant reviews, and the media moguls took that as a sign that it was now okay to treat the Vietnam War as History, not as some untouchable sore on the body politic that equated with box-office poison. I thought that movie was the most over-rated piece of shit I'd ever seen (and flayed it savagely in a critique for *Commentary* after my own novel had squatted on the bestseller list for a few months), but I can't deny the importance it had in paving the way for my book.

A lot of plum writing jobs fell my way after that, and of course the film Paramount made out of the Vietnam novel copped three Oscars. What followed was a predictable curve: three Trophy Wives (and three messy divorces), a long-running column in *Esquire*, six more novels (each received respectfully, but none, to my mind, on par with the first one), and a drinking habit that was probably spotting my liver by the time I was forty. And of course, the usual round of celebrity gigs at workshops and literary soirées, the most recent of which was the one at my Alma Mater, terminating in that sour encounter with the green-eyed coed and her proper little story.

Mine was a success story, to be sure. But there were nights when me and the Jack Daniels pulled out that old, yellowed, first-novel manuscript and I wept to see the untainted purity of so much that was in it, ached for the now-impossible dream of finishing that paean to pre-Vietnam innocence. If I had only known a tenth of what I knew now about my craft, what a fucking book that would have been!

But of course I could no more finish that book now than I could will myself to become eighteen again.

But no less could I leave my old campus without once more following that route to The Gardens. Would Virginia know of my career? Would she sometimes ache to remember our idyllic nights and our ravenous hunger for the feel and taste and (of course!) the smell of each other's flesh? She would be, what? Forty-five, forty-six, now? Had she found 'by instinct' another mate? Had she buried her mother, or merely repotted her?

After so many years, that period of my life had become a legend even to me. The pot-pourri bag was still with me, like a talisman, but I had never opened it again since the night it conjured, as though by magic, the shape and structure of my first, best, published book. Whatever other rewards and satisfactions I had known in my career, Magic had not been an ingredient – I used up the last of it from the pot-pourri bag like some latter-day Merlin who had hoarded one valedictory spell to cast at King Arthur's flaming burial-ship as it sailed into the mist between worlds.

Now, verging on fifty, I was a practical, world-weary man, and it was inconceivable that the things I thought I had seen and experienced in The Gardens had been real. Such things do not happen outside of fantasy tales . . . or dreams.

But just the same, I thought as I drove that once-familiar route towards The Gardens, *I had to know*. If I could, after so many years, reaffirm that my private mythology was indeed based on real events, a real and unforgettable love affair, perhaps the grace of Magic would touch me again. If it did, and my liver didn't give out, what strange and marvellous tales might I yet be able to write?

The hamlet of Haynesville – at whose only traffic light I had first seen that sign pointing towards The Gardens – was now a fair-sized town, the little general store was gone, replaced by a Wal-Mart and a Blockbuster video emporium. The hand-painted sign was also gone, of course, but that was no surprise. I was driving on automatic pilot, riding a tide of memory that flowed inexorably towards the site of my own personal shrine and, if she was still there, its priestess.

Once more, I drove through the narcotic opulence of honeysuckle, now in full riotous bloom. I parked on the highway's shoulder and approached the house quietly, instinctively going into that heightened state of sensory alert I had known on combat missions, although it struck me as slightly absurd that my body should react in such an extreme manner.

Evidently, Virginia, or somebody, was still in business, for The Gardens were as lush and well-tended as I remembered them. The house, however, when it finally came into view, had a dilapidated air to it: paint peeling in long dingy strips, one shutter hanging askew like a droopy eyelid. As I silently mounted the steps, I wondered: should I knock?

There was no need. The front door was open, and when I peered through the screen at the dark hallway, I saw her standing in silhouette at the entrance to the kitchen, arms folded placidly, as though my appearance after a quarter-century was neither surprising nor unexpected.

I entered and walked towards her, then stopped halfway, just looking at her. She had fleshed out some, but that only made her seem earthier, riper. Her cornsilk hair had turned a lustrous grey, but it still had the flow and fullness of youth. An astonishing sword-stroke of desire cut through me. We appraised each other for a moment, then she spoke:

'I knew you would be coming.'

'How did you know that, Virginia?'

She laughed, and there was just enough of an edge to the sound to make my skin prickle.

'You forget how much I know about genetics, about the power of blood and kin.'

'I haven't forgotten anything, and I have no idea what you're babbling about.'

Again that wise, knowing, sad and somehow chilling laugh.

'It's your son's birthday. What loving father would miss such an occasion?'

'What the fuck are you talking about, woman?'

'The last time we made love – the night before you destroyed some of my most precious plants by tearing yourself free of their embrace – that was the night, and part of the process, that made me pregnant.'

Now she sighed, with genuine regret.

'If only you had stayed unconscious for a little while longer, if only I had had a chance to explain things to you, my God, what a life we would have enjoyed together!'

She shook her head as though banishing the phantoms of memory.

'But enough of that! What's past is past, what's done is done. And now, it's time for you to meet your son.'

At that instant, my arms were pinned by a grip so fierce and unyielding that none of my rusty, basic training counter-moves could budge it. I did manage to drive one elbow into the chest of the powerful man who was restraining me, but I might as well have smashed it into a cinder-block.

Helpless, I watched Virginia come towards me, unscrewing the lid of a mason jar full of cotton wadding. As the first fumes of the chloroform seared my nostrils and napalm started bursting in my brain, I struggled like a gored bull, but the iron grip that held me never lessened.

The last thing I heard her say, as she clamped the jar over my mouth and nose, was surprisingly gentle:

'Welcome back to The Gardens, my only love.'

It has become difficult for me to think of 'time' in terms of days and weeks; now it seems more natural to think in seasons. With effort, however, I can for brief intervals reclaim some dim simulacrum of my consciousness as it was before the transformation, and during those brief, disturbing, spells, I estimate the passage of almost a year.

At first, until Virginia concocted the nostrums and aroma-blends that kept me both paralysed and numb to pain, I was restrained, by padded wires, to numerous stakes, like a vulnerable sapling. I was catheterised, of course, since urine, while I still produced it, is acidic and bad for my soil. My solid wastes, however, simply dropped from their usual orifice, fertilising the ground below. Virginia was always a believer in organic horticulture and during my frequent early moments of madness, the writer in me – still alive and kicking somewhere deep inside – found the very idea highly risible.

Now that I have taken root, of course, the wires and stakes are gone.

My son, who is indeed a strong young man, even though he cannot or will not speak, and might be judged by the outside world as a simpleton, proved to have a good heart. When I dropped my shit, he cleaned me tenderly and applied ointments to my frequent rashes.

Now he waters me, twice a day, and assists his mother, very efficiently, in preparing the nutrients that are regularly mixed with my soil. Virginia seems pleased with my development.

She still loves me, too. She plays classical music for me, an art form I have become very fond of in my present state. Sometimes she speaks to me tenderly and caresses my stems and kisses my new buds, of which I am very proud. She has also been kind enough never to hold a mirror up to the dwindling remnants of my vision. In the early months, when I was paralysed by her potions, I was unable to speak; now, even if I wanted to, I could not, for my mouth has become some sort of polyp-fringed orifice, not unlike – I assume from the sensations – the lips of a Venus Fly Trap.

Since the time when I no longer needed to be drugged or restrained, I have, in fact, known only one moment of terror: the night when she came towards me, her still-beautiful hands sheathed in gardening gloves, holding a bright pair of pruning shears.

'It's time to transplant those lovely buds into The Garden,' she said. 'I'm not certain, but I suspect you'll find the results interesting, something like being cloned and something like giving birth. I don't think it will hurt.'

But it did, and the thick, matter-clotted scream I produced startled her so much that she dropped the shears after the second cutting, apologised and hurriedly administered some sort of aromatic anaesthetic, so that the rest of the procedure was indeed painless.

I can no longer be positive, but I think that scream was the last recognisable human sound I ever made.

Now, although I can no longer 'see', I am discovering a whole new spectrum of senses. She tells me that my buds have matured nicely, out in The Gardens, and her intuition was correct: I *do* feel a growing sense of communal awareness with all the living, flowering, beautiful species that she tends so lovingly.

I sense that Spring is coming. It's a very pleasant sensation: a drowsy, slow, sensuous *awakening* – I would never have guessed that photosynthesis could feel so sexy.

I dream a lot, as the last of my formerly human senses atrophy into ghostly wisps. And in my dreams, I often seem to be floating through The Gardens, like one of those glorious fireflies whose golden arabesques lent true Magic to the first night when Virginia and I walked, hand in hand, through her world, when she first cast upon me the spell that would lure me into that world and bind me to her forever.

Even as I had wanted, from the first time she made love to me.

Yes, my dreams are often beautiful, and unbounded by any human measurement of Time.

I wonder what my flowers will look like in May, when the scent of honeysuckle is so very, very sweet.

William R. Trotter lives in Greensboro, North Carolina, with his wife, fantasy writer Elizabeth Lustig, and the youngest of their three sons. Since 1987 he has been Senior Writer for *PC Gamer Magazine* and in that capacity has published more than a thousand reviews and columns about entertainment software. The author of thirteen published books, including *Priest of Music: The Life and Times of Dimitri Mitropoulos*, *A Frozen Hell: The Russo-Finnish War of 1939–40* and the novel *Winter Fire* (currently being developed as a movie), his genre short fiction has appeared in such magazines and anthologies as *Fantasy Book*, *Night Cry*, *Deathrealm* and *The Song of Cthulhu*. About the preceding novella, he says: 'I've always wanted to blend, as seamlessly as possible, the mood and style of good literary fiction with the conventions of the horror genre. "Honeysuckle" is the latest experiment in that quest. And yes, I did know Norman Mailer during the 1960s.'

Final Departure
GAHAN WILSON

S'ki Tok paused in his thoughtful, careful study of the survivor's diary in order to glance up at its author and when he saw that the poor fellow was staring at him apprehensively he twitched his lower facial tentacles gently in order to make the species mask he was wearing show the chap a reassuring smile.

It was, as he knew from personal experience, which he still clearly and painfully remembered, a very hard thing to see a total stranger perusing intimate, confessional things you had written with what seemed at the time to be the sure and certain knowledge they would never be read.

'Please do not be concerned,' the face mask translated from S'ki Tok's original *N'yaktanese*. 'What you have written here will only be read by the most scrupulously protective professionals, such as myself. It will never be generally disseminated in anything like its original form and it will – as the accumulated information of prior diaries previously studied have done – greatly aid in assisting other survivors who will be finding themselves undergoing the same difficult emotional and intellectual transitions and adaptations which you are presently suffering.'

The survivor rubbed the thick hair growth on his lower face thoughtfully, cleared his throat a time or two as it was still proving difficult for him to take up the long-abandoned habit of talking, and spoke in a whisper which had already become noticeably less rasping than it had been when he was first discovered.

'I find it astounding that so many others have gone through what I've just experienced,' he said at last. 'I was certain I was undergoing something absolutely unique. It's still very hard to imagine that it . . . well, that it . . .'

S'ki Tok took pity on the poor fellow's groping for words. He opened and closed several lateral pincers, which caused the species suit to wave a consoling hand and shrug philosophically.

'Believe me, in a very short period of time you will discover that the whole business has almost automatically become much easier to deal with,' he said. 'Not only will you find that your own psychological processes are amazingly capable of dealing with what now appears to be an ungraspable position, but you will be enormously aided by personal contact with the many other survivors who you will shortly meet. I can see that your brief acquaintance with me, as another survivor, has already helped you to manage the situation.'

'Oh, it has!' said the survivor most emphatically. 'It truly has, and I do want you to understand that I really appreciate your being so helpful!'

He paused, obviously confused and flustered.

'Still, it's just that—' he began, and then broke off to look up at S'ki Tok with a suddenly stricken expression. 'You may think what I am going to say is terrible. I'm afraid you may even hate me for it!'

This time S'ki Tok caused his species suit to raise both hands in a gentle silencing gesture and the species mask to express the very tenderest of understanding smiles.

'Forgive me if I seem presumptuous,' he said, 'but I imagine I know what are you trying to tell me. Would you please be tolerant enough to let me speculate aloud?'

The survivor looked at him silently for a moment and then slowly nodded.

'Very well, then,' S'ki Tok said, 'I suspect you are thinking something very much along the lines of what *I* thought when, a long time ago, what has happened to you also happened to me.'

The survivor studied him intently, with burning eyes. He said nothing, but the clenching of his jaw and hands revealed his tension and suspense.

S'ki Tok, following the clear instructions of the declassification manual, let this vitally important moment stretch out a little longer before he spoke again.

'Please do not take offence,' he said, 'and please do not think I am in any way expressing disapproval of you. What I am going to say is based entirely on what I myself went through during trials and tribulations almost identical to those you have so recently experienced.'

The survivor swallowed violently. Sweat now beaded his brow. Both of these symptoms corresponded exactly to to those described in the species reactions subsection of the manual which was now scrolling helpfully in the interior of S'ki Tok's mask.

Thus encouraged, S'ki Tok proceeded.

'When I was found, as I found you,' he said, 'I, too, was astounded and amazed. I gaped at my visitor in absolute and complete bewilderment! I had never again expected to see such a sight! I found – and I am still embarrassed to have to confess this! – I was appalled to discover that I wanted to *kill* him!'

The survivor groaned deeply, then lowered his head and buried his face behind his knees and folded arms. After a pause, moving very carefully, S'ki Tok's suit reached out a hand and softly laid it on the poor fellow's shoulder.

'But I did not kill him,' S'ki Tok said. 'As you did not kill me.'

The survivor stiffened as his body squeezed in on itself.

'I observed you reach for your weapon when you saw me and thought I did not see you,' said S'ki Tok gently. 'I saw you grip it hard. And then I saw you take your hand away from it, just as I took my hand away from my weapon that long, long time ago.'

Slowly, almost cell by cell it seemed, the survivor's body began to relax.

'You passed the test,' said S'ki Tok, 'and you passed it well. But now there has come another, the one that presently tortures you. It is a far subtler test and one which is almost more painful because it is – dare I say it? – *humiliating*!'

As the manual warned, there was a distinct returning of the tenseness. S'ki Tok pressed the suit's hand on the fellow's shoulder as reassuringly as he could.

'Please do forgive me for using that word, but it is the only one that accurately applied to my condition, and that is why I suspect it may apply to yours.'

S'ki Tok leaned forward just a little to look more closely at his companion as the survivor raised his head from its hiding place in order to look back at him.

'You are haunted by an awful wish, are you not?' asked S'ki Tok.

The survivor blinked, gritted his teeth and nodded.

'You secretly wish it was as it was before I turned up, do you not?' asked S'ki Tok. 'That it was finally all done with. That the whole thing was at last completed. Settled. Finished. You do not *want* to wish it, oh, I know that, I know that well – but you still can't *help* wishing it.'

He took his hand from the poor fellow's shoulder and sat back, his mask smiling down.

'Do not worry,' said S'ki Tok, 'I had the exact same thought. We have *all* had the same thought, every one of us. And from personal experience I know it will go away. Believe me, for I speak the truth – it will go away.'

He studied the survivor's face and was pleased to see it was slowly relaxing and that the eyes were losing some of their furtiveness.

S'ki Tok picked up the survivor's precious diary and stood.

'And now I think it is time we left and boarded the ship,' he said, holding out the hand of the species suit.

After only a tiny pause the survivor took that hand and allowed himself to be helped to his feet.

'Ah, wait, till you see the ship,' said S'ki Tok. 'It is huge. And astoundingly well-equipped. It has everything for every one of us!'

He gave a comforting little laugh, then he opened the crude door of the survivor's hut and stepped outside.

'Come along,' said S'ki Tok.

And the last man alive on Earth obediently followed after.

Gahan Wilson was born in Evanston, Illinois, and now lives on Long Island. He is a winner of the World Fantasy Award and the Bram Stoker Award, and has been called 'a national treasure' by Erica Jong. His cartoons, which were once kindly described as 'genuinely traumatic', have appeared in a wide number of magazines, primarily *Playboy*, *The New Yorker*, *Punch*, *Paris Match* and *National Lampoon*, and something like twenty anthologies of them have been collected through the years, including *Still Weird* and *Gahan Wilson's Even Weirder*. The editor of such anthologies as *First World Fantasy Awards* and *Gahan Wilson's The Ultimate Haunted House* (with Nancy A. Collins, and based on the CD-ROM game), he has also written several children's books, a couple of mystery novels and an uncounted number of short stories, some of which were recently assembled in the collection *The Cleft and Other Odd Tales*, together with illustrations by the author. He writes a regular book review column for *Realms of Fantasy* magazine and is presently working on an animated special for television and a full-length animated film. About the preceding story he says: 'One of the things that is most obviously going to happen when we come into contact with an intelligent entity from another world is that we will have a lot of difficulty understanding one another. Not only will both be alien to the extreme, but so will our respective languages, the equipment we use to translate them and our basic assumptions about existence which essentially formed them. This last will probably be the most importantly misleading because each of us is likely to assume that they are shared with each other which, of course, they won't be.'

Pelican Cay

DAVID CASE

Prologue

They left another load of supplies down on the rocks this morning. I haven't bothered to pick them up yet, although I blinked out a message thanking them and letting them know I was still *all right*. There were three men in the boat. I think they were the same three as last time but they still appeared terrified. They kept looking up here and their faces were so white it seemed as if I'd turned the beam of the lamp onto them. They dropped the crates off – heaved them out, really – without ever touching the boat to shore. You'd think they'd know, by now, that I'm not infected. Still, I'm thankful for the supplies . . . they could just as well leave me, like the others.

I've been here two weeks now, in the lighthouse, and I'm getting much better at signalling with the big lamp and at receiving messages from the ships. They sent too fast, at first. But thank God for the light, there would be no way to communicate without it and it feels better to be in touch with the world, even if only by lamp – even if they won't believe me.

I wonder if my paper knows I'm here; if they've tried to contact me? What a story! And how absurd to think of it that way, now . . . as a newspaperman instead of . . . what I am. I wonder, too, what they'll do about me when the others are all dead? I don't think that will be too long now. I've been observing them through the glasses and they seem less furious, slower, weaker. They're all very thin. I saw three of them eating a dead one, earlier. I don't know if they killed him or not and I don't know if they are beginning to regain human instincts . . . like feeding. But they didn't seem ravenous or even very determined about it, they were just pulling ribbons of flesh off his bones and chewing them in a desultory manner, as if it were something they dimly recalled doing in the past.

A few of them are gathered on the docks now, not too near the water. They're terrified of water. They seem to be looking out at the patrolling ships or maybe beyond, to the dim line of the Keys. I can see the Keys quite clearly from the tower. It really is a remarkable vista, the lone line of islands spanned by the bridges. It was just over two weeks ago that I drove along those linked islands. A long time. I think about it often, too, for I have a great deal of time to think and, terrible as it was, it is better than thinking of the future...

I

United States Highway One begins in Fort Kent, Maine, at the borders of icy Canada, and ribbons all the way down the Eastern seaboard, spanning the islands in the tropical Gulf like concrete cartilage linking the spine of some coral sea beast. I'd followed that road from New York, spent the night in Miami and, in the early morning, with the bay on one hand and the straits on the other and the dew still sparkling on the tropical flowers, I motored slowly over the bridges. I had plenty of time and was enjoying the drive. I'd not been in the Keys for years and noticed the highway had developed in terms of human progress – at night, I feared, a neon holocaust threatened – but the morning mood was changeless. Like feathered boomerangs behind a screen of palm trees, the pelicans were banking and sliding sideways into the blue waters of the Straits of Florida. Behind the planing birds the sun climbed from the Atlantic and began its arc towards the Dry Tortugas and Mexico. A few early anglers were fishing from the bridges, not as efficiently as the pelicans; a shrimp boat parallelled my passage, high pronged masts distinctive, draped with net; a young couple wearing scuba gear basked on thrusting black rocks, drinking wine from the bottle and laughing with white teeth. It was a pleasant trip on a pleasant morning. I figured my stay would be pleasant, too. If I got a story out of it, that was fine and, if I didn't, that was fine, too. There are worse things than an expense account assignment in Florida, I thought.

And how wrong I was.

The Mangrove Inn was built out over the water, the outdoor platform at the back raised on wooden stilts. A tourist was on the platform, having his picture taken beside a hanging shark. The shark looked mildly embarrassed. I parked the car and went into the bar. It was air-conditioned and traditional, with fish nets on the walls and starfish ashtrays. I was a bit early and didn't think my contact was there yet, but as I moved to the bar the girl stood up from a dark corner booth and raised her eyebrows.

'Mister Harland?'

I nodded and she walked towards me, a pretty girl, blonde, wearing a light cotton dress. She had nice eyes and a nice smile. She said, 'I'm Mary Carlyle,' and held her hand out. 'Dr Elston asked me to meet you.'

'I'd expected him.'

'Yes. He was . . . well, busy, I suppose. Anyhow, I had to cross over and he thought perhaps I could bring you back to Pelican in my boat.'

'Yes, all right,' I said. Then: 'What's Pelican?'

She looked mildly surprised. 'You don't know?'

'No. Elston wrote me. He asked me to meet him here. He asked me not to write or phone – in fact, he made rather a point of that – just to be here, today.' I made a gesture, manifesting my presence. 'My paper seemed to think he was newsworthy – eminent biochemist and all that – and I wasn't inclined to pass up a trip to the Keys. I'm a bit intrigued by all the secrecy, I must say.'

'Oh, that. It's very secret on Pelican,' she said, smiling.

I had an idea that she didn't really feel like smiling when she said that. It was a shadowed smile . . . or, perhaps, a smile that foreshadowed something.

'It must be . . . since I have no idea what it is.'

'Pelican Cay. It's an island.'

'And that's where Elston is?'

'Um hum.'

The bartender came wandering down the bar, flicking at the polished surface with a towel. I asked Mary if she would like a drink and she said, 'Of course.' I liked her immediately. I also thought it could do no harm to talk to her. I had no idea how much she knew about why Elston had summoned me, but if it was anything at all, it was more than I knew. I was completely in the dark and curious about the things that – that no one should ever have to know. We got a couple of tall rum punches and went back to the booth. I sat opposite with a starfish ashtray between us, both of us in cool shadows.

'Are you his assistant?'

'Oh, no,' she said, laughing. 'Do I look like a biochemist?'

'Not really.'

'I'm relieved. Actually, I live on Pelican. I'm one of the few natives, a real Conch. I was born there and never saw much reason to leave. Until recently . . .' she added.

I waited but she didn't follow that up.

I said, 'Have you any idea what it's about?'

She shrugged and sipped her drink, gazing at me across the rim of the glass.

'Or why Elston chose me?'

'Ummm,' she said.

'I don't know if you're familiar with my sort of work . . .'

'Don't be modest.'

'. . . but I don't write scientific papers and it seems . . . well . . . strange that Elston wanted to talk to me. Intriguing, in point of fact. A biochemist contacting a scandalmonger . . .'

Mary was laughing again. She said, 'Dr Elston chose you because of your well-known discretion.'

'Hardly.'

'Oh, yes. When you refused to reveal your sources to the investigating committee after you broke the Warden scandal, and risked going to jail . . . well, he feels he can trust you.'

'It's like that, is it?'

'Like that,' she said, suddenly serious.

Well, she obviously knew something. But she was fencing. I thought I might engage her at an oblique angle. I said, 'You know, Mary, I don't like being an investigative reporter.' She blinked, surprised. I managed a sheepish grin. 'I've always wanted to write a novel,' I told her, and that was true enough, but to my purpose. 'I've tried. Not recently. Platitudes have bested me . . . and time . . . and following the course of least resistance. I make investigations and I write about them. I've acquired a certain reputation. And yet . . . the media deform truth. And that, in itself, is a truth. A fact, given to the masses, becomes malleable, as if the printed page were a distorted looking-glass, casting anamorphic reflections. The most blatant lie acquires an aura of truth, truth, in turn, is shadowed and pigeonholed and compartmented to fit the reader's mind.' I shrugged, not looking at her. I was turning the starfish ashtray on the table between us.

'Strange talk from a newspaperman,' she said.

'Not so very strange. I'm no Diogenes, holding up a lantern. And yet . . . I do write the truth, be that as it may. And I want people to be truthful with me.' I looked up. 'Mary?' I said.

She flushed slightly.

She leaned closer; said, 'Look, I'd better level with you, Mister Harland . . .'

'Jack,' I said. 'And yes, you had.'

'All right. Jack. It was my idea to write to you. I sort of talked Dr Elston into it, with the help of a few drinks and a little flirting. Oh, he wanted to. I didn't force the idea on him. But he would never have done it, on his own. What I'm saying is . . . you may have come down here for nothing. Elston may not go through with it. But I figured it was worth a chance.'

Then you do know what it's about?'

'No, I don't.' Now she was playing with the ashtray, turning it back and forth like the pointers in a game of chance. 'He wouldn't tell me. But I do know he's doing something, some sort of work, that he doesn't want to do. He let me know that much, no more. He was . . . disturbed. More than disturbed. I got the impression that he's in deeper than he intended, that his work is being applied in a manner of which he does not approve.' She had a way of gesturing when she spoke, as if punctuating her words and making her statements profound – but it didn't seem intentional or mannered. She was just a lively girl who got things done . . . who had got me to the Keys. 'Dr Elston is a timid man, the classic scientist who knows little of humanity. He can be manipulated just as he manipulates his chemicals – just as I manipulated him into writing you. He was afraid to meet you today, Jack . . . afraid someone would find out.' My eyebrows went up. 'Oh, no, he's not being restricted in any way, nothing like that. But he's afraid. Afraid of his employers, afraid of his work. He trusts me, probably because I have no connection with those employers . . . or perhaps because he needs to trust someone. But he's given me no details.'

'So you're just a catalyst, causing reactions.'

'That's about it.'

'Who are these employers?'

'The government. A government agency.'

'Which agency?'

'I don't know.'

I looked at her. She said, 'Really . . . I don't.'

'It's getting interesting.'

'It can get more than interesting, I think. This agency has taken over a large portion of Pelican . . . fenced it off in a compound, posted guards all around it . . . ruined the island. And this happened just after the ban on germ warfare.'

She gazed thoughtfully at me.

'Is that it? Germ warfare?'

'Not that, I think. But something . . . that should be stopped. Elston wants it stopped. I suggested you. He'd heard of you, vaguely; he's not the sort to read newspapers. I told him about the Warden thing and convinced him that you could let the world know what's being done here, and thereby halt it, without implicating Elston. So that's the story, so far. I can't guarantee that he will talk to you, after all. As I said, he's a timid man; he may well back out. He looked a bit sick after telling me as much as he did, in fact. But I think he will and I hope he does.' She smiled. 'I have an interest in this, you see. I bitterly resent them ruining Pelican. It was a paradise, now it's like a prison. Why, they even fenced off my favourite beach!' Then, serious again, she said, 'Whatever they're doing there, it's really very secret. Since the agency took over, we can't even get an open telephone line out; have to channel all calls through a switchboard within the compound. That island is my home, Jack; you can imagine how I – and the other residents – feel about it. Jack, I work for the Coast Guard. Just a part-time thing. There's a supply depot there and a lighthouse just off shore and . . . well, even the Coast Guard has to go through the switchboard, even the lighthouse is only connected to Pelican by a cable. No radio. One of my duties, in fact, is to talk to the lighthouse keeper. Sam Jasper. He's very talkative.'

'A talkative lighthouse keeper?'

'Yep. Phones in all the time. You think maybe he's in the wrong line of work?'

'Well, talking to you is . . . interesting.'

'I hope it pays off,' she said.

I nodded. Our drinks were finished. I would have liked another and she was looking at her glass, but she had piqued my interest; I figured this might be a bigger story than I'd planned on. I said, 'Shall we go, then?' and we went.

II

In the launch, which she handled expertly, she told me a bit about Pelican Cay. I took my shirt off and leaned against the gunwale, enjoying the spray and listening to her. Pelican, she told me, was a small island with one town looping in a crescent around a natural harbour. It had a colourful history. The first inhabitants had been wreckers, salvaging cargo from ships that had gone aground on the unmarked reefs – and were often lured onto those reefs by the wreckers. I raised an eyebrow at that; she shrugged; that was how it had been. Construction of the lighthouse had finished the wrecking industry in the mid nineteenth century, however, and the locals had turned their bloodstained hands to cigar-making, salt refining and, of course, fishing. It had been as populous and important as most of the

Keys, for a while, but had declined after the Overseas Highway was completed in 1938, when the linked islands became more accessible and convenient. Mary was pleased by that; she liked Pelican as it was – as it had been before the agency moved in.

'Of course, that's exactly why they did move in,' she said. 'It's an easy place to guard, to keep isolated and secure – and any stranger who showed up would be instantly noticed. Oh, the odd tourist makes the crossing . . . not enough to spoil things, though – they add to the local colour by contrast, bring in some money and, most important, give the locals an audience to which to play. We Conches are all born actors.' She turned to smile at me. I recalled the way she gestured when she spoke. 'Shrimpers, fishermen, Cuban refugees, retired smugglers . . . but they all play up to their images.'

She made Pelican sound pleasant and I could well understand why she resented the intruders.

'What about accommodation?' I asked.

'There's an inn. It functions mostly as a bar these days, but they'll give you a room. The Red Walls.'

'What?'

'That's the name of the place. The Red Walls. Red as in blood, don't you know? The walls awash with blood. Used to be a smugglers' den and the shrimpers drink there now . . . quite a history to the place, probably a story in itself. The locals will be pleased to give you all the gory details . . . embellished, no doubt; they're rather proud of the reputation, they cherish infamy. Anyhow, you can check in there and I'll let Dr Elston know where you are and try to get him to contact you, all right?'

I agreed.

'And maybe . . .' a spray of salt water slanted from her cheek; she paused; then: 'Maybe you'd better not tell anyone who you are . . . why you're here, I mean. Just pretend to be a tourist. I don't expect they'd like it, if they knew Elston was talking to you . . . and he will feel better about it, anyway.'

'Oh, I'll use my famous discretion,' I said.

'I don't know if they'd . . .' she hesitated, then shrugged. She didn't continue. A moment later she pointed. 'There's the lighthouse.'

I saw the grey tower rising up, mild surf breaking at the base. I could make out the low outline of the island. The launch was quick and the island came up fast. I saw a stretch of water between the island and the lighthouse and, anticipating my query, Mary said, 'The lighthouse is off shore . . . sort of. About a hundred yards out, but there's a rock reef connecting the two so that you can walk out at low tide, if you're nimble. A reef and . . .' she smiled . . . 'a cable, connecting Sam Jasper to me. He'll be getting twitchy by now, with no one to talk to all morning.'

'Well, you are nice to talk to.'

She looked at me, tilting an eyebrow.

'The sheriff thinks so, too,' she said. 'He's my boyfriend.'

I said, 'So much for that.'

Pelican Cay came up.

White as bleached bones in the sunlight, it dazzled; the glare made the shadows solid slabs of blackness so that, adjacent, they did not relate. Light and shade did not flow together through grey transition, they existed in separate dimensions . . . just as the island could be perceived on two levels – a pleasant, sunwashed isle . . . and the base whence wreckers had lured ships to destruction. Now, physically divided by the fenced compound, the dichotomy was truer than insight, more solid than a mood. Seagulls screamed as they dived at the water . . . and the timeless cry could have been the wail of doomed sailors drowning in the surf. The heat was so great it seemed to obey gravity, heavy on my shoulders and, in that glaring heat, I felt a chill . . .

Then we were moving into the harbour, gliding past shrimp boats and a few cabin cruisers and some naked kids who were jumping off the dock. I noticed at least three waterfront bars. The screaming of the gulls faded; there was nothing sinister in the happy cries of the children. My mood passed.

Mary brought the launch into the Coast Guard slot and jumped nimbly out. I figured she would have no trouble crossing over the reef to the lighthouse. I tossed my overnight bag onto the dock and stepped out with seemly caution. Since she was the sheriff's girl there was little sense in risking a soaking by feigning nimbleness. She tied the boat to the iron stanchion with a deft, intricate loop that looked, to me, like a Gordian knot. We walked up the wooden planking and I paused to put my shirt on. I had already started to burn. The docks were fenced off and there was a customs shed, but the gates were open and no one stopped us as we passed into the street. A pair of shore patrolmen sauntered past, all dazzling white. They looked into one of the bars. They appeared more wistful than dutiful. The dark interior was inviting, textured shadows unlike those black umbrae that had so strangely chilled me as we sailed. in. But Mary said she would walk me to the inn and we set off along the curved waterfront. Most of the town's business fronted on the harbour and we walked past a turtle kraal, a ship's chandler, a Cuban cigar-maker busy in his window and a couple more bars. Then we came to the jail and the sheriff came out.

He was a tall, fair-haired man with dark aviator glasses and a chin as big and square as a boot. He had a big, white Stetson in his hand and when he saw Mary he put the hat on, so that he could take it off again as he greeted her. He gave her a big smile and then looked suspiciously at me – not official suspicion.

'Jerry, this is Jack Harland. Jack, Jerry Muldoon, Pelican's only lawman.'

The suspicion left his face. He stuck his hand out and we shook. His hand was as big and square as his chin and I was surprised at how pleasant his smile was – one of those natural, easy smiles.

Mary said, 'Jerry knows why you're here.'

'Good thing, too,' he said. 'I saw the two of you a-walkin' together, took it to mind that he was bent on courtin' you.'

'Oh, no!' I said, hastily. 'I'm not even nimble.'

'Ummm. What I mean is, it's a good thing you're here, not that I knew why you were here.'

'Well, it's a nice change to be welcomed by the law,' I told him. I meant it, too. I had been advised to get out of town by sundown a few times. I said, 'I take it you resent this ... agency, too?'

'Sure do. Damn usurpers.'

'What?'

'Usurpers,' he said.

He put his hat on again and pulled the brim down to the top of his dark glasses, so that he had to tilt his head back to look at me.

'That's what they done, they done usurped my authority,' he told me. 'I was the only law on this here island and I admired to have it thataway, oh-yuh.' His jaw worked as if he were chewing tobacco, but he wasn't. Then he grinned and Mary giggled and I saw he was joking – playing his role. But joking on the square, I thought.

'Where are you staying?' he asked, dropping the accent.

'I was taking Jack to the Red Walls.'

Jerry laughed. 'You'll get your ear bent there, Jack. All those old boys that can't forget the old days – nor remember them with any accuracy, either. They get them a landlubber, they plumb wear his earholes out.' He slipped in and out of his rednecked accent and grace. 'It was quite a place, though, going back a few years, from what I hear. Had the plumbers in there, year or two back, they were fitting a new toilet. Had to rip the plaster out; found eighteen wallets that had been slipped down a hole in the wall, where the whores and pickpockets slung them after they took the money out. Shootin's, stabbin's . . . you name it. Not the same now, though; tamed down. Or so I hear. Couldn't say for sure, 'cause there's no way I'm gonna walk into that place on my own.'

'You'll scare Jack,' Mary chided him, embarrassing me and making me wish I had deboated more nimbly.

'Naw,' Jerry said. 'What I hear, Mr Harland is used to playing with the big boys. He won't scare. Although, come to think of it, I ain't so sure that these ain't the real big boys he come to play with here.'

He looked thoughtful, rubbing that incredible jaw.

'Might be sort of scary, at that,' he said.

Jerry Muldoon looked like he wouldn't be scared of a grizzly bear, and his point was well taken . . .

III

The Red Walls was a solid mahogany structure built to withstand hurricanes, which it had. My room was adequate and had an air-conditioning unit in the window. The bathroom was down the hall, but that was no inconvenience, for I was the only guest. I hadn't been asked to register. I took a cold shower, changed my clothing and went down to the bar to wait. Mary had to get in touch with Dr Elston in person, not trusting the telephone, and I had nothing to do but wait. The barroom was impressive, a huge chamber that would have made a passable cathedral, with arches and beams across the ceiling. The walls, disappointingly, weren't red. They were white. And they were slatted like Venetian blinds, so that they could be opened to take advantage of the sea breeze. They were open when I came down, laying bars of sunlight across the floor in a grid. I took a wicker stool at the bar and the barman was pleased to have a customer – the shrimpers and fishermen who made up the steady clientèle were plying their trade at that hour. I ordered a tall rum punch and the barman waited across the counter, fidgeting, obviously feeling obligated to entertain me with tales of the notorious Red Walls. I didn't feel much like talking. I was thinking about Elston and speculating on what he would, I hoped, tell me. But the bartender looked so hopeful that I figured it was only common decency to give him an opening.

'Sort of quiet here today,' I said.

He beamed.

'The place'll get livelier, later on,' he assured me. 'When the boats come in. Not as lively as it used to be, mind you. I could tell you a tale or two . . .'

'Which you no doubt will . . .'

'. . . about this place that'd curl your toes. Yessir. This here place was known far and wide. Why, I remember . . .'

He talked. It was quite interesting, really, and I listened and made proper responses and drank a second rum. He was still talking when Elston came in . . .

'. . . So, like I say, there was thirteen shrimpers standing at the bar here. This is going back ten, fifteen years. They was standing here, elbows on the bar, drinking away and minding their business, when what should happen but this jigaboo walks in. He's got him a gun. In he walks, bold as brass, says, "This is a stick-up!" Now, these thirteen shrimpers are all facing the bar, they don't pay him no mind. He waves the gun about. He's waving it, he says, "I say, this is a stick-up!" Well, sir, these thirteen shrimpers looks at one another and shakes their heads. Then they all turn around, nice and easy, all at the same time. There's thirteen of em, mind. And twelve of them got guns!' He chuckled. 'So there this jigaboo stands, he's got one gun and twelve shrimpers are all pointing guns at him. What's he do? Why, he puts his gun away and he says, "I guess I done robbed the wrong bar!" And he ups and buys a drink for the house. Yessir! Things was plenty lively in them days . . .'

The barman was chuckling merrily and preparing to launch into another story, but I shoved my glass out for a refill in order to distract him.

Elston was standing just inside the door.

I knew right away that it was Elston from Mary Carlyle's description of the man . . . timid. He had stepped to the side of the entrance, into the shadows, and his eyes shifted furtively around the big room. I raised my hand, casually, and he nodded with a quick, jerky movement. He looked out the door, then came across the room with a crablike, sidewinder gait.

'Harland?' he whispered.

'Yeah. Shall we go up to my room?'

He hesitated; then: 'Better stay here, just as if we had met socially, at the bar . . . as one does.'

He didn't strike me as the type to meet socially at a bar, but I nodded. The bartender, looking grieved that I had found another conversationalist, slid my drink across the counter. He looked at

Elston, but Elston didn't notice and didn't order a drink. His eyes still flitted about.

'Let's go down to the end of the bar,' I suggested.

I took another seat there. Elston stood. The bartender, glowering, began washing glasses.

'What's it all about?' I asked.

'You won't mention my name?'

'If you don't want me to.'

'You swear you won't bring me into it?'

'Boy Scout's oath and all that.'

'This isn't funny, Harland, not at all funny.'

'Sorry.'

He nodded. He said, 'I'm not so sure this is a good idea. I let Mary talk me into this. But ...' He took a deep breath, as if about to submerge under water, then very quickly he said, 'I want you to expose what is being done here before it goes any further. It must contravene the ban on germ warfare or something, some treaty or agreement ... I know nothing of such matters, but I'm sure that public outrage ...'

'I'm no scientist, so if this is technical ...'

'Technical? Well, of course it's technical ... my work, I mean. But ... gruesome, that's what it is. Gruesome. It was bad enough with the animals, but now that they have determined to use human volunteers—'

He shuddered and rolled his eyes. His whisper was a rasping thing in that great, vaulted chamber. It was eerie.

'Dr Elston ... if all you want is to prevent this research, or whatever it is, why don't you simply resign? Refuse?'

'It's too late for that!' he snapped. He had spoken loudly, and he shot a startled glance down the bar, but the bartender was taking no interest in our talk. In a lower tone, he said, 'It's done, God help me. My assistants could carry on without me, at this point ... assistants provided by them. And I'm not sure—' with his eyes flitting about '—that they'd let me resign. I'm afraid of them, Harland.'

'Who are they?'

'A branch of the government ... nameless. The navy provides ships and guards, but I'm not concerned with them, it's the others ... the civilians ... the ones who represent ... ruthless men, Harland. If you had seen what I have seen ...'

He seemed to be seeing those things now, looking through me. He was a shaken man, and frightened. I didn't like him, but I felt a touch of pity; perhaps some sympathetic vibration of his fear.

'You'll tell me?'

'Yes, yes. I will give you the details and you must reveal them to the world, without implicating me. Surely that will be enough, this fiendish thing will be stopped once it has come to light.'

I nodded. I took out my notepad and pen. Elston chewed his lip. He placed one hand flat on the counter and, not looking at me, he said, 'It began . . . it was pure research, my goal was to treat madness . . . not to create it.' He glanced at me and I moved my pen, just scribbling; waiting for details. He was grimacing as he continued, 'My research was in chemical lobotomy . . . not a pleasant thing in itself, but in certain cases . . . it is sometimes necessary to make the incurables . . . obedient. I trust you will understand that?' He looked at me doubtfully, the sort of man who must always preface an opinion by a justification. I sort of nodded. That he was taking such pains – and they were pains, they registered physically on his countenance – to excuse his involvement removed any lingering doubts I might have had, about this being a hoax, at any rate.

'I meant only good,' he went on, still staring at me, gauging my reaction or looking for scepticism. I kept my face blank. I had written one word: Lobotomy. A Pandora's Box of a word, opening up dark implications just as the lobotomist opened up a skull.

'Go on,' I said, unwilling to express the vindication he sought as he searched my face.

'My work came to their attention. This agency of the government. They saw possibilities that had never occurred to me – nor ever would have. I was not . . . given all the facts. I was given a government grant and brought to this place, provided with all the facilities to continue my research, assigned eager – too eager – assistants. I worked. That is what I have always done. I have few friends and little social life. I work. Naïvely, I still believed I was in control of my research, that I was working towards my own goals.' His lips tightened in a bitter smile. 'Well, gradually, I came to see what they intended.' He paused, twitching his cheek up several times, as if chewing and tasting his words. He did not relish the flavour of those syllables. 'If only I had renounced them then. I was still important to the project, it was still mine and without me . . . but I did not renounce them and there's no sense speaking of what has not been.'

He dropped his head. With his face still twitching, it seemed he was gnawing through his breast.

'They did not threaten me – but the threat was there; they spoke of the Russian menace – they were menacing. And then there were . . . volunteers . . .' My pen moved on the paper. I wrote: Volunteers. There were two words on the paper that should not have been linked and an icy sensation climbed up my spine.

'Volunteers,' he repeated. 'Say, rather, men to whom the alternative was worse. Well, who thought it worse, not knowing . . .' His head snapped up abruptly. He had to look directly at me as he said the next words. 'There are chemicals, Harland . . . chemicals that warp the fabric of the soul, that alter the structure of the mind as surely as the keenest scalpel. This treatment . . .'

He stopped.

Loudly, he said, 'So I don't get much time for fishing, but I understand it's good here . . . I'm sure you'll enjoy yourself, Mister . . . I didn't get your name . . .'

I blinked in surprise; Elston was very white.

'Well, it was pleasant meeting you,' he said, and he looked wildly about for a reason to be there. He snatched up my drink and gulped at it, then clutched it possessively, leaving *me* no reason for being there. Then he nodded curtly and brushed past me. Bewildered, I turned, getting an elbow on the bar and I saw the man who had just come in – the man Elston had seen a moment sooner.

He wore a dark suit and necktie in that blistering heat and he wasn't sweating. He had steel framed spectacles and his hair was close-cropped and he looked about ten pounds underweight – but it was underweight the way an athlete in training is underweight. He was heading for the bar, not looking at us. The open walls had laid a grid of sunlight across the floor and he moved through that grid as if describing an arc or a graph, not so much a man as – a statistic.

Elston crossed in front of him, nodding *en passant.*

The man nodded back.

Elston took two more steps, then turned jerkily back.

'Oh, hello, Larsen,' he said, as if he'd just identified the newcomer.

'Doctor,' said Larsen.

'I just stopped in for a drink, you know,' Elston said.

'Uh, huh,' said Larsen.

'Well . . . back to the grind,' Elston said and he walked to the door with his shoulders squared, like a man anticipating a bullet in the back. He went out. For a moment, framed in the doorway, he looked two-dimensional, a flat shadow of himself. Then he was gone and Larsen was standing at the bar.

I put my notebook away.

'Nice day,' I said.

'They're always nice here.'

'Hot, though. You must be boiling in that suit.'

'Not really.'

The barman came down and Larsen ordered a beer. The barman

served it without a word, the same barman who had talked nonstop to me. Larsen didn't touch the glass.

'Tourist, are you?'

'That's right. For the fishing.'

'Um. Staying long?'

'Just a day or two.'

'Uh huh,' he said.

He picked up the glass and turned to face me. His eyes were like lenses. I felt I was being filmed and filed away behind those steel-rimmed sockets. They drew me like a vacuum. He sipped his beer and I drank the last of my rum and all the while he watched me with his eyes glinting behind his spectacles.

IV

Larsen had the one beer and left.

I felt he was taking a part of me with him, that he had dragged some intangible segment from my spirit, unravelled a thread of my soul and wound it up again inside his skull, where he would dissect it at his leisure. I was sweating heavily and it had nothing to do with the heat now. It was the sweat of anxiety and Larsen had pulled it from my pores.

The bartender nodded at the door.

'One of them geezers from the compound, we don't care to have their trade. Damn liberty, it is, them comin' here. That guy you was talkin' to ... he was really filling you ear, eh? He come from the compound?'

'I don't know him,' I said.

'That a fact? Why, the way he was gibbering away, I figured you was old friends. Some folks is like that, though ... they'll bend anyone's ear, even a total stranger's.'

He proceeded to manifest that fact while I considered Elston and Larsen ... what Elston had managed to tell me and how Larsen had affected me. I was truly interested now ... and disturbed. The big room with the open walls had been cheerful: now it was atrabilious, Larsen had left gloom in his wake. The bright grid of sunlight remained, yet now those lines did not illuminate the cathedral distances – they segmented the room in a sequence of cramped oblongs, like crypts in a graveyard.

I wondered if Elston had been frightened off for good or if he would contact me again? Perhaps through Mary Carlyle, certainly not by telephone.

Then, thinking about the telephone and realising I might have to stay on Pelican longer than I'd expected, I asked the bartender to put me through to the Mangrove Inn. He did so, grumbling about the delay as the call went through the switchboard and, taking the phone, I felt sure that my call was being monitored. But that was all right. I told the owner of the Mangrove that I'd decided to spend a day or two on Pelican and asked if my car would be all right in his parking lot. He assured me it would and assumed I would be fishing. I didn't disabuse him – or the monitor – of that. The bartender had been listening as well, and after I hung up he spent some time telling me where to get the best value in hiring a boat. I told him I'd surely take his advice. I supposed that I should, too, to validate my cover story, but I didn't want to go fishing and cursed Elston for throwing that at me in his panic. I was no fisherman and my inept attempts would be a dead giveaway. But then, rationalising nicely, I figured that the average fisherman spends more time drinking than fishing and it would look odd were I to follow an aberrant routine. It would look . . . fishy. So I had another drink, quite in line with my cover – and needed it, after being in the line of Larsen's gaze . . .

In my room I stretched out on the bed and glanced at the meagre notes I'd taken. There wasn't much there, certainly nothing concrete, but the words were chilling. Lobotomy is a harsh word, not softened when prefaced by *chemical* . . . no more on the page than in the wreckage of a mind. I read the words, aware that my lips were moving as I mouthed the unsavoury syllables, then I tore the page out, and the two pages beneath where an impression might have been indented, and I burned them in the ashtray and flushed the ashes down the toilet in the hallway. I was taking this seriously now, absolutely. Larsen's ominous appearance had impressed me more than Elston's aborted statement. There was something cold and dangerous about Larsen. Not a viciousness so much as a void of compassion, a man to whom charity would be alien. He had the eye of a serpent and I'd fluttered like a bird, mesmerised by his gaze. I felt that, had he moved towards me, I would not have been able to retreat; that he'd pinned me with his eyes like a moth on a display board whilst he studied the texture of my spirit, traced the veins of my instincts and laid bare the articulation of my bones.

I was still sweating from the encounter.

I moved to the window and gazed out. A middle-aged man slowly and methodically pedalled past on a bicycle. He had a terrycloth sweatband around his high-domed, glabrous brow. His Adidas shoes went up and down on the pedals. His bony back was bent deeply over the dropped handlebars. The bike was a ten-speed, on an island devoid of hills where those multiple gearings were as useless as the fashion that compelled him to have them. Man had spent the long eons rising from the slime: he had learned to walk upright: now racing handlebars were pushing his face once more, unseeing, into the mud. I was feeling distinctly uncharitable towards the human race – a legacy, no doubt, of Larsen's gaze. I mourned Darwin. The industrial revolution had put paid to evolution; now giant, pea-brained athletes may outlast the dinosaurs and wizened accountants survive to breed; millions of joggers jarring their spines will fall in love over Perrier water and produce little joggers to trot through a world where trend has superceded evolution.

And men like Larsen existed.

Elston could well have been a bleeding heart, panicking for slight reason, but Larsen – there was a good reason for him to be there. I lay on the bed, waiting. I didn't expect Elston to contact me again so soon, probably not until Mary Carlyle inspired him once more, but I waited, anyhow, and after a while I slept and when I woke up I thought, for a moment, that the walls were vibrating or grating – as if all the violence that had taken place in this building in the past had somehow seeped into the fabric of the walls. I sat up. The vibrating slowed. It had been the drumming of my heart. Yet I had not been dreaming. I took a deep breath and smiled at my fanciful sensation. This strange island, with its sordid past, and its great panorama of pretence, was affecting me. But whatever was going on here, it was not supernatural.

Unnatural, perhaps.

My heartbeat was regular now.

I was hungry and decided to try the diner I'd noticed across the street . . .

V

The Fisherman's Café, a long, narrow building much ravaged by time, was diagonally across the street from the Red Walls. It wasn't elegant but it was handy. I went in, squinting from the dazzling sun, and took a seat at the chipped Formica counter. The Cuban counterman agreed to make a sandwich and served good coffee in a cracked mug. There was one other customer, an old fellow at the end of the counter. He had one eye, a greasy cap and leathery skin. After a while he walked down and stood beside me.

'I see you just come outta the Bloodbath.'

'I beg your pardon? What?'

He pointed across the street, his finger like a gnarled rope, his hand mangled from long years on the shrimp boats.

'Place there. See you come out.'

'Oh, the Red Walls? I did.'

'Yeah, that place. Bloodbath is what we calls it.'

I smiled at the idea that the Red Walls was too euphemistic for this old sailor.

'Ain't no place now like that was then. My oh my, that was a place. That surely was a place.'

'So I've heard.'

He squinted at me. Strangely enough, he squinted with the empty socket, not the eye.

'You'll be no Conch, then?'

'No.'

'Didn't think you was a Conch.'

'Coffee?'

'Wouldn't say no.'

He sat on the stool beside me. The Cuban slid a mug across and the old man enfolded it in his remarkable hand.

'Lost an eye in there,' he said.

He was peering down into his coffee mug and, for a moment, I thought that his eye had dropped in like a lump of sugar and he was wondering if he should stir it.

'In the Bloodbath,' he said. 'What you call the Red Walls. That's where I lost my eye. You notice I only got the one eye? That's 'cause I lost it in there. Fightin'.'

'Oh,' I said.

'Cuban fella and me, had to get at it. Over a woman, you know. Quite the woman. No better'n she ought to be, but a good old gal. Old Jenny what they called the Wolfgirl, on accounta how she used to howl. Howlin' fool, she was. Dead now, Jenny. Forget how she died. This big Cuban and me, we got down to it with fishknives. Not like you see in the moving pictures, no sir. We was sword fightin', up and down the bar. Hunks of flesh and bone flying all over the place. I flipped a big chunk of shoulder right off of him. That's how I lost my eye. Knife got wedged in his tendons, see, so that I had to sort of lever it out like haulin' in on an anchor. That's when he got my eye, while I was liftin' his shoulder off. Figured we was even. Neither of us relished fightin' much after that. Worse on him, really. Big, strappin' fella, worked on the docks, weren't much use there after he lost that big chunk of shoulder. Hanged hisself, in the end.'

He turned the mug around in his hand like the memories unwinding in his mind.

'That was in the Bloodbath, too, come to think of it. Nothin' to do with me, though, unless maybe he was broodin' and mopin' about his shoulder. Yep. Got to feelin' morose, the way some of these Cuban fellas get to feelin', got him a rope and walked in the bar, just plain announced he was aimin' to hang hisself. Plenty of fellas in there, friends of his, they tell him he hadn't ought to do that, but he says his mind is plumb made up. Don't even care if he has to go to Hell 'cause of it. Throws the rope over one of them big beams up to the ceiling, puts the noose around his neck and commences to haul away. Well, it was plain as day he was never gonna hang hisself that way. Plain as the nose on your face.' He squinted at me, the empty socket closing like an envelope. 'Say, I ain't borin' you, am I?'

'Not at all,' I told him.

He nodded and went on, 'We all got to feelin' sorry for him. He looked so danged foolish, tuggin' away with his eyes poppin' out, standin' on his tiptoes. One of his friends asked if he wanted some help. So he sort of nodded, looked like he nodded . . . hard to tell, his head in the noose and all. So three or four of his buddies got the end of the rope and give him a hand; hauled him off the floor and tied the end of the rope to the bar rail. Brass, it was. The bar rail. He kicked around awhile and we had some drinks. Then we got to thinkin' as he might of changed his mind and we cut him down but it was too late, if'n he did change his mind, 'cause he was already hanged. Be a bitch, he did change his mind.'

He giggled with fond memories, a man whose history was carved upon his body in runic scars and wrinkles and who added to his substance by subtracting an eye.

He saw I was fascinated.

'Say, can I get some rum in this coffee?'

'All right.'

The Cuban pulled an unlabelled bottle out and sloshed a healthy portion in his mug. The old man took a big gulp. He had a more interesting delivery than the bartender and I wanted to hear more. I said, 'Things like that don't happen so much these days, huh?'

'Not so much, not at the Bloodbath.' He gave me another eyeless squint. 'Strange things happen, though. Maybe even stranger than what usedta be. Not so natural, maybe.' Now he was squinting at his cup, with his good eye. I nodded to the Cuban, who poured some more rum in. There was more rum than coffee now, and the old man stared into the amber fluid as if seeking inspiration reflected in the surface. He looked vaguely uncomfortable.

'Things like fightin' and hangin', they is natural enough. Thing what I saw the other mornin', now ... that was strange. Happen it's the strangest thing I ever see ...'

His voice trailed off. I felt he wanted encouragement – a proud man who wished to pay for his rum with words – and said, 'What was that?' but he didn't seem to hear me. He was thinking, either choosing his words or gathering his recollections. Then he looked up and said, 'Say, now ... you wouldn't be connected with this government thing here, would you?'

'No. I'm just ...' I hesitated. I had been about to tell him that I was just a tourist, but somehow I couldn't bring myself to lie to this old man. 'No, I'm not.'

'Didn't figure you was. You don't look like most of them government Johnnies. Thought as I'd ask, though. On account of ... they got lots of security up to the compound,' he added. I realised that he was actually debating whether to continue; it didn't seem in character. For some reason he was wary. But then his basic nature won out and he began to speak.

'I got a boat,' he said. 'Used to be I did a bit of free trading, you take my point. Well, now, other side of the island there is this little cove, place you can land and nobody sees you. 'Cept you can't land there no more, they told me to bugger off. But they don't give a hoot what's on my boat, nothin' to do with customs duty, just don't want me there. Well, I tell you this 'cause it was around there I saw this strange thing. Maybe three weeks ago, it was after they told me not to land there no more, but I had to go sneakin' back. I'd left some crates there, things what I didn't want found. Nothin' bad, nothin' like dope or stuff, just some duty free stuff from the islands. Anyhow, I sneaked back there, took the dingy so I wouldn't make no noise and got to the cove all right; got ashore and dug up these crates. Then, just 'cause I was there, I went on up to the fence – this big fence they has built around the compound – just to have me a look. It was dawn. Just before dawn, sky sort of pearl-coloured and plenty of shadow for me to stand in. Well, that's when I see this strange thing.'

I was well and truly interested now. I nodded to the Cuban and got some rum in my own coffee.

'Happen you won't believe this I'm saying,' he went on. 'Tell you. My name's Tate. John Tate, although of late they's taken to callin' me One-Eye Tate. That don't matter. What I mean is, you can ask anyone about John Tate, they'll tell you he's an honest fella; might say he talks a piece too much but that what he says is straight. You can ask. Thing is, this I'm tellin' you, I don't believe it myself. I mean, I saw it, but I don't believe it, you follow me.'

I nodded. I had taken but a single bite from my sandwich. The Cuban was washing plates at the far end of the counter. Tate pulled a crumpled pack of cigarettes from his pocket and extracted one. It was wrinkled and a fine dust of dry tobacco spilled from the end.

'Well, while I'm standin' there in the shadows, just without the fence, a group of these Johnnies comes down from the big building. Laboratory, I guess it is. I was just about to light a cigarette, just stopped from strikin' the match in time; they'd of see me, I hit the match.' Now he lighted the crinkled cigarette, as if he'd been waiting to use it as evidence as he gave witness. Dry smoke writhed up around the grotto of his empty eye socket. 'So down they come, there's half a dozen of 'em, two of 'em got white coats like doctors or scientists and three of 'em are wearing dark suits. You see these dark suits guys around town, time to time. Don't like the weave of 'em, myself. But it's the other guy, the sixth guy, that takes my interest. He's wearin' a white thing, not like the doctors, more like a patient wears in hospital. And he looks ... unnatural. Looks like a robot, maybe. Or like one of them zombies what you get down to Haiti and Jamaica, them living dead Johnnies, you see it? Face all blank, eyes all rolled back white, he's to droolin' down his chin somewhat. Walks stiff. Knees and elbows ain't got much bend to 'em. Well, sir, I figure he's a pretty sick fella, and naturally I wonder why they's walkin' him down to the beach at dawn.'

He shifted on his stool. He had the mug in one hand and the wrinkled cigarette in the other and it appeared he couldn't decide which to lift to his mouth. And it seemed a monumental decision; he looked nervous and jumpy.

'I hunker down to have me a observation,' he said, speaking more slowly now. 'Down they come. They stop and then I see this big slab of concrete. It's real big, big square block with an iron ring set in the top. Thing must of weighed, I don't know ... must of weighed plenty more'n a ton. Well, they gather around it. One of the dark suits takes the ring, gives it a pretty hard tug. Them dark suits is sort of skinny, but they looks to be strong enough. Slab of concrete don't budge at all. Too heavy.'

Now Tate raised the coffee mug to his lips, very slowly, as if that, too, were too heavy. He sipped. Big veins stood out in his forearm and his hand was shaking slightly.

'Dark suit fella nods; he's satisfied.'

Tate nodded himself, not with satisfaction. He lowered the mug and raised the cigarette, both movements distinct, as if his arms were connected by a system of levers across his sunken chest. One went down and one went up. He moved by clockwork, timing his tale.

'Then one of the doctors says to the sick fella, "Lift it." No hemmin' nor hawin', just tells him to lift it. Now, I can see it ain't possible for a man to lift it. Anyone can see that. 'Ceptin' this sick lookin' Johnny. What's he to do but step right up and take the iron ring in his right hand and commence to lift. Matter-of-fact, like it was a pillow. Don't set his feet, don't take no deep breath, nothin'. Just commences to lift. It was awful funny. Strange funny, I mean. Got some ground mist rising around them, sky all grey, they look strange standin' around that concrete slab, like maybe they was worshippers at a tomb. And this guy is lifting!'

Tate lifted the mug, lowered it, lifted again; his leathery face was strained with the imagined effort.

'I mean, his face don't change none, it's blank, got no expression to it, but he is liftin' so hard I can hear his joints creak. He really thinks he can lift that slab!

'Now, ain't no man what could lift it, it's plain too heavy, but he don't know that. Ain't no big guy, neither. The others are all watchin' him and he's liftin' hard as he can and the slab ain't shiftin' at all, don't move an inch. The doctor says, "Lift it," again, but the guy is trying as hard as he can.

'Then the real strange thing happens.'

He put the mug down on the counter with a solid clunk, as if he wanted no further part of it. The Cuban looked up. His hands made slippery sounds in the soapy water.

'What I don't believe, 'ceptin' I see it. I've been a fisherman in my time, I've fought the big fish for hours, game as any man. I know when even the strongest guy has got to give in. But this guy don't know that. And all of a sudden there is this snap, just like a tree splitting in a hurricane. A loud crack . . .' the onomatopoeia of the word struck him: he repeated it, 'Crack,' relishing the word . . . but not the image behind it.

'And the guy has broke his own arm!'

Tate grimaced and gave a little shudder. 'Well, the bones are stickin' out from the elbow, where it has snapped.' He touched the inside of his own elbow. 'Blood is spoutin' out on the slab. And the guy is still liftin'. With his arm ruined, broke near in half and the bones all sticking out splintered, he is still trying to lift that concrete slab!'

He shook his head and peered at me. He looked down. I suddenly realised that I was gripping my own arm, rubbing it. It ached, tingling with some sympathetic vibration. I saw that concrete slab like a sacrificial altar, running with blood. My hand seemed to be stuck to my arm; it was hard to pull it away. When I did, the effort registered in my spine . . . my backbone seemed to be raising as if, set with rings, it was a handle by which his tale was hoisting me.

'I don't blame you, you don't believe it, but that is what I saw. Guy still had to expression, you could tell he was to feelin' no pain, he's heavin' with that bust flipper . . . Made me sort of sick. Ain't told no one about it before, 'count of I hadn't ought to be there and 'cause I maybe didn't have it all straight in my mind. But that's what happened. No, I don't blame you, you doubt it. Don't believe it, myself.

'But I saw it, though; that is the thing.'

I said, 'I believe you, Tate.'

'You do?' He looked pleased.

I said, 'Listen, could you take me to that place?'

Then he looked uncomfortable. He drained his cup and I nodded for a refill. The Cuban came down, his forearms lathered with soap-suds. He poured some rum. It didn't make Tate look any more comfortable.

Tate said, 'I don't believe I fancy going to there again.'

I didn't press him. I paid the tab and left without finishing the sandwich. Elston didn't contact me, I turned in early and had unquiet dreams . . .

There had been wreckers.

This island had been founded and prospered upon wreckage, they had drawn innocent ships onto the reefs with false lights and butchered the sailors as they foundered in the surf. They had not been sadistic men, those wreckers, nor cruel for the sake of cruelty. It was simply what they did, a way of life.

And there was wreckage now – the broken spar of a shattered arm, the breeched hull of a mind . . . drawn by the false light of science beamed from such as Larsen's eyes . . .

Unquiet dreams . . .

VI

The sun, too hot to be contained, spread in a pale curtain across the sky. It was ten in the morning and I was walking the pebbled beach south of the town with some vague idea of having a look at the compound, or at least the surrounding fence. Elston hadn't been in touch and I didn't fancy spending the day waiting for a contact that might not come. The bartender at the Red Walls, drawing with his index finger in some spilled beer, had given me a rough idea of how the compound was fenced off and I knew I should come to that barrier soon. I would have liked to have a look at the cove on the far side of the island, and that immovable concrete slab, but knew that was only possible by boat. Nor would there be anything to see now. Just a slab of concrete. But the image that John Tate had stamped into my mind was graphic. He knew how to deliver a tale and I could visualise those men standing around the slab; could hear, in my mind, the terrible sound of shattering bones. I remembered Elston's whispering, rasping voice, as well, and thought of the connection between the two ... and of Larsen, with his eyes magnified in the lenses of his spectacles, glinting at me.

I scrambled over some layered limestone and at the highest point of the island, which was not very high, paused to fill my pipe and gaze out over the sea. The water was very clear. I could see the sandy bottom some eight feet below and, further out, the water bubbled green over a coral reef. The lighthouse, from there, seemed to be on the island, a fold of the landscape hiding the stretch of water between. Seagulls looped around the grey tower and the beacon flashed with regularity, almost invisible in the glaring sunlight. I wondered why Sam Jasper left the light on in the daytime – if it was normal procedure, or if he had simply forgotten? Sitting on the limestone shelf I smoked contemplatively for a while. But it was too hot to enjoy the tobacco. I tapped the pipe out and walked on and, in a short time, came upon the tall, metal-meshed fence. It ran down to the edge of the water and I could go no further. Beyond, I knew, was the beach that Mary liked and which was now barred to her.

Then, suddenly, I laughed.

There was a hole in the fence.

With all that supposedly tight security and the monitored telephones and the secrecy, it struck me as very funny that the fence should be breached. Several strands of wire had been snapped off and bent back. The gap was large enough for a man to slip through and, for a moment, I was sorely tempted to do so – to enter that secret compound and see what I could see. I had actually moved up to the fence before I thought better of it. I would not be able to get into the buildings and would no doubt be apprehended before I'd gone very far and it was hardly worth compromising myself for the sake of a stroll through the grounds. I still thought it amusing that the security had been breached and wondered if someone, like Mary, resenting the barrier, had cut through to get to the further beach – or simply to aggravate the intruders.

I pulled a strand of the wire out and inspected the end. It hadn't been cut, it had been broken or twisted apart. It was heavy-gauge, hard to bend, and on one jagged end I noticed a dark stain. It looked like blood.

Then I heard voices.

I couldn't make out the words, but they sounded excited and they weren't far away. I looked around, thinking to secrete myself and eavesdrop, but there was no place to hide near the fence. I didn't care to be found there, by the break. Innocent of it, I nevertheless felt guilty. I turned away and went back over the limestone shelf and sat down on the far side. I felt excited, as if I were the quarry in a chase. The voices were yet closer and I risked a glance over the rocks.

Two men in naval whites were coming along the fence on the far side, following the line. As I looked, they came to the break. One of them cursed and both looked disturbed. They were armed and the flaps on their holsters were unsnapped. They looked around, standing back to back and whispering together over their shoulders. One shrugged. They were nervous and I caught a few snatches of their talk – enough to discern that they were arguing over who should remain guarding the break and who should report it. I wasn't sure which duty was the less desirable one. But then one, the one who had cursed, said, 'Well, what's the point? He's already got through, he won't be coming back this way.' They whispered some more, then both of them started back the way they'd come, heads turning as they looked around. I waited until they were out of sight. Then I slid down the limestone shelf and headed back to town.

The guards hadn't thought the break in the fence was funny at all.

Neither did I now.

Walking back, I passed close to the lighthouse.

The rock bridge leading out was just emerging from the water, like a fossilised spine excavated by the tide. At the end of that spine the lighthouse reared up and wailed its mournful warning and the regular, pale beat of the beacon flashed like a charm in a hypnotist's hand. I paused and gazed at that tall pharos rising from the sea. How like a symbol for man's conceit, I thought. The grey tower aspires to the heavens, yet is rooted in the rocks ... and man, considering the stars, disturbs the grass. What did man do, atop his shining towers, up there in those cloistered domains? Had he climbed there to a purpose, or was he no more than those swooping gulls who, having dined on filth, rise above the clouds?

I went on; I had decided to call on Mary Carlyle.

VII

The Coast Guard Depot was a small white building with green shutters on the windows and a step before the door. It looked more like a country cottage than anything else. The door was open and I looked in. There was an office at the front and a store room at the back. Mary Carlyle was sitting behind a desk with some papers spread out in front of her and Jerry Muldoon was balanced on the corner of the desk, one leg swinging back and forth, hands clasped over his knee. Mary gave me a bright smile. Jerry might possibly have looked a little annoyed at my entrance, but nothing serious. I supposed they had been flirting.

'I see you survived the night,' Jerry said.

'Neither stabbed nor shot, although I was well regaled with tales of stabbing and shooting.'

'Mostly true, probably.'

'Didn't you arrest a man there once, Jerry?' Mary put in, shifting some papers without looking at them.

'Why, yes. More than one, but only one that was serious. Shrimper that killed his wife, then got carried away and killed his wife's sister and carved his own brother up a mite. Had to point my gun at him.' He said that as if it distressed him. He shook his head once and his jaw was so heavy that it acted as a counterweight, so that his head swung a couple more times by inertia. 'I locked this fella up in the jail and he couldn't understand why. He kept asking me why in hell he had to get locked up. He was serious. I said, "For crissake, you just killed two women and wounded a guy," and he looked at me, sort of puzzled; said, "But that was family." And he meant it. Didn't think the law had any business interfering in a family matter. They're like that, shrimpers. He looked so puzzled that I felt sorry for him; for what he thought was unjust. Funny. Guy kills two women and I feel sorry for him.'

'You're all heart, Jerry.'

'Why . . . yes,' he said.

I said, 'I don't expect you've heard from Elston?'

'Didn't he see you? He promised . . .'

'He stopped at the inn yesterday. But just as he was starting to talk, a man came in . . . man called Larsen . . .' I saw that they both knew the man, or the name . . . 'and scared Elston off. Not, I hope, for good.'

'Oh. Damn,' she said. 'It's no wonder. Larsen is head of security. Nasty sort, I should think. Did he suspect anything?'

'I don't know. He's the sort of man that always looks suspicious. But Elston acted so damn flustered that he could have given it away.'

She gnawed at her lower lip.

'I'll talk to him . . .' she began, and then the phone rang. She smiled. 'But first I'll have to talk to Sam Jasper, I see. That's the direct line to the lighthouse.'

She reached for the phone. Jerry started to say something to me, then stopped. His teeth snapped shut. Mary's face had recoiled from the receiver as the shout came out. Jerry and I looked at each other. We had heard the words clearly enough. 'Help! For crissake, get some help out here . . .' Mary, looking startled, held the phone out and the sheriff took it. The cry for help came again, 'He's trying to get into the lamproom! He's trying to claw through the damn floor! Get me some help out here, Mary . . . fast!'

Jerry said, 'Hold on! This is Muldoon. What in hell are you yelling about, Sam?'

'Muldoon? Thank God. A berserker, Jerry. Tried to damn well kill me . . . after I went and saved his damn life, too . . . tell you he's trying to claw through the floor . . . he'd of killed me, he hadn't been full of water . . .' His voice was disjointed and terrified. 'Listen! You hear him clawing? Can't you hear it?'

'Hold on, old fella. I'll be right out.'

Jerry hung up the phone with Sam Jasper still shouting over the cable. The last words I heard were, '. . . bastard bit me!'

Jerry looked at Mary.

'Think he's slipped a cog?'

'No,' she said, definitely.

'Ummm. Fella that lives in a lighthouse . . . Well, I'd best get out there.' He looked at his wristwatch. 'How's the tide?'

'It's out,' she said. 'But wait. Take the launch from here, that'll be faster.'

He nodded. I touched his arm.

'Mind if I come with you?'

He hesitated. 'Can't do no harm,' he said. Then he said, 'You got some idea on this?' I shrugged. Mary was looking at me, her face clouded and worried, and she wasn't worried for Sam Jasper's sanity.

Jerry strode across the water from the dock to the launch and I jumped in right behind him, nimble as hell. Mary was pulling at the painter to cast us off as Jerry started the engines. She slipped on the wet dock and banged her knee against the iron staunchion. The skin split. It looked painful. She freed the line and tossed it to Jerry. 'Get that gash fixed,' he said. 'You get coral dust in that, it'll be nasty.' She nodded quickly and stepped back. A trickle of blood ran down her skin. She gave us a nervous sort of half-wave and then Jerry was taking the boat out of the harbour fast. A couple of red-sailed Sunfish were gliding across the roadstead and then bobbled perilously in our wash, one of the sailors shaking a fist at us. We turned towards the lighthouse. It thrust up beyond the slope of the island, then slid away as the angle changed. I could see the line of black rocks extending from the island to the larger rock on which the lighthouse rested. The sea was lashing around the rocks, white and foamy. They were slippery with seaweed. I was just as glad we had taken the boat; that rocky bridge was not to my liking. Jerry was watching the rocks carefully, coming in parallel with them on the shortest course to the lighthouse.

We both saw the figure at the same time.

'What the hell . . . ?' Jerry said.

The man was on the rocks, coming from the lighthouse, leaping and bounding as if unconcerned about the treacherous footing – or so terrified that panic dictated his movements. He wore a long white coat, the tails flapping behind him like broken wings, and his face was . . . terrible. His eyes were rolled back white and hollow and white foam sprayed from his lips like an echo of the foam breaking at his feet. He sprang to a rock, hunkered down for an instant, then bounded to the next; slipped but leaped forwards before he could fall. His mouth was open, lips squared back from his teeth, a grimace of torment.

'Is that Sam?' I asked.

'Not Sam,' Jerry said.

The launch had headed for the rocks as Jerry stared at the bounding figure. He corrected, swinging the prow back out. I could sense his indecision, whether to turn the boat after the fleeing figure. But then he looked at the lighthouse.

'We'd best see to Sam first,' he said.

He hadn't drawn his gun, either, and I liked him for his priorities.

Jerry went up the winding staircase first and I followed close behind. The staircase ended at a trap door which led up to the lamproom. The trap door was steel ... and it was smeared with lines of blood and tracks of gore. Pieces of flesh and fingernail were pasted, by blood, to the steel ... as if the man who had clawed at that door had been buried alive and was clawing at his crypt in final desperation. I tilted my head back, gaping upwards, and as I did so a shard of flesh dropped from the door and fell sluggishly past my face. I thought of John Tate's description of the man who had broken his arm against the unliftable weight. But it was not right ... the figure on the rocks had been more vigorous and his attack upon the trap door a thing of fury.

Jerry was shaking his head, looking at those gory tracks.

'Sam! It's Muldoon!' he called. There was no response. 'It's Jerry, Sam!'

'Jerry? You get him?' Sam called from above, his voice distorted through the floor between us, drawn out and quivering as if his words were elastic.

'He's gone. I saw him on the rocks.'

There was another pause while Sam considered this; then; 'You got a gun, Jerry?'

'Yeah, I got a gun. Open up.'

The bolt rasped slowly from the socket and the trap door lifted a few inches. Sam Jasper peered out, balanced at the edge, ready to slam the door closed again. He was an old man with wild white hair and darting fear in his eyes. Jerry stepped back to let Sam see him. Sam gave a little whine of relief and let the heavy door drop back with a clang. He was sitting on the floor. The big lamp was flashing behind him.

'He bit me, Jerry,' Sam said, quite calmly.

Then he began to rave ...

VIII

Dr Winston was a middle-aged, likeable fellow, who ran the local clinic. There was no hospital on the island and Winston was the only resident doctor – bar those, an unknown number, within the compound. He was not a native, but he had come there years before, simply because Pelican Cay needed a doctor and he needed nothing more than to practise his craft. Jerry Muldoon told me these things while we brought Sam Jasper back from the lighthouse, and I liked Winston the moment I saw him. He was fat; his belly hung over his belt and was obviously never subjected to exercise. He chainsmoked with nicotine-stained fingers and was short of breath. A certain colour to his cheeks and configuration of his nose hinted at a fondness for the vat. I figured straight off that this was a man one could trust.

When Jerry and I helped Sam Jasper into the clinic, Winston didn't seem surprised; seemed the sort that was seldom surprised by anything. Sam was between us, stumbling and twitching. He'd been in shock and mostly incoherent since we found him in the lamproom. Winston asked no questions. He looked at Sam's eyes and told us to get him onto a bed. Sam stretched out obediently, almost as if going to sleep, then sat up abruptly and looked around the room fearfully, turning his whole head while his eyes remained fixed in their sockets. Jerry kept a hand on his bony shoulder and Winston summoned his nurse; instructing her to administer a sedative. He examined Sam, his eyes darting about. Sam had a gash on his forearm and a slighter gash on the back of his hand, nothing that looked serious.

'Human?' Winston asked Jerry.

'What?'

'Those bites. Human, are they?'

'That's right.'

'Thought so. Seen a few of those.'

He spoke to the nurse again, telling her to give Sam an anti-tetanus shot and antibiotics. She bustled efficiently about, a matronly, grey-haired woman with kindly eyes, and Winston started to question Jerry about how it had happened.

Then Sam, sedated and calmer now, sat bolt upright.

'It was a hell of a thing,' he said.

'I'll get him, Sam,' Jerry said, but Sam didn't hear.

'Hell of a thing, I say,' he repeated.

'You ever see him before?'

'What? See him? Naw, not before I pulled him out of the water. He was from up there.'

'Up where?' Jerry asked.

Winston hovered near, hands clasped behind his back, ready to halt the questioning if Sam began to get agitated. I hoped that didn't happen, I wanted to hear what Sam Jasper had to say – to fit his story in with John Tate's and Elston's and – the break in the fence.

'Why, up the compound,' Jasper said.

'Now, Sam, how do you know that?'

'He was wearing one of them white kimonos, as sick people wear in hospitals, is how. Hell of a thing.'

'You say you saved him . . . pulled him out of the water?'

Jasper nodded. The nurse was standing beside the bed with a hypodermic. She looked at Dr Winston and Winston looked at Jerry. Jerry stepped back a pace, waiting for her to put the needle in before he continued his questioning, but Jasper was talking now and didn't stop. He said, 'First I saw of him, he was clinging to the rocks. On the seaward side, see, as if he's hiding from someone on the island. I see him from behind, see that white coat. Figured him for a drunk, but for that white coat. The water's lapping at his feet and he keeps shifting from one foot to the other, like he don't want to get his shoes wet. I called out to him but he didn't hear me, least he paid me no mind. A couple of seagulls started diving at him, flying around his head, he slapped at them like they was flies.' The nurse slipped the needle into his arm and pressed the plunger. Jasper glanced at her as if the process interested him, but he kept speaking to Jerry, from the side of his mouth. 'Well, then he slips off the rocks and falls into the water. Don't guess he could swim. He was clinging to the rocks with both hands and he's screaming, but he's screaming without making no noise, if you follow me. Screaming silent, mouth wide open but no sound coming out. Well, I didn't much fancy chancing my feet on them rocks, so I got out the rowboat. Time I rowed out he was still clinging to the rocks. Like a limpet, he was. I got the idea that he was too scared to pull himself out . . . scared of the water, see . . . like in a dream when you can't run away from what scares you. Must have been powerful strong, the way he was thrashing about you'd have thought he'd break his own grip. I got the boat up aside him, wedged up against the reef, and reached down to give him a hand. He looked up at me. Make you shudder, his face would. His mouth was wide open like his jaw was bust, I could see all his cavities and that little doodad what hangs down in your throat, but I couldn't see naught but white in his eyes, they was all rolled back like a horse in a fire. I pulled him into the boat. Wasn't a big man, nor heavy, but he was strong. Took a grip on my arm like a vice. But he never seemed to see me, he just sat in the boat all dumb. I figured it was best to row back to the lighthouse and phone in for help than to row to the island and have to walk the guy into town, and that's what I did. Had a job getting him out of the boat; had to pull the boat right up on the shore before he would step out. He could walk, all right, but he was wobbling, figured as he'd gulped down plenty of water. Soon as I get him into the lighthouse I take to pumping him out, got him coughing and spitting. All of a sudden he shakes himself like a wet dog.' Jasper shook himself as he said this, perhaps demonstrating what the other man had done – or perhaps shuddering involuntarily. 'Then he turns on me. Like a wild animal, all teeth and nails, and he's strong. I tried to hold him but he just throws me aside and bites me in the arm. Well, this puts a fright to me. He's crazy and he's plenty strong – it's a good thing he's still wobbly. I get away and run up the stairs with this guy snatching at my heels. Got into the lamproom and bolted the trap. Just in time, too. And what's he to do but try to claw right through the trap. I mean, it's steel, even a crazy fella ought to see that, but he claws away at it. I was so shook up I got to thinking he might claw through, at that. That's when I phoned in . . .'

'I think that's enough for now, Jerry,' Dr Winston said. 'I have to clean that wound and get some stitches into it.'

Jasper said, 'Terrible thing. That white coat, like that you see on a sick man . . . that was the worst of it, maybe – that and the silent screaming . . .'

'Take it easy now,' Jerry said.

He looked puzzled. Jasper lay back obediently and Winston started cleaning his torn arm. I followed Jerry into the office.

'What do you think of that?' he said.

Well, I was thinking of that. The man had tried to claw through solid steel . . . and John Tate had seen a man – a man in a white coat – try to lift an immovable object. Yet that man had broken his arm and the man who had attacked Sam Jasper had not had a broken arm; Tate's man had been obedient and devoid of emotion and Jasper's man had been ferocious. But both had been silent and immured to pain. Elston spoke of the chemicals that warp the fabric of the mind . . . and someone had torn through that heavy gauge fence. Chunks of the story that fitted together, not in a flat plane like a jigsaw puzzle but in a three-dimensional tableau – fitted together only roughly, but with contours that would dovetail once further knowledge had smoothed the rough edges. My thoughts flitted around through what I knew and I wondered how much I should tell Jerry. I liked and trusted him, and he was the sheriff, but I had an idea that this thing was far beyond his jurisdiction.

I turned to him, intending to speak.

But Jerry was on the phone.

*

'Yeah, yeah,' Jerry said. 'Yeah. Security, I guess.'

He waited impatiently, eyebrows raised. The phone made electric noises. Jerry started to say something to me, then paused and listened into the receiver.

'Yeah, got a problem here,' he said. 'Larsen? Yeah, this is Muldoon. Yeah, a guy run amuck, wearing a white coat . . . you be inclined to know anything about that? You do, huh? What? Naw, I don't need any assistance . . . it's only one guy. What the hell. I can handle it, just wanted to let you know. Sure, I know you got the authority, damn it. But I got a say in the matter, right? Damn right. I'll hold him for you but I ain't about to sit on my thumbs while he runs around loose. Forget it. Yeah, yeah, I know.' Jerry sighed. 'Okay, I'll expect a couple of your people. But in the meanwhile I'm gonna be looking. What? What?' he shouted. 'He's only one man, how in hell do I arrest him if I don't get close to him? Are you crazy?' Jerry set his jaw and glared at the phone. Then he slammed it down in the cradle.

He was angry.

He started to walk out without a word, then stopped and turned to me. He looked bewildered.

'Shoot him,' he said.

'What?'

'That's what Larsen told me to do. He said not to try to take the man alive, to shoot him. What the hell is happening on this island? He's only one man!'

Then he walked out.

I hadn't had a chance to tell him what I knew, but I didn't suppose it mattered. I figured it was time that I tried to use the telephone myself . . .

IX

'Sorry, sir . . . I really can't say,' the electronic voice chanted. The operator was nervous. Her words crackled with an electricity of their own. It was as exasperating as conversing with a recording.

'But surely you have some idea?'

'Sorry, sir . . . a difficulty with the lines.'

I said, 'Oh, hell,' and hung up. It was frustrating to have a story and be unable to phone the paper; it built up explosively inside me. Oh, it wasn't much of a story, really – not yet; not the important exposé I'd hoped to get from Elston. But it was certainly worth a phone call. There was something particularly gruesome about the affair, the isolation of a lighthouse, the old keeper trembling in the tower while a madman raged below. It would – I grimaced despite myself – sell newspapers. And that, for better or worse, was what my job was, what any newspaperman's job was, first and foremost – to sell papers. Whether one did this by revealing truth or popularising culture, by wallowing in scandal or spreading gossip or drawing comic strips, the job was the same. I was feeling cynical. Or maybe just honest with myself, knowing that my real success had come not because my exposé had put a halt to the Warden misappropriations, but because readers, thirsting for the blemished wine of scandal, had bought newspapers. Whatever good had come of it had been no more than a side effect and the public funds that had been saved had been saved for a public that preferred the vicarious thrill of being exploited. And mine was a respectable paper, at that.

Someday, I would write my novel.

Now I was going to write about what was happening on Pelican Cay. But what *was* happening? I had to find the hinge before I could open this mysterious box. I had uncovered graves of mouldering graft and unsealed Pandoran abuses in the past, but whatever I was looking for here did not deal with self-interest and the profit motive; it was deeper than greed, and more evil. Greed is a trait of living things, an integral slice of the will to survive and evolve, unpleasant, but part of the natural order. Whatever was being wrought behind those high fences had no place in nature.

There was no Western Union office on Pelican, but I thought maybe Mary Carlyle could help me. Surely the Coast Guard had communications not dependent on the switchboard and perhaps she could manage to patch me through to New York. With that in mind, I took leave of Dr Winston and headed down the waterfront.

It was then I became aware of how seriously the powers within the compound were taking the hunt for the escaped madman. Uniformed shore patrolmen were all over the place, walking in threes, and I spotted half a dozen civilians strolling about like tourists but with an intent they could not hide ... lean, fit, hard-faced men like Larsen. My nerves began to flash like beacons and my flesh crawled like the tide, carrying the flotsam of foreshadowed fear. I told myself this was a newspaperman's reaction to a story about to break, but in my heart I knew it was more than that ... I was scared.

'Jack!'

It was Mary, coming towards me. I noticed that she had a bandage on her knee, where she'd struck it against the stanchion. I said, 'I was just coming to see you,' and she said, 'I was just going to see Jerry. Is Sam all right?'

I told her, briefly and without the gory details, what had happened. She watched my face as I spoke. I added that Jerry wasn't likely to be in his office for a while and she looked around, as if she expected to see him.

'Poor Sam,' she said. 'I'm glad he's all right.'

'Listen, Mary . . . Is there any way you can connect me to the mainland from the Coast Guard depot? The telephone lines seem to be out.'

She nodded. 'I know. And I could, although we aren't supposed to use the radio now . . . except that I'm out, too.'

'What?'

'I've been given the day off. Dismissed, and quite curtly. Something very hush-hush is going on. I left the depot sort of flustered and forgot my handbag. When I went back for it there was a guard on the door. He wouldn't let me in. They sent the bag out to me, but for some reason they don't want anyone in there. The radio, I suppose. It figures, what with the telephones not working . . . or being worked . . .' She looked around again, looking for Jerry or, perhaps, determination. She said, 'Look, I have nothing to do now, Jack; I can run you over to the Keys in the launch, if you like. You can phone from there.'

I considered it. I have regretted my decision since, but at the time it seemed premature to leave Pelican before the madman had been captured . . . to rush off with the first half of a story only to be gone when the conclusion occurred. If I had . . . but perhaps, even then, they would not have let us go. At any rate, I said, 'Well . . . let me buy you a drink, Mary; I may take you up on your offer later.'

Now Mary seemed indecisive, fidgeting with her handbag and looking around.

She said, 'Do you think there's any connection?' I knew exactly what she meant, but she added, 'Between Elston and the attack on Sam Jasper?'

'Yes, I do.'

'So do I.'

'I must talk to him again.'

'It's more than a story, isn't it? I mean . . . something grotesque is going on here.' She gestured in that way she had, turning a hand over. 'Something that will affect us all.' It had already affected her; I saw the effect registered in her face, troubled and concerned. Two shore patrolmen walked past us with angular strides. A third came up behind, quickly; hurrying to catch up. Mary glanced at them. Then she smiled slightly and said, 'I'll take that drink, Jack. I've nothing to do. Nothing I *can* do,' she added.

I could tell she didn't feel like making any decisions, even in selecting a place to have a drink. I took her arm and guided her towards the nearest bar.

'How's your knee?' I asked.

'Ummm? Oh, it's okay. You have to be careful if you get any sort of break in the skin here. The coral dust is liable to get in it . . . keeps it from healing.' She touched her thigh, just above the bandage. 'Silly of me; I was in such a hurry to cast you off. I like Sam Jasper.'

'Well, he's all right, it wasn't serious; just scared him.'

I believed that to be true.

We were sitting in a pleasant dockside tavern. The bar was fashioned out of the side of a rowboat and we were sitting at the gunwales. A gunport had been cut out of the side of the boat in the middle and the snout of an old iron cannon thrust out. It made for a nice décor and I wondered if, in the wild days, loaded with grapeshot, it had ever been used to clear the premises of rowdies? The bartender wore a headrag and eyepatch and addressed the customers as landlubbers, but he seemed to enjoy his role so hugely that it didn't seem phony. A few locals were drinking rum at round wooden tables and a drunk slept, undisturbed, at the stern of the bar. Mary and I, by tacit agreement, were not talking about what we both were thinking and it made the conversation somewhat disjointed. She was a very pretty girl, but I didn't think about that, either. Then, by some strange alchemy, we knew that something had happened.

It came to us, and to the other customers, as if by a vibration sensed below the level of sound, just flirting with awareness. Drinking men looked up from their drinks, puzzled; Mary and I exchanged a glance. One does not explain these things. A moment later a young bait-cutter rushed in with the news that Sam Jasper's attacker had been captured. A sigh – silent but definite – passed through the drinkers, not so much because they hated or feared the madman, but because, independent men, they resented having the wharfs and streets crawling with shore patrol. The bait-cutter knew no details, he had only got the news a moment before, but no one doubted it.

I said, 'Let's go see Jerry. I'd like to get some details. Then you can run me across to the Keys, if you will.'

Mary agreed.

We finished our drinks and walked down the waterfront to the police station through crowded streets that hummed with excitement.

The police station was a small, concrete building with Jerry's office in the front and a single cell at the back. Jerry was sitting on the edge of his desk, the door to the cell was open and the cell was empty. Jerry looked bemused. He smiled when he saw Mary, but it was a serious sort of smile.

'We heard . . .' Mary started.

'You get that knee fixed up?' he asked.

'Yes. We heard . . .'

'Yeah, we got him.'

I glanced towards the cell again.

'Naw, he ain't here. They got him.' He slid from the desk and moved to the door, closing it for no apparent reason – just something to do. He said, 'I found him but I let them take him. I don't know. Something about the way Larsen talked on the phone . . . I don't like the guy, don't like men like him, but he impressed me . . . maybe that ain't the word I mean, but anyhow . . .' He reached up to his head, as if intending to adjust his hatbrim, but he wasn't wearing a hat. His hand hovered before his face and he looked embarrassed; he scratched his cheek, just as he'd closed the door – for something to do. Then he looked directly at us and said, 'I guess maybe I mean he scared me.' Then, wanting no comments on that admission, he went on, 'I found him hiding in a jumble of crates down on Third Wharf. Not hiding, exactly . . . just sort of sitting there. I was going to arrest him, I found him, Larsen be damned, but it was the damnedest thing . . .'

He hesitated. Mary and I said nothing, knowing he was wondering if he should continue. Then his jaw set. A look of distaste contorted his handsome countenance.

'He was eating a dead dog,' he said.

Mary gave a little gasp and her face twisted up. I felt faintly sick. Jerry said, 'A little brown dog. Just a stray. Don't know if he killed it or found it dead, but he was squatting there beside the crates just sort of picking at it . . . not really eating as if he were hungry, but just pulling a piece off from time to time and chewing it, sort of like he couldn't decide if it was to his taste . . . more curious than hungry. Just a little brown stray . . .'

'Eating a dog!' Mary rasped. 'The poor man!'

'Poor dog, the way I see it,' Jerry said.

'Oh my God . . .'

'Chemicals that warp the fabric of the mind ...' I whispered, but they didn't hear me.

Jerry said, 'Well, I saw that ... I didn't try to make the arrest. I called Larsen and then I just stayed back and watched the guy. I see what Sam meant about that white coat, it was sort of eerie ... worse than if he'd been naked, you know? Coat was all spattered with blood by then and the tails were dragging on the wharf. He'd tug at it from time to time, as if he would have liked to take it off but didn't know how. Then the damnedest thing happened ... they sent a truck down from the compound. Like a dog catcher's van, it was, with a cage in the back. And must of been a dozen guys with it. Not shore patrol. Some of them were Larsen's crew, dark suits and all, and some were ... well, doctors, I guess. They were all plenty scared. Even them hard-faced guys, they were scared. The guys in suits had rifles. And ... listen to this! The doctors had nets!'

'Nets?' I said, stupidly.

'Nets. Goddamn nets. Just like they was butterfly collectors ... just like in the cartoons, when the warders snag a crazy guy with butterfly nets. But the nets weren't like in cartoons, really ... they weren't on the end of poles, I mean. Just big nets with ropes on 'em, sort of like the gladiators, some of them, use in Hollywood films ... or in old Rome, far as I know. They ignored me and I didn't say a word. The guys with the nets whispered together, then began to move in on him from all sides – three sides, there was a big crate on one side.' I had the impression that Jerry was trying to be absolutely accurate in his description, as if he didn't think we would believe him – or didn't believe it, himself. 'The guys from Larsen's crew kept their rifles trained on him, the way they looked, all tense and tight jawed, I knew they would of shot him the moment he made a move. Just the one guy, but they would of shot him. I never had call to shoot a guy, myself,' he said irrelevantly; then, to the point: 'Seeing them that way, what did I do but draw my own gun. Didn't mean to. Just sort of had it in my hand before I knew it. Well ... they moved in and tossed the nets over him. He was preoccupied, he didn't seem to notice. They got about six nets onto him from all angles. Then, holding the ropes, they started to pull him towards the van. The minute he felt them tugging, he went berserk. He began to thrash about, he was rolling in the dead dog and tearing at the nets ... foaming at the mouth ... but he didn't make no sound. Lord, that fella was strong. He got to his feet, even though all six of the doctors were hauling to keep him off balance, and he sort of staggered in one direction while the men on that side backed off and those on the other side tried to hold him and got dragged along. He had one hand out from the nets, all hooked up like a talon, reaching for them. Made my flesh crawl. Few strands of the net parted and I could see they had wire inside the rope, no way he could break the nets, but he sure tried.' Jerry paused for breath. He was sweating. 'Finally they got him to the van, more by coaxing him that way than hauling him, and they prodded him with long poles until he tumbled inside, into the cage. They tossed the ropes in and slammed the doors and bolted them. He was hammering on the inside of the van and the metal was bulging out when he hit it. Then they drove off. Nobody said a word to me and I didn't ask.'

Jerry shrugged.

'He must have some terrible contagious disease,' Mary said.

'I guess. But nets? Not a very dignified way to treat a man, even a madman . . .'

Very quietly, I said, 'He bit Sam Jasper.'

'Oh, Christ!' Jerry said, we looked at each other, sharing an icy thrill of horror and, at that moment, Larsen burst in . . .

Larsen came through the door and his hard, cold face was vibrant with emotion now, his whole lean body taut and quivering.

Ignoring Mary and I, he confronted Jerry.

'Why in hell didn't you tell me someone was attacked!' he shouted.

'Take it easy,' Jerry said, thrusting his big jaw out.

'Who was attacked? You said he didn't get into the room with Jasper . . .'

'Well, now, is that what I said? Well, I guess I said it because it's true.' Jerry spoke with controlled fury; he didn't like Larsen and he didn't like the man's approach. Larsen was slightly taken aback.

Calmer, now, he said, 'I heard that the lighthouse keeper had been attacked.'

'Yeah. Well. That was before he bolted himself into the lamproom, right? He got hurt a bit before that.'

'Jesus! You should have told me, Muldoon!'

'That a fact? Well now, how was I supposed to know that? You never told me a thing. A guy gets attacked, he ain't hurt bad, I get him to the clinic . . . what's the problem?'

'The clinic? He there now?'

'Last I saw him.'

'How long ago was that?' Larsen snapped. Then he said, 'Think really carefully, Muldoon. Please.'

Jerry looked at his watch, then at me.

I said, 'About three hours.'

Larsen turned to me; said, 'Who the hell are you?'

Jerry said, 'Yeah, it was just on three hours.'

'Oh, Christ.' Larsen said. He was white-faced and his eyes, magnified by the spectacles, seemed huge. He turned, stiffly, as if his spine were fixed in the floor and he was rotating his body around it.

Then he rushed out.

Jerry leaned back against his desk, as if his energy had suddenly been spent. Then he grabbed his hat, slammed it on and started in pursuit of Larsen. Mary and I exchanged a glance and we started after Jerry. Mary called for him to wait and he stopped, waiting for us and watching Larsen. Larsen was running and he ran like a sprinter. I doubted that Jerry could have overtaken him. But Jerry didn't try, he was content to follow at a fast walk, with Mary and I at his heels. It was only a short distance and when we got there Larsen was standing in the doorway. He hadn't gone in. And he had a revolver in his hand . . .

'Now, that's a strange way to call on a sick man,' Jerry grunted. He wasn't being funny. We stepped up behind Larsen and looked past him – looked where he was looking. The matronly nurse was sitting on a bunk. Her uniform was open and there was a bandage on her neck. She was staring at the gun in Larsen's hand, looking bewildered. Then she saw Jerry move up behind him and figured everything was in hand. She remembered herself and modestly drew her uniform closed.

'No need for that, young man,' she said, nodding at Larsen's gun. She switched her gaze to Jerry. 'Didn't you see the doctor?'

'What happened?' Larsen asked.

'I have no idea who you are,' she said. 'Didn't the doctor tell you, Jerry?'

'I . . . haven't seen him.'

'Oh . . . I thought . . . well, it's certainly not a matter for firearms . . .'

Larsen put his gun away. He wore it in a holster on his hip. He left his coat unbuttoned. Jerry started to move past him, but he blocked the doorway, not going in. He said, 'What happened?' again and when the nurse looked at Jerry, the sheriff nodded.

She said, 'Well, it was an awful thing. Sam Jasper . . . he seems to have lost his mind. He was sleeping and I looked in on him just as he started having convulsions. Seemed to be in terrible pain. I called the doctor and went over to comfort Sam and all of a sudden he . . . he bit me. He sat right up in bed and bit me. Didn't know what he was doing, of course. He must have been allergic to one of the shots I gave him.' She fingered the bandage on her neck. 'It isn't serious, he just sort of snapped at me. Then he ran out.'

'Where's the doctor?'

'Why, he went looking for Sam. He looked at my neck and saw it wasn't bad, saw I could take care of it myself, so he set out to bring Sam back before he hurts himself.'

'How long ago was this ... when he bit you?' Larsen said, speaking each word distinctly.

'Why ... not more than ten, fifteen minures. I figured you'd run into the doctor, is that why you came along, Jerry?'

Larsen relaxed visibly. I could see his shoulders roll as they untensed. He stepped on into the room then. 'Was the doctor hurt ... wounded ... too?' he asked.

'Why, no. He was in his lab. I'm not really hurt, either ... it's just a scratch. Sam meant no harm.'

'He broke the skin, though?'

'Well, yes. Who is this man, Jerry?'

'I ain't sure, Ma'am,' Jerry said, looking at Larsen. Larsen had moved to the desk. He lifted the phone. The nurse said, 'Phone isn't working, young man; could have told you that had you asked permission to use it.' Larsen ignored her. He snapped something into the phone, a number or code. The phone squawked. A moment later Larsen was speaking.

They came for the nurse in an ambulance, three attendants and two of Larsen's men. She protested. 'Nothing wrong with me,' she said, 'and if there were the doctor could take care of it. I'm a trained nurse, I know when ...'

'Please don't be difficult,' Larsen said. 'This is for your own good. You ... you may have contracted a rare disease ... Well, it's best that we examine you, that's all.'

'Jerry?' she asked.

Jerry looked embarrassed. He said, 'Well, maybe you had ought to let them have a look, Julia.'

'Well ... if you say so. Lot of nonsense, you ask me. But I don't need the stretcher, I'm not in shock.'

'Please get on the stretcher,' Larsen said. He nodded and one of the attendants took her by the arm. She bristled. Jerry said, 'Now, see here, Larsen ... this woman is a civilian, you have no authority to order her around. She said she'd come and—'

Larsen wheeled on Jerry. I thought he was going to shout. But when he spoke, his voice was soft, almost pleading. He said, 'Muldoon, don't interfere in this. Please. There are things you don't understand.' Jerry's big jaw was sliding out like an avalanche, but something in Larsen's soft tone stopped his anger. He said, 'I guess you'd better do what he says, Julia. I'm sorry. I don't know what the hell's going on.'

The nurse made a huffing sound. She shook off the attendant's hand and climbed onto the stretcher as if mounting an inflated horse in the water, trying to be dignified about it. She lay back and the attendants pulled the straps around her, with her arms against her flanks. 'Ow! Not so tight,' she said. 'This is absurd. You don't need those . . .'

'Use 'em,' Larsen said. The nurse looked at Jerry and Jerry looked at Larsen. Jerry didn't like anything about this, but he was past protesting. His shoulders drooped. They carried the nurse out and loaded her into the back of the ambulance, still strapped tightly to the stretcher.

Larsen watched them drive off. Then he looked at his watch, lowered his arm and immediately raised it again, as if the time hadn't registered on the first look. His lips moved slightly, counting to himself . . . counting the minutes since or the minutes until . . . what?

Larsen went out of the door, buttoning his jacket. On the doorstep he turned back and said, 'Muldoon, you want to help, see if you can find the doctor. Keep him away from Sam Jasper. We'll find Jasper ourselves. I hope.' Without awaiting a reply, he moved off. Little eddies of dust swirled at his heels. As soon as he was out of sight I lifted the telephone, wanting desperately to get through to Elston. The switchboard that had just made contact for Larsen grated the same, 'I'm sorry, sir, the lines are out of order.'

Winking at Jerry, I said, 'This is Larsen.'

There was a pause.

Then the voice, sounding human for the first time, said, 'You're not Larsen. Who is this?'

I slammed the phone down.

'Well, it was worth a try,' I said, feeling silly. Jerry grinned, but not much. He was lost in thought . . . thinking about things that, as Larsen had said, he did not understand. It was a hell of a position for a sheriff to be in. It wasn't so good for a newspaperman, either.

'Mary,' I said, 'I think maybe you'd better run me over to the Keys . . .'

X

Mary and I walked down the cobbled street and turned into the docks. Mary looked at me, frowning, her step faltering. The gates were closed and locked and there was an armed guard on the other side of the wire. She raised her eyebrows and I shrugged. We walked on to the gate and the navy guard came to polite attention. 'Sorry, ma'am ... sir ... no one is permitted through until further notice.' I was going to speak, but Mary had her bag open; showed him her Coast Guard ID card. His eyes skimmed it. 'I have to use the launch,' she said. He was a young fellow and not too sure of himself. He said, 'Just a moment, please,' and went back to the guard house. Through the window we could see him talking on the telephone. He came back out, slightly flushed, as if he'd just been given a rocket. 'Sorry, no one is ...' He broke off the rote statement and grinned sheepishly. 'They said you couldn't go through,' he told us. 'Sorry.'

'You mean no one is allowed off the island?' I said.

'Well, I wouldn't know about that, sir. No one is allowed through this gate, is all I know.'

'What the hell is it all about?' I tried to sound formidable and authoritative. 'Some sort of quarantine?'

'Dunno, sir. Heard it was smallpox, or something.'

'Well, so much for that,' I said. Mary was still holding her ID card out in front of her. She tightened her fist, crumpling it. I nodded to the guard and he saluted and Mary and I walked back from the harbour.

I said, 'Well, whatever they're afraid of, they sure as hell can't keep it a secret now. Closing the island off ... that will have to be explained ...'

'Which means that they're more afraid than secretive,' she said. 'That it's more important to keep ... something ... contained on Pelican, than it is to keep it secret ...'

'I wonder how long?'

'I guess you'll get your story,' she said, smiling a little. 'I didn't get you down here for nothing, Jack. You'll have an exclusive ... if they ever let you write it.'

That disturbed me. We came out onto the waterfront. Quite a few men were standing about, shrimpers and fishermen and local shopkeepers, discussing the situation. No one seemed to know what it was all about, but they all thought it an unwarranted liberty. They were angry and surly and they glared at the shore patrolmen, who looked as confused as everyone else. Someone, loudly, said, 'I don't give a damn what they say, I'm taking my boat out in the morning and ain't nobody about to stop me.' Several other voices joined in, agreeing. '... burn the damn place down ...' 'Didn't want 'em here, the first place ...' They weren't a mob yet, they stood in individual clusters, but they were plenty angry. I said, 'Someone had better give them an explanation pretty damn soon or things could get ugly.'

'I'm going back to Jerry's; if they have decided to bring things out in the open they ought to let him know first. Coming?'

I hesitated. 'No, I think I'll go back to the Red Walls. I'd like to get my notes written up as much as I can ... have them ready as soon as the phones are working or I can get a boat.'

Mary walked off. I turned in the opposite direction. I had to pass several groups of men, but no one glared at me, they hadn't mistaken me for the enemy. Maybe they knew just who I was, as far as that went ... I hadn't been very subtle. Things had just moved too fast to even think about building a cover story. Well, I wasn't worried about that, now. Worried, yes. But not about that ...

XI

What were they playing at, those government bastards: what was Jerry Muldoon thinking of, letting them take Nurse Jeffries away? It was different with a crazy guy that ate dead dogs ... he was one of them and, anyhow, what harm could you do to a guy that already ate dead dogs? But Nurse Jeffries was a local; they were fiercely possessive. That was the thread that ran, embellished by rare obscenities, through the pattern of the talk in the bar of the Red Walls. The crowd was feasting on their resentment, a smorgasbord of rancour; indignation gurgled like a percolator and invective was chewed and savoured in lumps, like a fat sausage. 'Ain't the point. Maybe they has got proper doctors up to there, ain't the point; they didn't take her 'cause it was best for her, they took her 'cause Jerry let em!'

They were in an ugly mood, although it probably wasn't particularly ugly for such a gathering. I had intended to go straight to my room, avoiding the bar, but I heard the loud conversation from the doorway and it intrigued me. I figured I would be able to get some good background material from the outraged locals. I went past the stairs, but in the doorway of the bar, I hesitated. I wasn't sure I wanted to go in there, or that I should. The bar seemed to have become an informal sort of townhall for shrimpers and fishermen, a place where mobs are born and lynchings launched. This was as rough a group of men as I'd ever encountered. I'd heard talk of the old days, when things were rougher, but they were plenty rough for me, with their Buck knives and bill hooks in their belts and their leather skin all seamed with veins. Not sure of my welcome, I looked in from the doorway. A dozen men were strung out along the bar and one woman, with net stockings and a black eye, had hiked herself up on the counter.

A beefy, bearded man was saying, 'Like telling us we can't go to our boats. What the hell! They're our boats!'

'Like saying we can't fetch a little rum, a little Havana, up from the islands.'

'That's different. That's agin the law. It ain't right, but it ain't lawful.'

'Politicians!' said a thin man with long black hair drawn back in a ponytail and a scar down his cheek. 'Polititians, see, they got to be crooked by their nature. See it? They weren't crooked, they would never of riz in politics. Figures, don't it? But you or I do something what they ain't told us to do, they pass a law what makes us crooked.'

'These guys ain't politicians, though.'

'They're bastards, though . . .'

The bartender nodded in agreement with the piratical philosopher and, nodding, spotted me in the doorway. He sensed my uncertainty and waved me in. Everyone else, seeing his gesture, turned to look at me. They stopped talking and stared at me, grim and hard-eyed. I knew how the misguided stick-up man must have felt when they turned on him, aborting his crime. They didn't look hostile, exactly, but they looked infinitely capable of hostility.

I walked up to the bar and the bartender moved down to meet me, two ships joining on a charted course. I knew he was doing this to make me feel welcome and that embarrassed me. I was damned if I would act nervous and, instead of stopping at the end of the bar nearest the door, I walked right down the bar to the far end, running the gauntlet of their attention. The woman, laughing, swung a playful leg at me. The bartender passed me, going in the opposite direction, and now he had to retreat, parallelling my course along his own side of the bar. This struck me as funny and I laughed. The bartender laughed too, although he probably didn't know why. Greeting me by name, he asked if I wanted my usual and that broke the tension. The locals relaxed. One by one, they nodded, not so much to me as to the realisation that I was a neutral. I knew how a Swiss must feel. The bearded fellow nodded first, then the man beside him, then the pirate, and the nod ran down the line, heads rippling in sequence, like falling dominoes. Then they ignored me.

I stood at the end of the bar, by the stairs, listening to the talk and wondering if I should buy a round for the house, or if that would compromise my neutrality? I had a second drink. The bartender, my ally, kept looking down to make sure my glass was filled. The woman gave me a shy look that, with her black eye and coarse demeanour, was rather endearing. A gradual change altered the mood of the drinkers. They were men of abrupt rage never long sustained.

'Listen!' said one. He slapped his hand on the bar like a gavel. 'Listen, what if that dog-eater had walked in here?'

'Hey, that would of been something.'

'We'd of showed him what we does to dog-eaters, eh?'

'It would of been just like the old days!' cried an ancient mariner, gleefully.

This was rare good humour to them and everyone was laughing and drinking and taking turns in making lewd suggestions to the woman. Her replies outdid them. They had actually slipped from outrage to gaiety as abruptly as if they'd stepped from shadow into light and their levity depressed me far more than their resentment had. I finished my second drink and shook off the eager bartender. I didn't run the gauntlet again; I went up the back stairs to my room.

These were the descendents of the wreckers.

I could still hear the undulation of their mingled voices from my room. Laughter came in sudden bursts, punctuating the steady drone. They were speculating on how they would deal with a man who ate dead dogs and they spoke of that unfortunate man without the slightest sympathy, just as, I knew, a wrecker from the past would have joked with his peers, mocking the way some pitiful victim had squirmed and pleaded under his cudgel – and then, without the faintest feeling of wrongdoing, dutifully fetch his loot home to his adoring wife and happy children.

I felt a timeless despair.

XII

I dozed in depression and awoke to find the walls vibrating again. They seemed to pulse in and out like plastered lungs, billowing around me. It was not my heartbeat. A distant shouting sounded. I sat up, frightened, filmed by a pyrexia of dread. Then I realised the commotion came from below, running like fluids up the timbers of the building. There was a cry of anger ... a crash ... another cry that rose to a scream. It appeared that the ephemeral good humour of the crowd had turned surly again: autophagous anger devouring itself with ravenous rage. They had few tools, those rough men; they saw every frustration as a nail to be hammered by violence.

Then, of a sudden, the noise ceased.

There was no transition, no gradual ebbing of the uproar – there was bedlam and then there was a silence so absolute that it was sound in itself ... a cosmic boom. That void of sound roared in my ears. Fights do not end in such abrupt silence, unless ...

I went downstairs ...

From the balcony, gripping the banister, I looked into the barroom. The men were standing in a circle, looking inwards and down. The bartender was standing back, a broken truncheon in his hand. The woman was leaning against the counter, one hand at her throat. No one moved. I waited, scarcely breathing, knowing that there was some terrible centrepiece to that silent circle. I wanted to bear no witness to this scene: my impulse was to creep back up the stairs but I could not move. My legs seemed to grow from the floor, my hand was glued to the railing.

The big, bearded man moved. Something flashed silver in his hand – flashed silver and, turning, flashed red. His hand went to his pocket, he stepped aside. Another man moved. One by one they broke from that ring, cast off by the centrifugal force of shock; they went to the doors. I saw the body around which that motionless orbit had described its silent arc. Blood had spread out like melted wax; in that blood, the body was like a fossil, preserved forever in red amber.

It was Sam Jasper, and he was dead.

The woman walked out, stumbling, still holding her throat. Only the bartender remained. He still gripped the broken truncheon, like driftwood that kept him afloat in reality; his face was as bloodless as if he, too, had spilled his veins onto the floor.

I was able to move then – I had to move, for my trembling legs threatened to collapse. I went down the final steps into the room. The bartender turned towards me.

'I don't know,' he said.

He had anticipated my words; already launched from my throat, they came out, anyway: 'What happened?'

'I don't know,' he said, again.

I was trying not to look at Sam. I looked at the telephone and the bartender followed my gaze. He moved towards the phone and I stepped forwards. Then he came back towards me and I stopped. It was like some ritual dance choreographed in Hell. He moved the broken club like a baton, leading the silent music of our gavotte. Then he broke the pattern, leaning against the bar, his head lowered. He began to speak.

'Jasper,' he said. 'But not like Jasper. He came in the door. Someone asked him how he was, but he didn't answer. His mouth was open but not making any noise and ... drooling. He came at us. Not fast, he had a strange, deliberate step ... not like he was weak, like he was just remembering how to walk ...' The barman's throat worked convulsively, disgorging his words as if vomiting up poisoned food. '... His fingernails ... teeth ... like an animal ... Nobody did anything at first, we all knew old Sam ...' He looked at me as if he wanted confirmation. I nodded. I could imagine those men, confronted by the unknown, unable to react ... unable to identify the nail that had to be hammered. 'But then he grabbed Sally. She'd jumped up on top of the bar. Sometimes she used to dance on the bar,' he said, as if that were miraculous. 'Sam got her by the ankle ... pulled her off. Her back hit the edge of the bar and she screamed ... then everyone got hold of him ... it was because of Sally ... if she hadn't of moved ... that's when Sam went for her, when she jumped up on the bar ...' He stared at me. He was justifying it. An attack on a woman had played the catalyst to their stunned immobility, it was a thing to which they could react in their fashion. I nodded my understanding.

'But he was too strong,' he said, wonderingly.

'Just an old man everybody knew ... too strong. He was throwing men aside, snapping his teeth ... I thought he was going to kill Sally. I came over the bar and hit him ... with this—' he held up the truncheon '—and he didn't even feel it. It snapped over his shoulder ... Old Sam, but too strong ...'

He let the broken club roll from his hand onto the counter; his voice was hollow. 'Then there was a knife,' he said. 'I don't know who started it ... someone ... then they all had knives and hooks out, they were stabbing into Sam like they couldn't stop, like they was all crazy, like sharks when they get frenzied ... or like they was too scared to stop. And Sam didn't seem to know he was being stabbed. It went on and on. Then Sam was down on the floor, he must of been dead. All his blood has poured out, he's dead, and everyone steps back from him ... and Sam sits up!'

I flinched. The bartender's voice went into me as those knives had gone into Sam Jasper; I was bleeding sweat, congealed fear seeped from my pores The bartender gripped my arm; said, 'He sat up and his jaw dropped open; then he fell over again ... but all his blood was out and ... he moved after he was dead ...'

He was trembling. His hand shook on my arm and the trembling passed on into me. What terrible determination had caused Sam Jasper to move, to defy mortality with a final convulsion?

Locked together by the coupling of his hand, we shuddered face to face. Then he looked away.

'They left,' he said, as if aware for the first time that we were alone in the room. 'They all left.'

I understood that. Murder had been done and these were not men to plead self-defence or to stand trial ... nor to go, as Nurse Jeffries had, to the compound.

'It wasn't like the old days,' he said.

His hand dropped away from me. He went down the bar and hesitated by the telephone. Then he turned and went out the door. I waited for a few minutes. Then I went down to the phone. The switchboard said, 'Sorry, sir, the lines are still out of order ...' and I said, 'You'd better listen to me.' Ten minutes later Larsen arrived.

XIII

Even had the phone been working, it would never have occurred to me to call Jerry Muldoon, although, legally, Jasper's death should have been his concern. And I wasn't thinking of getting a story, either. I was lost in an emotional wilderness. I only hoped that Larsen would know what to do – that there was something that could be done. Waiting for him, I prayed that Mary Carlyle would not walk in, bearing some news for me. Mary had liked Sam Jasper. And that was not Sam on the floor, that sticky mould of red aspic ... nor, worse, had it been Sam in the moments before he died. I could never tell Mary what had happened here. But I could tell Larsen – in his way, he too was a dead man.

I went behind the bar and poured myself a huge brandy.

I was halfway through it when Larsen arrived. He came in with half a dozen men and, while they inspected the body – gingerly, at first – he came directly over to me.

He said, 'You were right to call me, Harland.'

'I thought I might be. Have a drink?'

His cold eyes flickered.

'The bartender left too,' I said.

'I'm going to need your help, Harland.'

I poured Larsen a drink. He didn't refuse it. When I'd first seen him, he'd sipped very slowly at a beer; things were changed. They were taking Sam Jasper out on a rubber sheet and, as they stepped, their heels made squishing sounds in the congealing blood.

'How can I help?'

'The men he fought with . . . who killed him. I want you to identify them.'

'I didn't see the fight. I told you, I—'

'The men who were in the bar earlier,' he said.

'I don't know if I can.'

'I guess you'll cooperate. You phoned me.'

'No, I don't mean I won't . . . I'm not sure I can. I didn't know any of them by name or—'

He nodded crisply; said, 'Understand this. You can't protect anyone. I'm not talking about a criminal charge here, this isn't crime and punishment. These locals are . . . independent types. They won't come in voluntarily, we'll have to find them. All of them. And they'll be hiding, thinking they are guilty of murder or—'

'Guilty? It strikes me that if anyone on this island is guilty of anything—'

'Don't be antagonistic,' he said. Then he took his spectacles off and rubbed his eyes. He looked at me, for the first time, without the lenses between us. He seemed more human. He said, 'Guilt? I know about guilt. I think every one of us, working on this thing, feels guilty. Sometimes, Harland . . . sometimes I feel guilt so heavy that it's like a shroud draped over me. I have to stop whatever I'm doing and take a deep breath. And doing that, I only manage to inhale the guilt, it gets in my lungs, inside me. I'm not a robot, Harland. I thought I was a patriot . . . but a guilty patriot. Now . . . well, now we do what we can.' He put the spectacles back on, as if hiding behind them. He took a slug of brandy. He was waiting for me to speak.

I said, 'I only know what the bartender told me . . .'

Larsen nodded impatiently.

'He ... Sam Jasper ... was inhumanly strong. He was insane, of course, but when the knives went into him he scarcely seemed to notice, he—'

'I know,' Larsen snapped. 'I don't need an account of the affair, I know what ... they ... can do.'

'They?'

He ignored that.

He said, 'Do you know if any of them were ... wounded?'

'No. But Sam was fighting with them ... and he had attacked a woman ... so I think we can assume he inflicted some damage.'

Larsen sighed, nodded; said, 'I want you to describe every one of the men who were in this room, as best you can. Then I'll want you to identify them as we bring them in. We have to find them, and we have to do it in the next couple hours.'

'Is that possible?'

'Probably not.'

'And if you don't?'

'I'm not at liberty to discuss that. Just in case we do. If we don't ... why, then, you'll know about it, just like everyone else. You won't like it.'

'This ... disease, this madness. It's infectious, right?'

'Of course it's infectious, goddamn it! You've seen what happens.'

'And you have to find these men in time to treat them, to give them an antidote or inoculate them or whatever ...'

'Whatever! You're wasting time.'

'I have to be sure just what I'm doing, just why I'm helping you, Larsen.'

'I told you, there will be no criminal charges. Isn't that enough?' He was looking at his watch. 'Please, Harland,' he said, quite softly.

'All right. I'll do the best I can.'

He nodded. 'We'll go up to the compound. You can dictate the descriptions in the car. I'm already having my men round up all the known regulars from this place, shrimpers, fishermen ... it's just possible ...'

One of the others came up to him, awaiting orders.

Larsen said, 'Get that blood up. All of it. We don't need ... Then seal the place.' The man nodded. The blood, too? I thought. Larsen turned back to me. 'Well, come on, then.'

I finished my drink and followed him towards the door.

Larsen grabbed my arm and maybe he said it to impress the urgency on me, or to frighten me, or maybe he just felt like saying it. He said:

'None of us may get out of this, Harland ... we may never leave this island. And, believe me, it won't be a tropical paradise then ...'

XIV

Drinking black coffee from a white mug, I sat behind a table in a small whitewashed room feeling depressed and sick and tired. I had described the men – and the woman – as best I could and, although the descriptions seemed pitifully inadequate to me, Larsen seemed satisfied. I expect he had a file on everyone who lived on Pelican. From time to time he nodded, as if in recognition. There was something almost intimate in our relationship as I confided in him in the back seat of the car. When I mentioned the woman, he said, 'That'll be Sally ... salad girl on the shrimp boats ... ship's whore, to speak plainly,' and he also put names to the bearded man and the long-haired philosopher ... several others – I paid little heed; perhaps I did not want these men to have names, to label those I was betraying and thereby make them individuals. My information was slight. My memory for details had been blurred, knocked out of focus, yet Larsen drew from me more than I thought I knew in the shadowed intimacy of that moving car. I had exhausted my recollections by the time we entered the compound.

We drove up to the main building, a single-storey affair with wings on either side, and Larsen escorted me to the whitewashed room. His men had not been idle. They started bringing the locals in as soon as I had taken my seat. Larsen stood beside me, behind the table. There was a gooseneck lamp there and he kept his hand on the flexible shaft, tilting it up and down. The bulb was very bright, very white against the wall. Larsen leaned forward; his face sprang out with an albedo to shame the moon, lips drawn back, clenched teeth geometrical. Dark veins in his neck defied the lurid glare. Then he leaned back into darkness and his face receded.

They brought the locals in one by one, two guards to each man and another guard on the door. They were angry, bewildered men, roused from bed or rousted from bars without explanation. The Cuban counterman from the Fisherman's Café was one of the first; he looked sullen and dejected. Others who had heard the news looked sly and cunning. They all stared directly at me and I felt the lowest form of traitor, but I neither flinched nor looked away, convinced that I was doing what had to be done, despite these secret police tactics. I recognised several of the locals, but not from the Red Walls. I spoke to no one and they just glared at me, their faces distorted by elongated shadows thrown up from the lamp. Perhaps they could not identify me as they looked into that glare. I shook my head each time and Larsen sighed. Knowing I had to identify the men who had been involved, I nevertheless felt satisfaction each time I was able to negate one.

Then they brought in an old man and my memory snatched his face from the crowd at the bar, moulding it to the frightened countenance that stood before me in this silent inquisition. It was the old man who had spoken fondly of the old days. I hesitated. I felt Larsen stiffen beside me. The old man was squinting in the direct beam of the lamp and I didn't know if he could see my features, but I knew he could see my head, at least in outline; that he would know if I nodded.

Larsen sensed my hesitation; he tilted the lamp higher and the old man's shadow sprang up the wall, crooked and distorted. The shadow seemed to have more substance than the man who cast it; there was a reality too dark to be illuminated in this room.

At last, I nodded.

The old man went rigid and Larsen's head snapped around towards me. I nodded again. Larsen flicked a glance at the guards. They took the old man by the arms and led him out. He was protesting in a high-pitched whine. I felt truly treacherous now and Larsen must have known this, for he placed his hand on my shoulder reassuringly and, as if to certify the humanity behind the gesture, he took his spectacles off for a moment.

Then they brought the next man in.

Twice more, I nodded.

I must have confronted forty or fifty men and only three of them had been in the bar. The bearded man had not been found, nor the long-haired fellow with the political views. The woman had not been brought in, nor had the bartender, but in those cases the identification was definite and they may have found them without bringing them before me in my stark chamber. They the steady stream of – what? Suspects? Victims? Carriers? . . . whatever, the stream of unfortunates brought there to stand before their tortured shadows began to taper off. In the first stormtrooper round-up Larsen's men had gathered up the unsuspecting and the innocent, but those who had been involved had already gone into hiding with, from their point of view, good reason – a man had been killed, one old, unarmed man had been stabbed to death by a mob and they had no desire to stand trial on that count. They were terrified by the bizarre aspects of the thing and, even discounting the murder, they knew that Nurse Jeffries had, under somewhat similar circumstances, been forced to go to the mysterious compound. They were not inclined to listen to the reasoning of authority and, even if they had, the time element was against that approach. I couldn't blame them for going into hiding. But while they hid, the disease was incubating.

'How long does it take?' I asked.

Larsen and I were alone behind the table. The guard on the door had his back to us, hands clasped, looking down the corridor. No one had been brought in for the last ten minues.

'What?'

'For the disease to take effect?'

'That's not . . .' He paused, leaning towards me so that his face came into the light as if he now were being identified, waiting for my dreaded nod. 'Oh, hell, it's a bit late in the game to play classified information, isn't it? I appreciate your help, Harland. The time . . . it varies according to the subject's weight and metabolism and, to a lesser degree, the body area where the . . . infection . . . was transferred. Say an average of . . . three hours.'

'That soon?'

'That soon,' he said, playing with the lamp, manipulating the shadows, twisting the flexible neck from side to side in his strong hands. I felt the same need to do something with my own hands. I got my pipe out and began to fill it carefully. He twisted the lamp and I stuffed tobacco in the bowl and lit it. A great cloud of smoke billowed out and hung over us. I remembered how Larsen had spoken of the cloud of guilt that often enveloped him. The drifting smoke made filigreed shadows up the wall. The shadows moved; they were not as enduring as guilt.

He was fairly strangling the lamp.

'It must be very virulent,' I said.

'Of course. Harland, it's a disease such as the world has never known. A disease that never should have been known . . . and we created it here.'

'What is it? Viral?'

'Chemical.'

Chemicals that warp the fabric of the mind . . . I said, 'Chemical? But how can that be contagious?'

Larsen dropped his head, twisting his own neck just as he'd twisted the lamp. He said, 'I don't know. But it is.' The light, reflecting from his taut face, seemed to come from within his skull. 'It's directly infectious, by contact. It's not . . . well, it's not the Black Death, say. It won't sweep across the world and decimate the population. Thank God for that. And yet, in its way it's far more horrible. It's so—' he sought the word '—so personal! Yes, that's it, exactly. Personal.' The word itself seemed anathema to this bureaucratic man. 'It goes beyond disease, Harland; it reaches into the realm of superstition and snatches up the stuff of legend, the dark fears that evolved with man. Werewolves, Harland . . . and vampires . . .' His face rose and fell as if under heavy blows. He looked sick. He said, 'These men . . . the man who contract this thing . . . officially, in the reports, they are termed subjects of Chemically Modified Behaviour. Informally . . .' he looked at me. 'We call them ghouls.'

I winced.

He said, 'An ugly word, and not just terminology. Yet when you've seen them . . . it is a word that caught on quite easily, amongst the guards and attendants, at first . . . until even the doctors use it. I use it. You . . .' He looked at me with a hint of a smile. 'You, no doubt, will use it in your story . . .'

'You know who I am, then?'

'. . . if you ever get to write it.'

No threat was intended in his words – no threat from him. I puffed and smoke flowed laterally across the table, crossing the lamp like clouds shredding before the face of the moon.

I said, 'How soon must the antidote be administered?'

Larsen looked as if he didn't understand the question. His thin lips drew back from his teeth and he snapped the light off. From the sudden shadows, he said, 'Not my field . . . I only know we have to have them before the damned thing takes effect. And . . .' he looked at his watch. 'I don't guess we're going to do it.'

He stood up and moved around the end of the table.

'I have things to arrange,' he told me. 'Will you wait here? They may bring a few more in before it's too late.'

'Of course,' I said.

He nodded and walked out. The guard saluted. I heard his footsteps drum hollow down the corridor and I didn't envy him his task . . . the arrangements he must make.

My pipe had gone out.

I struck a match and relit it and, as if that flare had been a signal, the guard on the door turned and stepped into the room. I had supposed he was there to make sure I didn't leave but, with proper deference, he said, 'What's going to happen next, sir?'

I gaped at him and he blushed. He was quite young.

'Oh, I realise I'm not cleared for classified information, sir, but . . . you know how it is . . . a man can't work in a place like this without getting a pretty good idea of what's going on. And my wife will be worried, I haven't been able to call her . . . I just wanted some idea of how long we'd be quarantined . . .'

I realised that Larsen and I had come in with such a flurry of haste that he had not explained the situation to the guard – or perhaps disdained informing a subordinate of anything. The young man obviously thought I was one of them. It was a natural enough mistake. Larsen and I had been collaborating as equals and he had even deferred to me on deciding which of the men brought in had been infected. The guard probably thought me an expert in detecting symptons of the disease before they became apparent to others. It was too good a chance to pass up.

I said, 'I can't tell you that,' trying to sound just curt enough to be authoritative without discouraging him.

'I'm sorry sir.'

He started to turn away.

'A bad business,' I said.

'Yes, sir. Very bad.'

'I just arrived . . . from the other laboratory . . .' I said. He showed no signs of disbelief. 'I've been in such a rush, I haven't had time to get the details. How did the first . . . subject . . . escape, do you know? The one who broke through the fence?' I held my breath. He didn't doubt me at all.

'Oh, Jefferson,' he said. 'Why, he broke the restraining straps. He'd been taken to the laboratory for an examination or something and someone slipped up; didn't use the reinforced straps, I guess.'

'Damned inefficiency.'

He blinked at me; said, 'Worse than inefficiency, if you'll pardon my saying so, sir. I guess maybe you don't know about Duncan?' I shook my head. 'Johnny Duncan. Friend of mind. Hell of a nice guy, Duncan. He was on the door, tried to stop the ghoul. Jefferson, I mean, sir. Only it's hard to call one of them by their name . . . by the name they had when they were human, you know? Makes it seem worse, somehow. Anyway, Duncan tried to stop him and the . . . and Jefferson tore his arm damn near off. It was just hanging there by a few ropes of tendon. Right arm, it was. Poor Duncan, he was right-handed; had to use his left hand when he shot himself . . .'

'Shot himself?'

'Lefthanded.'

He seemed to think this sinistral suicide more deplorable than had it been dextral; thus had morality been compromised and mutated in this place.

'Funny, you know . . . I was there by that time; I felt as if I ought to stop him from shooting himself, but he just looked at me and I couldn't do a thing. Even if it meant I got in trouble over it . . . couldn't do a thing. He put the gun to his head. He was in terrible pain, what with his arm torn off like that, but it wasn't the pain . . . it was knowing he was gonna turn ghoul. Hell of a guy. He said goodbye to me; made me feel awful. Then he blew his brains out. Wasn't married, Duncan; that's one thing.'

'But . . . the antidote . . .'

'Oh, you don't have to tell me that, sir.' He looked shy . . . maybe sly. He said, 'I know there's no antidote.'

I looked down at my glowing pipe and pretended that the alarm passing over my face was due to a congested stem. Slowly, I said, 'These subjects . . . the ones I was able to identify, and the nurse . . . how are they being . . . treated?'

'Oh, it's painless, sir. No need to worry about that. One of the docs gives 'em an injection, it's over in a few seconds.' He smiled at me. He was really quite young, his cheeks fuzzy, an innocent young man assuring me that murder was done efficiently and painlessly.

He said, 'That's what you meant when you said, antidote, huh? Funny how you scientists always use words that mean less than they ought. Meaning no offence, sir. Euphemism, is it? Well, anyhow, I guess that Duncan figured a bullet was just as painless as a shot in the arm, and a whole lot quicker. Or maybe he was afraid they wouldn't give him the shot, come to think of it; that they'd let him turn ghoul and study him in place of Jefferson . . .'

'Yes,' I said. I felt a band of sickness tighten across my diaphragm. I had just condemned, with a nod, three men to death. And yet, if I hadn't . . . it was mercy killing, benevolent condemnation, I could justify it . . . and yet—

The guard was saying, 'Maybe they would of, too, far as that goes. Of course, that was before all these other guys got infected. Got more ghouls than they know what to do with, now; can't study all of them. I don't know about the other lab . . . the one you come from . . . fact is, I didn't even know there was another one. But we only got three cells here strong enough to hold 'em and you can't put 'em in together or they'll eat each other. Guess they never reckoned on having more than three at once. So the only humane thing to do . . . but you know about that, sir.'

On abrupt impulse, I stood up. Yes, I knew about that . . . now; the knowledge was stalking around like a footpad in my soul.

'It seems to me that you know a good deal more than you're cleared for,' I said, jaws tight.

The guard looked frightened.

'I'm sorry, sir,' he said, blanching.

I pointed at him with my pipestem, paused, then sighed.

'Where is Elston now?' I asked.

'He's in his lab, sir. It's just down the hall, third door on the right,' he said quickly, hoping that other matters would intervene between us. I gave him a crisp nod and brushed past. He saluted. I walked down the corridor with my heels drumming just like Larsen's.

XV

Elston was in his laboratory, but he was not working; he was seated on a high stool, all sunk up in himself. I had the impression of a dunce at a blackboard. I closed the door and he looked up. 'You,' he said, without surprise. He was beyond surprise. I walked over to him and knocked my pipe out against the edge of a shelf. Test tubes rattled in a rack and arcane fluids sloshed about in beakers.

'You should have contacted me sooner,' I said.

'I wish to God I had.'

'Will you tell me about this . . . thing?'

'It's too late.'

'It could prevent a recurrence elsewhere.'

'I doubt . . .' he said, and paused, as if his doubt were a categorical statement. His eyes turned about, looking for some object deserving of that doubt. 'I doubt that even the government would attempt such a thing again. I am not a brave man, Harland . . . but there does not exist a torture that would ever again induce me to cooperate.'

'But you never intended this.'

'My God, no! I . . . never . . .' His voice trailed off. He lifted a murky beaker and looked into it, as if he expected to find resolution there, or courage; reading the runes of science. He moved the beaker and the fluid sloshed about; peering at it, he seemed to be contemplating a rare vintage, a distillate of evil. I felt that the fluid should be roiling and giving off vapours; had he suddenly drained it on a compulsive whim, I would not have been surprised.

Abruptly he began to speak, driven to explain and exonerate himself.

'In my research into chemical lobotomy, I discovered a process by which to make men mindless. I had not sought this result, it was a side-effect, accidental. These ... subjects ... were totally obedient and docile, but they were immensely powerful, for they no longer had inhibitions of any sort. They no longer knew the limitations of self preservation; were no longer confined by human instinct. They could, upon command, perform tasks that amazed me ...'

'The man who broke his arm lifting against an unliftable weight?'

'You know of that? Yes, that is an example. No normal man could exert enough pressure to break his own skeleton. But, feeling no pain and totally uninhibited, a man treated by this process became a superman.'

'But to what purpose?'

'To my purpose, to my intentions, it was merely a side-effect. I sought to make the incurable manageable, that was all. The purpose put to this by the agency, however ... the dark vision of those fiends ... they foresaw an army of living robots ...'

'Of course. Men without fear, unable to feel pain, totally obedient ...'

'That was the idea. An army that would walk through enemy fire, keep on walking even though they had been shot several times, had limbs blown off ... even crawling, legless, to carry out the attack ... only an absolutely mortal wound could stop them; even dead they could move for a few moments. It is shock that stops a wounded man, but only death itself could stop these poor creatures. But there was a flaw. Nearly mindless, they could make no decisions, could not discriminate between friend and foe; nor were they belligerent. They were unstoppable but they were useless. I believed that we had come to a dead end, and I was glad. But the devious minds that controlled me ... those minds must be as warped as those of my creations, their thoughts twisted through hideous configurations which bleed out humanity and distil pure evil ...' He looked directly at me. 'The next stage ... I balked at this, they threatened ... well, no matter; I am a coward; I did as they wished.'

Elston shook his head from side to side.

'Harland, I took the obedience out. I made these creatures savage and bestial, instilling bloodlust and ferocity ... the very factors that my original research had been designed to quell. It was not a difficult thing, merely a matter of finding the proper chemical balance. And again we seemed to have reached a dead end. Again I was glad. In taking the obedience from them, I made them unmanageable.'

'Then you were back where you started ...'

'Not quite. In one day, these men that controlled me, in one day those minds had realised a use for this . . . monstrosity.'

'I can see none.'

'Nor did I. But we are not like them. By this time, other scientists, scientists who thought like them, were working with me. They had access to all my material. It was one of those men who discovered that this state of mindless bloodlust could be transmitted from man to man, from host to victim. The chemicals that transfigured the mind ran rampant through the body. They infected the blood, the saliva . . . and could be transmitted, like any disease . . . like leprosy, like plague . . . but far, far more terrible. It was communicable madness.'

He put his hands to his face, dragging his fingers down his cheeks.

'I still don't see . . .'

'No, you wouldn't. I . . . again I protested. But by this time the work could have continued without me – or so I told myself, to justify what I did. And it was hideous. The first man we treated tore his eyes out. Obviously not a trait desirable in a soldier. We corrected that. We tested their aggression by putting them in a cage together.' He closed his eyes, remembering what he had seen in those cages. 'To find the proper balance, you see. They did not want these . . . ghouls, they call them . . . they did not want them to be so ferocious that they killed. That would have defeated their purpose . . .'

'And that purpose was?'

Elston ignored me. He continued, 'Like rabid dogs . . . that was the desirable condition . . . wounding and then leaving the victim alive, so that he, in turn, would become . . . one of them. The madness would spread by geometrical progression. I say madness, I might say bestiality . . . there is no term for them, really. Ghouls – they call them ghouls – they caused them to be created and then call them that. They are not cannibals, yet they would eat human flesh as any other . . . nor necrophagics, although they would devour a corpse . . . quite casually, these mindless things would devour . . . themselves.' He paused for a few moments, head cocked as though listening for the echo of his words from amongst the vials and beakers. 'But this is no more than a side-effect of their condition. They might just as well eat nothing and starve to death. A side effect, just as their fear of water. I could have removed that inhibition, of course. It was deemed wise to let it remain – a way to control them, surrounding them by water, confining them; useful on this island and later, in other places . . .'

'What places, Doctor?'

Again he ignored me. 'Well, it was done. I had regulated their fury to the proper degree. That fury was contagious. In the initial instance, when the disease is induced by injection, the time period between treatment and the onset of the violence can be regulated – that is, knowing the subject's weight and metabolism, I can regulate the dosage, leaving the disease like a slow fuse within him. But when it is transmitted directly from man to man, with the disease at full virulence in the host, it will take effect within hours in the victim. This was just as they wished it; it suited their scheme.'

'But what was that scheme?' I asked.

He looked at me, his fingers still dragging at his cheeks, drawing the flesh down.

'Their plan, Harland,' he said. 'Their plan was . . . to infect enemy prisoners of war!'

I saw it then. My flesh crawled.

'They would be treated to go berserk in, say, a month's time. Then allowed to escape, or be dealt in an exchange of prisoners, with the abomination smouldering in them. You can imagine the results. They laughed, those men . . . my masters . . . they laughed, thinking of a plague of ghouls behind the enemy lines. It would be most effective. The carriers would no doubt be killed, but not before inflicting wounds which would, in turn, create a second wave of monsters.'

'My God,' I whispered. 'The cold calculation . . .'

'Think of the panic, the confusion, the horror, when the enemy troops . . . and then the civilians . . . began to go berserk in ever-increasing numbers. By the time they realised what was causing it, if they ever did, it would be too late. The enemy army would be demoralised, if not destroyed. Perhaps the nation, itself . . . destroyed as surely as the minds of the infected. Then it would be a simple matter of quarantining the enemy country or holding the battle lines firm and waiting for the self-destruction. Such was their plan. They were greatly pleased with it . . .'

'It could escalate . . . to what proportions? Where would it stop?'

'We had to predict that. The . . . ghouls . . . would not survive for long. They cannot take care of themselves, they neglect the normal bodily needs. Those not killed outright would die, in due course, of accident, starvation, dehydration. But to say how long it would take . . .' He shrugged.

I heard a gun go off from somewhere without the compound.

'I guess we'll find that out now,' I said

Elston said, 'What?' and then he understood and said, 'Why, yes; so we shall . . .' Incredibly, there was a spark of scientific interest in his eyes . . . interest detached from guilt and regret. I turned and walked away and I don't think he even noticed. His motives in summoning me had been laudable, but he was yet a scientist interested in his work. The horror of it all...well, as Elston might have put it: that was a side-effect, no more. He had talked into me, as if I were a recording device and now, to him, I was switched off. I think, of the two, I respected Larsen more.

I wandered the corridors for awhile. There was a great deal of activity, both naval and civilian types rushing about; no one paid me any notice. From time to time I heard gunfire. Presently I returned to the whitewashed room. The guard was no longer on the door. I went in and sat down behind the table. A few minutes later Larsen came in.

'Where in hell have you been?' he asked.

'I took a walk. I don't suppose there was anything wrong in that, was there? Or am I under restraint?'

'What's eating you, Harland?'

'There is no antidote.'

'Oh. How did you . . . oh, it doesn't matter. Yes, we're killing them. What else can we do? We have no facilities to lock up so many, even if we wanted to. Can't lock them up together, you know. Anyhow, it's best for them. Wouldn't you wish to be killed, if the alternative was . . . becoming one of them?'

He was right, I supposed; or less wrong. I nodded, or shrugged. Right and wrong could not be taken in chunks, demarcated like the light and shadow of that room.

He said, 'We're shooting them as we find them; it's too late for anything else.'

'Are you finding many?'

'Too many.'

He leaned out into the corridor and said something. Then he stepped aside and two uniformed guards came in with a stretcher. There was a body on the stretcher, covered with a sheet; not moving. They slid the stretcher on the table and Larsen pulled the sheet down. I looked at a dead man's face.

'Recognise him? Was he in the Red Walls?'

I studied the face very carefully. In death, the man looked normal enough. But I had never seen him before.

'No,' I said.

'Are you sure?'

'Positive.'

'You know what that means?'

'Of course. The second stage has begun.'

'So we no longer need your help, Harland. It was worth a try. I never really expected . . .'

'How fast will it escalate?'

'God knows. If every one of the men Jasper infected – except for the three we got in time – if they infect even two more . . . I can't say. I suppose it's a matter of mathematics.' He turned to the guards. 'Take that away,' he said, and they jumped forwards and lifted the stretcher. 'Got to burn the bodies,' he said, to me. 'It can spread from a corpse. If a dog or a rat got at one of the bodies . . . the dead flesh still carries the change, you see. We learned that in the early experiments, before we were using human . . . volunteers. The catalyst, being chemical, doesn't need a living host. It can lurk in dead tissue and be ingested . . . got to burn them. I wouldn't even trust them to the worms.' The strain was showing on Larsen. He looked even thinner than before, his eyes were bigger behind his spectacles and his close-cropped hair stuck up in clumps.

'The worst part will be the women,' he said.

I didn't get that, for a moment; said, 'There was only the one woman, the salad girl . . .' but Larsen shook his head.

'No, the others. These men have wives, girlfriends . . . no bond of love will save them, if they are together when . . .' He paled suddenly. 'No, the worst part won't be the women,' he said.

'What, then?'

'The children,' Larsen said.

And horror ran, like malaria, in my veins . . .

XVI

Like demons in hell, the guards stood around the rim of the smouldering pit. They had dug the pit behind the laboratory, not far from the fence, and they were burning the corpses. The lab was equipped with an incinerator, but it was not large enough for the grisly task. As they had not anticipated needing cells for more than three at one time, so they had not figured on having to burn so many. The stench was appalling. I stood in the open back door of the building, staring out and smoking my pipe; fearful and wondering.

Black smoke, shot through with red flashes, billowed up from the pit. The sky was pale in the east, making the smoke seem blacker and thicker as it coiled up in ebony ropes and plumes, a Stygian cable anchored in the pit. I watched as two guards carried a corpse to the rim. They looked as if they stood at the doors to Hell, washed with the red glow. They threw the body into the inferno. A wave of increased heat struck me; sparks spun from the incandescent crater and threads of orange weaved through the writhing black funnel. One of the guards slapped at his thigh. A spark had struck him. And then they brushed their hands together, gazing down into the fiery pit for a moment before stepping away, workmen with a task well done. They might have been advertising beer on television . . . a hard job done and now it's time to relax with an ice cold . . .

Larsen stepped up beside me, his thin nostrils twitching.

'Jesus,' he said.

Then he grinned and said, 'That pipe of yours sure does stink.'

I blinked at him, astounded, and then, suddenly, we were both laughing at his joke. It wasn't forced laughter, we were honestly convulsed by his wit. He wrinkled his nose. Laughing, I said, 'If we get a midget ghoul, you can stuff him in my briar,' and Larsen howled with glee. I puffed away and the deep bowl of my pipe glowed and billowed in feeble imitation of the fiery pit.

Then, abruptly, we were not laughing.

It had been a strange impulse and only dimly grasped, yet I doubt I have ever laughed with such good humour as I did that night by the smouldering pit . . .

I said, 'How many?'

'Nine,' he told me. 'Not counting the nurse.'

He rubbed his lean jaw. One side of his face seemed to have ignited in the seething glow; the other was as dark as the smoke, the muscles in his cheek twisting in turbulent coils – a stormy face in a volcanic dawn. I knew that my own face reflected the same disunion, cleft by the chiaroscuro of the flames. Like carnal mirrors, we reflected one another.

'I don't know if we should be encouraged or discouraged by the numbers,' he said. 'Don't know what they signify. The more we get might mean the fewer left . . . or it might mean we are simply drawing from a larger pool . . .'

'I know. We don't know how many men Jasper actually wounded, but even if only three or four got away . . . three could become nine . . . or twelve . . . even with minimal numbers . . .' Even as I spoke, I was aware that I was thinking strictly of numbers as a statistic; not of the men they represented. And that I had to. '. . . And then, the third stage . . . Thank God we're on an island with a limited population.'

'I may decide to evacuate,' he said. He looked at me as if he wanted my advice. 'If we can't control the spread . . . but we'll have to make damned sure none of the evacuees is infected. Some system of quarantine before boarding the boat. I'm not sure I want that responsibility, that decision . . . Well, it may be a moot point. They may not let us leave.'

'If you do . . . we do . . . what about them? The . . . ghouls?' The word had a bitter taste; I was appalled that I'd used it. 'Will you just abandon them here?'

He looked at me with fire running down his profile.

'That decision will come from higher up . . . and I'm just as glad of that.' He rubbed his neck; his splayed fingers cast slender shadows and his hand glowed red; the heat rose and fell as if some terrible bellows pulsed in the pit.

'It's the ones who stayed in town that are hard to flush out . . . and have more opportunity to infect others,' he said. His lips twisted the words out. 'Most of the ones we got had come to the beach or inland. We've started a house-to-house search but the damnedest part is that we can't tell who is infected and who isn't until it takes effect.'

'Are there no symptons that show before?'

'I asked Elston about that, a few minutes ago. None that he knows of. He's . . . a dedicated man. He begged me not to burn all the corpses . . . to save a few for him to dissect.'

'Maybe he hopes to find an antidote.'

'That's a charitable supposition,' Larsen said.

He looked very human then, with his face inhumanly blazing in the glow. I wondered if he knew that Elston had written me. He knew who I was and maybe he'd known all along; maybe he, too, had wanted it stopped, wanting it helplessly from within the cage of his duty, the bureaucratic web that trapped his life. I felt the absolute helplessness of the man, the frustration; his life and his volition had been frozen in the ice of obedience, trapped as surely as a heart within a ribcage, a mind within a skull. I thought I might ask him – we had become friends, I think, in some twisted fashion – but as I was about to speak, gunfire sounded off to the side.

We both looked.

A man – a ghoul . . . the word asserted its rights in my mind . . . was running along the outside of the fence – not running as if frightened, for they knew no fear, but running as if he had started to run by pure chance and was too mindless to halt; running by inertia, as the planets run around the stars.

Three navy men in white uniforms were running after him, pausing to fire from time to time. They were hitting him. I saw blood spray out twice and once the impact of a bullet drove him to his knees, but he bounded up immediately and ran on. Immune to shock, he would run until the bullets broke his legs – and then he would crawl – until a shot pierced his heart or brain; he moved by descriptive law.

The fence took an outward turn just behind the pit. The ghoul ran into it. The three pursuers slowed and one went to his knees to take aim. Then the ghoul clenched his fist through the mesh of the fence and tore it open. I could hear the heavy metal snap. Beside me, Larsen snorted. The ghoul slid through the broken fence and bounded into the compound. The guards scattered back from the pit, darting silhouettes against the red glare and red-rimmed shadows against the smoke. The ghoul loped towards the inferno. He didn't see the pit, or he disregarded it. He ran right up to the rim and past it – not falling, but running into the flames. A moment later he came up from the other side, clothing ablaze and flesh melting from his bones. He was climbing out. He slipped and slid back, then came crawling out again. His hair was burning. The three navy men were through the broken fence now and, standing side by side, like a firing squad, they shot into his body. They backed off, shooting. Blood sizzled like fat in a frying pan. Slowly the creature slipped back into the pit and did not emerge again.

One of the guards laughed.

'Saves carrying that bugger,' he said.

I passed a hand across my eyes. I understood his jest, his coarse and callous attitude. God help me, I understood. It had been the same as laughing with Larsen at my pipe and I, too, had started to think of them as ghouls, to reason with the mentality of the Inquisition and to loathe them with instinctive fear and hatred that obscured all pity. This was primordial fear, a horror that should have been left behind when man evolved from the slime ... and now rose up again to brutalise and numb the emotions, as contagious as any disease.

The fire flared and crackled merrily as it fed on this new kindling. I was sickened. I felt I could stay there no longer. I turned to Larsen. His face was like a stone idol with living eyes. Sparks swirled and darted through the night; he looked on his fiery celebration as helplessly as any worshipped god.

'I'll go back to town,' I said.

Larsen looked at me; for a moment he didn't seem to know who I was or why I was there.

'If I may?'

'You're no prisoner, Harland. No more than are we all. But you'll be safer here.'

'No, I'll go.'

'As you like. I can't spare an escort.'

I hadn't thought of that. Numbed by the horror, I had forgotten the danger.

Or it was danger too grim to register on the mind.

Larsen said, 'I'll check out a rifle for you, if you like.'

He must have thought I might have qualms about that, for he added, 'It will be safer for you if you're carrying a gun. My men are scared. They might not be too hesitant about shooting a stranger walking alone. The rifle will be like a safe conduct, I guess.'

He stared directly at me.

The rifle was offered as a talisman, not a weapon.

'Thank you,' I said, not for the rifle.

I had never shot a man. I didn't know if I could. But it would be comfortable to have the option.

XVII

'Jack! Thank God you're all right!'

The front door of the jail had been locked and when Jerry opened it he stepped quickly back. He had a gun in his hand. I looked at his gun and he regarded my rifle. Mary spoke from behind him and, a bit sheepish, Jerry holstered the gun. Just a bit sheepish, like a thin veneer laid over grim determination. He said, 'I had a look for you at the Red Walls; place was swarming with . . . patrols, I guess. But they wouldn't tell me anything.'

'They don't know much.'

Jerry was locking the door again; said, 'Do you?'

'Yes; most of it.'

I leaned the rifle against the wall. I was drained with the tension of that solitary walk back from the compound, my nerves like vibrant webs under my skin. Jerry was waiting for me to tell him what I had discovered. Mary did not look so eager to hear it. I gazed out the window at the dawn through which I'd passed. It was a glorious morning, with sunrise ringing golden blows against the shield of dusk. A fan of pale light spread out in the eastern sky, opening slowly, as if reluctant to reveal the day. These things were better wrapped in darkness.

'You've seen Elston?' Mary asked.

'I saw him. And Larsen. I've been in the compound; I saw some other things that . . . I'd rather not have known.'

'What in hell is going on?' Jerry asked. He was fingering the bolt on the door. 'They've had vans down here with loudspeakers, telling everyone to stay inside and keep the doors locked.' He slid the bolt back and forth, as if playing a game of chance with the lock. 'I got a special visit from one of Larsen's men . . . polite sort of guy . . . but he sort of told me to stay right here and keep out of it. Whatever it is.'

'And he heard shooting,' Mary put in.

'There's nothing you can do, Jerry,' I told him. 'It's better to stay here. And keep Mary here. This thing . . . well, it's a highly contagious disease . . . of a sort . . .'

'Of a sort?'

And then, with Jerry swearing from time to time and Mary's eyes growing huge and frightened, I told them what I'd found out and what I'd seen. I was grabbing words in clumps and throwing them out, glad to be rid of them; but they left hollow impressions behind. When I finished we stood silent for a time. I could feel the pattern of my nerves tingling; felt as if the schematics of my nervous system were visible, glowing through my flesh.

Jerry twisted his hat brim. 'I wonder if they really would have done that?' he mused. 'If they really would have used it as a weapon?'

I said, 'Probably not. The people who develop these things aren't the ones who have the say on using them.'

He nodded, holding his hat so that his head dipped from it, exposing a wrinkled brow. He said, 'I was in the army. Didn't mind the idea of fighting. Never would of wanted to do a thing like that, though; ain't no enemy deserves a thing like that.'

'If only Elston had been more . . . courageous,' Mary said.

'A strange men, Elston. I'm not sure . . .'

'Well, I reckon we'd best get Mary off the island,' said the sheriff. He had slipped into his redneck accent; I wasn't sure if it was deliberate.

'I doubt they'll let anyone leave until . . .'

'Hell, they can't tell me not to go to the police cruiser. I'm still the law here . . . outside the compound, leastwise.'

'They wouldn't let me use the Coast Guard boat,' Mary said.

'Different thing, that is.'

'We could try,' I said.

'Why, sure. Anyone tries to stop us, I'll arrest him.' He gave us a grim smile. 'I'll run you two over to the Keys. Guess I ought to come back, myself . . . although I can't say I'm too damned keen on the idea.'

'There's no reason to; nothing you can do.'

'That's not the point, so much. Just that the sheriff hadn't ought to run out on a thing like this.' He was still mangling his Stetson; it was on the back of his head now, battered and twisted. His dedication was twisted, too; his sense of duty and obligation. I knew how he felt. Some insane part of my mind was telling me that I should stay on Pelican and see this out. It was more than getting a story, far more than a dedication to my work, but the turnings of such a resolve were too devious to follow, too sigmoidal to trace through the mind. I wanted to go.

Jerry said, 'There's no antidote at all, eh?'

'They've not found one.'

'And no one knows how long it will take for this thing to run its course?'

'No.'

He shook his head. 'Hell of a thing to do to a nice little island like this. Nice people. Well, let's go down to the boat, let's just see if we can . . .'

'Jerry . . . if they let us leave . . . I don't want you to come back here,' Mary said.

'Aw . . . we'll talk about that later.'

He moved to the door, drew the bolt and hesitated; then he threw the door open and stood back, with his gun ready. The street was empty. From the doorway we could look across the waterfront and out into the harbour. A large swordfish was hanging on a scale on the dock, hoisted up to be weighed and measured. Flecks of blue and green glinted in the drying skin. It would never be weighed now, never mounted. It seemed a shame. It was a big one; it had been caught at the wrong time, a death so vain it did not even bolster a fisherman's vanity. The harbour was jammed with bobbing boats and there were navy boats crossing back and forth across the approaches. Jerry stepped into the street and looked both ways. A patrol was moving down the front, going away from us. There was no one else in sight. Mary and I moved out behind Jerry. I had forgotten the rifle; I went back for it. I followed Mary out and, as I did so, a loudhailer boomed from a naval gunboat.

'Turn back! This island is under quarantine! Turn back at once!'

We saw the gunboat but we couldn't see the reason for the command. Then, as we watched, a fishing boat slid into view, coming from the south. Jerry squinted at it. He said, 'Why, that's John Tate's boat. What's he doing out there?'

I said, 'Tate? He told me he often ties up at one of the coves to the south, instead of using the harbour.'

'He still does that? Old Tate! Used to do some free trading. Never very much; little rum or Havana. Hasn't run a thing in ten years but he still clings to the image.'

Tate's boat continued on its course.

I could see him on the bridge, a spindly old man with one eye and plenty of memories. The gunboat had veered towards him, intersecting his course, a white bow wave breaking from the grey prow. Tate spun the wheel and his wooden boat cut sharply to starboard. I had only met him the one time, but he'd left an impression. I could imagine him grinning with ferocious glee as he pitted his seamanship against the power of authority once again. He had run contraband past customs before and it was just like the old days – except he must have thought it a game, now, when he was doing nothing he thought illegal and could toy with them without fear of punishment or confiscated cargo. His small boat seemed to stand up on its stern as it changed course. The gunboat cut back, ponderous by comparison, and massive. The two vessels were dangerously close. The loudhailer sounded again. I couldn't make out the words. Beside me, Jerry cursed violently.

'They're gonna ram him!' he shouted.

'Oh my God!' Mary cried.

I saw Tate raise his fist, shaking it vehemently at the man on the bridge of the gunboat. He didn't believe they were serious, I thought; he believed that some inexperienced navy captain was misjudging his approach and playing the game too close. Tate waved his gnarled fist, scolding the gunboat. The nimble wooden boat ducked down into a trough and the bow of the grey gunboat reared up. Tate's fist came down; he still thought it was a mistake, but he realised it was a serious mistake. Then the gunboat rammed him.

Tate's fishing boat went down within minutes.

The gunboat had taken the stern right off and veered away, like a bull hooking into a matador. I couldn't see Tate. He must have been knocked down by the impact. Fragments of wood and rope dragged back from the gunboat, festooning the high prow and the bows of Tate's boat pointed up to the sky and slid back and under. The water sighed as it closed.

The gunboat continued on.

Sailors looked back from the rails, but the boat never stopped.

Jerry's head was thrust forwards, the cords in his thick neck standing out like dark ropes, his throat rigged by rage.

He said, 'They aren't going to pick him up.'

'No,' I said softly. 'They wouldn't take him aboard ... that wasn't the idea.'

We looked, shading our eyes, but Tate never surfaced. Then we looked at one another.

'So much for that idea,' Jerry said.

We went back to the jail.

Mary had begun to sob hysterically. The sheriff put his hand on her shoulder and she clasped her own hand over his, her body vibrating. The tremors ran down Jerry's forearm.

'John Tate,' she whispered. 'Old pirate. He would have loved to live through this, wouldn't he? It would have made such a fine story ... better than how he lost his eye ... how he eluded the navy gunboat ...' She smiled sadly.

'Or how he helped hang a man in the Red Walls,' I said, not knowing why I said it; it seemed such an insignificant thing, viewed against the backdrop of his own death.

Jerry began to pace the room, like a prisoner in his own jail.

'We're safe enough here,' he said. 'We'll just have to wait it out.'

'But how long?' Mary sobbed.

We had no answer to that.

Jerry said, 'I guess it could be ... days ... maybe weeks, even.' He looked at me for confirmation. I didn't know. He said, 'We could always lock ourselves in the cell; they couldn't get at us there.'

'Weeks ...' I said. 'What about food? Supplies?'

'Lord! I never thought of that. We'll have to get some stuff in here.'

The thought of preparing for a seige was not appealing.

'They may decide to evacuate ...'

'Yeah, and they may not. We'd better not take a chance ... that chance. There's a shop just down the front.'

'I think, if we're going out again, we'd better do it now. This is likely to get worse before it gets better ... liable to spread until ... well, I'll go with you.'

'No, you stay here with Mary.'

'Nothing I'd like better than not going out there again. But Mary will be safe enough here, with the door barred, and the two of us can carry a lot more. There's no sense in making more than one forage. And ... we can watch each other's backs.'

'He's right, Jerry. I'll be okay here. Just ... don't be very long.'

'You sure?'

'Yes,' she whispered. Jerry regarded her for a moment, then he nodded.

'Let's go,' he said, and we went.

XVIII

I stepped deliberately, as if my footfalls were ticking off the moments, punctuating the passage of time. Jerry preceded me through the deserted streets. The low sun blocked sharp patterns on the buildings, as clearly defined as the light in the whitewashed room, but my own shadow dragged reluctantly at my heels, as if cast from a different source – thrown from me by the glow of my fear. A low fog was clinging against the walls and a heavier fog came rolling out from a sidestreet, curling like a cat across Jerry's boots. He stumbled, as if he'd tripped on the mist. He held his gun at his side, pointing down. I quickened my pace to catch him up and we moved on together. The walk was a hundred yards, no more. It seemed eternal. We met no one.

Mendoza's Market was a dusty storeroom with shelves and glass-fronted counters stocked with tins of almost everything. The door wasn't locked. Jerry stood just inside the entrance and shouted for Mendoza, who lived above. There was no response. We looked around the gloomy room.

Jerry said, 'We should of made us up a shopping list. Well, grab one of these boxes and fill 'er up with whatever takes your fancy; might as well dine to our taste.'

He began plucking tins from the shelves. I crossed to the other side of the room and began raiding the shelves myself, paying little attention to what I took, just tossing things into a big cardboard box. I didn't expect we'd have much appetite. The box was quite heavy when it was full; I had to tuck the rifle under my arm and use both hands to lift it. Jerry had filled his box before I finished; he held it easily under one arm. We moved back through the cluttered room, the tins rattling in the boxes. At the door, I paused.

'How about tobacco?'

'Why, yes . . . we might feel the urge to do some smoking, at that. I think Mendoza keeps the tobacco in the counter at the back. Might grab a couple bottles of rum from back there, too; can't do any harm to have some rum. Might help, even.'

'I'll get it,' I said.

I lowered my box to the dusty floor and stepped to the back of the room. I saw a variety of tobacco, in all forms, in a glass display case. The rum bottles were on a shelf behind. I filled my pockets with tobacco and stepped around the end of the counter ... and a white face loomed up from the shadows!

I tried to scream.

My vocal chords rebelled; they stiffened like frozen iron in my throat and only a strangled gasp came from me. I recoiled. The butt of the rifle struck the glass case, shattering it. I distinctly heard each splinter of glass fall out, the tinkling sounds echoed by the rattle of tins as Jerry shifted the box. He was shouting something from the door and I think I was shouting then, too; I know my mouth was open and a rushing filled my ears. I swung the rifle up before me, not aimed as a weapon but crossed against my breast like a crucifix against a vampire.

Jerry shouted again.

'Move!' He was advancing towards me along the shelves.

But then I slumped against the broken case, my vitality sucked from me in the deflation of sudden terror. Jerry was behind me, one hand on my shoulder; the other thrust the pistol past me. I could feel the big man tremble. I shook my head. It took great concentration, my skull was heavy, my neck limp. By then I'd realised there was no danger ... horror, yes, but no danger. The face had not moved towards me; I had inclined my head towards it as I reached for the rum and the white face had seemed to rise, thrown from the dark shadows as if buoyant from a heavy sea.

The man was dead, spread-eagled behind the counter as if nailed there by his final convulsions.

Jerry let his breath out slowly.

I was hollow. My energy, my life force, my very bones seemed to have been sucked from me into the vacuum of fear. I was still shaking my head – an act of inertia. I had thought the man alive, reaching for me – and I had been unable to flee, had never thought to use the rifle ... had waited for his touch ...

'Mendoza,' Jerry said.

The hand that had been trembling on my shoulder was firm now, solid as a stone, but the hand that gripped the gun had begun to shake as he lowered it.

He moved me aside and leaned over the corpse. He did not touch it.

'Looks like he might of died of natural causes,' he said. 'Heart attack, maybe ... he wasn't young ...'

'Yes, it looks that way.'

Jerry looked at me, face as white as Mendoza's.

'Isn't it remarkable?' he said. 'Here and now ... a man dying of natural causes ... it makes you see that life goes on.'

He paused, wondering if his statement had been absurd ... or profound.

'I never killed anyone,' he said. Nor had he yet. But the gun was in his hand ... he would have; he might have to. He was peering into my face. He said, 'Harland, do you think these ... things ... will go to heaven?'

I gaped dumbly at him and he flushed; the question had been genuine.

'Yes,' I said. I held no brief for the hereafter, but I said, 'Yes.'

And he said, 'I'd like to think so ...'

Walking back down the front with the heavy boxes, we met a patrol coming from the other direction. When they saw us they spread out and their rifles came up. They looked terrified – as terrified as we must have looked.

'Take it easy,' Jerry snapped.

'Don't come too close. Just move on.'

'Listen,' I said. 'There's a dead man in Mendoza's. We don't know if he's one of ... them ... but you'd better send someone to get the body.'

He didn't look as if he understood.

'To burn it,' I said.

'Oh. Yeah. You just move on.'

We moved on. The patrol turned, watching us. Then they went on in the other direction. When we had come to the jail, I looked back. The patrol had moved on down the street, past Mendoza's and, as I looked, they turned to the right, inland ... towards the compound. I hoped they wouldn't forget to send a van for Mendoza's body. I looked out at the harbour. There was some wood floating about, timber and planks, and an oily slick spreading slowly through the water. The swordfish still hung, neglected forever now, on the scales. The grey gunboats passed to and fro across the mouth of the harbour. How long? I wondered. How long would it be?

XIX

Mary was looking out the window as we approached.

Framed in the window, her face seemed to be disintegrating, dissolving with fear. Her cheeks were pinched in and her eyes were huge and staring. Jerry waved but she didn't acknowledge the gesture. She turned, looking back into the room. Her profile spread like a pale wash against the glass. Then we had passed the window and I heard the bolt rasp free. Mary opened the door and stepped out. Jerry's shoulders twitched as, instinctively, he tried to comfort her in his arms, but found the laden box between them. Mary was crying.

'Hey, now . . . it's okay,' the sheriff said.

'It's not okay; nothing is okay.'

'We'll be all right. Just a question of—'

'Doctor Winston is here,' she said.

'Hey, that's great,' Jerry said. He went through the door. Winston was standing in the corner, smoking a cigar, hands clasped behind his back. He looked as if he were thoughtfully considering a diagnosis.

'Glad you made it,' Jerry said. He put the box on the desk. 'That you thought to come here.'

'Mary doesn't seem to think it such a good idea,' Winston said. He was calm enough, but he'd been chewing on the cigar; the wrapper had started to uncurl.

Jerry looked at the girl, blinking.

'Doctor Winston has been . . . wounded,' she said.

Jerry started, all his big body going taut.

'He hasn't touched me,' Mary added, quickly. 'He came to the door. I let him in. I was glad to see him . . . I didn't know he had been hurt . . .'

'How'd it happen, Doc?'

'Why, it was one of these lunatics that seem to be about. That's why I came down here . . . to see if you had any idea what is going on here? Something to do with the research in the compound, is it? I tried to phone there but couldn't get past the switchboard and, by the way, I've heard nothing from my nurse . . .'

'How long, Doc?'

'What? Well, I phoned there at—'

'How long is it since you were attacked?'

'Well, what does . . . or *does* it?' Comprehension came into the doctor's face. He took the cigar from his teeth. 'It does matter, eh?

Apparently you know more about this than I. What is it, some sort of germ warfare?'

'Doc... how long?'

Winston winced at Jerry's tone. They were friends; he didn't understand it. He had paled slightly under his normal flush and Jerry's jaws were tight with great bands of muscle.

Winston said, 'Better part of an hour,' and he was watching the sheriff carefully, gauging his reaction. Winston was a big, heavy man; he looked to have a slow metabolism. I relaxed somewhat but, in relaxing, went icy cold. 'What is it, Jerry? What sort of thing is it? Am I liable to contaminate you by being here?'

Jerry didn't know what to say.

I said, 'Let's have a drink.'

I think I'd managed to keep my voice normal. Jerry shot me a grateful glance. I opened a bottle of Mendoza's rum and Jerry fetched glasses. We weren't going to share the bottle with Winston. He was standing behind the desk and we stood opposite. Winston took a large swallow and licked his lips.

'Excellent,' he said. Then: 'Well? Is it terminal?'

'Not terminal,' I said.

I had taken this upon myself and Jerry was glad enough to waive his authority. I sipped some rum. Winston watched me. I wasn't sure if I should deceive him or not. Every man has his own way of facing death and a right to face it that way and if this had been a natural disease, no matter how lethal or painful, I would have told him the truth. But it was not natural. This was a thing that created its own values and judgements.

I said, 'They have an antidote, at the compound.'

Jerry gave me a sharp look and I could tell he was thinking the same as me. Then he narrowed his eyes and looked down at his boots.

'That's why your nurse was taken to the compound,' I went on. 'We'll have to take you there, or bring the antidote here. That's all.'

'Well, that's a relief,' Winston said. 'The way you were all acting, I thought I was a goner. But what is it, anyway? The way these lunatics are running around... some new strain of rabies?'

'I believe it's something of that nature.'

'They shouldn't have been fooling around with that.'

'They know that... now.'

I refilled our glasses. I didn't flinch as I leaned across the desk to pour into the doctor's glass. Mary's glass was still full; she said, 'Is it wise to be drinking? I mean... hadn't we better keep our wits about us?'

'I think it's better if we have a few drinks,' Jerry said.

Mary knew what we were going to do, then. She said, 'Oh, yes. I'll have a drink as well.' Then she realised that she already had a full glass in her hand. She sipped. Tears streaked her cheeks, but she was no longer sobbing. We drank slowly and steadily. Doctor Winston seemed to be actually relishing the rum. Jerry and I needed it. We watched the doctor carefully, wondering what the first signs would be; whether it would be a sudden rage or a gradual transition? Unblinking, he gazed back over the rim of his glass. I started to pour some more rum.

'Hadn't we better see about this antidote, then?' Winston said. 'I suppose it should be administered as soon as possible. I'll prescribe a good healthy dosage of rum for all of us afterwards.'

He spoke slowly, as if deliberating each word. I wondered if he were getting drunk or if the process was starting to affect his ability to form the words. But he looked at us with clear, alert eyes. He looked almost amused. I had a terrible idea that we hadn't deceived him, after all; that he was playing the game with us, protecting our feelings as we tried to protect him from the truth.

Jerry snorted and slammed his glass down on the desk.

'I'll take the doc up to the compound now,' he said. 'You stay here with Mary. We won't be long.'

I said, 'I'll go with him, if you like.'

Jerry stared at me. He appreciated my offer and he knew the doctor a lot better than I did. I think he was tempted to let me do it. But maybe he didn't trust my nerve; he had seen me cringe from dead Mendoza, never even attempting to use the rifle.

'No, it's better if I go,' he said.

Winston was looking back and forth between us.

'I don't suppose I could go on my own?' he said.

Again I saw that look in his eyes. Jerry saw it, too.

'Come on, doc,' he said.

Mary was sitting with her face in her hands. She looked up at me once or twice, then lowered her face again immediately. We were not drinking now. I was taut as a tuning fork, waiting to vibrate to the sound of the gun . . . but no shot sounded.

Then Jerry came back in, his face a mask of anguish.

'Goddamn me!' he cried.

He slammed the door; across the room, the bars rattled.

I looked at Jerry, puzzled. I have never seen such torment on a face. He walked to the bars and gripped them, a prisoner outside the cell . . . inside a black despair.

'He knew,' Jerry said. 'He walked on ahead of me ... never looked back once. I guess he knew. I followed him. But I walked slower and slower ... and he just kept on at the same pace, so I was dropping behind ... and when he turned off towards the compound, I stopped ... and came back. I let him go. I couldn't do it! Goddamn me to hell!' he screamed, cursing himself ... for not killing his friend.

For a long while, no one spoke ...

XX

After a while Mary made a meal which none of us even pretented to eat. No shots had sounded for a long time. I looked out the window every few minutes but there was nothing to see. It was like a ghost town. A newspaper tumbled down the waterfront, starting to shred. A sea breeze had come up; it whined through the empty streets. From a wharf further down the front a door or shutter banged with a determined rhythm. The swordfish still hung from the scales, dry now; it looked like papier mâché. I felt sorry for the swordfish. It helped a bit to spread my sympathies. The others were looking out too, from time to time. We never looked out together, just took it in haphazard turns.

Jerry said, 'There's nobody ... nobody at all. Maybe it's tapering off. No patrols, either ... funny ...'

He came back from the window.

A little later, Mary looked out.

She saw the shore patrolman first ...

He was alone and looked relaxed.

He was standing down by the dock, looking out towards the patrol gunboats, not even watching his back. I breathed a sigh of relief. It must be over ... at least this particular patrolman believed it to be over, for he showed no signs of alertness or fear. He seemed interested in the boats, as if he were waiting for them to do something, perhaps for the blockade to disperse. Jerry opened the door and stepped out. He called to the man. The man didn't seem to hear. Jerry called again, louder. The patrolman heard then. He seemed to shake himself around inside his crisp white uniform, like a dog shaking off water. Then he turned to face us.

Jerry's breath went out in a rush.

I couldn't breath at all.

The ghoul in the white uniform made no move towards us; he stood, relaxed, watching us as he had watched the boats, with those blank, white eyes.

We went back in and barred the door.

We didn't look out for a while.

When we did, later, he was gone . . .

XXI

After that, we avoided the window. We did not look out, not wanting to see what was in the streets, and we did not look at it, not wanting to see what might . . . be looking in. From time to time we heard . . . things . . . shuffling past the building; once something banged against the wall. But there was no real effort to get in. We sat at the desk in the centre of the room and looked at our hands. We drank a little rum. At one point, Mary raised the question that had been troubling me – and perhaps Jerry, as well.

'What shall we do if someone . . . normal . . . wants to join us?'

She didn't wait for a reply; said, 'I mean, when Doctor Winston knocked on the door, I let him in as a matter of course . . . and then I found out . . . I mean, how will we know?' She spoke the last words in a strained voice that rose towards hysteria. I had no answer. She said, 'We can't refuse to let someone in, if there's a chance they might be all right . . .' She gestured with both hands, vehemently, as if we were arguing with her . . . 'We can't leave them out there . . .'

Jerry said, 'I guess what we'd do – will do, it happens – is lock 'em up in the cell. Keep 'em at gunpoint and explain that we're sorry but can't take any chances and get 'em in the cell. If they're still all right after . . . oh, say five hours, to be on the safe side . . . then we can let them out.'

Mary nodded. 'I hadn't thought of that.'

'There is a flaw, Jerry,' I said, shaking my head. When they both looked at me, I said, 'It's a good plan if only one person comes, but suppose two or three show up here? If they come separately – locking them up . . . would be like locking a man up with a time bomb, which might or might not explode . . . or a tiger, which might or might not be hungry. It would be torture.'

'Hell,' he said.

'Elston told me they had tested the ferocity of the subjects by locking them up together,' I added. 'It was not a pretty sight, although, no doubt, of great scientific interest,' I said, bitterly.

'Well . . . if one of us kept a constant watch . . . the moment one of them showed any signs of going berserk, we could kill him before the other was attacked . . .'

'Could we?' I asked.

Jerry dropped his head. He had not been able to kill Doctor Winston and I had not even aimed my rifle at Mendoza and Mary . . . yet, who knows what one can do? 'We might manage that,' I said.

'What else can we do?'

'There's one thing.' I hesitated, wishing that Mary had been sleeping; not wanting to disturb her even more. But she was listening carefully; she had an interest in the matter, after all. I said, 'We might need the cell for ourselves.'

'How do you mean?' Jerry asked.

'They're inhumanly strong. They could break in here, if they wanted to . . . no, not wanted to, they're too mindless for that . . . but if the urge takes them. I thought . . . well, if they do try to break in, we can lock ourselves in the cell.'

Jerry grimaced. He said, 'I don't like that idea at all . . . locked in there, cowering back from the bars . . . with things maybe reaching in, trying to get at us . . .' His great torso rippled; he shuddered like an earth tremor. 'I'd rather be mobile . . . run . . . shoot if we have to . . . Yeah, I can shoot them . . . and hell, we don't know how long we have to stay here.'

I hadn't relished the thought myself; it was an option I thought I should mention. I said, 'It may be a moot point. Maybe no one, normal or otherwise, will come. Let's wait and see.'

And maybe it was a moot point.

But I was to be reminded, in a terrible way, of our agonising dilemma . . . the problem was not unique to us . . .

We spoke no more, with nothing to say. Time moved ponderously. And very slowly the light changed at the window.

The long night had begun . . .

XXII

We sat in the lighted cube of our sanctuary and things moved in the darkness without. The sounds they made were soft, as if they caressed the walls lovingly, longingly, yearning to enter. They sensed we were within; they gently stroked the walls around us. We knew we should turn the light out . . . that it was drawing them to the jail like a beacon ... but knowing is one thing; we could not cherish darkness – by dawn we would have been inhuman.

Like a prisoner marking his passing sentence, Jerry drove his fist into his palm, not hard but as regular as a metronome; he winced with each soft blow, as if stung. Beside him, Mary sat with her face buried in her hands. From time to time she would shudder and look up, tearing her face from its shelter by main force ... from the hooks of her hands came her tormented countenance, haggard, white, ghastly, the flesh drawn from her fingers. I looked past them, at the bars and, beyond, the shadow of the bars on the wall of the cell. My backbone was like a bar, riveting me to my chair ... multiple bars, split by currents of fear and spreading like splintered bamboo through my torso – casting shadows on my soul. I was breathing heavily. We all were. And then something else was breathing heavily, at the door. Jerry looked up. His gun was on the table, but he did not touch it. The breath from without seemed to billow into the door; the door was solid, yet I felt as if it were fluttering like a sail, about to float open. A hand stroked the contours of the door, seeking, testing. Then it moved away; moving on, it drew with it shreds of my sanity ...

Suddenly, I was back in Mendoza's.

My mind out of time, I had just broken the glass case and the sound shattered in my ears. Mary's face was writhing; Jerry was vibrating; my mind snapped back and I knew I had heard glass break behind me. There was glass in the window. I remembered seeing Mary at the window, through the pane ... drawn against my will, I turned ...

Sally the salad girl was reaching in ...

Her face was framed in the window and her arm groped towards me, dripping blood where the glass had cut her. She was far more terrible than the men – somehow, she was still feminine and sensual, her painted lips drawn back as if smiling with lewd desire, her eyes rolling as if with passion, a mockery of what she had been; reaching out, it seemed she wished to fold me lovingly to her breast. I could not look away. Then she yielded, like a prostitute rejected; I did not go to her – she drifted away.

On the floor, shards of broken glass glinted in the light.

Within my body, my senses were shattered like the glass, cold splinters piercing my heart, sharp edges filing at the rim of my mind, jagged pieces rasping at my soul. I could almost hear fear grinding away at my guts. It was too much. The grinding horror wore away my humanity and polished my awareness to a smooth lump; I slipped into obfuscation. I did not move, I scarcely blinked. Things groped at the window and fondled the walls. And then the bars had double shadows. Dawn was at the window.

Mary shivered into reality, as if coming into focus from distortion or changing dimensions by some time warp. Jerry stood up, stiffly. I found I could move. I could think once more. The night had ended.

XXIII

From the window, we saw a destroyer standing off beyond the harbour. My first thought, such was my state of mind, was that the navy intended to shell the town. But that was foolish and I smiled – although grimly – at myself. I did wonder what they planned, however. A destroyer was hardly necessary to quarantine fishing boats and motor cruisers. Some decision had probably been reached – been forced upon them once the first member of the patrols had been infected. Maybe it was only the one – the one we had seen – but we had no way of knowing, nor, I suppose, did they. It had taken that option from them. The search-and-destroy mission had automatically failed the moment a single member of the patrols became one of the enemy ... to continue the patrols was to risk spreading the horror into the compound itself. They weren't likely to chance that. And it explained why the patrols had been withdrawn. But not what they intended to do.

Sometime later a helicopter came in.
   It was a big one and it passed over us, heading towards the compound. It didn't stay long. It vanished towards the west and then, half an hour later, a second 'copter came in – or the first one returned. It followed the same pattern, landing within the compound and flying off a short time afterwards. I wondered if reinforcements were being brought in, or if the compound was evacuating? Jerry, wondering the same thing, tried to phone through to the compound, but even the switchboard failed to answer now. The phone rang hollow and dead, a forlorn sound, as if the telephone itself knew it was not to be answered and sounded its despair.
   Jerry slammed it down, cursing.
   A few seconds later, it rang.
   The sound startled us and we gaped stupidly at each other. Then Jerry snatched it up. 'That's right,' he said, and at the same time I heard a loudspeaker blaring from somewhere in the streets behind us.

Jerry said, 'That's right. Three of us. Right, we'll be there at ten exactly. Well, sure ... but look ... how do we tell if they're ... all right? If we do find any others ... is there some way to tell?' He listened, tight-lipped. 'All right,' he said. He put the phone down.

'They're evacuating us from the navy pier,' he said.

'Thank God,' Mary whispered.

'We're to be there at ten o'clock, on the dot ... and they won't wait long.' Then, anticipating my question, he said, 'They didn't say how we could tell ... said that everyone would be checked by a doctor, at the pier.'

'Then they have found a way!' I said. 'Maybe Elston's damned autopsies proved fruitful.'

Jerry nodded doubtfully.

A van moved down the waterfront, going fast and not stopping. The loudspeaker sounded the message, the same message we had received over the telephone. I wondered if they were phoning every number in the town; I had an eerie echo of telephones ringing, unanswered, in empty houses; ringing in sequence up and down the streets, forlorn and futile. The van passed and I saw armed men holding their weapons ready at the windows; it turned up the cobbled streets and we heard the message repeated again and again as it wound through the town, making an effort to get through to anyone hiding there ... anyone who could understand. The message was given in Spanish on every third broadcast. I was cheered greatly by this, by the knowledge that something had been determined, something was being done, authority was taking measures. I suppose, without actually admitting it, I had feared that the compound had been overrun and that we were on our own. The authorities were responsible for this horror we were in, yet it was still reassuring to know they continued to function.

I said, 'Well, thank heaven.'

But Jerry said, 'It might not be so easy.'

He was at the window, looking out.

He said, 'Christ, they're all over the place!'

I felt my throat constrict. I joined him at the window and the hair came up stiff on my neck. The loudspeaker seemed to have attracted the ghouls, to have played the catalyst that brought them out of lethargy, summoning them from their various places and bringing them to the waterfront. There must have been twenty of them. They came filtering out of the sidestreets and from the warehouses, moving in the wake of the van ... some Pied Piper syndrome which Elston would have termed a side-effect, bringing them together. I recognised the bearded man from the Red Walls and, I think, two or three others from the initial infection. There were several women; one clutched a baby to her breast in a mockery of the maternal instinct. The baby was dead. They moved after the van and then, when it had vanished, milled about mindlessly. They did not attack one another. From time to time two or three of them, following their own paths, would come into contact – would bump or brush together – and then they would snap and slash at each other in a momentary bestial rage, but it was fleeting ferocity. An instant later they would wander apart again. They did not kill each other. Elston could be proud of the nicety with which he had regulated their instincts . . .

At nine o'clock a landing craft came wallowing into the harbour and dropped its ramp alongside the navy pier. The pier was some distance down the front and it was hard to see just what was happening, but we saw men in blue uniforms splashing through the shallow water and others running along the pier. They all carried automatic weapons. They deployed in a crescent around the pier. Several men in white coats detached themselves from the crescent and moved forward. They were all on the seaward side of the link fence. A group of men in khaki came through the defensive lines, carrying strange, bulky objects. They moved quickly and, within minutes, those objects had been transformed into a tent-like affair of poles and canvas. It looked like the shield they put around a broken-legged racehorse on the track, before they shoot it – letting the animal linger longer in agony so the spectators will not have their delicate sensibilities offended. This structure was erected near the fence, on the perimeter of the armed crescent. As soon as it was up, the men in khaki hurried back to the dock. The men in white vanished behind the canvas.

It was nine-thirty.

The navy pier was only ten minutes away – walking.

We were ready to go – waiting.

While this activity was going on, the ghouls were still wandering along the docks. They showed little interest in the proceedings at the pier. They didn't even look dangerous, somehow; demented, tormented, with the madness transfiguring their features, but not dangerous.

Jerry said, 'You know . . . it's funny . . . you'd think it would be more horrible with that whole load of things out there, but it don't seem as bad as it did with one – when Sally looked in the window. One thing, alone . . .' He was looking out, squinting, tight lines drawn around his mouth. 'Well, it ain't like snakes, is what I mean,' he said.

Mary and I looked at him.

I realised what he was doing – that he was just saying the first thing that came into his head, to hold our attention; to keep us from considering the gauntlet we soon must run.

He said, 'Now, you take your snakes. One snake, on his own . . . he ain't so scary. But you get a whole pit of snakes, all squirming together and wriggling about, that scares anybody. Now, you'd think that whole load of ghouls would be the same. But it ain't.' He paused. I thought he'd run dry, but he was just getting his words in order. He said, 'I guess they're more on the line of rats in a sack.'

Mary and I looked at each other, then at Jerry. But he knew what he was saying.

He said, 'Knew a fella once, used to make his living plucking rats out of a burlap bag. That's right. He'd go around the bars toting this big bag full of rats. He wasn't welcomed in restaurants, but he'd go in bars. He'd have fifteen, twenty rats in there. Well, he'd let everyone look in the sack, they'd see all them rats squirming around, they'd get pretty edgy. Then this fella, he'd wager he could reach down in that sack with his bare hand and pluck a rat out. Well, nobody would believe him. He'd get plenty of takers on his bet. Then, sure enough, he'd reach in and grab him a rat and pluck it right out, all wriggling and squealing. Saw him do it a dozen times. Never the once did he get bit.' Jerry looked at his hand, as if amazed that it had not been bitten. 'So one time I'm having a drink with him, I ask him what the secret is. He'd had some drink, he tells me there's no secret to it at all; he don't know why they don't bite him, they just don't. But here's the thing. He said that when he first started rat-plucking, he tried it with just one rat in the bag. Well, he got bit every time. But as long as there was more than one rat in there, he never got chawed. Now, that was the secret, although he didn't see it as a secret. When there was a whole squirming mass of rats, they just didn't bite. He could pluck them out one by one, fifteen, twenty in a row, never got nipped – but as soon as there was just one rat left in the sack, it bit him every time. Just something in the nature of rats in a sack. Well, you see what I mean . . .'

He had spoken slowly and thoughtfully.

It was nine-thirty-five.

The canvas shelter on the pier was billowing like a sail and the men who'd gone in there wearing white coats came out looking like astronauts or deep sea divers. They were bundled into thick, protective clothing, heavy leather gauntlets and helmets with black glass visors. The visors were lifted and their faced showed white in the openings. These were obviously the men who would examine prospective evacuees – who would, I hoped, examine us.

It was nine-forty and we were discussing whether we should walk steadily down the front, carefully avoiding the ghouls, or try to make it in one quick rush. We had already determined that we must make our approach down the waterfront, even though it was swarming with ghouls. The alternative was to sneak through the back streets and with narrow roads turning and intersecting that was too dangerous – we would have no warning if one of the things were lurking around a turning, in a doorway, in an alley. On the front we could, at least, see the danger.

But to run or walk . . .

Mary summed that up.

She said, 'I don't think I could walk,' and we knew what she meant. We decided to run. It might not be the safest policy, for quick movement might well draw their attention, just as the loudspeaker in the van had attracted them to it, but we doubted our nerve – doubted we could walk through that terrible throng. I felt my heart might explode if I denied my impulse to run . . . to maintain a moderate pace while my heart and brain screamed for the primordial solution, the flight that instinct demanded.

At nine-forty-five a van roared down to the gates.

The back opened and men jumped out, some in uniform and some in civilian clothing. The men in protective clothing opened the gates and the men from the van rushed through. The driver moved the van some ten yards down the barrier, then jumped out and ran back to the gates. A second van arrived, then a third. The occupants all passed through the gates and rushed directly out to the landing craft. There was no examination and I figured that must have already been done, at the laboratory. Examination at the pier was for us and any others who had remained in the town. I watched carefully but saw neither Elston nor Larsen. I figured they had left in the helicopters.

Then it was time for us to leave.

We went out the door fast, Jerry first and Mary next and I brought up the rear, shamefully close upon her heels. We went straight across the front to the fence, wanting that barrier on one side of our course. We passed within six feet of a ghoul. He turned stiffly, watching us, but did not offer pursuit. Two others took tentative steps towards us but, in doing so, they brushed against one another. They snarled in silence and snapped. Then we were running along the line of the fence and, for all our fear, it was easy. We made it to the gates with no more trouble than our labouring lungs and jangling nerves could claim.

We were not the first there.

Half a dozen others had come from the nearer streets of the town, joining at the fence, warily regarding one another. The gate was closed again and the men in protective suits had their visors down. Sunlight reflected from the black glass, glinting like stars in the void. They were faceless behind the glass, alien and inhuman. We drew up, panting, beside the others. Jerry spoke to a man he recognised. Three or four others came dashing from the streets, running hard. One was a woman, sobbing hysterically.

From behind his visor, one of the examiners said, 'All right. You'll come through one at a time. Go behind the canvas and take your clothing off. Take everything off.' He paused at the gate. 'The rest step back. Move it!'

Someone pushed the hysterical woman forward.

The visored man opened the gate and let her through. The men in blue uniforms had their automatic weapons trained on the rest of us. Two of them, standing apart from the line, held their guns on the woman. The visored man closed the gates again and the woman went behind the canvas. Two men in protective clothing followed her in.

Suddenly I felt like laughing . . . laughing wildly.

I realised that the canvas had not been erected to house some delicate instrument that could detect the latent disease but simply for the sake of modesty . . . so that we could undress in privacy! Modesty in the face of this horror! So was authority bound within their dimensions.

Then a darker realisation followed.

I knew we had hoped for too much from these saviours. They had found no way to detect the disease, they simply intended to examine us, naked, looking for any recent wound or break in the skin through which the disease might have got into our bodies.

I didn't, at first and with my mind jumping madly, see how this would affect us.

The woman emerged from behind the canvas and was directed to the pier. She moved on, stumbling and sobbing. She looked back once. The gate opened again and a man passed through. Jerry took a step forward and the guns all trained on him.

He stopped dead, raising his hands to shoulder-height.

'There's another woman here,' he said. 'For crissake let her go through next!'

The man at the gate nodded. Sunlight ran like black fire up his helmet.

None of the ghouls had come any distance towards us, they were still milling about back by the jail.

Jerry took Mary gently by the shoulder and pushed her towards the gates, then stepped back. She looked at him over her shoulder, trying to smile, as she moved forwards. The faceless man had his hand on the gate, ready to open it the moment the preceding man had been cleared behind the canvas.

Abruptly, he stiffened.

The instant he stiffened, I saw the reason . . . and tumultuous horror spun through my guts.

He had seen the bandage on her leg.

'Remove that,' he said.

Mary looked puzzled and Jerry hadn't yet understood. He still had his hands raised.

Mary said, 'What do you mean?' and the visored man said, 'The bandage.'

'What? Oh . . . no, that's all right. I cut myself the other day, it's not . . . what you think . . .' She had started speaking easily, as if confident the explanation would suffice, but her words trailed off weakly. The man with the black glass face was rigid. I knew that his features, behind the visor, would be as hard and as cold as the glass itself.

Mary bent down and pulled the bandage from her leg. The cut was red and ugly-looking. The man stared at her.

'I'm sorry,' he said.

'What the hell?' Jerry shouted.

The guns were trained on him from behind the fence and his hands were still raised, as if he'd thrown them up in amazement.

'They . . . won't . . .' I whispered.

'I'm sorry,' the faceless man said. 'There's no point in examining you further, miss. No one with an open wound can leave.'

'It isn't that!' Mary screamed.

Her cry drew the attention of the guns. They shifted from Jerry to her. The faceless man was shaking his head, perhaps in negation, strengthening his words with the gesture – or perhaps in pity. The second man had come out from behind the canvas and headed for the landing craft. The others were pressing forward, clamouring to get through the gate.

One of the visored men by the canvas called, 'What's the hold-up, Jim? Get them through here!'

Jim said, 'Please step back. You're holding things up . . . I don't want to have to . . .' He turned his helmeted head to the side, indicating the line of armed guards. They were quite ready to shoot.

Mary gasped and moved back from the gates.

Jerry stepped forward, past her. He faced the faceless man. Jerry's visage was like brittle glass itself. Had the visored man possessed a human countenance, Jerry might have argued with him, but they just looked at each other. Jerry had lowered his hands. I could tell what he was thinking as clearly as if my mind had been linked to his and the thought pulsing between us. He wanted to draw his gun and kill the faceless man who stood between Mary and safety. But he knew it would do no good – less than good, for he would be shot down in turn and Mary would still be on this side of the fence . . . without him.

After a long moment he turned back to us.

His face had shattered . . . just like glass.

XXIV

Mary was calm, remarkably calm. We stood back from the gates, watching the others go through one by one. None of them were turned back. Mary said, 'It's the same decision we faced . . . talked about facing . . . in the jail. If someone should come . . .'

'It's not the same,' Jerry rasped. But it was.

Then everyone else had gone through and the faceless man was looking at us.

Mary said, 'Jerry . . . please go through.'

'Well, I'm just likely to do that, ain't I?' he said.

Mary gave a little whimpering sigh. It was impossible to tell if it expressed relief or frustration; emotions were blurred in all of us now, our senses confused by anomie. It was worse for Mary, if anything, with an edge of guilt on her disorientation – without her, we could have gone through the gates.

The visored man said, 'Anyone else?' His voice was soft; he didn't like what he had to do.

'Jack . . . no sense in you staying,' Jerry said.

I wanted to go. My muscles actually lurched in the direction of the gates and I had to restrain my body. I could feel my bones distinctly within my flesh, the scaffold of my skeleton fixing me in place. I shook my head, refusing my own instincts rather than Jerry's suggestion.

'Please go,' Mary said. 'It will be easier for me . . .'

And Jerry said, 'Our supplies will last longer with just the two of us, Jack . . .'

It was so tempting I feared my honour would prove weak.

'No one else!' I called.

The visored man regarded us. Then he nodded and turned away. The line of men in uniform began to retreat, keeping formation and closing the crescent in around the pier. They moved as if executing a formal manoeuvre on the parade grounds, functioning exactly in a world gone mad. They had left the canvas shelter where it was; it snapped in the breeze, like a tent abandoned on a holiday in Hell.

Jerry's big hand closed on my shoulder in gentle gratitude.

'If it had been your girl . . .' he said.

Maybe, I thought.

One by one the guards were filtering out of the line and boarding the landing craft. The men in protective clothing were already aboard. The three of us stood there by the gates and a line of faces gazed at us from the boat. It looked like a row of disembodied heads posted around a stockade. The last uniformed man had started up the ramp when a ghoul came loping out of a sidestreet and flung himself onto the fence . . .

Like a demented monkey, the ghoul began to scale the barrier. He was moving with purpose and I was reminded of Jerry's tale of the solitary rat in the bag. His groping hand reached the top and clamped over the barbed wire. Blood ran down his arm. He jerked himself up. The other ghouls watched him, as if impressed by a virtuoso performance and envious of his agility.

The last guard was halfway up the boarding ramp when he looked back and saw the ghoul. His face set. The others, on board, were calling for him to hurry, but he turned back and sighted his weapon. He took aim as stolidly as if he'd been on the shooting range. I understood it. It was not a human target upon which he sighted. There was no need to kill the ghoul, the guard could have boarded in plenty of time, but he was guided by some instinct older than reason and deeper than logic. He squeezed off a burst from his automatic weapon. Cartridges spun over his shoulder, glinting in the sunlight. Splinters of bone and gore cascaded from the ghoul. Blood hung in a thin mist around him. He jerked; his body heaved up, then dropped back. He hung suspended from the top of the fence, his hand impaled on the barbed wire. Thick drops of blood fell from him and he swayed like some carnal fruit, bursting with red ripeness.

The guard grimaced – with satisfaction.

He turned back up the ramp. Spent cartridges were scattered at his feet and he looked down at them for a moment, as if they were runes which he had cast. Then he kicked at them. They spun off the ramp and dropped into the water. The guard went on up the ramp and then the ramp drew up and three of us were alone.

Mary buried her face in Jerry's chest, clinging there, as if using his body as a shield against the sight of the dead ghoul. He stroked her hair.

'We'd better get back to the jail,' he said.

'Again?' The word was muffled against his chest, carved into his body. 'Go through them again?'

'It's the safest place.'

I said, 'Jerry . . . when we left . . . I didn't close the door. I didn't think . . . they might be in there now.'

He winced.

'What about one of the vans?' Mary said.

'They seem attracted to them . . .' I said.

'Still, if we drive around without stopping,' Jerry said.

Mary said, 'I meant to drive back to the jail . . .'

'Jack left the door open, goddamn it!' Jerry snapped. Then: 'Why shouldn't he have left the door open? How did he know we'd be going back?'

He spoke as if it were an exercise in logics. He was looking around, standing with his back to the fence. Further down the fence, towards the jail, the dead ghoul was still hanging by his spiked hand . . . as if, like the swordfish, he had been suspended there to be weighed and measured and mounted. Blood still dripped from his erupted body, not spraying out – his heart no longer pumped – but falling in heavy globs obedient to gravity. The living ghouls still milled aimlessly about.

Jerry said, 'If we drive around they won't be able to catch us . . . as long as the gas holds out. But after that . . . those vans aren't as strong as the jail. They could break into a van and we'd be confined, unable to manoeuvre . . . Damn! If only we knew how long we have to hold out here . . . how long we'll be isolated before they . . . before they do whatever they're going to do about the island. We have to get to some place we can defend.'

'What about the compound?' Mary said. 'Take the van to the compound? The telephone is probably working from there, at least we could be in touch with . . . the world.'

Jerry considered that.

He was bareheaded now. He had lost his hat somewhere along the line. The sea breeze ruffled his fair hair.

'What's it like in the compound, Jack? Defensible?'

But I couldn't remember what the compound was like. I could remember only that small whitewashed room . . . and the stinking pit. Black smoke rose from that pit, a tower of smoke like . . .

'The lighthouse!' I cried.

'Why . . . yes. That's right!'

Mary was nodding enthusiastically. 'There'll even be supplies there. Sam Jasper's things. We won't have to go back to the jail . . .'

'The tide?' I asked.

'We'll take a boat,' Jerry said, then paused, glancing out at the harbour, where John Tate had been rammed. The destroyer stood at the approaches, attended by gunboats. It would not be wise to take a boat.

Mary thought for a moment; said, 'We can cross by the reef in half an hour.'

'And so can they,' said Jerry.

'But only one at a time . . . we can shoot them down one by one, if we have to . . . if they come . . .'

'If they come in daylight.'

'Oh, Christ . . . I don't know.'

'But wait!' Jerry said. 'They won't cross water, right? They won't go into water. That reef is none too solid. There must be a tyre iron or something in one of the vans . . . if we could lever a couple of rocks out of place, make a break in the line . . . it should work.'

'I think it's our best bet,' I said. 'I'd rather be there than here. And someone might be more inclined to rescue us from there . . . in a day or two they must realise we aren't infected . . . a boat or helicopter . . .'

'Mary?' the sheriff said.

'I . . . yes. Anything rather than staying here or going back to the jail . . . waiting for them to break in. Yes. The lighthouse.'

I think we all felt greatly cheered at having reached a decision. At least we were still in control of our own options. We moved to the nearest van.

The keys were in it.

We all got in the front, Jerry at the wheel and Mary between us. Jerry waited a few moments before he switched on the ignition but, once he did so, he started the van moving immediately.

We drove towards the ghouls.

The ghouls watched us come.

Jerry drove at them in first gear, steadily, and they made no attempt to get out of the way. They seemed fascinated by the van, by a large moving object . . . something of a magnitude to register on their dimmed perceptions. As we closed on the crowd, I saw Jerry's hand lift from the wheel and hover for a moment over the horn. It was a reaction from habit and he grinned grimly as he realised he had been about to sound the hooter.

'No way through them,' he muttered.

'We'll have to force our way through . . .'

Mary, tight-lipped and rigid between us, said, 'Can't you drive faster?'

She yearned for the sanctuary of the lighthouse.

Jerry said, 'Afraid to ram them too hard . . . don't want a fender jammed into a tyre or to bend the radiator back into the fan . . . just try to brush them aside . . .'

More ghouls were moving towards us. One was hanging on the fence, swinging by one hand, as if he'd discovered a new pleasure. I saw one come out of the open door of the jail and gaze up at the sun. He didn't blink. I wondered if they would soon be blind? I wondered if that would matter?

Jerry was saying, 'Why, there's Joe Wallace . . . used to play cards with him . . . Tim Carver . . . Ike Stanton . . . Hell, I know these people! Used to know them when they were people . . . There's Mrs Jones. Aw, hell . . . there's the Carpenter kid . . . he's only seven years old . . .'

I looked where he was looking and saw the child, its face preternaturally aged by drooling madness. I couldn't tell if it was a boy or a girl. Larsen had been right about that . . . the kids were the worst. I guessed there were about forty of them on the waterfront, men, women and children. I had no idea how many were in the town or how many had been killed . . . nor how long they would survive.

They were still individuals.

They shared the same mindless countenance, but they moved in different ways, not following a pattern, each affected differently. Some hopped and leaped like frogs, some crept along, some stood upright while others were hunched over, faces downcast as if ashamed of their condition. Most of them seemed to be injured in some way. I saw one youth whose arm had been torn off at the shoulder; perhaps he had torn it off himself, for he held the severed limb in his other hand. A woman had torn her hair out; her glabrous skull was dotted with hundreds of pinpoints of blood. One had no lower jaw. Two were naked. I stared at them in terrible fascination.

'Why, there's my hat!' Jerry said, and he brought his hand to his bare head.

The white Stetson was lying in the street just outside the jail. I thought, for a second, that Jerry was going to halt the van and retrieve it. But he drove steadily on, into them. The ghouls didn't move out of the way, but they allowed themselves to be brushed aside. They seemed quite passive and docile. I began to hope that the initial frenzy had worn off, that it had been a temporary rage that had burned itself out. That hope burned like acid in my heart.

Then they attacked the van.

A ghoulish face loomed up at my window.

Mary screamed. There was a loud banging on the side of the van, shaking it. Another bang came from the roof. Someone was hammering and pounding at the panels and the windscreen suddenly shattered in a jagged star.

Jerry cursed. He stepped on the accelerator and the tyres skidded and squealed. For a moment the van did not move; someone was holding the rear bumper. Then there was a screech of metal and the bumper peeled free from the van. We surged forward with a jolt . . . and the engine stalled.

Jerry snapped the ignition and it rasped. The engine didn't catch. I feared it was flooded. I think I was shouting at Jerry, and Mary was screaming over and over. But then the engine caught and we were moving again. As the van lurched forward the door on the driver's side was jerked completely off. A ghoul held it by the handle and he fell back as the door came free. The door sailed up like a steel kite, floating. Then we were through them and going fast. I looked back. The ghouls were coming, following after us. Jerry was hunched over the wheel and Mary and I were shouting for him to drive faster. He grunted and touched his forehead again. I figured he regretted losing his hat.

The lighthouse rose up like surging hope.

It was an ugly grey tower upon which gargoyles might have perched, but it looked beautiful to me. Jerry brought the van to a skidding halt, slewing sideways in the sand, just where the reef began. The tide was going out and the black rocks broke through the surface all the way to the lighthouse. For a moment we just sat there. Time was precious, but we had to sit for an instant as the void of our drained emotions filled.

Jerry reached into the toolbox behind the seat and came up with a tyre iron.

He said, 'This should do it.'

I was looking out the back, but we had gone beyond the sweep of the island. If the ghouls were still coming, I couldn't see them. I knew that their span of attention was too feeble to keep them going in pursuit of a vanished prey ... but feared that, once headed in our direction, inertia would keep them moving.

Jerry jumped out from his doorless side and stood, looking back. He had his gun in one hand and the tyre iron in the other. 'No sign of them,' he said. 'I reckon we made it.'

Then a hand reached down from the top of the van.

I remembered the bang I'd heard on the roof and my mouth sprang open. I shouted, leaning past Mary. The hand hovered, tilting at the wrist, delicately groping at the air. Then it descended onto Jerry's shoulder.

Jerry didn't react.

He had heard me shout and must have supposed it was my hand, seeking his attention. He was still looking back along our trail. Mary screamed and the sheriff looked towards us and then he looked up, just as the hand tightened on his shoulder. His face exploded with frenzy; he dropped the tyre iron and started to lift the gun; then the ghoul heaved his big body up and hauled him onto the roof of the van.

I saw the polished toe of his boot kicking wildly.

I threw open my door and rolled out, bringing the rifle up, seeming to move in slow motion. On the top of the van they were pressed together like lovers in a terrible embrace. The ghoul loomed over Jerry; Jerry was struggling, trying to throw the creature off. I didn't fire. In my horror, I did nothing. Jerry pressed his big revolver into the ghoul's midrift and, as I gaped at them, he began to fire into the thing. The ghoul's body jerked as the heavy-calibre slugs went into him. Jerry was cocking and firing the gun with terrible deliberation, fast but steady, and I saw the ghoul's spine unpeel from his back, the bony articulation coming out from his flesh like the backbone of a fish. The spine snapped in the middle and the bloody ends twanged apart. The ghoul's arms and legs went limp.

Jerry heaved him away and rolled from the van. The ghoul spread out across the roof, one hand hanging down on either side. His face was turned to me. He was still alive and, broken in half, trying to move.

I crossed behind the van. Jerry was sitting in the sand, panting. He was looking at his left arm. I moved towards him and we both looked at his arm and, as we did so, a red line appeared. His flesh was white, numbed by the ghoul's inhuman grip, and on that pale background a thin thread unravelled, as if slipping from a tapestry – and a trickle of blood oozed from the broken skin.

'Aw, hell,' he said, very softly. 'Aw, hell . . .'

And he looked at the lighthouse, so close now and so unobtainably far.

Grey and bleak, it rose up beyond him.

XXV

Mary clung to him.

She was gasping and sobbing and heaving violently at him, almost attacking him in her despair. Jerry was trying not to touch her. He held his left arm out to the side.

He said, 'I'll go back.'

She was crying. 'Jerry! Jerry! No!'

He said, 'I'll hold them for a while . . . stop as many as I can.' He looked down at Mary, then at me. I understood. I took her by the shoulders and dragged her from him. She struggled against me, babbling incoherently, her mouth forming words that had no meaning . . . sounds that arose from depths far beyond language, from feelings far more ancient than speech. She struck at me. I had to change my grip. Jerry was reloading his revolver, tucking the shells into the open chamber with amazing delicacy. He snapped the cylinder closed and began fingering the bullets remaining in his belt. His lips moved; he was counting. He wanted no mistakes in that enumeration. He would have a use for the final bullet.

'Jerry,' I said. Words were absurdly inadequate. I said, 'I'm sorry, Jerry. I . . . I'm glad I knew you.'

Mary was reaching for him, clawing for him.

And he couldn't even kiss her goodbye.

He said, 'Mary . . .' and his voice broke. His eyes were glazed over. He shook his massive body and turned. He didn't look back. He walked back the way we'd come with his shoulders square and I saw him raise his hand to his forehead. I knew he wished he had his Stetson as he walked back through the sunlight . . .

'Mary, please . . . go to the lighthouse!'

She ignored me.

She didn't even hear me. She stood on the rocks and looked back. Jerry had turned past the rim of the island. We couldn't see him. Mary had tried to go after him and three times I'd had to stop levering at the reef and drag her back to the rocks. I handed her the rifle and she took it, holding it by the barrel, not knowing what it was. Crazed with grief and horror, her mind had slipped out of focus. Keeping one eye on her, I attacked the reef again. It was a harder job than I'd thought. The rocks didn't roll off separately but splintered and came apart, spongy veins separating hard layers.

Jerry's gun sounded.

It went off six times and Mary's body jerked at every shot, just as if those bullets were slamming into her. I wondered if the sixth bullet had been for himself? But then he was firing again. He had reloaded, giving us all the time he could. He fired four more times. Then there was silence.

Mary sank down on a rock. One foot trailed in the water. I pried a black slice off and stepped back, wondering if the gap was wide enough. It wasn't. I knelt on the slippery reef and tried to lift a huge segment of stone. It was too heavy for me I wished that Jerry had stayed to help break the reef. I heaved with all my might and the rock would not move.

Then the ghouls were coming.

Loping, bounding, skulking . . . in their various fashions, they came for us. One was dragging a disembodied forearm at his side. I didn't want to know whose arm it had been. I heaved. The rock was far too heavy for me to lift, it was impossible that I should raise it and yet, ponderously, that great slab shifted. Fear had granted me strength as surely as mindless inhibition granted it to the ghouls. I rose up with the stone clasped to my breast; let it slide away, sideways, into the water. The water bubbled light green as the rock sank.

Mary screamed.

The first ghoul was on the reef, bounding from rock to rock. Blood streamed from an empty eyesocket. The other eye was fixed upon us. I backed away, reaching out for the gun, but Mary was too petrified to hand it to me; didn't even know she had it. She was so terrified that she took a step forwards, towards the ghoul.

I snatched the rifle from her, throwing us both off balance. Mary slipped forwards and I fell back. The ghoul sprang up from the rocks, he seemed to soar over the break as I fired from my knees, awkwardly, and the recoil shoved me over the slippery stone. Flailing wildly, I dropped backwards into the warm sea.

*

I surfaced, kicking and gasping. I had lost the rifle. I took one automatic stroke towards the rocks, then recoiled, pushing away. The ghoul's leap had fallen short . . . the gap had proved wide enough and the creature was in the water. His gory head bobbed up and down, water streaming from the open mouth, blood streaming from the open eyesocket, the other eye white and wild with terror. He was reaching for the rocks.

Mary stood there, staring down at the monster, frozen fast by her horror.

'Go back!' I cried.

Water swirled into my mouth, choking me.

The ghoul's hand slapped down on the rock, shifted . . . and clamped on Mary's ankle.

She never made a sound as the creature dragged her down into the sea. The water bubbled around them. She was trying to swim and the frenzied thing tore at her. Three or four other ghouls had come up to the break in the reef; they stood there, staring down at the ghoul in the water – and the woman. I stroked to the rocks beyond the gap and hauled myself out, gasping. I looked into the gap from my side of the break and the ghouls looked in from their side and in the water between there was blood.

Mary's face turned to me.

She pleaded with her eyes, silently.

She reached out towards me and my hand went out to her, but she was too far away. She was closer to the other side. The ghoul had gone under now and Mary was alone in the turbulent gap. She twisted violently, trying to kick off from the rocks, but she had drifted too close. The ghouls reached down.

She still made no sound, even as their hands closed over her and they drew her up onto the rocks. I would have shot her, of course . . . but I had lost the rifle. Mary was on the flat rock. She kicked spasmodically with one leg. The ghouls bent over her, slowly, solicitously, as if they had rescued her from drowning . . . bent to her, as if to give the kiss of life . . .

Epilogue

I thought I saw Mary amongst them today.

I was watching through the binoculars, a group of them were milling about by the rotting swordfish and one looked rather like Mary. But I stopped watching. I didn't want to know. I only want to know how much longer it will be, how many days or weeks I must sit here in my grey tower, rooted in the sea and rising towards the heavens. Not much longer, perhaps. They don't seem as frenzied now, they don't even fight amongst themselves when they make contact. I wonder if the madness is wearing off ... if they are recovering some human instinct ... or simply wasting away, weakening and dying? I hope it was not Mary I saw. When I looked later, most of them had gone. One was dead – lifeless, at least. The body had burst open and a length of intestine had uncoiled. I saw a seagull land on the ghoul's shoulder and dip its sharp beak into the gruesome cavity.

The gull's head came up and it seemed to shudder, as did I. Larsen's words came back to me. If a dog or a rat got at one of the bodies ... Again the gull's beak dipped; the plumed throat pulsed. Above the patrol boats the sky was clear and blue. The seagull was sated. It poised, wings lifted, then bore itself away.

David Case was born in New York but for the past few decades has lived in London as well as spending time in Spain and Greece. His acclaimed collection *The Cell: Three Tales of Horror* appeared in 1969, and it was followed by the novels *Fengriffen: A Chilling Tale* (1970), *Wolf Tracks* (1980) and *The Third Grave*, which appeared from Arkham House in 1981. More recently, a new collection entitled *Brotherly Love and Other Tales of Faith and Knowledge* was published by Pumpkin Books. Outside the horror genre, Case has written more than three hundred books under at least seventeen pseudonyms, ranging from porn to Westerns. Two of his short stories, 'Fengriffen' and the classic werewolf thriller 'The Hunter' were filmed as – *And Now the Screaming Starts!* (1973) and *Scream of the Wolf* (1974), respectively. 'Pelican Cay' was originally going to be published by the late James Turner in an anthology he planned to edit in the mid-1980s for Arkham House entitled *Summoning the Shadows*. When the horror market changed in America, the book was shelved and Case's powerful novella languished in a file for many years until its publication here. 'I wrote "Pelican Cay" in a seedy hotel in downtown Chicago,' remembers the author, 'but had lived in the Florida Keys before that, which inspired the atmosphere and setting. The Red Walls, or maybe Doors, was an upmarket place when I was there, but there were plenty of tales from when it was the haunt of shrimpers and salad girls (girls who signed on shrimp boats but didn't necessarily make salads). A fella was drowning his sorrows there once and, morose, said he would commit suicide if he dared. They hanged him from the rafters. My favourite: thirteen shrimpers are standing at the long bar. A guy runs in with a shooter and shouts "This is a stick-up!" The shrimpers turned around and twelve had shooters, the other had a bill-hook. The bandit says, "I guess I've robbed the wrong place." But he bought a round of drinks and they let him go.'